THE CAMBRIDGE EDITION OF
THE WORKS OF SAMUEL RICHARDSON 2

PAMELA: OR, VIRTUE REWARDED

THE CAMBRIDGE EDITION OF
THE WORKS AND CORRESPONDENCE OF
SAMUEL RICHARDSON

GENERAL EDITORS
Thomas Keymer *University of Toronto*
Peter Sabor *McGill University*

Thanks are expressed to the Social Sciences and Humanities
Research Council of Canada, the Leverhulme Trust, the Chancellor Jackman
Professorships Program, the Canada Research Chairs Program and Le
Fonds québécois de la recherche sur la société et la culture for
providing research funding towards the creation
of this edition.

THE CAMBRIDGE EDITION OF
THE WORKS AND CORRESPONDENCE OF
SAMUEL RICHARDSON

THE WORKS

1 Early Works
2 Pamela: or, Virtue Rewarded
3 Pamela in Her Exalted Condition
4–7 Clarissa: or, The History of a Young Lady
8–11 Sir Charles Grandison
12 Later Works and Index

In Preparation:
THE CORRESPONDENCE OF

SAMUEL RICHARDSON

PAMELA: OR, VIRTUE REWARDED

EDITED BY

Albert J. Rivero

CAMBRIDGE
UNIVERSITY PRESS

CAMBRIDGE UNIVERSITY PRESS
Cambridge, New York, Melbourne, Madrid, Cape Town,
Singapore, São Paulo, Delhi, Tokyo, Mexico City

Cambridge University Press
The Edinburgh Building, Cambridge CB2 8RU, UK

Published in the United States of America by Cambridge University Press, New York

www.cambridge.org
Information on this title: www.cambridge.org/9780521848954

First published 2011

Printed in the United Kingdom at the University Press, Cambridge

A catalogue record for this publication is available from the British Library

Library of Congress Cataloguing in Publication data
Richardson, Samuel, 1689–1761.
[Pamela]
Pamela, or, Virtue rewarded / Samuel Richardson ; edited by Albert J. Rivero.
p.   cm. – (The Cambridge edition of the works of Samuel Richardson ; 2)
Includes bibliographical references and index.
ISBN 978-0-521-84895-4
1. Master and servant – Fiction.   2. Kidnapping victims – Fiction.   3. Women household
employees – Fiction.   4.Virtue – Fiction.   5. England – Fiction.   I. Rivero, Albert J., 1953–
II. Title.   III. Title: Pamela.   IV. Title: Virtue rewarded.
PR3664.P35   2011
823'.6 – dc22   2011006850

ISBN 978-0-521-84895-4 Hardback

To Lisa and Albert

CONTENTS

ILLUSTRATIONS

GENERAL EDITORS' PREFACE

The Cambridge Edition of the Works of Samuel Richardson is the first fully annotated scholarly edition of Richardson's works, including his securely attributable minor works, ever to have been undertaken. Five substantial collected editions have been published before now: *The Works of Samuel Richardson*, with an introduction by Edward Mangin (19 volumes, 1811); *The Works of Samuel Richardson*, with an introduction by Leslie Stephen (12 volumes, 1883); *The Novels of Samuel Richardson*, with an introduction by William Lyon Phelps (19 volumes, 1901–2); *The Novels of Samuel Richardson*, with an introduction by Ethel M. McKenna (20 volumes, 1902); and finally *The Novels of Samuel Richardson* (18 volumes, 1929–31). None of these editions, however, contains any explanatory or textual apparatus, and none contains any of Richardson's writings beside his three major novels.

In the absence of any scholarly alternative, the last of these collected editions, the Shakespeare Head edition, has passed as standard for almost a century, though with no visible credentials for doing so. It is attractively printed, on fine paper, but suffers from several obvious shortcomings. First, it is extremely scarce; only five hundred copies were issued, many to individual subscribers, and few libraries possess copies. Second, it was anonymously edited, and a brief note on the text is ambiguous; to what extent, and if so on what principles, the text was modernized or corrected remains unclear. Third, the choice of copy-text for the novels, Richardson's octavo edition in each case, is highly questionable. A compulsive reviser and, unusually, his own printer, with complete and direct control over the production process, Richardson changed the texts of his novels with each edition that he printed. He issued one edition of each novel in octavo, in contrast to the smaller duodecimo size normally used. Intended for wealthier buyers, the octavo editions were printed on better paper, with more generous margins and leading, and, in the case of *Pamela*, with twenty-nine engravings by two of the foremost book-illustrators of the day. The octavo editions, however, represented a stage in the process of revision that was intermediate and in some respect tangential to the genealogy of the text: in the case of all three novels, Richardson went on to make extensive further changes, working from the previous duodecimo edition and losing many of the octavo revisions as he did so.[1] One might expect a standard edition to use as copy-text either the original version or the final revision, but not a text midway between – or aside from – these two significant states.

Groundbreaking annotated editions of individual works have appeared since the 1970s, notably in the Oxford English Novels, Oxford World's Classics and Penguin Classics series, but these have been limited in scope and ambition by their trade or textbook formats, and have not extended to significant works such as *Æsop's Fables* and the continuation of *Pamela*. Over the same period, other kinds of scholarship on Richardson – biographical, bibliographical, critical, historical – have flourished as never before, and large advances have also been made in relevant contextual fields. In light of all this work, and of the unprecedented research resources now available to editors of eighteenth-century literature, the time has come to provide Richardson's whole output with explanatory apparatus of the scale and depth that already exists for other major novelists of the period, such as Fielding, Smollett, and Sterne. The detailed introductions, comprehensive annotations, and bibliographical appendices of the Cambridge Edition provide comprehensive accounts of the composition, publication, and subsequent textual history of all his works, with the extensive commentary and additional material necessary to situate and understand them in their cultural, historical, linguistic, and literary contexts.

No perfect solution exists to the question of copy-text. The five previous collected editions all derive, with varying degrees of directness and accuracy, and without apparent awareness of the textual issues, from interim revised versions of all three novels. By contrast, most of the single-novel editions published since the 1970s revert to the earliest published state of each work, with an implied or explicit preference, critical or theoretical, for primary utterance over retrospective intervention, or for the version of each novel that generated controversy over the version that sought to allay it. Yet there is no simple choice to be made here between original and final authorial intentions or textual states, for neither can be clearly established. There is nothing particularly 'original' about the first edition of *Clarissa*, which in a process resembling scribal publication had already circulated for years in manuscript copies among at least a dozen readers, with several distinct stages of authorial revision undertaken during the process (the pre-publication

---

1 The exception here is the octavo edition of *Sir Charles Grandison*, which, though labelled the 'second' edition, was published simultaneously with the 'first' (duodecimo) edition. In effect, *Sir Charles Grandison* has two separate first editions in different states, with minor corrections incorporated in the octavo version (Robert Craig Pierson, 'The Revisions of Richardson's *Sir Charles Grandison*', *Studies in Bibliography* 21 (1966), 163–89).

manuscripts do not survive). There is nothing definitively 'final' about either the last octavo or the last duodecimo edition of *Pamela* published in Richardson's lifetime, each of which omits revisions included in the other, and both of which were followed decades later by a posthumous edition in which subsequent authorial revisions mingle, undetectably and inextricably, with alterations apparently made on their own initiative by Richardson's daughters. Strictly speaking, the first edition of Vol. V–VI of *Sir Charles Grandison* is not Richardson's own but a Dublin piracy, based on preliminary sheets of the novel stolen from his business premises, and here too, as in both *Pamela* and *Clarissa*, the authenticity of his final authorial revisions is obscured by intermingling familial interventions. From months or years before publication to decades after Richardson's death, all the novels were in a state of instability and flux that renders illegitimate any notion of a single authoritative text. At the same time, the swarming complexity of the textual situation makes clear not only the practical impossibility but also the theoretical undesirability of attempting to establish a composite or eclectic text. Numerous versions exist of the major works, all with a claim to validity and interest, none with a definitive claim to eclipse all other versions.

In these unusually complicated circumstances, the Cambridge Edition of the Works of Samuel Richardson takes as its copy-text the earliest version of each work to have been authorized and published. Richardson's subsequent rounds of revision are essential to complete understanding, and it may simplify the situation to say, as a previous editor has done of Richardson's characteristically deferential or precautionary practices as a reviser, that 'to the extent that he allowed outside pressure to influence his work, each edition is progressively less his own, further removed from the original conception, and often destructive of the spontaneity or colloquial tone of the first edition'.[2] But it is certainly true that much of Richardson's work as a reviser was palliative or defensive in the face of readerly incomprehension or conventional taste, and that cumulatively his revisions can dim our sense of his originality and distinctiveness as a writer, and of the impact made on his culture by the novels in their original published states. It is inevitable that competing trajectories are sometimes in play in the revision process, and among thousands of local adjustments, individual changes sometimes pull away from the larger trend. In comparison with later versions, however, the basic characteristics of a Richardson novel in its first edition are clear enough: in matters of linguistic, moral, and social decorum, it is typically more provocative and transgressive; and in matters of meaning and interpretation, it is typically more indeterminate and open. At a time when electronic databases now make all editions published

---

2 Samuel Richardson, *Sir Charles Grandison*, ed. Jocelyn Harris, 3 vols. (London: Oxford University Press, 1972), I, p. xxviii.

before 1800 available in digitized form, moreover, it makes more sense for readers interested in Richardson's revisions, or more generally in the pressures exerted on innovative works by conservative tastes, to work forward from a first-edition text rather than backward from a later version – the more so given the interrupted state of the revisions on Richardson's death, the ambiguous status of the posthumous editions, and the consequent impossibility of securely identifying final authorial intention in any published edition.

A further rationale for the choice of first-edition copy-texts is their direct link to Richardson's correspondence, in which the single most important topic is the composition, correction, publication, and interpretation of his novels. The vast majority of this protracted and, for the period, unprecedentedly rich and detailed debate on the art of fiction concerns either first editions or pre-publication versions, no longer extant, to which the earliest printed state is the closest surviving witness. Published alongside this edition is a companion edition of Richardson's complete known correspondence, most of it previously unpublished, in which his consultations, discussions and disputes with readers of the novels are recorded at length.

An important further component of the Cambridge Edition of the Works of Samuel Richardson, absent from previous collected editions, is Richardson's minor and occasional writing, in the first and last volumes of the edition. The first volume includes the two works from which Richardson's *Pamela* most immediately arose: his Æsopian collection of 1739 and *Letters Written to and for Particular Friends* (1741). These appear alongside other securely attributed writings of the same period and two substantial pamphlets of the mid-1730s: *The Apprentice's Vade Mecum* and *A Seasonable Examination of . . . Play-Houses*. All of these publications have generated considerable interest for some decades, but the absence of scholarly editions has impeded critical study of the works in their own right or in relation to the novels. The last volume includes an annotated text of Richardson's fragmentary attempt at a fourth novel, 'The History of Mrs. Beaumont', partly published by Anna Laetitia Barbauld in 1804 but edited here from the autograph manuscript in the Morgan Library, supplemented by additional fragments in the hand of Richardson's daughter Martha Bridgen, now at the Fondren Library, Rice University. The volume also contains Richardson's important *Rambler* essay of 1751 (approvingly cited by Austen in *Northanger Abbey*) and what appears to have been his final publication, an essay written for Smollett's *British Magazine* of April 1760, as well as a general index to the edition as a whole.

The Cambridge Edition of the Works of Samuel Richardson is designed to become the uniform scholarly edition. It has extensive historical and textual introductions, providing authoritative accounts of the composition, publication, early reception and subsequent revision of each work. Material on the personal and professional circumstances in which Richardson wrote the work, and on pre-publication circulation, consultation, and revision, is presented in full, as is whatever information can be established about the commercial practicalities of contracts, print runs, and sales. There are also ample linguistic and historical notes, addressing Richardson's use of language (the love for neologisms and puns, for example, that made him the most significant living presence in Johnson's *Dictionary*), as well as literary and cultural allusions. Emendation is conservative, and the meticulous preparation of the copy-texts by compositors under Richardson's direct supervision removes the need for more than very occasional minor correction. Textual apparatus includes, for each novel, tables of emendations, noting the source and authority of each emendation adopted; mid-production variants among different states of the first edition revealed by horizontal collation; tables of cancellantia and cancellanda, recording the variant text of the cancellanda where surviving evidence makes this possible; and other relevant appendices including descriptive bibliographies of principal editions and tables of word-division. Given the number of editions involved, and the thousands of changes typically made between each edition and the next, vertical collation, even if achievable, would be impossible to use. Instead, the significant additions in principal later editions of the novels will be included as substantive appendices, notably the new paratextual material added in the second and sixth editions of *Pamela* and the volume of *Letters and Passages Restored* published by Richardson in 1751 to provide readers of *Clarissa* in its first edition with the additions made in the third.

ACKNOWLEDGEMENTS

Many people and institutions have helped me in the preparation of this edition. First, I wish to thank Tom Keymer and Peter Sabor, my general editors, for their friendship, advice, and good humour; all that is valuable in this volume is owing to their superb guidance. Linda Bree and her editorial staff at Cambridge University Press, especially Maartje Scheltens, have offered their expert support throughout; they have been a pleasure to work with. David Vander Meulen taught me how to operate a Hinman Collator, access to which was provided by the University of Wisconsin–Milwaukee Golda Meir Library. I am grateful to Alex Pettit for being a great friend and for instituting the first version of the textual protocols followed in this edition; I thank Ashley Brookner Bender and Laura Thomason Wood for assisting Alex in the early editorial stages. Warm thanks are also due to Paula Backscheider, Martin C. Battestin, Nick Burckel, Christopher Daniel, John Dussinger, Michael Patrick Gillespie, Jocelyn Harris, Diane Hoeveler, Paul Hunter, George Justice, Steve Karian, Devoney Looser, Tim Machan, John Pauly, Kris Ratcliffe, Jeff Snell, Madeline Wake, and Howard Weinbrot for their personal and professional support during the years it took to complete this project. For granting me access to the collections in their care, I am indebted to the staffs of the American Antiquarian Society, Bodleian Library, British Library, Cornell University Library, Fondren Library (Rice University), Marquette University Library, McMaster University Library, Milwaukee Public Library, Morgan Library, National Art Library (Victoria and Albert Museum), National Library of Scotland, Newberry Library, New York Public Library, Princeton University Library, and the University of Chicago Library. Finally, I owe my most heartfelt gratitude to my wife, Lisa, and my son, Albert, for always being there with their love and encouragement; they both assisted in proofreading and Lisa, in addition, assembled the index.

CHRONOLOGY

1682

2 June   Marriage in London of SR's parents, Samuel Richardson, Sr (d. 1727), a master joiner, and Elizabeth Hall (d. 1736)

1687   Family leaves London for Derbyshire at about this time, perhaps for political reasons

1689

July–August   Born and baptized in Mackworth, near Derby, the fourth of nine children from the marriage

1695–9   Family returns to London during this period, settling in the Tower Hill district

1701–2   Probably educated at the Merchant Taylors' School, where his schoolfellows know him as '*Serious* and *Gravity*'

1706

1 July   Apprenticed to John Wilde, a printer of Aldersgate

1713

2 July   Completes apprenticeship with Wilde, where SR has become 'the Pillar of his House'

1715

13 June   Made freeman of the Stationers' Company and a citizen of London

1715–20   Works as a compositor and corrector in Wilde's business

1720   Manages the printing business of the Leake family on the corner of Blue Ball and Salisbury Courts; begins printing

xix

private bills for James Blew, a lawyer and parliamentary agent

1721   Buys 'Printing Presses and Letter Utensils of trade' from the Leakes and sets up as master printer in their former premises, where he resides until 1736; remains in the Salisbury Court district for his entire career

23 November   Marries Martha, daughter of John Wilde; five sons and a daughter from the marriage die in infancy

1722
5 March   Granted the livery of the Stationers' Company
6 August   Three Leake apprentices turned over to SR, the first of twenty-four apprentices bound to him during his career

1722–4   Denounced to the ministry by Samuel Negus, a printer, as one of the 'disaffected printers . . . Said to be High-Flyers'; continues printing Tory–Jacobite material, including the Duke of Wharton's periodical *The True Briton* (1723–4)

1725
December   Begins printing *The Daily Journal* (to 1737), one of several newspapers and periodicals printed by SR until the mid-1740s

1727
11 April   Elected to junior office as Renter Warden in the Stationers' Company

1728   Rents a second Salisbury Court house, opposite the first, for *Daily Journal* operations (to 1736)
September   Identified to the ministry by Edmund Curll as printer of a seditious number of *Mist's Weekly Journal*

1730
December   *The Infidel Convicted*, possibly by SR

1731
23 January   Death of Martha (Wilde) Richardson
February   Becomes a junior shareholder in the Stationers' Company, purchasing progressively more senior levels of stock in 1736, 1746, and 1751

October	Incurs financial losses on the collapse of the Charitable Corporation; embroiled until mid-1733 in related legal proceedings

1733

3 February	Marries Elizabeth Leake (d. 1773), sister of the Bath bookseller James Leake
February	Appointed first official printer to the House of Commons (to 1761), responsible for public bills and committee reports; SR thereby becomes 'more independent of Booksellers (tho' I did much Business for them) than any other Printer'
December	*The Apprentice's Vade Mecum*
23 December	Baptism of daughter Elizabeth, d. 1734

1734	Expands business premises into a third house, in Blue Ball Court (to 1740)

1735

2 January	Baptism of daughter Mary (Polly), m. 1757 (to Philip Ditcher), d. 1783
April	*A Seasonable Examination of the Pleas and Pretensions of the Proprietors of, and Subscribers to, Play-Houses*
June	Probably begins printing the pro-ministerial *Daily Gazetteer* (to 1746)

1736	Moves to 'House of a very grand outward Appearance' on Salisbury Square, which he occupies until 1756; also rents Corney House, a tenement of Sutton Court, Chiswick, as a weekend/summer retreat (to 1738)
January	*Gentleman's Magazine* publishes a light verse epistle by SR, noting that 'the Publick is often agreeably entertain'd with his Elegant Disquisitions in Prose'
16 July	Baptism of daughter Martha (Patty), m. 1762 (to Edward Bridgen), d. 1785

1737

16 August	Baptism of daughter Anne (Nancy), d. 1803

1738

Summer	Rents large semi-rural retreat at North End, Fulham (to 1754)

October	Edits and prints updated second edition of Defoe's *Tour*, also subsequent editions of 1742, 1748, 1753, and 1761–2

1739

26 April	Baptism of son Samuel, d. 1740
10 November	Starts writing *Pamela*
20 November	*Æsop's Fables*

1740

January	Completes draft of *Pamela*, revising the text over the ensuing months
29 March	*The Negotiations of Sir Thomas Roe in His Embassy to the Ottoman Porte*, edited and printed by SR for the Society for the Encouragement of Learning
17 July	Baptism of twelfth and last child, Sarah (Sally), m. 1763 (to Richard Crowther), d. 1773
6 November	*Pamela; or, Virtue Rewarded*

1741

	Expands his printing premises behind Salisbury Court
23 January	*Letters Written to and for Particular Friends*
28 May	Opening volume of John Kelly's *Pamela's Conduct in High Life*, a spurious continuation, published; SR starts planning his own authorized continuation
1 December	Elected to the Court of Assistants, ruling body of the Stationers' Company
7 December	*Pamela in Her Exalted Condition*, SR's continuation

1742

8 May	Sixth edition of *Pamela*, in octavo format and with twenty-nine engravings by Hubert Gravelot and Francis Hayman: the first simultaneous publication of both parts
May	Wins large contract to print the *Journals* of the House of Commons (to 1761)

1744	Begins printing the *Philosophical Transactions of the Royal Society* (to 1761), one of several major projects for learned societies
June–July	Earliest references in SR's correspondence to *Clarissa*, which already exists in some form of draft
December	Sends part of the novel in manuscript to Aaron Hill; manuscript copies in various states of revision circulate among SR's friends until 1747

1746

Summer   Assists the ministry in finding shorthand experts to help
              prosecute Jacobite rebels

December   Hill sends SR his 'Specimen of New Clarissa', a test
              abridgement of the novel's opening

1747

1 December   *Clarissa*, Vols. I and II

1748

28 April   *Clarissa*, Vols. III and IV

5 July   William Richardson, nephew, apprenticed to SR

2 August   Advertises in the *Whitehall Evening-Post* for contact with
              Lady Bradshaigh, who has been sending pseudonymous
              letters about *Clarissa*

6 December   *Clarissa*, Vols. V–VII

1749

June   Prints *Answer to the Letter of a Very Reverend and Worthy
              Gentleman*, a defence of *Clarissa*'s fire scene, for private
              distribution

August   Publishes notes responding to Albrecht von Haller's
              critique of *Clarissa* in the *Gentleman's Magazine*

December   Prints *Meditations Collected from the Sacred Books* for private
              distribution

1750

6 March   First face-to-face meeting with Lady Bradshaigh,
              thereafter his closest literary adviser

August   Death of SR's brother Benjamin; household joined by
              Benjamin's fourteen-year-old daughter Susanna (Sukey),
              'whom my Wife has in a manner adopted'

1751

January   Sections of *Sir Charles Grandison* start to circulate in
              manuscript among SR's friends

17 February   Publishes an essay (no. 97) on courtship and marriage in
              Samuel Johnson's periodical *The Rambler*, based on SR's
              letter of 8 September 1750 to Frances Grainger

20 April   Expanded third edition of *Clarissa*; new material separately
              published as *Letters and Passages Restored from the Original
              Manuscripts of the History of Clarissa*

1752

28 September   Fire at SR's printing house causes extensive damage and loss of stock; takes on additional Salisbury Court premises at about this time, probably as a warehouse and workmen's residence

1753

May   Begins distributing printed sheets of *Sir Charles Grandison* among friends

2 June   Writes autobiographical letter to Johannes Stinstra, his Dutch translator

30 June   Attains rank of Upper Warden in the Stationers' Company

August   Learns that four Dublin booksellers have stolen most of *Sir Charles Grandison* in printed sheets and plan to publish an unauthorized edition; halts printing and fires suspected employees

14 September   *The Case of Samuel Richardson, of London, Printer; with Regard to the Invasion of His Property* printed for free distribution

13 November   *Sir Charles Grandison*, Vols. I–IV, simultaneously published in duodecimo ('first') and octavo ('second') editions; Vols. I–VI of the piracy appear in Dublin the same month, before SR can bring out his authorized Vols. V–VI

11 December   *Sir Charles Grandison*, Vols. V–VI (duodecimo) and Vol. V (octavo)

1754

1 February   Prints *An Address to the Public*, a further attack on the Dublin pirates and on George Faulkner, an Irish bookseller, with whom he had failed to negotiate a solution

14 March   *Sir Charles Grandison*, Vol. VII (duodecimo) and Vol. VI (octavo)

19 March   Revised third edition of *Sir Charles Grandison* (duodecimo)

April   Prints two commentaries on *Sir Charles Grandison, Answer to a Letter from a Friend* and *Copy of a Letter to a Lady*, for private distribution; the latter explains that there will be no further volumes

6 July   Becomes Master of the Stationers' Company for a one-year term

July–October   Rents and renovates new weekend house at Parson's Green, which his wife and daughters make their main home

1755

February   Begins writing a fragmentary 'History of Mrs. Beaumont' (partly published in 1804), possibly as the basis for a new novel

6 March   *A Collection of the Moral and Instructive Sentiments, Maxims, Cautions, and Reflexions, Contained in the Histories of Pamela, Clarissa, and Sir Charles Grandison*

5 August   William Richardson completes apprenticeship and becomes SR's overseer

July–December   Builds expensive new business premises in Salisbury Court, renovating the adjoining house as a residence, which he occupies the following spring

1757

June   Approached by Erasmus Reich, a Leipzig bookseller, with proposals to bring out a German edition of his selected correspondence, which he starts to prepare

1758

May   Abandons the Reich project, but continues preparing letters for possible posthumous publication

August–September   Revises and corrects Urania Hill Johnson's novel *Almira*, which she publishes six months after SR's death, rejecting most of the revisions

1759

May   Prints Edward Young's *Conjectures on Original Composition*, composed by Young with SR's collaborative involvement

Summer   William Richardson leaves SR's employment to start his own printing business

1760

28 April   Revises and contributes to a translation of Marguerite de Lussan's *The Life and Heroic Actions of Balbe Berton*, printed by William Richardson

24 June   Enters partnership with Catherine Lintot, heir to the printer Henry Lintot, in a law patent with monopoly rights to print books on common law

1761

March   Borrows Lady Bradshaigh's annotated copies of *Pamela* and *Clarissa* to make further revisions

28 June   Suffers stroke during a visit from the portraitist Joseph Highmore

4 July   Dies, leaving an estate of £14,000 and bequeathing manuscripts to his daughters; buried in St Bride's, Fleet Street, beside his first wife and infant children

September   William Richardson returns to Salisbury Court, taking over SR's business with a partner, Samuel Clarke

1762   Posthumous revised editions of *Pamela* and *Sir Charles Grandison*

1765
March   'Six Original Letters upon Duelling' published in the *Candid Review and Literary Repository*

1771
25 January   Publication of Anna Meades's *The History of Sir William Harrington, written some years since, and revised and corrected by the late Mr. Richardson*; SR's daughters contest the claim, but he had indeed advised Meades in 1757–8

1780   William Richardson issues proposals for a uniform edition of the novels, 'with corrections', but the edition does not materialize

1784   Anne Richardson and Martha Bridgen plan a new edition of *Pamela*, based on unpublished final revisions by SR, to be 're-revised' by themselves

1786
January–February   Authorized 'Memoirs of Richardson', perhaps by Edward Bridgen, published in the *Universal Magazine*

1792   'New edition' of *Clarissa*, 'with the last corrections by the author', prepared with the involvement of Anne Richardson and SR's granddaughter Sarah Crowther Moodie

1801   Fourteenth edition of *Pamela*, prepared from Anne Richardson's copy, 'with numerous alterations . . . by the Author'

1803   Death of Anne, SR's last surviving child

1804

July   *The Correspondence of Samuel Richardson*, edited, with a
substantial biographical memoir, by Anna Laetitia
Barbauld

1810   'New edition' of *Sir Charles Grandison*, probably from
Anne Richardson's copy, 'with the last corrections by the
author'; fifteenth edition of *Pamela*, with further 'numerous
corrections and alterations', apparently from Anne's
annotated copy of the fourteenth edition

ABBREVIATIONS

Clarissa	Samuel Richardson, *Clarissa. Or, The History of a Young Lady*, 7 vols. (1747–8)
Eaves and Kimpel	T. C. Duncan Eaves and Ben D. Kimpel, *Samuel Richardson: A Biography* (Oxford: Clarendon Press, 1971)
ESTC	*English Short Title Catalogue* (online version)
EW	Samuel Richardson, *Early Works*, ed. Alexander Pettit (Cambridge University Press, 2011)
FM	Forster Collection, Victoria and Albert Museum
Johnson	Samuel Johnson, *A Dictionary of the English Language*, 2 vols. (1755)
Joseph Andrews	Henry Fielding, *Joseph Andrews*, ed. Martin C. Battestin (Middletown, CT: Wesleyan University Press, 1967)
Keymer	Samuel Richardson, *Pamela*, ed. Thomas Keymer and Alice Wakely, intro. Thomas Keymer (Oxford University Press, 2001)
Keymer and Sabor	Thomas Keymer and Peter Sabor, *Pamela in the Marketplace: Literary Controversy and Print Culture in Eighteenth-Century Britain and Ireland* (Cambridge University Press, 2005)
Maslen	Keith Maslen, *Samuel Richardson of London, Printer: A Study of His Printing Based on Ornament Use and Business Accounts* (Dunedin: University of Otago, 2001)
McKillop	Alan Dugald McKillop, *Samuel Richardson: Printer and Novelist* (Chapel Hill: University of North Carolina Press, 1936; repr. Shoe String Press, 1960)
ODEP	*The Oxford Dictionary of English Proverbs*, 3rd edn, rev. F. P. Wilson (Oxford: Clarendon Press, 1970)

OED	*O[xford] E[nglish] D[ictionary] Online* (Oxford University Press, 2008)
Pamela 2	Samuel Richardson, *Pamela; or, Virtue Rewarded . . . And afterwards, In her Exalted Condition*, vols 3–4 (1742)
Sabor	Samuel Richardson, *Pamela; or, Virtue Rewarded*, ed. Peter Sabor, intro. Margaret Anne Doody (Harmondsworth: Penguin, 1980)
Sale (1936)	William Merritt Sale, Jr, *Samuel Richardson: A Bibliographical Record of His Literary Career with Historical Notes* (New Haven, CT: Yale University Press, 1936)
Sale (1950)	William Merritt Sale, Jr, *Samuel Richardson: Master Printer* (Ithaca, NY: Cornell University Press, 1950)
SCG	Samuel Richardson, *The History of Sir Charles Grandison*, 2nd edn, 6 vols. (1753–4)
Shamela	Henry Fielding, *The Journal of a Voyage to Lisbon, Shamela, and Occasional Writings*, ed. Martin C. Battestin (Oxford: Clarendon Press, 2008)
Spectator	*The Spectator*, ed. Donald Bond, 5 vols. (Oxford: Clarendon Press, 1965)
Tilley	Morris Palmer Tilley, *A Dictionary of the Proverbs of England in the Seventeenth and Eighteenth Centuries* (Ann Arbor: University of Michigan Press, 1950)

GENERAL INTRODUCTION

Samuel Richardson's first full-length work of prose fiction, *Pamela: or, Virtue Rewarded*, was published anonymously on 6 November 1740 in two small duodecimo volumes; it became an instant bestseller and cultural event. Posing as 'editor' of a genuine correspondence, Richardson gave his readers, 'In a Series of Familiar Letters' (title page), the fascinating story of a young servant-girl who, withstanding the assaults of her late lady's rakish son, manages to convert him from his wicked ways and becomes his wife. Combining pious commentary with sexual titillation, and offering what its detractors affirmed was a recipe for social climbing, the novel spawned many publications, both from those who relished its religious message and from those who deplored its dubious morality. The so-called 'Pamela controversy', especially after Henry Fielding joined the fray with *Shamela* (first published on 2 April 1741, with a second edition appearing on 3 November 1741), has often been interpreted as one of the crucial events in the development of the English novel.[1] By May 1742, *Pamela: or, Virtue Rewarded* had reached its sixth edition (in

---

1 For the most comprehensive and accurate account of the events surrounding the novel's publication and reception, see Thomas Keymer and Peter Sabor, *Pamela in the Marketplace: Literary Controversy and Print Culture in Eighteenth-Century Britain and Ireland* (Cambridge University Press, 2005); I am deeply indebted to this work for my own account of the *Pamela* vogue. I am also indebted to Alan Dugald McKillop, *Samuel Richardson: Printer and Novelist* (Chapel Hill: University of North Carolina Press, 1936; repr. Shoe String Press, 1960), pp. 3–106, and T. C. Duncan Eaves and Ben D. Kimpel, *Samuel Richardson: A Biography* (Oxford: Clarendon Press, 1971), pp. 100–53. Still of some interest, but superseded by Keymer and Sabor's book, is Bernard Kreissman's monograph, *Pamela-Shamela: A Study of the Criticisms, Burlesques, Parodies, and Adaptations of Richardson's Pamela* (Lincoln: University of Nebraska Press, 1960). Most of the documents, including visual representations, generated by the novel's publication are conveniently reproduced in the six volumes of Thomas Keymer and Peter Sabor (eds.), *The Pamela Controversy: Criticisms and Adaptations of Samuel Richardson's Pamela, 1740–1750* (London: Pickering & Chatto, 2001). For an astute analysis of the cultural issues at stake, see James Grantham Turner, 'Novel Panic: Picture and Performance in the Reception of Richardson's *Pamela*', *Representations* 48 (1994), 70–96. Turner here follows Terry Eagleton, who views *Pamela* less as a novel than as 'a password or badge of allegiance, code for what became a whole cultural event'. For Eagleton, 'the modern equivalent of *Pamela* would . . . be . . . a phenomenon like Superman. The literary text . . . is merely the occasion or organizing principle of a multimedia affair, stretching all

octavo format, with illustrations). In an attempt to legitimize his heroine's social elevation and to reassert his right as the sole purveyor of her story, Richardson had published on 7 December 1741 a continuation in two volumes, detailing Pamela's life 'In her Exalted Condition'. An inveterate reviser, Richardson continued to tinker with both parts of the novel for the rest of his life, with an 'eighth edition' (the fourth of the sequel) being published on 18 October 1761, three months after his death. A 'new edition, being the fourteenth', claiming to incorporate the author's final 'corrections and alterations' (title page), was published in four volumes in 1801. Issued by what was essentially the same group of booksellers, a 'fifteenth' edition, also in four volumes and with further corrections, appeared in 1810.

Such, in short, is the history of the publication of what was arguably the most influential novel published in Britain in the eighteenth century. This history, as well as the history of the novel's initial critical reception, has often been told. It is not my purpose here to rehearse either one or both of these histories in detail, but instead to offer a brief general introduction to *Pamela: or, Virtue Rewarded* that will outline circumstances surrounding its composition, publication, early reception, and revisions. My aim is to sketch out, in so far as it is possible, the historical context of the novel's first appearance, not to offer a new critical interpretation or to engage in critical disputes. At the end of this introduction, I shall offer a brief rationale of the principles governing my annotations. Although in the ensuing pages I shall sometimes refer to the sequel, my focus throughout is on the original novel, reserving information on *Pamela in Her Exalted Condition* for my General Introduction to that work, published in a separate volume.

CIRCUMSTANCES OF COMPOSITION

Writing to Johannes Stinstra, the Dutch translator of *Clarissa*, on 2 June 1753, Richardson provides his own account of the genesis of *Pamela*:

You ask, 'If I had a Model before my Eyes, in some of my Pieces?' The Story of Pamela had some slight Foundation in Truth. Several Persons of Rank were guessed at, as having in my Mind sat for the two Principal Characters in that Piece: But no one Conjecture came near the Truth; nor was it likely that it should; for I myself knew no more of the Story, than what I recollected a Gentleman told me of it Fifteen Years before I sat down to write it; & as it was related to him by an Innkeeper in the

the way from domestic commodities to public spectacles, instantly recodable from one cultural mode to the next' (*The Rape of Clarissa: Writing, Sexuality and Class Struggle in Samuel Richardson* (Oxford: Basil Blackwell, 1982), p. 5). Building on the cultural analyses of Turner and Eagleton, William B. Warner examines what he calls 'The *Pamela* Media Event' in *Licensing Entertainment: The Elevation of Novel Reading in Britain, 1684–1750* (Berkeley: University of California Press, 1998), pp. 176–230.

Neighbourhood of the happy Pair; & which Gentleman had been, at the Time, several Years dead.

The writing it then, was owing to ye following Occasion: –Two Booksellers, my particular Friends, entreated me to write for them a little Volume of Letters, in a common Style, on such Subjects as might be of Use to those Country Readers who were unable to indite for themselves. Will it be any Harm said I, in a Piece you want to be written so low, if we should instruct them how they should think & act in common Cases, as well as indite? They were the more urgent with me to begin the little Volume for this Hint. I set about it, & in the Progress of it, writing two or three letters to instruct handsome Girls, who were obliged to go out to Service, as we phrase it, how to avoid the Snares that might be laid against their Virtue; the above story recurred to my Thought: And hence sprung Pamela.²

The 'little Volume' Richardson refers to here is *Letters Written to and for Particular Friends, On the Most Important Occasions*, commonly known as *Familiar Letters*, probably begun in September or October of 1739, though its publication was delayed until 23 January 1741, as Richardson turned his attention to completing the project that had so adventitiously 'sprung' from him.³ The one-paragraph Letter CXXXVIII, from 'A Father to a Daughter in Service, on hearing of her Master's attempting her Virtue', is clearly the germ of the second letter in *Pamela*, in which her parents advise Pamela to return to them 'if you find the least Attempt made upon your Virtue' (p. 12). But, unlike the daughter in *Familiar Letters*, who in her answer (Letter CXXXIX) succinctly apprises her father that 'I have this Day left the House', even though her master has not made another 'vile Attempt' (*EW*, p. 464), Pamela stays, a fateful decision not only for herself and her author but also for the history of the English novel. The two booksellers who persuaded Richardson to undertake *Familiar Letters* were his close friends and associates in the printing trade, John Osborn and Charles Rivington, who would also become the booksellers for *Pamela* and from whom, as he informs Stinstra, Richardson 'accepted of 20 Guineas for two Thirds of the Copy-Right; reserving to myself only one Third'.⁴ Given the spectacular success that lay ahead, it is evident, from this split in copyright shares, that Richardson, while cutting a relatively respectable deal for a first-time author of a novel, undersold himself.⁵

---

2 Richardson to Stinstra, 2 June 1753. All references to Richardson's correspondence are to the Cambridge Edition of the Correspondence of Samuel Richardson, gen. eds. Thomas Keymer and Peter Sabor, in progress.

3 Samuel Richardson, *Letters Written to and For Particular Friends, On the Most Important Occasions. Directing not only the Requisite Style and Forms To be Observed in Writing Familiar Letters; But How to Think and Act Justly and Prudently, in the Common Concerns of Human Life* (London, 1741). The full title of this work suggests that the stylistic and formal concerns of the traditional letter-writer are here secondary to issues of moral and ethical conduct.

4 Richardson to Stinstra, 2 June 1753.

5 Other than this figure, we have no other surviving evidence of how much money Richardson made from *Pamela*. William Merritt Sale, Jr, writes that 'an indication of how completely Richardson

A dozen years before his account to Stinstra, in late January or early February 1741, in reply to a query from Aaron Hill, Richardson had offered a similar version of the 'original groundwork of fact, for the general foundation of Pamela's story' but placed the gentleman's telling of it to him 'about twenty-five years ago'. In this earlier, fuller version, Richardson paints a detailed portrait of the lady, 'one of the greatest beauties in England; but the qualities of her mind had no equal: benevolent, prudent, and equally beloved and admired by high and low'. He continues:

That she had been taken at twelve years of age, for the sweetness of her manners and modesty, and for an understanding above her years, by Mr. B—'s mother, a truly worthy lady, to wait on her person. Her parents, ruined by suretiships, were remarkably honest and pious, and had instilled into their daughter's mind the best principles . . .

That the girl, improving daily in beauty, modesty, and genteel and good behaviour, by the time she was fifteen, engaged the attention of her lady's son, a young gentleman of free principles, who, on her lady's death, attempted, by all manner of temptations and devices, to seduce her. That she had recourse to as many innocent stratagems to escape the snares laid for her virtue; once, however, in despair, having been near drowning; that, at last, her noble resistance, watchfulness, and excellent qualities, subdued him, and he thought fit to make her his wife . . . [6]

The details of the original Mrs. B's story are so similar to those represented in *Pamela* that it is difficult to determine whether Richardson is reconstructing or obfuscating the historical origins of his novel, especially when one considers how the 'story' has been transmitted – from Richardson's recollection of a story told to him, 'many years before', by a friend, now dead, who, in turn, had heard it from the landlord of an inn. While it is entirely possible that Richardson, given

underestimated the value of the book as a publishing venture may be found in the fact that in 1776 a one-sixteenth share of *Pamela* sold for £18' (*Samuel Richardson: A Bibliographical Record of His Literary Career with Historical Notes* (New Haven, CT: Yale University Press, 1936), p. 16). But by then, though its popularity had waned, the novel was nonetheless still valuable 'as a publishing venture' precisely because of its initial spectacular success, not to mention Richardson's established reputation as the author of *Clarissa* and *Sir Charles Grandison*. Perhaps a more accurate measure of what a novelist might have expected as a lump sum payment for his work (as was the custom) in the early 1740s may be had in Henry Fielding's willingness (possibly prompted by the pressure of debt) to take only £25 for *Joseph Andrews* before James Thomson advised him to approach Thomson's own publisher, the bookseller Andrew Millar – even though, as Martin C. Battestin suggests, the details of the anecdote describing the selling of *Joseph Andrews* 'are suspiciously elaborate' (General Introduction, *Joseph Andrews*, ed. Martin C. Battestin (Middletown, CT: Wesleyan University Press, 1967), p. xxviii). That Fielding was actually paid £183 11s. might have been the result not only of Millar's munificence but also of the recent success of *Pamela*, which had very likely raised the price of that kind of literature. Millar later paid Fielding £600 for *Tom Jones* and £800–1000 for *Amelia*.

6 Richardson to Hill, [*c.*1 February 1741]. The original of this letter has not survived; the letter is quoted, undated, by Anna Laetitia Barbauld in the biographical preface to her six-volume edition of *The Correspondence of Samuel Richardson* (London, 1804), I, pp. lxix–lxxvi. The date given here is conjectural and derives from Eaves and Kimpel, p. 626. Richardson is answering Hill's letter of 15 January 1741; Hill replies to the letter cited here on 9 February 1741.

his remarkable memory, is accurately recollecting details that he had reused in his novel, it is just as plausible to hypothesize that he is taking details and phrases from the novel he has just published and making them part of his recollection, thus fashioning a 'historical' foundation for Pamela's fictional story. In short, unlike Henry Fielding, who would famously declare that *Joseph Andrews* (1742) had been 'Written in Imitation of The *Manner* of CERVANTES' (title page), Richardson does not identify a prior author or text as his model or inspiration. *Pamela*, he claims, owes its origins to his lucky recollection of a friend's anecdote, not to any tradition of prose fiction, domestic or foreign. Richardson's book does not derive from other books – except, of course, his own *Familiar Letters* – but from oral tradition.

Richardson's claim that his first novel was mostly self-generated has recently come under closer scrutiny. As a result, a critical consensus seems to be emerging that *Pamela* owes far more to earlier fiction – in particular the so-called 'amatory fiction' of such women authors as Aphra Behn, Delarivier Manley, and Eliza Haywood – than Richardson cared to acknowledge.[7] By his own admission, Richardson was not a learned man; his father, he tells Stinstra, had meant him for the clergy but, having sustained 'heavy Losses', was unable to support his son's education. Thus, 'at the Age of 15 or 16', the young man had to choose a 'Business' and chose that of printer because he thought that it 'would gratify my Thirst after Reading'.[8] Richardson devoted the rest of his life to the manufacturing of books, personally setting and proofreading some of them, especially at the beginning of his career. Although he eventually grew independent of the booksellers, he nonetheless continued, as he confides to Stinstra, to be sought by them 'because of the Readiness I shewed to oblige them, with writing Indexes, Prefaces, & sometimes, for their minor Authors, *honest* Dedications; abstracting, abridging, compiling, and giving my Opinion of Pieces offered them'.[9] Richardson, in short, was an active participant in the London publishing trade, both as printer and, in his other activities for the booksellers, as arbiter of what they published and, perhaps more important, of how they marketed those publications. While it is dangerous to assume that Richardson read every book he printed – or that he read only books that he printed and little else – a list of such books is a good place to start any inquiry into his reading.[10] The attribution of his authorship to an anonymous preface or dedication

---

7 See, for example, William B. Warner, 'The Elevation of the Novel in England: Hegemony and Literary History', *ELH* 59 (1992), 577–96. Warner argues that, in claiming to inaugurate a 'new species' of writing, Richardson and Fielding 'disavow' their debt to the novels of such women authors as Behn, Manley, and Haywood (p. 583). Warner offers a fuller exposition of his argument in *Licensing Entertainment*.

8 Richardson to Stinstra, 2 June 1753.   9 Ibid.

10 For the most up-to-date record of items, including books, newspapers, and parliamentary bills, printed by Richardson, see Keith Maslen, *Samuel Richardson of London, Printer: A Study of his*

is, of course, more difficult, though one can make some educated guesses based on content and style.

The evidence for Richardson's acquaintance with earlier amatory fiction is circumstantial and, therefore, to be interpreted with caution. The first piece of evidence is his printing of the first and fourth volumes of the third edition of Eliza Haywood's *Secret Histories, Novels, and Poems* in 1732.[11] The first volume contains the whole of Haywood's immensely popular first novel, *Love in Excess: or, the Fatal Enquiry*, originally published in three instalments in 1719–20; the fourth volume contains three novels – *The Rash Resolve: Or, The Untimely Discovery* (1724); *Lasselia: Or, The Self-Abandon'd* (1724); and *The Force of Nature: Or, The Lucky Disappointment* (1725) – and a 'secret history', *The Masqueraders: Or, Fatal Curiosity* (1725). None of these works can be regarded as a specific 'source' for Richardson's novel, except in the general sense that, like most of Haywood's early fiction, they all tell stories of seduction, of young virgins beset by predatory males, in suitably 'inflaming' language. Three years later, in 1735, Richardson printed an edition of Haywood's play, *A Wife to be Lett* (1724).[12] Haywood had also been part of Aaron Hill's literary circle in the 1720s; it was during that decade, when Richardson launched his career as printer and began to print Hill's works, that Haywood was the most prolific novelist in England.[13] There is little doubt, then, that though there is no evidence that he knew her personally, Richardson knew of Haywood and of her works. Thus, when he singles out for particular attack on *Pamela*'s title page the 'too many Pieces calculated for Amusement only, [that] tend to *inflame* the Minds they should *instruct*', we have good reason to suspect that he is very likely alluding to the kind of novel identified most closely – because of her prodigious rate of publication in the 1720s and 1730s – with Haywood, the 'Great Arbitress of Passion', as she is called in a poem by James Sterling fronting the first volume of *Secret Histories, Novels, and Poems*.[14]

The second piece of evidence, connecting Richardson with a woman novelist whose career may be read as the antithesis of Haywood's, is the anonymous preface to *A Collection of Entertaining Histories and Novels* (1739), a three-volume

Printing Based on Ornament Use and Business Accounts (Dunedin: University of Otago, 2001). Maslen greatly expands and sometimes corrects the pioneering bibliographical work of William Merritt Sale, Jr, *Samuel Richardson: Master Printer* (Ithaca, NY: Cornell University Press, 1950).

11 Maslen, p. 90, items 323–4 (not listed in Sale (1950)).

12 Ibid., item 325 (Sale (1950), pp. 173–4, item 171).

13 On Haywood's connections with Hill, see Christine Gerrard, *Aaron Hill: The Muses' Projector, 1685–1750* (Oxford University Press, 2003), pp. 66–77; see also Kathryn R. King, 'Eliza Haywood, Savage Love, and Biographical Uncertainty', *Review of English Studies* 59 (2008), 722–39.

14 'To Mrs. Haywood, On her Writings', *Secret Histories, Novels, and Poems, In Four Volumes. Written by Mrs. Eliza Haywood* (London, 1732), I, [p. ii]. Sterling also famously places Haywood within a tradition of eminent women writers: 'Pathetic *Behn*, or *Manley*'s greater Name; / Forget their Sex, and own when *Haywood* writ, / She clos'd the Fair Triumvirate of Wit' [p. iii].

compilation of the fictional works of Penelope Aubin, who seems to have died around 1731. Aubin's production in the 1720s had nearly matched Haywood's, if not in number certainly in variety of publications. 'Designed to promote the Cause of Virtue and Honor' (title page), the Aubin collection was published by a conger of booksellers, some of whom were closely associated with Richardson, such as Arthur Bettesworth, Charles Hitch, and the man soon to be instrumental in the publication of *Pamela*, Charles Rivington. In an article published in 1981, Wolfgang Zach presents a compelling argument for identifying this preface as one of those pieces Richardson, in his letter to Stinstra, claims to have written for the booksellers.[15] Zach finds parallels between views expressed in this preface and Richardson's repeated pronouncements on the moral aims of fiction, especially his own, in both his letters and publications; he also shows striking verbal similarities between the anonymous writer's style and Richardson's, including the presence of neologisms peculiar to Richardson. Short of discovering more convincing proof of authorship, such as a manuscript copy in his own hand, we can be reasonably confident that Richardson is indeed the author of this preface and can examine it to learn what he – or somebody who seems to have felt and written just like him – thought about the state of prose fiction near the end of the decade that would close with the publication of *Pamela*.

For the author of the preface, novels 'are principally of Use to divert and entertain the Minds of young Persons'.[16] Thus, just as Samuel Johnson would argue in the fourth *Rambler* (31 March 1750) at the end of the 1740s – a decade which, in the wake of *Pamela*, witnessed a surge in the publication of works of prose fiction – novels should be unequivocally moral. Unfortunately, 'those who have undertaken this Species of Writing' have not followed this didactic path and have 'brought a Disreputation on the very Name' of novels (*EW*, p. 95). These writers, identified as mostly female though no particular names are named, are 'like the *fallen Angels*, [who] having lost their own Innocence, seem, as one would think by their Writings, to make it their Study to corrupt the Minds of others, and render them as depraved, as miserable, and as lost as themselves' (*EW*, ibid.). In letter CXLVII of *Familiar Letters*, Richardson warns of the affective dangers of this kind of writing by focusing on a typically naïve female reader: 'The Maid may hope, may fansy much, in the Commerce between the Sexes, from her meditating on the heighten'd Scenes, which pernicious Novels, and idle Romances, the Poison of Female Minds, abound with' (*EW*, p. 480). Such was not

15 Wolfgang Zach, 'Mrs. Aubin and Richardson's Earliest Literary Manifesto (1739)', *English Studies* 62 (1981), 271–85.
16 Penelope Aubin, *A Collection of Entertaining Histories and Novels*, DESIGNED *To promote the Cause of VIRTUE and HONOUR. Principally founded on* FACTS, *and interspersed with a Variety of beautiful and instructive Incidents* (1739), *EW*, p. 94.

the case of Mrs Aubin, who 'had a far happier Manner of Thinking and Acting. She disdained to paint the guilty Scenes of Folly and Vanity in such Colours as might conceal their natural Deformity, and make the most unlovely and pernicious Vices amiable.'[17] A consummate practitioner of the 'good Novel', she makes 'her Heroes and Heroines . . . successful or unsuccessful, happy or unhappy, according to their Merit' (*EW*, p. 96). All of her writings, in short, tend 'to that one uniform End . . . the mending of the Hearts of her Readers; the Encouragement of Religion and Virtue; and the discountenancing of Impiety and Vice' (*EW*, pp. 95–6). These moral aims are precisely those Richardson professes to follow in *Pamela*, as he tacitly aligns his reforming efforts with those of 'good' novelists such as Aubin (whom, of course, he does not mention) and against the corrupting temptations of such 'fallen' novelists as the unnamed Haywood.

As he nears the end of his assessment of contemporary novels and of Aubin's exemplary opposition to their pernicious tendencies, the author of the preface notes her dedication of *The Life of Charlotta du Pont* (1723) to 'the celebrated Mrs. *Rowe*, with whom she had an Intimacy, as we there see, and may farther reasonably infer from the Tenor of both their Writings, for the Promotion of the Cause of Religion and Virtue, and from that Affinity and Kindred of Souls, which will always make the Worthy find out one another, and create stronger Ties of Union and Friendship than those of Blood' (*EW*, p. 97). The mention of Rowe at this point might reveal another clue as to the identity of the author of the preface. Richardson might have been thinking of Aubin's 'Kindred' spirit (who had died in 1737) at around this time, as he had recently printed part of the second volume of *The Miscellaneous Works in Prose and Verse of Mrs. Elizabeth Rowe*, published in 1738.[18] He would soon print the 1740 edition of her popular *Friendship in Death: In Twenty Letters from the Dead to the Living* (which Rowe had dedicated to Richardson's future friend, Edward Young), originally published in 1728 – the year when, coincidentally, Pope had famously skewered Eliza Haywood in the original *Dunciad* to expose, as Scriblerus explains in a note added in *The Dunciad Variorum* (1729), 'the profligate licenciousness of those shameless scriblers (for the most part of That sex, which ought least to be capable of such malice or impudence) who in libelous Memoirs and Novels, reveal the faults and misfortunes of both sexes . . .'[19] Thus, the author of the preface is echoing an old and well-known line of attack on scandalous women novelists. In this respect, one could argue that Richardson's project in writing *Pamela* derives, in some measure, from

---

17 Aubin, *A Collection of Entertaining Histories and Novels*, EW, p. 95.
18 Maslen, p. 133, item 718 (*Friendship in Death* is item 716).
19 Alexander Pope, *The Dunciad, Variorum. With the Prolegomena of Scriblerus* (London, 1729), p. 35.

Pope, who had memorably identified Haywood as the quintessentially immoral female novelist. By following Pope (who would later praise *Pamela*) in attacking disreputable novelists, and by advancing that Aubin and Rowe have, in essence, created a counter tradition, the author of the preface to *A Collection of Entertaining Histories and Novels* establishes the context – and offers a rationale – for the writing and publication of Richardson's own 'reforming' novel.

While *Pamela* might have 'sprung' from its author's lucky recollection of a twice-told tale, it can also be seen, then, as belonging to an English tradition of morally explicit novels, written mostly by women who are presented to the reading public – or represent themselves in their prefaces and dedications – as pious and virtuous. Richardson obliquely connects his work with this tradition by identifying on its title page and in its preface some of the 'inflaming' features of the type of novel he is *not* offering his young readers in the ensuing sheets. In this respect, he follows the marketing strategies of those 'good' novels, which are usually presented to the public as moral correctives to a corrupting genre. Richardson also studiously avoids the term 'novel' as a label for his 'little Work' (Preface), in a further strategic move to escape the Haywoodian taint, the 'Disreputation' of the name.

The revelation of a possible tradition for *Pamela* raises the intriguing question of whether Richardson was basing his novel on an earlier work – or group of works – which he also chose to leave unnamed. Several plausible sources for *Pamela* have been suggested but, so far, a fully convincing case remains to be made for any of them. As is well known, Richardson appears to have borrowed the (for the time) unusual name 'Pamela' from Sidney's *Arcadia*, possibly through Steele's *The Tender Husband*, a play Mr. and Mrs. B. attend in the sequel – though no such mediation needs to be posited, since Richardson had been one of the printers of a collected edition of Sidney's works published in 1724–5.[20] But, other than its country setting and vaguely pastoral romance themes, Richardson's work has little in common with Sidney's. The story of 'Amanda', told by John Hughes in *The Spectator*, no. 375 (Saturday, 10 May 1712), bears some resemblance to Pamela's, leading William Bowyer to assert, many years later, that 'Mr. Richardson's *Pamela*

---

20 *The Works of the Honourable Sir Philip Sidney*, 3 vols. (London, 1724). Maslen, p. 139, items 766–7. As Sale (1950) notes, Richardson printed the introductory matter in the first volume and all of the third volume; the five books of the *Arcadia* appear in the first two volumes (p. 204, item 41). Though he makes reference to Sale, who gets the information right, Maslen errs in claiming that Vol. III contains the *Arcadia*. Instead, the third volume opens with 'A Sixth book to the Countess of Pembroke's Arcadia. Written by R.B. of *Lincoln's-Inn*, Esq'; the volume concludes with a 'Postscript' ([pp. 185–7]), drawn from 'the Guardian (N°· 18)', featuring an English version of Psalm 137 (the same Psalm adapted by Pamela), supposedly left by Sidney in 'Manuscript' but 'never . . . printed' ([p. 185]). This number of *The Guardian*, originally published on Wednesday, 1 April 1713, was written by Sir Richard Steele.

is no other than the story in vol. V, No. 375. And perhaps it appears with as much advantage in its original brevity, as in its diffused length of a volume.'[21] But the resemblance is general and, though Richardson was familiar with *The Spectator*, there is no evidence that he was acquainted with this particular number or had it in mind when he wrote *Pamela*. Nor is there evidence that Richardson, though he had printed other works by Defoe, was familiar with *Moll Flanders* (1722) – a work not yet attributed to Defoe – in which Moll, finding herself in a situation similar to Pamela's, details how she withstood and then yielded to the blandishments of the elder brother in Colchester. Defoe's pose as 'editor' of 'historical' first person narratives, of course, anticipates Richardson's, but there is no warrant for supposing direct influence, given the commonplace nature of such a narrative strategy by Richardson's time.

While it is relatively easy, then, to adduce possible domestic sources for *Pamela*, it is far more difficult to prove that Richardson was specifically imitating any one of them. Even a work with the same phrase in its title – *Vertue Rewarded; or, The Irish Princess* (1693) – resembles *Pamela* only in so far as 'virtue rewarded' narratives featuring female protagonists tend to resemble each other.[22] But what about foreign sources? One contemporary reader, while not claiming direct influence, was certainly open to the possibility. The anonymous author of *Pamela Censured* (published on 25 April 1741), in answer to his own leading question, 'Was no Romance or Novel ever published with a Design to recommend moral Virtue? – Is *Pamela* the First of that Kind!', sneers that '*La Paysanne parvenu* now translated into *English*, a little *French* Novel, is something more modest, and as much calculated for the Encouragement of Virtue.'[23] The work alluded to, written by Charles de Fieux, chevalier de Mouhy, had indeed been recently translated as *The Fortunate Country Maid* (1740), but probably too late for Richardson (who could not read French) to be influenced by it – not to mention that, other than both heroines being country girls who marry up, the first person narrative of '*Jane*, Daughter of *John B*. Woodcutter' shares very little with Pamela's.[24]

---

21 John Nichols, *Literary Anecdotes of the Eighteenth Century*, 6 vols. (London, 1812), II, p. 443. Bowyer makes this observation in a letter, dated 14 June 1764, on the occasion of a forthcoming edition of *The Spectator*.

22 Paul Salzman appears to have been the first scholar to note the resemblance in titles. See his '"Vertue Rewarded" and "Pamela"', *Notes and Queries*, New Series 26 (1979), 554–6. Salzman raises the possibility of Richardson's indebtedness to *Vertue Rewarded*. Without acknowledging Salzman, Hubert McDermott makes a largely unconvincing attempt to prove that this Irish work is a 'credible source' for *Pamela* (*Novel and Romance: The Odyssey to Tom Jones* (Totowa, NJ: Barnes & Noble Books, 1989), pp. 157–69). McDermott repeats his argument in the introduction to his edition of the novel; see *Vertue Rewarded; or, The Irish Princess*, ed. Hubert McDermott (Gerrards Cross: Colin Smythe, 1992), pp. xxviii–xl.

23 *Pamela Censured: In a Letter to the Editor* (London, 1741), pp. 6–7.

24 Charles de Fieux, chevalier de Mouhy, *The Fortunate Country Maid. Being the Entertaining Memoirs of the Present Celebrated Marchioness of L. V.*, 2 vols. (London, 1740), I, p. 1.

There is, however, another possible French source that deserves consideration. *The Life of Marianne*, a translation of part of Marivaux's *La Vie de Marianne* (1731–41), had appeared in 1736, with a second volume following in 1741 and a third in 1742. This translation had been preceded, in 1735, by a translation of Marivaux's *Le Paysan parvenu*, the model of de Mouhy's work mentioned in *Pamela Censured* – suggesting, perhaps, an interest in Marivaux's fiction in the years surrounding the writing and publication of *Pamela*. Although we have no specific evidence that Richardson read Marivaux's fiction, either before writing *Pamela* or afterwards, from 1736 to 1743 he printed several books, including translations from French works, for Charles Davis, the bookseller responsible for *The Life of Marianne*.[25] One of these works, *The History of the Heavens* (1740–1), was translated from Noël Antoine Pluché's original by Richardson's friend, Jean Baptiste de Freval, whose involvement with *Pamela* we shall discuss below and who, though we have no proof that he did so, might have made Richardson acquainted with contemporary French fiction.[26] *The Life of Marianne*, we are told in the 'advertisement', is not a 'meer Fiction' but the autobiographical 'reflections' of its virtuous female protagonist, contained in a manuscript that the author 'had . . . from a Friend'[27] – a story of origins recalling that of *Pamela*. Without explicitly posing as such, the author professes to be nothing more than the editor of Marianne's first person story of her 'adventures': 'In short, this Work is intirely hers, the Alteration of a few Words excepted.'[28] While Marianne's story shares some similarities with Pamela's in narrative strategy and subject-matter – the destitute fifteen-year-old Marianne is also besieged by a man under whose protection she finds herself – there is little in the volume available to Richardson before writing *Pamela* that could be regarded as source material. Indeed, the portion of Marianne's story that might be read as potentially analogous to Pamela's does not begin until the second volume, not published (as noted above) until 1741. When, years later, William Warburton raised the possibility of the author's indebtedness to French sources in a preface he wrote for *Clarissa*, Richardson emphatically denied it: 'Then as to what you are pleased to hint, that I pursued in my former Piece the excellent Plan fallen upon lately by the French Writers, I would only observe that all that know me, know, that I am not acquainted in the least either with the French Language or Writers; and that it was Chance and not Skill or Learning, that made me fall into this way of Scribbling.'[29] If nothing else, Richardson stuck to his story of

25 On Richardson and Davis, see Sale (1950), p. 323.
26 Richardson printed the original two volumes of *The History of the Heavens* in 1740 and reissues of both volumes in 1741; see Maslen, p. 117, items 564–7.
27 Pierre Carlet de Chamblain de Marivaux, *The Life of Marianne: or, The Adventures of the Countess of* *** (London, 1736), p. 1.
28 Ibid., p. 2.   29 Richardson to Warburton, 14 April 1748.

xlii GENERAL INTRODUCTION

deriving his work from 'chance', from his own invention. Except for his reluctance to acknowledge, in more explicit terms, his general debt to the works of such 'good' novelists as Aubin and Rowe, which might have compromised his claims of authenticity regarding Pamela's letters, his still remains the most authoritative account of the origins of *Pamela* that we have.

By the time *Pamela* accidentally 'sprung' from him, then, Richardson had become a successful and well-respected member of the London printing world. He had established his printing business in 1721 in a house in Salisbury Court, off Fleet Street, in a solidly middle-class neighbourhood, inhabited mostly by tradesmen, where he would stay for the rest of his life.[30] A quick review of his principal printing activities and publications before he began writing *Familiar Letters* will round out this brief synopsis of the professional circumstances of the man who, at the age of fifty, was about to be surprised by the 'strange Success at Publication' of his first novel and to be 'complimented' as the founder of 'a New Species of Writing'.[31] As his biographers document, in the early 1720s Richardson printed several pamphlets by Archibald Hutcheson, a Tory Member of Parliament for Hastings, attacking the Walpole administration; Hutcheson, whose views are cited as those of an 'old friend' by Lord M. in *Clarissa*, might also be a source for Mr. B.'s professions of political impartiality in *Pamela*.[32] But while in the 1740s, especially after Walpole's fall in 1742, references to Hutcheson might have lost most of their political sting, such was not the case in the years when Richardson was printing for him, in the immediate aftermath of the collapse of the South Sea scheme. In fact, except for the first edition of Jonathan Smedley's *Poems on Several Occasions* and *Instructions for the Education of a Daughter* (translated from Fénelon), both published in 1721, Richardson seems to have printed almost exclusively for Hutcheson until 1723. Then, in 1723, in addition to three more pamphlets by Hutcheson, Richardson printed works by Francis Atterbury, Bishop of Rochester, and the Reverend George Kelly, both of whom had been imprisoned (with Bishop Atterbury being banished) after being convicted by Parliament of involvement in the failed Jacobite plot of 1722.[33] It was also in 1723 that Richardson began his association with the notorious Duke of Wharton, a stalwart opponent of the Walpole government, who had vigorously advocated the exoneration of Bishop Atterbury in a speech, printed by Richardson, given in the House of Lords on 15 May 1723.[34] Although he professed to espouse 'Old Whig' principles

---

30 See T. C. Duncan Eaves and Ben D. Kimpel, 'Samuel Richardson's London Houses', *Studies in Bibliography* 15 (1962), 135–48.
31 Richardson to Hill, 26 January 1746/7.   32 See p. 373 below as well as annotation to this passage.
33 For a chronology of works Richardson printed during these years, see Sale (1950), pp. 229–30.
34 *His grace the Duke of Wharton's speech in the house of Lords, on the third reading of the bill to inflict pains and penalties on Francis (late) lord bishop of Rochester* (1723). Richardson printed two editions of this speech (see Maslen, p. 152, items 883–4).

of individual liberty, Wharton revealed his true allegiances when he eventually joined the Jacobite court in exile. But, as Eaves and Kimpel sensibly advance, 'that the Duke of Wharton was later an open Jacobite does not, of course, imply that Richardson himself was one'.[35] A whiff of disloyalty seems nonetheless to have attached itself to Richardson, with his name being given sometime in 1722 to Lord Townshend, then Secretary of State, by Samuel Negus, a rival printer, as part of a group of printers 'Said to be High Flyers' – a term used to identify extreme Tories.[36] Whatever his true political leanings – though his voting for Tory candidates in the 1720s might give us a clue as to which side he favoured[37] – Richardson printed the whole run of Wharton's bi-weekly newspaper, *The True Briton*, from 3 June 1723 to 17 February 1724, and might even have contributed to it.[38] The man identified as its publisher, Thomas Payne, was prosecuted at various times, fined, and imprisoned, with Richardson posting a portion of his bail at least twice.[39] Although Richardson was not the object of such prosecution – his name never appearing in any of these inflammatory publications – there was, as Thomas Keymer has phrased it, 'a strongly dissident cast to [his] early output as a printer'.[40]

After Wharton's mounting debts and other personal difficulties led to the demise of *The True Briton*, Richardson began to move away from his association with Tory propaganda and, as his business grew, started to print less politically controversial material.[41] In 1724, for example, he printed part of the second edition of Nathan Bailey's *An Universal Etymological English Dictionary* for a group of printers that included Bettesworth and Rivington, as well as several numbers (32 to 60) of *The Plain Dealer*, a bi-weekly newspaper edited by William Bond and Aaron Hill, which, while beginning as the apparent successor to *The True Briton*,

---

35 Eaves and Kimpel, p. 30.   36 Ibid., p. 21.   37 Ibid., p. 31.

38 Ibid., p. 28: 'The factotums and arrangements of flowers in the periodical, however, show almost incontrovertibly that Richardson was the printer not only of the first numbers but of the whole run of the periodical.' Maslen agrees that 'all 74 numbers were printed by Richardson' (p. 299).

39 Eaves and Kimpel, p. 28.

40 Thomas Keymer, Introduction, *Pamela: or, Virtue Rewarded*, ed. Thomas Keymer and Alice Wakely (Oxford University Press, 2001), p. x.

41 But, even as late as 1728, Richardson found himself suspected of Jacobite associations, when the infamous bookseller Edmund Curll accused him of being involved in the printing of a virulent anti-government issue of *Mist's Weekly Journal* (Saturday, 24 August 1728). As Eaves and Kimpel write, 'this issue, reportedly sent from France by Wharton, immediately stimulated the government to the biggest prosecution of the press in the decade' (p. 33). Eaves and Kimpel suggest that Curll, while no doubt meaning to smear Richardson's reputation, might actually have been claiming that Richardson printed not the offending number of *Mist's* but the one published the following week, on 31 August, 'which was not objected to' (p. 32). McKillop observes that 'Curll's allegation was probably irresponsible, but shows that Richardson's connection with Wharton was still remembered. Before and after August, 1728, some of Richardson's advertisements appear in *Mist's Weekly Journal*, or, as it was renamed in consequence of this affair, *Fog's Weekly Journal*. Thus he had at least casual business relations with the offending newspaper, and may have had some sympathy with its politics as late as 1728' (p. 297). In the event, Richardson once again escaped prosecution.

did not concern itself with politics. The following year he printed the second half of Defoe's *A New Voyage Round the World* and began his long association with Defoe's *A Tour Thro' the Whole Island of Great Britain*, printing part of its second volume, which included indexes he probably compiled; he would print five more editions of this work (the last appearing in 1761, the year he died), becoming its 'editor' probably as early as 1738, with its second edition. Over the next few years, Richardson would also be involved in the printing of editions or reissues of other works by Defoe, including the second volume of the third edition of *The Complete English Tradesman* (1732, for Rivington), *A New Family Instructor* (1727; 1732, for Rivington; 1742), and the second edition of *Religious Courtship* (1729); these last two works, in their colloquial, circumstantial style and heavy-handed didacticism, look forward to *Pamela*. In 1725, he also printed the preface (written by Edmund Curll) to *Mrs. Manley's History of Her Own Life and Times* – a repackaging of the pseudo-biographical *Adventures of Rivella* (1714) by Delarivier Manley, who had recently died – a title no doubt meant to recall Bishop Gilbert Burnet's *History of His Own Time*, the first volume of which had been published in 1724. Other works of note Richardson printed either wholly or in part in the 1720s and 1730s included an abridgement of *Gulliver's Travels* (1727); *The Adventures of Telemachus* (1728, translated from Fénelon); two pamphlets of 'remarks' on Pope's works by John Dennis, on *The Rape of the Lock* (1728) and on 'preliminaries' to *The Dunciad* (1729); James Thomson's *Britannia* (1729) and *The Seasons* (1730); several works by his friend and physician, George Cheyne, including *The English Malady* (1733); two editions (1733, 1738) of William Law's *The Oxford Methodists*; Mary Barber's *Poems on Several Occasions* (1734, for Rivington), to which he subscribed and which was introduced by 'a recommendatory letter' from Swift to Lord Orrery; and two sermons by the Methodist George Whitefield, *The Benefits of An Early Piety* and *The Nature and Necessity of Our New Birth in Christ Jesus, in Order to Salvation* (both published in 1737 and printed for Rivington). During these two decades, he began to print for the House of Commons (which he would continue to do until his death) and was also involved in printing such periodicals as *The Daily Journal* (1725–37) and William Webster's *The Weekly Miscellany* (1732–6), *The Prompter* (1734–6; edited by Aaron Hill, William Popple, and others), *The Citizen* (1739); and, as the political affiliation of his printing press seemed to have fully shifted, he was very likely the printer of *The Daily Gazetteer* (1735–46), a vehicle for the Whig ministry.[42]

By the end of 1739, then, the output of Richardson's printing press was large, varied, and rather eclectic in subject-matter; it also included two anonymous

---

42 For a good analysis of Richardson's political views, see Margaret Anne Doody, 'Richardson's Politics', *Eighteenth-Century Fiction* 2 (1990), 113–26.

pamphlets, now attributed to him, as well as an edition of *Æsop's Fables*, which will be briefly described below. The first pamphlet, *The Apprentice's Vade Mecum: Or, Young Man's Pocket-Companion*, dated 1734 but published in late 1733, consists of three parts, with the second and third parts having their own title pages; a preface, detailed table of contents, and marginal glosses facilitate the young reader's progress through it. Part II seems to have derived from a 'familiar' letter of advice Richardson had written to his fifteen-year-old nephew, Thomas Verren Richardson, who had become his apprentice in August 1732 but who would die by November of that year.[43] Because the 'Time of Apprenticeship' is 'the most giddy and dangerous Period of Time in the whole Life of Man' (*EW*, p. 29), this part contains 'Summary Rules and Directions for the Behaviour of Young Men' which, if 'duly observ'd, Will lay a Foundation for their present Ease and Benefit, and their future Prosperity and Happiness' (Part II, title page). Part III specifically addresses the dangers of atheism and deism for 'a young Man' and offers 'some brief Cautions . . . against the Scepticism and Infidelity of the present Age' (*EW*, p. 44), including a warning against joining 'Clubs and Societies' erected for the purpose of encouraging 'Religious Doubts'; 'such Company', if not avoided by the impressionable youth, will become 'the Bane of his future Peace and Welfare' (*EW*, p. 59). Part I defines the terms of the 'Covenants entered into between Master and Servant' (*EW*, p. 15) and offers injunctions against fornication, marrying during apprenticeship, gaming, trafficking in goods without licence from one's master, and, most important perhaps, a 'double Restriction' not 'to haunt Taverns or Play-houses' (*EW*, p. 18). Although the author 'frankly' acknowledges that, if properly regulated, 'the *Stage* may be made subservient to excellent Purposes, and be an useful Second to the *Pulpit* itself' (*EW*, p. 19), he believes that playhouses are nonetheless to be avoided by the young tradesman or apprentice because, among other things, they encourage idleness, are 'the great Resort of lewd Women', and ridicule 'Men of Business' (*EW*, p. 20). In short, 'because of the shameful Depravity of the *British Stage*', playhouses are bad for 'all Ranks', but especially so for tradesmen (*EW*, ibid.). Thus, while playhouses 'at the gay End of the Town may be tolerated for the Amusement of Persons in upper Life', they 'must be of pernicious Consequence when set up in the City, or in those Confines of it, where the People of Industry generally inhabit' (*EW*, p. 23). Part I of *The Apprentice's Vade Mecum* forms the basis – with passages from it cited as corroboration – of the second anonymous pamphlet attributed to Richardson, *A Seasonable Examination of the Pleas and Pretensions of the Proprietors of, and Subscribers to, Play-houses* (1735). Written in support of a bill intended to regulate the number of playhouses, it was aimed specifically at 'the Subscribers to the Theatre in *Goodman's-Fields*'

---

43 Eaves and Kimpel, p. 51.

(*EW*, p. 66), one of the playhouses 'erected in Defiance of the Royal Licence' (*EW*, p. 64), whose corrupting influence on its working-class neighbourhood the author describes in great and damning detail. When in the sequel Pamela attends the theatre with Mr. B., she does so as a person 'in upper Life'; her mostly negative opinions on the plays she sees, however, are informed by the 'City' values Richardson expresses in these two pamphlets.[44]

Like *The Apprentice's Vade Mecum*, Richardson's edition of *Æsop's Fables* was intended for the instruction of young people – 'adapted to all capacities', as blazoned on its title page. It was undertaken, as Richardson explains to Stinstra, upon request from a bookseller – in this case, John Osborn, Jr, the son of the John Osborn responsible for *Familiar Letters* and *Pamela* – and was published on 20 November 1739, ten days after Richardson began writing the first draft of his novel.[45] Richardson acknowledges in his preface that, given that there are 'so many Editions' of the work, 'some Reasons should be given for the Appearance of a new one'.[46] 'Of all the *English* Editions', he considers 'only two, as worthy of Notice... That of the celebrated Sir *Roger Lestrange*, and that which appears under the Name of *S. Croxal*' (*EW*, p. 102). Although the Reverend Samuel Croxall's *Fables of Æsop and Others*, first published in 1722, would prove more popular than L'Estrange's version, on which it was based, racking up well over forty editions by the second half of the nineteenth century, it is Sir Roger's *Fables of Æsop and Other Eminent Mythologists*, published in two volumes in 1691 and 1699, that Richardson chooses as his model. As he argues, Croxall, whom he calls '*this tedious Declaimer*' (*EW*, p. 105), makes 'the depreciating' of L'Estrange's work 'the Corner-Stone of his own Building' (*EW*, p. 104), with all of his objections boiling down to a 'Quarrel... against the *Politicks* of Sir *Roger*' (*EW*, p. 105). While he 'heartily' agrees with Croxall that 'Sir *Roger* was certainly listed in a bad Cause as to Politicks, and his Reflections have many of them a pernicious Tendency', Richardson suggests that an impartial, 'charitable Mind' would regard the anarchical time in which L'Estrange wrote, immediately after the conclusion of the Civil Wars, 'if not in *Excuse*, yet in *Extenuation*, of the Fault' (*EW*, ibid.). However, Richardson does not agree with Croxall's more untenable charge, that Sir Roger was a Catholic, and mounts a spirited defence in a footnote: 'Not any of his Works, High-flier as he was, shew him to be a Papist' (*EW*, p. 104). In the event, though knowing what

44 It is important to stress that Richardson was not so much objecting to theatres as to theatres in the wrong neighbourhood. On this topic, see Tom Keymer, *Richardson's Clarissa and the Eighteenth-Century Reader* (Cambridge University Press, 1992), pp. 145–9.
45 Richardson to Stinstra, 2 June 1753. On the Osborns, see T. C. Duncan Eaves and Ben D. Kimpel, 'The Publisher of *Pamela* and its First Audience', *Bulletin of the New York Public Library* 64 (1960), 143–6 (pp. 143–4); and Sale (1950), pp. 332–4.
46 Samuel Richardson, *Æsop's Fables. With Instructive Morals and Reflections* (London, 1740), *EW*, p. 102.

has been 'said against Sir *Roger*'s Style', Richardson prefers his 'fine Original' over Croxall's 'bungling Imitation' because of its 'fine Humour, apposite Language, [and] accurate and lively Manner' (*EW*, p. 106). It is thus certain that the volume of *Æsop's Fables* Pamela finds among 'my Lady's Books' (p. 71), and in whose stories she finds several parallels to her own, is L'Estrange's, possibly the 'corrected' fifth edition published in 1708 – though 'the Æsop quoted in Pamela', is, of course, Richardson's, as noted, for example, in *The Daily Advertiser* (23 December 1742), in an advertisement that also includes the octavo *Pamela*. While Richardson claims to have muted or removed the 'Political Turn' (*EW*, p. 109) of L'Estrange's work from the fables he has selected or abridged for his own edition, he asserts that 'we have, in our Reflections . . . always given that Preference to the Principles of LIBERTY, which we hope will for ever be the distinguishing Characteristic of a *Briton*' (*EW*, ibid.). Richardson's professions of impartiality, of giving 'Preference to the Principles of LIBERTY', though reminiscent of some of Wharton's pronouncements in the 1720s, seem to provide evidence of a moderate, neutral political position at the time he begins writing *Pamela*; his eloquent, heartfelt advocacy of the work of the 'High-flier' L'Estrange against the partisan attacks of the virulently Whig Croxall might also suggest that there was (perhaps) still a Tory lurking in his heart.

Whether Richardson was ever a Tory or a Tory-sympathizer or, what is more relevant to our purposes here, held Tory or quasi-Tory views at the time he wrote *Pamela* remains a matter of speculation. To be sure, as we have seen, there are some tantalizing clues but we simply do not have enough of them. We know more of Richardson's private life after the publication of *Pamela*, when he becomes a celebrated author and begins to keep and catalogue his correspondence, than we know before it. Because of his reluctance to acknowledge antecedents for his work, we also find ourselves in the realm of speculation when it comes to searching for the literary origins of his first novel. One such possible – and obvious – antecedent might be previous epistolary fiction. The fully acknowledged influence of Sir Roger L'Estrange on his edition of *Æsop's Fables*, for example, has led critics to wonder whether Richardson, in the words of McKillop, 'may not have known one of L'Estrange's most important translations, his version of the *Five Love Letters from a Portuguese Nun to a Cavalier*'.[47] Purporting to be genuine letters written by a distraught Portuguese nun – who identifies herself as 'poor Mariane' – to a French officer, who has seduced and abandoned her, *Les Lettres portugaises* (1669), attributed to Gabriel Joseph de la Vergne, vicomte de Guilleragues, was 'Done out of *French* into *English*' (title page) by L'Estrange as *Five Love-Letters from a Nun to a Cavalier* (1678). The work had gone through several editions and

47 McKillop, p. 314.

adaptations (including one 'done into verse' in 1713) during the first four decades of the eighteenth century.[48] What made the Portuguese letters so popular and influential on subsequent European epistolary fiction was their powerful and apparently unmediated revelation of 'real' private passion. While Pamela does not write 'love letters', she does write, like the Portuguese nun, with a rawness, intensity, and immediacy that capture her emotions as they arise. We do not know (because he does not tell) whether Richardson was aware of, or influenced by, L'Estrange's translation or by the 'Portuguese' style of such epistolary novels as Aphra Behn's *Love-Letters between a Nobleman and His Sister*, published in three parts between 1684 and 1687, with a reissue of the 'sixth edition' (1721) appearing in 1735–6, at around the same time as the 'authentic' confessions of another 'poor' Marianne (Marivaux's) became available to the mere English reader.[49] What we do know, however, is that, while remaining typically evasive regarding the origins of his narrative method, Richardson deemed 'writing to the moment' – one of the most striking features of the 'Portuguese' style – the distinguishing characteristic of his epistolary art.[50]

PUBLICATION AND EARLY RECEPTION

As Richardson would later inform Aaron Hill, he wrote *Pamela* 'so diligently, through all my other business, that, by a memorandum on my copy, I began it Nov. 10 1739, and finished it Jan. 10 1739–40'.[51] As Eaves and Kimpel have calculated,

48 A 'seventh edition' of the *Five Love-Letters*, 'Done into Verse', was published in 1731 by the booksellers Arthur Bettesworth and Charles Hitch, for whom Richardson sometimes printed.
49 The 'sixth edition' of Behn's *Love-Letters* published in 1721, in three volumes, and the reissue of 1735–6, in two, were published by the same group of booksellers, except that Benjamin Motte (the publisher of *Gulliver's Travels*) replaces Benjamin Tooke in the colophon of the latter. Richardson printed for several of these booksellers (e.g., W. Mears, George Strahan, and Jacob Tonson). A 'seventh edition', in three volumes, appeared in 1759; among its publishers were Charles Hitch and Andrew Millar.
50 See the Preface to *SCG*: 'The Nature of Familiar Letters, written, as it were, to the *Moment*, while the heart is agitated by Hopes and Fears, on Events undecided, must plead an Excuse for the *Bulk* of a Collection of this Kind' (I, p. vi). Several volumes into the 'Collection', Lady G. writes, 'I love, Harriet, to write to the moment; that's a knack I had from you and my brother [Sir Charles Grandison]: And be sure continue it, on every occasion: No *pathetic* without it!' (*SCG*, V, p. 57). Cf. Preface to *Clarissa*: 'the Letters... are written while the Hearts of the Writers must be supposed to be wholly engaged in their Subjects: The Events at the Time generally dubious: – So that they abound, not only with critical Situations; but with what may be called *instantaneous* Descriptions and Reflections...' (I, p. v). In *Shamela*, as Fielding exposes the potential absurdity of this narrative device, the heroine writes not so much *to* the moment as *within* the moment: 'Mrs. Jervis and I are just in Bed, and the Door unlocked; if my Master should come – Odsbobs! I hear him just coming in at the Door. You see I write in the present Tense, as Parson *Williams* says. Well, he is in Bed between us, we both shamming a Sleep, he steals his Hand into my Bosom, which I, as if in my Sleep, press close to me with mine, and then pretend to awake' (*Shamela*, p. 165).
51 Richardson to Hill, [*c*.1 February 1741].

Richardson was writing 'over three thousand words a day, in the intervals of a busy life'[52] that included not only the 'inditing' of *Familiar Letters* but also the meticulous, time-consuming job of editing *The Negotiations of Sir Thomas Roe*, for which he wrote a long preface and compiled a detailed table of contents running to about 90,000 words; this impressive folio of over 900 pages, published in March 1740, was printed by Richardson 'At the Expence of the Society for the Encouragement of Learning' (title page) and sold by, among others, John Osborn, Jr, and Charles Rivington. Richardson had been encouraged in the prosecution of his novel, he tells Hill, by 'my worthy-hearted wife, and the young lady who is with us'[53] (Elizabeth Midwinter, whose father, the bookseller Edward Midwinter, had died in 1736), with these two women thus becoming the first of several groups of admirers, in his later years mostly female, whose approval and advice he would eagerly seek and make an integral part of his writing process. He recalls a pleasant scene of readerly solicitude: 'when I had read them some part of the story, which I had begun without their knowing it, [they] used to come in to my little closet every night, with – "Have you any more of Pamela, Mr. R? We are come to hear a little more of Pamela," &c'.[54] He had also been spurred along by the 'approbation' of 'two more' friends, 'who were so kind as to give me prefaces for it, but which were much too long and circumstantial', so that he resolved to write his own: 'I therefore, spirited by the good opinion of these four, and knowing that the judgments of nine parts in ten of readers were but in hanging-sleeves, struck a bold stroke in the preface you see, having the umbrage of the editor's character to screen myself behind.'[55]

We do not know the identities of these 'two more' friends, whose prefaces Richardson (acting with a restraint against prolixity he rarely exercised) rejected, but we do know of two other friends who must have been told of the work-in-progress: Jean Baptiste de Freval, whose letter in praise of the novel appears immediately after the editor's preface in the first edition, and the Reverend William Webster, who had published a letter addressed '*To my worthy Friend, the Author of* PAMELA, *&c.*' in *The Weekly Miscellany* on Saturday, 11 October 1740, the first public hint of the novel's existence.[56] Purportedly sent to 'Mr. Hooker' (Webster's

---

52 Eaves and Kimpel, p. 90.
53 Richardson to Hill, [*c.*1 February 1741]. On the identification of the 'young lady' as Elizabeth Midwinter, see Eaves and Kimpel, 'Publisher of *Pamela*', pp. 144–6.
54 Ibid.   55 Ibid.
56 Both men were indebted to Richardson. Richardson had published de Freval's translation of *The History of the Heavens* (as noted above) and had apparently helped Webster out of financial difficulties, including recently forgiving him a debt of £90 (see Keymer and Sabor, pp. 26–7). Richardson had printed the first 209 issues of *The Weekly Miscellany*, from 16 December 1732 to 11 December 1736 (Maslen, p. 300). *The Apprentice's Vade Mecum* had been heavily advertised in *The Weekly Miscellany* in 1733 (see, e.g., 15 and 29 September, 8 December) and throughout 1734 (over a

pseudonym) to help him in his paper's promotion of 'Virtue', this letter, with 'Author' corrected to 'Editor', is reprinted virtually unchanged after de Freval's as the last of three panegyric pieces launching Pamela's writings into the world. Its author, very likely Webster or (as Fielding would insinuate in *Shamela*) perhaps Richardson himself hiding behind yet another 'screen', praises his 'worthy Friend' – in an introductory address omitted from *Pamela* – for having 'written an *English Novel*, with a truly *English Spirit* of unaffected good Sense, and yet with a great deal of Invention and Ingenuity'. 'I chuse this publick Manner of giving the Author my Sentiments upon it', he concludes, 'in hopes by this Means to quicken the Publication of it, and excite Peoples Attention to it when it does come out.' Nearly a month before its coming out, the way was being thus prepared for the publication of a work that would 'excite Peoples Attention' beyond any 'hopes' even the most enthusiastic friends of the 'worthy Author' could have reasonably entertained.

On Tuesday, 4 November 1740, to secure their rights to the work, Richardson, together with Osborn and Rivington, entered *Pamela: or, Virtue Rewarded* at the Stationers' Company. On Thursday, 6 November 1740, *The Daily Gazetteer* carried the novel's first advertisement, prominently placed at the top of the middle column of book notices, but otherwise typically worded: '*This Day is Published*, | In Two Neat Pocket Volumes. | (Priced 6s. bound)' – with these three lines followed by the title of the book in large capitals and, right below that, reproduced from its title page, the short paragraphs outlining its contents and didactic purpose. The novel was again advertised in *The Daily Gazetteer* on Monday, 10 November (with a notice for the Roe volume, which was not selling well, appearing on Friday, 7 November) and in several other papers, ranging in their political sympathies from government to opposition to neutral, over the next month, including *The London Evening Post* (8, 18, 27 November, 2 December); *The Universal Spectator and Weekly Journal* (8 November); *The London Daily Post and General Advertiser* (11 November); *Common Sense or The Englishman's Journal* (15, 22 November); and *The Country Journal or The Craftsman* (15, 22 November). Having already puffed the 'new Performance' before its publication, *The Weekly Miscellany* rejoined the advertising campaign on Saturday, 13 December 1740, with a letter from an anonymous admirer who, asserting that 'the Design is undeniably laudable, and . . . the Execution shews a Genius', asks 'Mr. Hooker' to publish (which he does, in their entirety) the editor's preface as well as '*Recapitulation*', found in the closing pages of the second volume, 'of the Uses that the Reader may make of' what

---

dozen times, from 12 January to 2 November), no doubt because of Richardson's connection with the paper as printer, but also because both publications had the same publisher, James Roberts. Roberts was also the publisher of *Pamela Censured*.

he or she has read. Though it concludes by taking note of lapses in the heroine's language, a mostly positive appraisal – padded with extensive extracts from the preface and epistolary 'Encomiums', as well as a plot summary of the novel – appeared in December 1740 in *The History of the Works of the Learned*, a publication that had, in May, commended the printer and editor of *The Negotiations of Sir Thomas Roe* for having 'executed his Part so well in both Capacities'.[57] We do not know whether this review was an 'inside job', as Thomas Keymer and Peter Sabor suggest, though *'a sort of Novel'* (as the volume's indexer calls it) was certainly unusual fare for a publication presumably concerned with more high-minded material.[58] On the other hand, given the apparent friendship between its publisher, Edward Cave, and Richardson, an item appearing at the end of the register of books in *The Gentleman's Magazine* in January 1741, commenting on what Fielding's Parson Oliver would soon call the 'epidemical Phrenzy' (*Shamela*, p. 157) then raging over *Pamela*, might be suspected of being part of what appeared to be an orchestrated effort to pump up interest in the novel, especially since the writer of it seems to have 'inside' information that *'a Second Edition'* will soon *'come out to supply the Demands in the Country'*. But the state of affairs he describes – *'it being judged in Town as great a Sign of Want of Curiosity not to have read* Pamela, *as not to have seen the* French *and* Italian *Dancers'* – seems to have been exactly what was happening.[59]

Pamela was indeed a spectacular success. The book was selling briskly, with *'a large Impression having been carried off in less than Three Months'*, as Richardson boasts in his expanded introduction to the second edition published on 14 February 1741, with three more editions appearing within a year of its initial publication: a third (less than a month after the second) on 12 March, a fourth on 5 May, and a fifth on 22 September. It was also being praised by nearly everyone who read it – or claimed to have read it. For example, as Hill wrote to Richardson in early January 1741, Dr Benjamin Slocock, chaplain of St Saviour's church, had recommended the novel from his Southwark pulpit, for which recommendation some of his contemporaries suspected he was paid a bribe; he would soon be 'rewarded' in a far more dubious way, when *Pamela Censured* was dedicated to him.[60] Pope, visiting

---

57 For the appraisal of *Pamela*, see *The History of the Works of the Learned* (December 1740), article XXVIII, 433–9. For the much longer notice on the *Roe* folio, see article XXV, 346–60, in the May 1740 volume; the quoted material is from p. 346.

58 Keymer and Sabor, pp. 28–9. The *Pamela* article was sandwiched between a review of a book on logarithms and a review of the theologian George Turnbull's *Three Dissertations*, a monograph containing essays on such 'learned' subjects as sculpture, painting, and theatrical masks.

59 *The Gentleman's Magazine: and Historical Chronicle* XI (January 1741), [p. 56?]; this section of the volume is not paginated.

60 Hill to Richardson, 6 January 1741. A portion of this letter appears in the introduction to the second edition of the novel. The passage in which Hill alludes to Slocock's recommendation is quoted by Peter Sabor in his 'Did Richardson Bribe Dr. Slocock?', *Notes and Queries*, New Series 26

Bath in early 1741, 'charged' Dr George Cheyne 'to make his warm Compliments' to Richardson 'as an honest good Man', and to tell him 'that he had read Pamela with great Approbation and Pleasure, and wanted a Night's Rest in finishing it, and says it will do more good than a great many of the new Sermons'; we do not know if Cheyne followed up on his promise to Richardson of making 'you and him acquainted', but such high praise from the age's leading man of letters, however ironic it might sound to modern ears, must have pleased.[61] Even those far down the social scale, who could not perhaps read it or afford to buy the book, found joy in Pamela's uplifting story; the villagers of Slough reportedly rang church bells upon hearing of her wedding.[62] It seems that people from every walk of life, male and female, young and old, learned and unlearned, were reading the book, most of them with 'approbation', though there were some, in a vocal minority that would soon include both Henry Fielding and Eliza Haywood, who found fault with, among other things, its 'warm' scenes, its 'low' writing, and, perhaps most egregious of all, its how-to, do-it-yourself approach to social climbing.

Not all those who objected disliked the book. While no reader was as unswervingly enthusiastic in his approval as Hill, who believed that not 'one Word *can* be chang'd for a better',[63] others offered qualified praise and, in some cases, made possible suggestions for revision. Of these readers, one seems to have struck a particular chord with Richardson. A 'good-natured Letter' (as Richardson characterized it on the original manuscript), dated 15 November 1740, had been sent to Rivington by an 'anonymous Gentleman' who, while 'pleased with a Book publish'd under the Title of Pamela', proceeds to provide the bookseller with a detailed account of its flaws.[64] Often citing the number of the page where the offending passage occurs, he ranges widely, from Pamela's 'Style', which should be raised 'from about the 4th Day after Marriage' to suit her new rank, to the lurking bawdry

---

(1979), 29–31. In his Dedication, the anonymous author of *Pamela Censured* reminds Slocock that 'No Divine, I imagine, would recommend any Thing in his Sacred Function, but what might be repeated there [the pulpit], without Offence to Decency and Morality', adding that 'I think *Pamela* is deficient in both' ([p. 3]). The author of *Pamela Censured* does not seem to know about the 'bribe' – which, given his animosity, he would certainly have mentioned as further evidence of Slocock's venality – but the author of *The Life of Pamela* (1741), published about three months later, treats it as an apparently well-known fact. In a note lamenting the '*Boldness*' with which Pamela, '*this modest young Creature*', speaks in Richardson's original, he asserts: '*Such monstrous Inconsistencies must be shocking to a judicious Reader, and destroy the Character that so much Pains have been taken with, even tho' a Parson should have ten Guineas to recommend it from the Pulpit*' (*The Life of Pamela*, p. 340). Sabor refutes the possibility of a bribe in his article, but Keymer and Sabor (p. 24) leave it as an open question.

61   Cheyne to Richardson, 12 February 1741.
62   See Alan Dugald McKillop, 'Wedding Bells for Pamela', *Philological Quarterly* 28 (1949), 323–5.
63   Introduction to the second edition, p. 472 below. At this point, Richardson is excerpting a letter from Hill, dated 15 January 1741 (FM XIII, 2, fols 40–4; two ms folios are missing from this letter).
64   The original manuscript of this four-page letter is in FM XVI, I, fols. 33–4.

of her trembling 'betwixt Fear and Delight' at the wedding ceremony as well as later having 'no Appetite to any thing else' after 'I had made shift to eat a bit of the &c.' – as the letter-writer innocently wanders off in the direction of the abbreviation Fielding would have so much fun with in *Shamela* (the actual phrasing in the novel is somewhat more decorous: 'a bit of Apple-pie, and a little Custard'). In a paragraph inserted at the end of an advertisement for the novel on 20 November in *The Daily Gazetteer*, Richardson, anonymous himself in his editor's pose, 'most heartily' thanks 'the Gentleman for his *Candid* and *Judicious* Observations' and begs 'the Favour of a further Correspondence', but, despite repeating this appeal in several subsequent advertisements, he apparently received no response. In the event, the gentleman's objections found their way into the prefatory matter to the second edition of *Pamela*, where, boiled down to a list of seven items, they become fodder for yet another anonymous 'gentleman' correspondent, who vehemently defends the novel against this and other detractors. The language of this defence is at times so derogatory that it, in turn, prompted an anonymous clergyman to pen a terse one-paragraph letter to Osborn, sent sometime in February 1741, in which he berates the bookseller for having been 'bewitched to Print that bad Stuff in the Introduction'; the clerical letter-writer seems particularly incensed because he and his 'Brethren of the Cloth', being 'great Admirers of Pamela', have been recommending the book, in Slocockian fashion, 'in all' their 'Visits'.[65] The author of the 'bad Stuff' was none other than Aaron Hill, to whom Richardson had sent the letter from the 'anonymous Gentleman' for 'remarks'.[66] Hill had finally extracted from Richardson an admission that he was indeed 'the wonderful author' of the anonymous book he had sent Hill's daughters, Astræa and Minerva.[67] Having apparently been reading the book incessantly and exclusively since its arrival ('It has witchcraft in every page of it'), Hill was only too happy to oblige.[68]

In its presentation of extracts from the letters of 'anonymous' correspondents, the introduction to the second edition thus makes public the main points of an epistolary debate over the novel that had been going on behind the scenes. If the triple commendation constituting the prefatory matter to the first edition had been meant to shape the reception of a work that had been read only by a handful of

---

65 FM XVI, I, fol. 45.
66 Richardson wrote, in his later trembling hand, 'See Remarks on this good-natured Letter, p. 89', at the bottom of the last page of the 'anonymous' gentleman's letter (see n. 64 above), referring to Hill's letters of 6 and 15 January 1741.
67 Hill to Richardson, 17 December 1740.
68 Ibid. Hill was still asking Richardson about the identity of the author ('Pray who is he, dear Sir?') in this letter. In modestly coy fashion, Richardson would soon remove all doubt: 'After the inimitably fine Character and high Praises you have given to the simple Piece, which I took the Liberty to present to your excellent young Ladies, how can I comply with your Commands, and name the Writer?' (Richardson to Hill, 22 December 1740).

'friends' before publication, the introduction to the second records the responses of several readers (including some not 'friends' of the author) after it. In this respect, the introduction to the second edition gives its readers a summary of the reception history of the first (at least Richardson's version of it) and, in doing so, attempts to condition the responses of readers to this edition and – so long as Richardson continued to reprint this material – of editions yet to come. It is also significant that all these readers are identified as 'gentlemen', indicating that the work is not just a 'novel', the reading matter of untutored and impressionable maids, but serious enough to gain the attention of 'gentleman' readers, as Richardson moved to expand both the size and social standing of his audience. He took to heart some of the objections of the 'anonymous Gentleman', as well as those of others, and began incrementally to revise the novel to make its language more proper, its potentially 'inflaming' scenes less objectionable, and, by clarifying the social rank of Pamela's parents, its controversial endorsement of marriage between high and low less revolutionary; by the 'fourteenth' edition of 1801, it is clear that Pamela's writing has lost much of its original demotic power. But, by also letting his readers peruse what he must have regarded as Hill's demolition of those objections – indeed printing the objections surrounded by Hill's aggressive words of praise – Richardson manages to demonstrate, while acknowledging that some readers have found fault with some passages in his work, that their objections are themselves objectionable, that such readers have misunderstood what they have read. In short, Richardson does not ignore objections to his work but places them in an interpretive context that serves his own promotional purposes, that allows him both to encourage and to control his readers' responses. By foregrounding the critical debate over the novel, the introduction to the second edition thus became part of a marketing strategy that would continue to fuel itself – and thereby sales of the book – so long as readers were willing to join the conversation. No doubt much to his delight, Richardson had learned from the initial reaction to his work – a lesson he now wanted readers of the second edition to learn – that *Pamela* was not only a book to be bought and read, but also to be discussed, to be talked and written about. *Pamela*, in short, had created its own book club.

It was a strategy that would eventually lead to some unintended consequences. Having thus encouraged his readers to comment on his work, Richardson soon discovered that some of them would not be content only with sending letters or commendatory verses to the booksellers or the 'editor', or with posting favourable notices in the newspapers. A former playwright, turned hackney writer, finding himself in a sponging house for debt, decided to make some much needed money by writing a parody of *Pamela* – the first of several publications attempting to cash in on the novel's popularity – that would unmask its heroine as a sham. The author of *An Apology for the Life of Mrs. Shamela Andrews* did not need to look far for objections to the work or its heroine because Richardson had obligingly listed them in his introduction to the second edition. In fact, most of the objections made by early readers, including Fielding, were already part of the text of the novel. Before being converted by Pamela's virtue, both Mr. B. and Lady Davers, for example, suspect that 'she is a subtle artful Gypsey' (p. 26) and acting a 'Theatrical Part' (p. 356). Richardson seemed to have anticipated objections to his work as he was writing it and thus included in it both those objections and Pamela's refutations of them, in a dialectic that would be replicated by his first readers. In short, Richardson in many ways defined the critical framework within which his novel would be read and thus began a process, which he might not have yet fully understood or consciously worked out, that would become the basis of his contract with readers of his novels. As he wrote to Lady Bradshaigh on 25 February 1754, following his not entirely facetious suggestion (given his prior experience) that the 'debate' over the inconclusive conclusion of *Sir Charles Grandison* might lead 'some other officious Pen (as in Pamela in High Life, as it was called), [to] prosecute the Story': 'It is not an unartful Management to interest the Readers so much in the Story, as to make them differ in Opinion as to the Capital Articles, and by Leading one, to espouse one, another, another, Opinion, make them all, if not Authors, Carvers.'[69] This memorable description, written at the end of his novelistic career, seems to sum up what he was trying to do at its beginning, when *Pamela* prompted many of its readers to set their 'officious' pens to work.

Fielding, of course, was not alone in trying to capitalize on *Pamela*'s success, though his satirical distillation of all that made the novel appear so ridiculous to some of its early readers, from its stylistic gaffes to its semi-pornographic scenes of virtue-in-distress to its brazen self-promotion, still haunts our appreciation of it, while virtually all other *Pamela* spin-offs are now largely forgotten. Richardson tried to keep count of his work's progeny, later estimating, in a note he scribbled (in the trembling hand of his last years) at the end of a letter he had sent to his brother-in-law, the Bath bookseller James Leake, in August 1741, that 'The Publication of the History of Pamela gave Birth to no less than 16 Pieces, as Remarks, Imitations, Retailings of the Story, Pyracies, &c.'[70] As the evidence shows, Richardson

69 Richardson to Lady Bradshaigh, 25 February 1754. In his edition of the *Selected Letters of Samuel Richardson* (Oxford: Clarendon Press, 1964), John Carroll changes 'Carvers' – clearly the correct word in the original manuscript – to 'Carpers' (p. 296). Richardson is encouraging the active participation of his readers, asking them to 'carve', to choose for themselves according to their own discretion, rather than to 'carp', to find fault. Some of the first readers of *Pamela* obviously chose to do both.

70 Richardson to Leake, August 1741, FM XVI, I, fols. 55–6. Richardson offers the same estimate of 'no less than 16 Pieces' (again in his later trembling hand) at the bottom of the first page of a letter in which Solomon Lowe, writing thirteen months after the novel's publication, congratulates him on *Pamela* not only 'answering the great . . . End you had in View', but also proving 'of so much Service to your very Brethren; witness the Labours of the press in Piracies, in Criticisms, in Cavils, in Panegyricks, in Supplements, in Imitations, in Transformations, in Translations, &c, beyond anything I know of' (Lowe to Richardson, 21 December 1741, FM XVI, I, fol. 78).

underestimated the number of pieces spawned by his work, even if he was taking into account only those pieces that were actually published. As Keymer and Sabor have put it, *Pamela* inspired 'a Grubstreet gabfest in which a hungry succession of entrepreneurial opportunists and freeloading hacks...moved in for a slice of the action'.[71] Because Keymer and Sabor have so magisterially (if not definitively) documented the fortunes and misfortunes of *Pamela* in the marketplace, we need only to comment here on the principal items that swarmed from the presses in the immediate aftermath of its publication. Prior to the publication of *Shamela* on 2 April 1741, sometime in March, the novel began to be serialized in *Robinson Crusoe's London Daily Evening Post*; an Irish edition (published by George Faulkner and George Ewing) had been issued in January in Dublin, with a second following in March; and a French translation, very likely by Jean Baptiste de Freval, to be 'Printed by J. Osborn' and therefore authorized, had been advertised as being '*In the* PRESS' on 27 March in *The Daily Post*, though it was not actually published until 23 October. Though this translation adopts some readings from the fifth edition, it seems to be based on earlier editions of the novel. However, as Eaves and Kimpel point out, this translation is noteworthy because it includes a passage, added to a scene in which Pamela is visited by a group of 'fine ladies', not to appear in English until the octavo edition of May 1742 – suggesting that the translator had inside knowledge of Richardson's ongoing revisions.[72] A work we have already mentioned, *Pamela Censured*, appeared on 25 April; its ostensible purpose, as announced on its title page, was to demonstrate 'That under the Specious Pretence of Cultivating the Principles of Virtue in the Minds of the Youth of both Sexes, the MOST ARTFUL and ALLURING AMOROUS IDEAS are convey'd'. It is difficult to determine whether its author was really so offended as he claims by the Richardsonian scenes he quotes from in such salacious detail, or whether, as Hill wrote to Richardson (supposedly citing the suspicions of a friend), *Pamela Censured* was nothing more than 'a Bookseller's Contrivance' to recommend *Pamela* to 'Light and Loose Readers'.[73] This is certainly an intriguing possibility, one that Richardson strongly denied. That the novel could be read as pornography, and advertised as such, suggests that its enormous popularity

71 Keymer and Sabor, p. 2.
72 A publication notice for the translation, entitled *Pamela; ou la Vertue Recompensée* and published by Thomas Woodward and 'Jean' Osborn, appeared in *The Daily Gazetteer* on 23 October 1741. It parenthetically touted the work's pedagogical purpose – '(*For the Use of* SCHOOLS)' – as Richardson and his publishers found yet another way of repackaging (and cashing in on) their literary property. Though there is no definitive proof regarding the identity of the translator, the consensus seems to be that it was Jean Baptiste de Freval, the author of one of the epistolary puffs included in the novel's preface and an associate of Richardson at this time. The French *Pamela* was placed on the *Index Librorum Prohibitorum* in June 1744 (see McKillop, p. 99).
73 Hill to Richardson, 25 May 1741, FM XIII, 2, fols. 48–9. Richardson writes 'Quite mistaken!' next to Hill's comment.

must have derived from its appeal to readers of varied tastes and proclivities. Rather than a satirical characterization, Fielding's Parson Tickletext, who ejaculates pieties while savouring the smut, might have actually been a fairly typical reader.

Another reader inspired by the publication of *Pamela* to take up her pen was Eliza Haywood, who, as the market for novels dried up by the end of the 1720s, had turned her energies to the theatre in the 1730s, writing (or co-writing) several plays and acting as a member of Fielding's company at the Little Theatre on the Haymarket. With the passage of the Licensing Act in 1737, Haywood, like the author of *Shamela*, found herself in search of new outlets for her talent. Published anonymously on 16 June, 'as a necessary Caution to all Young Gentlemen' (title page), *Anti-Pamela: or, Feign'd Innocence Detected* mounts a direct attack on the dangerous attraction of Richardson's heroine, in particular her hypocritical performance of virtue. As Haywood portrays her, Syrena Tricksy is an unsentimental, vicious predator who, impervious to the risks she runs in the pursuit of her 'adventures', is finally unmasked for her many impositions and ends up not being 'rewarded' with wealth and marriage, as she and her conniving mother had hoped, but punished with exile into 'the farther part of *Wales*'.[74] While Fielding, Haywood, and the author of *Pamela Censured* had attempted to cash in on *Pamela* by exposing its faults, under the cover of presumably loftier purposes of moral reformation, there were others who just wanted to cash in. Beginning around May and ending in September, the bookseller Mary Kingman published a piracy of the novel in three instalments; in late September, she issued the first of three numbers of *Pamela in High Life: Or, Virtue Rewarded*, which, promising to give 'an Account of Pamela' until her death, was advertised on 29 September, in *The London Daily Post and General Advertiser*, as having been 'Carefully extracted from Original Manuscripts, communicated to the Editor by her Son'. Sometime in August, another serialization, *The Life of Pamela*, began to appear. Published by Charles Whitefield, possibly a relation of George Whitefield as well as bookseller of a collection of his 'discourses' issued in 1739 as well as of individual sermons appearing in 1739 and 1740, this third-person narrative invokes a *Shamela*-like project, aiming to rectify the many mistakes of Richardson's novel by following '*the original Papers now in the Hands of the Reverend Mr. Perkins of Shendisford Abbey*'.[75] This spin-off is

74 Eliza Haywood, *Anti-Pamela: or, Feign'd Innocence Detected; In a Series of Syrena's Adventures* (1741), p. 280.
75 *The Life of Pamela*, p. 2. I have not found any biographical information on Charles Whitefield, who, according to the *ESTC*, seems to have been in business between 1739 and 1749. He published around fifty works, among them two editions of Defoe's *Roxana* (1745, 1749) and a translation of Marivaux's *La Vie de Marianne*, under the title *The Life and Adventures of Indiana, the Virtuous Orphan* (1746). The bulk of his publications, however, was by George Whitefield, giving his press, especially at the time of the publication of *The Life of Pamela*, a decidedly Methodist profile. The coincidence

also noteworthy because it featured a frontispiece and eleven illustrations by John Carwitham, the first visual representations of the novel still extant.[76] Previous visual representations of scenes from the novel, which unfortunately have not survived, appeared on a fan, advertised for sale in *The Daily Advertiser* on 28 April and 2 May.[77]

Before looking more closely at the work that led Richardson to undertake his own continuation, we should briefly mention a few more items inspired by *Pamela* in the first year after its publication. Following the example of Hill's poetic panegyric on the 'Unknown Author' at the end of the introduction to the second edition – reprinted two weeks later as part of the promotional material featured in *The Weekly Miscellany* on 28 February – verses commending (or condemning) the novel began to appear in the newspapers. Five days after the publication of *Shamela*, on 7 April, *The Daily Advertiser* published a four-line epigram, 'Advice to Booksellers (After reading *Pamela*)'; suggesting that a 'printer' is the author of the novel ('Let printers write, and let your writers print'), this seems to have been the first public hint of Richardson's authorship and was reprinted in the April issue of *The Gentleman's Magazine*. *The London Magazine: or, Gentleman's Monthly Intelligencer* published two anti-*Pamela* 'poetical essays' in two successive numbers: 'Remarks on *Pamela*. By a Prude' (May; reprinted in *The Scots Magazine* in July); and 'To the Author of *Shamela*' (June). The following month, it printed 'An Apology for the Censorious. In a familiar Epistle to a Female Friend', signed by 'R.D.' and dated 'July 8, 1741', which contains a brief defence of the novel. The first part of George Bennet's *Pamela Versified*, a 'heroic poem' projected to run for fifteen parts, was advertised on 24 July in *The Daily Advertiser* (an advertisement for the second part appeared on 12 August); no copy has survived, though an excerpt from it was reprinted in *The Scots Magazine* in October, with the wistful comment that 'the work now seems dropt'. Pamela's story also found its way onto the stage. The first *Pamela* play to be acted in London (and later in Dublin) was Henry Giffard's *Pamela. A Comedy*. It opened on 9 November at Goodman's Fields Theatre – the playhouse Richardson had disapproved of in *A Seasonable Examination* in 1735 – and had run for seventeen performances

of surname has confused a prominent Whitefield scholar, who suggests that the preacher's eight sermons published in 1739 and 'printed for C. Whitefield' must have been self-published, as 'the initial appears to be a misprint' (Frank Lambert, *'Pedlar in Divinity': George Whitefield and the Transatlantic Revivals, 1737–1770* (Princeton University Press, 1994), p. 89).

76 Carwitham's frontispiece and illustrations are reproduced in Keymer and Sabor (eds.), *Pamela Controversy*, II, pp. 249–71. For Sabor's perceptive remarks on Carwitham's engravings, see Introduction to this volume, pp. xxx–xxxiii.

77 The advertisement for 'PAMELA, a new Fan', posted by 'M. Gamble', promises scenes 'Design'd and engraved by the best Masters', 'representing the principal Adventures of her Life, in Servitude, Love, and Marriage'. Pamela would also be celebrated in a series of waxworks in 1745 and 1746 (see Keymer and Sabor, pp. 167–9).

by 18 December; published on 17 November, the play featured a young David
Garrick (identified only as 'a Gentleman' in the dramatis personae) as speaker
of the prologue and in the role of the foppish Jack Smatter.[78] Another dramatic
comedy, *Pamela: or, Virtue Triumphant*, 'intended to be acted at the Theatre
Royal in *Drury-Lane*' (title page), was published anonymously on 16 November.
This might have been the *Pamela* performed between parts of a concert on 28
December at the French Theatre, Haymarket; it is also possible that this was a
different, still unidentified play.[79] To conclude this list of *Pamela*-inspired items
for the year 1741, we should mention three more prose works. James Parry's *The
True Anti-Pamela: Or, Memoirs of Mr. James Parry*, a slight book related to *Pamela*
only by its title, appeared on 27 June (with a second edition on 26 September).
Charles Povey's *The Virgin in Eden: or, the State of Innocency*, which includes a
section denouncing 'Pamela's Letters' as 'Immodest Romances painted in Images
of Virtue' (p. 68), was published on 23 November. Finally, *Memoirs of the Life of
Lady H —— ,* a hasty summary of Richardson's novel issued anonymously on 4
December, suggests that 'The Celebrated *PAMELA*' was actually Hannah Sturges
(1709–65), a coachman's daughter who had become the wife of Sir Arthur Hesilrige
(1705–63), seventh baronet of Northampton, in June 1725, as the guessing-game
over the true identity of Richardson's heroine and the time-frame of the story –
which Richardson would address publicly three days later, in the preface to *Pamela
in Her Exalted Condition*[80] – gave further evidence of the continuing interest in
Pamela's rags-to-riches tale.

Although a fuller examination of the events that compelled Richardson to
publish *Pamela in Her Exalted Condition* will appear in the General Introduction
to that novel, a brief summary of his dealings with the 'High-Life Men', as he
called them, will round out this account of the early reception of *Pamela: or, Virtue
Rewarded.* The first public acknowledgement that Richardson was working on a
continuation appeared in a paragraph added on 7 May to the advertisement for

78 For London performances of *Pamela. A Comedy*, see Arthur H. Scouten (ed.), *The London Stage,
1660–1800* (Carbondale: Southern Illinois University, 1961), Part 3: 1729–1747, II, pp. 941–52. Garrick
had made his debut on the London stage on 19 October 1741 at Goodman's Fields, playing the part
of Richard III (*The London Stage*, Part 3, II, p. 935). Giffard's play opened in Dublin on 7 December
1741, the same day Richardson's continuation of *Pamela* was published in London.
79 For the *Pamela* performance on 28 December 1741, see Scouten (ed.), *The London Stage*, Part 3,
II, p. 954. Two ballad operas followed in 1742. On dramatic adaptations of *Pamela* in 1741–2, see
Keymer and Sabor, pp. 115–25.
80 See the last paragraph of the Preface: '*The Editor has been much press'd with Importunities and
Conjectures in relation to the Person and Family of the incomparable Lady, who is the Subject of these
Volumes: All that he thinks himself at Liberty to say, or is necessary to be said, is only to repeat what has
been already hinted, That the Story has its Foundation in Truth: That the most material Incidents (as
will be collected from several Passages in the Letters) happen'd between the Years 1717 and 1730: And that
there was a Necessity, for obvious Reasons, to vary and disguise some Facts and Circumstances, as also the
Names of Persons, Places,* &c.' (*Pamela 2*, III, pp. iii–iv).

the fourth edition of the novel in *The Daily Gazetteer* (the advertisement had appeared without the paragraph on 5 May). To warn as many readers as possible against 'a spurious Continuation', the expanded advertisement was posted several times through the rest of May in *The Daily Gazetteer* and was reprinted at least once in another paper, *The London Evening Post*, on 14 May 1741, curiously enough right below a notice for *Pamela Censured*. Richardson was clearly upset by what he viewed as the theft of his property '*against* his Consent', but he was also a savvy businessman who was about to take advantage of an opportunity to profit further from Pamela's story (as many others were doing) while professing that he was writing a sequel only because he had been forced to do so. Dropping his editorial mask, 'the Author' reveals 'that he is actually continuing the Work himself, from Materials, that, perhaps, but for such a notorious Invasion of his Plan, he should not have published'.[81] 'Perhaps' is a telling word. Given the enormous success of the original, Richardson might have been contemplating a sequel, but he also understood the dynamics of the London book market, the importance of publishing a work, especially a 'continuation', at the right time and under the right circumstances. As he wrote to James Leake, in the letter at the end of which he appended his estimate of *Pamela* 'pieces' cited above, 'Second Parts are generally received with Prejudice, and it was treating the Public too much like a Bookseller to pursue a Success till they tired out the buyers.' But second parts can be justified, in imitation of the manner of Cervantes, when an author's 'Characters [are] likely to be debased' and his 'whole Purpose inverted'.[82] The 'High-Life Men' had unwittingly given Richardson the opening he needed, however reluctant he might have been – or professed to have been – to take it. Beginning with an address '*To the PUBLICK*', posted on 30 May in *The Daily Gazetteer*, *Pamela in Her Exalted Condition* would be marketed as the 'GENUINE CONTINUATION' its aggrieved author had no choice but to write.

But who were the 'High-Life Men' and what had they done to upset 'the Author'? Richardson gave Leake 'a Short Acc^t of the Affair' in an angry letter of complaint from which we have been quoting, and, so far as surviving evidence corroborates, he seems to have been telling the truth. This letter is interesting not only because of what it tells us about this 'Affair' but also because the manuscript has several lines crossed out, with interlinear and marginal additions (in Richardson's

---

81 The additional paragraph is worth quoting in full: 'Certain Booksellers having in the Press a spurious Continuation of these Two Volumes (in Letters from Pamela to Mrs. Jervis her *Housekeeper*) the Author thinks it necessary to declare, that the same is carrying on *against* his Consent, and without any other Knowledge of the Story than what they are able to collect from the Two Volumes already printed: And that he is actually continuing the Work himself, from Materials, that, perhaps, but for such a notorious Invasion of his Plan, he should not have published.'
82 Richardson to Leake, August 1741.

later trembling hand) providing information an insider such as Leake would not have needed, as Richardson revised to turn this into the official 'account' of his side of the story. As Richardson originally wrote, he had 'heard that Chandler had employed one Kelly, a Bookseller's Hackney, who never wrote any thing that was tolerably receiv'd, and had several of his Performances refused by the Stage', later adding the clause 'to continue my Pamela'.[83] Richard Chandler (1713?–44), together with his partner Caesar Ward (1710–59), owned bookshops in London, Scarborough, and York; their publishing list featured law and travel books but also included such 'literary' works as editions of Defoe's *Colonel Jacque* (1738, 1739, 1743) and translations of Cervantes's *Persiles and Sigismunda* (1741) and Quevedo's *Comical Works* (1742). Unfortunately for Chandler, things did not turn out too well; overwhelmed by business losses, he shot himself in the head in early 1744. His hired hand, John Kelly (1680?–1751), a West Indian heir down on his luck, was not quite the 'Bookseller's Hackney' that Richardson painted him out to be; in fact, he had had a relatively successful career as a playwright when he, like Fielding and Haywood, became a casualty of the Licensing Act of 1737.[84] When Chandler approached him to write a continuation to *Pamela*, he no doubt (like Fielding and Haywood) welcomed what seemed like a promising opportunity to make some money. According to Richardson, after he 'remonstrated against' this 'base' proceeding 'to a Friend of Kelly's', he was visited by Chandler, who made several proposals, including cancelling the '4 Sheets he had printed' and taking the loss of the '9 Guineas' he and his associates 'had advanced to their Author', and then having Richardson write the continuation for them.[85] An indignant Richardson turned down this proposal and thought that Chandler had left 'convinced of this Baseness, wishing he had not ingaged in it, and saying he would consult his Partners, and give me an Answer'. But, Richardson continues, 'I never heard further from him only of his Boasts how well written their Piece was, and how determined they were to prosecute it, braving it out that if I did Advertise against them, they had Authors who c^d give me Advertisement for Advertisement let me say what I wou'd, and that I was like the Dog in the Manger wou'd neither eat myself nor let them eat.'[86] An advertising free-for-all did indeed follow, with Chandler advertising his continuation in such opposition newspapers as *The Champion* (which he partly owned) on 28 May and *The Craftsman* and *Common Sense* on 30 May, and Richardson launching his pre-emptive strike in *The Daily Gazetteer* on 7 May, with more attacks and counterattacks following over the next

---

83 Ibid.
84 For a sympathetic – and excellent – account of John Kelly's career and of his continuation of *Pamela*, see Keymer and Sabor, pp. 66–82. Information on publications by Chandler and Ward is drawn from *ESTC*.
85 Richardson to Leake, August 1741.   86 Ibid.

weeks and months.[87] *Pamela's Conduct in High Life*, claiming to be 'Publish'd from her ORIGINAL PAPERS' (title page), was published on 28 May, with a second volume, 'To the Time of her Death' (title page), following on 12 September. By the time Richardson's own two-volume continuation appeared on 7 December, readers had several versions of Pamela to choose from, all of them vouching for their authenticity. Having inaugurated the book-length appropriation of Pamela's story with *Shamela* in April, Fielding would publish another one the following year, on 22 February 1742. Featuring a cameo by a prissy Pamela, smugly enjoying the privileges of her exalted condition as Squire Booby's lady, *The History of the Adventures of Joseph Andrews, And of his Friend Mr. Abraham Adams* concludes with the tongue-in-cheek (and actually kept) promise that its hero will not 'be prevailed on by any Booksellers, or their Authors, to make his Appearance in *High-Life*' (*Joseph Andrews*, p. 344).

Pamela would also make her appearance on the Continent, especially in France, where the French translation seems to have divided readers as much as the original had done at home.[88] The author of *Lettre sur Pamela* (1742), for example, finds fault with the novel's unpolished language and manners but also shows some grudging appreciation for the simple rusticity of its heroine and, allowing for the crudeness of the English, for its depiction of the universal 'politeness of the heart' ('politesse du cœur'); more specifically, he harps on Pamela's ludicrous decision not to quit Milord's 'dangereuse maison' when she finds herself in sexual danger in order to finish embroidering his waistcoat, pokes fun at her attempts to 'parody' the Psalms, and (while condemning his officiousness) expresses mock 'pity' for the travails of 'le pauvre Williams'.[89] A more enthusiastic reader, Pierre Desfontaines, writes a Hill-like panegyric on the novel in *Observations sur les écrits modernes* in June 1742, only to be attacked, in August, by the anonymous author of *Lettre à Monsieur l'Abbé Des Fontaines sur Pamela*, who rebukes Desfontaines for praising a nation with which France was then at war. Under these circumstances, not to mention the gratuitous swipes at French morals and taste in the novel's preface, it is understandable why some French readers treated *Pamela* with hostility. Though

87 On the advertising war, see Keymer and Sabor, pp. 59–66. Competing advertisements sometimes appeared together. For example, a notice for the fourth edition of *Pamela* is followed by a publication announcement for the first part of *Pamela's Conduct in High Life*, followed in turn by two denunciations from Richardson, with his promise that 'the genuine Continuation' is forthcoming (*London Evening Post*, 23–5 June 1741); Keymer and Sabor reproduce this advertising cluster (p. 60) as well as another one (*London Evening Post*, 8–10 October 1741) featuring the fifth edition of *Pamela* and the (by now) two volumes of *Pamela's Conduct* (p. 65).

88 For this brief summary of the *Pamela* vogue on the Continent, I am indebted to Keymer and Sabor, pp. 132–42; McKillop, pp. 92–106; and Henry Seidel Canby, '*Pamela* ABROAD', *Modern Language Notes* 18 (1903), 206–13.

89 *Lettre sur Pamela*, pp. 11, 16, 22, 23. Though this work has sometimes been attributed to the Abbé Marquet and bears a London (Londres) imprint, we do not know for certain either the identity of the author or the place of publication.

the French translation seems to have been the main conduit through which *Pamela* was transmitted to the Continent, there were also early Dutch (1742–4) and German (1742) translations, followed by later translations into Danish (1743–6), Italian (1744–6), Russian (1787), Portuguese (179?), and Spanish (1794). The Dutch, in particular, seem to have taken a special interest in the *Pamela* controversy brewing in London. An anonymous attack on the novel, *Pamela Bespiegeld* ('Pamela Exposed'), was published in Amsterdam in 1741; its contents include not only the author's own exposure of the work's moral and stylistic deficiencies, but also a translation of *Pamela Censured*. A Dutch translation of Haywood's *Anti-Pamela* appeared in 1743.[90] But nowhere on the Continent was the *querelle de Pamela* so spirited as in France.

Just as in London, *Pamela* was adapted for the stage in Paris, with three plays produced in 1743: Louis de Boissy's *Paméla en France, ou la vertu mieux éprouvée* in March and, in December, Nivelle de La Chaussée's *Pamela* and Claude Godard d'Acour's *La Déroute des Paméla*.[91] A recently discovered work, *Les mémoires de Pamela, écrits par elle-même*, a third person abridgement of both parts of *Pamela*, was also published in 1743.[92] Towards the end of the decade, *Pamela* caught the attention of two of Europe's most celebrated writers. Voltaire's three-act play, *Nanine, ou le préjugé vaincu*, premiered in June 1749 at the Comédie-Française. Goldoni's comedy, *Pamela nubile*, debuted in the spring of 1750 in Mantua and was also performed in November in Venice.[93] Goldoni followed up *Pamela nubile* with *Pamela maritata* (1760), as well as operatic versions of both plays, with music by Nicolo Piccini, *La buona figliuola* (1760) and *La buona figliuola maritata* (1761). Perhaps to make her story more agreeable to sophisticated Italian audiences, Goldoni, in imitation of the manner of the 'High-Life Men', had exalted Pamela's condition by making her the daughter of an aristocrat. Based on Goldoni's *Pamela nubile*, Nicolas François de Neufchâteau's comedy, *Paméla, ou la Vertu récompensée*, opened in Paris in August 1793.[94] Deemed to run against the egalitarian sentiments

---

90 On the novel's translations and reception in European countries other than France, see McKillop, pp. 100–1, 323–4. The Spanish translation, which includes all four volumes of the novel, misnames the author of the English original as 'Thomás Richárdson' on its title page; the second edition (1799) retains the error but changes the spelling of the first name to 'Tomas'.

91 For a perceptive analysis of de Boissy's *Paméla en France*, see Turner, 'Novel Panic', pp. 88–90.

92 For an edition of this work, see *Les mémoires de Pamela, écrits par elle-même*, ed. Franco Piva (Fasano: Schena Editore, 2007).

93 As McKillop documents, Goldoni was especially influential in spreading Pamela's story throughout the Continent, with versions of *Pamela nubile*, for example, appearing in German (1756, 1758), French (1759), Norwegian (1765), Portuguese (1766), Spanish (1787), Greek (1791), Russian (1812), Armenian (1866), and Czech (1887); see McKillop, pp. 104–6. John Nourse published *Pamela nubile*, in the original Italian with an English translation, in London in 1756.

94 For an edition of Neufchâteau's play, see *Paméla, ou La Vertu récompensée*, ed. Martial Poirson (Oxford: Voltaire Foundation, 2007). For Peter Sabor's informative review of this edition, as well as the edition of *Les mémoires de Pamela* cited above (n. 92), see *Eighteenth-Century Fiction* 21 (2009), 660–3.

of the Revolution, the play was closed by the Committee of Public Safety after eight performances and its author arrested. To save his play and possibly his neck, de Neufchâteau restored Pamela to her lowly condition; the play was eventually rehabilitated, with a revival mounting the boards in 1795, a year after the fall of Robespierre. Of course, we do not know whether Pamela in her original 'Country Apparel' might have avoided prosecution. Still, it is one of the ironies of literary history that a work that had ruffled aristocratic feathers in the early 1740s in both England and France was, by century's end, considered not revolutionary enough. As some readers had grasped in London immediately after the novel's initial publication, the Terror authorities in Paris recognized that the story of Pamela was not so much a comic romance as a potentially dangerous political statement.

REVISIONS

Richardson began revising his novel soon after publication, partly to answer the objections of such readers as the 'anonymous Gentleman', but also to deal with difficulties which, given the criticisms of Pamela already present in the first edition, he seems to have been aware of as he wrote. To that end, he consulted several of his learned friends, pre-eminent among them Aaron Hill, whose advice to leave *Pamela* alone he chose not to take. But he also had plans to enhance the quality and appearance of the actual physical book, to make it more attractive to potential buyers. As he reveals near the end of the introduction to the second edition, he had intended '*to prefix two neat Frontispieces to this Edition, (and to present them to the Purchasers of the first)*', but, unhappy with the engraving of the one actually completed and cognizant that '*Demand for the new Impression*' required him to expedite publication, he chose not to include them.[95] We do not

95 See Introduction to the second edition, p. 475 below. We do not know the number of copies printed for the first edition of *Pamela*, other than Richardson's self-congratulatory comment in this introduction about 'a large Impression having been carried off in less than Three Months' (p. 463). We also do not know the size of the print run for the second edition. An entry for 2 March 1741 in one of William Bowyer's ledgers (B354, 408) recording the printing of 3,000 copies of two sheets ('Sam. Richardson, Pamela, 2 shts SP 12°') for what was probably the third edition of the novel – an edition exhausted within two months – might give us a sense of the number of copies being snapped up by eager buyers at the height of the novel's popularity; see *The Bowyer Ledgers: The Printing Accounts of William Bowyer Father and Son*, ed. Keith Maslen and John Lancaster (London: The Bibliographical Society; New York: The Bibliographical Society of America, 1991), item 2907, p. 223. J. D. Fleeman cites what appears to be a variant of this entry, from a complementary set of Bowyer's ledgers he discovered at the Grolier Club in New York, in '18th-Century Printing Ledgers', *Times Literary Supplement* (Thursday, 19 December 1963), 1056. We do not know whether these 3,000 copies were the whole run for the edition or supplements to copies (number unknown) of the same edition being printed by other printers or by Richardson, whose press could not supply enough product on its own to meet the overwhelming demand. For more information on this edition, see the section on bibliographical description below. Bowyer printed signatures B and C of the first volume of this edition, which matches the two sheets recorded in the ledgers.

know if William Hogarth, apparently Richardson's first choice for the job, was responsible for the illustration(s) in question, but what we do know is that a little over a year later, in May 1742, Richardson did issue a magnificent four-volume octavo edition, 'Embellish'd with COPPER PLATES, Design'd and Engrav'd' (title page) by Francis Hayman and Hubert Gravelot.[96] But that was still to come. In the meantime, his initial efforts to illustrate his novel thus frustrated, he focused his attention on 'improving' his heroine's language. But first he added to the second edition the lengthy introduction, printed after the original prefatory matter to the first edition, in which he allows Hill to defend the novel against its 'gentlemen' detractors while fulsomely praising 'the Beauties of PAMELA'. In the fourth edition, Richardson began to tone down the excessive language of Hill's defence, with each subsequent edition, especially the fifth, removing or rephrasing more of 'that bad Stuff' that had given offence to some and prompted others to ridicule the author for puffing his work in such clumsy, self-serving fashion. It should be noted, however, that, in all the duodecimo editions in which Richardson had a direct hand, up until the eighth (dated 1762), published soon after his death, the praise of the novel, while substantially muted, is still allowed to stand as the reader's introduction to Pamela's letters and journal.

As one would expect, it is Pamela's 'low' and at times ungrammatical language that undergoes the most revision.[97] Most of the 841 changes that Richardson made in the second edition aimed to raise the 'Style' of the heroine, as the 'anonymous Gentleman' had recommended. For example, 'Curchee' becomes 'Court'sey' throughout (or 'curtesy', as when the word appears as a verb in the first letter); the rustic "Squire' is often substituted with the less regional 'Mr. B.' or 'Gentleman' (though Richardson to the end resisted the gentleman's recommendation to 'procure' for Mr. B. 'the Title of a Baronet'); 'God' either disappears or is modified to the more general 'Heaven' or, as in the first letter, 'Providence', thus introducing

---

96 On Hogarth's possible involvement in the discarded frontispiece(s) for the second edition, Hayman and Gravelot's twenty-nine illustrations for the octavo edition, various engravings appearing in other *Pamela* editions up to 1810, and Joseph Highmore's series of twelve oil paintings (completed in 1744) depicting scenes from the novel, see T. C. Duncan Eaves, 'Graphic Illustration of the Novels of Samuel Richardson, 1740–1810', *Huntington Library Quarterly* 14 (1950–1), 349–69.

97 This section is indebted to T. C. Duncan Eaves and Ben D. Kimpel's indispensable 'Richardson's Revisions of *Pamela*', *Studies in Bibliography* 20 (1967), 61–88. I have adopted Eaves and Kimpel's figures for numbers of changes made to each edition of the first two volumes because, while not precise (Eaves and Kimpel do not claim that they are so), they nonetheless 'suggest the extent of revision' (p. 62). In doing so, I follow the precedent of other textual critics who accept these figures, such as Philip Gaskell ('Example 3: Richardson, *Pamela*, 1741', *From Writer to Reader: Studies in Editorial Method* (Oxford: Clarendon Press, 1978), pp. 63–79) and Tom Keymer ('Assorted Versions of Assaulted Virgins; or, Textual Instability and Teaching', in Lisa Zunshine and Jocelyn Harris (eds.), *Approaches to Teaching the Novels of Samuel Richardson* (New York: The Modern Language Association of America, 2006), pp. 24–31). My own examination of the evidence corroborates that Eaves and Kimpel's figures are roughly accurate and, therefore, useful to characterize the type and scope of the corrections appearing in each of the editions I discuss here.

the novel's providential theme at the outset of the narrative; such verb tenses as 'have broke' and 'have wrote', associated with lower-class speech, are corrected to 'have broken' and 'have written'; a colloquialism like 'seeing me frighted' (first letter) is dropped in favour of 'seeing me tremble' – a change that also cleans up the redundancy of three versions of 'fright' in such close proximity. Yet a more overt instance of 'low' speech singled out by the gentleman, 'foolish thing that I am', is retained in all editions, including that of 1801, probably because Richardson agreed with Hill's persuasive argument against this '*Dutch Emendation*'.[98] Two passages that might lead readers (especially after being alerted) to suppose 'a double Entendre', partially transcribed (as earlier noted) by the gentleman in his original letter to Rivington but referred to in the introduction only by their page numbers, are also emended. Pamela at her wedding no longer trembles 'betwixt Fear and Delight' but 'betwixt Fear and Joy' (II, p. 175), presumably on the supposition that 'Joy' is not a sexually transmitted emotion; Richardson rephrases her later comments, immediately preceding her wedding night, from 'I made shift to eat a bit of Apple-pie, and a little Custard; but I had no Appetite to any thing else' to 'I made shift to get down a bit of Apple-pie, and a little Custard; but that was all' (II, p. 181), a change which, while intended to put a full stop to sexual imaginings at one end ('that was all'), seems (at least to modern ears) to violate linguistic decorum at the other ('get down'). In short, as Thomas Keymer summarizes the cumulative effect of Richardson's revisions, 'Pamela is increasingly made to speak in the voice of the fine lady she will later become, and not of the servant she initially is.'[99]

Richardson continued the process of linguistic elevation through subsequent editions, with fifty-nine minor changes made in the third (12 March) and forty-eight in the fourth (5 May), the relatively low number of revisions in these texts probably due to his need to print two new editions as quickly as possible to meet public demand. In the four months between the fourth and fifth edition (22 September), he revised the novel, especially the editor's preface, more extensively, implementing 950 changes, 45 of them in the introduction. As Eaves and Kimpel have noted, these are 'changes of phrasing, rather than grammatical changes or changes of single words, as in the second edition'.[100] In the first letter, for example, Richardson erases the phrase 'in my Fright' ('He, in my Fright, took it', in all editions up to the fourth), thereby curbing Pamela's tendency to repeat the same word when 'frightened' by whittling the original three versions of 'fright' down to one; he also adds two clauses, after 'I am not angry with you', in which Mr. B. urges Pamela to exercise discretion in her letter-writing, as Richardson glances in the direction of one of Parson Oliver's major objections in *Shamela*: 'for writing such innocent Matters as these; tho' you ought to be wary what Tales you send out of a Family' (I, p. 4). These changes show that Richardson is editing his original text to answer not only some of the objections of the 'anonymous Gentleman' but also those made by other readers, in particular readers who had published books or pamphlets attacking his novel. The author of *Pamela Censured*, for instance, had fulminated that the scene in which Mr. B. looks through a keyhole at the unconscious body of Pamela 'stretch'd out at my Length', while it 'may indeed be read by one in his *grand Climacteric* without ever wishing to see one in the same Situation', 'must naturally excite Passions of Desire' in the 'young Men' for whom the novel had been presumably intended.[101] In the fifth edition, Richardson attempts to wiggle his way out of this ticklish situation by having Pamela appear 'stretch'd out at Length, on my Face' (I, p. 31), a not entirely successful solution, to say the least; Pamela remained on her face until the 1801 edition, when, omitting specifics about her posture, she simply writes that Mr. B. "spy'd me upon the floor' (I, p. 30). There are also two additions that look forward to the sequel, which Richardson by then had nearly completed. Where in the first four editions Pamela 'lov'd Writing,' in the fifth she loves 'Writing as well as Reading'; told by Mrs. Jewkes that 'below is my Master's Library; you may take out what Books you will', Pamela picks out 'some Books... with which I filled a Shelf in the Closet she gave me Possession of; and from these I hope to receive Improvement, as well as Amusement' (I, p. 143). Richardson thus gives his readers a plausible explanation for the philosophical, 'masculine' learning that the young servant maid, having begun her education by reading her late lady's books, will display in her exalted condition. In a new paragraph, Richardson also mentions that Pamela has 'agreed upon a Correspondence' with Miss Darnford, 'an admirable young Lady' who has 'a happy Talent in Writing, and is learned, and well-read, for so young a Lady' (II, p. 333). Like Anna Howe for Clarissa, or Lucy Selby for Harriet Byron in *Grandison*, Polly Darnford will become for Pamela the correspondent – of about her own age and roughly of the same rank into which Pamela will marry – to whom she can entrust her secrets, seek and offer advice, and otherwise (as demanded by the conventions of epistolary fiction) disclose the narrative of her life.

Published in four volumes on 8 May 1742, the octavo edition was the first to include both parts of the novel. Its title page indicates that it is 'The SIXTH EDITION, Corrected', but that is true only of the first part, volumes III and IV actually being the third edition of the second part. There are 633 changes in the first two volumes; very likely to avoid repagination, these changes do not carry over

101 *Pamela Censured*, p. 31.

into the sixth, seventh, and eighth duodecimo editions. In addition to its larger print, better paper, and the twenty-nine engravings (seven in each of the first three volumes, eight in the fourth) by Gravelot and Hayman, the octavo edition is noteworthy because, while retaining the editor's preface (as corrected since the first edition) '*to the Two first Volumes of this Piece*', it omits the 'Two Recommendatory Letters' and 'Introductory Preface' from '*the* Four *Latter Impressions*' (p. vii). As the editor explains, '*the kind Reception which these Volumes have met with, renders the* Recommendatory Letters *unnecessary*' (p. viii); the introduction answering '*some Objections, made by well-meaning Persons, to a few Passages in the Work*' (pp. vii–viii) is also not needed '*because the most material of the Objections . . . are taken notice of and obviated in the Third Volume, in Letters from the fair Writer to Lady* Davers, *and others of her Correspondents*' (p. viii). Instead, '*their Place is supply'd . . . by* [an] *Epitome of the Work*' (ibid.), running to thirty-six pages of closely printed text, reminiscent of the index introducing *The Negotiations of Sir Thomas Roe*. Also rendered 'unnecessary' by the continuing volumes, and therefore eliminated, are the editor's concluding remarks and 'observations' originally appearing at the end of the second volume. To make the first two volumes equivalent in number of pages, some material from volume II is moved into volume I – a change that also has the dramatic effect of making Pamela's departure from the Lincolnshire estate occur at the end of the first volume, with the heroine asking, as Colbrand prepares the coach and horses, 'What will be the End of all this?' (I, p. 407). Richardson also corrects the first of two successive entries in Pamela's journal dated '*TUESDAY Morning*' to '*MONDAY Morning, Eleven o'Clock*' (II, p. 233). The scene in which Pamela meets with the 'fine Ladies' is considerably expanded, from two pages in the original first edition volume (I, pp. 59–60) to eight (I, pp. 71–8), as Pamela somewhat self-consciously hopes that she will not 'tire' her parents in her 'Account of the Characters and Persons of these Four Ladies' (I, p. 72), an account very much in the conversational, comedy-of-manners style Richardson had begun to master in parts of the continuation and would deploy again in *Grandison*. Other revisions of the octavo text are relatively minor and consist of changes of words and phrases, as well as corrections of verb tenses, similar to those made in previous editions.

The sixth duodecimo edition, published in October 1746, has only twenty-six changes, all of them minor, indicating that, after the major revisions of the octavo edition, Richardson had decided to let the text of the fifth edition stand as the basis of subsequent reissues of the novel, especially since he was now busy with *Clarissa*, the first two volumes of which would appear in December 1747. Dated 1754, the seventh duodecimo edition, the last to be published in his lifetime, is also very lightly revised, with only thirty-five minor changes. As Eaves and Kimpel have surmised, it is entirely possible that changes made in this edition might not even be by Richardson,[102] who, trying to stay ahead of Irish pirates, was then occupied with printing and revising *Grandison*, which would be published in a third edition of seven duodecimo volumes on 19 March 1754, only five days after the publication of the final volume of the first and second editions. In short, as his other writing projects took more of his time and attention, Richardson seems to have put aside his plans to improve his first novel beyond its octavo state, though, as his correspondence of these years attests, Pamela continued to be very much on his mind. Writing to Lady Bradshaigh on 5 October 1753, in a letter in which he informs her that one of his reasons for delaying publication of *Grandison* is to keep Irish 'Rapparees' from completing 'their Edition from mine', he vows that 'I will give Pamela my last Correction, if my Life be spared; that, as a Piece of Writing only, she may not appear, for her Situation, unworthy of her Younger Sisters.'[103] He had expressed the same intention in June of that year, in his autobiographical letter to Johannes Stinstra, from which we have earlier quoted: 'I should say, that I intend to give to my good Pamela, my last Hand. I find I shall correct it much; but shall leave a particular Regard to preserve ye Simplicity of the Character.'[104] A year later, on 28 June 1754, he tells Stinstra that 'I shall retouch Pamela, as I have Opportunity; having gone a good way in it', at the same time informing him that he is now collecting the 'Sentiments' of his first and last novel (having already done so for *Clarissa*) for 'a kind of Vade Mecum' to those who have read (or not read) his stories.[105] As he worked on *A Collection of the Moral and Instructive Sentiments, Maxims, Cautions, and Reflexions, Contained in the Histories of Pamela, Clarissa, and Sir Charles Grandison*, published in March 1755, Richardson must have been going over the text of the novel once again, so that, writing to Stinstra on 26 November 1755, he could declare that 'I have actually retouched Pamela.'[106] Although he adds that in the edition (1754) he has recently printed the first two volumes remain 'as they were', that does not necessarily argue against his having made corrections to those volumes which he saved for inclusion in future editions.[107] One possible

---

102 Eaves and Kimpel, 'Richardson's Revisions of *Pamela*', p. 71.

103 Richardson to Lady Bradshaigh, 5 October 1753.   104 Richardson to Stinstra, 2 June 1753.

105 Richardson to Stinstra, 28 June 1754.   106 Richardson to Stinstra, 26 November 1755.

107 Having told Stinstra that he has 'actually retouched Pamela', Richardson adds a somewhat confusing clarification: 'But there being a Number of the 3^d and 4th Volumes of that Work in hand, more than of the 1st and 2^d. I only, printed as many of the two latter, as would make perfect Setts; and was therefore obliged to keep the two former as they were.' Though it is difficult to tell whether 'former' here refers to the volumes Richardson has mentioned first (III and IV) or to the volumes *published* first (I and II) and thus *former* to III and IV, this comment might support the hypothesis that the minor corrections in the first two volumes of the 1754 edition might have been made not by Richardson but by one of his compositors as the text was being set at the press. In short, Richardson's 'retouching' of *Pamela* – his phrasing seeming to indicate major revision – appears not to have been implemented in this edition, suggesting that there were corrections that Richardson kept in reserve for future editions.

agent of correction might have been Lady Bradshaigh. Having confessed to her his 'Ignorance of Proprietys of those Kinds' (such as 'the Titles of Characters') in October 1753, he had sought her advice to correct his 'Mistakes'.[108] To that end, she agreed, in a letter she began on 23 December 1753 but did not complete until 14 January 1754, to 'write my marginal notes, in an old Edition of Pamela that I have by me', adding 'it will be great amusement to me. tho' of no great Benefit to anybody, but myself'.[109] We do not know on which 'old Edition' of the novel Lady Bradshaigh wrote her marginalia or if Richardson was actually able to use them to shape his revisions. The next surviving reference in their correspondence to this annotated copy occurs in a letter from one of Richardson's daughters to Lady Bradshaigh, sent in early March 1761, requesting that she 'will favour him with the Perusal of your Observations . . . as may make ye future Edition more perfect than otherwise it can be',[110] a request with which she complied on 13 March. Whether the increasingly frail Richardson had time, in the three and a half months he had left to live (he died on 4 July), to benefit from his friend's 'Observations' is debatable. However, given that many of the changes made in the next 'future Edition', the duodecimo eighth published on 28 October 1761 (dated 1762), concern forms of address and the manners of the upper ranks, it is plausible to infer her influence.

Though published posthumously, the eighth edition is the last that can confidently be regarded as fully authoritative, with most of its 251 changes following patterns of revision evident in previous lifetime editions and, therefore, very likely by Richardson himself. Thus, for example, the twenty-seven changes in the introduction continue the process of moderating Hill's excessive praise of the novel, a few more ''Squires' and stylistic lapses disappear from the letters and journal, and more of the information in the original conclusion at the end of volume II, rendered redundant or inaccurate by the continuation, is eliminated or altered. Nevertheless, though this edition has the largest number of changes of all the post-octavo duodecimo editions, most of them are not substantive and leave the first two volumes essentially as they were in the fifth edition of September 1741. Several more editions appeared before 1800, none claiming any textual authority, though published by descendants or associates of the original publishers of the novel: the ninth in 1767 (volume I reads 'eighth'; all other volumes, 'ninth'); tenth in

---

108 Richardson to Lady Bradshaigh, 5 October 1753.
109 Lady Bradshaigh to Richardson, 14 January 1754.
110 [Martha?] Richardson to Lady Bradshaigh, [early March?] 1761, FM XI, fol. 270. As Eaves and Kimpel point out (p. 704), the surviving draft of this letter in the Forster Collection is in Richardson's hand. I accept here Eaves and Kimpel's conjectures regarding which one of Richardson's daughters transcribed the letter as well as its date. Lady Bradshaigh's reply of 13 March (FM XI, fol. 276) is addressed to Richardson.

1771; another 'tenth' in 1775; eleventh in 1776; twelfth in 1785; and thirteenth in 1792. A reissue of the 1742 octavo edition, with new title pages, was 'sold' by William Otridge in 1772. In 1785, James Harrison published all four volumes of the novel and also issued them together in volume XX of *The Novelist's Magazine*.[111] There were also several abridgements, including *The Paths of Virtue Delineated* (1768; second edition, 1773; third, 1777), containing 'in miniature' versions of all three of Richardson's novels, a work sometimes attributed to Oliver Goldsmith, and *The History of Pamela; or, Virtue Rewarded* (1792; reissued, 1795), 'comprized in one large volume octavo', published by Alexander Hogg. Abridgements, sometimes illustrated with 'cuts', also appeared in the United States in the 1790s, not only in Boston, Philadelphia, and New York, but also in such smaller towns as Worcester (Massachusetts), Norristown (Pennsylvania), and Fairhaven (Vermont), indicating that interest in Pamela's story remained high in the former colony, half a century after Benjamin Franklin had published a so-called 'fifth edition' (based on Richardson's fourth) of the first two volumes in Philadelphia (1742–4), thereby making *Pamela: or, Virtue Rewarded* the first English novel printed in North America.[112]

---

111 It is highly significant that James Harrison, a savvy observer of publishing trends, included *Pamela* in *The Novelist's Magazine*, as he chose only blockbusters for his collection, thus assuring the continued popularity and canonization of many of them. See Richard C. Taylor, 'James Harrison, *The Novelist's Magazine*, and the Early Canonizing of the English Novel', *Studies in English Literature* 33 (1993), 629–43. For an overview of this type of publication, see Robert D. Mayo, *The English Novel in the Magazines, 1740–1815* (Evanston, IL: Northwestern University Press, 1962). In *The Business of Books: Booksellers and the English Book Trade 1450–1850* (New Haven and London: Yale University Press, 2007), James Raven summarizes Harrison's publishing career: 'James Harrison was an author and literary innovator as well as a highly successful entrepreneur. Among his 120 or so eighteenth-century titles were several part-book periodicals and weekly magazines. In November 1779, Harrison commenced his *Novelist's Magazine* in octavo with double columns and stitched in small weekly numbers... [A]t their peak, 10000 copies or more of the *Novelist's Magazine* sold each week, with twenty-three volumes extant by the date of completion. The *Novelist's Magazine* opened with John Hawkesworth's oriental *Almoran and Hamet* and Henry Fielding's *Joseph Andrews* and *Amelia* (the numbers of these three comprised the first volume). Later reprinted works included Tobias Smollett's *Peregrine Pickle* and *Humphry Clinker* and Samuel Richardson's *Pamela* and *Clarissa* (among sixty-one novels in all). In 1785, Harrison launched his *British Classicks* over eight volumes, ending in 1787 (and reprinted again beginning in 1793...). Harrison's *Sacred Classicks* began in 1786, followed by his *New Novelist's Magazine*, which ran monthly from May 1786 to early 1788...' (p. 245).

112 The colophon of Franklin's edition reads: '*LONDON*, Printed: PHILADELPHIA; Reprinted, and Sold by B. FRANKLIN.'; the second volume is dated 1743. On Richardson and Franklin, see Paul Giles, *Transatlantic Insurrections: British Culture and the Foundation of American Literature, 1730–1860* (Philadelphia: University of Pennsylvania Press, 2001), pp. 70–91; Giles asserts that *Pamela* 'remained the most widely read of Richardson's novels in the New World' (p. 72). For a discussion of the 'American Richardson', see Leonard Tennenhouse, *The Importance of Feeling English: American Literature and the British Diaspora, 1750–1850* (Princeton University Press, 2007), pp. 43–72. Back in Britain, the London bookseller Charles Cooke included both parts of *Pamela*, unabridged, in his *Pocket Edition of Select Novels* in 1801–3; the text resembles that of the posthumous 'eighth' edition published in 1761. Cooke also published an abridgement of the novel in 1811, again based on the 1761 edition, which, reissued at least ten times before 1838, was not only the most widely available version of the novel in the early nineteenth century, but also provided the text for the Everyman

Except for the 1742 octavo, on which it seems to be based, the most important and textually significant of the revised editions of *Pamela* is the fourteenth, published in four duodecimo volumes in 1801.[113] Because this edition appeared forty years after Richardson's death, readers need to exercise caution before accepting as 'authorial' any changes in this edition not found in (or clearly derived from) editions up to the eighth. Simply put, we do not know, with certainty, which of the new changes were made by Richardson and which by his two daughters, Martha Bridgen (who died in February 1785) and Anne Richardson, both of whom seem to have made attempts to correct the copy of the novel left in their possession – a copy which had, in Anne's words to her sister on 31 July 1784, 'received' their 'Father's last hand', but was still 'not enough perfect to be published'.[114] In short, though it can claim a direct line of descent from Richardson – '*THE Booksellers*' assuring '*the Public*' in the 'Advertisement' that they were '*favoured with the copy, from which this Edition is printed, by his only surviving daughter, Mrs. Anne Richardson*' – this edition is not fully authoritative. Nonetheless, so long as the possibly mixed authority of this edition is acknowledged, its value in the textual and publication history of the novel cannot be discounted. Whatever the extent of his daughters' editorial interventions, the 1801 edition presents *Pamela* in the exalted textual condition towards which Richardson's own revisions had been pointing since the second edition of February 1741. The elevation of Pamela's language and

edition of 1914. Thus, for most of the nineteenth century and well into the twentieth, readers of *Pamela* read the novel in a truncated state neither authored nor authorized by Richardson. On this subject, see Peter Sabor, 'The Cooke-Everyman Edition of *Pamela*', *The Library*, 5th Series, 32 (1977), 360–6.

113 Anne Richardson, who died in 1803, informed a correspondent in October 1801 that she was correcting 'errors of printing &c.' in the 1801 edition of *Pamela*. Published by essentially the same group of booksellers as the 1801 edition, a 'fifteenth' edition, correcting typographical and other stylistic errors, appeared in 1810. Because this is the last edition in what might be called the Richardson–Bridgen line of textual transmission, it is of some significance. However, just as the 1801 edition, it must be used with caution. For information on the 1810 edition, see Eaves and Kimpel, 'Richardson's Revisions of *Pamela*', pp. 76–7. Eaves and Kimpel surmise that 'the 1810 edition was printed from a copy of the 1801 corrected by Anne Richardson. It is not impossible that she consulted the copy in her father's hand, but none of the changes are beyond her abilities' (p. 77). In short, we do not know who is responsible for changes in the 1810 text.

114 Quoted in Eaves and Kimpel, 'Richardson's Revisions of *Pamela*', p. 75; Eaves and Kimpel cite excerpts from the correspondence between the sisters from 28 June to 31 July 1784 (see pp. 74–5). A longer passage from Anne's letter of 28 June to Martha conveys a sense of the kinds of revision the sisters have been discussing to 'perfect' their father's work: 'Mr. Bridgen [Martha's husband] likewise mentioned the publication of the corrected Pamela, which, if you approve, I think wou'd be very proper: But my Love farther Corrections *by you* wou'd be *necessary* and make it infinitely more perfect. – I remember that I thot the conversation at the farmer's on her journey from the Bedford to the Lincoln house was *not* an improvement, as the stile is different from the rest of the two first vols: and that therefore it was better before' (quoted in McKillop, pp. 59–60). These letters, once owned by McKillop, are now at Fondren Library, Rice University; see 'Richardson family papers, 1714–1802', MS. 279.

social circumstances, begun by Richardson six decades earlier, reaches its fullest expression in these volumes.[115]

With over 8,400 changes in the first two volumes, the fourteenth edition is by far the most extensively revised; contrary to Richardson's usual patterns of revision, it is actually shorter than the original and – again, atypical of his usual practice – lighter in overt moral commentary. As Eaves and Kimpel observe, with only minor exaggeration, 'hardly a paragraph is untouched'.[116] The editor's preface appears as it was in the octavo; as in the octavo, the prefatory letters and introduction are omitted, as are the two paragraphs in the octavo accounting for such omission. The table of contents from the octavo is considerably reduced and no longer appears in its entirety before Pamela's first letter; instead, each volume has its own table of contents. As in the octavo, the summary paragraphs concluding the second volume, kept in all duodecimo editions, are eliminated. While many changes are imported from the octavo, there are also some adopted from the duodecimos, suggesting that Richardson, as he gave his 'last Hand' to *Pamela* during the 1750s, might have been reviewing his corrections to previous editions to determine which ones were worth preserving. But thousands of changes are new and, while their provenance might be disputable, they are, for the most part, consistent with Richardson's plan to improve Pamela's style and social standing. For example, in the opening letter, revised in ways typical of the whole work, Pamela hopes not 'to be a burden to my dear parents' (I, p. 2) rather than 'a Clog upon' them. A more extensive alteration in this letter is also of a piece with Richardson's previous practice. After Pamela mentions that she is sending to her parents the four guineas 'which were in my lady's pocket' – a more refined phrasing of 'my old Lady's Pocket' of prior editions – a sentence is added to fend off the suspicion that Mr. and Mrs. Andrews might be habitual free-loaders on their daughter's occasional charity; the old couple, while 'low' in their circumstances, do not behave in a 'low' fashion: 'I formerly sent you such little matters as arose from my lady's bounty, loth as you was always to take any thing from me' (ibid.). Following her reassurance to them that 'Providence will not let me want', a few additional clauses reveal not only the young girl's precocious good sense in monetary matters but also her prudence and self-importance in her dealings with members of her own class: 'and I have made, in case of sudden occasions, a little reserve (besides the silver now given me) that I may not be obliged to borrow, and look little in the eyes of my fellow-servants' (ibid.). She then wraps the guineas in paper 'that they may not chink'

---

115 Few copies of this edition have survived, but all four volumes are available in facsimile (New York: Garland, 1974). For an excellent modern edition of the first two volumes, incorporating corrections from the 1810 edition, see Samuel Richardson, *Pamela; or, Virtue Rewarded*, ed. Peter Sabor, intro. Margaret A. Doody (Harmondsworth: Penguin, 1980).

116 Eaves and Kimpel, 'Richardson's Revisions of *Pamela*', p. 78.

(I, p. 3), expanding the contraction from prior editions ('that they mayn't chink'), thus eliminating another trace of 'low' speech. In the postscript to the letter, Mr. B. notices that Pamela spells 'very well' (I, p. 4) rather than 'tolerably'; he no longer comments on his mother's 'Care' in Pamela's 'Learning' or the girl's love of reading, though he still encourages her to 'look into any of my mother's books to improve yourself, so you take care of them' (ibid.). Finally, the overly cheery 'Indeed, he is the best of Gentlemen, I think!' from the octavo – 'Indeed he is the best of Gentlemen, I think!' in all the duodecimos – becomes the somewhat more ominous (and syntactically complex) 'Indeed, he was once thought to be wildish; but he is now the best of gentlemen, I think!' (ibid.), so that readers, from the very beginning, are alerted that Mr. B., having already earned a reputation as a dangerous rake, is not quite the fumbling booby squire that Fielding and others had laughed at.

Richardson's goal as he revised – a goal also aimed at by his daughters – was to 'perfect' the novel and its heroine, to answer the objections of past readers and to prevent future criticism and ridicule, to make, in short, the 'low' Pamela of the first two volumes fit better with the 'exalted' Pamela of the last two. When, in her 'biographical account' of the author introducing her edition of Richardson's correspondence (1804), Anna Laetitia Barbauld astutely observed that the second part of the novel 'aims to palliate, by counter criticism, the faults which had been found in the first part', adding that 'it is less a continuation than the author's defence of himself',[117] she could well have been speaking of the revisions to the first two volumes, especially in the fourteenth edition, which had been published three years earlier. Although the rustic Pamela of the first edition does not entirely disappear from the fourteenth, she loses something vital to Richardson's original conception of her character when, for example, she is made to drop such spontaneous verbal bursts as 'For what I do, must be at a Jirk, to be sure' (8vo, I, p. 182) in favour of more proper expressions or (as is in this particular instance) silence. Whether this excision was made by Richardson or by one of his daughters, it bespeaks a fundamental misunderstanding of what attracted so many readers to the novel in late 1740 and early 1741. Pamela's original strength, the catalyst of the 'epidemical Phrenzy' decried by Fielding's dour Parson Oliver, was precisely her 'low' speech, her unaffected manners, her humble 'Country-habit'. As Aaron Hill correctly asserted in his enthusiastic defence of the work in the introduction to the second edition, 'In *Pamela*, in particular, we owe All to her *Lowness*' (p. 468 below). It was indeed her lowness that captured London in November 1740. Readers of the more stylistically proper 1801 edition might well have wondered what all the fuss had been about.

---

117 *The Correspondence of Samuel Richardson*, p. lxxvii.

PRINCIPLES OF ANNOTATION

Because *Pamela: or, Virtue Rewarded* remains relatively accessible to the modern reader, it does not require extensive, specialized annotation. Unlike Henry Fielding, who aimed to dazzle the 'Classical Reader' with the range of his learning, Richardson was content, especially at the beginning of his career as a novelist, with writing for 'the mere *English* Reader'.[118] As a result, where the editor of Fielding's novels will need to write many learned annotations to explain his author's many learned allusions, the editor of Richardson's novels, especially of his first, does not need to be familiar with the works of Homer and Virgil or with the curriculum of Eton College. *Pamela: or, Virtue Rewarded* rarely strays beyond knowledge plausibly available to its fifteen-year-old, unschooled female narrator or to its intended audience of young readers. But even 'the mere *English* Reader' of 1740 would have known certain things that we do not know. Richardson's original readers, learned or unlearned, inhabited a world and a linguistic space different from ours. The main purpose of my annotations, then, is to recover as much of their world as possible and thus make intelligible to modern readers aspects of Richardson's first novel obscured by the passage of time.[119] To that end, I have consulted contemporary documents, such as newspapers, histories, pamphlets, and Richardson's correspondence, to identify or explain Pamela's references to notable persons or to cultural, historical, and political events. As is well known, Richardson liked to coin words or to use them in peculiar or idiosyncratic ways; when necessary to clarify the sense, I have derived definitions of words and phrases both from eighteenth-century dictionaries, such as Johnson's, and from the *Oxford English Dictionary*.[120] In addition, for legal terms I sometimes cull my definitions from contemporary law dictionaries. Pamela's language is characterized by biblical allusions and proverbial expressions. For biblical allusions, I have relied primarily on the King James Bible, but also on contemporary editions of hymnals and the Book of Common Prayer; for proverbial expressions, I draw upon Tilley's venerable *A Dictionary of the Proverbs in England in the Sixteenth and Seventeenth Centuries* as well as *The Oxford Dictionary of English Proverbs*. Quotations of Shakespeare's plays are from

118 *Joseph Andrews*, Preface, p. 3 (the 'Classical Reader' is mentioned on p. 4).
119 My views on annotation are indebted to Arthur Friedman, 'Principles of Historical Annotations in Critical Editions of Modern Texts', *English Institute Annual 1941* (New York: Columbia University Press, 1942), pp. 115–28; and Martin C. Battestin, 'A Rationale of Literary Annotation: The Example of Fielding's Novels', *Studies in Bibliography* 34 (1981), 1–22.
120 Johnson draws on Richardson for some of his illustrative quotations. Although Richardson is the 'living' author (after Johnson himself) most often cited in Johnson's *Dictionary*, there are only three references to *Pamela*: *glisten* ('The ladies eyes glistened with pleasure'); *key* ('Pamela loves to handle the spinet, and touch the keys'); and *romance* ('This is strange romancing'). *Clarissa*, however, is a different matter, with nearly 100 citations. See William R. Keast, 'The Two *Clarissas* in Johnson's *Dictionary*', *Studies in Philology* 54 (1957), 429–39; Keast's actual number is 96.

The Riverside Shakespeare, ed. G. Blakemore Evans, 2nd edn (Boston: Houghton Mifflin, 1997). Because Richardson often returns to the same concepts or ideas throughout his career, I also record in my annotations parallels with his other works, especially *Clarissa* and *Grandison*. Whenever appropriate in identifying a possible source or illuminating a particular point, I quote from books Richardson himself printed, on the assumption that he might have been familiar with their contents – a daunting task made easier by William Sale's pioneering *Samuel Richardson: Master Printer* (1950) and Keith Maslen's superb *Samuel Richardson of London, Printer* (2001). Although I have examined all the primary and secondary sources listed or cited in my annotations, I am greatly indebted to the work of previous editors of the novel, especially T. C. Duncan Eaves and Ben D. Kimpel (Riverside), Peter Sabor (Penguin), and Thomas Keymer and Alice Wakely (Oxford World's Classics).

TEXTUAL INTRODUCTION

In accordance with the usual textual policy of the Cambridge Edition of the Works of Samuel Richardson (CEWSR), this edition of *Pamela: or, Virtue Rewarded* offers a critical unmodernized text of the first edition of the novel, published on 6 November 1740 (dated 1741); the text is based on a copy of this edition at the Newberry Library in Chicago (Call Number: VAULT Case 3A 881, v. 1–2). In preparing the text, I collated four copies of the first edition (British Library, National Library of Scotland, Newberry Library, and the University of Chicago Library) and discovered no press-variants. Because Richardson was his own printer, the distinctions in authority between substantives and accidentals advanced in classical textual theory do not entirely apply.[1] Although it is possible that somebody other than Richardson made changes in this and subsequent editions – especially in such house-style matters as punctuation, as the texts were being set from manuscript or corrected copy – we can reasonably assume that all editions of the novel appearing during Richardson's lifetime were issued with his approval, if not his supervision, and are thus 'authoritative'.[2] With some caution, we can add to this group the 'eighth' duodecimo edition, published on 28 October 1761 (dated 1762), three months after Richardson's death, because the changes in it are consistent with those found in previous lifetime editions. More problematic in terms of its authority is the 'fourteenth' edition of 1801. Published forty years after Richardson's death, it claims to incorporate the author's final 'corrections and alterations' (title page). But, as

---

1 See W. W. Greg, 'The Rationale of Copy-Text', *Studies in Bibliography* 3 (1950), 19–36. As Greg writes, 'we need to draw a distinction between the significant, or as I shall call them "substantive," readings of the text, those namely that affect the author's meaning or the essence of his expression, and others, such in general as spelling, punctuation, word-division, and the like, affecting mainly its formal presentation, which may be regarded as the accidents, or as I shall call them "accidentals," of the text' (p. 22).
2 There is evidence that Richardson printed only parts of the third and fourth editions because the demand for the novel was exceeding the capabilities of his press; see the section on bibliographical description below. Several printers were also involved in the production of the octavo edition.

their surviving correspondence seems to suggest, this edition was contaminated, to an extent we cannot now recover, by the editorial interference of his daughters.[3] Thus, any case that might be made for this edition as incorporating Richardson's 'final' intentions for his work is undercut by the uncertain provenance of its corrections.

What we know for certain is that Richardson had intended to give his first novel his 'last Hand', as he writes to Johannes Stinstra on 2 June 1753, but that he died before he could publish that final version.[4] There is, then, no edition of *Pamela: or, Virtue Rewarded* that can legitimately claim to contain Richardson's 'final' intentions, with the eight editions issued after the first – the 'sixth' edition existing in textually different octavo (1742) and duodecimo (1746) versions – serving only as provisional stages on the way to an ideal text that Richardson did not live to print. Under these circumstances, and in keeping with recent trends in textual scholarship, choosing the first edition as copy-text makes the most sense because it stands as the purest expression of Richardson's original and, at the date of its original publication, 'final' intentions for his work, the closest in time to the moment when Pamela 'sprung' from his imagination.[5] It is also the first edition of the novel that is the most historically significant, capturing the public's attention and giving rise to a vigorous debate over its moral, social, and literary value. This debate, because often focused on the 'lowness' of his heroine, caused Richardson to have second thoughts regarding the propriety of her language and led him to undertake revisions to smooth out the rough edges of her rustic speech. The first edition, in short, gives us '*Pamela* as *Pamela* wrote it; in her own Words', not in the words that Richardson later thought she should have used; it presents Pamela

---

3 On this topic, see General Introduction, pp. lxxii–lxxiv.

4 Richardson to Stinstra, 2 June 1753: 'Only, I should say, that I intend to give my good Pamela, my last Hand. I find I shall correct it much; but shall leave a particular Regard to preserve the Simplicity of the Character.' For a fuller account of the textual history summarized here, see General Introduction, pp. lxiv–lxx.

5 Greg (see n. 1 above) favoured first editions because closest to the author's original manuscript, before the work became contaminated by the process of publication. Greg derived his rationale of copy-text from his experience as editor of sixteenth- and seventeenth-century printed books. Fredson Bowers, Greg's disciple, also preferred first editions but, in editing post-Renaissance works, he also took into account revisions in subsequent editions that could be confidently attributed to the author, thus producing an 'eclectic' text based on the first edition but incorporating into it 'final' intentions, as exemplified in his text for the Wesleyan Edition *Tom Jones* (1974). Bowers enunciated his editorial principles in many essays published over his long career, the most important of them up to 1976 conveniently collected in *Essays in Bibliography, Texts, and Editing* (Charlottesville: Bibliographical Society of the University of Virginia, 2003); see also his 'Greg's Rationale of Copy-Text Revisited', *Studies in Bibliography* 31 (1978), 90–161. For a brief review of some of the issues involved in the choice and treatment of the copy-text in critical editions, see my 'Whose Work Is It Anyway? Or, How We Learned to Stop Worrying about the Author and Love the Text', in Alexander Pettit (ed.), *Textual Studies and the Common Reader: Essays on Editing Novels and Novelists* (Athens, GA, and London: University of Georgia Press, 2000), pp. 180–97.

as she originally appeared, dressed in 'her neat Country Apparel' (Preface, p. 7) rather than in the more genteel clothing her author attempted to fashion for her in subsequent editions.[6]

TREATMENT OF THE COPY-TEXT

Richardson was a careful printer and, as a result, the first edition of *Pamela: or, Virtue Rewarded* is relatively free of typographical and other errors. Therefore, the text presented here is conservatively edited and faithful to the copy-text, except for those changes in format and presentation implemented according to the guidelines of the CEWSR. In recognition of the orthographic fluidity of eighteenth-century English, no attempt has been made to regularize the spelling of words variously spelled within the copy-text or to make them conform to modern British usage. Emendations made to the copy-text are presented in the list of Emendations below, with each entry noting the edition from which the emendation has been adopted as well as recording the rejected reading from the copy-text. Falling outside the scope of the list of Emendations, a change in the setting of a letter needs special mention here. I have moved the postscript dating the letter ending on p. 232 ('*Monday* Morn. near three o'Clock.') from its confusing position, wedged left next to the complimentary closing in the copy-text and other duodecimo editions, to a slot right below it, as it appears in the octavo edition (II, p. 15).[7]

A table of word-division lists compounds or possible compounds that are hyphenated at the end of the line in the Cambridge edition; it also lists compounds or possible compounds that are hyphenated at the end of the line in the copy-text. Forms of compounds hyphenated at the end of the line in the copy-text follow the usual practice of the copy-text when appearing within the line in the Cambridge edition; subsequent editions printed by Richardson have been consulted if no instance of the compound exists within the line in the copy-text. The

---

6 On the elevation of Pamela's diction in subsequent editions, see, for example, Eaves and Kimpel, 'Richardson's Revisions of *Pamela*'; Philip Gaskell, *From Writer to Reader: Studies in Editorial Method* (Oxford: Clarendon Press, 1978), pp. 63–79; Peter Sabor, 'Richardson's Correspondence and His Final Revision of *Pamela*', *Transactions of the Samuel Johnson Society of the Northwest* 12 (1981), 114–31; and Keymer, 'Assorted Versions of Assaulted Virgins'. Richardson's tendency to elevate the language of the first edition is also evident in his revisions of *Clarissa* and *Sir Charles Grandison*; see Shirley Van Marter, 'Richardson's Revisions of *Clarissa* in the Second Edition', *Studies in Bibliography* 26 (1973), 107–32, and 'Richardson's Revisions of *Clarissa* in the Third and Fourth Editions', *Studies in Bibliography* 28 (1975), 119–52; and Robert Craig Pierson, 'The Revisions of Richardson's *Sir Charles Grandison*', *Studies in Bibliography* 21 (1968), 163–89.

7 This change in the octavo, however, seems to have confused G. Woodfall, the printer of the 1801 edition, who, setting his page from the octavo page, moves the postscript date forward, to become the heading of the next journal entry, 'MONDAY *Morning, near Three o-Clock.*' (II, p. 12). Woodfall restores the postscript date to its correct octavo position in the 1810 edition (II, p. 11).

redundant 'e' in present participles and other words hyphenated at the end of a line (e.g., 'breathe-ing', 'pleasure-able', 'Assure-ance') has been removed, to reflect the usual spelling of those words in the copy-text. Original line-divisions in the copy-text are reproduced in titles, subtitles, and section headings (as in 'PREFACE | BY THE | EDITOR'), except in those instances where such divisions do not seem to be meaningful and apparently occur only to accommodate the length of the line of Richardson's original page (for example, the headings of both letters in the preface, which are set as two lines in the copy-text).

While the layout of the text generally follows that of the copy-text, the Cambridge edition aims for a certain degree of uniformity. Thus, a three-line space appears between letters or journal entries; a two-line space after letter or journal headings; a two-line space when a gap in the copy-text signals a pause in writing; and a one-line space after datelines and salutations as well as before complimentary closes and postscripts. Datelines are set one em from the right margin. Salutations are indented from the left margin by one em, with the opening line of each letter flushed left. Display capitals in the opening lines ('I Have great Trouble'; 'YOUR Letter was indeed a great Trouble') are set in lower case ('I have great Trouble'; 'Your Letter was indeed a great Trouble'). Decorative initials or drop capitals are normalized and the factota in which they are inserted are not reproduced, though the factota will be identified, along with other ornaments, in the bibliographical description of the copy-text.[8] Complimentary closes and signatures are set flush right, staggered by one em per line if running to two or more lines. Postscripts are set flush left, without the hanging indents often used in the copy-text. In the rare instances in which a postscript extends beyond one sentence or paragraph, the second and subsequent sentences or paragraphs are set one em from the left margin. Block passages of poetry (such as Pamela's 'VERSES on my going away') are centred. Though the long 's' is normalized and running marginal quotation marks eliminated, most typographical features – roman/italic/bold font; large/small caps; ligatures; superscripts; marginal indices, bullets, and other symbols; single or double quotation marks; different styles of parentheses – are presented as they appear in the copy-text. Missing quotation marks have been silently added when it is clear that they were accidentally omitted. Following the common but not always consistent practice of the copy-text, italics are used for all punctuation occurring within

---

8 Bibliographical descriptions of all editions of *Pamela: or, Virtue Rewarded* up to 1762, including the French edition published with Richardson's approval in October 1741, appear in the bibliographical section below. This also includes bibliographical descriptions of the 1801 and 1810 editions because, though published decades after Richardson's death, they nonetheless belong to a line of textual transmission that can be traced back to Richardson. Editions or abridgements of the novel appearing in Dublin, North America (including Benjamin Franklin's), or London (after 1762) are not described because there is no evidence that Richardson was involved in their publication.

italicized phrases, and for question marks and exclamation points appearing at the end of italicized words and phrases; other punctuation, including the possessive apostrophe (as in *Pamela*'s), is roman. Opening and closing quotation marks are not italicized. The abbreviation '&c.' is set to reflect the general tendency of the copy-text, where italic '*&c.*' usually precedes or follows roman text and roman '&c.' precedes or follows *italic text*. Variations in size of types are reproduced only when different sizes are mixed within a line, thereby indicating a clear distinction between small and large capitals or between capitals and lower-case letters (e.g., '*the* YOUTH *of* both Sexes').

Recognizing the possible validity of recent arguments made for the expressive significance of dash lengths in the printed texts of some eighteenth-century novels, this edition will not attempt to regularize the presentation of hyphens and dashes found in the copy-text.[9] At the same time, a close examination of the copy-text reveals that the length of interruptive hyphens or dashes, while sometimes appearing to be expressive, often seems to be dictated by nothing more than the number or length of words that can be accommodated within Richardson's original line. Thus, while the usual practice of the copy-text is to signal an interruption in the narrative with an em dash or three hyphens ('---'), sometimes Richardson's compositors insert a longer dash, or add four or (rarely) five or more hyphens to the

9 On the interpretive significance of 'accidentals', see, for example, Janine Barchas, 'Sarah Field-ing's Dashing Style and Eighteenth-Century Print Culture', *ELH* 63 (1996), 633–56; and Kathryn Sutherland, 'Speaking Commas/Reading Commas: Punctuating *Mansfield Park*', *TEXT* 12 (1999), 101–22. Both Barchas and Sutherland argue for a return to the first editions of, respectively, *The Adventures of David Simple* (published May 1744) and *Mansfield Park* (1814) to recuperate significant expressive features of the authors' style obscured in later editions by attempts to eliminate what Sutherland calls 'apparently "bad" punctuation' (p. 104). Both Barchas and Sutherland agree that this editorial cleansing seems particularly insidious in the case of women authors, with apparently well-intentioned male editors (Henry Fielding and R. W. Chapman) 'improving' the work by cor-recting what they perceived as defective grammar, syntax, and orthography. Barchas takes to task Malcolm Kelsall for using the second edition of *The Adventures of David Simple*, corrected by Henry Fielding and published in July 1744, as the copy-text for his 1969 edition of the novel, published by Oxford University Press, and looks forward to an edition, then in preparation by Peter Sabor, based on the 'uncorrected' first edition. Sabor's edition, published by the University Press of Kentucky in 1998, meticulously reproduces the 'accidentals' of the first edition, restoring, for example, not only the dashes of that edition but also their various lengths. Sutherland had earlier published an edition of *Mansfield Park* (Penguin, 1996) according to the editorial principles she describes in her *TEXT* article, based on the first edition of 1814, rather than the second of 1816. Both of these editions are discussed in Jeanine Casler, 'The Primacy of the "Rougher" Version: Neo-Conservative Editorial Practices and Clara Reeve's *Old English Baron*', *Papers on Language and Literature* 37 (2001), 404–37. Although pointing out 'a few questionable assumptions' (p. 411) in Barchas's methodology, Casler nonetheless agrees that the 'accidentals' of earlier states of women's novels should be recovered. This is why she argues for the recuperation of the more expressive text of the first edition of Reeve's *Old English Baron*, published under a different title, *The Champion of Virtue* (1777), before the novel was revised by Martha Bridgen, Reeve's 'patroness' and Richardson's daughter, for a presumably more 'correct' second edition. Casler's characterization of Bridgen's 'editorial technique' as tending 'toward the heavily interventionist' (p. 419) further reinforces caution in accepting as authoritative alterations in the 1801 *Pamela*.

usual sequence of three, for no other apparent reason than to fill in a gap in the line. Without occluding these features of the copy-text, on the assumption that some of them might be of expressive significance, this edition nonetheless aims for some pragmatic standardization in their presentation, in keeping with what appears to have been the practice of Richardson's printing house. Interruptive hyphens, then, are set as rules of varying lengths depending on the number of hyphens (em for the 'standard' three hyphens; 2-em for four to six hyphens; 3-em for seven or more hyphens), closed to both the previous and the succeeding characters in the line. Dashes are also set in these three categories (em, 2-em, 3-em) to reflect the three different lengths commonly found in the copy-text (measuring approximately 4 mm, 5.5 mm, 7 mm), with broken dashes (i.e., two em dashes in a row) set as a single 2-em rule; these are also closed to the surrounding elements in the line.

Elliptical hyphens are reproduced exactly in number as they appear in the copy-text, closed to surrounding characters within a word ('B----n-hall'), open to both sides when denoting a word ('my Lord ------ who'), and closed only to the previous element when completing a word ('here is Mr. *B*-----'). However, there are some instances where the number of hyphens in the copy-text does not correspond to the number of letters needed to complete an obviously familiar word (e.g., in Letter XXIV, 'D---d Impertinence' and 'by G---- I will have her!'); in such cases, where elliptical correctness is apparently not intended, the number of hyphens has not been expanded or reduced to account for the exact number of letters missing from the word as conventionally spelled, but set as rules of appropriate length in accordance with the criteria outlined above. Readers of the present edition will thus be apprised of those places in the copy-text where dashes and interruptive and elliptical hyphens do not follow the standard length or sequence; whether these variations are of critical or interpretive significance lies outside the province of the textual editor to determine.

PAMELA;

OR,

VIRTUE Rewarded

PAMELA:
OR,
VIRTUE Rewarded.

In a SERIES of

FAMILIAR LETTERS

FROM A

Beautiful Young DAMSEL,
To her PARENTS.

Now first Published

In order to cultivate the Principles of
VIRTUE and RELIGION in the Minds of
the YOUTH of BOTH SEXES.

A Narrative which has its Foundation in TRUTH
and NATURE; and at the same time that it agreeably entertains, by a Variety of *curious* and *affecting*
INCIDENTS, is intirely divested of all those Images,
which, in too many Pieces calculated for Amusement
only, tend to *inflame* the Minds they should *instruct*.

In TWO VOLUMES.

VOL. I.

LONDON:

Printed for C. RIVINGTON, in *St. Paul's Church-
Yard*; and J. OSBORN, in *Pater-noster Row*.
MDCCXLI.

1 *Pamela: or, Virtue Rewarded.* Reproduced by kind permission of the
Newberry Library, Chicago

PREFACE
BY THE
EDITOR.

If to Divert *and* Entertain, *and at the same time to* Instruct, *and* Improve *the Minds of the* YOUTH *of* both Sexes:

If to inculcate Religion *and* Morality *in so easy and agreeable a manner, as shall render them equally* delightful *and* profitable *to the* younger Class *of Readers, as well as worthy of the Attention of Persons of* maturer *Years and Understandings:*

If to set forth in the most exemplary Lights, the Parental, *the* Filial, *and the* Social *Duties,*[1] *and that from* low *to* high *Life:*

If to paint VICE *in its proper Colours, to make it* deservedly Odious; *and to set* VIRTUE *in its own amiable Light, to make it* truly Lovely:

If to draw Characters justly, *and to support them* equally:

If to raise a Distress from natural *Causes, and to excite Compassion from* proper *Motives:*

If to teach the Man of Fortune *how to* use *it; the Man of* Passion *how to* subdue *it; and the Man of* Intrigue, *how, gracefully, and with Honour to himself, to* reclaim:

If to give practical *Examples, worthy to be followed in the most* critical *and affecting Cases, by the modest* Virgin, *the chaste* Bride, *and the obliging* Wife:

If to effect all these good Ends, in so probable, so natural, so lively a manner, as shall engage the Passions of every sensible Reader,[2] *and strongly interest them in the edifying Story:*

And all without raising a single Idea *throughout the Whole, that shall shock the exactest Purity, even in those tender Instances where the exactest Purity would be most apprehensive:*

If these, (embellished with a great Variety of entertaining Incidents) be laudable or worthy Recommendations of any Work, the Editor of the following Letters, which have their Foundation in Truth *and* Nature, *ventures to assert, that all these desirable Ends are obtained in these Sheets: And as he is therefore confident of the favourable Reception which he boldly bespeaks for this little Work; he thinks any* further Preface *or* Apology *for it, unnecessary: And the rather for two Reasons,* 1st. *Because he can Appeal from his own Passions, (which have been uncommonly* moved *in perusing these engaging Scenes) to the Passions of* Every one *who shall read them with the least Attention: And, in the next place, because an* Editor *may reasonably be supposed to judge with an Impartiality which is rarely to be met with in an* Author *towards his own Works.*

The Editor.

To the Editor of the Piece intitled, PAMELA; *or,* VIRTUE Rewarded.

Dear SIR,

I have had inexpressible Pleasure in the Perusal of your PAMELA. It intirely answers the Character you give of it in your Preface; nor have you said one Word too much in Commendation of a Piece that has Advantages and Excellencies peculiar to itself. For, besides the beautiful Simplicity of the Style, and a happy Propriety and Clearness of Expression (the Letters being written under the immediate Impression of every Circumstance which occasioned them, and that to those who had a Right to know the fair Writer's most secret Thoughts) the several Passions of the Mind must, of course, be more affectingly described, and Nature may be traced in her undisguised Inclinations with much more Propriety and Exactness, than can possibly be found in a Detail of Actions long past, which are never recollected with the same Affections, Hopes, and Dreads, with which they were felt when they occurred.

This little Book will infallibly be looked upon as the hitherto much-wanted Standard or Pattern for this Kind of Writing. For it abounds with lively Images and Pictures; with Incidents natural, surprising, and perfectly adapted to the Story; with Circumstances interesting to Persons in common Life, as well as to those in exalted Stations. The greatest Regard is every where paid in it to Decency, and to every Duty of Life: There is a constant Fitness of the Style to the Persons and Characters described; Pleasure and Instruction here always go hand in hand: Vice and Virtue are set in constant Opposition, and Religion every-where inculcated in its native Beauty and chearful Amiableness; not dressed up in stiff, melancholy, or gloomy Forms, on one hand, nor yet, on the other, debased below its due Dignity and noble Requisites, in Compliment to a too fashionable but depraved Taste. And this I will boldly say, that if its numerous Beauties are added to its excellent Tendency, it will be found worthy a Place, not only in all Families (especially such as have in them young Persons of either Sex) but in the Collections of the most curious and polite Readers. For, as it borrows none of its Excellencies from the romantic Flights of unnatural Fancy, its being founded in Truth and Nature, and built upon Experience, will be a lasting Recommendation to the Discerning and Judicious; while the agreeable Variety of Occurrences and Characters, in which it abounds, will not fail to engage the Attention of the gay and more sprightly Readers.

The moral Reflections and Uses to be drawn from the several Parts of this admirable History, are so happily deduced from a Croud of different Events and Characters, in the Conclusion of the Work, that I shall say the less on that Head. But I think, the Hints you have given me, should also prefatorily be given to the Publick; *viz.* That it will appear from several Things mentioned in the Letters, that the Story must have happened within these Thirty Years past: That you have been obliged to vary some of the Names of Persons, Places, *&c.* and to disguise a few of the Circumstances, in order to avoid giving Offence to some Persons, who would not chuse to be pointed out too plainly in it; tho' they would be glad it may do the Good so laudably intended by the Publication.[1] And as you have in Confidence submitted to my Opinion some of those Variations, I am much pleased that you have so managed the Matter, as to make no Alteration in the Facts; and, at the same time, have avoided the digressive Prolixity too frequently used on such Occasions.

Little Book, charming PAMELA! face the World, and never doubt of finding Friends and Admirers, not only in thine own Country, but far from Home; where thou mayst give an Example of Purity to the Writers of a neighbouring Nation;[2] which now shall have an Opportunity to receive *English* Bullion in Exchange for its own Dross, which has so long passed current among us in Pieces abounding with all the Levities of its volatile Inhabitants. The reigning Depravity of the Times has yet left Virtue many Votaries. Of their Protection you need not despair. May every head-strong Libertine whose Hands you reach, be reclaimed; and every tempted Virgin who reads you, imitate the Virtue, and meet the Reward of the high-meriting, tho' low-descended, PAMELA. I am, Sir,

Your most Obedient,
and Faithful Servant,
J.B.D.F.[3]

To my worthy Friend, the Editor of PAMELA, *&c.*

SIR,

I return the Manuscript of *Pamela* by the Bearer, which I have read with a
great deal of Pleasure. It is written with that Spirit of Truth and agreeable
Simplicity, which, tho' much wanted, is seldom found in those Pieces
which are calculated for the Entertainment and Instruction of the Publick.
It carries Conviction in every Part of it; and the Incidents are so natural and
interesting, that I have gone hand-in-hand, and sympathiz'd with the pretty
Heroine in all her Sufferings, and been extremely anxious for her Safety,
under the Apprehensions of the bad Consequences which I expected, every
Page, would ensue from the laudable Resistance she made. I have interested
myself in all her Schemes of Escape; been alternately pleas'd and angry with
her in her Restraint; *pleas'd* with the little Machinations and Contrivances
she set on foot for her Release, and *angry* for suffering her Fears to defeat
them; always lamenting, with a most sensible Concern, the Miscarriages
of her Hopes and Projects. In short, the whole is so affecting, that there is
no reading it without uncommon Concern and Emotion. Thus far only as
to the *Entertainment* it gives.

As to *Instruction* and *Morality*, the Piece is full of both. It shews Virtue in
the strongest Light, and renders the Practice of it amiable and lovely. The
beautiful Sufferer keeps it ever in her View, without the least Ostentation,
or Pride; she has it so strongly implanted in her, that thro' the whole
Course of her Sufferings, she does not so much as hesitate once, whether
she shall sacrifice it to Liberty and Ambition, or not; but, as if there were
no other way to free and save herself, carries on a determin'd Purpose to
persevere in her Innocence, and wade with it throughout all Difficulties and
Temptations, or perish under them. It is an astonishing Matter, and well
worth our most serious Consideration, that a young beautiful Girl, in the
low Scene of Life and Circumstance in which Fortune placed her, without
the Advantage of a Friend capable to relieve and protect her, or any other
Education than what occurr'd to her from her own Observation and little
Reading, in the Course of her Attendance on her excellent Mistress and
Benefactress, could, after having a Taste of Ease and Plenty in a higher
Sphere of Life than what she was born and first brought up in, resolve
to return to her primitive Poverty, rather than give up her Innocence.
I say, it is surprizing, that a young Person, so circumstanced, could, in
Contempt of proffer'd Grandeur on the one side, and in Defiance of
Penury on the other, so happily and prudently conduct herself thro' such a

Series of Perplexities and Troubles, and withstand the alluring Baits, and almost irresistible Offers of a fine Gentleman, so universally admired and esteemed, for the Agreeableness of his Person and good Qualities, among all his Acquaintance; defeat all his Measures with so much Address, and oblige him, at last, to give over his vain Pursuit, and sacrifice his Pride and Ambition to Virtue, and become the Protector of that Innocence which he so long and so indefatigably labour'd to supplant: And all this without ever having entertain'd the least previous Design or Thought for that Purpose: No Art used to inflame him, no Coquetry practised to tempt or intice him, and no Prudery or Affectation to tamper with his Passions; but, on the contrary, artless and unpractised in the Wiles of the World, all her Endeavours, and even all her Wishes, tended only to render herself as un-amiable as she could in his Eyes: Tho' at the same time she is so far from having any Aversion to his Person, that she seems rather prepossess'd in his Favour, and admires his Excellencies, whilst she condemns his Passion for her. A glorious Instance of Self-denial! Thus her very Repulses became Attractions: The more she resisted, the more she charm'd; and the very Means she used to guard her Virtue, the more indanger'd it, by inflaming his Passions: Till, at last, by Perseverance, and a brave and resolute Defence, the Besieged not only obtain'd a glorious Victory over the Besieger, but took him Prisoner too.

I am charmed with the beautiful Reflections she makes in the Course of her Distresses; her Soliloquies and little Reasonings with herself, are exceeding pretty and entertaining: She pours out all her Soul in them before her Parents without Disguise; so that one may judge of, nay, almost see, the inmost Recesses of her Mind. A pure clear Fountain of Truth and Innocence, a Magazine[1] of Virtue and unblemish'd Thoughts!

I can't conceive why you should hesitate a Moment as to the Publication of this very natural and uncommon Piece. I could wish to see it out in its own native Simplicity, which will affect and please the Reader beyond all the Strokes of Oratory in the World; for those will but spoil it: and, should you permit such a murdering Hand to be laid upon it, to gloss and tinge it over with superfluous and needless Decorations, which, like too much Drapery in Sculpture and Statuary, will but incumber it; it may disguise the Facts, marr the Reflections, and unnaturalize the Incidents, so as to be lost in a Multiplicity of fine idle Words and Phrases, and reduce our Sterling Substance into an empty Shadow, or rather *frenchify* our *English* Solidity into Froth and Whip-syllabub.[2] No; let us have *Pamela* as *Pamela* wrote it; in her own Words, without Amputation, or Addition. Produce her to us in her neat Country Apparel, such as she appear'd in, on her intended Departure to her Parents; for such best becomes her Innocence and beautiful Simplicity. Such a Dress will best edify and entertain. The flowing Robes of Oratory may indeed amuse and amaze, but will never strike the Mind with solid Attention.

In short, Sir, a Piece of this Kind is much wanted in the World, which is but too much, as well as too early debauched by pernicious *Novels*. I know nothing Entertaining of that Kind that one might venture to recommend to the Perusal (much less the Imitation) of the Youth of either Sex: All that I have hitherto read, tends only to corrupt their Principles, mislead their Judgments, and initiate them into Gallantry and loose Pleasures.

Publish then, this good, this edifying and instructive little Piece for their Sakes. The Honour of *Pamela's* Sex demands *Pamela* at your Hands, to shew the World an Heroine, almost beyond Example, in an unusual Scene of Life, whom no Temptations, or Sufferings, could subdue. It is a fine, and glorious Original, for the Fair to copy out and imitate. Our own Sex, too, require it of you, to free us, in some measure, from the Imputation of being incapable of the Impressions of Virtue and Honour; and to shew the Ladies, that we are not inflexible while they are so.

In short, the Cause of Virtue, calls for the Publication of such a Piece as this. Oblige then, Sir, the concurrent Voices of both Sexes, and give us *Pamela* for the Benefit of Mankind: And as I believe its Excellencies cannot be long unknown to the World, and that there will not be a Family without it; so I make no Doubt but every Family that has it, will be much improv'd and better'd by it. 'Twill form the tender Minds of *Youth* for the Reception and Practice of Virtue and Honour; confirm and establish those of *maturer Years* on good and steady Principles; reclaim the Vicious, and mend the Age in general; insomuch that as I doubt not *Pamela* will become the bright Example and Imitation of all the fashionable young Ladies of *Great Britain*; so the truly generous Benefactor and Rewarder of her exemplary Virtue, will be no less admired and imitated among the *Beau Monde* of our own Sex. I am,

Your affectionate Friend, &c.[1]

PAMELA;

OR,

VIRTUE Rewarded.

In a Series of FAMILIAR LETTERS, &c.

LETTER I.

Dear Father and Mother,

I have great Trouble, and some Comfort, to acquaint you with. The Trouble is, that my good Lady died of the Illness I mention'd to you, and left us all much griev'd for her Loss; for she was a dear good Lady, and kind to all us her Servants. Much I fear'd, that as I was taken by her Goodness to wait upon her Person, I should be quite destitute again, and forc'd to return to you and my poor Mother, who have so much to do to maintain yourselves; and, as my Lady's Goodness had put me to write and cast Accompts,[1] and made me a little expert at my Needle, and other Qualifications above my Degree, it would have been no easy Matter to find a Place that your poor *Pamela* was fit for: But God, whose Graciousness to us we have so often experienc'd at a Pinch, put it into my good Lady's Heart, on her Death-bed, just an Hour before she expir'd, to recommend to my young Master all her Servants, one by one; and when it came to my Turn to be recommended, for I was sobbing and crying at her Pillow, she could only say, My dear Son!—and so broke off a little, and then recovering—Remember my poor *Pamela!*—And these were some of her last Words! O how my Eyes run!—Don't wonder to see the Paper so blotted![2]

Well, but God's Will must be done!—and so comes the Comfort, that I shall not be oblig'd to return back to be a Clog[3] upon my dear Parents! For my Master said, I will take care of you all, my Lasses; and for you, *Pamela*, (and took me by the Hand; yes, he took me by the Hand before them all) for my dear Mother's sake, I will be a Friend to you, and you shall take care of my Linen.[4] God bless him! and pray with me, my dear

Father and Mother, for God to bless him: For he has given Mourning[1]
and a Year's Wages to all my Lady's Servants; and I having no Wages as
yet, but what my Lady said she would do for me as I deserv'd, order'd
the House-keeper to give me Mourning with the rest, and gave me with
his own Hand Four golden Guineas,[2] besides lesser Money, which were
in my old Lady's Pocket when she dy'd; and said, If I was a good Girl,
and faithful and diligent, he would be a Friend to me, for his Mother's
sake. And so I send you these four Guineas for your Comfort; for God
will not let me want: And so you may pay some old Debt with Part; and
keep the other Part to comfort you both. If I get more, I am sure it is
my Duty, and it shall be my Care to love and cherish you both; for you
have lov'd me and cherish'd me, when I could do nothing for myself: And
so you have for us all, or what must have become of us! I send it by *John*
our Footman, who goes your way; but he does not know what he carries;
because I seal it up in one of the little Pill-boxes which my Lady had,
wrapt close in Paper, that it mayn't chink; and be sure don't open it before
him.

I know, dear Father and Mother, I must give you both Grief and Pleasure; and so I will only say, Pray for your *Pamela*; who will ever be,

Your most dutiful Daughter.

I have been scared out of my Senses; for just now, as I was folding this
Letter, in my late Lady's Dressing-room, in comes my young Master!
Good Sirs! how was I frightned! I went to hide the Letter in my Bosom,
and he seeing me frighted, said, smiling, Who have you been writing to,
Pamela?—I said, in my Fright, Pray your Honour forgive me!—Only to my
Father and Mother. He said, Well then, Let me see how you are come on
in your Writing! O how I was sham'd!—He, in my Fright, took it, without
saying more, and read it quite thro', and then gave it me again;—and I
said, Pray your Honour forgive me;—yet I know not for what. For he was
always dutiful to his Parents; and why should he be angry, that I was so to
mine! And indeed he was not angry; for he took me by the Hand, and said,
You are a good Girl, *Pamela*, to be kind to your aged Father and Mother. I
am not angry with you. Be faithful, and diligent; and do as you should do,
and I like you the better for this. And then he said, Why, *Pamela*, you write
a very pretty Hand, and spell tolerably too. I see my good Mother's Care
in your Learning has not been thrown away upon you. My Mother used
to say, you lov'd reading; you may look into any of her Books to improve
yourself, so you take care of them. To be sure I did nothing but curchee
and cry, and was all in Confusion, at his Goodness. Indeed he is the best

of Gentlemen, I think! But I am making another long Letter. So will only say more, I shall ever be,

Your dutiful Daughter,
PAMELA ANDREWS.

LETTER II.

In Answer to the preceding.

Dear PAMELA,

Your Letter was indeed a great Trouble and some Comfort to me, and your poor Mother. We are troubled, to be sure, for your good Lady's Death, who took such care of you, and gave you Learning, and for Three Years past has always been giving you Cloaths and Linen, and every thing that a Gentlewoman need not be asham'd to appear in. But our chief Trouble is, and indeed a very great one, for fear you should be brought to any thing dishonest or wicked, by being set so above yourself. Every body talks how you have come on, and what a genteel Girl you are, and some say, you are very pretty; and indeed, Six Months since, when I saw you last, I should have thought so too, if you was not our Child. But what avails all this, if you are to be ruin'd and undone!—Indeed, my dear Child, we begin to be in great Fear for you; for what signifies all the Riches in the World with a bad Conscience, and to be dishonest? We are, 'tis true, very poor, and find it hard enough to live; tho' once, as you know, it was better with us. But we would sooner live upon the Water and Clay of the Ditches I am forc'd to dig, than to live better at the Price of our dear Child's Ruin.

I hope the good 'Squire has no Design; but when he has given you so much Money, and speaks so kindly to you, and praises your coming on; and Oh! that fatal Word, that he would be kind to you, if you would do as *you should do*, almost kills us with Fears.

I have spoken to good old Widow *Mumford* about it, who, you know, has formerly lived in good Families, and she puts us in some Comfort; for she says, it is not unusual, when a Lady dies, to give what she has about her to her Waiting-maid, and to such as sit up with her in her Illness. But then, why should he smile so kindly upon you? Why should he take such a poor Girl as you by the Hand, as your Letter says he has done twice? Why should he stoop to read your Letter to us; and commend your Writing and Spelling? And, why should he give you Leave to read his Mother's Books!—Indeed, indeed, my dearest Child, our Hearts ake for you; and then you seem so full of Joy at his Goodness, so taken with his kind Expressions, which truly are very great Favours, if he means well, that we fear—Yes, my dear Child, we fear—you should be *too* grateful,—and reward him with that Jewel, your Virtue, which no Riches, nor Favour, nor any thing in this Life, can make up to you.

I, too, have written a long Letter; but will say one Thing more; and that is, That in the Midst of our Poverty and Misfortunes, we have trusted in God's Goodness, and been honest, and doubt not to be happy hereafter, if we continue to be good, tho' our Lot is hard here; but the Loss of our dear Child's Virtue, would be a Grief that we could not bear, and would bring our grey Hairs to the Grave at once.

If you love *us* then, if you value *God*'s Blessing, and *your own* future Happiness, we both charge you to stand upon your Guard; and, if you find the least Attempt made upon your Virtue, be sure you leave every thing behind you, and come away to us; for we had rather see you all cover'd with Rags, and even follow you to the Church-yard, than have it said, a Child of ours preferr'd worldly Conveniencies to her Virtue.

We accept kindly of your dutiful Present; but 'till we are out of our Pain, cannot make use of it, for fear we should partake of the Price of our poor Daughter's Shame: So have laid it up in a Rag among the Thatch, over the Window, for a while, lest we should be robb'd. With our Blessings and our hearty Prayers for you, we remain,

Your careful, but loving Father and Mother,
JOHN *and* ELIZABETH ANDREWS.

LETTER III.

Dear Father,

I must needs say, that your Letter has fill'd me with much Trouble. For it has made my Heart, which was overflowing with Gratitude for my young Master's Goodness, suspicious and fearful; and yet, I hope I never shall find him to act unworthy of his Character; for what could he get by ruining such a poor young Creature as me? But that which gives me most Trouble is, that you seem to mistrust the Honesty of your Child. No, my dear Father and Mother, be assur'd, that, by God's Grace, I never will do any thing that shall bring your grey Hairs with Sorrow to the Grave. I will die a thousand Deaths, rather than be dishonest any way. Of that be assur'd, and set your Hearts at rest; for altho' I have liv'd above myself for some Time past, yet I can be content with Rags and Poverty, and Bread and Water, and will embrace them rather than forfeit my good Name, let who will be the Tempter. And of this rest satisfy'd, and think better of

Your dutiful Daughter till Death.

My Master continues to be very affable to me. As yet I see no Cause to fear any thing. Mrs. *Jervis* the House-keeper too is very civil to me, and I have the Love of every body. Sure they can't *all* have Designs against me because they are civil. I hope I shall always behave so as to be respected by every one; and hope nobody would do me more hurt, than I am sure I would do them. Our *John* so often goes your way, that I will always get him to call that you may hear from me, either by Writing, for it brings my Hand in, or by Word of Mouth.

LETTER IV.

Dear Mother,

For the last Letter was to my Father, in Answer to his Letter; and so I will now write to you; tho' I have nothing to say but what will make me look more like a vain Hussy, than any thing else: Yet I hope I shan't be so proud as to forget myself. Yet there is a secret Pleasure one has to hear one's self prais'd. You must know then, that my Lady *Davers*, who, you know, is my Master's Sister, has been a whole Month at our House, and has taken great Notice of me, and given me good Advice to keep myself to myself; she told me I was a very pretty Wench, and that every body gave me a very good Character, and lov'd me; and bid me take care to keep the Fellows at a Distance; and said, *that* I might do, and be more valu'd for it, even by themselves. But what pleas'd me much, was, that at Table, as

Mrs. *Jervis* was telling me, my Master and her Ladyship were talking of me, and she told him, she thought me the prettiest Wench she ever saw in her Life; and that I was too pretty to live in a Batchelor's House; and that no Lady he might marry, would care to continue me with her. He said, I was vastly improv'd, and had a good Share of Prudence, and Sense above my Years; and it would be Pity, that what was my Merit, should be my Misfortune.—No, says my good Lady, *Pamela* shall come and live with me, I think. He said, With all his Heart, he should be glad to have me so well provided for. Well, said she, I'll consult my Lord about it. She ask'd how old I was; and Mrs. *Jervis* said, I was Fifteen last *February*. O! says she, if the Wench (for so she calls all us Maiden Servants) takes care of herself, she'll improve yet more and more, as well in her Person as Mind.

Now, my dear Father and Mother, tho' this may look too vain to be repeated by me, yet are you not rejoic'd as well as I, to see my Master so willing to part with me?—This shews that he has nothing bad in his Heart. But *John* is just going away, and so I have only to say, that I am, and will always be,

Your honest, as well as dutiful Daughter.

Pray make use of the Money; you may now do it safely.

LETTER V.

My dear Father and Mother,

John being going your way, I am willing to write, because he is so willing to carry any thing for me. He says it does him good at his Heart to see you both, and to hear you talk. He says you are both so good, and so honest, that he always learns something from you to the Purpose. It is a thousand Pities, he says, that such honest Hearts should not have better Luck in the World. But this is more Pride to me, that I am come of such honest Parents, than if I had been born a Lady.

I hear nothing yet of going to Lady *Davers*. And I am very easy at present here. For Mrs. *Jervis* uses me as if I was her own Daughter, and is a very good Woman, and makes my Master's Interest her own. She is always giving me good Counsel, and I love her, next to you two, I think, best of any body. She keeps so good Rule and Order, she is mightily respected by us all; and takes Delight to hear me read to her; and all she loves to hear read, is good Books, which we read whenever we are alone; so that I think I am at home with you. She heard one of our Men, *Harry*, who is no better than he should be, speak freely to me; I think he call'd me his pretty *Pamela*, and took hold of me, as if he would have kiss'd me; for which you may be sure I was very angry; and she took him to Task, and was as angry at him as could be, and told me she was very well pleas'd to see my Prudence and Modesty, and that I kept all the Fellows at a Distance. And indeed I am sure I am not proud, and carry it civil to every body; but yet, methinks I can't bear to be look'd upon by these Men-servants; for they seem as if they would look one thro'; and, as I almost always breakfast, dine, and sup with Mrs. *Jervis*, so good she is to me, so I am very easy that I have so little to say to them. Not but they are very civil to me in the main, for Mrs. *Jervis*'s sake, who they see loves me; and they stand in Awe of her, knowing her to be a Gentlewoman born, tho' she has had Misfortunes. I am going on again with a long Letter; for I love Writing, and shall tire you. But when I began, I only intended to say, that I am quite fearless of any Danger now: And indeed can but wonder at myself, (tho' your Caution to me was your watchful Love) that I should be so foolish as to be so uneasy as I have been: For I am sure my Master would not demean himself so, as to think upon such a poor Girl as I, for my Harm. For such a Thing would ruin his Credit as well as mine, you know: For, to be sure, he may expect one of the best Ladies in the Land. So no more at present; but that I am

Your ever dutiful Daughter.

LETTER VI.

Dear Father and Mother,

My Master has been very kind since my last; for he has given me a Suit of my old Lady's Cloaths, and half a Dozen of her Shifts, and Six fine Handkerchiefs, and Three of her Cambrick Aprons, and Four Holland ones:[1] The Cloaths are fine Silks, and too rich and too good for me, to be sure. I wish it was no Affront to him to make Money of them, and send it to you: it would do me more good.

You will be full of Fears, I warrant now, of some Design upon me, till I tell you, that he was with Mrs. *Jervis* when he gave them me; and he gave her a Mort¹ of good Things at the same Time, and bid her wear them in Remembrance of her good Friend, my Lady, his Mother. And when he gave me these fine Things, he said, These, *Pamela*, are for you; have them made fit for you, when your Mourning is laid by, and wear 'em for your good Mistress's sake. Mrs. *Jervis* gives you a very good Word; and I would have you continue to behave as prudently as you have done hitherto, and every body will be your Friend.

I was so surpris'd at his Goodness, that I could not tell what to say. I curcheed to him, and to Mrs. *Jervis* for her good Word; and said, I wish'd I might be deserving of his Favour, and his Kindness: And nothing should be wanting in me, to the best of my Knowledge.

O how amiable a Thing is doing good!—It is all I envy great Folks for!

I always thought my young Master a fine Gentleman, as every body says he is: But he gave these good Things to us both with such a Graciousness, as I thought he look'd like an Angel.

Mrs. *Jervis* says, he ask'd her, If I kept the Men at a Distance; for he said, I was very pretty, and to be drawn in to have any of them, might be my Ruin, and make me poor and miserable betimes. She never is wanting to give me a good Word, and took Occasion to launch out in my Praise, she says. But I hope she said no more than I shall try to deserve, tho' I mayn't at present. I am sure I will always love her next to you and my dear Mother. So I rest,

Your ever dutiful Daughter.

LETTER VII.

Dear Father,

Since my last, my Master gave me more fine Things. He call'd me up to my old Lady's Closet,² and pulling out her Drawers, he gave me Two Suits of fine *Flanders* lac'd Headcloths,³ Three Pair of fine Silk Shoes, two hardly the worse, and just fit for me; for my old Lady had a very little Foot; and several Ribbands and Topknots of all Colours, and Four Pair of fine white Cotton Stockens, and Three Pair of fine Silk ones; and Two Pair of rich

Stays, and a Pair of rich Silver Buckles in one Pair of the Shoes. I was quite astonish'd, and unable to speak for a while; but yet I was inwardly asham'd to take the Stockens; for Mrs. *Jervis* was not there: If she had, it would have been nothing. I believe I receiv'd them very awkwardly; for he smil'd at my Awkwardness; and said, Don't blush, *Pamela*: Dost think I don't know pretty Maids wear Shoes and Stockens?

I was so confounded at these Words, you might have beat me down with a Feather. For, you must think, there was no Answer to be made to this: So, like a Fool, I was ready to cry; and went away curcheeing and blushing, I am sure, up to the Ears; for, tho' there was no Harm in what he said, yet I did not know how to take it. But I went and told all to Mrs. *Jervis*, who said, God put it into his Heart to be good to me; and I must double my Diligence. It look'd to her, she said, as if he would fit me in Dress for a Waiting-maid's Place on his Sister Lady *Davers's* own Person.

But still your kind fatherly Cautions came into my Head, and made all these Gifts nothing near to me what they would have been. But yet I hope there is no Reason; for what Good could it do him to harm such a simple Maiden as me? Besides, to be sure, no Lady would look upon him, if he should so disgrace himself. So I will make myself easy; and indeed, I should never have been otherwise, if you had not put it into my Head; for my Good, I know very well. But, may be, without these Uneasinesses to mingle with these Benefits, I might be too much puff'd up: So I will conclude, All that happens is for our Good; and so God bless you, my dear Father and Mother; and I know you will pray to God to bless me; who am, and shall always be,

Your dutiful Daughter.

LETTER VIII.

Dear PAMELA,

I cannot but renew my Cautions to you on your Master's Kindness to you, and his free Expression to you about the Stockens. Yet there may not be, and I hope there is not, any thing in it. But when I reflect, that there *possibly* may, and that if there should, no less depends upon it than my Child's everlasting Happiness in this World and the next; it is enough to make one fearful of the worst. Arm yourself, my dear Child, for the worst; and resolve to lose your Life sooner than your Virtue. What tho' the Doubts I fill'd you with, lessen the Pleasure you would have had in your Master's Kindness, yet what signify the Delights that arise from a few paltry fine Cloaths, in Comparison with a good Conscience?

These are indeed very great Favours that he heaps upon you, but so much the more to be suspected; and when you say he look'd so amiable, and like an Angel, how afraid I am, that they should make too great an Impression upon you! For, tho' God has bless'd you with Sense and Prudence above your Years, yet, I tremble to think what a sad Hazard a poor Maiden of no more than Fifteen Years of Age stands against the Temptations of this World, and a designing young Gentleman, if he should prove so, who has so much Power to oblige, and has a kind of Authority to command as your Master.

I charge you, my dear Child, on both our Blessings, poor as we are, to be on your Guard; there can be no Harm in that: and since Mrs. *Jervis* is so good a Gentlewoman, and so kind to you, I am the easier a great deal, and so is your Mother; and we hope you will hide nothing from her, and take her Counsel in every thing. So with our Blessings and assured Prayers for you, more than for ourselves, we remain

Your loving Father and Mother.

Besure don't let People's telling you you are pretty, puff you up: for you did not make yourself, and so can have no Praise due to you for it. It is Virtue and Goodness only, that make the true Beauty. Remember that, *Pamela.*

LETTER IX.

Dear Father and Mother,

I am sorry to write you word, that the Hopes I had of going to wait on Lady *Davers* are quite over. My Lady would have had me; but my Master, as I hear by the bye, would not consent to it. He said, Her Nephew might be taken with me, and I might draw him in, or be drawn in by him; and he thought, as his Mother lov'd me, and committed me to his Care, he ought to continue me with him; and Mrs. *Jervis* would be a Mother to me. Mrs. *Jervis* tells me, the Lady shook her Head, and said, *Ah! Brother!* and that was all. And as you have made me fearful by your Cautions, my Heart at times misgives me. But I say nothing yet of your Caution, or my own Uneasiness, to Mrs. *Jervis*; not that I mistrust her, but for fear she should think me presumptuous, and vain, and conceited, to have any Fears about the matter, from the great Distance between so great a Man, and so poor a Girl. But yet Mrs. *Jervis* seem'd to build something upon Lady *Davers'* shaking her Head, and saying, *Ah! Brother*, and no more! God, I hope, will give me his Grace; and so I will not, if I can help it, make myself too uneasy; for I hope there is no Occasion. But every little matter that happens, I will acquaint you with, that you shall continue to me your good Advice, and pray for

Your sad-hearted PAMELA.

LETTER X.

Dear Mother,

You and my good Father may wonder that you have not had a Letter from me in so many Weeks; but a sad, sad Scene has been the Occasion of it. For, to be sure, now it is too plain, that all your Cautions were well-grounded. O my dear Mother! I am miserable, truly miserable!—But yet, don't be frighted, I am honest!—God, of his Goodness, keep me so!

O this Angel of a Master! this fine Gentleman! this gracious Benefactor to your poor *Pamela!* who was to take care of me at the Prayer of his good dying Mother; who was so careful of me, lest I should be drawn in by Lord *Davers's* Nephew; that he would not let me go to Lady *Davers's*: This very Gentleman (yes, I must call him Gentleman, tho' he has fallen from the Merit of that Title) has degraded himself to offer Freedoms to his poor Servant! He has now shew'd himself in his true Colours, and to me, nothing appears so black and so frightful.

I have not been idle; but have writ from time to time how he, by sly mean Degrees, exposed his wicked Views: But somebody stole my Letter, and I know not what is become of it. It was a very long one. I fear he that was mean enough to do bad things, in one respect, did not stick at this; but be it as it will, all the Use he can make of it will be, that he may be asham'd of *his* Part; I not of *mine*. For he will see I was resolv'd to be honest, and glory'd in the Honesty of my poor Parents. I will tell you all, the next Opportunity; for I am watch'd, and such-like, very narrowly; and he says to Mrs. *Jervis*, This Girl is always scribbling; I think she may be better employ'd. And yet I work all Hours with my Needle, upon his Linen, and the fine Linen of the Family; and am besides about flowering¹ him a Waistcoat.—But, Oh! my Heart's broke almost; for what am I likely to have for my Reward, but Shame and Disgrace, or else ill Words, and hard Treatment! I'll tell you all soon, and hope I shall find my long Letter.

Your most afflicted Daughter.

I must *he* and *him* him now; for he has lost his Dignity with me!

LETTER XI.

Dear Mother,

Well, I can't find my Letter, and so I'll tell you all, as briefly as I can. All went well enough in the main for some time after my last Letter but one. At last, I saw some Reason to suspect; for he would look upon me, whenever he saw me, in such a manner, as shew'd not well; and at last he came to me, as I was in the Summer-house in the little Garden, at work with my Needle, and Mrs. *Jervis* was just gone from me; and I would have gone out; but he said, No, don't go, *Pamela*; I have something to say to you; and you always fly me so, whenever I come near you, as if you was afraid of me.

I was all confounded; and said at last; It does not become your poor Servant to stay in your Presence, Sir, without your Business requir'd it; and I hope I shall always know my Place.

Well, says he, my Business does require it sometimes, and I have a mind you should stay to hear what I have to say to you.

I stood all confounded, and began to tremble, and the more when he took me by the Hand; for now no Soul was near us.

My Sister *Davers*, said he, (and seem'd, I thought, to be as much at a Loss for Words as I) would have had you live with her; but she would not do for you what I am resolv'd to do, if you continue faithful and obliging. What say'st thou, my Girl, said he, with some Eagerness, hadst thou not rather stay with me than go to my Sister *Davers?* He look'd so, as fill'd me with Affrightment; I don't know how; wildly I thought.

I said, when I could speak, Your Honour will forgive your poor Servant; but as you have no Lady for me to wait upon, and my good Lady has been now dead this Twelve-month, I had rather, if it would not displease you, wait upon Lady *Davers, because*——

I was proceeding; and he said a little hastily—*Because* you're a little Fool, and know not what's good for yourself. I tell you, I will make a Gentlewoman of you, if you be obliging, and don't stand in your own Light;[1] and so saying, he put his Arm about me, and kiss'd me!

Now you will say, all his Wickedness appear'd plainly. I struggled, and trembled, and was so benumb'd with Terror, that I sunk down, not in a Fit, and yet not myself; and I found myself in his Arms, quite void of Strength, and he kissed me two or three times, as if he would have eaten me.—At last I burst from him, and was getting out of the Summer-house; but he held me back, and shut the Door.

I would have given my Life for a Farthing. And he said, I'll do you no Harm, *Pamela*; don't be afraid of me. I said, I won't stay! You won't, Hussy, said he! Do you know who you speak to! I lost all Fear, and all Respect, and said, Yes, I do, Sir, too well!—Well may I forget that I am your Servant, when you forget what belongs to a Master.

I sobb'd and cry'd most sadly. What a foolish Hussy you are, said he, have I done you any Harm?—Yes, Sir, said I, the greatest Harm in the World: You have taught me to forget myself, and what belongs to me, and have lessen'd the Distance that Fortune has made between us, by demeaning yourself, to be so free to a poor Servant. Yet, Sir, said I, I will be so bold to say, I am honest, tho' poor; And if you was a Prince, I would not be otherwise.

He was angry, and said, Who would have you otherwise, you foolish Slut! Cease your blubbering! I own I have demean'd myself; but it was only to try you: If you can keep this Matter secret, you'll give me the better Opinion of your Prudence; and here's something, said he, putting some Gold in my Hand, to make you Amends for the Fright I put you to. Go, take a Walk in the Garden, and don't go in till your blubbering is over: And I charge you say nothing of what has past, and all shall be well, and I'll forgive you.

I won't take the Money, indeed, Sir, said I; poor as I am! I won't take it: for to say Truth, I thought it look'd like taking Earnest;[2] and so I put it upon the Bench; and as he seem'd vex'd and confus'd at what he had done, I took the Opportunity to open the Door, and went out of the Summer-house.

He called to me, and said, Be secret, I charge you, *Pamela*; and don't go in yet, as I told you.

O how poor and mean must these Actions be, and how little must they make the best of Gentlemen look, when they offer such things as are unworthy of themselves, and put it into the Power of their Inferiors to be greater than they!

I took a Turn or two in the Garden, but in Sight of the House for fear of the worst, and breathed upon my Hand to dry my Eyes, because I would not be too disobedient. My next shall tell you more.

Pray for me, my dear Father and Mother; and don't be angry I have not yet run away from this House, so late my Comfort and Delight, but now my Anguish and Terror. I am forc'd to break off, hastily,

Your dutiful and honest Daughter.

LETTER XII.

Dear Mother,

Well, I will now proceed with my sad Story. And so after I had dry'd my Eyes, I went in, and begun to ruminate with myself what I had best to do. Sometimes I thought I would leave the House, and go to the next Town, and wait an Opportunity to get to you; but then I was at a Loss to resolve whether to take away the Things he had given me or no, and how to take them away: Sometimes I thought to leave them behind me, and only go with the Cloaths on my Back; but then I had two Miles and a half, and a By-way, to go to the Town; and being pretty well dress'd, I might come to some harm, almost as bad as what I would run away from; and then may-be, thought I, it will be reported, I have stolen something, and so was forc'd to run away; and to carry a bad Name back with me to my dear poor Parents, would be a sad thing indeed!—O how I wish'd for my grey Russet¹ again, and my poor honest Dress, with which you fitted me out, and hard enough too you had to do it, God knows, for going to this Place, when I was but twelve Years old, in my good Lady's Days! Sometimes I thought of telling Mrs. *Jervis*, and taking her Advice, and only feared his Command, to be secret; for, thought I, he may be ashamed of his Actions, and never attempt the like again: And as poor Mrs. *Jervis* depended upon him, thro' Misfortunes that had attended her, I thought it would be a sad thing to bring his Displeasure upon her for my sake.

In this Quandary, now considering, now crying, and not knowing what to do, I pass'd the Time in my Chamber till Evening; when desiring to be excused going to Supper, Mrs. *Jervis* came up to me; and said, Why must I sup without you, *Pamela?* Come, I see you are troubled at something; tell me what is the Matter.

I begg'd I might be permitted to lie with her on Nights; for I was afraid of Spirits, and they would not hurt such a good Person as she. That was a silly Excuse, she said; for why was you not afraid of Spirits before? Indeed I did not think of that. But you shall be my Bedfellow with all my Heart, said she, let your Reason be what it will; only come down to Supper. I begg'd to be excus'd; for, said I, I have been crying so, that it will be taken Notice of by my Fellow-servants; and I will hide nothing from you, Mrs. *Jervis*, when we are a-bed.

She was so good to indulge me, and went down to Supper; but made more haste to come up to-bed; and told the Servants, that I should lie with her, because she said she could not rest well, and she would get me to read her to sleep, because she knew I lov'd reading, as she said.

When we were alone, I told her every bit and crumb of the Matter; for I thought, tho' he had bid me not, yet if he should come to know I had told, it would be no worse; for to keep a Secret of such a Nature, I thought would be to deprive myself of the good Advice which I never wanted more; and might encourage him to think I did not resent it as I ought, and would keep worse Secrets, and so make him do worse by me. Was I right, my dear Mother?

Mrs. *Jervis* could not help mingling Tears with my Tears; for I cry'd all the Time I told her the Story; and begg'd her to advise me what to do; and I shew'd her my dear Father's two Letters, and she praised the Honesty and Inditing of them; and said pleasing things to me of you both. But she begg'd I would not think of leaving my Service; for, says she, in all Likelihood, you behav'd so virtuously, that he will be asham'd of what he has done, and never offer the like to you again: Tho', my dear *Pamela*, said she, I fear more for your Prettiness than for any thing else; because the best Man in the Land might love you; so she was pleased to say. She said she wished it was in her Power to live independent; that then she would take a little private House, and I should live with her like her Daughter.

And so, as you order'd me to take her Advice, I resolved to tarry to see how things went, without he was to turn me away; altho', in your first

Letter, you order'd me to come away the Moment I had any Reason to be apprehensive. So, dear Father and Mother, it is not Disobedience, I hope, that I stay; for I could not expect a Blessing, or the good Fruits of your Prayers for me, if I was disobedient.

All the next Day I was very sad, and began to write my long Letter. He saw me writing, and said (as I mention'd) to Mrs. *Jervis*, That Girl is always scribbling; methinks she might find something else to do, or to that purpose. And when I had finish'd my Letter, I put it under the Toilet,[1] in my late Lady's Dressing-room, where nobody comes but myself and Mrs. *Jervis*, besides my Master; but when I came up again to seal it up, to my great Concern it was gone; and Mrs. *Jervis* knew nothing of it; and nobody knew of my Master's having been near the Place in the time; so I have been sadly troubled about it: But Mrs. *Jervis*, as well as I, thinks he has it some how or other; and he appears cross and angry, and seems to shun me, as much as he said I did him. It had better be so than worse!

But he has order'd Mrs. *Jervis* to bid me not spend so much time in writing; which is a poor Matter for such a Gentleman as he to take notice of, as I am not idle otherways, if he did not resent what he thought I wrote upon. And this has no very good Look.

But I am a good deal easier since I lie with Mrs. *Jervis*; tho' after all, the Fears I live in on one side, and his Frowning and Displeasure at what I do on the other, makes me more miserable than enough.

O that I had never left my Rags nor my Poverty, to be thus expos'd to Temptations on one hand, or Disgusts on the other! How happy was I a-while ago! How miserable now!—Pity and pray for

Your afflicted PAMELA.

LETTER XIII.

My dearest Child,

Our Hearts bleed for your Distress, and the Temptations you are tried with. You have our hourly Prayers; and we would have you flee this evil Great House and Man, if you find he renews his Attempts. You ought to have done it at first, had you not had Mrs. *Jervis* to advise with. We can find no Fault in your Conduct hitherto: But it makes our Hearts ake for fear of the worst. O my Child! Temptations are sore things; but yet without them, we know not our selves, nor what we are able to do.

Your Temptations are very great; for you have Riches, Youth, and a fine Gentleman, as the World reckons him, to withstand; but how great will be your Honour to withstand them! And when we consider your past Conduct, and your virtuous Education, and that you have been bred to be more asham'd of Dishonesty than Poverty, we trust in God that he will enable you to overcome. Yet, as we can't see but your Life must be a Burden to you, through the great Apprehensions always upon you; and that it may be presumptuous to trust too much to your own Strength; and that you are but very young; and the Devil may put it into his Head to use some Stratagem, of which great Men are full, to decoy you; I think you had best come home to share our Poverty with Safety, than to live with so much Discontent in a Plenty, that itself may be dangerous. God direct you for the best. While you have Mrs. *Jervis* for an Adviser, and Bedfellow, (and, O my dear Child, that was prudently done of you) we are easier than we should be; and so committing you to God's blessed Protection, remain

> *Your truly loving,*
> *but careful, Father and Mother.*

LETTER XIV.

Dear Father and Mother,

Mrs. *Jervis* and I have liv'd very comfortably together for this Fortnight past; for my Master was all that time at his *Lincolnshire* Estate, and at his Sister's the Lady *Davers*. But he came home Yesterday. He had some Talk with Mrs. *Jervis* soon after he came home; and mostly about me. He said to her, it seems, Well, Mrs. *Jervis*, I know *Pamela* has your good Word; but do you think her of any Use in the Family? She told me, she was surpris'd at the Question; but said, That I was one of the most virtuous and industrious young Creatures that ever she knew. Why that Word *virtuous*, said he, I pray you? Was there any Reason to suppose her otherwise? Or has any body taken it into their Heads to try her?—I wonder, Sir, says she, you ask me such a Question! Who dare offer any thing to her in such an orderly and well-govern'd House as yours, and under a Master of so good a Character for Virtue and Honour? Your Servant, Mrs. *Jervis*, says he, for your good Opinion; but pray, if any body did, do you think *Pamela* would let you know it? Why, Sir, said she; she is a poor innocent young Thing, and I believe has so much Confidence in me, that she would take my Advice as soon as she would her Mother's. *Innocent!* again; and *virtuous*, I warrant! Well, Mrs. *Jervis*, you abound with your Epithets; but 'tis my Opinion, she is an artful young Baggage;[1] and had I a young handsome Butler or Steward, she'd soon make her Market of one of them, if she thought it worth while to snap at him for a Husband. Alack-a-day, Sir, said she, 'tis early Days with *Pamela*, and she does not yet think of a Husband, I dare say: And your Steward and Butler are both Men in Years, and think nothing of the Matter. No, said he, if they were younger, they'd have more Wit than to think of such a Girl. I'll tell you my Mind of her, Mrs. *Jervis*, I don't think this same Favourite of yours so very artless a Girl, as you imagine. I am not to dispute with your Honour about her, said Mrs. *Jervis*; but I dare say, if the Men will let her alone, she'll never trouble herself about them. Why, Mrs. *Jervis*, said he, are there any Men that will not let her alone that you know of? No, indeed, Sir, said she; she keeps herself so much to herself, and yet behaves so prudently, that they all esteem her, and shew her as great Respect as if she was a Gentlewoman born.

Ay, says he, that's her Art, that I was speaking of: But let me tell you, the Girl has Vanity and Conceit, and Pride too, or I am mistaken; and I could give you perhaps an Instance of it. Sir, said she, you can see further than such a poor silly Woman as me; but I never saw any thing but Innocence in her.—And *Virtue* too, I'll warrant ye, said he. But suppose I could give you an Instance, where she has talk'd a little too freely of the Kindnesses that have been shew'd her from a *certain Quarter*; and has had the Vanity to impute a few kind Words utter'd in mere Compassion to her Youth and Circumstances, into a Design upon her, and even dar'd to make free with Names that she ought never to mention but with Reverence and Gratitude; what would you say to that?—Say, Sir! said she, I cannot tell what to say. But I hope *Pamela* incapable of such Ingratitude.

Well, no more of this silly Girl, says he; you may only advise her, as you are her Friend, not to give herself too much Licence upon the Favours she meets with; and if she stays here, that she will not write the Affairs of my Family purely for an Exercise to her Pen and her Invention. I tell you, she is a subtle artful Gypsey,[2] and time will shew it you.

Was ever the like heard, my dear Father and Mother? It is plain he did not expect to meet with such a Repulse, and mistrusts that I have told Mrs.

Jervis, and has my long Letter too that I intended for you; and so is vex'd to the Heart. But, however, I can't help it. So I had better be thought artful and subtle, than be so, in *his* Sense; and as light as he makes of the Words *Virtue* and *Innocence* in me, he would have made a less angry Construction, had I less deserved that he should do so; for then, may be, my *Crime* would have been my *Virtue* with him; naughty Gentleman as he is!—I will soon write again; but must now end with saying, That I am, and shall always be,

Your honest Daughter.

LETTER XV.

Dear Mother,

I broke off abruptly my last Letter; for I fear'd he was coming; and so it happen'd. I thrust the Letter into my Bosom, and took up my Work, which lay by me; but I had so little of the Artful, as he called it, that I look'd as confused, as if I had been doing some great Harm.

Sit still, *Pamela*, said he, and mind your Work, for all me.—You don't tell me I am welcome home after my Journey to *Lincolnshire*. It would be hard, Sir, said I, if you was not always welcome to your Honour's own House.

I would have gone; but he said, Don't run away, I tell you. I have a Word or two to say to you. Good Sirs, how my Heart went pit-a-pat! When I was a *little kind*, said he, to you in the Summer-house, and you carry'd yourself so *foolishly* upon it, as if I had intended to do you great harm, did I not tell you, you should take no Notice of what pass'd, to any Creature? And yet you have made a common Talk of the Matter, not considering either my Reputation or your own.—I made a common Talk of it, Sir, said I! I have nobody to talk to, hardly!

He interrupted me, and said, *Hardly!* you little Equivocator! what do you mean by *hardly?* Let me ask you, Have you not told Mrs. *Jervis* for one? Pray your Honour, said I, all in Agitation, let me go down; for 'tis not for me to hold an Argument with your Honour. Equivocator, again! said he, and took my Hand, what do you talk of an *Argument?* Is it holding an Argument with me, to answer a plain Question? Answer me what I asked.

O good, Sir, said I, let me beg you will not urge me further, for fear I forget myself again, and be sawcy.

Answer me then, I bid you, says he, Have you told Mrs. *Jervis?* It will be sawcy in you, if you don't answer me directly to what I ask. Sir, said I, and fain would have pulled my Hand away, may be I should be for answering you by another Question, and that would not become me. What is it, says he, you would say? Speak out!

Then, Sir, said I, why should your Honour be so angry I should tell Mrs. *Jervis*, or any body else, what passed, if you intended no harm?

Well said, pretty *Innocent* and *Artless!* as Mrs. *Jervis* calls you, said he; and is it thus you taunt and retort upon me, insolent as you are! But still I will be answered directly to my Question? Why then, Sir, said I, I will not tell a Lye for the World: I did tell Mrs. *Jervis*; for my Heart was almost broke; but I open'd not my Mouth to any other. Very well, Boldface, said he, and Equivocator, again! You did not open your Mouth to any other; but did you not *write* to some other? Why now, and please your Honour, said I, (for I was quite courageous just then) you could not have asked me this Question, if you had not taken from me my Letter to my Father and Mother, in which, I own, I had broke my Mind freely to them, and asked their Advice, and poured forth my Griefs!

And so I am to be exposed, am I, said he, *in* my House, and *out* of my House, to the whole World, by such a Sawcebox as you? No, good Sir, said I, and I hope your Honour won't be angry with me; it is not me that expose you if I say nothing but the Truth. So, taunting again! Assurance as you are, said he! I will not be thus talk'd to.

Pray, Sir, said I, who can a poor Girl take Advice of, if it must not be of her Father and Mother, and such a good Woman as Mrs. *Jervis*, who for her Sex-sake, should give it me when asked? Insolence! said he, and stamp'd with his Foot, Am I to be question'd thus by such a one as you? I fell down on my Knees, and said, For God's sake, your Honour, pity a poor distressed Creature, that knows nothing of her Duty, but how to cherish her Virtue and good Name! I have nothing else to trust to; and tho' poor and friendless here, yet I have always been taught to value Honesty above my Life. Here's ado with your Honesty, said he, foolish Girl! Is it not one Part of Honesty, to be dutiful and grateful to your Master, do you think? Indeed, Sir, said I, it is impossible I should be ingrateful to your Honour, or disobedient, or deserve the Names of Boldface and Insolent, which you call me, but when your Commands are contrary to that first Duty, which shall ever be the Principle of my Life!

He seem'd to be moved, and rose up, and walked into the great Chamber two or three Turns, leaving me on my Knees; and I threw my Apron over my Face, and laid my Head on a Chair, and cry'd as if my Heart would break, having no Power to stir.

At last he came in again, but, alas! with Mischief in his Heart! and raising me up, he said, Rise, *Pamela*, rise; you are your own Enemy. Your perverse Folly will be your Ruin! I tell you this, that I am very much displeased with the Freedoms you have taken with my Name to my House-keeper, as also to your Father and Mother; and you may as well have *real* Cause to take these Freedoms with me, as to make my Name suffer for imaginary ones: And saying so, he offer'd to take me on his Knee, with some Force. O how I was terrify'd! I said, like as I had read in a Book a Night or two before, Angels, and Saints, and all the Host of Heaven, defend me!¹ And may I never survive one Moment, that fatal one in which I shall forfeit my Innocence. Pretty Fool! said he, how will you forfeit your Innocence, if you are oblig'd to yield to a Force you cannot withstand? Be easy, said he; for let the worst happen that can, you'll have the Merit, and I the Blame; and it will be a good Subject for Letters to your Father and Mother, and a Tale into the Bargain for Mrs. *Jervis*.

He by Force kissed my Neck and Lips; and said, Who ever blamed *Lucretia*,² but the *Ravisher* only? and I am content to take all the Blame upon me; as I have already borne too great a Share for what I have deserv'd. May I, said I, *Lucretia* like, justify myself with my Death, if I am used barbarously? O my good Girl! said he, tauntingly, you are well read, I see; and we shall make out between us, before we have done, a pretty Story in Romance,³ I warrant ye!

He then put his Hand in my Bosom, and the Indignation gave me double Strength, and I got loose from him, by a sudden Spring, and ran out of the Room; and the next Chamber being open, I made shift to get into it, and threw-to the Door, and the Key being on the Inside, it locked; but he follow'd me so close, he got hold of my Gown, and tore a Piece off, which hung without the Door.

I just remember I got into the Room; for I knew nothing further of the Matter till afterwards; for I fell into a Fit with my Fright and Terror, and there I lay, till he, as I suppose, looking through the Key-hole, spy'd me lying all along upon the Floor, stretch'd out at my Length;⁴ and then he call'd Mrs. *Jervis* to me, who, by his Assistance, bursting open the Door, he went away, seeing me coming to myself; and bid her say nothing of the Matter, if she was wise.

Poor Mrs. *Jervis* thought it was worse, and cry'd over me like as if she was my Mother; and I was two Hours before I came to myself; and just as I got a little up on my Feet, he coming in, I went away again with the Terror; and so he withdrew again: But he staid in the next Room to let nobody come near us, that his foul Proceedings might not be known.

Mrs. *Jervis* gave me her Smelling-bottle,[1] and had cut my Laces, and sat me in a great Chair, and he call'd her to him: How is the Girl, said he? I never saw such a Fool in my Life. I did nothing at all to her. Mrs. *Jervis* could not speak for crying. So, he said, she has told you, it seems, that I was kind to her in the Summer-house, tho' I'll assure you, I was quite innocent then as well as now; and I desire you to keep this Matter to yourself, and let me not be nam'd in it.

O Sir, said she, for your Honour's sake, and for Christ's sake—But he would not hear her, and said—For your own sake, I tell you, Mrs. *Jervis*, say not a Word more. I have done her no harm. And I won't have her stay in my House; prating, perverse Fool, as she is! But since she is so apt to fall into Fits, or at least pretend to do so, prepare her to see me To-morrow after Dinner, in my Mother's Closet, and do you be with her, and you shall hear what passes between us.

And so he went out in a Pet, and order'd his Chariot and Four[2] to be got ready, and went away a Visiting somewhere.

Mrs. *Jervis* then came to me, and I told her all that had happen'd, and said I was resolv'd not to stay in the House; and she saying, He seem'd to threaten as much; I said, Thank God; then I shall be easy: So she told me all he had said to her, as I have said above.

Mrs. *Jervis* is very loth I should go; and yet, poor Woman! she begins to be afraid for herself; but would not have me ruin'd for the World. She says, To be sure he means no good; but may be, now he sees me so resolute, he will give over all Attempts: And that I shall know what to do better after To-morrow, when I am to appear before a very bad Judge, I doubt!

O how I dread this To-morrow's Appearance! But be assured, my dear Parents, of the Honesty of your poor Child! As I am sure I am of your Prayers for

Your dutiful Daughter.

Oh! this frightful To-morrow! how I dread it!

LETTER XVI.

My dear Parents,

I know you longed to hear from me soon. I send as soon as I could.

Well, you may believe how uneasily I passed the Time till his appointed Hour came. Every Minute, as it grew nearer, my Terrors increased; and sometimes I had great Courage, and sometimes none at all; and I thought I should faint when it came to the Time my Master had dined. I could neither eat nor drink, for my part; and do what I could, my Eyes were swell'd with crying.

At last he went up to the Closet, which was my good Lady's Dressing-room; a Room I once lov'd, but then as much hated.

Don't your Heart ake for me?—I am sure mine flutter'd about like a Bird in a Cage new caught. O *Pamela,* said I to my self, why art thou so foolish and fearful! Thou hast done no harm! what, if thou fearest an unjust Judge,[1] when thou art innocent, wouldst thou do before a just one, if thou wert guilty? Have Courage, *Pamela,* thou knowest the worst! And how easy a Choice Poverty and Honesty is, rather than Plenty and Wickedness?

So I chear'd myself; but yet my poor Heart sunk, and my Spirits were quite broken. Every thing that stirred, I thought was to call me to my Account. I dreaded it, and yet I wished it to come.

Well, at last he rung the Bell; O thought I, that it was my Passing-bell![2] Mrs. *Jervis* went up, with a full Heart enough, poor good Woman! He said, Where's *Pamela?* let her come up, and do you come with her. She came to me; I was ready to come with my Feet, but my Heart was with my dear Father and Mother, wishing to share your Poverty and Happiness. But I went.

O how can wicked Men look so steddy and untouch'd, with such black Hearts, while poor Innocents look like Malefactors before them!

He looked so stern, that my Heart failed me, and I wish'd myself any-where but there, tho' I had before been summoning up all my Courage. Good God of Heaven, said I to myself, give me Courage to stand before this naughty Master! O soften him! or harden me!

Come in, Fool, said he, angrily, as soon as he saw me (and snatch'd my Hand with a Pull); you may well be asham'd to see me, after your Noise and Nonsense, and exposing me as you have done. *I* ashamed to see *you!* thought I: Very pretty indeed!—But I said nothing.

Mrs. *Jervis*, said he, here you are both together. Do you sit down; but let her stand if she will: Ay, thought I, if I *can*; for my Knees beat one against another. Did you not think, when you saw the Girl in the way you found her in, that I had given her the greatest Occasion that could possibly be given any Woman? And that I had actually ruin'd her, as she calls it? Tell me, could you think any thing less? Indeed, says she, I fear'd so at first. Has she told you what I did to her, and *all* I did to her, to occasion all this Folly, by which my Reputation might have suffer'd in your Opinion, and in that of all the Family?—Tell me, what has she told you?

She was a little too much frighted, as she owned afterwards, at his Sternness, and said, Indeed she told me you only pulled her on your Knee, and kissed her.

Then I plucked up my Spirit a little. *Only!* Mrs. *Jervis*, said I, and was not that enough to shew me what I had to fear! When a Master of his Honour's Degree demeans himself to be so free as that to such a poor Servant as me, what is the next to be expected?—But your Honour went further, so you did; and threaten'd what you would do, and talk'd of *Lucretia*, and her hard Fate.—Your Honour knows you went too far for a Master to a Servant, or even to his Equal; and I cannot bear it! So I fell a crying most sadly.

Mrs. *Jervis* began to excuse me, and to beg he would pity a poor Maiden, that had such a Value for her Reputation. He said, I speak it to her Face, I think her very pretty, and I thought her humble, and one that would not grow upon my Favours, or the Notice I took of her; but I abhor the Thought of forcing her to any thing. I know myself better, said he, and what belongs to me: And to be sure I have enough demean'd myself to take so much Notice of such a one as she; but I was bewitch'd, I think, by her, to be freer than became me; tho' I had no Intention to carry the Jest farther.

What poor Stuff was all this, my dear Mother, from a Man of his Sense! But see how a bad Cause and bad Actions confound the greatest Wits!—It gave me a little more Courage then; for Innocence, I find, in a weak Mind, has many Advantages over Guilt, with all its Riches and Wisdom!

So I said, Your Honour may call this Jest or Sport, or what you please; but indeed, Sir, it is not a Jest that becomes the Distance between a Master and a Servant! Do you hear, Mrs. *Jervis*, said he? Do you hear the Pertness of the Creature? I had a good deal of this Sort before in the Summer-house, and Yesterday too, which made me rougher to her than perhaps I had otherwise been.

Says Mrs. *Jervis*, *Pamela*, don't be pert to his Honour! You should know your Distance; you see his Honour was only in jest!—O dear Mrs. *Jervis*, said I, don't you blame me too! It is very difficult to keep one's Distance to the greatest of Men, when they won't keep it themselves to their meanest Servants!

See again, said he; could you believe this of the young Baggage, if you had not heard it. O good your Honour, said the well-meaning Gentlewoman, pity and forgive the poor Girl; she is but a Girl; and her Virtue is very dear to her; and I will pawn my Life for her, she will never be pert to your Honour, if you'll be so good as to molest her no more, nor frighten her again. Said she, You see how, by her Fit, she was in Terror; she could not help it; and tho' your Honour intended her no harm; yet the Apprehension was almost Death to her: And I had much ado to bring her to herself again. O the little Hypocrite, said he! she has all the Arts of her Sex; they are born with her; and I told you a-while ago, you did not know her. But, said he, this was not the Reason principally of my calling you before me both together: I find I am likely to suffer in my Reputation by the Perverseness and Folly of this Girl. She has told you all, and perhaps more than all; nay, I make no doubt of it; and she has written Letters; for I find she is a mighty Letter-writer! to her Father and Mother, and others, as far as I know; in which she makes herself an Angel of Light, and me, her kind Master and Benefactor, a Devil incarnate!—(O how People will sometimes, thought I, call themselves by the right Names!—) And all this I won't bear; and so I am resolv'd she shall return to the Distresses and Poverty she was taken from; and let her take care how she uses my Name with Freedom, when she is gone from me.

I was brighten'd up at once upon these welcome Words: And I threw myself upon my Knees at his Feet, with a most sincere, glad Heart; and I said, God Almighty bless your Honour for your Resolution: Now I shall be happy; and permit me, on my bended Knees, to thank your Honour for all the Benefits and Favours you have heaped upon me: For the Opportunities I have had of Improvement and Learning; through my good Lady's Means, and yours. I will now forget all your Honour has done to me: And I promise you, that I will never take your Name in my Lips, but with Reverence and Gratitude: And so God Almighty bless your Honour, for ever and ever, *Amen!*—And so I got up, and went away with another-guise sort of Heart than I came into his Presence with. And so I fell to writing this Letter. And thank God all is over.

And now my dearest Father and Mother, expect to see soon your poor Daughter, with an humble and dutiful Mind, return'd to you: And don't fear but I know how to be happy with you as ever: For I will lie in the Loft, as I used to do; and pray let the little Bed be got ready; and I have a little

Money, which will buy me a Suit of Cloaths, fitter for my Condition than what I have; and I will get Mrs. *Mumford* to help me to some Needle-work; and fear not that I shall be a Burden to you, if my Health continues; and I know God will bless me, if not for my own sake, for both your sakes, who have, in all your Trials and Misfortunes, preserved so much Integrity, as makes every body speak well of you both. But I hope he will let good Mrs. *Jervis* give me a Character, for fear it should be thought I was turn'd away for Dishonesty.

And so God bless you both, and may you be blest for me, and I blest for you: And I will always bless my Master and Mrs. *Jervis*. And so good Night; for it is late, and I shall be soon called to-bed.

I hope Mrs. *Jervis* is not angry with me, because she has not called me to Supper with her; tho' I could eat nothing if she had. But I make no doubt I shall sleep purely to Night, and dream that I am with you, in my dear, dear, happy Loft once more.

So, good Night again, my dear Father and Mother, says

Your honest poor Daughter.

May-hap I mayn't come this Week, because I must get up the Linen, and leave every thing belonging to my Place in Order. So send me a Line if you can, to let me know if I shall be welcome, by *John*, who'll call for it as he returns. But say nothing of my coming away to him, as yet. For it will be said I blab every thing.

LETTER XVII.

My dearest Daughter,

Welcome, welcome, ten times welcome, shall you be to us; for you come to us innocent, and happy, and honest; and you are the Staff of our Old-age, and our Comfort too.[1] And tho' we cannot do for you as we would, yet we doubt not we shall live comfortably together, and what with my diligent Labour, and your poor Mother's Spinning, and your Needle-work, I make no doubt we shall live better and better. Only your poor Mother's Eyes begin to fail her; tho' I bless God, I am as strong, and able, and willing to labour as ever; and Oh my dear Child, your Virtue has made me, I think, stronger and better than I was before. What blessed Things are Trials and Temptations to us, when they be overcome!

But I am thinking about those same four Guineas: I think you should give them back again to your Master; and yet I have broke them. Alas! I have only three left; but I will borrow it if I can, Part upon my Wages, and Part of Mrs. *Mumford*, and send it to you, that you may return it, against[^1] *John* comes next, if he comes again, before you.

I want to know how you come. I fansy honest *John* will be glad to bear you Company Part of the Way, if your Master is not so cross as to forbid him. And if I know time enough, your Mother will go one five Miles, and I will go ten on the Way, or till I meet you, as far as one Holiday will go: For that I can get Leave for; and we shall receive you with more Pleasure than we had at your Birth, when all the worst was over; or than we ever had in our Lives.

And so God bless you, till the happy Time comes; say both your Mother and I; which is all at present, from

Your truly loving Parents.

LETTER XVIII.

Dear Father and Mother,

I thank you a thousand times for your Goodness to me, express'd in your last Letter. I now long to get my Business done, and come to my New-Old Lot, again, as I may call it. I have been quite another thing since my Master has turn'd me off; and as I shall come to you an honest Daughter, what Pleasure it is to what I should have, if I could not have seen you but as a guilty one! Well, my writing Time will soon be over, and so I will make Use of it now, and tell you all that has happen'd since my last Letter.

I wonder'd Mrs. *Jervis* did not call me to sup with her, and fear'd she was angry; and when I had finish'd my Letter, I long'd for her coming to Bed. At last she came up, but seem'd shy and reserv'd; and I said, O my dear Mrs *Jervis*, I am glad to see you: you are not angry with me, I hope. She said she was sorry Things went so far; and that she had a great deal of Talk with my Master after I was gone. She said, he seem'd mov'd at what I said, and at my falling on my Knees to him, and my Prayer for him, at my going away. He said, I was a strange Girl; he knew not what to make of me: And is she gone? said he: I intended to say something else to her, but she behav'd so oddly, that I had not Power to stop her. She ask'd if she should call me again. He said, Yes; and then, No, let her go; it is best for her and me too, that she shall go now I have given her Warning. But where she had it, I can't tell; but I never met with the Fellow of her in my Life, at any Age. She said, he had order'd her not to tell me all: but she believ'd he never would offer any thing to me again, and I might stay, she fansy'd, if I would beg it as a Favour; tho' she was not sure neither.

I stay! dear Mrs. *Jervis*, said I, why 'tis the best News that could have come to me, that he will let me go. I do nothing but long to go back again to my Poverty and Distress, as he said I should; for, tho' I am sure of the Poverty, I shall not have Half the Distress I have had for some Months past, I'll assure you.

Mrs. *Jervis*, dear good Soul, wept over me, and said, Well, well, *Pamela*, I did not think I had shew'd so little Love to you, as that you should express so much Joy to leave me. I am sure I never had a Child half so dear to me as you!

I cry'd to hear her so good to me, as indeed she has always been; and said, What would you have me to do, dear Mrs. *Jervis?* I love you next to my own Father and Mother, and you are the chief Concern I have to leave this Place; but I am sure it is certain Ruin if I stay. After such Offers, and such Threatenings, and his comparing himself to a wicked Ravisher, in the very Time of his last Offer; and making a Jest of me, that we should make a pretty Story in Romances; can I stay, and be safe? Has he not demean'd himself twice? and it behoves me to beware of the third Time, for fear he should lay his Snares surer; for may-hap he did not expect a poor Servant would resist her Master so much. And must it not be look'd upon as a sort of Warrant for such Actions, if I stay after this? for I think, when one of our Sex finds she is attempted, it is an Encouragement to a Person to proceed, if one puts one's self in the Way of it, when one can help it; and it shews one can forgive what in short ought not to be forgiven. Which is no small Countenance to foul Actions, I'll assure you.

She hugg'd me to her, and said, *I'll assure you!* Pretty-face, where gottest thou all thy Knowledge, and thy good Notions, at these Years? Thou art a Miracle for thy Age, and I shall always love thee! But, do you resolve to leave us, *Pamela?*

Yes, my dear Mrs. *Jervis*, said I; for as Matters stand, how can I do otherwise?—But I'll do all the Duties of my Place first, if I may. And I hope you'll give me a Character as to my Honesty, as it may not look as if

I was turn'd away for any Harm. Ay, that I will, said she; I will give thee such a Character as never Girl at thy Years deserv'd. And I am sure, said I, I will always love and honour you, as my third best Friend, whenever I go, or whatever becomes of me.

And so we went to Bed, and I never wak'd 'till 'twas Time to rise; which I did, as blyth as a Bird, and went about my Business with great Pleasure.

But I believe my Master is fearfully angry with me; for he past by me two or three times, and would not speak to me; and towards Evening he met me in the Passage, going into the Garden, and said such a Word to me as I never heard in my Life from him, to Man, Woman or Child; for he first said, This Creature's always in my way, I think! I said, standing up as close as I could, and the Entry was wide enough for a Coach[1] too, I hope I shan't be long in your Honour's Way. D—n you! said he, (that was the hard Word) for a little Witch; I have no Patience with you.

I profess I trembled to hear him say so; but I saw he was vex'd, and as I am going away, I minded it the less. But I see, my dear Parents, that when a Person will do wicked Things, it is no Wonder he will speak wicked Words. And so I rest

Your dutiful Daughter.

LETTER XIX.

Dear Father and Mother,

Our *John* having no Opportunity to go your Way, I write again, and send both Letters at once. I can't say yet when I can get away, nor how I shall come; because Mrs. *Jervis* shew'd my Master the Waistcoat I am flowering for him, and he said, It looks well enough, I think the Creature had best stay till she has finish'd it.

There is some private Talk carry'd on betwixt him and Mrs. *Jervis*, that she don't tell me of; but yet she is very kind to me, and I don't mistrust her at all. I should be very base if I did. But to be sure she must oblige him, and keep all his lawful Commands; and other, I dare say, she won't keep; she is too good, and loves me too well; but she must stay when I am gone, and so must get no Ill-will.

She has been at me again to ask to stay, and humble myself, as she says. But what have I done, Mrs. *Jervis*, said I? If I have been a Sawce-box, and a Bold-face, and Pert, and a Creature, as he calls me, have I not had Reason? Do you think I should ever have forgot myself, if he had not forgot to act as my Master? Tell me, from your own Heart, dear Mrs. *Jervis*, said I, if you think I could stay and be safe? What would you think, or how would you act in my Case?

My dear *Pamela*, said she, and kiss'd me, I don't know how I should act, or what I should think. I hope I should act as you do. But I know nobody else that would. My Master is a fine Gentleman; he has a great deal of Wit and Sense, and is admir'd, as I know, by half a dozen Ladies, who would think themselves happy in his Addresses. He has a noble Estate; and yet I believe he loves my good Maiden, tho' his Servant, better than all the Ladies in the Land; and he has try'd to overcome it, because he knows you are so much his Inferior; and 'tis my Opinion he finds he can't; and that vexes his proud Heart, and makes him resolve you shan't stay; and so he speaks so cross to you, when he sees you by Accident.

Well, but, Mrs. *Jervis*, said I, let me ask you, if he can stoop to like such a poor Girl as I, as may be he may, for I have read of Things almost as strange, from great Men to poor Damsels; What can it be for?—He may condescend, may-hap, to think I may be good enough for his Harlot; and those Things don't disgrace Men, that ruin poor Women, as the World goes. And so, if I was wicked enough, he would keep me till I was undone, and 'till his Mind changed; for even wicked Men, I have read, soon grow weary of Wickedness of one Sort, and love Variety. Well then, poor *Pamela* must be turn'd off, and look'd upon as a vile abandon'd Creature, and every body would despise her; ay, and justly too, Mrs. *Jervis*; for she that can't keep her Virtue, ought to live in Disgrace.

But, Mrs. *Jervis*, said I, let me tell you, that I hope, if I was sure he would always be kind to me, and never turn me off at all, that God will give me his Grace, so as to hate and withstand his Temptations, were he not only my Master, but my King, for the Sin's sake; and this my poor dear Parents have always taught me; and I should be a sad wicked Creature indeed, if, for the sake of Riches or Favour, I should forfeit my good Name: yea, and worse than any other young body of my Sex; because I can so contentedly return to my Poverty again, and think it less Disgrace to be oblig'd to wear Rags, and live upon Rye-bread and Water, as I use to do, than to be a Harlot to the greatest Man in the World.

Good Mrs. *Jervis* lifted up her Hands, and had her Eyes full of Tears: God bless you, my dear Love, said she; you are my Admiration and Delight!—How shall I do to part with you?

Well, good Mrs. *Jervis*, said I, let me ask you now:—You and he have some Talk, and you mayn't be suffer'd to tell me all. But, do you think, if I was to ask to stay, that he is sorry for what he has done! ay, and *asham'd* of it too! for I am sure he ought, considering his high Degree, and my low Degree, and how I have nothing in the World to trust to but my Honesty! Do you think in your own Conscience now, pray answer me truly; that he would never offer any thing to me again; and that I could be safe?

Alas! my dear Child, said she, don't put thy home Questions to me, with that pretty becoming Earnestness in thy Look. I know this, that he is vex'd at what he has done; he was vex'd the *first* Time, more vex'd the *second* Time.

Yes, said I, and so he will be vex'd I suppose the *third*, and the *fourth* Time too, 'till he has quite ruin'd your poor Maiden, and who will have Cause to be vex'd then?

Nay, *Pamela*, said she, don't imagine that I would be accessary to your Ruin for the World. I only can say, that he has yet done you no Hurt; and 'tis no Wonder that he should love you, you are so pretty; tho' so much beneath him: But I dare swear for him, he never will offer you any Force.

You say, said I, that he was sorry for his *first* Offer in the Summer-house; well, and how long did his Sorrow last?—Only 'till he found me by myself; and then he was worse than before: and so became sorry *again*. And if he has deign'd to love me, and you say can't help it, why he can't help it neither, if he should have an Opportunity, a *third* time to distress me. And I have read, that many a Man has been asham'd at a Repulse, that never would, had they succeeded. Besides, Mrs. *Jervis*, if he *really* intends to offer no *Force*, What does that mean?—While you say he can't help liking me, for *Love* it cannot be!—Does not it imply, that he hopes to ruin me by my own *Consent?* I *think*, said I, (and I hope God would give me Grace to *do* so) that I should not give way to his Temptations on any Account; but it would be very presumptuous in me to rely upon my own Strength, against a Gentleman of his Qualifications and Estate, and who is my Master; and thinks himself intitled to call me Bold-face, and what not; only for standing on my necessary Defence? And that where the Good of my Soul and Body, and my Duty to God, and my Parents, are all concerned. How then, Mrs. *Jervis*, said I, can I *ask* or *wish* to stay?

Well, well, says she; as he seems very desirous you should not stay, I hope it is from a good Motive; for fear he should be tempted to disgrace himself as well as you. No, no, Mrs. *Jervis*, said I; I have thought of that too, for I would be glad to think of him with that Duty that becomes me; but then he would have let me gone to Lady *Davers*, and not have hinder'd my Preferment. And he would not have said, I should return to my *Poverty* and *Distress*, when I had been, by his Mother's Goodness, lifted out of it; but that he intended to fright me, and *punish* me, as he thought, for not complying with his Wickedness: And this shews me enough what I have to expect from his future Goodness, except I will deserve it at his own dear, dear Price!

She was silent, and I said, Well there's no more to be said; I must go, that's certain; All my Concern will be how to part with you: And indeed, next to you; with every body; for all my Fellow-servants have lov'd me, and you and they will cost me a Sigh and a Tear too now-and-then, I am sure; and so I fell a-crying. I could not help it. For it is a pleasant Thing to one to be in a House among a great many Fellow-servants, and be belov'd by them all.

Nay, I should have told you before now, how kind and civil Mr. *Longman* our Steward is: Vastly courteous indeed on all Occasions, and he said, once to Mrs. *Jervis*, he wish'd he was a young Man for my sake, I should be his Wife, and he would settle all he had upon me on Marriage; and, you must know, he is reckon'd worth a Power[1] of Money.

I take no Pride in this; but bless God, and your good Example, my dear Parents, that I have been enabled to have every body's good Word. Not but that our Cook one Day, who is a little snappish and cross sometimes, said once to me, Why this *Pamela* of ours goes as fine as a Lady. See what it is to have a fine Face!—I wonder what the Girl will come to at last!

She was hot with her Work; and I sneak'd away; for I seldom went down in the Kitchen; and I heard the Butler say, Why, *Jane*, nobody has your good Word! What has Mrs. *Pamela* done to you? I am sure she offends no body. And what, said the peevish Wench, have I said to her, *Foolatum*;[2] but that she was pretty? They quarrel'd afterwards, I heard; but I was sorry for it, and troubled myself no more about it. Forgive this silly Prattle, from

Your dutiful Daughter.

O! I forgot to say, that I would stay to finish the Waistcoat; I never did a prettier Piece of Work; and I am up early and late to get it finish'd; for I long to come to you.

LETTER XX.

My dear Father and Mother,

I did not send my last Letters so soon as I would, because *John* (whether my Master mistrusts or no, I can't say) had been sent to Lady *Davers*'s, instead of *Isaac*, who used to go; and I could not be so free with, nor so well trust *Isaac*; tho' he is very civil to me too. So I was forced to stay till *John* return'd.

As I may not have Opportunity to send again soon, and yet as I know you keep my Letters, and read them over and over (so *John* told me) when you have done Work, so much does your Kindness make you love all that comes from your poor Daughter; and as it may be some little Pleasure to me, may-hap, to read them myself, when I am come to you, to remind me what I have gone thro', and how great God's Goodness has been to me (which, I hope, will rather strengthen my good Resolutions, that I may not hereafter, from my bad Conduct, have Reason to condemn myself from my own Hand, as it were): For all these Reasons, I say, I will write as I have Time, and as Matters happen, and send the Scribble to you as I have Opportunity; and if I don't every time, in Form, subscribe as I ought, I am sure you will always believe that it is not for want of Duty. So I will begin where I left off about the Talk between Mrs. *Jervis* and me, for me to ask to stay.

Unknown to Mrs. *Jervis*, I put a Project, as I may call it, in Practice. I thought with myself some Days ago, Here I shall go home to my poor Father and Mother, and have nothing on my Back, that will be fit for my Condition; for how should your poor Daughter look with a Silk Night-gown, Silken Petticoats, Cambrick Head-cloaths, fine Holland Linen, lac'd Shoes, that were my Lady's, and fine Stockens! And how in a little while must they have look'd, like old Cast-offs indeed, and I look'd so for wearing them! And People would have said, (for poor Folks are envious, as well as rich) See there Goody *Andrews*'s Daughter, turn'd home from her fine Place! What a tawdry Figure she makes! And how well that Garb becomes her poor Parents Circumstances!—And how would they look upon me, thought I to myself, when they come to be in Tatters, and worn out? And how should I look, even if I could get homespun Cloths, to dwindle into them one by one, as I could get them?—May-be, an old Silk Gown, and a new Linsey-woolsey[1] Petticoat, and so on. So, thinks I, I had better get myself at once 'quipt in the Dress that would become my

Condition; and tho' it might look but poor to what I was us'd to wear of late Days, yet it would serve me, when I came to you, for a good Holiday and Sunday Suit, and what by God's Blessing on my Industry, I might, may-be, make shift to keep up to.

So, as I was saying, unknown to any body, I bought of Farmer *Nichols*'s Wife and Daughters, a good sad-colour'd Stuff, of their own Spinning, enough to make me a Gown and two Petticoats; and I made Robings and Facings of a pretty Bit of printed Calicoe,[1] I had by me.

I had a pretty good Camlet[2] quilted Coat, that I thought might do tolerably well; and I bought two Flannel Under-coats, not so good as my Swan-skin[3] and fine Linen ones; but what would keep me warm, if any Neighbour should get me to go out to help 'em to milk, now-and-then, as sometimes I us'd to do formerly; for I am resolv'd to do all your good Neighbours what Kindness I can; and hope to make myself as much belov'd about you, as I am here.

I got some pretty good *Scots* Cloth,[4] and made me at Mornings and Nights, when nobody saw me, two Shifts, and I have enough left for two Shirts, and two Shifts, for you, my dear Father and Mother. When I come home, I'll make 'em for you, and desire your Acceptance as my first Present.

Then I bought of a Pedlar, two pretty enough round-ear'd Caps,[5] a little Straw Hat, and a Pair of knit Mittens, turn'd up with white Calicoe; and two Pair of ordinary blue Worsted Hose, that make a smartish Appearance, with white Clocks,[6] I'll assure you; and two Yards of black Ribbon for my Shift Sleeves, and to serve as a Necklace; and when I had 'em all come home, I went and look'd upon them once in two Hours, for two Days together: For, you must know, tho' I lay with Mrs. *Jervis*, I kept my own little Apartment still for my Cloaths; and nobody went thither but myself. You'll say, I was no bad Housewife to have sav'd so much Money; but my dear good Lady was always giving me something.

I believ'd myself the more oblig'd to do this, because as I was turn'd away for what my good Master thought Want of Duty; and, as he expected other Returns for his Presents, than I intended, I bless God, to make him; so I thought it was but just to leave his Presents behind me when I went away: for, you know, if I would not earn his Wages, why should I have them?

Don't trouble yourself, now I think of it, about the Four Guineas, nor borrow to make them up; for they were given me, with some Silver, as I told you, as a Perquisite, being what my Lady had about her when she dy'd; and, as I hope for no other Wages, I am so vain as to think I have deserv'd them in the fourteen Months, since my Lady's Death: For she, good Soul!

overpaid me before in Learning and other Kindnesses.—O had she liv'd, none of these Things might have happen'd!—But God be prais'd, 'tis no worse. Every thing turns about for the best, that's my Confidence.

So, as I was saying, I have provided a new and more suitable Dress, and I long to appear in my new Cloaths, more than ever I did in any new Cloaths in my Life; for then I shall be soon after with you, and at Ease in my Mind.—But mum—I am, &c.

LETTER XXI.

My dear Father and Mother,

I was forc'd to break off; for I fear'd my Master was coming; but it prov'd to be only Mrs. *Jervis.* She came to me, and said, I can't endure you should be so much by yourself, *Pamela.* And I, said I, dread nothing so much as Company; for my Heart was up at my Mouth now, for fear my Master was coming. But I always rejoice to see my dear Mrs. *Jervis.*

Said she, I have had a world of Talk with my Master about you. I am sorry for it, said I; that I am made of so much Consequence as to be talk'd of by him. O, said she, I must not tell you all; but you are of more Consequence to him, than you think for—

Or *wish* for, said I; for the Fruits of being of Consequence to him, would make me of none to myself, or any body else.

Said she, thou art as witty as any Lady in the Land. I wonder where thou gottest it. But they must be poor Ladies, with such great Opportunities, I am sure, if they have no more than I.—But let that pass.

I suppose, said I, that I am of so much Consequence, however, as to vex him, if it be but to think, he can't make a Fool of such a one as I; and that is nothing at all, but a Rebuke to the Pride of his high Condition, which he did not expect, and knows not how to put up with.

There is something in that, may-be, says she; but indeed, *Pamela*, he is very angry at you *too*; and calls you twenty perverse Things; wonders at his own Folly, to have shewn you so much Favour, as he calls it; which he was first inclin'd to, he says, for his Mother's sake, and would have persisted to shew you for your own, if you was not your own Enemy.

Nay, now, I shan't love you, Mrs. *Jervis*, said I; you are going to persuade me to ask to stay, tho' you know the Hazards I run.—No, said she, he says you shall go; for he thinks it won't be for his Reputation to keep you: But he wish'd (don't speak of it for the World, *Pamela*) that he knew a Lady of Birth, just such another as yourself, in Person and Mind, and he would marry her To-morrow.

I colour'd up to the Ears at this Word; but said, Yet if I was the Lady of Birth, and he would offer to be rude first, as he has twice done to poor me, I don't know whether I would have him: For she that can bear an Insult of that kind, I should think not worthy to be any Gentleman's Wife; any more than he would be a Gentleman that would offer it.

Nay, now, *Pamela*, said she, thou carriest thy Notions a great way. Well, dear Mrs. *Jervis*, said I, very seriously, for I could not help it, I am more full of Fears than ever. I have only to beg of you as one of the best Friends I have in the World, to say nothing of my asking to stay. To say my Master likes me, when I know what End he aims at, is Abomination to my Ears; and I shan't think myself safe till I am at my poor Father's and Mother's.

She was a little angry at me, 'till I assur'd her, that I had not the least Uneasiness on her Account, but thought myself safe under her Protection and Friendship. And so we dropt the Discourse for that Time.

I hope to have finish'd this ugly Waistcoat in two Days; after which, I have only some Linen to get up, and do something to, and shall then let you know how I shall contrive as to my Passage; for the heavy Rains will make it sad travelling on Foot: But may-be I may get a Place to ----, which is ten Miles of the Way, in Farmer *Nichols*'s close Cart; for I can't sit a Horse well at all. And may-be nobody will be suffer'd to see me on upon the Way. But I hope to let you know more,

From, &c.

LETTER XXII.

My dear Father and Mother,

All my Fellow-servants have now some Notion, that I am to go away; but can't imagine for what. Mrs. *Jervis* tells them, that my Father and Mother growing in Years, cannot live without me; and so I go to them to help to comfort their old Age; but they seem not to believe it.

What they found it out by, was, the Butler heard him say to me, as I pass'd by him, in the Entry leading to the Hall, Who's that? *Pamela*, Sir, said I. *Pamela!* said he, How long are you to stay here!—Only, please your Honour, said I, till I have done the Waistcoat; and it is almost done.—You might, says he, (very roughly indeed) have finish'd that long enough ago, I should have thought! Indeed, and please your Honour said I, I have work'd early and late upon it; there is a great deal of Work in it! Work in it! said he; yes, you mind your Pen more than your Needle; I don't want such idle Sluts to stay in my House.

He seem'd startled, when he saw the Butler. As he enter'd the Hall, where Mr. *Jonathan* stood, What do *you* here, said he?—The Butler was as much confounded as I; for I never having been tax'd so roughly, could not help crying sadly; and got out of both their ways to Mrs. *Jervis*, and told my Complaint. This Love, said she, is the D—l! in how many strange Shapes does it make People shew themselves! And in some the farthest from their Hearts.

So one, and then another, has been since whispering, Pray, Mrs. *Jervis*, are we to lose Mrs. *Pamela?* as they always call me—What has she done? And then she tells them as above, about going home to you.

She said afterwards to me, Well, *Pamela*, you have made our Master from the sweetest-temper'd Gentleman in the World, one of the most peevish. But you have it in your Power to make him as sweet-temper'd as ever; tho' I hope in God you'll never do it on his Terms!

This was very good in Mrs. *Jervis*; but it intimated, that she thought as ill of his Designs as I; and as she knew his Mind more than I, it convinc'd me, that I ought to get away as fast as I could.

My Master came in, just now, to speak to Mrs. *Jervis* about Houshold Matters, having some Company to dine with him To-morrow; and I stood up, and having been crying, at his Roughness in the Entry, I turn'd away my Face.

You may well, said he, turn away your cursed Face; I wish I had never seen it!—Mrs. *Jervis*, how long is she to be about this Waistcoat?

Sir, said I, if your Honour had pleased, I would have taken it with me; and tho' it will be now finish'd in a few Hours, I will do so still; and remove this hateful poor *Pamela* out of your House and Sight for ever.

Mrs. *Jervis*, said he, not speaking to me, I believe this little Slut has the Power of Witchcraft, if ever there was a Witch; for she inchants all that come near her. She makes even you, who should know better what the World is, think her an Angel of Light.

I offer'd to go away; for I believ'd he wanted me to ask to stay in my Place, for all this his great Wrath; and he said, Stay here, stay here, when I bid you; and snatch'd my Hand. I trembled, and said, I will! I will! for he hurt my Fingers, he grasp'd me so hard.

He seem'd to have a mind to say something to me; but broke off abruptly; and said, Begone! And away I tripp'd, as fast as I could; and he and Mrs. *Jervis* had a deal of Talk, as she told me; and among the rest, he express'd himself vex'd to have spoke in Mr. *Jonathan's* Hearing.

Now you must know, that Mr. *Jonathan* our Butler, is a very grave good sort of old Man, with his Hair as white as Silver! and an honest worthy Man he is. I was hurrying out, with a Flea in my Ear, as the Saying is, and going down Stairs into the Parlour, met him. He took hold of my Hand, in a gentler manner tho', than my Master, with both his; and he said, Ah! sweet, sweet Mrs. *Pamela!* what is it I heard just now!—I am sorry at my Heart; but I am sure I will sooner believe any body in Fault than you. Thank you, Mr. *Jonathan,* said I; but as you value your Place, don't be seen speaking to such a one as me. I cry'd too; and slipt away as fast as I could from him, for his own sake, lest he should be seen to pity me.

And now I will give you an Instance how much I am in Mr. *Longman's* Esteem also.

I had lost my Pen some how; and my Paper being wrote out, I stepp'd to Mr. *Longman's* our Steward's Office, to beg him to give me a Pen or two, and a Sheet or two of Paper. He said, Aye, that I will, my sweet Maiden! And gave me three Pens, some Wafers,[1] a Stick of Wax, and twelve Sheets of Paper; and coming from his Desk, where he was writing, he said, Let me have a Word or two with you, my sweet little Mistress (for so these two good old Gentlemen often call me; for I believe they love me dearly): I hear bad News; that we are going to lose you: I hope it is not true. Yes, it is, Sir, said I; but I was in Hopes it would not be known till I went away.

What a D—l, said he, ails our Master of late! I never saw such an Alteration in any Man in my Life! He is pleas'd with nobody, as I see; and by what Mr. *Jonathan* tells me just now, he was quite out of the way with you. What could you have done to him, tro'?[2] Only Mrs. *Jervis* is a very good Woman, or I should have fear'd *she* had been your Enemy.

No, said I, nothing like it. Mrs. *Jervis* is a just good Woman, and next to my Father and Mother, the best Friend I have in the World.—Well then, says he, it must be worse. Shall I guess? You are too pretty, my sweet Mistress, and, may-be, too virtuous. Ah! have I not hit it? No, good Mr.

Longman, said I, don't think any thing amiss of my Master; he is cross and angry with me indeed, that's true; but I may have given Occasion for it, may-be; and because I am oblig'd to go to my Father and Mother, rather than stay here, may-hap, he may think me ungrateful. But you know, Sir, said I, that a Father and Mother's Comfort is the dearest thing to a good Child that can be. Sweet Excellence! said he, this becomes you; but I know the World and Mankind too well; tho' I must hear, and see, and say nothing! But God bless my little Sweeting, said he, where-ever you go! And away went I, with a Curchee and Thanks.

Now this pleases one, my dear Father and Mother, to be so beloved.— How much better, by good Fame and Integrity, is it to get every one's good Word but *one*, than by pleasing *that one*, to make *every one else* one's Enemy, and be an execrable Creature besides! I am, &c.

LETTER XXIII.

My dear Father and Mother,

We had a great many neighbouring Gentlemen, and their Ladies, this Day at Dinner; and my Master made a fine Entertainment for them. And *Isaac*, and Mr. *Jonathan*, and *Benjamin* waited at Table. And *Isaac* tells Mrs. *Jervis*, that the Ladies will by-and-by come to see the House, and have the Curiosity to see me; for it seems, they said to my Master, when the Jokes flew about, Well Mr. *B*—, we understand that you have a Servant-maid, who is the greatest Beauty in the County; and we promise ourselves to see her before we go.

The Wench is well enough, said he; but no such Beauty as you talk of, I'll assure ye. She was my Mother's Waiting-maid, and she on her Death-bed engag'd me to be kind to her. She is young, and every thing is pretty that is young.

Aye, aye, says one of the Ladies, that is true; but if your Mother had not recommended her so strongly, there is so much Merit in Beauty, that I make no doubt such a fine Gentleman would have wanted no such strong Inducement to be kind.

They all laugh'd at my Master: And he, it seems, laugh'd for Company; but said, I don't know how it is; but I see with different Eyes from other People; for I have heard much more Talk of her Prettiness, than I think she deserves: She is well enough, as I said; but I think her greatest Excellence is, that she is humble, and courteous, and faithful, and makes all her Fellow-servants love her; my House-keeper in particular doats upon her, and you know, Ladies, she is a Woman of Discernment; and, as for Mr. *Longman*, and *Jonathan*, here, if they thought themselves young enough, I am told, they would fight for her. Is it not true, *Jonathan?* Troth, Sir, said he, an't please your Honour, I never knew her Peer, and all your Honour's Family are of the same Mind. Do ye hear now? said my Master—Well, said the Ladies, we will make a Visit to Mrs. *Jervis* by-and-by, and hope to see this Paragon.

Well, I believe, they are coming, and I will tell you more by-and-by. I wish they had come, and were gone. Why can't they make their Game without me!

Well, these fine Ladies have been here, and gone back again. I would have been absent if I could, and did step into the Closet, so they saw me not when they came in.

There were four of them, Lady *Arthur* at the great white House on the Hill, Lady *Brooks*, Lady *Towers*, and the other, it seems, a Countess, of some hard Name, I forget what.

So, Mrs. *Jervis*, says one of the Ladies, how do you do? We are all come to inquire after your Health. I am much oblig'd to your Ladyships, said Mrs. *Jervis*: Will your Ladyships please to sit down? But, said the Countess, we are not only come to ask after Mrs. *Jervis*'s Health neither; but we are come to see a Rarity besides. Aye, says Lady *Arthur*, I have not seen your *Pamela* these two Years, and they tell me she is grown wondrous pretty in that Time.

Then I wish'd I had not been in the Closet; for when I came out, they must needs know I heard them: but I have often found, that bashful Bodies owe themselves a Spight,[1] and frequently confound themselves more, by endeavouring to avoid Confusion.

Why, yes, says Mrs. *Jervis*, *Pamela* is very pretty indeed; she's but in the Closet there:—*Pamela*, pray step hither. I came out, all cover'd with Blushes; and they smil'd at one another.

The Countess took me by the Hand: Why, indeed, she was pleas'd to say, Report has not been too lavish, I'll assure you. Don't be asham'd, Child (and star'd full in my Face); I wish I had just such a Face to be asham'd of! O how like a Fool I look'd!—

Lady *Arthur* said, Aye, my good *Pamela*, I say as her Ladyship says: Don't be so confus'd; tho' indeed it becomes you too. I think your good Lady departed made a sweet Choice of such a pretty Attendant. She would have been mighty proud of you, as she always was praising you, had she liv'd till now.

Ah! Madam, said Lady *Brooks*, do you think, that so *dutiful* a Son as our Neighbour, who always *admir'd* what his Mother *lov'd*, does not pride himself, for all what he said at Table, in such a pretty Maiden?

She look'd with such a malicious sneering Countenance, I cannot abide her.

Lady *Towers* said, with a free Air; for it seems she is call'd a Wit; Well, Mrs. *Pamela*, I can't say, I like you so well as these Ladies do; for I should never care, if you were my Servant, to see you and your Master in the same House together. Then they all set up a great Laugh.

I know what I could have said, if I durst. But they are Ladies—and Ladies may say any thing.

Says Lady *Towers*, Can the pretty Image speak, Mrs. *Jervis?* I vow she has speaking Eyes! O you little Rogue, says she, and tapt me on the Cheek, you seem born to undo, or to be undone!

God forbid, and please your Ladyship, said I, it should be either!—I beg, said I, to withdraw; for the Sense I have of my Unworthiness, renders me unfit for such a Presence.

I then went away, with one of my best Curchees; and Lady *Towers* said, as I went out, Prettily said, I vow!—And Lady *Brooks* said, See that Shape! I never saw such a Face and Shape in my Life; why she must be better descended than you have told me!

And so, belike, their Clacks¹ run for half an Hour in my Praises, and glad was I, when I got out of the Hearing of them.

But it seems they went down with such a Story to my Master, and so full of me, that he had a hard Life to stand it; but as it was very little to my Reputation, I am sure I could take no Pride in it; and I fear'd it would make no better for me. This gives me another Cause for leaving this House.

This is *Thursday* Morning, and next *Thursday* I hope to set out; for I have finish'd my Task, and my Master is horrid cross: And I am vex'd, his Crossness affects me so. If ever he had any Kindness towards me, I believe he now hates me heartily.

Is it not strange, that Love borders so much upon Hate? But this wicked Love is not like the true virtuous Love, to be sure: That and Hatred must be as far off, as Light and Darkness. And how must this Hate have been increased, if he had met with a base Compliance, after his wicked Will had been gratify'd?

Well, one may see by a little, what a great deal means: For if Innocence cannot attract common Civility, what must Guilt expect, when Novelty had ceas'd to have its Charms, and Changeableness had taken place of it? Thus we read in Holy Writ, that wicked *Amnon*, when he had ruin'd poor *Tamar*, hated her more than ever he lov'd her, and would have turn'd her out of Door!¹

How happy am I, to be turn'd out of Door, with that sweet Companion my Innocence!—O may that be always my Companion! And while I presume not upon my own Strength, and am willing to avoid the Tempter, I hope the Divine Grace will assist me.

Forgive me, that I repeat in my Letter Part of my hourly Prayer. I owe every thing, next to God's Goodness, to your Piety and good Examples, my dear Parents; my dear *poor* Parents, I will say, because your *Poverty* is my *Pride*, as your Integrity shall be my Imitation.

As soon as I have din'd, I will put on my new Cloaths. I long to have them on. I know I shall surprise Mrs. *Jervis* with them; for she shan't see me till I am full-dress'd.—*John* is come back, and I'll soon send you some of what I have written.—I find he is going early in the Morning; and so I'll close here, that I am

Your most dutiful Daughter.

Don't lose your Time in meeting me; because I am so uncertain. It is hard, if some how or other, I can't get a Passage to you. But may-be my Master won't refuse to let *John* bring me. I can ride behind him, I believe, well enough; for he is very careful, and very honest; and you know *John* as well as I; for he loves you both. Besides, may-be, Mrs. *Jervis* can put me in some way.

LETTER XXIV.

Dear Father and Mother,

I shall write on, as long as I stay, tho' I should have nothing but Sillinesses to write; for I know you divert yourselves at Nights with what I write, because it is mine. *John* tells me how much you long for my coming; but he says, he told you, he hop'd something would happen to hinder it.

I am glad you did not tell him the Occasion of my coming away; for *if* they should guess, it were better so, than to have it from you or me: Besides, I really am concern'd that my poor Master should cast such a Thought upon such a Creature as me; for besides the Disgrace, it has quite turn'd his Temper; and I begin to think he likes me, and can't help it; and yet strives to conquer it, and so finds no way but to be cross to me.

Don't think me presumptuous and conceited; for it is more my Concern than my Pride, to see such a Gentleman so demean himself, and lessen the Regard he used to have in the Eyes of all his Servants on my Account.—But I am to tell you of my new Dress to Day.

And so, when I had din'd, up Stairs I went, and lock'd myself into my little Room. There I trick'd myself up as well as I could in my new Garb, and put on my round-ear'd ordinary Cap; but with a green Knot however, and my homespun Gown and Petticoat, and plain-leather Shoes; but yet they are what they call *Spanish* Leather, and my ordinary Hose, ordinary I mean to what I have been lately used to; tho' I shall think good Yarn may do very well for every Day, when I come home. A plain Muslin Tucker[1] I put on, and my black Silk Necklace, instead of the *French* Necklace my Lady gave me, and put the Ear-rings out of my Ears; and when I was quite 'quip'd, I took my Straw Hat in my Hand, with its two blue Strings, and look'd about me in the Glass, as proud as any thing.——To say Truth, I never lik'd myself so well in my Life.

O the Pleasure of descending with Ease, Innocence and Resignation! ——Indeed there is nothing like it! An humble Mind, I plainly see, cannot meet with any very shocking Disappointment, let Fortune's Wheel turn round as it will.

So I went down to look for Mrs. *Jervis*, to see how she lik'd me.

I met, as I was upon the Stairs, our *Rachel*, who is the House-maid, and she made me a low Curchee, and I found did not know me. So I smil'd, and went to the House-keeper's Parlour. And there sat good Mrs. *Jervis* at Work, making a Shift: And, would you believe it? she did not know me at first; but rose up, and pull'd off her Spectacles; and said, Do you want me, forsooth? I could not help laughing, and said, Hey-day! Mrs. *Jervis*, what! don't you know me?——She stood all in Amaze, and look'd at me from Top to Toe; Why you surprise me, said she; what! *Pamela!* Thus metamorphos'd! How came this about? As it happen'd, in stept my Master, and my Back being to him, he thought it was a Stranger speaking to Mrs. *Jervis*, and withdrew again; and did not hear her ask if his Honour had any Commands with her?———She turn'd me about and about, and I shew'd her all my Dress, to my Under-petticoat; and she said, sitting down, Why I am all in Amaze! I must sit down. What can all this mean? I told her, I had no Cloaths suitable to my Condition when I return'd to my Father's; and so it was better to begin here, as I was soon to go away, that all my Fellow-servants might see, I knew how to suit myself to the State I was returning to.

Well, said she, I never knew the like of thee. But this sad Preparation for going away (for now I see you are quite in Earnest) is what I know not how to get over. O my dear *Pamela*, how can I part with you!

My Master rung in the back Parlour, and so I withdrew, and Mrs. *Jervis* went to attend him. It seems he said to her, I was coming in to let you know that I shall go to *Lincolnshire*, and may-be to my Sister *Davers's*, and be absent some Weeks. But, pray, what pretty neat Damsel was that with you? She says, she smil'd, and ask'd if his Honour did not know who it was? No, said he, I never saw her before. Farmer *Nichols*, or Farmer *Brady*, have neither of them such a tight prim Lass for a Daughter; have they?—Tho' I did not see her Face neither, said he. If your Honour won't be angry, said she, I will introduce her into your Presence; for I think, says she, she out-does our *Pamela*.

Now I did not thank her for this, as I told her afterwards (for it brought a great deal of Trouble upon me, as well as Crossness, as you shall hear). That can't be, he was pleased to say. But if you can find an Excuse for it, let her come in.

At that she stept to me, and told me, I must go in with her to my Master; but, said she, for Goodness sake, let him find you out; for he don't know you. Good Sirs! Mrs. *Jervis*, said I, how could you serve me so? Besides, it looks too free both *in me*, and *to him*. I tell you, said she, you shall come in; and pray don't reveal yourself till he finds you out.

So I went in, foolish as I was; tho' I must have been seen by him another time, if I had not then. And she would make me take my Straw-hat in my Hand.

I dropt a low Curchee, but said never a Word. I dare say, he knew me as soon as he saw my Face; but was as cunning as *Lucifer*. He came up to me, and took me by the Hand, and said, Whose pretty Maiden are you?—I dare say you are *Pamela*'s Sister, you are so like her. So neat, so clean, so pretty! Why, Child, you far surpass your Sister *Pamela*!

I was all Confusion, and would have spoken; but he took me about the Neck; Why, said he, you are very pretty, Child; I would not be so free with your *Sister*, you may believe; but I must kiss *you*.

O Sir, said I, I am *Pamela*, indeed I am: Indeed I am *Pamela, her own self!*

He kissed me for all I could do; and said, Impossible! you are a lovelier Girl by half than *Pamela*; and sure I may be innocently free with you, tho' I would not do her so much Favour.

This was a sad Bite¹ upon me indeed, and what I could not expect; and Mrs. *Jervis* look'd like a Fool as much as I, for her Officiousness.—At last I got away, and ran out of the Parlour, most sadly vex'd, as you may well think.

He talk'd a good deal to Mrs. *Jervis*, and at last order'd me to come in to him. Come in, said he, you little Villain! for so he call'd me; good Sirs! what a Name was there! Who is it you put your Tricks upon? I was resolved never to honour your Unworthiness, said he, with so much Notice again; and so you must disguise yourself, to attract me, and yet pretend, like an Hypocrite as you are—

I was out of Patience, then; Hold, good Sir, said I; don't impute Disguise and Hypocrisy to me, above all things; for I hate them both, mean as I am. I have put on no Disguise.——What a-plague, said he, for that was his Word, do you mean then by this Dress?——Why, and please your Honour, said I, I mean one of the honestest things in the World. I have been in Disguise indeed ever since my good Lady, your Mother, took me from my poor Parents. I came to her Ladyship so poor and mean, that these Cloaths I have on, are a princely Suit, to those I had then. And her Goodness heap'd upon me rich Cloaths, and other Bounties: And as I am now returning to my poor Parents again so soon, I cannot wear those good things without being whooted at; and so have bought what will be more suitable to my Degree, and be a good Holiday Suit too, when I get home.

He then took me in his Arms, and presently push'd me from him. Mrs. *Jervis*, said he, take the little Witch from me; I can neither bear, nor forbear her!² (Strange Words these!)——But stay, you shan't go!——Yet begone!——No, come back again.

I thought he was mad, for my Share; for he knew not what he would have. But I was going however, and he stept after me, and took hold of my Arm, and brought me in again: I am sure he made my Arm black and blue; for the Marks are upon it still. Sir, Sir, said I, pray have Mercy; I will, I will come in!

He sat down, and look'd at me, and look'd as silly as such a poor Girl as I, I thought afterwards.——At last, he said, Well, Mrs. *Jervis*, as I was telling you, you may suffer her to stay a little longer, till I see if my Sister *Davers* will have her; if, mean time, she humble herself, and ask this as a

Favour, and is sorry for her Pertness, and the Liberty she has taken with my Character, out of the House and in the House. Your Honour indeed told me so, said Mrs. *Jervis*; but I never found her inclinable to think herself in Fault. Pride and Perverseness, said he, with a Vengeance! Yet this is your Doating-piece!——Well, for once I'll submit myself, to tell you, Hussy, said he to me, you may stay a Fortnight longer, till I see my Sister *Davers*: Do you hear what I say to you, Statue! can you neither speak, nor be thankful?—Your Honour frights me so, said I, that I can hardly speak: But I will venture to say, that I have only to beg, as a Favour, that I may go to my Father and Mother.—Why, Fool, says he, won't you like to go to wait on my Sister *Davers?* Sir, said I, I was once fond of that Honour; but you was pleased to say, I might be in Danger from her Ladyship's Nephew, or he from me?—D—d Impertinence! said he; do you hear, Mrs. *Jervis*, do you hear, how she retorts upon me? Was ever such matchless Assurance!——

I then fell a weeping; for Mrs. *Jervis* said, Fie, *Pamela*, fie!—And I said, My Lot is very hard indeed! I am sure I would hurt nobody; and I have been, it seems, guilty of Indiscretions, which have cost me my Place, and my Master's Favour, and so have been turn'd away. And when the Time is come, that I should return to my poor Parents, I am not suffer'd to go quietly. Good your Honour, what have I done, that I must be used worse than if I had robb'd you!——Robb'd me! said he, why so you have, Hussy; you *have* robb'd me. Who! I! Sir, said I, have I robb'd you? Why then you are a Justice of Peace,[1] and may send me to Gaol, if you please, and bring me to a Tryal for my Life! If you can prove that I have robb'd you, I am sure I ought to die!

Now I was quite ignorant of his Meaning; tho' I did not like it when it was afterwards explain'd, neither; and, well, thought I, what will this come to at last, if poor *Pamela* is thought a Thief! Then I thought, in an Instant, how I should shew my Face to my honest poor Parents, if I was but suspected.

But, Sir, said I, let me ask you but one Question, and pray don't let me be call'd Names for it; for I don't mean disrespectfully; Why, if I have done amiss, am I not left to be discharged by your House-keeper, as the other Maids have been? And if *Jane*, or *Rachel*, or *Hannah*, were to offend, would your Honour stoop to take Notice of them? And why should you so demean yourself to take Notice of me? Pray, Sir, if I have not been worse than others, why should I suffer more than others? and why should I not be turn'd away, and there's an End of it? For indeed I am not of Consequence enough for my Master to concern himself and be angry about such a Creature as me.

Do you hear, Mrs. *Jervis*, cry'd he again, how pertly I am interrogated by this sawcy Slut? Why, Sauce-box, says he, did not my good Mother desire me to take care of you? and have you not been always distinguish'd by me, above a common Servant? and does your Ingratitude upbraid me for this?

I said something mutteringly, and he vow'd he would hear it. I begg'd Excuse; but he insisted upon it. Why then, said I, if your Honour must know, I said, That my good Lady did not desire your Care to extend to the Summer-house and her Dressing-room.

Well, this was a little sawcy, you'll say!——And he flew into such a Passion, that I was forced to run for it; and Mrs. *Jervis* said, It was happy I got out of his way.

Why, what makes him provoke one so, then?—I'm almost sorry for it; but I would be glad to get away at any rate. For I begin to be fearful now.

Just now Mr. *Jonathan* sent me these Lines—(Lord bless me! what shall I do?)

"Dear Mrs. *Pamela*, Take care of yourself; for *Rachel* heard my Master say to Mrs. *Jervis*, who, she believes, was pleading for you, Say no more, Mrs. *Jervis*; for by G—— I will have her! Burn this instantly."

O pray for your poor Daughter! I am called to go to-bed by Mrs *Jervis*, for it is past Eleven; and I am sure she shall hear of it; for all this is owing to her, tho' she did not mean any Harm. But I have been, and am, in a strange Fluster; and I suppose too, she'll say, I have been full-pert.

O my dear Father and Mother, Power and Riches never want Advocates! But, poor Gentlewoman! she cannot live without him. And he has been very good to her.

So, Good-night. May-be I shall send this in the Morning; but may-be not; so won't conclude; tho' yet I must say, I am

Your most dutiful Daughter.

LETTER XXV.

My dear Parents,

O let me take up my Complaint, and say, Never was poor Creature so unhappy, and so barbarously used, as your *Pamela!* O my dear Father and Mother, my Heart's just broke! I can neither write as I should do, nor let it alone; for to whom but you can I vent my Griefs, and keep my poor Heart from bursting! Wicked, wicked Man!—I have no Patience left me!—But yet, don't be frighted—for,—I hope—I hope, I am honest!—But if my Head and my Heart will let me, you shall hear all.—Is there no Constable nor Headborough, tho', to take me out of his House? for I am sure I can safely swear the Peace against him:[1] But, alas! he is greater than any Constable, and is a Justice himself; such a Justice, deliver me from!—But God Almighty, I hope, in time, will right me!—For he knows the Innocence of my Heart!—

John went your way in the Morning; but I have been too much distracted to send by him; and have seen nobody but Mrs. *Jervis,* and *Rachel,* and one I hate to see: And indeed I hate now to see any body. Strange things I have to tell you, that happen'd since last Night, that good Mr. *Jonathan's* Letter, and my Master's Harshness put me into such a Fluster. But I will no more *preambulate.*

I went to Mrs. *Jervis's* Chamber; and Oh! my dear Father and Mother, my wicked Master had hid himself, base Gentleman as he is! in her Closet, where she has a few Books, and Chest of Drawers, and such-like. I little suspected it; tho' I used, till this sad Night, always to look into that Closet, and another in the Room, and under the Bed, ever since the Summer-house Trick, but never found any thing; and so I did not do it then, being fully resolv'd to be angry with Mrs. *Jervis* for what had happen'd in the Day, and so thought of nothing else.

I sat myself down on one side of the Bed, and she on the other, and we began to undress ourselves; but she on that side next the wicked Closet, that held the worst Heart in the World. So, said Mrs. *Jervis,* you won't speak to me, *Pamela!* I find you are angry with me. Why, Mrs. *Jervis,* said I, so I am, a little; 'tis a Folly to deny it. You see what I have suffer'd by your forcing me in to my Master! And a Gentlewoman of your Years and Experience must needs know, that it was not fit for me to pretend to be any body else for my own sake, nor with regard to my Master.

But, said she, who would have thought it would have turn'd out so? Ay, said I, little thinking who heard me, *Lucifer* always is ready to promote his own Work and Workmen. You see, presently, what Use he made of it, pretending not to know me, on purpose to be free with me: And when he took upon himself to know me, to quarrel with me, and use me hardly: And you too, said I, to cry, Fie, fie, *Pamela!* cut me to the Heart: For that encourag'd him.

Do you think, my Dear, said she, that I would encourage him?—I never said so to you before; but since you force it from me, I must tell you, that ever since you consulted me, I have used my utmost Endeavours to divert him from his wicked Purposes; and he has promised fair; but, to say all in a Word, he doats upon you; and I begin to see it is not in his Power to help it.

I luckily said nothing of the Note from Mr. *Jonathan*; for I began to suspect all the World almost: But I said, to try Mrs. *Jervis*, Well then, what would you have me do? You see he is for having me wait on Lady *Davers* now.

Why, I'll tell you freely, my dear *Pamela*, said she, and I trust to your Discretion to conceal what I say: My Master has been often desiring me to put you upon asking him to let you stay.—

Yes, said I, Mrs. *Jervis*, let me interrupt you: I will tell you why I could not think of that: It was not the Pride of my Heart; but the Pride of my Honesty: For what must have been the Case? Here my Master has been very rude to me, once and twice; and you say he cannot help it, tho' he pretends to be sorry for it: Well, he has given me Warning to leave my Place, and uses me very harshly; may-hap, to frighten me to his Purposes, as he supposes I would be fond of staying (as indeed I should, if I could be safe; for I love you and all the House, and value him, if he would act as my Master). Well then, as I know his Designs, and that he owns he cannot help it; must I not have asked to stay, knowing he would attempt me again? for all you could assure me of, was, he would do nothing by *Force*; so I, a poor weak Girl, was to be left to my own Strength, God knows! And was not this to allow him to tempt me, as one may say? and to encourage him to go on in his wicked Devices?—How then, Mrs. *Jervis*, could I ask or wish to stay?

You say well, my dear Child, says she; and you have a Justness of Thought above your Years; and for all these Confederations,[1] and for what I have heard this Day, after you run away, (and I am glad you went as you did) I cannot persuade you to stay; and I shall be glad, which is what I never thought I could have said, that you was well at your Father's; for if Lady *Davers* will entertain you, she may as well have you from thence as here. There's my good Mrs. *Jervis*! said I; God will bless you for your good Counsel to a poor Maiden that is hard beset. But pray what did he say, said I, when I was gone? Why, says she, he was very angry with you. But he would hear it, said I! I think it was a little bold; but then he provoked me to it. And had not my Honesty been in the Case, I would not by any means have been so sawcy. Besides, Mrs. *Jervis*, consider, it was the Truth; if he does not love to hear of the Summer-house and the Dressing-room, why should he not be asham'd to continue in the same Mind. But, said she, when you had mutter'd this to yourself, you might have told him any thing else. Well, said I, I cannot tell a wilful Lye, and so there's an End of it. But I find you now give him up, and think there's Danger in staying!—Lord bless me, I wish I was well out of the House; so it was at the Bottom of a wet Ditch, on the wildest Common in *England!*

Why, said she, it signifies nothing to tell you all he said; but it was enough to make me fear you would not be so safe as I could wish; and upon my Word, *Pamela,* I don't wonder he loves you; for, without Flattery, you are a charming Girl! and I never saw you look more lovely in my Life, than in that same new Dress of yours. And then it was such a Surprize upon us all!—I believe truly, you owe some of your Danger to the lovely Appearance you made. Then, said I, I wish the Cloaths in the Fire. I expected no Effect from them; but if any, a quite contrary one.

Hush! said I, Mrs. *Jervis,* did you not hear something stir in the Closet? No, silly Girl, said she! your Fears are always awake!—But indeed, says I, I think I heard something rustle!—May-be, says she, the Cat may be got there: But I hear nothing.

I was hush; but she said, Pr'ythee, my good Girl, make haste to-bed. See if the Door be fast. So I did, and was thinking to look in the Closet; but hearing no more Noise, thought it needless, and so went again and sat myself down on the Bedside, and went on undressing myself. And Mrs. *Jervis* being by this time undrest, stept into Bed, and bid me hasten, for she was sleepy.

I don't know what was the Matter; but my Heart sadly misgave me; but Mr. *Jonathan*'s Note was enough to make it do so, with what Mrs. *Jervis* had said. I pulled off my Stays, and my Stockens, and my Gown, all to an Under-petticoat; and then hearing a rustling again in the Closet, I said, God protect us! but before I say my Prayers, I must look into this Closet. And so was going to it slip-shod, when, O dreadful! out rush'd my Master, in a rich silk and silver Morning Gown.[1]

I scream'd, and run to the Bed; and Mrs. *Jervis* scream'd too; and he said, I'll do you no harm, if you forbear this Noise; but otherwise take what follows.

Instantly he came to the Bed; for I had crept into it, to Mrs. *Jervis,* with my Coat on, and my Shoes; and taking me in his Arms, said, Mrs. *Jervis,* rise, and just step up Stairs, to keep the Maids from coming down at this Noise; I'll do no harm to this Rebel.

O, for God's sake! for Pity's sake! Mrs. *Jervis,* said I, if I am not betray'd, don't leave me; and, I beseech you, raise all the House. No, said Mrs. *Jervis,* I will not stir, my dear Lamb; I will not leave you. I wonder at you, Sir, said she, and kindly threw herself upon my Coat, clasping me round the

Waist, you shall not hurt this Innocent, said she; for I will lose my Life in her Defence. Are there not, said she, enough wicked ones in the World, for your base Purpose, but you must attempt such a Lamb as this!

He was desperate angry, and threaten'd to throw her out of the Window; and to turn her out of the House the next Morning. You need not, Sir, said she; for I will not stay in it. God defend my poor *Pamela* till To-morrow, and we will both go together.—Says he, let me but expostulate a Word or two with you, *Pamela*. Pray, *Pamela*, said Mrs. *Jervis*, don't hear a Word, except he leaves the Bed, and goes to the other End of the Room. Aye, out of the Room! said I; expostulate To-morrow, if you must expostulate!

I found his Hand in my Bosom, and when my Fright let me know it, I was ready to die; and I sighed, and scream'd, and fainted away. And still he had his Arms about my Neck; and Mrs. *Jervis* was about my Feet, and upon my Coat. And all in a cold, clammy Sweat was I. *Pamela, Pamela!* said Mrs. *Jervis*, as she tells me since, O—h, and gave another Shriek, my poor *Pamela* is dead for certain!——And so, to be sure, I was for a time; for I knew nothing more of the Matter, one Fit following another, till about three Hours after, as it prov'd to be, I found myself in Bed, and Mrs. *Jervis* sitting up on one side, with her Wrapper about her, and *Rachel* on the other; and no Master, for the wicked Wretch was gone. But I was so over-joy'd, that I hardly could believe myself; and I said, which were my first Words, Mrs. *Jervis*, Mrs. *Rachel*, can I be sure it is you? God be prais'd! God be prais'd!——Where have I been? Hush, my Dear, said Mrs. *Jervis*, you have been in Fit after Fit. I never saw any body so frightful in my Life!

By this I judg'd Mrs. *Rachel* knew nothing of the Matter; and it seems my wicked Master had, upon Mrs. *Jervis's* second Noise on my going away, slipt out, and, as if he had come from his own Chamber, disturbed by the Screaming, went up to the Maids Room, (who hearing the Noise, lay trembling, and afraid to stir) and bid them go down and see what was the Matter with Mrs. *Jervis* and me. And he charged Mrs. *Jervis*, and promised to forgive her for what she had said and done, if she would conceal the Matter. So the Maids came down; for the Men lie in the Out-houses; and all went up again, when I came to myself a little, except *Rachel*, who staid to sit up with me, and bear Mrs. *Jervis* Company. I believe they all guess the Matter to be bad enough; tho' they dare not say any thing.

When I think of my Danger, and the Freedoms he actually took, tho' I believe Mrs. *Jervis* saved me from worse, and she says she did, (tho' what can I think, who was in a Fit, and knew nothing of the Matter?) I am almost distracted.

At first I was afraid of Mrs. *Jervis*; but I am fully satisfied she is very good, and I should have been lost but for her; and she takes on grievously about it. What would have become of me, had she gone out of the Room, to still the Maids, as he bid her. He'd certainly have shut her out, and then, Mercy on me! what would have become of your poor *Pamela!*

I must leave off a little, for my Eyes and my Head are sadly bad.—O this was a dreadful Trial! This was the worst of all! God send me safe from this dreadful wicked Man! Pray for

Your distressed Daughter.

LETTER XXVI.

My dear Father and Mother,

I did not rise till Ten o'Clock, and I had all the Concerns and Wishes of the Family, and Multitudes of Enquiries about me. My wicked Master went out early to hunt; but left word, he would be in to breakfast. And so he was.

He came up to our Chamber about Eleven, and had nothing to do to be sorry: for he was our *Master*, and so put on sharp Anger at first.

I had great Emotions at his entring the Room, and threw my Apron over my Head, and fell a crying, as if my Heart would break.

Mrs. *Jervis*, said he, since I know you, and you me so well, I don't know how we shall live together for the future. Sir, said she, I will take the Liberty to say what I think is best for us. I have so much Grief, that you should attempt to do any Injury to this poor Girl, and especially in my Chamber, that I should think myself accessary to the Mischief, if I was not to take Notice of it. Tho' my Ruin therefore may depend upon it, I desire not to stay; but pray let poor *Pamela* and I go together. With all my Heart, said he, and the sooner the better. She fell a crying. I find, says he, this Girl has made a Party of the whole House in her Favour against me. Her Innocence deserves it of us all, said she very kindly: And I never could have thought that the Son of my dear good Lady departed, could have so forfeited his Honour, as to endeavour to destroy what he ought to protect. No more of this, Mrs. *Jervis*, said he, I will not bear it. As for *Pamela*, she has a lucky Knack at falling into Fits, when she pleases. But the cursed Yellings of you both made me not my self. I intended no Harm to her, as I told you both, if you'd have left your Squallings; and I did no Harm neither, but to myself; for I rais'd a Hornet's Nest about my Ears, that, as far as I know, may have stung to Death my Reputation. Sir, said Mrs. *Jervis*, then I beg Mr. *Longman* may take my Accounts, and I will go away, as soon as I can. As for *Pamela*, she is at Liberty, I hope, to go away next *Thursday*, as she intends.

I sat still, for I could not speak nor look up, and his Presence discompos'd me extremely; but I was sorry to hear myself the unhappy Occasion of Mrs. *Jervis*'s losing her Place, and hope that may be made up.

Well, said he, let Mr. *Longman* make up your Accounts, as soon as you will; and Mrs. *Jewkes* (his House-keeper in *Lincolnshire*) shall come hither in your Place, and won't be less obliging, I dare say, than you have been. Said she, I have never disoblig'd you till now, and let me tell you, Sir, if you knew what belong'd to your own Reputation or Honour—No more, no more, said he, of these antiquated Topicks. I have been no bad Friend to you; and I shall always esteem you, tho' you have not been so faithful to my Secrets, as I could have wish'd, and have laid me open to this Girl, which has made her more afraid of me than she had Occasion. Well, Sir, said she, after what pass'd Yesterday, and last Night, I think I went rather too far in favour of your Injunctions than otherwise; and I should have deserv'd every body's Censure for the basest of Creatures, had I been capable of contributing to your lawless Attempts. Still, Mrs. *Jervis*, still reflecting upon me, and all for imaginary Faults! for what Harm have I done the Girl?—I won't bear it, I'll assure you. But yet, in respect to my Mother, I am willing to part friendly with you. Tho' you ought both of you to reflect on the Freedom of your Conversation, in relation to me; which I should have resented more than I do; but that I am conscious I had no Business to demean myself so as to be in your Closet, where I might expect to hear a multitude of Impertinence between you.

Well Sir, said she, you have no Objection, I hope, to *Pamela*'s going away on *Thursday* next? You are mighty sollicitous, said he, about *Pamela*: But, no, not I, let her go as soon as she will: She is a naughty Girl, and has brought all this upon herself; and upon me more Trouble than she can have had from me; but I have overcome it all; and will never concern myself about her.

I have a Proposal made me, added he, since I have been out this Morning, that I shall go near to embrace; and so wish only that a discreet Use may be made of what is past; and there's an End of every thing with me, as to *Pamela*, I'll assure you.

I clasp'd my Hands together thro' my Apron, over-joy'd at this, tho' I was so soon to go away: For, naughty as he has been to me, I wish his Prosperity with all my Heart, for my good old Lady's sake.

Well, *Pamela*, said he, you need not now be afraid to speak to me; tell me what you lifted up your Hands at? I said not a Word. Says he, If you like what I have said, give me your Hand upon it. I held my Hand thro' my Apron; for I could not speak to him, and he took hold of it, and press'd it, tho' less hard than he did my Arm the Day before. What does the little Fool cover her Face for, said he? Pull your Apron away; and let me see how you look, after your Freedom of Speech of me last Night! No wonder you're asham'd to see me. You know you were very free with my Character.

I could not stand this barbarous Insult, as I took it to be, considering his Behaviour to me; and I then spoke, and said, O the Difference between the Minds of thy Creatures, good God! How shall some be cast down in their Innocence, while others shall triumph in their Guilt!

And so saying, I went up Stairs to my Chamber, and wrote all this; for tho' he vex'd me, at his Taunting, yet I was pleas'd to hear he was likely to be marry'd, and that his wicked Intentions were so happily overcome as to me; and this made me a little easier. And, I hope I have pass'd the worst; or else it is very hard: And yet I shan't think my self at Ease quite, till I am with you. For methinks, after all, his Repentance and Amendment are mighty suddenly resolv'd upon. But God's Grace is not confin'd to Space;[1] and Remorse may, and I hope has, smote him to the Heart at once, for his Injuries to poor me! Yet I won't be too secure neither.

Having Opportunity, I send now what I know will grieve you to the Heart. But I hope I shall bring my next Scribble myself; and so conclude, tho' half broken-hearted,

Your ever dutiful Daughter.

LETTER XXVII.

Dear Father and Mother,

I am glad I desir'd you not to meet me, and *John* says you won't; for he says, he told you, he is sure I shall get a Passage well enough, either behind some one of my Fellow-servants on Horseback, or by Farmer *Nichols*'s Means:

But as for the Chariot he talk'd to you of, I can't expect that Favour, to be sure; and I should not care for it, because it would look so much above me. But Farmer *Brady*, they say, has a Chaise[1] with one Horse, and we hope to borrow that, or hire it rather than fail; tho' Money runs a little lowish, after what I have laid out; but I don't care to say so here, tho' I warrant I might have what I would of Mrs. *Jervis*, or Mr. *Jonathan*, or Mr. *Longman*; but then how shall I pay it, you'll say? And besides, I don't love to be beholden.

But the chief Reason I am glad you don't set out to meet me is the Uncertainty; for it seems I must stay another Week still, and hope certainly to go *Thursday* after. For poor Mrs. *Jervis* will go at the same time, she says, and can't be ready before.

God send me with you!—Tho' he is very civil now, at present, and not so cross as he was; and yet he is as vexatious another way, as you shall hear. For Yesterday he had a rich Suit of Cloaths brought home, which they call a Birth-day Suit;[2] for he intends to go to *London* against next Birth-day, to see the Court, and our Folks will have it he is to be made a Lord.—I wish they may make him an honest Man, as he was always thought; but I have not found it so, God help me!

And so, as I was saying, he had these Cloaths come home, and he try'd them on. And before he pull'd them off, he sent for me, when nobody else was in the Parlour with him: *Pamela*, said he, you are so neat and so nice in your own Dress, (Alas! for me, I did'n't know I was!) that you must be a Judge of ours. How are these Cloaths made? Do they fit me!—I am no Judge, said I, and please your Honour; but I think they look very fine.

His Waistcoat stood an End with Gold Lace, and he look'd very grand. But what he did last, has made me very serious, and I could make him no Compliments. Said he, Why don't you wear your usual Cloaths? Tho' I think every thing looks well upon you. For I still continue in my new Dress. I said, I have no Cloaths, Sir, I ought to call my own, but these: And it is no Matter what such a one as I wears! Says he, Why you look very serious, *Pamela*. I see you can bear Malice.—Yes, so I can, Sir, said I, according to the Occasion! Why, said he, your Eyes always look red, I think. Are you not a Fool to take my last Freedom so much to Heart? I am sure you, and that Fool Mrs. *Jervis*, frightened me, by your hideous Squalling, as much as I could frighten you. That is all we had for it, said I; and if you could be so afraid of your own Servants knowing of your Attempts upon a poor unworthy Creature, that is under your Protection while I stay, surely your Honour ought to be more afraid of God Almighty, in whose Presence we all stand, in every Action of our Lives, and to whom the greatest as well as the least, must be accountable, let them think what they list.

He took my Hand, in a kind of good-humour'd Mockery, and said, Well said, my pretty Preacher! when my *Lincolnshire* Chaplain dies, I'll put thee on a Gown and Cassock, and thou'lt make a good Figure in his Place!—I wish, said I, a little vex'd at his Jeer, your Honour's Conscience would be your Preacher, and then you would need no other Chaplain. Well, well, *Pamela*, said he, no more of this unfashionable Jargon. I did not send for you so much for your Opinion of my new Suit, as to tell you, you are welcome to stay, since Mrs. *Jervis* desires it, till she goes. I welcome! said I; I am sure I shall rejoice when I am out of the House!

Well, said he, you are an ungrateful Baggage; but I am thinking it would be Pity, with these fair soft Hands, and that lovely Skin (as he call'd it) that you should return again to hard Work, as you must, if you go to your Father's; and so I would advise her to take a House in *London*, and let Lodgings to us Members of Parliament, when we come to Town, and such a pretty Daughter as you may pass for, will always fill her House, and she'll get a great deal of Money.

I was sadly vex'd at this barbarous Joke; but was ready to cry before, and I gush'd out into Tears, and said, I can expect no better from such a rude Gentleman! Your Behaviour, Sir, to me has been just of a Piece with these Words; nay, I will say't tho' you was to be ever so angry.—I angry, *Pamela*, no, no, said he, I have overcome all that; and as you are to go away, I look upon you now as Mrs. *Jervis*'s Guest, while you both stay, and not as my Servant, and so you may say what you will. But I'll tell you, *Pamela*, why you need not take this Matter in such high Disdain!— You have a very pretty romantic Turn for Virtue, and all that!—And I don't suppose but you'll hold it still; and no body will be able to prevail upon you. But, my Child, (fleeringly he spoke it) do but consider what a fine Opportunity you will then have, for a Tale every Day to good Mother *Jervis*, and what Subjects for Letter-writing to your Father and Mother, and what pretty Preachments you may hold forth to the young Gentlemen. Ad's my Heart,[1] I think it would be the best Thing you and she could do.

You do well, Sir, said I, to even your Wit to such a poor Maiden as me! But, Sir, let me say, that if you was not rich and great, and I poor and little, you would not insult me so in my Misery!—Let me ask you, Sir, if you think this becomes your fine Cloaths! and a Master's Station? Why so serious, my pretty *Pamela?* said he; why so grave? and would kiss me; but my Heart was full, and I said, Let me alone! I will tell you, if you was a King, and said to me as you have done, that you are no Gentleman: And I won't stay to be used thus! I will go to the next Farmer's, and there wait for

Mrs. *Jervis*, if she must go: And I'd have you know, Sir, that I can stoop to the ordinary'st Work of your Scullions, for all these nasty soft Hands, sooner than bear such ungentlemanly Imputations.

Well, said he, I sent for you in, in high good Humour; but 'tis impossible to hold it with such an Impertinent: However I'll keep my Temper. But while I see you here, pray don't put on those dismal grave Looks: Why, Girl, you should forbear 'em, if it were but for your Pride-sake; for the Family will think you are grieving to leave the House. Then, Sir, said I, I will try to convince them of the contrary, as well as your Honour; for I will endeavour to be more chearful while I stay, for that very Reason.

Well, said he, I will set this down by itself, as the first Time that ever what I advis'd had any Weight with you. And I hope, said I, as the first Advice you have given me of late, that was fit to be follow'd!—I wish, said he, (I'm almost asham'd to write it, impudent Gentleman as he is! I wish) I had thee as quick another Way,[1] as thou art in thy Repartees—And he laugh'd, and I tripp'd away as fast as I could. Ah! thinks I, marry'd! I'm sure 'tis time you was marry'd, or at this Rate no honest Maiden will live with you.

Why, dear Father and Mother, to be sure he grows quite a Rake! Well, you see, how easy it is to go from bad to worse, when once People give way to Vice!

How would my poor Lady, had she liv'd, have griev'd to see it! But may-be he would have been better then!—Tho', it seems, he told Mrs. *Jervis*, he had an Eye upon me in his Mother's Life-time; and he intended to let me know as much by the Bye, he told her! Here's Shamelessness for you!—Sure the World must be near an End! for all the Gentlemen about are as bad as he almost, as far as I can hear!—And see the Fruits of such bad Examples: There is 'Squire *Martin* in the Grove, has had three Lyings-in,[2] it seems, in his House, in three Months past, one by himself; and one by his Coachman; and one by his Woodman; and yet he has turn'd none of them away. Indeed, how can he, when they but follow his own vile Example. There is he, and two or three more such as he, within ten Miles of us; who keep Company and hunt with our fine Master, truly; and I suppose he's never the better for their Examples. But, God bless me, say I, and send me out of this wicked House!

But, dear Father and Mother, what Sort of Creatures must the Womenkind be, do you think, to give way to such Wickedness? Why, this it is that makes every one be thought of alike: And, alack-a-day! what a World we live in! for it is grown more a Wonder that the Men are resisted, than that the Women comply. This, I suppose, makes me such a Sawce-box, and Boldface, and a Creature; and all because I won't be a Sawce-box and Boldface indeed.

But I am sorry for these Things; one don't know what Arts and Stratagems these Men may devise to gain their vile Ends; and so I will think as well as I can of these poor Creatures, and pity them. For you see by my sad Story, and narrow Escapes, what Hardships poor Maidens go thro', whose Lot is to go out to Service; especially to Houses where there is not the Fear of God, and good Rule kept by the Heads of the Family.

You see I am quite grown grave and serious; so it becomes

Your dutiful Daughter.

LETTER XXVIII.

Dear Father and Mother,

John says you wept when you read my last Letters, that he carry'd. I am sorry you let him see that; for they all mistrust already how Matters are; and as it is no Credit, that I have been *attempted*; tho' it is that I have *resisted*; yet I am sorry they have Cause to think so evil of my Master from any of us.

Mrs. *Jervis*, has made up her Accounts with Mr. *Longman*; and I believe will stay again. I am glad of it, for her own sake, and for my Master's; for she has a good Master of him; so indeed all have, but poor me!—and he has a good Housekeeper in her.

Mr. *Longman*, it seems, took upon him to talk to my Master, how faithful and careful of his Interests she was, and how exact in her Accounts; and he told him, there was no Comparison between her Accounts and Mrs. *Jewkes*'s, at the *Lincolnshire* Estate. He said so many fine Things, it seems, of Mrs. *Jervis*, that my Master sent for her in Mr. *Longman*'s Presence, and said, I might come along with her: I suppose to mortify me, that I must go while she was to stay: But as, when I go away, I am not to go with her, nor she with me; so I did not matter it much; only it would have been creditable to such a poor Girl, that the House-keeper would bear me Company, if I went.

Said he, to her, Well Mrs. *Jervis*, Mr. *Longman* says you have made up your Accounts with him, with your usual Fidelity and Exactness. I had a good mind to make you an Offer of continuing with me, if you can be a little sorry for your hasty Words, which indeed were not so respectful as I have deserv'd at your Hands. She seem'd at a sad Loss what to say, because Mr. *Longman* was there, and she could not speak of the Occasion of those Words, which was me.

Indeed, said Mr. *Longman*, I must needs say before your Face, that since I have known my Master's Family, I have never found such good Management, and so much Love and Harmony too. I wish the *Lincolnshire* Estate was as well serv'd!—No more of that, said my Master; but Mrs. *Jervis* may stay, if she will; and here, Mrs. *Jervis*, pray accept of this, which at the Close of every Year's Accounts I will present you with, besides your Salary, as long as I find your Care so useful and agreeable. And he gave her five Guineas!—She made him a low Curchee, and pray'd God to bless him; and look'd to me, as if she would have spoken of me.

He took her Meaning, I believe; for he said,—Indeed I love to encourage Merit and Obligingness, Mr. *Longman*; but I can never be equally kind to those who don't deserve it at my Hands; and then he look'd full at me; Mr. *Longman*, continued he, I said that Girl might come in with Mrs. *Jervis*; because they love to be always together. For Mrs. *Jervis* is very good to her, as if she was her Daughter. But else—Mr. *Longman*, interrupting him, said, *Good* to Mrs. *Pamela!* Aye, Sir, and so she is, to be sure! But every body must be good to her,—

He was going on. But my Master said, No more, no more, Mr. *Longman*. I see old Men are taken with pretty young Girls, as well as other Folks; and fair Looks hide many a Fault, where a Person has the Art to behave obligingly. Why, and please your Honour, said Mr. *Longman*, every body— and was going on, I believe to say something more in my Praise; but he interrupted him, and said, Not a Word more of this *Pamela*. I can't let her stay, I'll assure you; not only for her own Freedom of Speech; but her Letter-writing of all the Secrets of my Family. Aye, said the good old Man! I'm sorry for that too! But Sir,—No more, I say, said my Master; for my Reputation's so well known (mighty fine, thought I!) that I care not what any body writes or says of me: But to tell you the Truth, not that it need go further, I think of changing my Condition soon; and, you know, young Ladies of Birth and Fortune will chuse their own Servants, and that's my chief Reason why *Pamela* can't stay. As for the rest, said he, the Girl is a good sort of Body, take her all together; tho' I must needs say, a little pert, since my Mother's Death, in her Answers, and gives me two Words for one; which I can't bear; nor is there Reason I should, says he, you know, Mr. *Longman*. No, to be sure, Sir, said he; but 'tis strange methinks, she should be so mild and meek to every one of us in the House, and forget herself so where she should shew most Respect! Very true, Mr. *Longman*, said he, I'll assure you; and it was from her Pertness that Mrs. *Jervis* and I had the Words: And I should mind it the less; but that the Girl (there she stands, I say it to her Face)! has Wit and Sense above her Years, and knows better.

I was in great Pain to say something; but yet I knew not what, before Mr. *Longman*; and Mrs. *Jervis*, look'd at me, and walk'd to the Window to hide her Concern for me. At last, I said, It is for *You*, Sir, to say what you please; and for *me* only to say, God bless your Honour!

Poor Mr. *Longman* falter'd in his Speech, and was ready to cry. Said my insulting Master to me; why pr'ythee, *Pamela*, now, shew thy self as thou art, before Mr. *Longman*. Canst not give him a Specimen of that Pertness which thou hast exercis'd upon me sometimes? Did not he, my dear Father and Mother, deserve all the Truth to be told; yet I overcame myself, so far, as to say, Well, your Honour may play upon a poor Girl, that you know *can* answer you, but *dare* not. Why pr'ythee now, Insinuator, said he, say the worst you can before Mr. *Longman* and Mrs. *Jervis!*—I challenge the utmost of thy Impertinence; and as you are going away, and have the Love of every body, I would be a little justify'd to my Family, that you have no Reason to complain of Hardships from me, as I have of pert saucy Answers from you, besides exposing me by your Letters.

Well, Sir, said I, I am of no Consequence equal to this, sure, in your Honour's Family, that such a great Gentleman as you, my Master, should need to justify yourself about me. I am glad Mrs. *Jervis* stays with your Honour; and I know I have *not deserv'd* to stay; and more than that, I don't *desire* to stay.

Ads-bobbers!ᴵ said Mr. *Longman*, and ran to me; don't say so, don't say so, dear Mrs. *Pamela!* We all love you dearly; and pray down of your Knees, and ask his Honour Pardon, and we will all become Pleaders in a Body, and I, and Mrs. *Jervis* too, at the Head of it, to beg his Honour's Pardon, and to continue you, at least till his Honour marries.—No, Mr. *Longman*, said I, I cannot ask; nor will I stay, if I might. All I desire is to return to my poor Father and Mother, and tho' I love you all, I won't stay;—O well-a-day, well-a-day! said the good old Man, I did not expect this!—When I had got Matters thus far, and had made all up for Mrs. *Jervis*, I was in Hopes to have got a double Holiday of Joy for all the Family, in your Pardon too. Well, said my Master, this is a little Specimen of what I told you, Mr. *Longman*. You see there's a Spirit you did not expect.

Mrs. *Jervis* told me after, that she could stay no longer to hear me so hardly used, and must have spoke, had she stay'd, what would never have been forgiven her; so she went out. I look'd after her to go too; but my Master said, Come, *Pamela*, give another Specimen, I desire you, to Mr. *Longman*: I am sure you must, if you will but speak. Well, Sir, said I, since it seems your Greatness wants to be justified by my Lowness, and I have no Desire you should suffer in the Sight of your Family, I will say, on my bended Knees (and so I kneeled down) that I have been a very faulty, and a very ingrateful Creature to the *best* of Masters! I have been very perverse, and sawcy; and have deserv'd nothing at your Hands, but to be turn'd out of your Family with Shame and Disgrace. I, therefore, have nothing to say for myself, but that I am not worthy to stay, and so cannot wish to stay, and will not stay: And so God Almighty bless you, Sir, and you, Mr. *Longman*, and good Mrs. *Jervis*, and every living Soul of the Family! and I will pray for you all as long as I live.—And so I rose up, and was forc'd to lean upon my Master's Elbow Chair,[1] or I should have sunk down.

The poor old Man wept more than I, and said, Ads-bobbers! was ever the like heard! 'Tis too much, too much; I can't bear it. As I hope to live, I am quite melted. Dear Sir, forgive her: The poor Thing prays for you; she prays for us all! She owns her Fault; yet won't be forgiven! I profess I know not what to make of it.

My Master himself, harden'd Wretch as he was, seem'd a little mov'd, and took his Handkerchief out of his Pocket, and walk'd to the Window: What Sort of a Day is it, said he?—And then getting a little more Hardheartedness, he said, Well, you may be gone from my Presence, thou strange Medley of Inconsistence! but you shan't stay after your Time in the House.

Nay, pray Sir, pray Sir, said the good old Man, relent a little! Adsheartlikins,[2] you young Gentlemen are made of Iron and Steel, I think: I'm sure, said he, my Heart's turn'd into Butter, and is running away at my Eyes. I never felt the like before.—Said my Master, with an imperious Tone, Get out of my Presence, Hussy, I can't bear you in my Sight. Sir, said I, I'm going as fast as I can.

But indeed, my dear Father and Mother, my Head was so giddy, and my Limbs trembled so, that I was forc'd to go holding by the Wainscot all the way, with both my Hands, and thought I should not have got to the Door: But when I did, as I hop'd this would be my last Interview with this terrible hard-hearted Master; I turn'd about, and made a low Curchee, and said, God bless you, Sir! God bless you, Mr. *Longman!* And I went into the Lobby leading to the great Hall, and dropt into the first Chair; for I could get no further a good while.

I leave all these Things to your Reflection, my dear Parents; but I can write no more. My poor Heart's almost broke! Indeed it is.—O when shall I get away!—Send me, good God, in Safety, once to my poor Father's peaceful Cot![1]—and there the worst that can happen will be Joy in Perfection to what I now bear!—O pity

Your distressed Daughter.

LETTER XXIX.

My dear Father and Mother,

I must write on, tho' I shall come so soon; for now I have hardly any thing else to do. For I have finish'd all that lay upon me to do, and only wait the good Time of setting out. Mrs. *Jervis* said, I must be low in Pocket, for what I had laid out; and so would have presented me with two Guineas of her Five; but I could not take them of her, because, poor Gentlewoman! she pays old Debts for her Children that were extravagant, and wants them herself. This, tho', was very good in her.

I am sorry, I shall have but little to bring with me; but I know you won't; you are so good!—and I will work the harder when I come home, if I can get a little Plain-work,[2] or any thing to do. But all your Neighbourhood is so poor, that I fear I shall want Work; but may-be Dame *Mumford* can help me to something, from some good Family she is acquainted with.

Here, what a sad Thing it is! I have been brought up wrong, as Matters stand. For, you know, my Lady, now with God, lov'd Singing and Dancing; and, as she would have it I had a Voice, she made me learn both; and often and often has she made me sing her an innocent Song, and a good Psalm too, and dance before her. And I must learn to flower and draw too, and to work fine Work with my Needle; why, all this too I have got pretty tolerably at my Finger's End, as they say, and she us'd to praise me, and was a good Judge of such Matters.

Well now, what is all this to the Purpose, as Things have turn'd about?

Why, no more nor less, than that I am like the Grashopper in the Fable,[1] which I have read of in my Lady's Books; and I will write it down, in the very Words.

"As the Ants were airing their Provisions one Winter, a hungry Grashopper (as suppose it was poor I!) begg'd a Charity of them. They told him, that he should have wrought in Summer, if he would not have wanted in Winter. Well, says the Grashopper, but I was not idle neither; for I sung out the whole Season. Nay, then, said they, you'll e'en do well to make a merry Year of it, and dance in Winter to the Tune you sung in Summer."

So I shall make a fine Figure with my Singing and my Dancing when I come home to you. Nay, even I shall be unfit for a May-day Holiday-time; for these Minuets, Rigadoons, and *French* Dances, that I have been practising, will make me but ill Company for my rural Milk-maid Companions that are to be. Besure I had better, as Things stand, have learn'd to wash and scour, and brew and bake, and such-like. But I hope, if I can't get Work, and can get a Place, to learn these soon, if any body will have the Goodness to bear with me, till I can learn. For I bless God! I have an humble, and a teachable Mind, for all what my Master says; and, next to his Grace, that is all my Comfort: For I shall think nothing too mean that is honest. It may be a little hard at first, but woe to my proud Heart, if I shall find it so, on Tryal! for I will make it bend to its Condition, or will break it.

I have read of a good Bishop that was to be burnt for his Religion; and he try'd how he could bear it, by putting his Fingers into the lighted Candle:[2] So I, t'other Day, try'd, when *Rachel*'s Back was turn'd, if I could not scour the Pewter Plate she had begun. I see I could do't by Degrees; tho' I blister'd my Hand in two Places.

All the Matter is, if I could get Needle-work enough, I would not spoil my Fingers by this rough Work. But if I can't, I hope to make my Hands as red as a Blood-pudden, and as hard as a Beechen Trencher,[3] to accommodate them to my Condition.—But I must break off, here's some-body coming!—

'Twas only our *Hannah* with a Message from Mrs. *Jervis!*—But, good Sirs, there is some body else!—Well, it is only *Rachel*. I am as much frighted as were the City Mouse and the Country Mouse in the same Book of Fables,[4] at every thing that stirs. Oh! I have a Power of these

Things to entertain you with in Winter Evenings, when I come home. If I can but get Work, with a little Time for reading,[1] I hope we shall be very happy, over our Peat Fires!

What made me hint to you, that I should bring but little with me, is this.

You must know, I did intend to do, as I have this Afternoon done: And that is, I took all my Cloaths, and all my Linen, and I divided them into three Parcels; and I said, It is now *Monday*, Mrs. *Jervis*, and I am to go away on *Thursday* Morning betimes; so, tho' I know you don't doubt my Honesty, I beg you will look over my poor Matters, and let every one have what belongs to them; for, said I, you know, I am resolv'd to take with me only what I can properly call my own.

Said she, (I did not know her Drift then; to be sure, she meant well; but I did not thank her for it, when I did know it) Let your Things be brought down into the green Room, and I will do any thing you would have me do.

With all my Heart, said I, green Room or any where; but I think you might step up, and see 'em as they lie.

However, I fetch'd 'em down, and laid them in three Parcels, as before; and, when I had done, I went down to call her up to look at them.

Now, it seems, she had prepar'd my Master for this Scene, unknown to me; and in this green Room was a Closet, with a Sash-door[2] and a Curtain before it; for there she puts her Sweet-meats and such Things; and she did it, it seems, to turn his Heart, as knowing what I intended, I suppose that he should make me take the Things; and if he had, I should have made Money of them, to help us when we got together; for, to be sure, I could never have appear'd in them.

Well, as I was saying, he had got unknown to me in this Closet; I suppose while I went to call Mrs. *Jervis*: And she since told me, it was at his Desire, when she told him something of what I intended, or else she would not have done it. Tho' I have Reason, I am sure, to remember the last Closet-work!

So I said, when she came up, Here, Mrs. *Jervis*, is the first Parcel; I will spread it all abroad. These are the Things my good Lady gave me.—In the first place, said I,—and so I went on describing the Cloaths and Linen my Lady had given me, mingling Blessings, as I proceeded, for her Goodness to me; and when I had turn'd over that Parcel, I said, Well, so much for the first Parcel, Mrs. *Jervis*, that was my Lady's Presents.

Now I come to the Presents of my dear virtuous Master: Hay, you know, *Closet* for that, Mrs. *Jervis!* She laugh'd, and said, I never saw such a comical

Girl in my Life. But go on. I will, Mrs. *Jervis*, said I, as soon as I have
open'd the Bundle; for I was as brisk and as pert as could be, little thinking
who heard me.

Now here, Mrs. *Jervis*, said I, are my ever worthy Master's Presents; and
then I particulariz'd all those in the second Bundle.

After which, I turn'd to my own, and said,

Now, Mrs. *Jervis*, comes poor *Pamela*'s Bundle, and a little one it is,
to the others. First, here is a Calicoe Night-gown,¹ that I used to wear o'
Mornings. 'Twill be rather too good for me when I get home; but I must
have something. Then there is a quilted Callimancoe² Coat, and a Pair of
Stockens I bought of the Pedlar, and my Straw-hat with blue Strings; and
a Remnant of *Scots* Cloth, which will make two Shirts and two Shifts, the
same I have on, for my poor Father and Mother. And here are four other
Shifts, one the Fellow to that I have on; another pretty good one, and the
other two old fine ones, that will serve me to turn and wind with at home,
for they are not worth leaving behind me; and here are two Pair of Shoes, I
have taken the Lace off, which I will burn, and may-be will fetch me some
little Matter at a Pinch, with an old Shoe-buckle or two.

What do you laugh for, Mrs. *Jervis?* said I.—Why you are like an *April-*
day; you cry and laugh in a Breath.

Well, let me see; aye, here is a Cotton Handkerchief I bought of the
Pedlar; there should be another somewhere. O here it is! And here too
are my new-bought knit Mittens. And this is my new Flannel Coat, the
Fellow to that I have on. And in this Parcel pinn'd together, are several
Pieces of printed Callicoe, Remnants of Silks, and such-like, that, if good
Luck should happen, and I should get Work, would serve for Robings and
Facings, and such-like Uses. And here too are a Pair of Pockets; they are
too fine for me; but I have no worse. Bless me! said I, I didn't think I had
so many good Things!

Well, Mrs. *Jervis*, said I, you have seen all my Store, and I will now sit
down, and tell you a Piece of my Mind.

Be brief then, said she, my good Girl; for she was afraid, she said
afterwards, that I should say too much.

Why then the Case is this: I am to enter upon a Point of Equity and
Conscience,³ Mrs. *Jervis*, and I must beg, if you love me, you'd let me have
my own Way. Those Things there of my Lady's, I can have no Claim to,
so as to take them away; for she gave them me, supposing I was to wear
them in her Service, and to do Credit to her bountiful Heart. But since I

am to be turn'd away, you know, I cannot wear them at my poor Father's; for I should bring all the little Village upon my Back: And so I resolve not to have them.

Then, Mrs. *Jervis*, said I, I have far less Right to these of my worthy Master's. For you see what was his Intention in giving them to me. So they were to be the Price of my Shame, and if I *could* make use of them, I should think I should never prosper with them; and besides, you know, Mrs. *Jervis*, if I would not do the good Gentleman's Work, why should I take his Wages? So in Conscience, in Honour, in every thing, I have nothing to say to thee, thou second wicked Bundle!

But, said I, come to my Arms, my dear third Parcel, the Companion of my Poverty, and the Witness of my Honesty; and may I never deserve the least Rag that is contained in thee, when I forfeit a Title to that Innocence that I hope will ever be the Pride of my Life; and then I am sure it will be my highest Comfort at my Death, when all the Riches and Pomps of the World will be worse than the vilest Rags that can be worn by Beggars! And so I hugg'd my third Bundle.—

But, said I, Mrs. *Jervis*, (and she wept to hear me) one thing I have more to trouble you with, and that's all.

There are four Guineas, you know, that came out of my good Lady's Pocket, when she dy'd, that, with some Silver, my Master gave me: Now those same four Guineas I sent to my poor Father and Mother, and they have broke them; but would make them up, if I would. And if you think it should be so, it shall. But pray tell me honestly your Mind: As to the three Years before my Lady's Death, do you think, as I had no Wages, I may be supposed to be Quits?—By Quits, I cannot mean, that my poor Services should be equal to my Lady's Goodness; for that's impossible. But as all her Learning and Education of me, as Matters have turn'd, will be of little Service to me now; for it had been better for me to have been brought up to hard Labour, to be sure; for that I must turn to at last, if I can't get a Place; (and you know, in Places too, one is subject to such Temptations as are dreadful to think of): So I say, by Quits, I only mean, as I return all the good Things she gave me, whether I may not set my little Services against my Keeping; because, as I said, my Learning is not now in the Question; and I am sure my dear good Lady would have thought so, had she liv'd: But that, too, is now out of the Question. Well then, if so, I would ask, whether in above this Year that I have liv'd with my Master; as I am resolv'd to leave all his Gifts behind me, I may not have earn'd besides my Keeping, these four Guineas; and these poor Cloaths here upon my Back, and in my third Bundle? Now tell me your Mind freely, without Favour or Affection.

Alas! my dear Maiden, said she, you make me unable to speak to you at all: To be sure, it will be the highest Affront that can be offer'd, for you to leave any of these Things behind you; and you must take all your Bundles with you, or my Master will never forgive you.

Well, well, Mrs. *Jervis*, said I, I don't care; I have been too much used to be snubb'd and hardly treated by my Master: Of late I have done him no Harm; and I shall always pray for him, and wish him happy. But I don't deserve these Things, I know I don't. Then I can't wear 'em, if I should take them; so they can be of no Use to me: And I trust God will provide for me, and not let me want the poor Pittance, that is all I desire, to keep Life and Soul together. Bread and Water I can live upon, Mrs. *Jervis*, with Content. Water I shall get any-where; and if I can't get me Bread, I will live like a Bird in Winter upon Hips and Haws,[1] and at other times upon Pig-nuts,[2] and Potatoes or Turneps, or any thing. So what Occasion have I for these Things?—But all I ask is about these four Guineas, and if you think I need not return them, that is all I want to know?—To be sure, my Dear, you need not, said she, you have well earn'd them by that Waistcoat only. No, I think not *so*, in that only; but in the Linen, and other Things, do you think I have? Yes, yes, said she, and more. And my Keeping allow'd for, I mean, said I, and these poor Cloaths on my Back, besides? remember that Mrs. *Jervis*. Yes, my dear Odd-ones, no doubt you have! Well then, said I, I am as happy as a Princess. I am quite as rich as I wish to be! And, once more, my dear third Bundle, I will hug thee to my Bosom. And I beg you'll say nothing of all this till I am gone, that my Master mayn't be so angry, but that I may go in Peace; for my Heart, without other Matters, will be ready to break to part with you all.

Now, Mrs. *Jervis*, said I, as to one Matter more: And that is my Master's last Usage of me, before Mr. *Longman*.—Said she, Pr'ythee, dear *Pamela*, step to my Chamber, and fetch me a Paper I left on my Table. I have something to shew you in it. I will, said I, and stept down; but this was only a Fetch[3] to take the Orders of my Master, I found; it seems he said, he thought two or three times to have burst out upon me; but he could not stand it, and wish'd I might not know he was there. But I tript up again so nimbly, for there was no Paper, that I just saw his Back, as if coming out of that green Room, and going into the next to it, the first Door, that was open.—I whipt in, and shut the Door, and bolted it. O Mrs. *Jervis*, said I, what have you done by me?—I see I can confide in nobody. I am beset on all Hands! Wretched, wretched *Pamela!* where shalt thou expect a Friend, if Mrs. *Jervis* joins to betray me thus?—She made so many Protestations, telling me all; and that he own'd I had made him wipe his Eyes two or three times, and said she hop'd it would have a good Effect, and remember'd me, that I had said nothing but would rather move Compassion than Resentment, that I forgave her. But oh! that I was safe from this House! for never poor Creature sure was so fluster'd as I have been, for so many Months together!—I am called down from this most tedious Scribble. I wonder what will next befall

Your dutiful Daughter.

Mrs. *Jervis* says, she is sure I shall have the Chariot to carry me home to you. Tho' this will look too great for me, yet it will shew as if I was not turn'd away quite in Disgrace. The travelling Chariot is come from *Lincolnshire*, and I fansy I shall go in that; for the other is quite grand.

LETTER XXX.

My dear Father and Mother,

I write again, tho', may-be, I shall bring it to you in my Pocket myself. For I shall have no Writing, nor Writing-time, I hope, when I come to you. This is *Wednesday* Morning, and I shall, I hope, set out to you To-morrow Morning; but I have had more Trials, and more Vexation; but of another Complexion too a little, tho' all from the same Quarter.

Yesterday my Master, after he came from Hunting, sent for me. I went with great Terror; for I expected he would storm, and be in a fine Passion with me for my Freedom of Speech before: So I was resolv'd to begin first, with Submission, to disarm his Anger; and I fell upon my Knees as soon as I saw him; and I said, For God's Sake, good Sir, and for the Sake of my dear good Lady your Mother, who recommended me to you with her last Words, let me beg you to forgive me all my Faults, as you hope to be forgiven yourself: And only grant me this Favour, the last I have to ask you, that you will let me depart your House with Peace and Quietness of Mind, that I may take such a Leave of my dear Fellow-servants as befits me; and that my Heart be not quite broken.

He took me up, in a kinder Manner, than ever I had known from him; and he said, Shut the Door, *Pamela*, and come to me in my Closet: I want to have a little serious Talk with you. How can I, Sir, said I, how can I? and wrung my Hands! O pray, Sir, let me go out of your Presence, I beseech you. By the God that made me, said he, I'll do you no Harm. Shut the Parlour Door, and come to me in my Library.

He then went into his Closet, which is his Library, and full of rich Pictures besides, a noble Apartment, tho' called a Closet, and next the private Garden, into which it has a Door that opens. I shut the Parlour Door, as he bid me; but stood at it irresolute. Place some Confidence in me surely, said he, you may, when I have spoken thus solemnly. So I crept towards him with trembling Feet, and my Heart throbbing thro' my Handkerchief. Come in, said he, when I bid you. I did so. Pray, Sir, said I, pity and spare me. I will, said he, as I hope to be sav'd. He sat down upon a rich Settee; and took hold of my Hand, and said, Don't doubt me, *Pamela*. From this Moment, I will no more consider you as my Servant; and I desire you'll not use me with Ingratitude for the Kindness I am going to express towards you. This a little embolden'd me; and he said, holding both my Hands in his, You have too much Wit and good Sense not to discover that I, in spite of my Heart, and all the Pride of it, cannot but love you. Yes, look up to me, my sweet-fac'd Girl! I must say I love you; and have put on a Behaviour to you, that was much against my Heart, in hopes to frighten you to my Purposes. You see I own it ingenuously; and don't play your Sex upon me for it.

I was unable to speak, and he saw me too much oppress'd with Confusion to go on in that Strain; and he said, Well, *Pamela*, let me know in what Situation of Life is your Father; I know he is a poor Man; but is he as low and as honest as he was when my Mother took you?

Then I could speak a little; and with a down Look, (and I felt my Face glow like Fire) I said, Yes, Sir, as poor and as honest too; and that is my Pride. Says he, I will do something for him, if it be not your Fault, and make all your Family happy. Ah! Sir, said I, he is happier already than ever he can be, if his Daughter's Innocence is to be the Price of your Favour. And I beg you will not speak to me on the only Side that can wound me. I have no Design of that sort, said he. O Sir, said I, tell me not so, tell me not so!—'Tis easy, said he, for me to be the Making of your Father, without injuring you. Well, Sir, said I, if this can be done, let me know how; and all I can do with Innocence shall be the Study and Practice of my Life.—But Oh! what can such a poor Creature as I do, and do my Duty?—Said he, I would have you stay a Week or Fortnight only, and behave yourself with Kindness to me: I stoop to beg it of you, and you shall see all shall turn out beyond your Expectation. I see, said he, you are going to answer otherwise than I would have you; and I begin to be vex'd I should thus meanly sue; and so I will say, that your Behaviour before honest *Longman*, when I used you as I did, and you could so well have vindicated yourself, has quite charm'd me. And tho' I am not pleased with all you said Yesterday while I was in the Closet, yet you have mov'd me more to admire you than before; and I am awaken'd to see more Worthiness in you than ever I saw in any Lady in the World. All the Servants, from the highest to the lowest, doat upon you, instead of envying you; and look upon you in so superior a Light, as speaks what you ought to be. I have seen more of your Letters than you imagine, (This surpriz'd me!) and am quite overcome with your charming manner of Writing, so free, so easy, and so much above your Sex; and all put together, makes me, as I tell you, love you to Extravagance. Now, *Pamela*, when I have stoop'd so low as to acknowledge all this, oblige me only to stay another Week or Fortnight, to give me Time to bring about some certain Affairs; and you shall see how much you shall find your Account in it.

I trembled to find my poor Heart giving way!—O good Sir, said I, pray your Honour, spare a poor Maiden, that cannot look up to you, and speak. My Heart is full! And why should you wish to undo me!—Only oblige me, said he, to stay a Fortnight longer, and *John* shall carry word to your Father, that I will see him in the Time, either here or at the *Swan* in his Village. O my Heart will burst, said I! but, on my bended Knees, I beg you, Sir, to let me go to-morrow, as I design'd! And don't offer to tempt a poor Creature, whose whole Will would be to do yours, if my Virtue and my Duty would permit.—They will, they shall permit it, said he; for I intend no Injury to you, God is my Witness!——Impossible, said I; I cannot, Sir, believe you after what has pass'd! How many Ways are there to undo poor Creatures! Good God, protect me this one time, and send me but to my dear Father's Cot in Safety!——Strange, damn'd Fate! says he, that when I speak so solemnly, I can't be believ'd!—What should I believe, Sir? said I; what can I believe? What have you said, but that I am to stay a Fortnight longer? and what then is to become of me!——My Pride of Birth and Fortune, (damn them both! said he, since they cannot obtain Credit with you, but must add to your Suspicions) will not let me stoop at once; and I ask you but for a Fortnight's Stay, that after this Declaration, I may pacify those proud Demands upon me.

O how my Heart throbbed! and I begun, for I did not know what I did, to say the Lord's Prayer. None of your Beads to me, *Pamela*, said he, thou art a perfect Nun, I think.

But I said aloud, with my Eyes lifted up to Heaven, *Lead me not into Temptation. But deliver me from Evil*, O my good God!——He hugg'd me in his Arms, and said, Well, my dear Girl, then you stay this Fortnight, and you shall see what I will do for you.—I'll leave you a Moment, and walk into the next Room, to give you Time to think of it, that you shall see I have no Design upon you. Well, this, I thought, did not look amiss.

He went out, and I was tortur'd with twenty different Thoughts in a Minute; sometimes I thought, that to stay a Week or Fortnight longer in this House to obey him, while Mrs. *Jervis* was with me, could do no great Harm: But then, thinks I, how do I know what I may be able to do? I have withstood his Anger; but may I not relent at his Kindness?—How shall I stand that!—Well, I hope, thought I, by the same protecting Grace in which I will always confide!—But then, what has he promised?—Why he will make my poor Father and Mother's Life comfortable. O, said I to myself, that is a rich Thought; but let me not dwell upon it, for fear I should indulge it to my Ruin.—What can he do for me, poor Girl as I am!—What can his Greatness stoop to! He talks, thought I, of his Pride of Heart, and Pride of Condition; O these are in his Head, and in his Heart too, or he would not confess them to me at such an Instant. Well then, thought I, this can be only to seduce me!—He has promis'd nothing.—But I am to *see* what he will do, if I stay a Fortnight; and this Fortnight, thought I again, is no such great Matter; and I shall see, in a few Days, how he carries it.—But then, when I again reflected upon the Distance between us, and his now open Declaration of Love, as he called it, and that after this he would talk with me on that Subject more plainly than ever, and I should be less arm'd, may be, to withstand him; and then I bethought myself, why, if he meant no Dishonour, he should not speak before Mrs. *Jervis*; and the odious frightful Closet came again into my Head, and my narrow Escape upon it; and how easy it might be for him to send Mrs. *Jervis* and the Maids out of the way; and so that all the Mischief he design'd me might be brought about in less than that Time; I resolved to go away, and trust all to Providence, and nothing to myself. And O how ought I to bless God for this Resolution! as you shall hear.

But just as I have writ to this Place, *John* sends me word, that he is going this Minute your way; and so I will send so far as I have written, and hope, by to-morrow Night, to ask your Blessings, at your own poor, but happy Abode, and tell you the rest by word of Mouth; and so I rest, till then, and for ever,

Your dutiful Daughter.

LETTER XXXI.

My dear Father and Mother,

I will continue my Writing still, because, may-be, I shall like to read it, when I am with you, to see what Dangers God has enabled me to escape; and tho' I bring it in my Pocket.

I told you my Resolution, my happy Resolution, which, to be sure God inspired me with. And just then he came in again, with great Kindness in his Looks, and said, I make no doubt, *Pamela*, you will stay this Fortnight to oblige me. I knew not how to frame my Words so as to deny, and yet not make him storm. But, said I, Forgive, Sir, your poor distressed Maiden. I know I cannot possibly deserve any Favour at your Hands, consistent with my Honesty; and I beg you will let me go to my poor Father. Why, said he, thou art the veriest Fool that I ever knew. I tell you I will see your Father; I'll send for him here to-morrow, in my Travelling Chariot, if you will; and I'll let him know what I intend to do for him and you. What, Sir, may I ask you, can that be? Your Honour's noble Estate may easily make him happy, and not unuseful perhaps to you in some respect or other. But what Price am I to pay for all this?—You shall be happy as you can wish, said he, I do assure you: And here I will now give you this Purse, in which are Fifty Guineas, which I will allow your Father yearly, and find an Employ suitable to his Liking, to deserve that and more: *Pamela*, he shall never want, depend upon it. I would have given you still more for him; but that perhaps you'd suspect I intended it as a Design upon you.—O Sir, said I, take back your Guineas, I will not touch one, nor will my Father, I am sure, till he knows what is to be done for them; and particularly what is to become of me. Why then, *Pamela*, said he, suppose I find a Man of Probity and genteel Calling for a Husband for you, that shall make you a Gentlewoman as long as you live?—I want no Husband, Sir, said I; for now I begun to see him in all his black Colours!—But being in his Power so, I thought I would a little dissemble. But, said he, you are so pretty, that go where you will, you will never be free from the Designs of some or other of our Sex; and I shall think I don't answer the Care of my dying Mother for you, who committed you to me, if I don't provide you a Husband, to protect your Virtue and your Innocence; and a worthy one I have thought of for you.

O black, perfidious Creature, thought I! what an Implement art thou in the Hands of *Lucifer*, to ruin the innocent Heart!—But still I dissembled;

for I fear'd much both him and the Place I was in. But who, pray Sir, have you thought of?—Why, said he, young Mr. *Williams*, my Chaplain in *Lincolnshire*, who will make you happy. Does he know, Sir, said I, any thing of your Honour's Intentions?—No, my Girl, said he, and kissed me (much against my Will; for his very Breath was now Poison to me!) but his Dependence on my Favour, and your Beauty and Merit, will make him rejoice at my Goodness to him.—Well, Sir, said I, then it is time enough to consider of this Matter; and this cannot hinder me from going to my Father's: For what will staying a Fortnight longer signify to this? Your Honour's Care and Goodness may extend to me *there* as well as *here*; and Mr. *Williams*, and all the World, shall know that I am not ashamed of my Father's Poverty.

He would kiss me again, and I said, If I am to think of Mr. *Williams*, or any body else, I beg *you'll* not be so free with me: That is not pretty I'm sure. Well, said he, but you stay this next Fortnight, and in that time I'll have both *Williams* and your Father here; for I will have the Match concluded in my House; and when I have brought it on, you shall settle it as you please together. Mean time take and send only these Fifty Pieces to your Father, as an Earnest of my Favour, and I'll make you all happy.—Sir, said I, I beg at least two Hours to consider of this. I shall, said he, be gone out in one Hour, and I would have you write to your Father, what I propose, and *John* shall carry it on purpose; and he shall carry the Purse with him for the good old Man, if you approve it. Sir, said I, I will let you know in one Hour then my Resolution. Do so, said he; and gave me another Kiss, and let me go.

O how I rejoiced I had got out of his Clutches!—So I write you this, that you may see how Matters stand; for I am resolv'd to come away, if possible. Base, wicked, treacherous Gentleman, as he is!

So here was a Trap laid for your poor *Pamela!* I tremble to think of it!—O what a Scene of Wickedness was here laid down for all my wretched Life. Black-hearted Wretch! How I hate him!—For at first, as you'll see by what I have written, he would have made me believe other things; and this of Mr. *Williams*, I believe, came into his Head after he walked out from his Closet, as I suppose, to give himself time to think, as well as me, how to delude me better: But the Covering was now too thin, and easy to be seen through.

I went to my Chamber, and the first thing I did, was to write to him; for I thought it was best not to see him again, if I could help it; and I put it under his Parlour-door, after I had copy'd it, as follows:

'*Honour'd Sir,*

'Your last Proposal to me, convinces me, that I ought not to stay; but to go to my Father, if it were but to ask his Advice about Mr. *Williams*. And I am so set upon it, that I am not to be persuaded. So, honour'd Sir, with a thousand Thanks for all Favours, I will set out to-morrow early; and the Honour you design'd me, as Mrs. *Jervis* tells me, of your Chariot, there will be no Occasion for; because I can hire, I believe, Farmer *Brady*'s Chaise. So begging you will not take it amiss, I shall ever be

'*Your dutiful Servant.*

'As to the Purse, Sir, my poor Father, to be sure, won't forgive me, if I take it, till he can know how to deserve it. Which is impossible.'

So he has since sent Mrs. *Jervis* to tell me, that since I am resolv'd to go, go I may, and the Travelling Chariot shall be ready; but it shall be worse for me; for that he will never trouble himself about me as long as he lives. Well, so I get out of the House, I care not; only I should have been glad I could, with Innocence, have made you, my poor Parents, happy.

I cannot imagine the Reason of it, but *John*, who I thought was gone with my last, is but now going; and he sends to know if I have any thing else to carry. So I break off to send you this with the former.

I am now preparing for my Journey; and about taking Leave of my good Fellow-servants. And if I have not time to write, I must tell you the rest, when I am so happy as to be with you.

One Word more, I slip in a Paper of Verses, on my going; sad poor Stuff! but as they come from me, you'll not dislike them, may-be. I shew'd them to Mrs. *Jervis*, and she liked them; and took a Copy; and made me sing them to her, and in the green Room too; but I looked into the Closet first. I will only add, that I am

Your dutiful Daughter.

Let me just say, that he has this Moment sent me five Guineas by Mrs. *Jervis*, as a Present for my Pocket; so I shall be very rich; for as *she* brought them, I thought I might take them. He says he won't see me: And I may go when I will in the Morning. And *Lincolnshire Robin* shall drive me; but he is so angry, he orders that nobody shall go out at the Door with me, not so much as into the Court-yard. Well! I can't help it, not I! but does not this expose him more than me?

But *John* waits, and I would have brought this and the other myself; but he says, he has put it up among other things, and so can take both as well as one.

John is very good, and very honest, God reward him! I'd give him a Guinea, now I'm so rich, if I thought he'd take it. I hear nothing of my Lady's Cloaths, and those my Master gave me: For I told Mrs. *Jervis*, I would not take them; but I fansy, by a Word or two that was dropt, they will be sent after me. Dear Sirs! what a rich *Pamela* you'll have, if they should! But as I can't wear them, if they do, I don't desire them; and will turn them into Money, as I can have Opportunity. Well, no more—I'm in a fearful Hurry!

VERSES on my going away.

I.

My Fellow-servants, dear, attend
To these few Lines, which I have penn'd:
I'm sure they're from your honest Friend,
And Wisher-well, poor Pamela.

II.

I from a State of low Degree
Was taken by our good Lady.
Some say it better had been for me,
I'd still been rustick Pamela.

III.

But yet, my Friends, I hope not so:
For, tho' I to my Station low
Again return, I joyful go,
And think no Shame to Pamela.

IV.

For what makes out true Happiness,
But Innocence, and inward Peace?
And that, thank God, I do possess:
O happy, happy Pamela!

V.

My future Lot I cannot know:
But this, I'm sure, where-e'er I go,
What-e'er I am, what-e'er I do,
I'll be the grateful Pamela!

VI.

No sad Regrets my Heart annoy.
I'll pray for all your Peace and Joy

From Master high, to Scullion Boy,
For all your Loves to Pamela.

VII.

One thing or two I've more to say;
God's holy Will, be sure obey;
And for our Master always pray;
As ever shall poor Pamela.

VIII.

For, Oh! we pity should the Great,
Instead of envying their Estate;
Temptations always on 'em wait,
   Exempt from which are such as we.

IX.

Their Riches often are a Snare;
At best, a pamper'd weighty Care:
Their Servants far more happy are:
   At least, so thinketh Pamela.

X.

Your Parents and Relations love:
Let them your Duty ever prove;
And you'll be blessed from above,
   As will, I hope, poor Pamela.

XI.

For if ashamed I could be
Of my poor Parents low Degree,
I'm sure it would been worse for me,
   God had not blessed Pamela.

XII.

Thrice happy may you ever be,
Each one in his and her Degree;
And, Sirs, whene'er you think of me,
   Pray for Content to Pamela.

XIII.

Yes, pray for my Content and Peace;
For, rest assur'd, I'll never cease
To pray for all your Joys Increase,
   While Life is lent to Pamela.

XIV.
On God all future Good depends:
Him let us serve. My Sonnet ends;
With Thank-ye, Thank-ye, honest Friends,
For all your Loves to Pamela.

Here it is necessary to observe, that the fair *Pamela*'s Tryals were not yet over; but the worst of all were to come, at a Time when she thought them all at an End, and that she was returning to her Father: For when her Master found her Virtue was not to be subdu'd, and that he had in vain try'd to conquer his Passion for her, being a Gentleman of Pleasure and Intrigue, he had order'd his *Lincolnshire* Coachman to bring his Travelling Chariot from thence, not caring to trust his Body Coachman,[1] who, with the rest of the Servants, so greatly loved and honour'd the fair Damsel; and having given him Instructions accordingly, and prohibited his other Servants, on Pretence of resenting *Pamela*'s Behaviour, from accompanying her any Part of the Way, he drove her five Miles on the Way to her Father's; and then turning off, cross'd the Country, and carried her onward towards his *Lincolnshire* Estate.

It is also to be observ'd, that the Messenger of her Letters to her Father, who so often pretended Business that way, was an Implement in his Master's Hands, and employ'd by him for that Purpose; and who always gave her Letters first to him, and his Master used to open and read them, and then send them on; by which means, as he hints to her (as she observes in one of her Letters, *p.* 78) he was no Stranger to what she wrote. Thus every way was the poor Virgin beset: And the Whole will shew the base Arts of designing Men to gain their wicked Ends; and how much it behoves the Fair Sex to stand upon their Guard against their artful Contrivances, especially when Riches and Power conspire against Innocence and a low Estate.

A few Words more will be necessary to make the Sequel better understood. The intriguing Gentleman thought fit, however, to keep back from her Father her three last Letters; in which she mentions his concealing himself to hear her partitioning out her Cloaths, his last Effort to induce her to stay a Fortnight, his pretended Proposal of the Chaplain, and her Hopes of speedily seeing them, as also her Verses; and to send himself a Letter to her Father, which is as follows.

'*Goodman* ANDREWS,

'You will wonder to receive a Letter from me. But I think I am obliged to let you know, that I have discover'd the strange Correspondence carry'd on between you and your Daughter, so injurious to my Honour and Reputation, and which I think you should not have encourag'd till you knew the Truth of it. Something, possibly, there might be in what she has wrote from time to time; but, believe me, with all her pretended Simplicity and Innocence, I never knew so much romantick Invention as she is Mistress of. In short, the Girl's Head's turn'd by Romances, and such idle Stuff, which she has given herself up to, ever since her kind Lady's Death. And she assumes such Airs, as if she was a Mirror of Perfection, and believ'd every body had a Design upon her. Nay, she has not, I understand, spared me, who used to joke and divert myself with her Innocence, as I thought it.

'Don't mistake me however; I believe her very honest, and very virtuous; but I have found out also, that she is carrying on a sort of Correspondence, or Love Affair, with a young Clergyman, that I hope in time to provide for; but who, at present, is destitute of any Subsistence but my Favour: And what would be the Consequence, can you think of two young Folks, who have nothing in the World to trust to of their own, to come together, with a Family multiplying upon them, before they have Bread to eat?

'For my Part, I have too much Kindness to them both, not to endeavour to prevent it, if I can: And for this Reason I have sent her out of his Way for a little while, till I can bring them to better Consideration; and I would not therefore have you surpriz'd you don't see your Daughter so soon as you might possibly expect.

'Yet, I do assure you, upon my Honour, that she shall be safe and inviolate; and I hope you don't doubt me, notwithstanding any Airs she may have given herself, upon my jocular Pleasantry to her, and perhaps a little innocent Romping with her, so usual with young Folks of the two Sexes, when they have been long acquainted, and grown up together; for Pride is not my Talent.

'As she is a mighty Letter-writer, I hope she has had the Duty to apprise you of her Intrigue with the young Clergyman; and I know not whether it meets with your Countenance: But now she is absent for a little while, (for I know he would have follow'd her to your Village, if she had gone home; and there perhaps they would have ruin'd one another, by marrying) I doubt not I shall bring him to see his Interest, and that he engages not before he knows how to provide for a Wife: And when that can be done, let them come together in God's Name, for me.

'I expect not to be answer'd on this Head, but by your good Opinion, and the Confidence you may repose in my Honour; being

'Your hearty Friend to serve you.

'*P.S.* I find my Man *John* has been the Manager of the Correspondence, in which such Liberties have been taken with me. I shall soon let the sawcy Fellow know how much I resent his Part of the Affair, in a manner that becomes me. It is a hard thing, that a Man of my Character in the World, should be used thus freely by his own Servants.'

It is easy to guess at the poor old Man's Concern upon reading this Letter, from a Gentleman of so much Consideration. He knew not what Course to take, and had no manner of Doubt of his poor Daughter's Innocence, and that foul Play was design'd her. Yet he sometimes hoped the best, and was ready to believe the surmised Correspondence between the Clergyman and her, having not receiv'd the Letters she wrote, which would have clear'd up that Affair.

But after all, he resolved, as well to quiet his own as his Wife's Uneasiness, to undertake a Journey to the 'Squire's; and leaving his poor Wife to excuse him to the Farmer who imploy'd him, he sat out[1] that very Night, late as it was; and travelling all Night, he found himself soon after Day-light, at the Gate of the Gentleman, before the Family was up: And there he sat down to rest himself, till he should see somebody stirring.

The Grooms were the first he saw, coming out to water their Horses; and he ask'd, in so distressful a manner, what was become of *Pamela*, that they thought him crasy; and said, Why, what have you to do with *Pamela*, old Fellow? Get out of the Horse's Way.—Where is your Master? said the poor Man; pray, Gentlemen, don't be angry: My Heart's almost broke.— He never gives any thing at the Door, I assure you, says one of the Grooms; so you'll lose your Labour.—I am not a Beggar yet, said the poor old Man; I want nothing of him, but my *Pamela!*—O my Child! my Child!

I'll be hang'd, says one of them, if this is not Mrs. *Pamela*'s Father!— Indeed, indeed, said he, wringing his Hands, I am; and weeping, Where is my Child? Where is my *Pamela?*—Why, Father, said one of them, we beg your Pardon; but she is gone home to you! How long have you been come from home?—O but last Night, said he; I have travelled all Night! Is the 'Squire at home, or is he not?—Yes, but he is not stirring tho', said the Grooms, as yet. Thank God for that, said he! thank God for that! then I hope I may be permitted to speak to him anon. They asked him to go in, and he stept into the Stable, and sat down on the Stairs there, wiping his Eyes, and sighing so sadly, that it grieved the Servants to hear him.

The Family was soon raised, with the Report of *Pamela*'s Father coming to inquire after his Daughter; and the Maids would fain have had him go into the Kitchen. But Mrs. *Jervis* having been told of his coming, got up, and hasten'd down to her Parlour, and took him in with her, and there heard all his sad Story, and read the Letter. She wept bitterly; but yet endeavoured to hide her Concern; and said, Well, Goodman *Andrews*, I cannot help weeping at your Grief; but I hope there is no Occasion; let nobody see this Letter, whatever you do. I dare say your Daughter's safe.

Well, but said he, I see you, Madam, know nothing about her!—If all was right, so good a Gentlewoman as you are, would not have been a Stranger to this. To be sure you thought she was with me!

Said she, My Master does not always inform his Servants of his Proceedings; but you need not doubt his Honour. You have his Hand for it. And you may see he can have no Design upon her, because he is not from hence, and does not talk of going hence. O that is all I have to hope for, said he! that is all, indeed!—But, said he, and was going on, when the Report of his coming had reach'd the 'Squire, who came down in his Morning-gown and Slippers, into the Parlour, where he and Mrs. *Jervis* was.

What's the Matter, Goodman *Andrews?* said he; what's the Matter? O my Child, said the good old Man, give me my Child, I beseech you, Sir.—Why, I thought, says the 'Squire, that I had satisfy'd you about her; sure you have not a Letter I sent you, written with my own Hand. Yes, yes, but I have, Sir, said he, and that brought me hither; and I have walked all Night. Poor Man! return'd he, with great seeming Compassion, I am sorry for it truly! Why your Daughter has made a strange Racket in my Family; and if I thought it would have disturb'd you so much, I would have e'en let her gone home; but what I did was to serve her and you too. She is very safe, I do assure you, Goodman *Andrews*; and you may take my Honour for it, I would not injure her for the World. Do you think I would, Mrs. *Jervis?* No, I hope not, Sir, said she!—*Hope not!* said the poor Man, so do I; but pray, Sir, give me my Child; that is all I desire; and I'll take care no Clergyman shall come near her.

Why, *London* is a great way off, said the 'Squire, and I can't send for her back presently. What then, said he, have you sent my poor *Pamela* to *London?* I would not have it said so, says the 'Squire; but I assure you, upon my Honour, she is quite safe and satisfied, and will quickly inform you of as much by Letter. I am sure she is in a reputable Family, no less than a Bishop's, and will wait on his Lady till I get this Matter over, that I mentioned to you!

O how shall I know this! reply'd he.—What, said the 'Squire, pretending Anger, am I to be doubted?—Do you believe I can have any View upon your Daughter! And if I had, do you think I would take such Methods as these to effect it? Why, Man, you know not who you talk to!—O Sir, said he, I beg your Pardon; but consider my dear Child is in the Case: Let me know what Bishop, and where, and I will travel to *London* barefoot, to see my Daughter, and then shall be satisfied.

Why, Goodman *Andrews*, I think thou hast read Romances as well as thy Daughter, and thy Head's turn'd with them. May I not have my Word taken? Do you think, once more, I would offer any thing to your Daughter! Is there any thing looks like it?—Pr'ythee, Man, consider a little who I am; and if I am not to be believ'd, what signifies talking? Why, Sir, said he, pray forgive me; but there is no Harm to say, What Bishop's, or whereabouts? What, and so you'd go troubling his Lordship with your impertinent Fears and Stories! Will you be satisfied if you have a Letter from her within a Week, it may be less, if she be not negligent, to assure you all is well with her? Why that, said the poor Man, will be a Comfort. Well then, said the 'Squire, I can't answer for her Negligence, if she don't; but she will send a Letter to you, Mrs. *Jervis*, for I desire not to see it; I have had Trouble enough about her already; and be sure you send it by a Man and Horse the Moment you receive it. To be sure I will, said she. Thank your Honour, said the good Man. And then I must wait with as much Patience as I can for a Week, which will be a Year to me.

I tell you, said the 'Squire, it must be her own Fault if she don't; for 'tis what I insisted upon for my own Reputation; and I shan't stir from this House, I assure you, till she is heard from, and that to Satisfaction. God bless your Honour, said the poor Man, as you say and mean Truth. *Amen*, *Amen*, Goodman *Andrews*, said he; you see I am not afraid to say *Amen*. So, Mrs. *Jervis*, make the good Man as welcome as you can; and let me have no Uproar about the Matter.

He then, whispering her, bid her give him a couple of Guineas to bear his Charges home; telling him, he should be welcome to stay there till the Letter came, if he would; and he should be a Witness, that he intended honourably, and not to stir from his House for one while.

The poor old Man staid and din'd with Mrs. *Jervis*, with some tolerable Ease, in hopes to hear from his beloved Daughter in a few Days, and then accepting the Present, return'd for his own House; and resolv'd to be as patient as possible for a few Days.

Mean time Mrs. *Jervis*, and all the Family, were in the utmost Grief for the Trick put upon the poor *Pamela*, and she and the Steward represented it to the 'Squire in as moving Terms as they durst: But were forced to rest satisfy'd with his general Assurances of intending her no Harm; which however Mrs. *Jervis* little believ'd from the Pretence he had made in his Letter, of the Correspondence between *Pamela* and the young Parson; which she knew to be all Invention; tho' she durst not say any thing of it.

But the Week after she went away, they were made a little more easy, by the following Letter, brought by an unknown Hand, and left for Mrs. *Jervis*; which how procur'd, will be shewn in the Sequel.

'*Dear Mrs.* Jervis,

'I have *been vilely trick'd, and,* instead of being driven by *Robin* to my dear Father's, *I am* carry'd off, to where I have no Liberty to tell. However, I am at present not used hardly *in the main*; and I write to beg of you to let my dear Father and Mother (whose Hearts must be well-nigh broken) know, That I am well, and that I am, and, by the Grace of God, ever will be, their dutiful and honest Daughter, as well as

'*Your obliged Friend,*
'PAMELA ANDREWS.

'I must neither send Date nor Place. But have most solemn Assurances of honourable Usage. *This is the only Time my low Estate has been troublesome to me, since it has subjected me to the Frights I have undergone. Love to your good self, and all my dear Fellow-servants. Adieu! Adieu! But pray for poor* PAMELA.'

This, tho' it quieted not intirely their Apprehensions, was shewn to the whole Family, and to the 'Squire himself, who pretended to know not how it came; and Mrs. *Jervis* sent it away to the good old Folks; who at first suspected it was forged, and not their Daughter's Hand; but finding the contrary, they were a little easier to hear she was alive and well. And having inquir'd of all their Acquaintance, what could be done, and no one being able to put them in a way how to proceed, with Effect, on so extraordinary an Occasion, against so rich and daring a Gentleman; and being afraid to make Matters worse, (tho' they saw plainly enough, that by this Letter she was in no Bishop's Family, and so mistrusted all the rest of his Story) they apply'd themselves to Prayers for their poor Daughter, and for a happy Issue to an Affair that almost distracted them.

We shall now leave the honest old Pair, praying for their dear *Pamela*; and return to the Account she herself gives of all this; having written it Journal-wise, to amuse and employ her Time, in hopes some Opportunity might offer to send it to her Friends, and, as was her constant View, that she might afterwards thankfully look back upon the Dangers she had escaped, when they should be happily over-blown, as in time she hoped they would be; and that then she might examine, and either approve of, or repent for, her own Conduct in them.

LETTER XXXII.

O my dearest Father and Mother,

Let me write and bewail my miserable hard Fate, tho' I have no Hope that what I write will be convey'd to your Hands!—I have now nothing to do but write, and weep, and fear, and pray; and yet, What can I pray for, when God Almighty, for my Sins, to be sure, vouchsafes not to hear my Prayers; but suffers me to be a Prey to a wicked Violator of all the Laws of God and Man!—But, gracious Heaven, forgive me my Rashness! O let me not sin against thee; for thou best knowest what is fittest for thy poor Handmaid!—And as thou sufferest not thy poor Creatures to be tempted above what they can bear; I will resign, thro' thy Grace assisting me, to thy good Pleasure. But since these Temptations are not of my own seeking, the Effects of my Presumption and Vanity, O enable me to withstand them all, and deliver me from the Dangers that hang over my poor Head, and make me perfect thro' Sufferings, and, in thy own good Time, deliver me from them!

Thus do I pray, imperfectly as I am forced by my distracting Fears and Apprehensions; and O join with me, my dear Parents!—But, alas! how can you know, how can I reveal to you, the dreadful Situation of your poor Daughter! The unhappy *Pamela* may be undone, (which God forbid, and sooner deprive me of Life!) before you can know my hard Lot!

O the unparallel'd Wickedness, and Stratagems, and Devices of those who call themselves Gentlemen, and pervert the Design of Providence, in giving them ample Means to do good, to their own Perdition, and to the Ruin of poor oppressed Innocence!

But let me tell you what has befallen me; and yet, How shall you receive it? For I have now no honest *John* to carry my Letters to you; but am likely to be watch'd in all my Steps, till my hard Fate ripens his wicked Projects for my Ruin. I will every Day now write my sad State; and some way, perhaps, may be open'd to send the melancholy Scribble to you. But if you know it, what will it do but aggravate your Troubles: For, Oh! what can the abject Poor do against the mighty Rich, when they are determin'd to oppress?

Well, but I will proceed to write what I had hoped to tell you in a few Hours, that I believed I should be blessed by you on my Return to you, from so many Hardships.

I will begin here with my Account from the last Letter I wrote you, in which I inclosed my poor Stuff of Verses, and continue it at times, as I have Opportunity; tho' as I said, I know not how it can reach you now.

The long hop'd-for *Thursday* Morning came, that I was to set out. I had taken my Leave of my Fellow-servants over-night; and a mournful Leave it was to us all: For Men, as well as Women-servants, wept much to part with me; and, for my Part, I was overwhelm'd with Tears, and the Instances of their Esteem. They all would have made me little Presents, as Tokens of their Love; but I would not take any thing from the lower Servants, to be sure. But Mr. *Longman* made me a Present of several Yards of *Holland*, and a silver Snuff-box, and a gold Ring, which he desir'd me to keep for his sake; and he wept over me; but said, I am sure, so good a Maiden God will bless; and tho' you return to your poor Father again, and his low Estate; yet Providence will find you out, and one Day, tho' I mayn't live to see it, you will be rewarded.

I said, O dear Mr. *Longman*, you make me too rich, and too mody;[1] and yet I must be a Beggar before my Time: For I shall want often to be scribbling, (little thinking it would be my only Employment so soon) and I will beg you, Sir, to favour me with some Paper; and as soon as I get home, I will write you a Letter, to thank you for all your Kindness to me; and a Letter to good Mrs. *Jervis* too.

This was lucky; for I should have had none else, but at pleasure of my rough-natur'd Governess, as I may call her; but now I can write to ease my Mind, tho' I can't send it to you; and write what I please, for she knows not how well I am provided. For good Mr. *Longman* gave me above forty Sheets of Paper, and a dozen Pens, and a little Phial of Ink; which last I wrapt in Paper, and put in my Pocket; and some Wax and Wafers.

O dear Sir, said I, you have set me up. How shall I requite you? He said, By a Kiss, my fair Mistress; and I gave it very willingly; for he is a good old Man.

Rachel and *Hannah* cry'd sadly when I took my Leave, and *Jane*, who sometimes used to be a little crossish, and *Cicely* too, wept sadly, and said they would pray for me; but poor *Jane*, I doubt, seldom says her Prayers for herself: More's the pity!

Then *Arthur* the Gardener, our *Robin* the Coachman, and *Lincolnshire Robin* too, who was to carry me, were very civil; and both had Tears in their Eyes; which I thought then very good-natur'd in *Lincolnshire Robin*, because he knew but little of me.—But since, I find he might well be concern'd, for he had then his Instructions, it seems, and knew how he was to be a Means to intrap me.

Then our other three Footmen, *Harry, Isaac,* and *Benjamin,* and Grooms, and Helpers too, were very much affected likewise; and the poor little Scullion-boy, *Tommy,* was ready to run over for Grief.

They had got all together over-night, expecting to be differently imploy'd in the Morning; and they all begg'd to shake Hands with me, and I kiss'd the Maidens; and pray'd to God to bless them all; and thanked them for all their Love and Kindnesses to me: And indeed I was forced to leave them sooner than I would, because I could not stand it: indeed I could not! *Harry* (I could not have thought it, for he is a little wildish, they say) cry'd till he sobb'd again. *John,* poor honest *John,* was not then come back from you. But as for the Butler, Mr. *Jonathan,* he could not stay in Company.

I thought to have told you a deal about this; but I have worse things to employ my Thoughts.

Mrs. *Jervis,* good Mrs. *Jervis,* cry'd all Night long; and I comforted her all I could: and she made me promise, that if my Master went to *London* to attend Parliament, or to *Lincolnshire,* I would come and stay a Week with her. And she would have given me Money; but I would not take it.

Well, next Morning came, and I wonder'd I saw nothing of poor honest *John;* for I waited to take Leave of him, and thank him for all his Civilities to me and to you: But I suppose he was sent further by my Master, and so could not return; and I desired to be remember'd to him.

And when Mrs. *Jervis* told me, with a sad Heart, the Chariot was ready, with four Horses to it, I was just upon sinking into the Ground, tho' I wanted to be with you.

My Master was above Stairs, and never asked to see me. I was glad of it in the main; but he knew, false Heart as he is! that I was not to be out of his Reach!—O preserve me, Heaven, from his Power, and from his Wickedness!

Well, they were not suffer'd to go with me one Step, as I writ you before; for he stood at the Window to see me go. And in the Passage to the Gate, out of his Sight, there they stood all of them, in two Rows; and we could say nothing on both sides, but God bless you! and God bless you! But *Harry* carried my own Bundle, my third Bundle, as I was used to call it, to the Coach, and some Plum-cakes, and Diet-bread,[1] made for me over-night, and some Sweet-meats, and six Bottles of Canary Wine, which Mrs. *Jervis* would make me take in a Basket, to chear our Hearts now-and-then when we got together, as she said. And I kiss'd all the Maids again, and shook Hands with the Men again; but Mr. *Jonathan* and Mr. *Longman* were not there; and tript down Steps to the Chariot, Mrs. *Jervis* crying most sadly.

I look'd up when I got to the Chariot, and I saw my Master at the Window, in his Gown; and I curchee'd three times to him very low, and pray'd for him with my Hands lifted up, for I could not speak; and he bow'd his Head to me, which made me then very glad he would take such Notice of me; and in I stept, and was ready to burst with Grief; and could only, till *Robin* begun to drive, wave my white Handkerchief to them, wet with my Tears: And at last away he drove, Jehu-like[1] as they say, out of the Court-yard; and I too soon found I had Cause for greater and deeper Grief.

Well, says I to myself, at this rate I shall soon be with my dear Father and Mother; and till I had got, as I supposed, half way, I thought of the good Friends I had left. And when, on stopping for a little Bait[2] to the Horses, *Robin* told me, I was near half-way, I thought it was high time to wipe my Eyes, and think to whom I was going; as then, alack for me! I thought. So I began to ponder what a Meeting I should have with you; how glad you'd both be to see me come safe and innocent to you, after all my Dangers; and so I began to comfort myself, and to banish the other gloomy Side from my Mind; tho' too it return'd now-and-then; for I should be ingrateful not to love them for their Love.

Well, I believe, I sat out about Eight o'Clock in the Morning; and I wonder'd, and wonder'd, when it was about Two, as I saw by a Church-dyal in a little Place we pass'd thro', that I was still more and more out of my Knowledge. Hey-day! thinks I, to drive this strange Pace, and to be so long a-going little more than twenty Miles, is very odd! But, to be sure, thought I, *Robin* knows the Way.

At last he stopt, and look'd about him, as if he was at a Loss for the Way; and I said, Mr. *Robert*, sure you are out of the Way!—I'm afraid I am, said he. But it can't be much; I'll ask the first Person I see. Pray do, said I; and he gave his Horses a Mouthful of Hay; and I gave him some Cake, and two Glasses of Canary Wine; and stopt about half an Hour in all. Then he drove on very fast again.

I had so much to think of, of the Dangers I now doubted not I had escaped, of the loving Friends I had left, and my best Friends I was going to, and the many things I had to relate to you, that I the less thought of the Way, till I was startled out of my Meditations by the Sun beginning to set, and still the Man driving on, and his Horses sweating and foaming; and then I begun to be alarm'd all at once, and called to him; and he said, he had horrid ill Luck; for he had come several Miles out of the Way, but was now right, and should get in still before it was quite dark. My Heart began then to misgive me a little; and I was very much fatigued; for I had no Sleep for several Nights before to signify; and at last, I said, Pray, Mr. *Robert*, there is a Town before us, What do you call it?—If we are so much out of the Way, we had better put up there; for the Night comes on apace; and, Lord protect me! thought I, I shall have new Dangers, may-hap, to encounter with the Man, who have escaped the Master?—Little thinking of the base Contrivance of the latter. Says he, I am just there; 'tis but a Mile on one side of the Town before us.—Nay, said I, I may be mistaken, for it is a good while since I was this way; but I am sure the Face of the Country here is nothing like what I remember it.

He pretended to be much out of Humour with himself for mistaking the Way, and at last stopt at a Farm-house, about two Miles beyond the Village I had seen, and it was then almost dark, and he alighted, and said, We must make shift here; for I am quite out.

Lord, thought I, be good to the poor *Pamela!* More Tryals still!—What will befal me next?

The Farmer's Wife, and Maid, and Daughter, came out, and said, What brings you this way at this time of Night, Mr. *Robert?* And with a Lady too?—Then I began to be frighten'd out of my Wits; and laying Middle and both Ends together,[1] I fell a-crying, and said, God give me Patience! I am undone for certain!—Pray, Mistress, said I, do you know Esquire *B.* of *Bedfordshire?*

The wicked Coachman would have prevented the answering me; but the simple Daughter said, Know his Worship! yes, surely! why he is my Father's Landlord!—Well, said I, then I am undone, undone for ever!—O wicked Wretch! what have I done to you, said I to the Coachman, to serve me thus?—Vile Tool of a wicked Master! Faith, said the Fellow, I'm sorry this Task was put upon me: But I could not help it. But make the best of it now; Here are very civil, reputable Folks; and you'll be safe here, I'll assure you.—Let me get out, said I, and I'll walk back to the Town we came thro', late as it is!—For I will not enter here.

Said the Farmer's Wife, You'll be very well used here, I'll assure you, young Gentlewoman, and have better Conveniencies than any where in the Village. I matter not Conveniencies, said I, I am betray'd and undone! As you have a Daughter of your own, pity me, and let me know, if your Landlord, as you call him, be here!—No, I'll assure you, he is not, said she.

And then came the Farmer, a good-like sort of Man, grave, and well-behav'd; and he spoke to me in such sort, as made me a little more pacify'd; and seeing no Help for it, I went in; and the Wife immediately carry'd me up Stairs to the best Apartment, and told me that was mine as long as I staid; and nobody should come near me but when I called! I threw myself on the Bed in the Room, tir'd, and frighten'd to Death almost, and gave way to the most excessive Fit of Grief that I ever had!

The Daughter came up, and said, Mr. *Robert* had given her a Letter to give me; and there it was. I raised myself, and saw it was the Hand and Seal of the wicked Wretch my Master, directed To Mrs. *Pamela Andrews.*— This was a little better than to have him here; tho' if he had, he must have been brought thro' the Air; for I thought I was.

The good Woman (for I begun to see things about a little reputable, and no Guile appearing in them, but rather a Face of Grief for my Grief) offered me a Glass of some cordial Water,[1] which I accepted, for I was ready to sink; and then I sat up in a Chair a little, tho' very faintish: And they brought me two Candles, and lighted a Brush-wood Fire; and said, if I call'd, I should be waited upon instantly, and so left me to ruminate on my sad Condition, and to read my Letter, which I was not able to do presently. After I had a little come to myself, I found it to contain these Words:

'*Dear* PAMELA,

'The Passion I have for you, and your Obstinacy, have constrained me to act by you in a manner that I know will occasion you great Trouble and Fatigue, both of Mind and Body. Yet, forgive me, my dear Girl; for tho' I have taken this Step, I will, by all that's good and holy, use you honourably. Suffer not your Fears to transport you to a Behaviour that will be disreputable to us both. For the Place where you'll receive this, is a Farm that belongs to me; and the People civil, honest and obliging.

'You will be by this time far on your way to the Place I have allotted for your Abode for a few Weeks, 'till I have manag'd some Affairs, that will make me shew myself to you in a much different Light than you may possibly apprehend from this rash Action. And to convince you that I mean you no Harm, I do assure you, that the House you are going to, shall be so much at your Command, that even I myself will not approach it without Leave from you. So make yourself easy; be discreet and prudent; and a happier Turn shall reward these your Troubles, than you may at present apprehend.

'Mean time I pity the Fatigue you will have, if this comes to your hand in the Place I have directed. And will write to your Father, to satisfy him, that nothing but what is honourable shall be offer'd to you, by

'*Your passionate Admirer, (so I must style myself)* ———

'Don't think hardly of poor *Robin*: You have so possess'd all my Servants in your Favour, that I find they had rather serve you than me; and 'tis reluctantly the Fellow undertook this Task; and I was forced to submit to assure him of my honourable Intentions to you, which I am fully resolved to make good, if you compel me not to a Conduct abhorrent to me at present.'

I but too well apprehended, that this Letter was only to pacify me for the present; but as my Danger was not so immediate as I had reason to dread, and he had promised to forbear coming to me, and to write to you, my dear Parents, to quiet your Concern, I was a little more easy than I was before: And I made shift to eat a little Bit of boil'd Chicken they had got for me, and drank a Glass of my Sack, and made them do so too.

But after I had so done, I was again a little fluster'd; for in came the Coachman with the Look of a Hangman, I thought, and Madam'd me up strangely; telling me, he would beg me to get ready to pursue my Journey by Five in the Morning, or else he should be late in. I was quite griev'd at this; for I began not to dislike my Company, considering how Things stood, and was in hopes to get a Party among them, and so to put myself into any worthy Protection in the Neighbourhood, rather than go forward.

When he withdrew, I began to tamper with the Farmer and his Wife. But, alas! they had had a Letter deliver'd them at the same time I had; so securely had *Lucifer* put it into his Head to do his Work; and they only shook their Heads, and seem'd to pity me; and so I was forced to give over that Hope.

However, the good Farmer shew'd me his Letter; which I copy'd as follows: For it shews the deep Arts of this wicked Master; and how resolv'd he seem'd on my Ruin, by the Pains he took to deprive me of all Hopes of freeing myself from his Power.

'Farmer N O R T O N,

'I send to your House, *for one Night only*, a young Gentlewoman, much against her Will, who has deeply imbark'd in a Love Affair, which will be her Ruin, as well as the Person's to whom she wants to betroth herself. I have, *to oblige her Father*, order'd her to be carry'd to one of my Houses, where she will be well us'd, to try if by Absence, and Expostulation with both, they can be brought to know their own Interest. And I am sure you will use her kindly for my sake. For excepting this Matter, *which she will not own*, she does not want Prudence and Discretion. I will acknowledge any Trouble you shall be at in this Matter, the first Opportunity, and am

'*Your Friend and Servant.*'

He had said, too cunningly for me, that I would not own this pretended Love Affair; so that he had provided them not to believe me, say what I would; and as they were his Tenants, who all love him, (for he has some good Qualities, and so he had need!) I saw all my Plot cut out; and so was forc'd to say the less.

I wept bitterly, however; for I saw he was too hard for me, as well in his Contrivances as Riches; and so had Recourse again to my only Refuge, that God who takes the innocent Heart into his Almighty Protection, and is alone able to baffle and confound the Devices of the Mighty. Nay, the Farmer was so prepossess'd with the Contents of his Letter to him, that he began to praise his Care and Concern for me, and to advise me against entertaining Addresses without my Friends Advice and Consent, and made me the Subject of a Lesson for his Daughter's Improvement. So I was glad to shut up this Discourse; for I saw I was not likely to be believ'd.

I sent, however, to tell my Driver, that I was so fatigued, I could not set out so soon the next Morning. But he insisted upon it, and said it would make my Day's Journey the lighter; and I found he was a more faithful Servant to his Master, notwithstanding what he wrote of his Reluctance, than I could have wish'd: So I saw still more and more, that all was deep Dissimulation, and Contrivance worse and worse.

Indeed I might have shewn them his Letter to me as a full Confutation of his to them; but I saw no Probability of engaging them in my Behalf; and so thought it signify'd little, as I was to go away so soon, to enter more particularly into the Matter with them; and besides, I saw they were not inclinable to let me stay longer for fear of disobliging him; so I went to Bed, but had very little Rest; and they would make their Servant-maid bear me Company in the Chariot five Miles, early in the Morning, and she was to walk back.

I had contriv'd in my Thoughts, when I was on my Way in the Chariot, on *Friday* Morning, that when we came into some Town, to bait,[1] as he must do for the Horses sake, that I would at the Inn apply myself, if I saw I any way could, to the Mistress of the Inn, and tell her the Case, and refuse to go further, having nobody but this wicked Coachman to contend with.

Well, I was very full of this Project, and was in great Hopes, some how or other, to extricate myself this way. But Oh! the artful Wretch had provided for even this last Resource of mine; for when we came to put up at a large Town on the Way, to eat a Morsel for Dinner, and I was fully resolv'd to execute my Project, who should be at the Inn that he put up at, but the wicked Mrs. *Jewkes* expecting me, and her Sister-in-law was the Mistress of it; and she had provided a little Entertainment for me.

And this I found, when I desir'd, as soon as I came in, to speak with the Mistress of the House. She came to me, and I said, I am a poor unhappy young Body that wants your Advice and Assistance, and you seem to be a good sort of Gentlewoman, that would assist an oppressed innocent Person. Yes, Madam, said she, I hope you guess right, and I have the Happiness to know something of the Matter before you speak. Pray call my Sister *Jewkes.*—*Jewkes! Jewkes!* thought I, I have heard of that Name; I don't like it.

Then the wicked Creature appear'd, whom I had never seen but once before, and I was terrify'd out of my Wits. No Stratagem, thought I, not one! for a poor innocent Girl; but every thing to turn out against me; that is hard indeed!

So I began to pull in my Horns, as they say; for I saw I was now worse off than at the Farmer's.

The naughty Woman came up to me with an Air of Confidence, and kiss'd me, See, Sister, said she, here's a charming Creature! would not she tempt the best Lord in the Land to run away with her! O frightful, thought I! here's an Avowal of the Matter at once! (for she would not part with me out of her Sight) I am now gone, that's certain! And so was quite silent and confounded; and seeing no Help for it, I was forc'd to set out with her in the Chariot; for she came thither on Horseback with a Man-servant, who rode by us the rest of the Way, with her Horse; and now I gave over all Thoughts of Redemption, and was in a desponding Condition indeed.

Well, thought I, here are strange Pains taken to ruin a poor innocent, helpless, and even worthless young Body. This Plot is laid too deep, and has been too long a hatching to be baffled, I fear. But then I put my Trust in God, who I knew was able to do every thing for me, when all other possible Means should fail: And in Him I was resolv'd to confide.

You may see!—Yet, oh! that kills me, for I know not whether ever you may see what I now write, or no!—Else you may see, what sort of Woman this Mrs. *Jewkes* is, compar'd to good Mrs. *Jervis*, by this—

Every now-and-then she would be staring in my Face, in the Chariot, and squeezing my Hand, and saying, Why, you are very pretty, my silent

Dear! and once she offer'd to kiss me. But I said, I don't like this Sort of Carriage, Mrs. *Jewkes*; it is not like two Persons of one Sex.

She fell a laughing very confidently, and said, That's prettily said, I vow; then thou hadst rather be kiss'd by the other Sex? If 'ackins,[1] I commend thee for that! I was sadly teaz'd with her Impertinence, and bold Way; but no wonder, she was an Inn-keeper's House-keeper before she came to my Master; and those Sort of Creatures don't want Confidence, you know. And indeed she made nothing to talk confidently on twenty Occasions, and said two or three times, when she saw the Tears every now-and-then, as we rid, trickle down my Cheeks, I was sorely hurt, truly, to have the handsomest and finest young Gentleman in five Counties in Love with me!

So I find I am got into the Hands of a wicked Procuress, and if I was not safe with good Mrs. *Jervis*, and where every body lov'd me, what a dreadful Prospect have I now before me, in the Hands of a Woman that seems to delight in Filthiness!

O dear Sirs! what shall I do! What shall I do!—Surely, I shall never be equal to all these Things!

About Eight at Night, we enter'd the Court-yard of this handsome, large, old, and lonely Mansion, that looks made for Solitude and Mischief, as I thought, by its Appearance, with all its brown nodding Horrors[2] of lofty Elms and Pines about it; And here, said I to myself, I fear, is to be the Scene of my Ruin, unless God protect me, who is all-sufficient!

I was very sick at entring it, partly from Fatigue, and partly from Dejection of Spirits: And Mrs. *Jewkes* got me some mull'd Wine, and seem'd mighty officious to welcome me thither. And while she was absent, ordering the Wine, the wicked *Robin* came in to me, and said, I beg a thousand Pardons for my Part in this Affair, since I see your Grief, and your Distress, and I do assure you, that I am sorry it fell to my Task.

Mighty well, Mr. *Robert!* said I; I never saw an Execution but once, and then the Hangman ask'd the poor Creature's Pardon, and wip'd his Mouth,[3] as you do, and pleaded his Duty, and then calmly tuck'd up the Criminal: But I am no Criminal, as you all know: And if I could have thought it my Duty to obey a wicked Master, in his unlawful Commands, I had sav'd you all the Merit of this vile Service.

I am sorry, said he, you take it so. But every body don't think alike. Well, said I, you have done your Part, Mr. *Robert*, towards my Ruin, very faithfully; and will have Cause to be sorry, may-be, at the Long-run, when you shall see the Mischief that comes of it.—Your Eyes were open, and you knew I was to be carry'd to my Father's, and that I was barbarously trick'd and betray'd, and I can only once more, thank you for your Part of it. God forgive you!

So he went away a little sad. What have you said to *Robin*, Madam, said Mrs. *Jewkes*, who came in as he went out? The poor Fellow's ready to cry. I need not be afraid of your following his Example, Mrs. *Jewkes*, said I: I have been telling him, that he has done his Part to my Ruin: And he now can't help it! So his Repentance does me no good; I wish it may him.

I'll assure you, Madam, said she, I should be as ready to cry as he, if I should do you any Harm. It is not in his Power to help it now, said I; but your Part is to come, and you may chuse whether you'll contribute to my Ruin or not.—Why, look ye, look ye, Madam, said she, I have a great Notion of doing my Duty to my Master; and therefore you may depend upon it, if I can do that, and serve you, I will: But you must think, if your Desire and his Will come to clash once, I shall do as he bids me, let it be what it will.

Pray, Mrs. *Jewkes*, said I, don't Madam me so; I am but a silly poor Girl, set up by the Gambol of Fortune, for a May-game;[1] and now am to be something, and now nothing, just as that thinks fit to sport with me: And let you and I talk upon a Foot together; for I am a Servant inferior to you, and so much the more as I am turn'd out of Place.

Ay, ay, says she, I understand something of the Matter; you have so great Power over my Master, that you may be soon Mistress of us all; and so I would oblige you, if I could. And I must and will call you Madam; for I am instructed to shew you all Respect, I'll assure you.

Who instructed you to do so, said I? Who! my Master, to be sure, said she. Why, said I, how can that be, you have not seen him lately. No, that's true, said she; but I have been expecting you here some time (O! the deep-laid Wickedness thought I!) and besides, I have a Letter of Instructions by *Robin*; but may-be, I should not have said so much. If you would shew them to me, said I, I should be able to judge how far I could, or could not, expect Favour from you, consistent with your Duty to our Master. I beg your Pardon, fair Mistress, for that, said she; I am sufficiently instructed, and you may depend upon it, I will observe my Orders; and so far as they will let me, so far will I oblige you; and there's an End of it.

Well, said I, you will not, I hope, do an unlawful or wicked Thing, for any Master in the World! Look-ye, said she, he is my Master, and if he bids me do a Thing that I can do, I think I ought to do it, and let him, who has Power, to command me, look to the Lawfulness of it. Why, said

I, suppose he should bid you cut my Throat, would you do it? There's no Danger of that, said she; but to be sure I would not; for then I should be hang'd; for that would be Murder. Well, said I, and suppose he should resolve to insnare a poor young Creature, and ruin her, would you assist him in that? For to rob a Person of her Virtue, is worse than cutting her Throat.

Why now, says she, how strangely you talk! Are not the two Sexes made for one another? And is it not natural for a Gentleman to love a pretty Woman? And suppose he can obtain his Desires, is that so bad as cutting her Throat? And then the Wretch fell a laughing, and talk'd most impertinently, and shew'd me, that I had nothing to expect from her Virtue or Conscience. And this gave me great Mortification; for I was in hopes of working upon her by degrees.

So we ended our Discourse here, and I bid her shew me where I must lie?—Why, said she, lie where you list, Madam; but I can tell you, I must lie with you for the present. *For the present*, said I, and Torture then wrung my Heart!—But is it in your Instructions that you must lie with me? Yes, indeed, said she. I am sorry for it, said I. Why, said she, I am wholsome and cleanly too, I'll assure you. Yes, said I, I don't doubt that; but I love to lie by myself. Why, said she, Mrs. *Jervis* was your Bed-fellow at t'other House.

Well, said I, quite sick of her, and my Condition, you must do as you are instructed, I think. I can't help myself; and am a most miserable Creature. She repeated her insufferable Nonsense, Mighty miserable indeed, to be so well belov'd by one of the finest Gentlemen in *England!*

*I am now come down in my Writing to this present
SATURDAY, and a deal I have written.*

My wicked Bed-fellow has very punctual Orders it seems; for she locks me and herself in, and ties the two Keys (for there is a double Door to the Room) about her Wrist, when she goes to Bed. She talks of the House having been attempted to be broke open two or three times; whether to fright me, I can't tell; but it makes me fearful; but not so much as I should be, if I had not other and greater Fears.

I slept but little the preceding Night, and got up, and pretended to sit by the Window, which looks into the spacious Gardens; but I was writing all the time, from Break of Day to her getting up, and after, when she was absent.

At Breakfast she presented the two Maids to me, the Cook and House-maid, poor awkward Souls, that I can see no Hopes of, they seem so devoted to her and Ignorance. Yet I am resolv'd, if possible, to find some way to escape, before this wicked Master comes.

There are besides, of Servants, the Coachman *Robert*, a Groom, a Helper, a Footman; all but *Robert* (and he is accessary to my Ruin) strange Creatures, that promise nothing; and all likewise devoted to this Woman. The Gardener looks like a good honest Man; but he is kept at a Distance; and seems reserv'd.

I wonder'd I saw not Mr. *Williams* the Clergyman, but would not ask after him, apprehending it might give her some Jealousy; but when I had beheld the rest, he was the only one I had Hopes of; for I thought his Cloth would set him above assisting in my Ruin.—But, in the Afternoon he came; for it seems he has a little *Latin* School in the neighbouring Village, which he attends, and this brings him in a little Matter, additional to my Master's Favour, till something better falls, of which he has Hopes.

He is a sensible, sober young Gentleman, and when I saw him, I con-firm'd myself in my Hopes of him; for he seem'd to take great Notice of my Distress and Grief; for I could not hide it; tho' he appear'd fearful of Mrs. *Jewkes*, who watch'd all our Motions and Words.

He has an Apartment in the House; but is mostly at a Lodging in the Town, for Conveniency of his little School; only on *Saturday* Afternoons and *Sundays*; and he preaches sometimes for the Parson of the Village, which is about three Miles off.

I hope to go to Church with him to-morrow: Sure it is not in her Instruc-tions to deny me. He can't have thought of every thing. And something may strike out for me there.

I have ask'd her, for a Feint, (because she shan't think I am so well provided) to indulge me with Pen and Ink, tho' I have been using my own so freely when her Absence would let me; for I begg'd to be left to myself as much as possible. She says she will let me have it, but then I must promise not to send any Writing out of the House, without her seeing it. I said, It was only to divert my Grief, when I was by myself, as I desired to be; for I lov'd Writing; but I had nobody to send to, she knew well enough.

No, not at present, may-be, said she; but I am told you are a great Writer, and it is in my Instructions to see all you write; so, look you here, said she, I will let you have a Pen and Ink, and two Sheets of Paper; for this Employment will keep you out of worse Thoughts: but I must see them always when I ask, written or not written. That's very hard, said I; but may I not have the Closet in the Room where we lie, to myself, with the Key to lock up my Things? I believe I may consent to that, said she, and I will set it in Order for you, and leave the Key in the Door. And there is a Spinnet too, said she; if it be in Tune, you may play to divert you now-and-then; for I know my old Lady learnt you.

So I resolv'd to hide a Pen of my own here, and another there, for fear I should come to be deny'd, and a little of my Ink in a broken China Cup, and a little in another Cup; and a Sheet of Paper here-and-there among my Linen, with a little Wax and a few Wafers in several Places, lest I should be search'd; and something I thought might happen to open a Way for my Deliverance, by these or some other Means. O the Pride, thought I, I shall have, if I can secure my Innocence, and escape the artful Wiles of this wicked Master! For, if he comes hither, I am undone to be sure! For this naughty Woman will assist him, rather than fail, in the worst of his Attempts, and he'll have no Occasion to send her out of the Way, as he would have done Mrs. *Jervis* once. So I must set all my little Wits at Work!

It is a Grief to me to write, and not to be able to send to you what I write; but now it is all the Diversion I have, and if God will favour my Escape with my Innocence, as I trust he graciously will, for all these black Prospects, with what Pleasure shall I read them afterwards!

I was going to say, Pray for your dutiful Daughter, as I used; but, alas! you cannot know my Distress! tho' I am sure I have your Prayers. And I will write on as Things happen, that if a Way should open, my Scribble may be ready to send. For what I do, must be at a Jirk,[1] to be sure.

O how I want such an obliging honest-hearted Man as *John!*

I am now come to SUNDAY.

Well, here is a sad Thing! I am deny'd by this barbarous Woman, to go to Church, as I had built upon I might. And she has huffed poor Mr. *Williams* all to-pieces, for pleading for me. I find he is to be forbid the House, if she pleases. Poor Gentleman! all his Dependence is upon my Master, who has a very good Living for him, if the Incumbent die, and he has kept his Bed these four Months, of old Age and Dropsy.

He pays me great Respect; and I see pities me; and would perhaps assist my Escape from these Dangers, but I have nobody to plead for me; and why should I wish to ruin a poor Gentleman, by engaging him against his Interest? Yet one would do any thing to preserve one's Innocence; and God Almighty would, may-be, make it up to him!

O judge (but how shall you see what I write!) my distracted Condition, to be reduc'd to such a Pass as to desire to lay Traps for Mankind!—But he wants sadly to say something to me, as he whisperingly hinted.

The Wretch (I think I will always call her the *Wretch* henceforth) abuses me more and more. I was but talking to one of the Maids just now, indeed a little to tamper with her by degrees; and she popt upon us, and said—Nay, don't offer, Madam, to tempt poor innocent Country Maidens from doing their Duty. You wanted, I hear, she should take a Walk with you. But I charge you, *Nan*, never stir with her, nor obey her, without letting me know it, in the smallest Trifles.—I say, walk with you! why, where would you go, I trow? Why, barbarous Mrs. *Jewkes*, said I, only to look a little up the Elm-walk, as you would not let me go to Church.

Nan, said she, to shew me how much they were all in her Power, pull off Madam's Shoes, and bring them to me. I have taken care of her others——Indeed she shan't, said I—Nay, said *Nan*, but I must, if my Mistress bids me; so pray, Madam, don't hinder me: And so indeed, (would you believe it?) She took my Shoes off, and left me barefoot: And, for my Share, I have been so frighten'd at this, that I have not Power even to relieve my Mind by my Tears. I am quite stupify'd, to be sure! Here I was forc'd to leave off.

Now I will give you a Picture of this Wretch! She is a broad, squat, pursy,[1] fat Thing, quite ugly, if any thing God made can be ugly; about forty Years old. She has a huge Hand, and an Arm as thick as my Waist, I believe. Her Nose is flat and crooked, and her Brows grow over her Eyes; a dead, spiteful, grey, goggling Eye, to be sure, she has. And her Face is flat and broad; and as to Colour, looks like as if it had been pickled a Month in Salt-petre: I dare say she drinks!—She has a hoarse man-like Voice, and is as thick as she's long; and yet looks so deadly strong, that I am afraid she would dash me at her Foot in an Instant, if I was to vex her.—So that with a Heart more ugly than her Face, she frightens me sadly; and I am undone, to be sure, if God does not protect me; for she is very, very wicked——indeed she is.

This is but poor helpless Spight in me!—But the Picture is too near the Truth notwithstanding. She sends me a Message just now, that I shall have my Shoes again, if I will accept of her Company to walk with me in the Garden—To *waddle* with me, rather, thought I.

Well, 'tis not my Business to quarrel with her downright. I shall be watch'd the narrower, if I do; and so I will go with the hated Wretch.—O for my dear Mrs. *Jervis!* or rather, to be safe with my dear Father and Mother!

Oh I'm out of my Wits, for Joy! Just as I have got my Shoes on, I am told, *John,* honest *John,* is come, on Horseback!—God bless him! What Joy is this! But I'll tell you more by-and-by. I must not let her know, I am so glad to see this dear blessed *John,* to be sure!—O but he looks sad, as I see him out of the Window! What can be the Matter!—I hope my dear Parents are well, and Mrs. *Jervis,* and Mr. *Longman,* and every body, my naughty Master not excepted—for I wish him to live and repent of all his Wickedness to poor me.

O dear Heart! what a World do we live in!—I am now to take up my Pen again! But I am in a sad Taking truly! Another puzzling Tryal, to be sure!

Here is *John,* as I said; and the poor Man came to me, with Mrs. *Jewkes,* who whisper'd, that I would say nothing about the Shoes, for my own sake, as she said. The poor Man saw my Distress, and my red Eyes, and my haggard Looks, I suppose; for I had had a sad Time of it, you must needs think; and he would have hid it, but his Eyes run over. Oh Mrs. *Pamela!* said he; Oh Mrs. *Pamela!*—Well, honest Fellow-servant, said I, I cannot help it at present! I am oblig'd to your Honesty and Kindness, to be sure; and then he wept more. Said I, (for my Heart was ready to break to see his Grief; for it is a touching thing to see a Man cry) Tell me the worst! Is my Master coming? No, no, said he, and sobb'd.—Well, said I, is there any News of my poor Father and Mother? how do they do?—I hope, well, said he; I know nothing to the contrary: There is no Mishap, I hope, to Mrs. *Jervis,* or Mr. *Longman,* or my Fellow-servants! No—said he, poor Man! with a long N—o, as if his Heart would burst. Well, thank God then! said I.

The Man's a Fool, said Mrs. *Jewkes,* I think; what ado is here! why sure thou'rt in Love, *John.* Dost thou not see young Madam is well? what ails thee, Man? Nothing at all, said he, but I am such a Fool, as to cry for Joy to see good Mrs. *Pamela:* But I have a Letter for you.

I took it, and saw it was from my Master; so I put it in my Pocket. Mrs. *Jewkes,* said I, you need not, I hope, see this. No, no, said she, I see who it comes from, well enough; or else, may-be, I must desire to see it.

And here is one for you, Mrs. *Jewkes*, said he; but yours, said he to me, requires an Answer, which I must carry back early in the Morning, or to-night, if I can.

You have no more, *John*, said Mrs. *Jewkes*, for Mrs. *Pamela*, have you? No, said he, I have not. But every body's kind Love and Service. Ay, to us both, to be sure, said she. *John*, said I, I will read the Letter, and pray take care of yourself; for you are a good Man. God bless you; and I rejoice to see you, and hear from you all. But I long'd to say more, only that nasty Mrs. *Jewkes*——

So I came up hither, and lock'd myself in my Closet, and open'd the Letter; and this is a Copy of it.

'*My dearest* PAMELA,

'I send purposely to you on an Affair that concerns you very much, and me something, but chiefly for your sake. I am conscious that I have proceeded by you in such a manner as may justly alarm your Fears, and give Concern to your honest Friends: And all my Pleasure is, that I can and will make you Amends for all the Disturbance I have given you. As I promis'd, I sent to your Father the Day after your Departure, that he might not be too much concern'd for you, and assured him of my Honour to you; and made an Excuse, such a one as ought to have satisfy'd him, for your not coming to him. But this was not sufficient, it seems; for he, poor Man! came to me next Morning, and set my Family almost in an Uproar about you.

'O my dear Girl, what Trouble has not your Obstinacy given me, and yourself too! I had no way to pacify him, but to promise, that he should see a Letter wrote from you to Mrs. *Jervis*, to satisfy him you were well.

'Now all my Care in this Case, is for your aged Parents, lest they should be fatally touched with Grief; and for you, whose Duty and Affection for them I know to be so strong and laudable: For this Reason I beg you will write a few Lines to them, and let me prescribe the Form for it; which I have done, putting myself as near as I can in your Place, and expressing your Sense, with a Warmth that I doubt will have too much possess'd you.

'After what is done, and which cannot now be help'd, but which, I assure you, shall turn out honourably for you, I expect not to be refus'd; because I cannot possibly have any View in it, but to satisfy your Parents; which is more your Concern than mine; and so I must beg you will not alter one Tittle of the underneath. If you do, it will be impossible for me to send it, or that it should answer the good End I propose by it.

'I have promis'd to you, that I will not approach you without your Leave: If I find you easy, and not attempting to dispute or avoid your present Lot,

I will keep to my Word, tho' 'tis a Difficulty upon me. Nor shall the present Restraint upon you last long: For I will assure you, that I am resolv'd very soon to convince you, how ardently I am

'*Yours, &c.*'

The Letter he prescribed for me was this:

'*Dear Mrs.* JERVIS,

'I have, instead of being driven, by *Robin*, to my dear Father's, been carry'd off, to where I have no Liberty to tell. However, at present, I am not us'd hardly; and I write to beg you to let my dear Father and Mother, whose Hearts must be well-nigh broken, know, that I am well; and that I am, and, by the Grace of God, ever will be, their dutiful and honest Daughter, as well as

'*Your obliged Friend.*

'I must neither send Date nor Place; but have most solemn Assurances of honourable Usage.'

I knew not what to do on this most strange Request and Occasion. But my Heart bled so much for you, my dear Father, who had taken the Pains to go yourself and inquire after your poor Daughter, as well as for my dear Mother, that I resolv'd to write, and pretty much in the above[a] Form, that it might be sent to pacify you, till I could let you, some how or other, know the true State of the Matter. And I wrote this to this strange wicked Master himself:

'SIR,

'If you knew but the Anguish of my Mind, and how much I suffer by your dreadfully strange Usage of me, you would surely pity me, and consent to my Deliverance. What have I done, that I should be the only Mark of your Cruelty! I can possibly have no Hope, no Desire of living left me, because I cannot have the least Dependence, after what has pass'd, upon your solemn Assurances—It is impossible, surely, they should be consistent with the honourable Designs you profess.

'Nothing but your Promise of not seeing me here in my deplorable Bondage, can give me the least Ray of Hope.

'Don't drive the poor distressed *Pamela* upon a Rock, I beseech you, that may be the Destruction both of her Body and Soul! You don't know, Sir, how dreadfully I *dare*, weak as I am of Mind and Intellect, when my

a See p. 90; her Alterations are in a different Character.

Virtue is in Danger. And, oh! hasten my Deliverance, that a poor unworthy Creature, below the Notice of so great a Man, may not be made the Sport of a high Condition, for no Reason in the World, but because she is not able to defend herself, nor has a Friend that can right her.

'I have, Sir, in part to shew my Obedience to you, but indeed, I own, more to give Ease to the Minds of my poor distressed Parents, whose Poverty, one would think, should screen them from Violences of this sort, as well as their poor Daughter, follow'd pretty much the Form you have prescrib'd for me, to Mrs. *Jervis*; and the Alterations I have made, (for I could not help a few) are of such a Nature, as, tho' they shew my Concern a little, yet must answer the End you are pleas'd to say you propose by this Letter.

'For God's sake, good Sir, pity my lowly Condition, and my present great Misery; and let me join with all the rest of your Servants to bless that Goodness, which you have extended to every one, but the poor afflicted, heart-broken

'PAMELA.'

I thought, when I had written this Letter, and that which he had pre-scrib'd, it would look like placing a Confidence in Mrs. *Jewkes*, to shew them to her; and I shew'd her at the same time my Master's Letter to me; for I believ'd, the Value he express'd for me, would give me Credit with one who profess'd in every thing to serve him right or wrong; tho' I had so little Reason, I fear, to pride myself in it: And I was not mistaken; for it has seem'd to influence her not a little, and she is at present mighty obliging, and runs over in my Praises; but is the less to be minded, because she praises as much the Author of all my Miseries, and his honourable Intentions, as she calls them; when I see, that she is capable of thinking, as I fear *he* does, that every thing that makes for his wicked Will, is honourable, tho' to the Ruin of the Innocent. Pray God I may find it otherwise. I hope, whatever the naughty Gentleman may intend, that I shall be at least rid of her impertinent bold Way of Talk, when she seems to think, by his Letter, that he means honourably.

I am now come to MONDAY, *the 5th Day of my Bondage and Misery.*

I was in Hope to have an Opportunity to see *John*, and have a little private Talk with him before he went away; but it could not be. The poor Man's excessive Sorrow made Mrs. *Jewkes* take it into her Head, to think he lov'd me, and so she brought up a Message to me from him this Morning, that he was going. I desir'd he might come up to my Closet, as I call'd it; and she came with him: And the honest Man, as I thought him, was as full of Concern as before, at taking Leave. And I gave him my two Letters, the one for Mrs. *Jervis*, inclos'd in that for my Master: But Mrs. *Jewkes* would see me seal them up, for fear of any other—I was surpriz'd, at the Man's going away, to see him drop a Bit of Paper, just at the Head of the Stairs, which I took up without Mrs. *Jewkes's* seeing me; but I was a thousand times more surpriz'd, when I return'd to my Closet, and opening it, read as follows:

'*Good Mrs.* PAMELA,

'I am griev'd to tell you how much you have been deceiv'd and betray'd, and that by such a vile Dog as I. Little did I think it would come to this. But I must say, if ever there was a Rogue in the World, it is me. I have all along shew'd your Letters to my Master: He employ'd me for that Purpose; and he saw every one before your Father and Mother, and then seal'd them up, and sent me with them. I had some Business that way; but not half so often as I pretended. And as soon as I heard how it was with you, I was ready to hang myself. You may well think I could not stand in your Presence. O vile, vile Wretch, to bring you to this! If you are ruin'd, I am the Rogue that caus'd it. All the Justice I can do you, is, to tell you, you are in vile Hands; and I am afraid will be undone in spite of all your sweet Innocence; and I believe I shall never live after I know it. If you can forgive me, you are exceeding good; but I shall never forgive myself, that's certain. Howsomever, it will do you no good to make this known; and may-hap I may live to do you Service. If I can, I will. I am sure I ought—Master kept your last two or three Letters, and did not send them at all. I am the most abandon'd Wretch of Wretches.

J. ARNOLD.

'You see your Undoing has been long hatching. Pray take care of your sweet Self. Mrs. *Jewkes* is a Devil. But in my Master's t'other House you have not one false Heart, but myself. Out upon me for a Villain!'

My dear Father and Mother, when you come to this Place, I make no doubt your Hair will stand an End, as mine does!—O the Deceitfulness of the Heart of Man!—This *John*, that I took to be the honestest of Men; that you took for the same; that was always praising you to me, and me to you, and for nothing so much as for our honest Hearts; this very Fellow was all the while a vile Hypocrite, and a perfidious Wretch, and helping to carry on my Ruin!

But he says enough of himself; and I can only sit down with this sad Reflection, That Power and Riches never want Tools to promote their vilest Ends, and that there is nothing so hard to be known as the Heart of Man!—Yet I can but pity the poor Wretch, since he seems to have some Remorse, and I believe it best to keep his Wickedness secret; and, if it lies in my way, to encourage his Penitence; for I may possibly make some Discoveries by it.

One thing I should mention in this Place; he brought down, in a Portmanteau, all the Cloaths and Things my Lady and Master had presented me, and moreover two Velvet Hoods, and a Velvet Scarf, that used to be worn by my Lady; but I have no Comfort in them!

Mrs. *Jewkes* had the Portmanteau brought into my Closet, and she shew'd me what was in it; but then locked it up, and said, she would let me have what I would out of it, when I asked; but if I had the Key, it might set me a wanting to go abroad, may-be; and so the insolent Woman put it in her Pocket.

I gave myself over to sad Reflections upon this strange and surprizing Discovery of *John*'s, and wept much for him, and for myself too; for now I see, as he says, my Ruin has been so long a hatching, that I can make no Doubt what my Master's honourable Professions will end in. What a Heap of Names does the poor Fellow call himself! But what must they deserve, who set him to work? O what has this wicked Master to answer for, to be so corrupt himself, and to corrupt others, who would have been innocent; and all to carry on further a more corrupt Scene, and to ruin a poor Creature, who never did him Harm, nor wish'd him any; and who can still pray for his Happiness, and his Repentance?

I can but wonder what these Gentlemen, as they are called, can think of themselves for these vile Doings? *John* had some Inducement; for he hoped to please his Master, who rewarded him, and was bountiful to him; and the same may be said, bad as she is, for this same odious Mrs. *Jewkes*. But what Inducement has my Master for taking so much Pains to do the Devil's Work?—If he loves me, as 'tis falsely called, must he therefore ruin me, and lay Traps for me, and endeavour to make me as bad as himself? I cannot imagine what good the Undoing of such a poor Creature as I can procure him!—To be sure, I am a very worthless Body. People indeed say I am handsome; but if I was so, should not a Gentleman prefer an honest Servant to a guilty Harlot?—And must he be *more* earnest to seduce me, because I dread of all things to be seduced, and would rather lose my Life than my Honesty!

Well, these are strange things to me! I cannot account for them, for my Share; but sure nobody will say, that these fine Gentlemen have any Tempter but their own wicked Wills!—This naughty Master could run away from me, when he thought none but his Servants should know his base Attempts, in that sad Closet Affair; but is it not strange, that he should not be afraid of the All-seeing Eye, from which even that black poisonous Heart of his, and its most secret Motions, could not be hid?—But what avail me these sorrowful Reflections? He is and will be wicked; and I am, I fear, to be a Victim to his lawless Attempts, if the God in whom I trust, and to whom I hourly pray, prevent it not!

TUESDAY and *WEDNESDAY.*

I have been hinder'd, by this wicked Woman's watching me too close, from writing on *Tuesday*; and so I will put both these Days together. I have been a little Turn with her, for an Airing, in the Chariot, and walked several times in the Garden; but have always her at my Heels.

Mr. *Williams* came to see us, and took a Walk with us once; and while her Back was just turn'd, (encourag'd by the Hint he had before given me) I said, Sir, I see two Tiles upon that Parsley-bed; cannot one cover them with Mould, with a Note between them, on Occasion?—A good Hint, said he; let that Sun-flower by the Back-door of the Garden be the Place; I have a Key to that; for it is my nearest way to the Town.

So I was forced to begin. O what Inventions will Necessity be the Parent of! I hugg'd myself with the Thought; and she coming to us, he said, as if he was continuing the Discourse we were in; No, not extraordinary pleasant. What's that? what's that? said Mrs *Jewkes*—Only, said he, the Town, I'm saying, is not very pleasant. No, indeed, said she, 'tis not; 'tis a poor Town, to my thinking. Are there any Gentry in it? said I. And so we chatted on about the Town, to deceive her. But my Deceit intended no Hurt to any body.

We then talked of the Garden, how large and pleasant, and the like; and sat down on the turfted Slope of the fine Fish-pond, to see the Fishes play upon the Surface of the Water; and she said, I should angle if I would.

I wish, said I, you'd be so kind to fetch me a Rod and Baits. Pretty Mistress! said she—I know better than that, I'll assure you! at this time!—I mean no Harm, said I, indeed. Let me tell you, said she, I know nobody has their Thoughts more about them than you. A body ought to look to it, where you are. But we'll angle a little to-morrow. Mr. *Williams*, who is much afraid of her, turn'd the Discourse to a general Subject. I saunter'd in, and left them to talk by themselves; but he went away to Town, and she was soon after me.

I had got to my Pen and Ink; and I said, I want some Paper (putting what I was about in my Bosom): You know I have wrote two Letters, and sent them by *John* (O how his Name, poor guilty Fellow! grieves me). Well, said she, you have some left; one Sheet did for those two Letters. Yes, said I, but I used half another for a Wrapper, you know; and see how I scribbled the other Half; and so I shewed her a Parcel of broken Scraps of Verses, which I had try'd to recollect, and which I had wrote purposely that she might see, and think me usually employ'd to such idle Purposes. Ay, said she, so you have; well, I'll give you two Sheets more; but let me see how you dispose of them, either written or blank. Well, thinks I, I hope still, *Argus*,[1] to be too hard for thee. Now *Argus*, the Poets say, had an hundred Eyes, and was made to watch with them all, as she is.

She brought me the Paper, and said, Now, Madam, let me see you write something. I will, said I; and took the Pen, and wrote, "I wish Mrs. *Jewkes* would be as good to me, as I would be to her, if I had it in my Power!"— That's pretty now! said she; well, I hope I am; but what then? "Why then (*wrote I*) she would do me the Favour to let me know, what I have done to be made her Prisoner; and what she thinks is to become of me." Well, and what then, said she? "Why then, of Consequence, (*scribbled I*) she would let me see her Instructions, that I may know how far to blame her, or acquit her."

Thus I fooled on, to shew her my Fondness for scribbling; for I had no Expectation of any Good from her; that so she might suppose I employ'd myself, as I said, to no better Purpose at other times: For she will have it, that I am upon some Plot, I am so silent, and love so much to be by myself.—She would have had me go on a little further. No, said I, you have not answer'd me. Why, said she, what can you doubt, when my Master himself assures you of his Honour? Ay, says I; but lay your Hand to your Heart, Mrs. *Jewkes*, and tell me, if you yourself believe him. Yes, said she, to be sure I do. But, said I, what do you call Honour?—Why, said she, what does he call Honour, think you?—Ruin! Shame! Disgrace! said I, I fear!—Pho, pho, said she; if you have any Doubt about it, he can best explain his own Meaning!—I'll send him word to come to satisfy you, if you will!—Horrid Creature! said I, all in a Fright!—Can'st thou not stab me to the Heart? I'd rather thou wouldst, than say such another Word!—But I hope there is no Thought of his coming.

She had the Wickedness to say, No, no; he don't intend to come, as I know of—But if I was he, I would not be long away!—What means the Woman, said I?—Means! said she (turning it off); why I mean, I would come, if I was he, and put an End to all your Fears—by making you as happy as you wish. 'Tis out of his Power, said I, to make me happy, great and rich as he is, but by leaving me innocent, and giving me Liberty to go to my dear Father and Mother.

She went away soon after, and I ended my Letter, in Hopes to have an Opportunity to lay it in the appointed Place. So I went to her, and said; I suppose, as it is not dark, I may take another Turn in the Garden. 'Tis too late, said she; but if you will go, don't stay, and, *Nan*, see and attend Madam, as she called me.

So I went towards the Pond, the Wench following me, and dropt purposely my Hussy:[1] And when I came near the Tiles, I said, Mrs. *Ann*, I have dropt my Hussy; be so kind to look for it. I had it by the Pond-side. The Wench went to look, and I slipt the Note between the Tiles, and cover'd them as quick as I could with the light Mould, quite unperceiv'd; and the Maid finding the Hussy, I took it, and saunter'd in again, and met Mrs. *Jewkes* coming to see after me. What I wrote was this:

'*Reverend Sir,*

'The want of Opportunity to speak my Mind to you, I am sure will excuse this Boldness in a poor Creature that is betray'd hither, I have Reason to think, for the worst Purposes. You know something, to be sure, of my Story, my native Poverty, which I am not ashamed of, my late Lady's Goodness, and my Master's Designs upon me. 'Tis true, he promises Honour, and all that; but the Honour of the Wicked is Disgrace and Shame to the Virtuous. And he may think he may keep his Promises according to the Notions he may allow himself to hold; and yet, according to mine, and every good Body's beside, quite ruin me.

'I am so wretched, and ill treated by this Mrs. *Jewkes*, and she is so ill-principled a Woman, that as I may soon want the Opportunity which the happy Hint of this Day affords to my Hopes; so I throw myself at once upon your Goodness, without the least Reserve; for I cannot be worse than I am, should *that* fail me; which, I dare say, to your Power, it will not: For I see it, Sir, in your Looks, I hope it from your Cloth, and I doubt it not from your Inclination, in a Case circumstanced as my unhappy one is. For, Sir, in helping me out of my present Distress, you perform all the Acts of Religion in one; and the highest Mercy and Charity, both to a Body and a

Soul of a poor Wretch, that, believe me, Sir, has, at present, not so much as in Thought, swerv'd from her Innocence.

'Is there not some way to be found out for my Escape, without Danger to yourself? Is there no Gentleman or Lady of Virtue in this Neighbourhood, to whom I may fly, only till I can find a way to get to my poor Father and Mother? Cannot Lady *Davers* be made acquainted with my sad Story, by your conveying a Letter to her? My poor Parents are so low in the World, they can do nothing but break their Hearts for me; and that, I fear, will be the End of it.

'My Master promises, if I will be easy, as he calls it, in my present Lot, he will not come down without my Consent. Alas! Sir, this is nothing. For what's the Promise of a Person, who thinks himself at Liberty to act as he has done by me? If he comes, it must be to ruin me; and come, to be sure, he will, when he thinks he has silenc'd the Clamours of my Friends, and lulled me, as no doubt he hopes, into a fatal Security.

'Now, therefore, Sir, is all the Time I have to work and struggle for the Preservation of my Honesty. If I stay till he comes, I am undone. You have a Key to the back Garden-door; I have great Hopes from that. Study, good Sir, and contrive for me. I will faithfully keep your Secret.—Yet I should be loth to have you injur'd for me!

'I say no more, but commit this to the happy Tiles, and to the Bosom of that Earth from which I hope my Deliverance will take Root, and bring forth such Fruit, as may turn to my inexpressible Joy, and your eternal Reward, both here and hereafter. As shall ever pray,

> '*Your most oppressed humble Servant.*'

THURSDAY.

This completes a fatal Week since my setting out, as I hoped, to see you, my dear Father and Mother. O how different my Hopes then, from what they are now! Yet who knows what these happy Tiles may produce!

But I must tell you, first, how I have been beaten by Mrs. *Jewkes!* 'Tis very true!

My Impatience was great to walk in the Garden, to see if any thing had offer'd, answerable to my Hopes. But this wicked Mrs. *Jewkes* would not let me go without her; and she said she was not at Leisure. We had a great many Words about it; for I said, it was very hard I could not be trusted to walk by myself in the Garden for a little Air; but must be dogg'd and watch'd worse than a Thief.

She still pleaded her Instructions, and said she was not to trust me out of her Sight: And you had better, said she, be easy and contented, I assure you. For I have worse Orders than you have yet found; and if you remember, said she, what you said when Mr. *Williams* was with us, asking if there were any Gentry in the Neighbourhood, it makes me suspect you want to get away to them, to tell your sad dismal Story, as you call it.

My Heart was at my Mouth; for I fear'd by that Hint, she had seen my Letter under the Tiles: O how uneasy I was! At last she said, Well, since you take on so, you may take a Turn, and I will be with you in a Minute.

I went out; and when I was out of the Sight of her Window, I speeded towards the hopeful Place; but was soon forced to slacken my Pace, by her odious Voice; Hey-day, why so nimble, and so fast? said she: What! are you upon a Wager? I stopt for her, till her pursy Sides were waddled up to me; and she held by my Arm, half out of Breath: So I was forced to pass by the dear Place, without daring to look at it.

The Gardener was at work a little further, and so we looked upon him, and I began to talk about his Art; but she said softly, My Instructions are, not to let you be so familiar with the Servants. Why, said I, are you afraid I should confederate with them to commit a Robbery upon my Master? May-be I am, said the odious Wretch; for to rob him of yourself, would be the worst that could happen to him, in his Opinion.

And pray, said I, walking on, how came I to be his Property?[1] What Right has he in me, but such as a Thief may plead to stolen Goods?—Why, was ever the like heard, says she!—This is downright Rebellion, I protest! Well, well, Lambkin, (which the Foolish often calls me) if I was in his Place, he should not have his Property in you long questionable. Why, what would you do, said I, if you was he?—Not stand shill-I, shall-I, as he does; but put you and himself both out of your Pain.—Why, *Jezebel*,[2] said I, (I could not help it); would you ruin me by Force?—Upon this she gave me a deadly Slap upon my Shoulder: Take that, said she; who do you call *Jezebel?*

I was so scar'd, (for you never beat me, my dear Father and Mother, in your Lives) that I was as one thunder-struck; and looked round, as if I wanted somebody to help me; but, alas! I had nobody; and said, at last, rubbing my Shoulder, Is this too in your Instructions?—Alas! for me! am I to be beaten too? and so I fell a crying, and threw myself upon the Grass-walk we were upon.—Said she, in a great Pet, I won't be call'd such Names, I'll assure you. Marry come up! I see you have a Spirit! You must and shall be kept under. I'll manage such little provoking Things as you, I warrant ye! Come, come, we'll go in Doors, and I'll lock you up, and you shall have no Shoes, nor any thing else, if this is to be the Case!

I didn't know what to do. This was a cruel thing to me, and I blam'd myself for my free Speech; for now I had given her some Pretence; and Oh! thinks I, here I have, by my Malapertness, ruin'd the only Project I had left.

The Gardener saw this Scene; but she called to him, Well, *Jacob*, what do you stare at! Pray mind what you're upon. And away he walk'd, to another Quarter, out of Sight.

Well, thinks I, I must put on the Dissembler a little, I see. She took my Hand roughly; Come, get up, said she, and come in Doors.—I'll *Jezebel* you, I warrant ye!—Why, dear Mrs. *Jewkes*, said I—None of your Dears and your Coaxing, said she; why not *Jezebel* again!—She was in a fearful Passion, I saw, and I was half out of my Wits. Thinks I, I have often heard Women blam'd for their Tongues; I wish mine had been shorter. But I can't go in, said I, indeed I can't!—Why, said she, can't you? I'll warrant I can take such a thin Body as you are under my Arm, and carry you in, if you won't walk. You don't know my Strength—Yes, but I do, said I, too well; and will you not use me worse when I come in?—So I arose, and she mutter'd to herself all the way, She to be a *Jezebel* with me, that had used me so well! and such-like.

When I came near the House, I said, sitting down upon a Settle-bench,[1] Well, I will not go in, till you say, you will forgive me, Mrs. *Jewkes*—If you will forgive my calling you that Name, I will forgive your beating me—She sat down by me, and seem'd in a great Pucker,[2] and said, Well, come, I will forgive you for this time; and so kissed me, as a Mark of Reconciliation—But pray, said I, tell me where I am to walk, and go, and give me what Liberty you can; and when I know the most you can favour me with, you shall see I will be as content as I can; and not ask you for more.

Why, said she, that's something like: I wish I could give you all the Liberty you desire; for you must think it is no Pleasure to me to tie you to my Petticoat, as it were, and not to let you stir without me—But People that will do their Duties, must have some Trouble; and what I do, is to serve as good a Master, to be sure, as lives—Ay, says I, to every body but me!—He loves you too well, to be sure, said she, and that's the Reason; so you ought to bear it. I say, *love*, said I! Come, said she, don't let the Wench see you have been crying, nor tell her any Tales; for you won't tell them fairly, I am sure; and I'll send her, and you shall take another Walk in the Garden, if you will. May-be, said she, it will get you a Stomach to your Dinner; for you don't eat enough to keep Life and Soul together. You

are Beauty to the Bone, said the strange Wretch, or you could not look so
well as you do, with so little Stomach, so little Rest, and so much pining
and whining for nothing at all. Well, thought I, say what thou wilt, so I
can be rid of thy bad Tongue and Company: And I hop'd to find some
Opportunity now, to come at my Sun-flower. But I walked the other way,
to take that in my Return, to avoid Suspicion.

I forced my Discourse to the Wench; but it was all upon general things;
for I find she is asked after every thing I say and do. When I came near the
Place, as I had been devising, I said, Pray, step to the Gardener, and ask
him to gather a Sallad for me to Dinner. She called out, *Jacob!*—Said I, he
can't hear you so far off; and pray tell him, I should like a Cucumber too, if
he has one. When she had stept about a Bow-shot from me, I popt down,
and whipt my Fingers under the upper Tile, and pulled out a little Letter,
without Direction, and thrust it in my Bosom, trembling for Joy. She was
with me before I could well secure it; and I was in such a taking, that
I feared I should discover myself. You seem frighted, Madam, said she:
Why, said I, with a lucky Thought, (alas! your poor Daughter will make
an Intriguer by-and-by; but I hope an innocent one!) I stoopt to smell at
the Sun-flower, and a great nasty Worm run into the Ground, that startled
me; for I don't love Worms. Said she, Sun-flowers don't smell. So I find,
said I. And so we walked in; and Mrs. *Jewkes* said, Well, you have made
haste in—You shall go another time.

I went up to my Closet, lock'd myself in, and opening my Letter, found
in it these Words:

'I am infinitely concern'd for your Distress. I most heartily wish it may be
in my Power to serve and save so much Innocence, Beauty and Merit. My
whole Dependence is upon the 'Squire; and I have a near View of being
provided for by his Goodness to me. But yet, I would sooner forfeit all
my Hopes upon him, and trust in God for the rest, than not assist you, if
possible. I never look'd upon Mr. *B.* in the Light he now appears to me in,
in your Case. To be sure, he is no profess'd Deboshee. But I am intirely
of Opinion, you should, if possible, get out of his Hands, and especially as
you are in very bad ones in Mrs. *Jewkes's.*

'We have here the Widow Lady *Jones,* Mistress of a good Fortune,
and a Woman of Virtue, I believe. We have also old Sir *Simon Darnford,*
and his Lady, who is a good Woman; and they have two Daughters. All
the rest are but middling People, and Traders, at best. I will try, if you
please, either Lady *Jones,* or Lady *Darnford,* if they will permit you to
take Refuge with them. I see no Probability of keeping myself conceal'd

in this Matter; but will, as I said, risque all things to serve you; for I never saw a Sweetness and Innocence like yours; and your hard Case has attached me intirely to you; for I know, as you so happily express, if I can serve you in this Case, I shall thereby perform all the Acts of Religion in one.

'As to Lady *Davers*, I will convey a Letter, if you please, to her; but it must not be from our Post-house, I give you Caution; for the Man owes all his Bread to the 'Squire, and his Place too; and I believe, by something that dropt from him, over a Can^r of Ale, has his Instructions. You don't know how you are surrounded; all which confirms me in your Opinion, that no Honour is meant you, let what will be professed; and I am glad you want no Caution on that Head.

'Give me Leave to say, that I had heard much in your Praise, both as to Person and Mind; but I think greatly short of what you deserve: My Eyes convince me of the one, your Letter of the other. For fear of losing the present lucky Opportunity, I am longer than otherwise I should be. But I will not inlarge, only to assure you, that I am, to the best of my Power,

> '*Your faithful Friend and Servant*
> 'ARTHUR WILLIAMS.

'I will come once every Morning, and once every Evening, after School-time, to look for your Letters. I'll come in, and return without going into the House, if I see the Coast clear: Otherwise, to avoid Suspicion, I'll come in.'

I instantly, to this pleasing Letter, wrote as follows:

'*Reverend Sir*,

'O how answerable to your Function, and your Character, is your kind Letter! God bless you for it. I now think I am beginning to be happy. I should be sorry you should suffer on my Account; but I hope it will be made up to you an hundred-fold, by that God whom you so faithfully serve. I should be too happy, could I ever have it in my Power to contribute in the least to it. But, alas! to serve me, must be for God's sake only; for I am poor and lowly in Fortune; though in Mind, I hope, too high to do a mean or unworthy Deed, to gain a Kingdom. But I lose Time.

'Any way you think best, I shall be pleased with; for I know not the Persons, nor in what manner it is best to apply to them. I am glad of the Hint you so kindly give me of the Man at the Post-house. I was thinking of opening a way for myself by Letter, when I could have Opportunity; but I see more and more, that I am indeed strangely surrounded with Dangers; and that there is no Dependence to be made on my Master's Honour.

'I should think, Sir, if either of those Ladies would give Leave, I might some way get out by Favour of your Key; and as it is impossible, watched as I am, to know when it can be, suppose, Sir, you could get one made by it, and put it, by the next Opportunity, under the Sun-flower?—I am sure no Time is to be lost; because it is rather my Wonder, that she is not thoughtful about this Key, than otherwise; for she forgets not the minutest thing. But, Sir, if I had this Key, I could, if these Ladies would *not* shelter me, run away any-where. And if I was once out of the House, they could have no Pretence to force me in again; for I have done no Harm, and hope to make my Story good to any compassionate Body; and by this way *you* need not be known. Torture should not wring it from me, I assure you.

'One thing more, good Sir. Have you no Correspondence with my Master's Family? By that means, may-be, I could be informed of his Intentions of coming hither, and when. I inclose you a Letter of a deceitful Wretch; for I can trust you with any thing, poor *John Arnold*. Its Contents will tell why I inclose it. Perhaps, by his means something may be discover'd; for he seems willing to atone for his Treachery to me, by the Intimation of future Service. I leave the Hint for you to improve upon, and am, Reverend Sir,

'*Your for ever obliged*
'*and thankful Servant.*

'I hope, Sir, by your Favour, I could send a little Packet, now-and-then, some how, to my poor Father and Mother. I have a little Stock of Money, about five or six Guineas: Shall I put half in your Hands, to defray a Man and Horse, or any other Incidents?'

I had time but just to transcribe this, before I was called to Dinner; and I put that for Mr. *Williams*, with a Wafer in it, in my Bosom, to get an Opportunity to lay it in the dear Place.

O good Sirs! Of all the Flowers in the Garden, the Sun-flower, sure, is the loveliest!—It is a propitious one to me! How nobly my Plot succeeds! But I begin to be afraid my Writings may be discover'd; for they grow large! I stitch them hitherto in my Under-coat, next my Linen. But if this Brute should search me!—I must try to please her, and then she won't.

Well, I am but just come off from a Walk in the Garden; and have deposited my Letter by a simple Wile. I got some Horse-beans;[1] and we took a Turn in the Garden, to angle, as Mrs. *Jewkes* had promis'd me. She baited the Hook, and I held it, and soon hooked a lovely Carp. Play it, play it, said she; I did, and brought it to the Bank. A sad Thought just then came into my Head; and I took it, and threw it in again; and O the Pleasure it seem'd to have, to flounce in, when at Liberty!—Why this? says she. O Mrs. *Jewkes!* said I, I was thinking this poor Carp was the unhappy *Pamela.* I was likening you and myself to my naughty Master. As we hooked and deceived the poor Carp, so was I betrayed by false Baits; and when you said, Play it, play it, it went to my Heart, to think I should sport with the Destruction of the poor Fish I had betray'd; and I could not but fling it in again: And did you not see the Joy with which the happy Carp flounced from us! O! said I, may some good merciful Body procure me my Liberty in the same manner; for, to be sure, I think my Danger equal!

Lord bless thee! said she, what a Thought is there!—Well, said I, I can angle no more. I'll try *my* Fortune, said she, and took the Rod. Well, said I, I will plant Life then, if I can, while you are destroying it. I have some Horse-beans here, and I'll go and stick them into one of the Borders, to see how long they will be coming up; and I will call them my Garden.

So you see, dear Father and Mother (I hope now you will soon see; for, may-be, if I can't get away so soon myself, I may send my Papers, some how) I say, you will see, that this furnishes me a good Excuse to look after my Garden another time; and if the Mould should look a little freshish, it won't be so much suspected. She mistrusted nothing of this; and I went and stuck in here and there my Beans, for about the Length of five Ells,[1] of each side of the Sun-flower; and easily reposited my Letter. And not a little proud am I of this Contrivance. Sure something will do at last. God grant it!

FRIDAY, SATURDAY.

I have just now told you a Trick of mine; now I'll tell you a Trick of this wicked Woman's. She comes up to me; says she, I have a Bill I cannot change till to-morrow; and a Tradesman wants his Money most sadly; and I don't love to turn poor Tradesfolks away without their Money: Have you any about you? How much will do, said I? I have a little! Oh! said she, I want eight Pounds. Alack, said I, I have but between five and six. Lend me that, said she, till to-morrow. I did so; and she went down Stairs: And when she came up, she laugh'd, and said, Well, I have paid the Tradesman: Said I, I hope you'll give it me again to-morrow. At that, the Assurance, laughing loud, said, Why, what Occasion have you for Money? To tell you the Truth, Lambkin, I didn't want it. I only fear'd you might make a bad Use of it; and now I can trust *Nan* with you a little oftener, especially as I have got the Key of your Portmanteau; so that you can neither corrupt her with Money or fine things. Never did any body look more silly than I!—O how I fretted to be so foolishly outwitted!—And the more, as I had hinted to Mr. *Williams*, to have some to defray the Charges of my sending to you. I cry'd for Vexation!—And now I have not five Shillings left to support me, if I *can* get away!—Was ever such a Fool as I! I must be priding myself in my Contrivances indeed! Said I, was this in your Instructions, *Wolfkin?* for she called me *Lambkin. Jezebel*, you mean, Child, said she!—Well, I now forgive you heartily; let's buss, and be Friends!—Out upon you, said I! I cannot bear you. But I durst not call her Names again; for I dread her huge Paw most sadly. The more I think of this thing, the more do I regret it!

This Night the Man from the Post-house brought a Letter for Mrs. *Jewkes*, in which was one inclosed to me: She brought it me up. Said she, Well, my good Master don't forget us. He has sent you a Letter; and see what he writes to me. So she read, That he hoped her fair Charge was well, happy, and contented: Ay to be sure, said I, I can't chuse!—That he did not doubt her Care and Kindness to me; that I was very dear to him, and she could not use me too well; and the like. There is a Master for you, said she! Sure you will love and pray for him. I desir'd her to read the rest. No, no, said she, but I won't. Said I, Are there any Orders for taking my Shoes away, and for beating me? No, said she, nor about *Jezebel* neither. Well, said I, I cry Truce; for I have no mind to be beat again. I thought, said she, we had forgiven one another.

My Letter is as follows:

'*My dearest* PAMELA,

'I begin to repent already, that I have bound myself, by Promise, not to see you till you give me Leave; for I think the Time very tedious. Can you place so much Confidence in me, as to invite me down? Assure yourself that your Generosity shall not be thrown away upon me. I the rather would press this, as I am uneasy for your Uneasiness; for Mrs. *Jewkes* acquaints me that you take your Restraint very heavily; and neither eat, drink, nor rest well; and I have too great an Interest in your Health, not to wish to shorten the Time of this Trial to you; which will be the Consequence of my coming down to you. *John* too, has intimated to me your Concern,

with a Grief that hardly gave him Leave for Utterance; a Grief that a
little alarm'd my Tenderness for you. Not that I fear any thing, but that
your Disregard to me, which yet my proud Heart will hardly permit me
to own, may throw you upon some Rashness, that might encourage a
daring Hope: But how poorly do I descend, to be anxious about such a
Menial as he?—I will only say one thing, that if you will give me Leave
to attend you at the Hall, (consider who it is that requests this from you
as a Favour) I solemnly declare, that you shall have Cause to be pleased
with this obliging Mark of your Confidence in me, and Consideration for
me; and if I find Mrs. *Jewkes* has not behaved to you with the Respect
due to one I so dearly love, I will put it intirely into your Power to dis-
charge her the House, if you think proper; and Mrs. *Jervis*, or who else
you please, shall attend you in her place. This I say on a Hint *John* gave
me, as if you resented something from that Quarter. Dearest *Pamela*,
answer favourably this earnest Request of one that cannot live without
you, and on whose Honour to you, you may absolutely depend; and so
much the more, as you place a Confidence in it. I am, and assuredly ever
will be,

'*Your faithful and affectionate*, &c.

'You will be glad, I know, to hear your Father and Mother are well, and
easy upon your last Letter. That gave me a Pleasure that I am resolved you
shall not repent. Mrs. *Jewkes* will convey to me your Answer.'

I but slightly read this Letter for the present, to give way to one I had
hopes of finding by this time, from Mr. *Williams*. I took, in Mrs. *Jewkes*'s
Company, an Evening Turn, as I call'd it, and walking by the Place, I
said, Do you think Mrs. *Jewkes*, any of my Beans can have struck since
Yesterday? She laugh'd, and said, You are a poor Gardener; but I love to see
you divert yourself. She passing on, I found my good Friend had provided
for me, and slipping it in my Bosom, for her Back was towards me, Here,
said I, having a Bean in my Hand, is one of them; but it has not stirr'd. No,
to be sure, said she; and turn'd upon me a most wicked Jest, unbecoming
the Mouth of a Woman, about Planting, &c.[1]—When I came in, I hy'd to
my Closet, and read as follows.

'I am sorry to tell you, that I have a Repulse from Lady *Jones*. She is
concerned at your Case, she says, but don't care to make herself Enemies.
I apply'd to Lady *Darnford*, and told her in the most pathetick manner I
could, your sad Story, and shew'd her your more pathetick Letter. I found
her well dispos'd; but she would advise with Sir *Simon*, who, by-the-bye,
is

not a Man of extraordinary Character for Virtue; but he said to his Lady, in my Presence, Why, what is all this, my Dear, but that the 'Squire our Neighbour has a mind to his Mother's Waiting-maid? And if he takes care she wants for nothing, I don't see any great Injury will be done her. He hurts no Family by this.' (So, my dear Father and Mother, it seems that poor Peoples Honesty is to go for nothing). 'And I think, Mr. *Williams*, you, of all Men, should not engage in this Affair, against your Friend and Patron. He spoke this in so determin'd a manner, that the Lady had done; and I had only to beg no Notice should be taken of the Matter as from me.

'I have hinted your Case to Mr. *Peters*, the Minister of this Parish, but I am concern'd to say, that he imputed selfish Views to me, as if I would make an Interest in your Affections, by my Zeal. And when I represented the Duties of our Function, &c. and protested my Disinterestedness, he coldly said, I was very good; but was a young Man, and knew little of the World. And tho' 'twas a Thing to be lamented, yet when he and I set about to reform the World in this respect, we should have enough upon our Hands; for, he said, it was too common and fashionable a Case to be withstood by a private Clergyman or two: And then he utter'd some Reflections upon the Conduct of the Fathers of the Church, in regard to the first Personages of the Realm, as a Justification of his Coldness on this score.

'I represented the different Circumstances of your Affair; that other Women liv'd evilly by their own Consent, but to serve you, was to save an Innocence that had but few Examples; and then I shew'd him your Letter.

'He said, It was prettily written; and he was sorry for you; and that your good Intentions ought to be encourag'd; but what, said he, would you have me do, Mr. *Williams*? Why, suppose Sir, said I, you give her Shelter in your House, with your Spouse and Niece, till she can get to her Friends?—What, and imbroil myself with a Man of the 'Squire's Power and Fortune! No, not I, I'll assure you!—And he would have me consider what I was about. Besides, she owns, said he, that he promises to do honourably by her; and her Shyness will procure her good Terms enough; for he is no covetous nor wicked Gentleman; except in this Case; and 'tis what all young Gentlemen will do.

'I am greatly concern'd for him, I assure you; but am not discourag'd by this ill Success, let what will come of it, if I can serve you.

'I don't hear, as yet, that the 'Squire is coming; I am glad of your Hint as to that unhappy Fellow *John Arnold*; something, perhaps, will strike out from that, which may be useful. As to your Pacquets, if you seal them up, and lay them in the usual Place, if you find it not mistrusted, I will watch an Opportunity to convey them; but if they are large, you had best be very cautious. This evil Woman, I find, mistrusts me much.

'I just hear that the Gentleman is dying, whose Living the 'Squire has promis'd me. I have almost a Scruple of taking it, as I am acting so contrary to his Desires; but I hope he'll one Day thank me for it. As to Money, don't think of it at present. Be assured you may command all in my Power to do for you, without Reserve.

'I believe, when we hear he is coming, it will be best to make use of the Key, which I shall soon procure you; and I can borrow a Horse for you, I believe, to wait within half a Mile of the Back-Door, over the Pasture; and will contrive by myself, or somebody, to have you conducted some Miles distant, to some one of the Villages thereabouts; so don't be discomforted, I beseech you. I am, excellent Mrs. *Pamela*,

'Your faithful Friend, &c.'

I made a thousand sad Reflections upon the former Part of this honest Gentleman's kind Letter; and but for the Hope he gave me at last, should have given up my Case as quite desperate. I then wrote to thank him most gratefully for his kind Endeavour; to lament the little Concern the Gentry had for my deplorable Case; the Wickedness of the World to first give way to such iniquitous Fashions, and then plead the Frequency of them against the Offer to amend them; and how unaffected People were to the Distresses of others. I recall'd my former Hint as to writing to Lady *Davers*, which I fear'd, I said, would only serve to apprize her Brother, that she knew his wicked Scheme, and more harden him in it, and make him come down the sooner, and to be the more determin'd on my Ruin; besides, that it might make Mr. *Williams* guess'd at, as a means of conveying my Letter; and being very fearful, that if that good Lady would interest herself in my Behalf, (which was a Doubt, because she both lov'd and fear'd her Brother) it would have no Effect upon him; and that, therefore, I would wait the happy Event I might hope for from his kind Assistance in the Key and the Horse, &c. I intimated my Master's Letter, begging to be permitted to come down; was fearful it might be sudden; and that I was of Opinion no Time was to be lost; for we might lose all our Opportunities, &c. telling him the Money-trick of this vile Woman, &c.

I had not time to take a Copy of this Letter, I was so watch'd. But when I had it ready in my Bosom, I was easy. And so I went to seek out Mrs. *Jewkes*, and told her I would have her Advice upon the Letter I had receiv'd from my Master, which Point of Confidence in her, pleas'd her not a little. Ay, said she, now this is something like. Why, we'll take a Turn in the Garden, or where you please. I pretended it was indifferent to me; and so we walk'd into the Garden. I began to talk to her of the Letter; but was far from acquainting her with all the Contents; only that he wanted my Consent to come down, and hop'd she us'd me kindly, &c. And I said, Now, Mrs. *Jewkes*, let me have your Advice as to this. Why then, said she, I will give it you freely. E'en send to him to come down. It will highly oblige him, and I dare say you'll fare the better for it. How the better? said I—I dare say, you think yourself that he intends my Ruin. I hate, said she, that foolish Word; *your Ruin!*—Why ne'er a Lady in the Land may live happier than you, if you will, or be more honourably used.

Well, Mrs. *Jewkes*, said I, I shall not at this time dispute with you about the Words *Ruin* or *honourable*. I thank God, we have quite different Notions of both; but now I will speak plainer than ever I did. Do you think he intends to make Proposals to me, as to a kept Mistress, or kept Slave rather; or do you not?—Why, Lambkin, said she, what dost thou think thyself?—I fear, said I, he does. Well, said she, but if he does, for I know nothing of the Matter, I assure you; you may have your own Terms—I see that; for you may do any thing with him.

I could not bear this to be spoken, tho' it was all I fear'd of a long time; and began to exclaim most sadly. Nay, said she, he may marry you, as far as I know.—No, no, said I, that cannot be—I neither desire nor expect it. His Condition don't permit me to have such a Thought, and that, and the whole Series of his Conduct to me, convinces me of the contrary; and you would have me invite him to come down, would you? Is not this to invite my Ruin?

'Tis what I would do, said she, in your Place; and if it was to be as you *think*, I should rather be out of my Pain, than live in continual Frights and Apprehensions, as you do. No, said I, an Hour of Innocence is worth an Age of Guilt; and were my Life to be made ever so miserable by it, I should never forgive myself, if I were not to lengthen out to the longest Minute my happy Time of Honesty. Who knows what God may do for me!

Why, may-be, said she, as he loves you so well, you may prevail upon him by your Prayers and Tears; and for that Reason, I should think you'd better let him come down. Well, said I, I will write him a Letter, because he expects an Answer, or may-be he will make that a Pretence to come down. You'll send it for me. How can it go?

I'll take care of that, said she; it is in my Instructions—Ay, thought I, so I doubt, by the Hint Mr. *Williams* gave me, about the Post-house.

The Gardener coming by, I said, Mr. *Jacob* I have planted a few Beans, and I call it my Garden. It is just by the Door out-yonder, I'll shew it you; pray don't dig them up. So I went on with him; and when we had turn'd the Alley out of her Sight, and were near the Place, said I, Pray step to Mrs. *Jewkes*, and ask her if she has any more Beans for me to plant? He smil'd, I suppose at my Foolishness, and I popt the Letter under the Mould, and stept back, as if waiting for his Return; which being near, was immediate, and she follow'd him. What should I do with Beans? said she—and sadly scar'd me; for she whisper'd me, I am afraid of some Fetch! you don't use to send of such simple Errands—What Fetch? said I; it is hard I can neither stir, nor speak, but I must be suspected—Why, said she, my Master writes me, that I must have all my Eyes about me; for, tho' you are as innocent as a Dove, yet you're as cunning as a Serpent.[1] But I'll forgive you if you cheat me!

Then I thought of my Money, and could have call'd her Names, had I dar'd: And I said, Pray, Mrs. *Jewkes*, now you talk of forgiving me if I cheat you; be so kind as to pay me my Money; for tho' I have no Occasion for it, yet I know you was but in Jest, and intended to give it me again. You shall have it in a proper time, said she; but, indeed, I was in earnest to get it out of your Hands, for fear you should make an ill Use of it. And so we cavilled upon this Subject as we walk'd in, and I went up to write my Letter to my Master; and, as I intended to shew it her, I resolved to write accordingly as to her Part of it; for I made little Account of the Offer of Mrs. *Jervis* to me, instead of this wicked Woman, (tho' the most agreeable thing that could have befallen me, except my Escape from hence) nor indeed of any thing he said: For to be honourable, in the just Sense of the Word, he need not have caus'd me to be run away with, and confin'd as I am. I wrote as follows:

'*Honoured Sir*,

'When I consider how easily it is for you to make me happy, since all I desire is to be permitted to go to my poor Father and Mother: When I reflect upon your former Proposal to me, in relation to a certain Person, not one Word of which is now mentioned; and upon my being in that strange manner run away with, and still kept here a miserable Prisoner; do you think, Sir, (pardon your poor Servant's Freedom; my Fears make me bold; do you think, I say) that your general Assurances of Honour to me, can have the Effect upon me, that, were it not for these Things, all your Words ought to have?—O good Sir! I too much apprehend, that *your* Notions of Honour and *mine* are very different from one another: And I have no other Hope but in your continued Absence. If you have any Proposals to make

me, that are consistent with your honourable Professions, in my humble
Sense of the Word, a few Lines will communicate them to me, and I will
return such an Answer as befits me. But, Oh! what Proposals can one in
your high Station have to make to one in my low one! I know what belongs
to your Degree too well, to imagine, that any thing can be expected but
sad Temptations, and utter Distress, if you come down; and you know not,
Sir, when I am made desperate, what the wretched *Pamela dares to do!*

'Whatever Rashness you may impute to me, I cannot help it, but I wish
I may not be forced upon any, that otherwise would never enter into my
Thoughts. Forgive me, Sir, my Plainness; I should be loth to behave to
my Master unbecomingly; but I must needs say, Sir, my Innocence is so
dear to me, that all other Considerations are, and, I hope, shall ever be,
treated by me as Niceties, that ought, for that, to be dispensed with. If you
mean honourably, why, Sir, should you not let me know it plainly? Why
is it necessary to imprison me, to convince me of it? And why must I be
close watch'd and attended, hinder'd from stirring out, from speaking to
any body, from going so much as to Church to pray for you, who have been
till of late so generous a Benefactor to me? Why, Sir, I humbly ask, why all
this, if you mean honourably?—It is not for me to expostulate so freely, but
in a Case so near to me, with you, Sir, so infinitely my Superior. Pardon
me, I hope you will; but as to any the least Desire of seeing you, I cannot so
much as bear the dreadful Apprehension. Whatever you have to propose,
whatever you intend by me, let my Assent be that of a free Person, mean
as I am, and not of a sordid Slave, who is to be threatened and frightened
into a Compliance, that your Conduct to her seems to imply would be
otherwise abhorr'd by her.——My Restraint is indeed hard upon me. I am
very uneasy under it. Shorten it, I beseech you, or—But I will not dare to
say more, than that I am

'Your greatly oppressed unhappy Servant.'

After I had taken a Copy of this, I folded it up, and Mrs. *Jewkes* coming
up, just as I had done, sat down by me, and said, when she saw me direct
it, I wish you would tell me if you have taken my Advice, and consented to
my Master's coming down. If it will oblige you, said I, I will read it to you.
That's good, said she, then I'll love you dearly.—Says I, then you must not
offer to alter one Word. I won't, said she; so I read it to her, and she prais'd
me much for my Wording it; but said, she thought I push'd the Matter
very close; and it would better bear talking of, than writing about. She
wanted an Explanation or two, as about the Proposal to a *certain Person*;
but I said she must take it as she heard it. Well, well, said she, I make no

doubt you understand one another, and will do so more and more. I seal'd up the Letter, and she undertook to convey it.

SUNDAY.

For my part, I knew it in vain, to expect to have Leave to go to Church now, and so I did not ask; and I was the more indifferent, because, if I might have had Permission, the Sight of the neighbouring Gentry, who had despis'd my Sufferings, would have given me great Regret and Sorrow, and it was impossible I should have edify'd under any Doctrine preached by Mr. *Peters*: So I apply'd myself to my private Devotions.

Mr. *Williams* came Yesterday, and this Day, as usual, and took my Letter; but having no good Opportunity, we avoided one another's Conversation, and kept at a Distance: But I was concern'd I had not the Key; for I would not have lost a Moment in that Case, had it been me. When I was at my Devotions, Mrs. *Jewkes* came up, and wanted me sadly to sing her a Psalm, as she had often on common Days importun'd me for a Song upon the Spinnet; but I declin'd it, because my Spirits were so low, I could hardly speak, nor car'd to be spoke to; but when she was gone, I remembering the 137th Psalm to be a little touching, turn'd to it, and took the Liberty to alter it to my Case more; I hope I did not sin in it: But thus I turn'd it.[1]

I.
When sad I sat in B———n-hall,[2]
All watched round about,
And thought of ev'ry absent Friend,
The Tears for Grief burst out.

II.
My Joys and Hopes all overthrown,
My Heart strings almost broke,
Unfit my Mind for Melody,
Much more to bear a Joke;

III.
Then she to whom I Prisoner was,
Said to me tauntingly,
Now chear your Heart, and sing a Song,
And tune your Mind to Joy.

IV.

Alas! said I, how can I frame
My heavy Heart to sing;
Or tune my Mind, while thus inthrall'd
By such a wicked Thing!

V.

But yet, if from my Innocence
I, ev'n in Thought, should slide,
Then let my Fingers quite forget
The sweet Spinnet to guide.

VI.

And let my Tongue within my Mouth
Be lock'd for ever fast,
If I rejoice, before I see
My full Deliv'rance past.

VII.

And thou, Almighty, recompence
The Evils I endure,
From those who seek my sad Disgrace,
So causeless, to procure.

VIII.

Remember, Lord, this Mrs. Jewkes,
When with a mighty Sound,
She cries, Down with her Chastity,
Down to the very Ground!

IX.

Ev'n so shalt thou, O wicked One,
At length to Shame be brought;
And happy shall all those be call'd
That my Deliv'rance wrought.

X.

Yea, blessed shall the Man be call'd
That shames thee of thy Evil,
And saves me from thy vile Attempts,
And thee, too, from the D—l.

MONDAY, TUESDAY, WEDNESDAY.

I write now with a little more Liking, tho' less Opportunity, because Mr. *Williams* has got a large Parcel of my Papers safe, in his Hands, to send them to you, as he has Opportunity; so I am not quite uselesly employ'd; and I am deliver'd, besides, from the Fear of their being found, if I should be search'd, or discover'd. I have been permitted to take an Airing five or six Miles, with Mrs. *Jewkes*: But, tho' I know not the Reason, she watches me more closely than ever; so that we have discontinued, by Consent, for these three Days, the Sun-flower Correspondence.

The poor Cook-maid has had a bad Mischance; for she has been hurt much by a Bull in the Pasture, by the Side of the Garden, not far from the Back-door. Now this Pasture I am to cross, which is about half a Mile, and then comes to a Common, and near that a private Horse-road, where I hope to find an Opportunity for escaping, as soon as Mr. *Williams* can get me a Horse, and has made all ready for me: For he has got me the Key, which he put under the Mould, just by the Door, as he found an Opportunity to hint to me.

He just now has signify'd, that the Gentleman is dead, whose Living he has had Hope of, and he came pretendedly to tell Mrs. *Jewkes* of it, and so could speak this to her, before me. She wish'd him Joy; see what the World is! one Man's Death is another Man's Joy: Thus we thrust out one another!—My hard Case makes me serious. He found means to slide a Letter into my Hands, and is gone away: He look'd at me with such Respect and Solemnness at Parting, that Mrs. *Jewkes* said, Why, Madam, I believe our young Parson is half in Love with you—Ah! Mrs. *Jewkes*, said I, he knows better. Said she, (I believe to sound me) Why I can't see you can either of you do better; and I have lately been so touch'd for you, seeing how heavily you apprehend Dishonour from my Master, that I think it is Pity you should not have Mr. *Williams*.

I knew this must be a Fetch of hers, because, instead of being troubled for me, she had watched me closer, and him too; and so I said, There is not the Man living, that I desire to marry; if I can but keep myself honest, it is all my Desire; and to be a Comfort and Assistance to my poor Parents, if it should be my happy Lot to be so, is the very Top of my Ambition. Well, but, said she, I have been thinking very seriously, that Mr. *Williams* would make you a good Husband, and as he will owe all his Fortune to my Master, he will be very glad, to be sure, to be oblig'd to him for a Wife of his chusing: Especially, said she, such a pretty one, and one so ingenious and genteelly educated.

This gave me a Doubt, whether she knew of my Master's Intimation of that sort formerly; and I asked her, if she had Reason to surmize, that that was in View? No, she said; it was only her own Thought; but it was very likely that my Master had either that in View, or something better for me. But, if I approv'd of it, she would propose such a thing to her Master directly; and gave a detestable Hint, that I might take Resolutions upon it, of bringing such an Affair to Effect. I told her, I abhorr'd her Insinuation; and as to Mr. *Williams*, I thought him a civil good sort of Man; but as on one side, he was above me; so on the other, of all Things, I did not love a Parson. So finding she could make nothing of me, she quitted the Subject.

I will open his Letter by-and-by, and give you the Contents of it; for she is up and down, so much, that I am afraid of her catching me.

Well, I see Providence has not abandon'd me. I shall be under no Necessity to make Advances to Mr. *Williams*, if I was, as I am sure I am not, dispos'd to it. This is his Letter.

'I know not how to express myself, lest I should appear to you to have a selfish View in the Service I would do you. But I really know but one effectual and honourable Way to disengage yourself, from the dangerous Situation you are in. It is that of Marriage with some Person that you could make happy in your Approbation. As for my own part, it would be, as Things stand, my apparent Ruin; and, worse still, I should involve you in Misery too. But yet, so great is my Veneration for you, and so intire my Reliance in Providence, on so just an Occasion, that I should think myself but too happy, if I might be accepted. I would, in this Case, forego all my Expectations, and be your Conductor to some safe Distance. But why do I say, *in this Case?* That I will do, whether you think fit to reward me so eminently or not. And I will, the Moment I hear of the 'Squire's setting out, (and I think now I have settled a very good Method of Intelligence of all his Motions) get the Horse ready, and myself to conduct you. I refer myself wholly to your Goodness and Direction, and am, with the highest Respect,

'Your most faithful humble Servant.

'Don't think this a sudden Resolution. I always admir'd your hear-say Character; and the Moment I saw you, wish'd to serve so much Excellence.'

What shall I say, my dear Father and Mother, to this unexpected Declaration? I want now more than ever your Blessing and Direction. But after all, I have no Mind to marry. I had rather live with you. But yet, I would marry a Man who begs from Door to Door, and has no Home nor Being, rather than indanger my Honesty. Yet, I cannot, methinks, hear of being a Wife.—After a thousand different Thoughts, I wrote as follows.

'*Reverend Sir*,

'I am much confused at the Contents of your last. You are much too generous, and I can't bear you should risque all your future Prospects for so unworthy a Creature. I cannot think of your Offer without equal Concern and Gratitude; for nothing but to avoid my utter Ruin can make me think of a Change of Condition; and so, Sir, you ought not to accept of such an involuntary Compliance, as mine would be, were I, upon the last Necessity, to yield to your very generous Proposal. I will rely wholly upon your Goodness to me, in assisting my Escape; but shall not, on your account principally, think of the Honour you propose for me, at present; and never, but at the Pleasure of my Parents, who, poor as they are, in such a weighty Point, are as much intitled to my Obedience and Duty, as if they were ever so rich. I beg you therefore, Sir, not to think of any thing from me, but everlasting Gratitude, which will always bind me to be

'*Your most obliged Servant.*'

THURSDAY, FRIDAY, SATURDAY, *the 14th, 15th and 16th of my Bondage.*

Mrs. *Jewkes* has received a Letter, and is much civiller to me, and Mr. *Williams* too, than she used to be. I wonder I have not one in Answer to mine to my Master. I suppose I press'd the Matter too home to him; and he is angry. I am not the more pleas'd for her Civility; for she is horrid cunning, and is not a bit less watchful. I laid a Trap to get at her Instructions, which she carries in the Bosom of her Stays, but it has not succeeded.

My last Letter is come safe to Mr. *Williams*, by the old Conveyance, so that is not suspected. He has intimated, that tho' I have not come so readily as he hop'd into his Scheme, yet his Diligence shall not be slacken'd, and he will leave it to Providence and myself, to dispose of him as he shall be found to deserve. He has signify'd to me, that he shall soon send a special Messenger with the Pacquet to you, and I have added to it what has occurr'd since.

SUNDAY.

I am just now quite astonish'd!—I hope all is right!—But I have a strange Turn to acquaint you with. Mr. *Williams* and Mrs. *Jewkes* came to me both together; he in Ecstacies, she with a strange fluttering sort of Air. Well, said she, Mrs. *Pamela*, I give you Joy! I give you Joy!—Let nobody speak but me! Then she sat down, as out of Breath, puffing and blowing. Why every thing turns as I said it would, said she! Why there is to be a Match between you and Mr. *Williams!* Well, I always thought it. Never was so good a Master! Go to, go to, naughty mistrustful Mrs. *Pamela*, nay, Mrs. *Williams*, said the forward Creature, I may as good as call you, you ought on your Knees to beg his Pardon a thousand times for mistrusting him.

She was going on; but I said, Don't torture me thus, I beseech you, Mrs. *Jewkes*. Let me know all!—Ah! Mr. *Williams*, said I, take care, take care!—Mistrustful again, said she! why, Mr. *Williams*, shew her your Letter; and I will shew her mine: They were brought by the same Hand.

I trembled at the Thoughts of what this might mean; and said, You have so surpriz'd me, that I cannot stand, nor hear, nor read! Why did you come up in such a manner to attack such weak Spirits? Said he, to Mrs. *Jewkes*, Shall we leave our Letters with Mrs. *Pamela*, and let her recover from her Surprize? Ay, said she, with all my Heart; here is nothing but flaming Honour and Good-will! And so saying, they left me their Letters, and withdrew.

My Heart was quite sick with the Surprize; so that I could not presently read them, notwithstanding my Impatience; but after a while, recovering, I found the Contents thus strange and wonderful.

'*Mr.* WILLIAMS,

'The Death of Mr. *Fownes* has now given me the Opportunity I have long wanted to make you happy, and that in a double respect. For I shall soon put you in Possession of his Living, and, if you have the Art of making yourself well receiv'd, of one of the loveliest Wives in *England*. She has not been used (as she has reason to think) according to her Merit; but when she finds herself under the Protection of a Man of Virtue and Probity, and a happy Competency to support Life in the manner to which she has been of late Years accustom'd, I am persuaded she will forgive those seeming Hardships which have pav'd the Way to so happy a Lot, as I hope it will be to you both. I have only to account for and excuse the odd Conduct I have been guilty of, which I shall do, when I see you: But as I shall soon set out for *London*, I believe it will not be yet this Month. Mean time, if you can prevail with *Pamela*, you need not suspend for that your mutual Happiness; only, let me have Notice of it first, and that she approves of it; which ought to be, in so material a Point, intirely at her Option, as I assure you, on the other hand, I would have it on yours, that nothing may be wanting to complete your Happiness. I am

'*Your humble Servant.*'

Was ever the like heard!—Lie still, my throbbing Heart, divided, as thou art, between thy Hopes and thy Fears!—But this is the Letter Mrs. *Jewkes* left with me.

'*Mrs.* JEWKES,

'You have been very careful and diligent in the Task, which, for Reasons I shall hereafter explain, I had impos'd upon you. Your Trouble is now almost at an End; for I have wrote my Intentions to Mr. *Williams* so particularly, that I need say the less here, because he will not scruple, I believe, to let you know the Contents of my Letter. I have only one Thing to mention, that if you find what I have hinted to him in the least measure disagreeable to either, that you assure them both that they are at intire Liberty to pursue their own Inclinations. I hope you continue your Civilities to the mistrustful, uneasy *Pamela*, who now will begin to think better of hers and

'*Your Friend,* &c.'

I had hardly time to transcribe these Letters, tho' writing so much, I write pretty fast, before they both came up again, in high Spirits; and Mr. *Williams* said, I am glad at my Heart, Madam, that I was *before-hand* in my Declarations to you: This generous Letter has made me the happiest Man on Earth; and, Mrs. *Jewkes*, you may be sure, that if I can procure this Fair-one's Consent, I shall think myself—I interrupted the good Man, and said, Ah! Mr. *Williams*, take care, take care; don't let—There I stopt, and Mrs. *Jewkes* said, Still mistrustful!—I never saw the like in my Life!—But I see, said she, I was not wrong while my old Orders lasted, to be wary of you both.—I should have had a hard Task to prevent you, I find; for, as the Saying is, *Nought can restrain Consent of Twain.*[1]

I doubted not her taking hold of his joyful Indiscretion.—I took her Letter, and said, Here, Mrs. *Jewkes*, is yours; I thank you for it; but I have been so long in a Maze, that I can say nothing of this for the present. Time will bring all to Light.—Sir, said I, here is yours: May every thing turn to your Happiness! I give you Joy of my Master's Goodness in the Living—It will be *dying*, said he, not a *Living*, without you.—Forbear, Sir, said I: While I've a Father and Mother, I am not my own Mistress, poor as they are: And I'll see myself quite at Liberty before I shall think myself fit to make a Choice.

Mrs. *Jewkes* held up her Eyes and Hands, and said, Such Art, such Caution, such Cunning for thy Years!—Well!—Why, said I, (that he might be more on his Guard, tho' I hope there cannot be Deceit in this; 'twould be strange Villainy, and that is a hard Word, if there should!) I have been so used to be made a Fool of by Fortune, that I hardly can tell how to govern myself; and am almost an Infidel as to Mankind.—But I hope, I may be wrong; henceforth, Mrs. *Jewkes*, you shall regulate my Opinions as you please, and I will consult you in every thing——(that I think proper, said I to myself)—for to be sure, tho' I may forgive her, I can never love her.

She left Mr. *Williams* and me, a few Minutes, together; and I said, Consider, Sir, consider what you have done. 'Tis impossible, said he, there can be Deceit. I hope so, said I; but what Necessity was there for you to talk of your *former* Declaration? Let this be as it will, that could do no Good, especially before this Woman. Forgive me, Sir; they talk of Womens Promptness of Speech; but indeed I see an honest Heart is not always to be trusted with itself in bad Company.

He was going to reply; but, tho' her Task is said to be ALMOST (I took Notice of that Word) at an End, she came up to us again; and said, Well, I had a good mind to shew you the way to Church to-morrow. I was glad of this, because, tho', in my present doubtful Situation, I should not have chosen it, yet I would have encourag'd her Proposal, to be able to judge by her being in Earnest or otherwise, whether one might depend upon the rest. But Mr. *Williams* again indiscreetly help'd her to an Excuse; by saying, that it was now best to defer it one *Sunday*, and till Matters were riper for my Appearance; and she readily took hold of it.

After all, I hope the best; but if this should turn out to be a Plot, I fear nothing but a Miracle can save me. But, sure the Heart of Man is not capable of such black Deceit. Besides, Mr. *Williams* has it under his own Hand, and he dare not but be in Earnest; and then again, tho' to be sure he has been very wrong to me, yet his Education, and Parents Example, have neither of them taught him such very black Contrivances. So I will hope for the best!—

Mr. *Williams*, Mrs *Jewkes* and I, have been all three walking together in the Garden; and she pull'd out her Key, and we walk'd a little in the

Pasture to look at the Bull, an ugly, grim, surly Creature, that hurt the poor Cook-maid, who is got pretty well again. Mr. *Williams* pointed at the Sun-flower, but I was forc'd to be very reserved to him; for the poor Gentleman has no Guard, no Caution at all.

We have just supp'd together, all three; and I cannot yet think but all must be right.—Only I am resolv'd not to marry, if I can help it; and I will give no Encouragement, I am resolv'd, at least, till I am with you.

Mr. *Williams* said, before Mrs. *Jewkes*, he would send a Messenger with a Letter to my Father and Mother!—I think the Man has no Discretion in the World: But I desire you will give no Answer till I have the Pleasure and Happiness, which now I hope for soon, of seeing you. He will, in sending my Pacquet, send a most tedious Parcel of Stuff, of my *Oppressions*, my *Distresses*, my *Fears*; and so I will send this with it (for Mrs. *Jewkes* gives me Leave to send a Letter to my Father, which looks well); and I am glad I can conclude, after all my Sufferings, with my *Hopes*, to be soon with you, which I know will give you Comfort; and so I rest, begging the Continuance of your Prayers, and Blessings,

Your ever dutiful Daughter.

My dear Father and Mother,

I have so much Time upon my Hands, that I must write on to employ myself. The *Sunday Evening*, where I left off, Mrs. *Jewkes* asked me, If I chose to lie by myself? I said, Yes, with all my Heart, if she pleased. Well, said she, after to-night you shall. I ask'd her for more Paper, and she gave me a little Bottle of Ink, eight Sheets of Paper, which she said was all her Store, (for now she would get me to write for her to our Master, if she had Occasion) and six Pens, with a Piece of Sealing-wax. This looks mighty well!

She press'd me, when she came to Bed, very much, to give Encouragement to Mr. *Williams*, and said many Things in his Behalf, and blam'd my Shyness to him, &c. I told her, I was resolv'd to give no Encouragement till I had talk'd to my Father and Mother. She said, she fancy'd I thought of somebody else, or I could never be so insensible. I assur'd her, as I could do very safely, that there was not a Man on Earth I wish'd to have; and, as to Mr. *Williams*, he might do better by far, and I had proposed so much Happiness in living with my poor Father and Mother, that I could not think of any Scheme of Life, with Pleasure, till I had try'd that. I ask'd her for my Money; and she said it was above in her strong Box, but that I shall have it to-morrow. All these Things look well, as I said.

Mr. *Williams* would go home this Night, tho' late, because he would dispatch a Messenger to you with a Letter he had propos'd from himself, and my Pacquet. But pray don't encourage him, as I said; for he is much too heady and precipitate as to this Matter, in my way of thinking; tho', to be sure, he is a very good Man, and I am much oblig'd to him.

MONDAY Morning.

Alas-a-day! we have bad News from poor Mr. *Williams*. He has had a sad Mischance; fallen among Rogues in his Way home last Night; but by good Chance has sav'd my Papers. This is the Account he gives of it to Mrs. *Jewkes*.

'*Good Mrs.* JEWKES,

'I have had a sore Misfortune in going from you; when I had got as near the Town as the Dam, and was going to cross the Wooden-bridge, two Fellows got hold of me, and swore bitterly they would kill me, if I did not give them what I had. They romag'd my Pockets, and took from me my Snuff-Box, my Seal-ring, and Half a Guinea, and some Silver, and Half-pence; also my Handkerchief, and two or three Letters I had in my Pocket. By good Fortune the Letter Mrs. *Pamela* gave me was in my Bosom, and so that escap'd; but they bruis'd my Head, and Face, and cursing me for having no more Money, tipt me into the Dam, Crying, Lie there, Parson, till to-morrow! My Shins and Knees were bruis'd much in the Fall against one of the Stumps; and I had like to have been suffocated in Water and Mud. To be sure, I shan't be able to stir out this Day or two. For I am a fearful Spectacle! My Hat and Wig I was forc'd to leave behind me, and go home a Mile and a Half without; but they were found next Morning, and brought me, with my Snuff-box, which the Rogues must have dropt. My Cassock is sadly torn, as is my Band.[1] To be sure, I was much frighted; for a Robbery in these Parts has not been known many Years. Diligent Search is making after the Rogues. My humblest Respects to good Mrs. *Pamela*. If she pities my Misfortunes, I shall be the sooner well, and fit to wait on her and you. This did not hinder me in writing a Letter, tho' with great Pain, as I do this;' [*To be sure this good Man can keep no Secret!*] 'and sending it away by a Man and Horse, this Morning. I am, good Mrs. *Jewkes*,

'*Your most obliged humble Servant.*

'God be prais'd it is no worse! and I find I have got no Cold, tho' miserably wet from Top to Toe. My Fright, I believe, prevented me catching Cold;

for I was not rightly myself for some Hours, and know not how I got home. I will write a Letter of Thanks this Night, if I am able, to my kind Patron for his inestimable Goodness to me. I wish I was enabled to say all I hope, with regard to the *better Part* of his Bounty to me, incomparable Mrs. *Pamela*.'

The wicked Brute fell a laughing when she had read this Letter, till her fat Sides shook; said she, I can but think how the poor Parson look'd, after parting with his pretty Mistress in such high Spirits, when he found himself at the Bottom of the Dam! And what a Figure he must cut in his tatter'd Band and Cassock, and without Hat and Wig, when he got home. I warrant, said she, he was in a sweet Pickle!¹—I said, I thought it was very barbarous to laugh at such a Misfortune: But she said, As he was safe, she laughed; otherwise she should have been sorry: And she was glad to see me so concern'd for him.—It look'd *promising*, she said.

I heeded not her Reflection; but as I have been used to Causes for Mistrusts, I cannot help saying, that I don't like this thing: And their taking his Letters most alarms me.—How happy it was, they miss'd my Pacquet! I know not what to think of it!—But why should I let every Accident break my Peace? But yet it will do so while I stay here.

Mrs. *Jewkes* is mightily at me, to go with her in the Chariot, to visit Mr. *Williams*. She is so officious to bring on the Affair between us, that being a cunning, artful Woman, I know not what to make of it: I have refused her absolutely; urging, that except I intended to encourage his Suit, I ought not to do it. And she is gone without me.

I have strange Temptations to get away in her Absence, for all these fine Appearances. 'Tis sad to have no body to advise with!—I know not what to do. But, alas for me! I have no Money, if I should, to buy any body's Civilities, or to pay for Necessaries or Lodging. But I'll go into the Garden, and resolve afterwards.—

I have been in the Garden, and to the Back-door; and there I stood, my Heart up at my Mouth.² I could not see I was watch'd; so this looks well. But if any thing should go bad afterwards, I should never forgive myself, for not taking this Opportunity. Well, I will go down again, and see if all is clear, and how it looks out at the Back-door in the Pasture.

To be sure, there is Witchcraft in this House; and I believe *Lucifer* is bribed, as well as all about me, and is got into the Shape of that nasty grim

Bull, to watch me!—For I have been down again; and ventur'd to open the Door, and went out about a Bow-shoot into the Pasture; but there stood that horrid Bull, staring me full in the Face, with fiery Saucer Eyes, as I thought. So, I got in again; for fear he should come at me. Nobody saw me, however.—Do you think there are such things as Witches and Spirits? if there be, I believe in my Heart, Mrs. *Jewkes* has got this Bull of her Side. But yet, what could I do without Money or a Friend?—O this wicked Woman! to trick me so! Every thing, Man, Woman and Beast, is in a Plot against your poor *Pamela*, I think!—Then I know not one Step of the Way, nor how far to any House or Cottage; and whether I could gain Protection, if I got to a House: And now the Robbers are abroad too, I may run into as great Danger, as I want to escape from; nay, greater much, if these promising Appearances hold: And sure my Master cannot be so black as that they should not!—What can I do?—I have a good mind to try for it once more; but then I may be pursued and taken; and it will be worse for me; and this wicked Woman will beat me, and take my Shoes away, and lock me up.

But after all, if my Master should mean *well*, he can't be angry at my Fears, if I should escape; and nobody can blame me; and I can more easily be induced with you, when all my Apprehensions are over, to consider his Proposal of Mr. *Williams*, than I could here; and he pretends he will leave me at my Choice: Why then should I be afraid? I will go down again, I think! But yet my Heart misgives me, because of the Difficulties before me, in escaping; and being so poor and so friendless!——O good God! the Preserver of the Innocent! direct me what to do!—Well, I have just now a sort of strange Persuasion upon me, that I ought to try to get away, and leave the Issue to Providence. So, once more!—I'll see, at least, if this Bull be still there!

Alack-a-day! what a Fate is this! I have not the Courage to go, neither can I think to stay. But I must resolve. The Gardener was in Sight last time! so made me come up again. But I'll contrive to send him out of the way, if I can!—For if I never should have such another Opportunity, I could not forgive myself. Once more I'll venture. God direct my Footsteps, and make smooth my Path and my Way to Safety!

Well, here I am, come back again! frighted like a Fool, out of all my Purposes! O how terrible every thing appears to me! I had got twice as far again, as I was before, out of the Back-door; and I looked, and saw the

Bull, as I thought, between me and the Door; and another Bull coming
towards me the other way: Well, thought I, here is double Witchcraft, to
be sure! Here is the Spirit of my Master in one Bull; and Mrs. *Jewkes*'s in
the other; and now I am gone, to be sure! O help! cry'd I, like a Fool, and
run back to the Door, as swift as if I flew. When I had got the Door in my
Hand, I ventur'd to look back, to see if these supposed Bulls were coming;
and I saw they were only two poor Cows, a grazing in distant Places, that
my Fears had made all this Rout about. But as every thing is so frightful
to me, I find I am not fit to think of my Escape: For I shall be as much
frighted at the first strange Man that I meet with. And I am persuaded,
that Fear brings one into more Dangers, than the Caution, that goes along
with it, delivers one from.

I then locked the Door, and put the Key in my Pocket, and was in a sad
Quandary; but I was soon determined; for the Maid *Nan* came in Sight,
and asked, If any thing was the matter, that I was so often up and down
Stairs? God forgive me; but I had a sad Lye at my Tongue's End; said I,
Tho' Mrs. *Jewkes* is sometimes a little hard upon me, yet I know not where
I am without her: I go up, and I come down to walk about in the Garden;
and not having her, know scarcely what to do with myself. Ay, said the
Idiot, she is main good Company, Madam; no wonder you miss her.

So here I am again; and here likely to be; for I have no Courage to help
myself any-where else. O why are poor foolish Maidens try'd with such
Dangers, when they have such weak Minds to grapple with them!—I will,
since it is so, hope the best: But yet I cannot but observe how grievously
every thing makes against me: For here are the Robbers; tho' I fell not into
their Hands myself, yet they gave me as much Terror, and had as great an
Effect upon my Fears, as if I had: And here is the Bull; it has as effectually
frighten'd me, as if I had been hurt by it instead of the Cook-maid; and so
they join'd together, as I may say, to make a very Dastard of me. But my
Folly was the worst of all; for that depriv'd me of my Money; for had I had
that, I believe I should have ventur'd the other Two.

MONDAY *Afternoon.*

So, Mrs. *Jewkes* is returned from her Visit: Well, said she, I would have
you set your Heart at Rest; for Mr. *Williams* will do very well again. He
is not half so badly off as he fancy'd. O these Scholars, said she, they

have not the Hearts of Mice! He has only a few Scratches on his Face; which, said she, I suppose he got by grabbling[1] among the Gravel, at the Bottom of the Dam, to try to find a Hole in the Ground, to hide himself from the Robbers. His Shin and his Knee are hardly to be seen to ail any thing. He says in his Letter, he was a frightful Spectacle: He might be so indeed, when he first came in a-doors; but he looks well enough now; and, only for a few Groans now-and-then, when he thinks of his Danger, I see nothing is the matter with him. So, Mrs. *Pamela*, said she, I would have you be very easy about it. I am glad of it, said I, for all your Jokes, Mrs. *Jewkes*.

Well, said she, he talks of nothing but you; and when I told him, I would fain have persuaded you to come with me, the Man was out of his Wits with his Gratitude to me; and so has laid open all his Heart to me, and told me all that has passed, and was contriving between you two. This alarm'd me prodigiously; and the rather, as I saw, by two or three Instances, that his honest Heart could keep nothing, believing every one as undesigning as himself. I said, but yet with a heavy Heart, Ah, Mrs. *Jewkes*, Mrs. *Jewkes*, this might have done with me, had he had any thing that he could have told you of! But you know well enough, that had we been disposed, we had no Opportunity for it, from your watchful Care and Circumspection. No, said she, that's very true, Mrs. *Pamela*; not so much as for that Declaration that he own'd before me, he had found Opportunity, for all my Watchfulness, to make you. Come, come, said she, no more of these Shams with me! You have an excellent Head-piece[2] for your Years; but may-be I am as cunning as you.—However, said she, all is well now; because my *Watchments* are now over, by my Master's Direction. How have you employ'd yourself in my Absence?

I was so troubled at what might have passed between Mr. *Williams* and her, that I could not hide it. And she said, Well, Mrs. *Pamela*, since all Matters are likely to be so soon and so happily ended, let me advise you to be a little less concern'd at his Discoveries; and make me your Confident, as *he* has done, and I shall think you have some Favour for me, and Reliance upon me; and perhaps you might not repent it.

She was so earnest, that I mistrusted she did this to pump me; and I knew how, now, to account for her Kindness to Mr. *Williams*, in her Visit to him; which was only to get out of him what she could. Why, Mrs. *Jewkes*, said I, is all this fishing about for something, where there is nothing, if there be an End of your *Watchments*, as you call them? Nothing, said she, but Womanish Curiosity, I'll assure you; for one is naturally led to find out

Matters, where there is such Privacy intended. Well, said I, pray let me know what he has said; and then I'll give you an Answer to your Curiosity. I don't care, said she, whether you do or not; for I have as much as I wanted from him; and I despair of getting out of you any thing you han't a mind I should know, my little cunning Dear.—Well, said I, let him have said what he would, I care not; for I am sure he can say no Harm of me; and so let us change the Talk.

I was the easier indeed; because, for all her Pumps, she gave no Hints of the Key and the Door, &c. which had he communicated to her, she would not have forborn giving me a Touch of.—And so we gave up one another, as despairing to gain our Ends of each other. But I am sure he must have said more than he should.—And I am the more apprehensive all is not right, because she has now been actually, these two Hours, shut up a-writing; tho' she pretended she had given me up all her Stores of Paper, &c. and that I should write for her. I begin to wish I had ventur'd every thing, and gone off, when I might. O when will this State of Doubt and Uneasiness end!

She has just been with me, and says she shall send a Messenger to *Bedfordshire*; and he shall carry a Letter of Thanks for me, if I will write it, for my Master's Favour to me. Indeed, said I, I have no Thanks to give, till I am with my Father and Mother: And besides, I sent a Letter, as you know; but have had no Answer to it. She said, she thought that his Letter was sufficient to Mr. *Williams*; and the least I could do, was to thank him, if but in two Lines. No need of it, said I; for I don't intend to have Mr. *Williams*: What then is that Letter to me?—Well, said she, I see thou art quite unfathomable!

I don't like all this. O my foolish Fears of Bulls and Robbers!—For now all my Uneasiness begins to double upon me. O what has this uncautious Man said? That, no doubt, is the Subject of her long Letter.

I will close this Day's writing, with just saying, that she is mighty silent and reserved, to what she was, and says nothing but No, or Yes, to what I ask. Something must be hatching, I doubt!—I the rather think so, because I find she does not keep her word with me, about lying by myself, and my Money; to both which Points, she return'd suspicious Answers, saying, as to the one, Why you are mighty earnest for your Money: I shan't run away with it: And to the other, Good lack! you need not be so willing, as I know of, to part with me for a Bedfellow, till you are sure of one you *like better*. This cut me to the Heart!—And at the same time stopt my Mouth.

TUESDAY, WEDNESDAY.

Mr. *Williams* has been here; but we have had no Opportunity to talk together: He seem'd confounded at Mrs. *Jewkes*'s Change of Temper, and Reservedness, after her kind Visit, and their Freedom with one another, and much more at what I am going to tell you. He asked, if I would take a Turn in the Garden with Mrs. *Jewkes* and him. No, said she, I can't go. Said he, May not Mrs. *Pamela* take a Walk?—No, said she; I desire she won't. Why, said he, Mrs. *Jewkes?* I am afraid I have some-how disobliged you. Not at all, said she; but I suppose you will soon be at Liberty to walk together as much as you please: And I have sent a Messenger for my last Instructions, about *this* and *more* weighty Matters; and when they come, I shall leave you to do as you both will; but till then, it is no matter how little you are together. This alarm'd us both; and he seem'd quite struck of a Heap, and put on, as I thought, a self-accusing Countenance. So I went behind her Back, and held my two Hands together, flat, with a Bit of Paper, I had, between them, and looked at him; and he seemed to take me, as I intended, intimating the renewing of the Correspondence by the Tiles.

So I left them both together, and retired to my Closet, to write a Letter for the Tiles; but having no Time for a Copy, I will give you the Substance only.

I expostulated with him on his too great Openness and Easiness to fall into Mrs. *Jewkes*'s Snares; told him my Apprehensions of foul Play; and gave briefly the Reasons which moved me: Begg'd to know what he had said; and intimated, that I thought there was the highest Reason to resume our Project of the Escape by the Back-door. I put this in the usual Place, in the Evening, and now wait with Impatience for an Answer.

THURSDAY.

I have the following Answer:

'*Dearest Madam,*

'I am utterly confounded, and must plead guilty to all your just Reproaches. O that I was Master of half your Caution and Discretion! I hope, after all, this is only a Touch of this ill Woman's Temper, to shew her Power and Importance: For I think Mr. *B.* neither can nor dare deceive me in so black a manner. I would expose him all the World over, if he did. But it is not, cannot be in him. I have received a Letter from *John Arnold*; in which he tells me, that the 'Squire is preparing for his *London* Journey; and believes, afterwards, he will come into these Parts. But he says, Lady *Davers* is at their House, and is to accompany her Brother to *London*, or meet him there, he knows not which. He professes great Zeal and Affection to your Service. But I find he refers to a Letter he sent me before, but which is not come to my Hand. I think there can be no Treachery; for it is a particular Friend at *Gainsborough*,[1] that I have order'd him to direct to; and this is come safe to my Hands by this means; for well I know, I durst trust nothing to *Brett*, at the Post-house here. This gives me a little Pain; but I hope all will end well, and we shall soon hear, if it be necessary to pursue our former Intentions. If it be, I will lose no Time to provide a Horse for you, and another for myself; for I can never do either God or myself better Service, tho' I were to forego all my Expectations for it here. I am

> '*Your most faithful humble Servant.*

'I was too free indeed with Mrs. *Jewkes*, led to it by her Dissimulation, and by her Concern to make me happy with you. I hinted, that I would not have scrupled to have procured your Deliverance by any means; and that I had proposed to you, as the only honourable one, Marriage with me. But I assured her, tho' she would hardly believe me, that you discouraged my Application. Which is too true! But not a Word of the Back-door, Key, *&c.*'

Mrs. *Jewkes* continues still sullen and ill-natur'd; and I am afraid, almost, to speak to her. She watches me as close as ever, and pretends to wonder why I shun her Company as I do.

I have just put under the Tiles these Lines; inspired by my Fears, which are indeed very strong; and, I doubt, not without Reason.

'*Sir*,

'Every thing gives me additional Disturbance. The miss'd Letter of *John Arnold*'s makes me suspect a Plot. Yet am I loth to think myself of so much Importance, as to suppose every one in a Plot against me. Are you sure, however, the *London* Journey is not to be a *Lincolnshire* one? May not *John*, who has been once a Traitor, be so again?—Why need I be thus in doubt?—If I could have this Horse, I would turn the Reins on his Neck, and trust to Providence to guide him for my Safeguard! For I would not indanger you, now just upon the Edge of your Preferment. Yet, Sir, I fear your fatal Openness will make you suspected as accessary, let us be ever so cautious.

'Were my Life in question, instead of my Honesty, I would not wish to involve you, or any body, in the least Difficulty for so worthless a poor Creature. But, O Sir! my Soul is of equal Importance with the Soul of a Princess; though my Quality is inferior to that of the meanest Slave.[1]

'Save then, my Innocence, good God, and preserve my Mind spotless; and happy shall I be to lay down my worthless Life, and see an End to all my Troubles and Anxieties!

'Forgive my Impatience: But my presaging Mind bodes horrid Mischiefs!—Every thing looks dark around me; and this Woman's impenetrable Sullenness and Silence, without any apparent Reason, from a Conduct so very contrary, bids me fear the worst.—Blame me, Sir, if you think me wrong; and let me have your Advice what to do: which will oblige

'Your most afflicted Servant.'

FRIDAY.

I have this half-angry Answer; but, what is more to me than all the Letters in the World could be, yours, my dear Father, inclosed.

'Madam,

'I think you are too apprehensive by much. I am sorry for your Uneasiness. You may depend upon me, and all I can do. But I make no doubt of the *London* Journey, nor of *John*'s Contrition and Fidelity. I have just received, from my *Gainsborough* Friend, this Letter, as I suppose, from your good Father, in a Cover, as directed for me, as I had desired. I hope it contains nothing to add to your Uneasiness. Pray, dearest Madam, lay aside your Fears, and wait a few Days for the Issue of Mrs. *Jewkes*'s Letter, and mine of Thanks to the 'Squire. Things, I hope, must be better than you expect. God Almighty will not desert such Piety and Innocence; and be this your Comfort and Reliance. Which is the best Advice that can at present be given, by

'Your most faithful humble Servant.'

N. B. The Father's Letter was as follows:

'My dearest Daughter,

'God has at length heard our Prayers, and we are overwhelmed with his Goodness. O what Sufferings, what Trials hast thou gone thro'! and, blessed be God, who enabled thee, what Temptations hast thou withstood! We have not yet had Leisure to read thro' your long Accounts of all your

Hardships. I say *long*, because I wonder how you could find Time and Opportunity for them; but otherwise, they are the Delight of our spare Hours; and we shall read them over and over, as long as we live, with Thankfulness to God, who has given us so virtuous and so discreet a Daughter. How happy is our Lot, in the midst of our Poverty! O let none ever think Children a Burden to them; when the poorest Circumstances can produce so much Riches in a *Pamela!* Persist, my dear Daughter, in the same excellent Course; and we shall not envy the highest Estate, but defy them to produce such a Daughter as ours.

'I said, we had not read thro' all yours in Course. We were too impatient, and so turn'd to the End; where we find your Virtue within View of its Reward, and your Master's Heart turn'd to see the Folly of his Ways, and the Injury he had intended to our dear Child. For, to be sure, my Dear, he would have ruin'd you, if he could. But seeing your Virtue, God has touched his Heart; and he has, no doubt, been edified by your good Example.

'We don't see that you can do any way so well, as to come into the present Proposal, and make Mr. *Williams*, the worthy Mr. *Williams*, God bless him!—happy. And tho' we are poor, and can add no Merit, no Reputation, no Fortune to our dear Child, but rather must be a Disgrace to her, as the World will think; yet I hope I do not sin in my Pride, to say, that there is no good Man, of a common Degree (especially as your late Lady's Kindness gave you such good Opportunities, which, by God's Grace, you have so well improv'd) but may think himself happy in you. But, as you say, you had rather *not* marry at present, far be it from us to offer Violence to your Inclinations. So much Prudence as you have shewn in all your Conduct, would make it very wrong in us to mistrust it in this, or to offer to direct you in your Choice. But, alas! my Child, what can we do for you?—To partake our hard Lot, and involve yourself into as hard a Life, would not help us; but add to our Afflictions. But it is time enough to talk of these things, when we have the Pleasure you now put us in Hope of, of seeing you with us; which God grant. *Amen, Amen*, say

'Your most indulgent Parents, Amen!

'Our humblest Service and Thanks to the worthy Mr. *Williams*. Again, we say, God bless him for ever!

'O what a deal have we to say to you! God give us a happy Meeting! We understand the 'Squire is setting out for *London*. He is a fine Gentleman, and has Wit at Will. I wish he was as good. But I hope he will now reform.'

O what inexpressible Comfort, my dear Father, has your Letter given me. You ask, What can you do for me!—What is it you cannot do for your

Child!—You can give her the Advice she has so much wanted, and still wants, and will always want; you can confirm her in the Paths of Virtue, into which you first initiated her; and you can pray for her, with Hearts so sincere and pure, that are not to be met with in Palaces!—Oh! how I long to throw myself at your Feet, and receive, from your own Lips, the Blessings of such good Parents!—But, alas! how are my Prospects again over-clouded to what they were when I closed my last Parcel!—More Trials, more Dangers, I fear, must your poor *Pamela* be engaged in: But thro' God's Goodness, and your Prayers, I hope, at last, to get well out of all my Difficulties; and the rather, as they are not the Effect of my own Vanity or Presumption!

But I will proceed with my hopeless Story. I saw Mr. *Williams* was a little nettled at my Impatience; and so I wrote to assure him I would be as easy as I could, and directed by him; especially as my Father, whose Respects I mentioned, had assured me, my Master was setting out for *London*; which he must have some-how from his own Family, or he would not have written me word of it.

SATURDAY, SUNDAY.

Mr. *Williams* has been here both these Days, as usual; but is very indifferently received still by Mrs. *Jewkes*; and, to avoid Suspicion, I left them together, and went up to my Closet, most of the Time he was here. He and she, I found by her, had a Quarrel; and she seems quite out of Humour with him; but I thought it best not to say any thing. And he said, he would very little trouble the House, till he had an Answer to his Letter from the 'Squire. And she return'd, The less, the better. Poor Man! he has got but little by his Openness, and making Mrs. *Jewkes* his Confident, as she bragged, and would have had me to do likewise. I am more and more satisfied there is Mischief brewing, and shall begin to hide my Papers, and be circumspect. She seems mighty impatient for an Answer to her Letter to my Master.

MONDAY, TUESDAY, the 25th and 26th Days of my heavy Restraint.

Still more and more strange things to write. A Messenger is return'd, and now all is out! O wretched, wretched *Pamela!* What, at last, will become of me!—Such strange Turns and Trials sure never poor Creature of my Years, experienced. He brought two Letters, one to Mrs. *Jewkes*, and one to me: But as the greatest Wits may be sometimes mistaken, they being folded and sealed alike, that for me, was directed to Mrs. *Jewkes*; and that for her, was directed to me. But both are stark naught, abominably bad! She brought me up that directed for me, and said, Here's a Letter for you: Long look'd-for is come at last. I will ask the Messenger a few Questions, and then I will read mine. So she went down, and I broke it open in my Closet, and found it directed, *To Mrs.* PAMELA ANDREWS. But when I open'd it, it began, Mrs. *Jewkes*. I was quite confounded; but, thinks I, this may be a lucky Mistake; I may discover something. And so I read on these horrid Contents:

'*Mrs.* JEWKES,

'What you write me, has given me no small Disturbance. This wretched *Fool's Plaything*,[1] no doubt, is ready to leap at any thing that offers, rather than express the least Sense of Gratitude for all the Benefits she has received from my Family, and which I was determined more and more to heap upon her. I reserve her for my future Resentment; and I charge you double your Diligence in watching her, to prevent her Escape. I send this by an honest *Swiss*, who attended me in my Travels; a Man I can trust; and so let him be your Assistant: For the *artful Creature* is enough to corrupt a Nation by her seeming Innocence and Simplicity; and she may have got a Party, perhaps, among my Servants with you, as she has here. Even *John Arnold*, whom I confided in, and favour'd more than any, has proved an execrable Villain; and shall meet his Reward for it.

'As to that *College Novice Williams*, I need not bid you take care he sees not this *painted Bauble*; for I have order'd Mr. *Shorter*, my Attorney, to throw him instantly into Gaol, on an Action of Debt,[2] for Money he has had of me, which I had intended never to carry to account against him; for I know all his rascally Practices; besides what you write me of his perfidious Intrigue with that Girl, and his acknowledged Contrivances for her Escape; when he knew not, for certain, that I design'd her any Mischief; and when, if he had been guided by a Sense of Piety, or Compassion for injured Innocence, as he pretends, he would have expostulated with me, as his Function, and my Friendship for him, might have allow'd him. But to enter into a vile Intrigue! charm'd, like a godly Sensualist, with the *amiable Gewgaw!*[3] to favour her Escape in so base a manner, (to say nothing of his disgraceful Practices against me, in Sir *Simon Darnford*'s Family; of which Sir *Simon* himself has inform'd me) is a Conduct that, instead of preferring the ingrateful Wretch, as I had intended, shall pull down upon him utter Ruin.

'Monsieur *Colbrand*,[1] my trusty *Swiss*, will obey you without Reserve, if my other Servants refuse.

'As for her denying that she encouraged his Declaration, I believe it not. 'Tis certain the *speaking Picture*,[2] with all that pretended Innocence and Softness of Heart, would have run away with him. Yes, she would have run away with a Fellow that she had been acquainted with (and that not intimately, if you was as careful as you ought to be) but few Days; at a time, when she had the strongest Assurances of my Honour to her.

'Well, I think I now *hate her* perfectly; and tho' I will do nothing to her *myself*, yet I can bear, for the sake of my Revenge, and my *injur'd Honour*, and *slighted Love*, to see any thing, even what *she most fears*, be *done to her*; and then she may be turned loose to her evil Destiny, and echo to the Woods and Groves her piteous Lamentations for the Loss of her fantastical Innocence,[3] which the romantick Idiot makes such a work about. I shall go to *London*, with my Sister *Davers*; and the Moment I can disengage myself, which perhaps may be in three Weeks from this time, I will be with you, and decide *her Fate*, and put an End to your Trouble. Mean time, be doubly careful; for this Innocent, as I have warn'd you, is full of Contrivances. I am

'Your Friend.'

I had but just read this dreadful Letter thro', when Mrs. *Jewkes* came up, in a great Fright, guessing at the Mistake, and that I had her Letter; and she found me with it open in my Hand, just sinking away. What Business, said she, had you to read my Letter? and snatch'd it from me. You see, said she, looking upon it, it says, *Mrs. Jewkes*, at top: You ought, in Manners, to have read no further. O add not, said I, to my Afflictions! I shall be soon out of all your ways! This is too much! too much! I never can support this!—and threw myself upon the Couch, in my Closet, and wept most bitterly. She read it in the next Room, and came in again afterwards; Why this, said she, is a sad Letter indeed! I am sorry for it: But I fear'd you would carry your Niceties too far!—Leave me, dear Mrs. *Jewkes*, said I, for a-while: I cannot speak nor talk!—Poor Heart! said she; well, I'll come up again presently, and hope to find you better. But here, take your own Letter; I wish you well; but this is a sad Mistake! And so she laid down by me, that that was intended for me. But I had no Spirit to read it presently. O Man! Man! hard-hearted, cruel Man! what Mischiefs art thou not capable of, unrelenting Persecutor as thou art!

I sat ruminating, when I had a little come to myself, upon the Terms of this wicked Letter; and had no Inclination to look into my own. The bad Names, *Fool's Plaything, artful Creature, painted Bauble, Gewgaw, speaking Picture*, are hard things for your poor *Pamela*; and I began to think, whether I was not indeed a very naughty Body, and had not done vile Things: But when I thought of his having discover'd poor *John*, and of Sir *Simon's* base Officiousness, in telling him of poor Mr. *Williams*, with what he had resolved against him, in Revenge for his Goodness to me, I was quite mortified; and yet still more, about that fearful *Colbrand*, and what he could *see done to me*; for then I was ready to gasp for Breath, and my Spirits quite failed me. Then how dreadful are the Words, that he will *decide my Fate* in three Weeks! Gracious Heaven, said I, strike me dead before that time, with a Thunderbolt, or provide some way for my escaping these threaten'd Mischiefs! God forgive me if I sinned.

At last, I took up the Letter directed for Mrs. *Jewkes*, but designed for me; and I find *that* little better than the other. These are the hard Terms it contains:

'Well have you done, perverse, forward, artful, yet foolish *Pamela*, to convince me, before it was too late, how ill I had done to place my Affections on so unworthy an Object. I had vow'd Honour and Love to your Unworthiness, believing you a Mirror of bashful Modesty, and unspotted Innocence; and that no perfidious Designs lurked in so fair a Bosom. But now I have found you out, you specious Hypocrite! and see, that tho' you could not repose the least Confidence in one you had known for Years, and who, under my good Mother's misplaced Favour for you, had grown up, in a manner, with you; when my Passion, in spite of my Pride, and the Difference of our Condition, made me stoop to a Meanness that now I despise myself for; yet you could enter into an Intrigue with a Man you never knew, till within these few Days past, and resolve to run away with a Stranger, whom your fair Face, and insinuating Arts, had bewitched to break thro' all the Ties of Honour and Gratitude to me, even at a Time when the Happiness of his future Life depended upon my Favour.

'Henceforth, for *Pamela's* sake, whenever I see a lovely Face, will I mistrust a deceitful Heart: And whenever I hear of the greatest Pretences to Innocence, will I suspect some deep-laid Mischief. You were determin'd to place no Confidence in me, tho' I have solemnly, over and over, engaged my Honour to you. What, tho' I had alarm'd your Fears, in sending you one way, when you hoped to go another; yet, had I not, to convince you of my Resolution to do justly by you, (altho' with infinite Reluctance, such then was my Love for you) engaged not to come near you without your own Consent? Was not this a voluntary Demonstration of the Generosity of my Intentions to you? Yet how have you requited me? The very first Fellow that your charming Face, and insinuating Address, could influence, you have practis'd upon, corrupted too, I may say, (and even ruin'd, as the ingrateful Wretch shall find) and thrown your *forward* Self upon him. As therefore you would place no Confidence in me, my Honour owes you nothing; and in a little time you shall find how much you have err'd in treating, as you have done, a Man, who was once

'Your affectionate and kind Friend.

'Mrs. *Jewkes* has Directions concerning you; and if your Lot is now harder than you might wish, you will bear it the easier, because your own rash Folly has brought it upon you.'

Alas! for me, what a Fate is mine, to be thus thought artful and forward, and ingrateful! when all I intended, was to preserve my Innocence; and when all the poor little Shifts, which his superior wicked Wit and Cunning have render'd ineffectual, were forced upon me in my own necessary Defence!

Mrs. *Jewkes* came up to me again, and found me bathed in Tears. She seemed, as I thought, to be moved to some Compassion; and finding myself now intirely in her Power, and that it is not for me to provoke her, I said, It is now, I see, in vain for me to contend against my evil Destiny, and the superior Arts of my barbarous Master. I will resign myself to God's Will, and prepare to expect the worst. But you see how this poor Mr. *Williams* is drawn in and undone; I am sorry I am made the Cause of *his* Ruin:—Poor, poor Man!—to be taken in thus, and for my sake too!—But, if you'll believe me, said I, I gave no Encouragement to what he proposed, as to Marriage; nor would he have proposed it, I believe, but as the only honourable way he thought was left to save me: And his principal Motive to it all, was Virtue and Compassion to one in Distress. What other View could he have? You know I am poor and friendless. All I beg of you, is to let the poor Gentleman have Notice of my Master's Resentment; and let him flee the Country, and not be thrown into Gaol: This will answer my Master's End as well; for it will as effectually hinder him from assisting me, as if he was in a Prison.

Ask me, said she, to do any thing that is in my Power, consistent with my Duty and Trust, and I will do it; for I am sorry for you both. But, to be sure, I shall keep no Correspondence with him, nor let you. I offer'd to talk of a Duty superior to that she talked of, which would oblige her to help distressed Innocence, and not permit her to go the Lengths injoin'd by lawless Tyranny;[1] but she plainly bid me be silent on that Head; for it was in vain to attempt to persuade her to betray her Trust.—All I have to advise you, said she, is to be easy; lay aside all your Contrivances and Arts to get away; and make me your Friend, by giving me no Reason to suspect you; for, said she, I glory in my Fidelity to my Master: And you have both practised some strange sly Arts, to make such a Progress as he has own'd there was between you, so seldom as, I thought, you saw one another; that I must be more circumspect than I have been.

This doubled my Concern; for I now apprehended I should be much closer watch'd than before.

Well, said I, since I have, by this strange Accident, discover'd my hard Destiny, let me read over again that fearful Letter of yours, that I may get it by heart, and feed my Distress upon it; for now I have nothing else to think of, and must familiarize myself to Calamity. Then, said she, let me read yours again. I gave her mine, and she lent me hers; and so I took a Copy of it, with her Leave; because, as I said, I would, by it, prepare myself for the worst. And when I had done, I pinn'd it on the Head of the Couch: This, said I, is the Use I shall make of this wretched Copy of your Letter; and here you shall always find it wet with my Tears.

She said, She would go down to order Supper, and insisted upon my Company to it: I would have excused myself; but she begun to put on a commanding Air, that I durst not oppose. And when I went down, she took me by the Hand, and presented me to the most hideous Monster I ever saw in my Life. Here, Monsieur *Colbrand*, said she, here is your pretty Ward and mine; let us try to make her Time with us easy. He bow'd, and put on his foreign Grimaces, and seem'd to bless himself! and, in broken *English*, told me, I was happy in de Affections of de vinest Gentleman in de Varld!—I was quite frighten'd, and ready to drop down; and I will describe him to you, my dear Father and Mother, if now you will ever see this; and you shall judge if I had not Reason, especially not knowing he was to be there, and being appriz'd, as I was, of his hated Employment, to watch me closer.

He is a Giant of a Man, for Stature; taller by a good deal, than *Harry Mawlidge*, in your Neighbourhood, and large-bon'd, and scraggy; and a Hand!—I never saw such an one in my Life. He has great staring Eyes, like the Bull's that frighten'd me so. Vast Jaw-bones sticking out; Eyebrows hanging over his Eyes; two great Scars upon his Forehead, and one on his left Cheek; and two huge Whiskers, and a monstrous wide Mouth; blubber Lips; long yellow Teeth, and a hideous Grin. He wears his own frightful long Hair, ty'd up in a great black Bag;[1] a black Crape Neckcloth, about a long ugly Neck; and his Throat sticking out like a Wen. As to the rest, he was drest well enough, and had a Sword on, with a nasty red Knot to it; Leather Garters, buckled below his Knees; and a Foot—near as long as my Arm, I verily think.

He said, He fright de Lady, and offer'd to withdraw; but she bid him not; and I told Mrs. *Jewkes*, That as she knew I had been crying, she should not have called me to the Gentleman without letting me know he was there. I soon went up to my Closet; for my Heart aked all the time I was at Table; not being able to look upon him without Horror, and this Brute of a Woman, tho' she saw my Distress, before this Addition to it, no doubt did it on purpose to strike me more into Terror. And indeed it had its Effect; for when I went to-bed, I could think of nothing but his hideous Person, and my Master's more hideous Actions; and thought them too well pair'd; and when I dropt asleep, I dream'd they were both coming to my Bed-side, with the worst Designs; and I jump'd out of Bed in my Sleep, and frighted Mrs. *Jewkes*; till, waking with the Terror, I told her my Dream: And the wicked Creature only laughed, and said, All I fear'd was but a Dream, as well as that; and when it was over, and I was well awake, I should laugh at it as such!

And now I am come to the Close of WEDNESDAY, *the 27th Day of my Distress.*

Poor Mr. *Williams* is actually arrested, and carried away to *Stamford*.[2] So there is an End of all my Hopes in him. Poor Gentleman! his Over-security and Openness, have ruin'd us both! I was but too well convinced, that we ought not to have lost a Moment's time; but he was half angry, and thought me too impatient; and then his fatal Confessions, and the detestable Artifice of my Master!—But one might well think, that he who had so cunningly, and so wickedly, contrived all his Stratagems hitherto, that it was impossible to avoid them, would stick at nothing to complete them. I fear I shall soon find it so!

But one Stratagem I have just invented, tho' a very discouraging one to think of; because I have neither Friends nor Money, nor know one Step of the Way, if I was out of the House. But let Bulls, and Bears, and Lions, and Tygers,[3] and, what is worse, false, treacherous, deceitful Men, stand in my Way, I cannot be in more Danger than I am; and I depend nothing upon his three Weeks: For how do I know, now he is in such a Passion, and has already begun his Vengeance on poor Mr. *Williams*, that he will not change his Mind, and come down to *Lincolnshire* before he goes to *London?*

My Stratagem is this; I will endeavour to get Mrs. *Jewkes* to-bed without me, as she often does, while I sit lock'd up in my Closet; and as she sleeps very sound in her first Sleep, of which she never fails to give Notice by snoring, if I can then but get out between the two Bars of the Window, (for you know, I am very slender, and I find I can get my Head thro') then I can drop upon the Leads[1] underneath, which are little more than my Height, and which Leads are over a little Summer-parlour, that juts out towards the Garden, and which, as I am light, I can easily drop from; for they are not high from the Ground: Then I shall get into the Garden; and then, as I have the Key of the Back-door, I will get out. But I have another Piece of Cunning still; good Heaven, succeed to me my dangerous, but innocent Devices!—I have read of a great Captain,[2] who being in Danger, leaped over-board, into the Sea; and his Enemies shooting at him with Bows and Arrows, he got off his upper Garment, and swam away, while they stuck that full of their Darts and Arrows; and he escaped, and triumphed over them all. So what will I do, but strip off my upper Petticoat, and throw it into the Pond, with my Neck-handkerchief; for, to be sure, when they miss me, they will go to the Pond first, thinking I have drowned myself; and so, when they see some of my Cloaths floating there, they will be all employ'd in dragging the Pond, which is a very large one; and as I shall not, perhaps, be miss'd till the Morning, this will give me Opportunity to get a great way off; and I am sure I will run for it when I am out. And so, I trust, that God will direct my Steps to some good Place of Safety, and make some worthy Body my Friend; for sure, if I suffer ever so, I cannot be in more Danger, nor in worse Hands, than where I am; and with such avow'd bad Designs.

O my dear Parents! don't be frighted when you come to read this!—But all will be over before you can see it; and so God direct me for the best. My Writings, for fear I should not escape, I will bury in the Garden; for, to be sure, I shall be search'd, and used dreadfully, if I can't get off. And so I will close here, for the present, to prepare for my Plot. Prosper thou, O gracious Protector of oppressed Innocence! this last Effort of thy poor Handmaid! that I may escape the crafty Devices and Snares that have already begun to entangle my Virtue! and from which, but by this one Trial, I see no way of escaping! And Oh! whatever becomes of me, bless my dear Parents, and protect poor Mr. *Williams* from Ruin! for he was happy before he knew me!

Just now, just now! I heard Mrs. *Jewkes*, who is in her Cups, own, to the horrid *Colbrand*, that the robbing of poor Mr. *Williams*, was a Contrivance of hers, and executed by the Groom and a Helper, in order to seize my Letters upon him, which they miss'd. They are now both laughing at the dismal Story, which they little think I heard—O how my Heart akes! for what are not such Wretches capable of! Can you blame me for endeavouring, thro' any Danger, to get out of such Clutches?

Past Eleven o'Clock.

Mrs. *Jewkes* is come up, and gone to-bed; and bids me not stay long in my Closet, but come to-bed. O for a dead Sleep for the treacherous Brute! I never saw her so tipsy, and that gives me Hopes. I have try'd again, and find I can get my Head thro' the Iron Bars. I am now all prepared, as soon as I hear her fast;[1] and now I'll seal up these and my other Papers, my last Work: And to thy Providence, O my gracious God, commit the rest!—Once more, God bless you both! and send us a happy Meeting; if not here, in his heavenly Kingdom. *Amen.*

THURSDAY, FRIDAY, SATURDAY, SUNDAY, the 28th, 29th, 30th, and 31st Days of my Distress.

And Distress indeed! For here I am still! And every thing has been worse and worse! Oh! the poor unhappy *Pamela!*—Without any Resource left, and ruin'd in all my Contrivances. But, Oh! my dear Parents, rejoice with me, even in this low Plunge of my Distress; for your poor *Pamela* has escap'd from an Enemy worse than any she ever met with; an Enemy she never thought of before; and was hardly able to stand against. I mean, the Weakness and Presumption, both in one, of her own Mind! which had well nigh, had not divine Grace interposed, sunk her into the lowest last Abyss of Misery and Perdition! I will proceed, as I have Opportunity, with my sad Relation: For my Pen and Ink (in my now doubly secur'd Closet) is all that I have, besides my own Weakness of Body, to employ myself with: And, till yesterday Evening, I have not been able to hold a Pen.

I took with me but one Shift, besides what I had on, and two Hand-kerchiefs, and two Caps, which my Pocket held, (for it was not for me to incumber myself) and all my Stock of Money, which was but five or six

Shillings, to set out for I knew not where; and got out of the Window, not without some Difficulty, sticking a little at my Shoulders and Hips; but I was resolv'd to get out, if possible. And it was further from the Leads than I thought, and I was afraid I had sprain'd my Ancle; and when I had dropt from the Leads to the Ground, it was still further off; but I did pretty well there; at least, I got no Hurt to hinder me from pursuing my Intentions: So being now on the Ground, I hid my Papers under a Rose-bush, and cover'd them over with Mould, and there they still lie, as I hope. Then I hy'd away to the Pond: The Clock struck Twelve, just as I got out; and it was a dark misty Night, and coldish; but I felt none then.

When I came to the Pond-side, I flung in my Upper-coat, as I had design'd, and my Neck-handkerchief, and a round-ear'd Cap, with a Knot; and then with great Speed ran to the Door, and took the Key out of my Pocket, my poor Heart beating all the Time against my Bosom, as if it would have forc'd its way out: And beat it well might! For I then, too late, found, that I was most miserably disappointed; for the wicked Woman had taken off that Lock, and put another on; so that my Key would not open it. I try'd and try'd, and feeling about, I found a Padlock besides, on another Part of the Door. O then how my Heart sunk!—I dropt down with Grief and Confusion, unable to stir or support myself for a while. But my Fears awakening my Resolution, and knowing that my Attempt would be as terrible for me, as any other Danger I could then encounter, I clamber'd up upon the Ledges of the Door, and the Lock, which was a great wooden one, reaching the Top of the Door with my Hands; and little thinking I could climb so well, made shift to lay hold on the Top of the Wall with my Hands; but, alas for me! nothing but ill Luck!—no Escape for poor *Pamela!* The Wall being old, the Bricks I held by, gave way, just as I was taking a Spring to get up, and down came I, and received such a Blow upon my Head, with one of the Bricks, that it quite stunn'd me; and I broke[1] my Shins and my Ancle besides, and beat off the Heel of one of my Shoes.

In this dreadful way, flat upon the Ground, lay poor I, for I believe five or six Minutes; and when I would have got up, I could hardly stand; for I found I had bruis'd my left Hip and Shoulder, and was full of Pain with it; and besides my Head bled, and ak'd with the Blow I had with the Brick.—Yet this I valued not! but crawl'd a good way, upon my Feet and Hands, in Search of a Ladder, I just recollected to have seen against the Wall two Days before, on which the Gardener was nailing a Nectarine Branch, that was blown off from the Wall: But no Ladder could I find, and the Wall was very high. What now, thinks I, must become of the poor miserable *Pamela!*—Then I began to wish myself most heartily again in my Closet, and to repent of my Attempt, which I now censur'd as rash, because it did not succeed.

God forgive me! but a sad Thought came just then into my Head!—I tremble to think of it! Indeed my Apprehensions of the Usage I should meet with, had like to have made me miserable for ever! O my dear, dear Parents, forgive your poor Child; but being then quite desperate, I crept along till I could get up on my Feet, tho' I could hardly stand; and away limp'd I!—What to do, but to throw myself into the Pond, and so put a Period to all my Griefs in this World!—But, Oh! to find them infinitely aggravated (had I not, by God's Grace, been with-held) in a miserable *Eternity!* As I have escap'd this Temptation, (blessed be God for it!) I will tell you my Conflicts on this dreadful Occasion, that God's Mercies may be magnify'd in my Deliverance, that I am yet on this Side the dreadful Gulph, from which there can be no Redemption.

It was well for me, as I have since thought, that I was so maim'd, as made me the longer before I got to the Water; for this gave me some Reflection, and abated that Liveliness of my Passions, which possibly might otherwise have hurry'd me, in my first Transport of Grief, (on my seeing no way to escape, and the hard Usage I had Reason to expect from my dreadful Keepers) to throw myself in without Consideration; but my Weakness of Body made me move so slowly, that it gave Time for a little Reflection, a Ray of Grace, to dart in upon my benighted Mind; and so, when I came to the Pond-side, I sat myself down on the sloping Bank, and began to ponder my wretched Condition: And thus I reason'd with myself.

Pause here a little, *Pamela,* on what thou art about, before thou takest the dreadful Leap; and consider whether there be no Way yet left, no Hope, if not to escape from this wicked House, yet from the Mischiefs threatened thee in it.

I then consider'd, and after I had cast about in my Mind, every thing that could make me hope, and saw no Probability; a wicked Woman devoid of all Compassion! a horrid Helper just arriv'd in this dreadful *Colbrand!* an angry and resenting Master, who now hated me, and threaten'd the most afflicting Evils! and, that I should, in all Probability, be depriv'd even of the Opportunity I now had before me, to free myself from all their Persecutions—What hast thou to do, distressed Creature, said I to myself, but throw thyself upon a merciful God, (who knows how innocently I suffer) to avoid the merciless Wickedness of those who are determin'd on my Ruin?

And then thought I, (and Oh! that Thought was surely of the Devil's Instigation; for it was very soothing and powerful with me) these wicked Wretches, who now have no Remorse, no Pity on me, will then be mov'd to lament their Misdoings; and when they see the dead Corpse of the unhappy *Pamela* dragg'd out to these slopy Banks, and lying breathless at their Feet, they will find that Remorse to wring their obdurate Hearts, which now has no Place there!—And my Master, my angry Master, will then forget his Resentments, and say, O this is the unhappy *Pamela!* that I have so causelesly persecuted and destroy'd! Now do I see she preferr'd her Honesty to her Life, will he say, and is no Hypocrite, nor Deceiver; but really was the innocent Creature she pretended to be! Then, thinks I, will he, perhaps, shed a few Tears over the poor Corse of his perse-cuted Servant; and, tho' he may give out, it was Love and Disappoint-ment, and that too, (in order to hide his own Guilt) for the unfortunate Mr. *Williams*, perhaps, yet will he be inwardly griev'd, and order me a decent Funeral, and save me, or rather this Part of me, from the dreadful Stake, and the Highway Interrment;[1] and the young Men and Maid-ens all around my dear Father's, will pity poor *Pamela*; but O! I hope I shall not be the Subject of their Ballads and Elegies; but that my Mem-ory, for the sake of my dear Father and Mother, may quickly slide into Oblivion!

I was once rising, so indulgent was I to this sad way of thinking, to throw myself in: But again, my Bruises made me slow; and I thought, What art thou about to do, wretched *Pamela?* how knowest thou, tho' the Prospect be all dark to thy short-sighted Eye, what God may do for thee, even when all human Means fail? God Almighty would not lay me under these sore Afflictions, if he had not given me Strength to grapple with them, if I will exert it as I ought: And who knows, but that the very Presence I so much dread, of my angry and designing Master, (for he has had me in his Power before, and yet I have escap'd) may be better for me, than these persecuting Emissaries of his, who, for his Money, are true to their wicked Trust, and are harden'd by that, and a long Habit of Wickedness, against Compunction of Heart? God can touch his Heart in an Instant; and if this should not be done, I can then but put an End to my Life, by some other Means, if I am so resolved.

But how do I know, thought I, that even these Bruises and Maims that I have gotten, while I pursu'd only the laudable Escape I had meditated, may not kindly furnish me with the Opportunity I now am tempted to precipitate myself upon, and of surrendering up my Life, spotless and unguilty, to that merciful Being who gave it!

Then, thought I, who gave thee, presumptuous as thou art, a Power over thy Life? Who authoriz'd thee to put an End to it, when the Weakness of thy Mind suggests not to thee a Way to preserve it with Honour? How knowest thou what Purposes God may have to serve, by the Trials with which thou art now tempted? Art *thou* to put a Bound to God's Will, and to say, Thus much will I bear, and no more? And, wilt thou *dare* to say, that if the Trial be augmented, and continued, thou wilt sooner die than bear it?

This Act of Despondency, thought I, is a Sin, that, if I pursue it, admits of no Repentance, and can therefore claim no Forgiveness.[1]—And wilt thou, for shortening thy transitory Griefs, *heavy* as they are, and *weak* as thou fanciest thyself, plunge both Body and Soul into everlasting Misery? Hitherto, *Pamela*, thought I, thou art the innocent, the suffering *Pamela*; and wilt thou be the guilty Aggressor? and, because wicked Men persecute thee, wilt thou fly in the Face of the Almighty, and bid Defiance to his Grace and Goodness, who can still turn all these Sufferings to thy Benefits? And how do I know, but that God, who sees all the lurking Vileness of my Heart, may not have permitted these Sufferings on that very Score, and to make me rely solely on his Grace and Assistance, who perhaps have too much prided myself in a vain Dependence on my own foolish Contrivances? Then again, thought I, wilt thou suffer in *one* Moment all the good Lessons of thy poor honest Parents, and the Benefit of their Example, (who have persisted in doing their Duty with Resignation to the Divine Will, amidst the extremest Degrees of Disappointment, Poverty and Distress, and the Persecutions of an ingrateful World, and merciless Creditors) to be thrown away upon thee; and bring down, as in all Probability this thy Rashness will, their grey Hairs with Sorrow to the Grave, when they shall understand that their beloved Daughter, slighting the Tenders of Divine Grace, desponding in the Mercies of a gracious God, has blemish'd, in this *last Act*, a *whole* Life, which they had hitherto approv'd and delighted in?

What then, presumptuous *Pamela*, dost thou here, thought I? Quit with Speed these guilty Banks, and flee from these dashing Waters, that even in their sounding Murmurs, this still Night, reproach thy Rashness! Tempt not God's Goodness on the mossy Banks, that have been Witnesses of thy guilty Intentions; and while thou hast Power left thee, avoid the tempting Evil, lest thy grand Enemy, now repuls'd by Divine Grace, and due Reflection, return to the Charge with a Force that thy Weakness may not be able to resist! And lest one rash Moment destroy all the Convictions, which now have aw'd thy rebellious Mind into Duty and Resignation to the Divine Will!

And so saying, I arose; but was so stiff with my Hurts, so cold with the moist Dew of the Night, and the wet Banks on which I had sat, as also the Damps arising from so large a Piece of Water, that with great Pain I got from the Banks of this Pond, which now I think of with Terror; and bending my limping Steps towards the House, refug'd myself in the Corner of an Out-house, where Wood and Coals are laid up for Family Use, till I should be found by my cruel Keepers, and consign'd to a wretched Confinement, and worse Usage than I had hitherto experienc'd; and there behind a Pile of Fire-wood I crept, and lay down, as you may imagine, with a Mind just broken, and a Heart sensible to nothing but the extremest Woe and Dejection.

This, my dear Father and Mother, is the Issue of your poor *Pamela's* fruitless Enterprize; and God knows, if I had got out at the Back-door, whether I had been at all in better Case, moneyless, friendless, as I am, and in a strange Place!—But blame not your poor Daughter too much: Nay, if ever you see this miserable Scribble, all bathed and blotted with my Tears, let your Pity get the better of your Blame! But I know it will.—And I must leave off for the present—For, Oh! my Strength and my Will are at present very far unequal to one another.—But yet, I will add, that tho' I should have prais'd God for my Deliverance, had I been freed from my wicked Keepers, and my designing Master; yet I have more abundant Reason to praise God, that I have been deliver'd from a worse Enemy, *myself!*

I will continue my sad Relation.

It seems Mrs. *Jewkes* awaked not till Day-break, and not finding me in Bed, she call'd me; and no Answer being return'd, she relates, that she got out of Bed, and run to my Closet; and not finding me, searched under the Bed, and in another Closet, finding the Chamber-door as she had left it, quite fast, and the Key, as usual, about her Wrist. For if I could have got out at the Chamber-door, there were two or three Passages, and Doors to them all, double lock'd and barr'd, to go thro', into the great Garden; so that if I would escape, there was no Way but that of the Window; and that very Window, because of the Summer-parlour under it; for the other Windows were a great way from the Ground.

She says, she was excessively frighted, and instantly rais'd the *Swiss*, and the two Maids, who lay not far off; and finding every Door fast, she said, I must be carry'd away, as St. *Peter* was out of Prison, by some Angel.[1] It is a Wonder she had not a worse Thought!

She says, she wept and wrung her Hands, and took on sadly, running about like a mad Woman, little thinking I could have got out of the Closet Window, between the Iron Bars; and indeed I don't know if I could do so again. But at last finding that Casement open, they concluded it must be so; and so they ran out into the Garden, and found, it seems, my Footsteps in the Mould of the Bed which I dropt down upon from the Leads: And so speeded away, all of them, that is to say, Mrs. *Jewkes, Colbrand* and *Nan*, towards the Back-door, to see if that was fast, while the Cook was sent to the Out-offices¹ to raise the Men, and make them get Horses ready, to take each a several way to pursue me.

But it seems, that finding that Door double-lock'd and padlock'd, and the Heel of my Shoe, and the broken Bricks, they verily concluded I was got away by some Means, over the Wall; and then, they say, Mrs. *Jewkes* seem'd like a distracted Woman: Till at last, *Nan* had the Thought to go towards the Pond, and there seeing my Coat, and Cap and Handkerchief in the Water, cast almost to the Banks by the dashing of the Waves, she thought it was me, and screaming out, run to Mrs. *Jewkes*, and said, O Madam, Madam! here's a piteous Thing!——Mrs. *Pamela* lies drown'd in the Pond!—Thither they all ran! and finding my Cloaths, doubted not I was at the Bottom; and they all, *Swiss* among the rest, beat their Breasts, and made most dismal Lamentations; and Mrs. *Jewkes* sent *Nan* to the Men, to bid them get the Drag-net ready, and leave the Horses, and come to try to find the poor Innocent! as she, it seems, *then* call'd me, beating her Breast, and lamenting my hard Hap;² but most what would become of them, and what Account they should give to my Master.

While every one was thus differently employ'd, some weeping and wailing, some running here and there, *Nan* came into the Wood-house; and there lay poor I; so weak, so low, and dejected, and withal so stiff with my Bruises, that I could not stir nor help myself to get upon my Feet. And I said, with a low Voice, (for I could hardly speak) Mrs. *Ann*, Mrs. *Ann!*—The Creature was sadly frighted, but was taking up a Billet³ to knock me on the Head, believing I was some Thief, as she said; but I cry'd out, O Mrs. *Ann*, Mrs. *Ann*, help me, for Pity's sake, to Mrs. *Jewkes!* for I cannot get up!—Bless me, said she, what! you, Madam!—Why our Hearts are almost broke, and we were going to drag the Pond for you, believing you had drown'd yourself. Now, said she, you'll make us all alive again!

And, without helping me, she run away to the Pond, and brought all the Crew to the Wood-house.—The wicked Woman, as she entered, said, Where is she?—Plague of her Spells, and her Witchcrafts! She shall dearly repent of this Trick, if my Name be *Jewkes*; and coming to me, took hold of my Arm so roughly, and gave me such a Pull, as made me squeal out, (my Shoulder being bruis'd on that Side) and drew me on my Face. O cruel Creature! said I, if you knew what I had suffer'd, it would move you to pity me!

Even *Colbrand* seem'd to be concern'd, and said, Fie, Madam, fie! you see she is almost dead! You must not be so rough with her. The Coachman *Robin* seem'd to be sorry for me too, and said, with Sobs, What a Scene is here! Don't you see she is all bloody in her Head, and cannot stir?—Curse of her Contrivances! said the horrid Creature; she has frighted me out of my Wits, I'm sure. How the D—l came you here?—O! said I, ask me now no Questions, but let the Maids carry me up to my Prison; and there let me die decently, and in Peace! For indeed I thought I could not live two Hours.

The still more inhuman Tygress said, I suppose you want Mr. *Williams* to pray by you, don't you? Well, I'll send for my Master this Minute; let him come and watch you himself, for me; for there's no such thing as holding you, I'm sure!

So the Maids took me up between them, and carry'd me to my Chamber; and when the Wretch saw how bad I was, she began a little to relent— while every one wonder'd (at what I had neither Strength nor Inclination to tell them) how all this came to pass; which they imputed to Sorcery and Witchcraft.

I was so weak, when I had got up Stairs, that I fainted away, with Dejection, Pain and Fatigue; and they undress'd me, and got me to Bed, and Mrs. *Jewkes* order'd *Nan* to bathe my Shoulder, and Arm, and Ancle, with some old Rum warm'd; and they cut the Hair a little from the back Part of my Head, and wash'd that; for it was clotted with Blood, from a pretty long, but not deep Gash; and put a Family Plaister[1] upon it; for if this Woman has any good Quality, it is, it seems, in a Readiness and Skill to manage in Cases, where sudden Misfortunes happen in a Family.

After this, I fell into a pretty sound and refreshing Sleep, and lay till Twelve o'Clock, tolerably easy, considering I was very feverish and aguishly inclin'd; and she took a good deal of Care to fit me to undergo more Trials, which I had hop'd would have been more happily ended: But Providence did not see fit.

She would make me rise about Twelve; but I was so weak, I could only sit up till the Bed was made, and went into it again; and was, as they said, delirious some Part of the Afternoon. But having a tolerable Night on *Thursday*, I was a good deal better on *Friday*, and on *Saturday* got up, and eat a little Spoon-meat,[2] and my Feverishness seem'd to be gone, and I was so pick'd up by Evening, that I begg'd her Indulgence in my Closet, to be left to myself; which she consented to, it being double-barr'd the Day before, and I assuring her that all my Contrivances, as she call'd them, were at an End. But first she made me tell her the whole Story of my Enterprize; which I did, very faithfully, knowing now that nothing could stand me in any stead, or contribute to my Safety and Escape: And she seem'd full of Wonder at my Resolution and Venturesomeness; but told me frankly, that I should have found a hard Matter to get quite off; for, that she was provided with a Warrant from my Master, (who is a Justice of Peace in this County, as well as the other) to get me apprehended, if I *had* got away, on Suspicion of wronging him, let me have been where I would.

O how deep-laid are the Mischiefs designed to fall on my devoted Head!—Surely, surely, I cannot be worthy all this Contrivance!—This too well shews me the Truth of what was hinted to me formerly at the other House, that my Master swore he would *have* me! O preserve me, Heaven! from being his, in his own wicked Sense of the Adjuration!

I must add, that now this Woman sees me pick up so fast, she uses me worse, and has abridg'd me of Paper all but one Sheet, which I am to shew her written or unwritten on Demand, and has reduc'd me to one Pen; yet my hidden Stores stand me in stead. But she is more and more snappish and cross; and tauntingly calls me Mrs. *Williams*, and any thing that she thinks will vex me.

SUNDAY Afternoon.

Mrs. *Jewkes* has thought fit to give me an Airing, for three or four Hours this Afternoon, and I am much better; and should be much more so, if I knew for what I am reserv'd. But Health is a Blessing hardly to be coveted in my Circumstances, since that fits me for the Calamity I am in continual Apprehensions of; whereas a weak and sickly State might possibly move Compassion for me. O how I dread the coming of this angry and incensed Master; tho' I am sure I have done him no Harm!

Just now we heard, that he had like to have been drown'd in crossing a Stream, a few Days ago, in pursuing his Game. What is the Matter, with all his ill Usage of me, that I cannot hate him? To be sure, I am not like other People! I am sure he has done enough to make me hate him; but yet when I heard his Danger, which was very great, I could not in my Heart forbear rejoicing for his Safety; tho' his Death would have ended my Afflictions. Ungenerous Master! if you knew this, you surely would not be so much my Persecutor! But for my late good Lady's sake, I must wish him well; and O what an Angel would he be in my Eyes yet, if he would cease his Attempts, and reform.

Well, I hear by Mrs. *Jewkes*, that *John Arnold* is turn'd away, being detected in writing to Mr. *Williams*; and that Mr. *Longman*, and Mr. *Jonathan* the Butler, have incurr'd his Displeasure, for offering to speak in my Behalf. Mrs. *Jervis* too is in Danger; for all these three, belike, went together to beg in my Favour; for now it is known where I am.

Mrs. *Jewkes* has, with the News about my Master, receiv'd a Letter; but she says the Contents are too bad for me to know. They must be bad indeed, if they be worse than what I have already known.

Just now the horrid Creature tells me, as a Secret, that she has reason to think he has found out a Way to satisfy my Scruples: It is, by marrying me to this dreadful *Colbrand*, and buying me of him on the Wedding-day, for a Sum of Money!—Was ever the like heard?—She says that it will be my Duty to obey my Husband; and that Mr. *Williams* will be forc'd, as a Punishment, to marry us; and that when my Master has paid for me, and I am surrender'd up, the *Swiss* is to go home again, with the Money, to his former Wife and Children, for she says, it is the Custom of those People to have a Wife in every Nation.

But this, to be sure, is horrid romancing! but abominable as it is, it may possibly serve to introduce some Plot now hatching!—With what strange Perplexities is my poor Mind agitated! Perchance, some Sham-marriage may be design'd, on purpose to ruin me: But can a Husband sell his Wife,[1] against her own Consent?—And will such a Bargain stand good in Law?

MONDAY, TUESDAY, WEDNESDAY, *the 32d, 33d, and 34th Days of my Imprisonment.*

Nothing offers these Days but Squabblings between Mrs. *Jewkes* and me. She grows worse and worse to me. I vexed her yesterday, because she talked nastily, and told her she talk'd more like a vile *London* Prostitute, than a Gentleman's Housekeeper; and she cannot use me bad enough for it. Bless me! she curses and storms at me like a Trooper, and can hardly keep her Hands off me. You may believe she must talk sadly to make me say such harsh Words: Indeed it cannot be repeated; and she is a Disgrace to her Sex. And then she ridicules me, and laughs at my Notions of Honesty; and tells me, impudent Creature that she is! what a fine Bedfellow I shall make for my Master, and such-like, with such whimsical Notions about me!—Do you think this is to be borne! And yet she talks worse than this, if possible!—Quite filthily! O what vile Hands am I put into!

THURSDAY.

I have now all the Reason that can be, to apprehend my Master will be here soon; for the Servants are all busy in setting the House to rights; and a Stable and Coach-house are cleaning out, that have not been us'd some time. I ask Mrs. *Jewkes*; but she tells me nothing, nor will hardly answer me when I ask her a Question. Sometimes I think she puts on these strange wicked Airs to me, purposely to make me wish for what I dread most of all Things, my Master's coming down. *He* talk of Love!—If he had any the least Notion of Regard for me, to be sure he would not give this naughty Body such Power over me:—And if he does come, where is his Promise of not seeing me without I consent to it? But it seems *His Honour owes me nothing!* So he tells me in his Letter; and why? Because I am willing to keep mine. But, indeed, he says, *he hates me perfectly*; and it is plain he does, or I should not be left to the Mercy of this Woman; and, what is worse, to my woful Apprehensions.

FRIDAY, *the 36th Day of my Imprisonment.*

I took the Liberty yesterday Afternoon, finding the Gates open, to walk out before the House; and before I was aware, had got to the Bottom of the long Row of Elms; and there I sat myself down upon the Steps of a sort of broad Stile, which leads into the Road, that goes towards the Town. And as I sat musing about what always busies my Mind, I saw a whole Body of Folks, running towards me from the House, Men and Women, as in a Fright. At first I wonder'd what was the Matter, till they came nearer; and I found they were all alarm'd, thinking I had attempted to get off. There was first the horrible *Colbrand*, running with his long Legs, well nigh two Yards at a Stride; then there was one of the Grooms, poor Mr. *Williams*'s Robber; then I spy'd *Nan*, half out of Breath; and the

Cook-maid after her; and lastly, came waddling, as fast as she could, Mrs. *Jewkes*, exclaiming most bitterly, as I found, against me. *Colbrand* said, O how have you frighted us all!—And went behind me, lest I should run away, as I suppose.

I sat still, to let them see I had no View to get away; for, besides the Improbability of succeeding, my last sad Attempt had cur'd me of enterprizing again. And when Mrs. *Jewkes* came within hearing, I found her terribly incens'd, and raving about my Contrivances. Why, said I, should you be so concerned? Here I have sat a few Minutes, and had not the least Thought of getting away, or going further; but to return as soon as it was duskish. She would not believe me; and the barbarous Creature struck at me with her horrid Fist, and, I believe, would have felled me, had not *Colbrand* interposed, and said, He saw me sitting still, looking about me, and not seeming to have the least Inclination to stir. But this would not serve: She order'd the two Maids to take me each by an Arm, and lead me back into the House, and up Stairs; and there have I been locked up ever since, without Shoes. In vain have I pleaded that I had no Design, as, indeed I had not the least; and, last Night I was forced to lie between her and *Nan*; and I find she is resolved to make a Handle¹ of this against me, and in her own Behalf—Indeed, what with her Usage, and my own Apprehensions of still worse, I am quite weary of my Life.

Just now she has been with me, and given me my Shoes, and has laid her imperious Commands upon me, to dress myself in a Suit of Cloaths out of the Portmanteau, which I have not seen lately, against three or four o'Clock; for, she says, she is to have a Visit from Lady *Darnford's* two Daughters, who come purposely to see me; and so she gave me the Key of the Portmanteau. But I will not obey her; and I told her I would not be made a Shew of, nor see the Ladies. She left me, saying, It should be worse for me, if I did not. But how can that be?

Five o'Clock is come,

And no young Ladies!—So that, I fansy—But, hold, I hear their Coach, I believe. I'll step to the Window.—I won't go down to them, I am resolv'd.—

Good Sirs! good Sirs! What will become of me! Here is my Master come in his fine Chariot!—Indeed he is!—What shall I do? Where shall I hide myself!—Oh! what shall I do!—Pray for me! But Oh! you'll not see this!—Now, good Heaven preserve me! if it be thy blessed Will!

Seven o'Clock.

Tho' I dread to see him, yet do I wonder I have not. To be sure something is resolved against me, and he stays to hear all her Stories. I can hardly write; yet, as I can do nothing else, I know not how to forbear!—Yet I cannot hold my Pen!—How crooked and trembling the Lines!—I must leave off, till I can get quieter Fingers!—Why should the Guiltless tremble so, when the Guilty can possess their Minds in Peace!

SATURDAY *Morning.*

Now let me give you an Account of what passed last Night; for I had no Power to write, nor yet Opportunity, till now.

This naughty Woman held my Master till half an Hour after seven; and he came hither about five in the Afternoon. And then I heard his Voice on the Stairs, as he was coming up to me. It was about his Supper; for he said, I shall chuse a boil'd Chicken, with Butter and Parsley.—And up he came!

He put on a stern and majestick Air; and he can look very majestick when he pleases. Well, perverse *Pamela*, ungrateful Runaway, said he, for my first Salutation!—You do well, don't you, to give me all this Trouble and Vexation? I could not speak; but throwing myself on the Floor, hid my Face, and was ready to die with Grief and Apprehension.—He said, Well may you hide your Face! well may you be ashamed to see me, vile forward one, as you are!—I sobb'd, and wept, but could not speak. And he let me lie, and went to the Door, and called Mrs. *Jewkes.*—There, said he, take up that fallen Angel!—Once I thought her as innocent as one!—But I have now no Patience with her. The little Hypocrite prostrates herself thus, in hopes to move my Weakness in her Favour, and that I'll raise her from the Floor myself. But I shall not touch her: No, said he, cruel Gentleman as he was! let such Fellows as *Williams* be taken in by her artful Wiles; I know her now, and see that she is for any Fool's Turn, that will be caught by her.

I sighed, as if my Heart would break!—And Mrs. *Jewkes* lifted me up upon my Knees; for I trembled so, I could not stand. Come, said she, Mrs. *Pamela*, learn to know your best Friend; confess your unworthy Behaviour, and beg his Honour's Forgiveness of all your Faults. I was ready to faint;

and he said, She is Mistress of Arts, I'll assure you; and will mimick a Fit, ten to one, in a Minute.

I was struck to the Heart at this; but could not speak presently; only lifted up my Eyes to Heaven!—And at last made shift to say—God forgive you, Sir!—He seem'd in a great Passion, and walked up and down the Room, casting sometimes an Eye to me, and seeming as if he would have spoken, but check'd himself.—And at last he said, When she has acted this her first Part over, perhaps I will see her again, and she shall soon know what she has to trust to.

And so he went out of the Room: And I was quite sick at Heart!—Surely, said I, I am the wickedest Creature that ever breath'd! Well, said the Impertinent, not so wicked as that neither; but I am glad you begin to see your Faults. Nothing like being humble!—Come, I'll stand your Friend, and plead for you, if you'll promise to be more dutiful for the future: Come, come, added the Wretch, this may be all made up by to-morrow Morning, if you are not a Fool.—Begone, hideous Woman! said I; and let not my Afflictions be added to by thy inexorable Cruelty, and unwomanly Wickedness!

She gave me a Push, and went away in a violent Passion. And it seems, she made a Story of this; and said, I had such a Spirit, there was no bearing it.

I laid me down on the Floor, and had no Power to stir, till the Clock struck Nine; and then the wicked Woman came up again. You must come down Stairs, said she, to my Master; that is, if you please, Spirit!—Said I, I believe I cannot stand. Then, said she, I'll send Monsieur *Colbrand* to carry you down.

I got up, as well as I could, and trembled all the way down Stairs. And she went before me into the Parlour; and a new Servant, that he had waiting on him instead of *John*, withdrew as soon as I came in.

I thought, said he, when I came down, you should have sat at Table with me, when I had not Company; but when I find you cannot forget your Original, but must prefer my Menials to me, I call you down to wait on me, while I sup, that I may have a little Talk with you, and throw away as little Time as possible upon you.

Sir, said I, you do me Honour to wait upon you—And I never shall, I hope, forget my Original. But I was forced to stand behind his Chair, that I might hold by it. Fill me, said he, a Glass of that *Burgundy*. I went to do it; but my Hand shook so, that I could not hold the Plate with the Glass in it, and spilt some of the Wine. So Mrs. *Jewkes* pour'd it for me, and I carry'd it as well as I could; and made a low Curchee. He took it, and said, Stand behind me, out of my Sight!

Why, Mrs. *Jewkes*, said he, you tell me, she remains very sullen still, and eats nothing. No, said she, not so much as will keep Life and Soul together.—And is always crying, you say, too? said he. Yes, Sir, said she, I think she is, for one thing or another. Ay, said he, your young Wenches will feed upon their Tears; and their Obstinacy will serve them for Meat and Drink. I think I never saw her look better, tho', in my Life!—But I suppose she lives upon Love. This sweet Mr. *Williams*, and her little villainous Plots together, have kept her alive and well, to be sure. For Mischief, Love, and Contradiction, are the natural Aliments of a Woman.

Poor I was forced to hear all this, and be silent; and indeed my Heart was too full to speak.

And so you say, said he, that she had another Project, but Yesterday, to get away? She denies it herself, said she; but it had all the Appearance of one. I'm sure she made me in a fearful Pucker about it. And I am glad your Honour is come, with all my Heart; and I hope, whatever be your Honour's Intention concerning her, you will not be long about it; for you'll find her as slippery as an Eel, I'll assure you!

Sir, said I, and clasped his Knees with my Arms, not knowing what I did, and falling on my Knees, Have Mercy on me, and hear me, concerning that wicked Woman's Usage of me.—

He cruelly interrupted me, and said, I am satisfy'd she has done her Duty: It signifies nothing what you say against Mrs. *Jewkes*. That you are here, little Hypocrite as you are, pleading your Cause before me, is owing to her Care of you; else you had been with the Parson.— Wicked Girl! said he, to tempt a Man to undo himself, as you have done him, at a Time when I was on the Point of making him happy for his Life!

I arose, but said, with a deep Sigh, I have done, Sir, I have done! I have a strange Tribunal to plead before. The poor Sheep, in the Fable, had such an one; when it was try'd before the Vultur, on the Accusation of the Wolf![1]

So, Mrs. *Jewkes*, said he, you are the Wolf, I the Vultur, and this the poor innocent Lamb, on her Trial before us.—Oh! you don't know how well this Innocent is read in Reflection.[2] She has Wit at Will, when she has a mind to display her own romantick Innocence, at the Price of other People's Characters.

Well, said the aggravating Creature, this is nothing to what she has called me; I have been a *Jezebel*, a *London* Prostitute, and what not?—But I am contented with her ill Names, now I see it is her Fashion, and she can call your Honour a Vultur.

Said I, I had no Thought of comparing my Master—And was going to say on: But he said, Don't prate, Girl!—No, said she, it don't become you, I'll assure you.

Well, said I, since I must not speak, I will hold my Peace: But there is a righteous Judge, who knows the Secrets of all Hearts![1] and to him I appeal.

See there! said he: Now this meek, good Creature is praying for Fire from Heaven upon us! O she can curse most heartily, in the Spirit of Christian Meekness, I'll assure you!—Come, Sawcy-face, give me another Glass of Wine!

So I did, as well as I could; but wept so, that he said, I suppose I shall have some of your Tears in my Wine!

When he had supp'd, he stood up, and said, O how happy for you it is, that you can, at Will, thus make your speaking Eyes overflow in this manner, without losing any of their Brilliancy! you have been told, I suppose, that you are most beautiful in your Tears!—Did you ever, said he to her, (who all this while was standing in one Corner of the Parlour) see a more charming Creature than this? Is it to be wonder'd at, that I demean myself thus to take Notice of her!—See, said he, and took the Glass with one Hand, and turn'd me round with the other, What a Shape! what a Neck! what a Hand! and what a Bloom in that lovely Face!—But who can describe the Tricks and Artifices, that lie lurking in her little, plotting, guileful Heart! 'Tis no Wonder the poor Parson was infatuated with her!—I blame him less than her; for who could expect such Artifice in so young a Sorceress!

I went to the further Part of the Room, and held my Face against the Wainscot; and, in spite of all I could do to refrain crying, sobb'd, as if my Heart would break. He said, I am surpriz'd, Mrs. *Jewkes*, at the Mistake of the Letters you tell me of! But, you see, I am not afraid any body should read what I write. I don't carry on private Correspondencies, and reveal every Secret that comes to my Knowledge, and then corrupt People to carry my Letters, against their Duty, and all good Conscience.

Come hither, Hussy, said he; you and I have a dreadful Reckoning to make.—Why don't you come, when I bid you?—Fie upon it! Mrs. *Pamela*, said she, what! not stir, when his Honour commands you to come to him!—Who knows but his Goodness will forgive you?

He came to me, (for I had no Power to stir) and put his Arms about my Neck, and would kiss me; and said, Well, Mrs. *Jewkes*, if it were not for the Thought of this cursed Parson, I believe in my Heart, so great is my Weakness, that I could yet forgive this intriguing little Slut, and take her to my Bosom.

O, said the Sycophant, you are very good, Sir, very forgiving, indeed!—But come, added the profligate Wretch, I hope you will be so good, as to take her to your Bosom; and that, by to-morrow Morning, you'll bring her to a better Sense of her Duty!

Could any thing, in Womanhood, be so vile! I had no Patience: But yet Grief and Indignation choaked up the Passage of my Words; and I could only stammer out a passionate Exclamation to Heaven, to protect my Innocence. But the Word was the Subject of their Ridicule. Was ever poor Creature worse beset!

He said, as if he had been considering whether he could forgive me or not, No, I cannot yet forgive her neither—She has given me great Disturbance; has brought great Discredit upon me, both abroad and at home; has corrupted all my Servants at the other House; has despised my honourable Views and Intentions to her, and sought to run away with this ingrateful Parson—And surely I ought not to forgive her all this!—Yet, with all this wretched Grimace,[1] he kissed me again, and would have put his Hand in my Bosom; but I struggled, and said, I would die before I would be used thus.—Consider, *Pamela*, said he, in a threatening Tone, consider where you are! and don't play the Fool: If you do, a more dreadful Fate awaits you than you expect. But, take her up Stairs, Mrs. *Jewkes*, and I'll send a few Lines to her to consider of; and let me have your Answer, *Pamela*, in the Morning. Till then you have to resolve upon: And after that, your Doom is fix'd.—So I went up Stairs, and gave myself up to Grief and Expectation of what he would send: But yet I was glad of this Night's Reprieve!

He sent me, however, nothing at all. And about Twelve o'Clock, Mrs. *Jewkes* and *Nan* came up, as the Night before, to be my Bedfellows; and I would go to-bed with two of my Petticoats on; which they mutter'd at sadly; and Mrs. *Jewkes* railed at me particularly: Indeed I would have sat up all Night, for Fear, if she would have let me. For I had but very little Rest that Night, apprehending this Woman would let my Master in. She did nothing but praise him, and blame me; but I answer'd her as little as I could.

He has Sir *Simon Tell-tale*, alias *Darnford*, to dine with him to-day, whose Family sent to welcome him into the Country; and it seems, the old Knight wants to see me; so I suppose I shall be sent for, as *Samson* was,[1] to make Sport for him—Here I am, and must bear it all!

Twelve o'Clock Saturday Noon.

Just now he has sent me up, by Mrs. *Jewkes*, the following Proposals. So here are the honourable Intentions all at once laid open. They are, my dear Parents, to make me a vile kept Mistress: Which God, I hope, will always enable me to detest the Thoughts of. But you'll see how they are accommodated to what I should have most lov'd, could I have honestly promoted it, your Welfare and Happiness. I have answer'd them, as you'll, I'm sure, approve; and I am prepared for the worst: For tho' I fear there will be nothing omitted to ruin me, and tho' my poor Strength will not be able to defend me, yet I will be innocent of Crime in my Intention, and in the Sight of God; and to him leave the avenging of all my Wrongs, in his own good Time and Manner. I shall write to you my Answer against his Articles; and hope the best, tho' I fear the worst. But if I should come home to you ruin'd and undone, and may not be able to look you in the Face; yet pity and inspirit the poor *Pamela*, to make her little Remnant of Life easy; for long I shall not survive my Disgrace. And you may be assured it shall not be my Fault, if it be my Misfortune.

'To Mrs. PAMELA ANDREWS.

'The following ARTICLES are proposed to your serious Consideration; and let me have an Answer, in Writing, to them; that I may take my Resolutions accordingly. Only remember, that I will not be trifled with; and what you give for Answer, will absolutely decide your Fate, without Expostulation or further Trouble.

This is my ANSWER.

Forgive, good Sir, the Spirit your poor Servant is about to shew in her Answer to your ARTICLES. Not to be warm, and in earnest, on such an Occasion as the present, would shew a Degree of Guilt, that, I hope, my Soul abhors. I will not trifle with you, nor act like a Person doubtful of her own Mind; for it wants not one Moment's Consideration with me; and I therefore return the ANSWER following, let what will be the Consequence.

'I. If you can convince me, that the hated Parson has had no Encouragement from you in his Addresses; and that you have no Inclination for him, in Preference to me; then I will offer the following Proposals to you, which I will punctually make good.

I. As to the first Article, Sir, it may behove me, that I may not deserve, in your Opinion, the opprobrious Terms of *forward* and *artful*, and the like, to declare solemnly, that Mr. *Williams* never had the least Encouragement from me, as to what you hint; and I believe his principal Motive was the apprehended Duty of his Function, quite contrary to his apparent Interest, to assist a Person he thought in Distress. You may, Sir, the rather believe me, when I declare, that I know not the Man breathing I would wish to marry; and that the only one I could honour more than another, is the Gentleman, who, of all others, seeks my everlasting Dishonour.

'II. I will directly make you a Present of 500 *Guineas*, for your own Use, which you may dispose of to any Purpose you please: And will give it absolutely into the Hands of any Person you shall appoint to receive it; and expect no Favour in Return, till you are satisfy'd in the Possession of it.

II. As to your second Proposal, let the Consequence be what it will, I reject it with all my Soul. Money, Sir, is not my chief Good: May God Almighty desert me, whenever it is; and whenever, for the sake of that, I can give up my Title to that blessed Hope which will stand me in stead, at a Time when Millions of Gold will not purchase one happy Moment of Reflection on a past mis-spent Life!

'III. I will likewise directly make over to you a Purchase I lately made in *Kent*, which brings in 250 *l. per Annum*, clear of all Deductions. This shall be made over to you in full Property for your Life, and for the Lives of any Children,

III. Your third Proposal, Sir, I reject, for the same Reason; and am sorry you could think my poor honest Parents would enter into their Part of it, and be concerned for the Management of an Estate, which would be owing to the to Perpetuity, that you may happen to have: And your Father shall be immediately put into Possession of it, in Trust for these Purposes. And the Management of it will yield a comfortable Subsistence to him and your Mother, for Life; and I will make up any Deficiencies, if such should happen, to that clear Sum, and allow him 50 *l. per Annum* besides, for his Life, and that of your Mother, for his Care and Management of this your Estate.

'IV. I will, moreover, extend my Favour to any other of your Relations, that you may think worthy of it, or that are valued by you.

'V. I will, besides, order Patterns to be sent you for chusing four complete Suits of rich Cloaths, that you may appear with Reputation, as if you was my Wife. And I will give you the two Diamond Rings, and two Pair of Ear-rings, and Diamond Necklace, that were bought by my Mother, to present to Miss *Tomlins*, if the Match had been brought to Effect, that was proposed between her and me: And I will confer upon you

Prostitution of their poor Daughter. Forgive, Sir, my Warmth on this Occasion; but you know not the poor Man, and the poor Woman, my ever dear Father and Mother, if you think that they would not much rather chuse to starve in a Ditch, or rot in a noisome Dunghil, than accept of the Fortune of a Monarch, upon such wicked Terms. I dare not say all that my full Mind suggests to me on this grievous Occasion.—But indeed, Sir, you know them not; nor shall the Terrors of Death, in its most frightful Forms, I hope, thro' God's assisting Grace, ever make me act unworthy of such poor honest Parents.

IV. Your fourth Proposal, I take upon me, Sir, to answer as the third. If I have any Friends that want the Favour of the Great, may they ever want it, if they are capable of desiring it on unworthy Terms!

V. Fine Cloaths, Sir, become not me; nor have I any Ambition to wear them. I have greater Pride in my Poverty and Meanness, than I should have in Dress and Finery. Believe me, Sir, I think such things less become the humble-born *Pamela*, than the Rags your good Mother raised me from. Your Rings, Sir, your Necklace, and your Ear-rings, will better befit Ladies of Degree, than me: And to lose the best Jewel, my still other Gratuities, as I shall find myself obliged, by your good Behaviour and Affection.

'VI. Now, *Pamela*, will you see by this, what a Value I set upon the Free-will of a Person already in my Power; and who, if these Proposals are not accepted, shall find that I have not taken all these Pains, and risqued my Reputation, as I have done, without resolving to gratify my Passion for you, at all Adventures, and if you refuse, without making any Terms at all.

'VII. You shall be Mistress of my Person and Fortune, as much as if the foolish Ceremony had passed. All my Servants shall be yours; and you shall chuse any two Persons to attend yourself,

Virtue, would be poorly recompensed by those you propose to give me. What should I think, when I looked upon my Finger, or saw, in the Glass, those Diamonds on my Neck, and in my Ears, but that they were the Price of my Honesty; and that I wore those Jewels outwardly, because I had none inwardly?

VI. I know, Sir, by woful Experience, that I am in your Power: I know all the Resistance I can make will be poor and weak, and perhaps stand me in little stead: I dread your Will to ruin me is as great as your Power: Yet, Sir, will I dare to tell you, that I will make no Free-will Offering of my Virtue. All that I can do, poor as it is, I will do, to convince you, that your Offers shall have no Part in my Choice; and if I cannot escape the Violence of Man, I hope, by God's Grace, I shall have nothing to reproach myself, for not doing all in my Power to avoid my Disgrace; and then I can safely appeal to the great God, my only Refuge and Protector, with this Consolation, That my Will bore no Part in my Violation.

VII. I have not once dared to look so high, as to such a Proposal as your seventh Article contains. Hence have proceeded all my little, abortive Artifices to escape from the Confinement either Male or Female, without any Controul of mine; and if your Conduct be such, that I have Reason to be satisfied with it, I know not (but will not engage for this) that I may, after a Twelvemonth's Cohabitation, marry you; for if my Love increases for you, as it has done for many Months past, it will be impossible for me to deny you any thing.

'And now, *Pamela*, consider well, it is in your Power to oblige me on such Terms, as will make yourself, and all your Friends, happy: But this will be over this very Day, irrevocably over; and you shall find all you would be thought to fear, without the least Benefit arising from it to yourself.—And I beg you'll well weigh the Matter, and comply with my Proposals; and I will instantly set about securing to you the full Effect of them: And let me, if you value yourself, experience a grateful Return on this Occasion; and I'll forgive all that's past.'

you have put me in; altho' you promised to be honourable to me. Your Honour, well I knew, would not let you stoop to so mean and so unworthy a Slave, as the poor *Pamela*: All I desire is, to be permitted to return to my native Meanness unviolated. What have I done, Sir, to deserve it should be otherwise? For the obtaining of this, tho' I would not have *marry'd* your Chaplain, yet would I have *run away* with your meanest Servant, if I had thought I could have got safe to my beloved Poverty. I heard you once say, Sir, That a certain great Commander,[1] who could live upon Lentils, might well refuse the Bribes of the greatest Monarch; and, I hope, as I can contentedly live at the meanest Rate, and think not myself above the lowest Condition, that I am also above making an Exchange of my Honesty for all the Riches of the *Indies*. When I come to be proud and vain of gaudy Apparel, and outside Finery; then, (which, I hope, will never be) may I rest my principal Good in such vain Trinkets, and despise for them the more solid Ornaments of a good Fame, and a Chastity inviolate!

Give me Leave to say, Sir, in Answer to what you hint, That you may, in a Twelvemonth's Time, marry me, on the Continuance of my good Behaviour; that this weighs less with me, if possible, than any thing else you have said. For, in the first Place, there is an End of all Merit, and all good Behaviour, on my Side, if I have now any, the Moment I consent to your Proposals. And I should be so far from expecting such an Honour, that I will pronounce, that I should be most unworthy of it. What, Sir, would the World say, were you to marry your Harlot?—That a Gentleman of your Rank in Life, should stoop, not only to the base-born *Pamela*, but to a base-born Prostitute?—Little, Sir, as I know of the World, I am not to be caught by a Bait so poorly cover'd as this!

Yet, after all, dreadful is the Thought, that I, a poor, weak, friendless, unhappy Creature, am too fully in your Power! But permit me, Sir, to pray, as I now write, on my bended Knees, That before you resolve upon my Ruin, you will weigh well the Matter. Hitherto, Sir, tho' you have taken large Strides to this crying Sin, yet are you on this Side the Commission of it—When once it is done, nothing can recal it! And where will be your Triumph?—What Glory will the Spoils of such a weak Enemy yield you? Let me but enjoy my Poverty with Honesty, is all my Prayer; and I will bless you, and pray for you every Moment of my Life! Think, O think! before it is yet too late! what Stings, what Remorse will attend your dying Hour, when you come to reflect, that you have ruin'd, perhaps Soul and Body, a wretched Creature, whose only Pride was her Virtue! And how pleas'd you will be, on the contrary, if in that tremendous Moment you shall be able to acquit yourself of this foul Crime, and to plead in your own Behalf, that you suffer'd the earnest Supplications of an unhappy Wretch to prevail with you to be innocent yourself, and let her remain so!—May God Almighty, whose Mercy so lately sav'd you from the Peril of perishing in deep Waters, (on which, I hope, you will give me Cause to congratulate you!) touch your Heart in my Favour, and save you from this Sin, and me from this Ruin!—And to Him do I commit my Cause; and to Him will I give the Glory, and Night and Day pray for you, if I may be permitted to escape this great Evil!—From

> *Your poor, oppressed,*
> *broken-spirited Servant.*

I took a Copy of this for your Perusal, if I shall ever be so happy to see you again, my dear Parents (for I hope my Conduct shall be approved of by you); and at Night, when Sir *Simon* was gone, he sent for me down. Well, said he, have you considered my Proposals? Yes, Sir, said I, I have: And there is my Answer. But pray let me not see you read it. Is it your Bashfulness, said he, or your Obstinacy, that makes you not chuse I should read it before you?

I offer'd to go away; and he said, Don't run from me; I won't read it till you are gone. But, said he, tell me, *Pamela*, whether you comply with my Proposals, or not? Sir, said I, you will see presently; pray don't hold me; for he took my Hand. Said he, Did you well consider before you answer'd?—I did, Sir, said I. If it be not what you think will please me, said he, dear Girl, take it back again, and reconsider it; for if I have this as your absolute Answer, and I don't like it, you are undone; for I will not sue meanly, where I can command.¹ I fear, said he, it is not what I like, by your Manner. And, let me tell you, That I cannot bear Denial. If the Terms I have offer'd are not sufficient, I will augment them to two Thirds of my Estate; for, said he, and swore a dreadful Oath, I cannot live without you: And since the thing is gone so far, I *will not!*—And so he clasped me in his Arms, in such a manner as quite frighted me; and kissed me two or three times.

I got from him, and run up Stairs, and went to the Closet, and was quite uneasy and fearful.

In an Hour's time, he called Mrs. *Jewkes* down to him; and I heard him very high in Passion: And all about poor me! And I heard her say, It was his own Fault; there would be an End of all my Complaining and Perverseness, if he was once resolved; and other most impudent Aggravations. I am resolved not to go to-bed this Night, if I can help it—Lie still, lie still, my poor fluttering Heart!—what will become of me!

Almost Twelve o'Clock SATURDAY Night.

He sent Mrs. *Jewkes*, about Ten o'Clock, to tell me to come to him. Where? said I. I'll shew you, said she. I went down three or four Steps, and saw her making to his Chamber, the Door of which was open: So I said, I cannot go there!—Don't be foolish, said she; but come; no Harm will be done to you!—Well, said I, if I die, I cannot go there. I heard him say, Let her come, or it shall be worse for her. I can't bear, said he, to speak to her myself!—Well, said I, I cannot come, indeed I cannot; and so I went up again into my Closet, expecting to be fetch'd by Force.

But she came up soon after, and bid me make haste to-bed: Said I, I will not go to-bed this Night, that's certain!—Then, said she, you shall be made to come to-bed; and *Nan* and I will undress you. I knew neither Prayers nor Tears would move this wicked Woman: So, I said, I am sure you will let my Master in, and I shall be undone! Mighty Piece of Undone, she said! But he was too exasperated against me, to be so familiar with me, she would assure me—Ay, said she, you'll be disposed of another way soon, I can tell you for your Comfort; And I hope your *Husband* will have your Obedience, tho' nobody else can. No Husband in the World, said I, shall make me do an unjust or base thing.—She said, That would be soon try'd; and *Nan* coming in, What, said I, am I to have two Bedfellows again, these warm Nights? Yes, said she, Slippery-ones, you are, till you can have one good one instead of us. Said I, Mrs. *Jewkes*, don't talk nastily to me. I see you are beginning again; and I shall affront you, may-be; for next to bad Actions, are bad Words; for they could not be spoken, if they were not in the Heart.—Come to-bed, Purity! said she. You are a Nonsuch,[1] I suppose. Indeed, said I, I can't come to-bed; and it will do you no harm to let me sit all Night in the great Chair. *Nan*, said she, undress my young Lady. If she won't let you, I'll help you: And if neither of us can do it quietly, we'll call my Master to do it for us; tho', said she, I think it an Office worthier of Monsieur *Colbrand!*—You are very wicked, said I. I know it, said she: I am a *Jezebel*, and a *London* Prostitute, you know. You did great Feats, said I, to tell my Master all this poor Stuff! But you did not tell him how you beat me: No, Lambkin, said she, (a Word I had not heard a good while) that I left for you to tell; and you was going to do it, if the Vultur had not taken the Wolf's Part, and bid the poor innocent Lamb be silent!—Ay, said I, no matter for your Fleers, Mrs. *Jewkes*; tho' I can have neither Justice nor Mercy here, and cannot be heard in my Defence, yet a Time will come, may-be, when I shall be heard, and when your own Guilt will strike you dumb—Ay, Spirit! said she; and the Vultur too! Must we both be dumb? Why that, Lambkin, will be pretty!—Then, said the wicked one, you'll have all the Talk to yourself!—Then how will the Tongue of the pretty Lambkin bleat out Innocence, and Virtue, and Honesty, till the whole Trial be at an End!—You're a wicked Woman, that's certain, said I; and if you thought any thing of another World, could not talk thus. But no Wonder!—It shews what Hands I am got into!—Ay, so it does, said she; but I beg you'll undress, and come to-bed, or I believe your Innocence won't keep you from still worse Hands. I will come to-bed, said I, if you will let me have the Keys in my own Hand; not else, if I can help it. Yes, said she, and then, hey! for another Contrivance, another Escape!—No, no, said I, all my Contrivances are over, I'll assure you! Pray let me have the Keys, and I will come to-bed. She came to me, and took me in her huge Arms, as if I was a Feather; said she, I do this to shew you, what a poor Resistance you can make against me, if I pleased to exert myself; and so, Lambkin, don't say to your Wolf, I *won't* come to-bed!—And set me down, and tapped me on the Neck: Ah! said she, thou art a pretty Creature, it's true; but so obstinate! so full of Spirit! If thy Strength was but answerable to that, thou wouldst run away with us all, and this great House too on thy Back! but undress, undress, I tell you.

Well, said I, I see my Misfortunes make you very merry, and very witty too: But I will love you, if you will humour me with the Keys of the Chamber-doors.—Are you sure you will love me, said she?—Now speak your Conscience!—Why, said I, you must not put it so close; neither would you, if you thought you had not given Reason to doubt it!—But I will love you as well as I can!—I would not tell a wilful Lye: And if I did, you would not believe me, after your hard Usage of me. Well, said she, that's all fair, I own!—But *Nan*, pray pull off my young Lady's Shoes and Stockens.—No, pray don't, said I; I will come to-bed presently, since I must.

And so I went to the Closet, and scribbled a little about this idle Chit-chat. And she being importunate, I was forced to go to-bed; but with two of my Coats on, as the former Night; and she let me hold the two Keys; for there are two Locks, there being a double Door; and so I got a little Sleep that Night, having had none for two or three Nights before.

I can't imagine what she means; but *Nan* offer'd to talk a little once or twice; and she snubbed her, and said, I charge you, Wench, don't open your Lips before me! And if you are asked any Questions by Mrs. *Pamela*, don't answer her one Word, while I am here!—But she is a lordly Woman to the Maid-servants, and that has always been her Character. O how unlike good Mrs. *Jervis* in every thing!

SUNDAY Morning.

A Thought came into my Head; I meant no Harm; but it was a little bold. For seeing my Master dressing to go to Church, and his Chariot getting ready, I went to my Closet, and I writ,

> The Prayers of this Congregation are earnestly desired for a Gentleman of great Worth and Honour, who labours under a Temptation to exert his great Power to ruin a poor, distressed, worthless Maiden.
> And also,
> The Prayers of this Congregation are earnestly desired, by a poor distressed Creature, for the Preservation of her Virtue and Innocence.

Mrs. *Jewkes* came up; Always writing, said she! and would see it. And strait, all that ever I could say, carry'd it down to my Master.—He look'd upon it, and said, Tell her, she shall soon see how her Prayers are answer'd. She is very bold. But as she has rejected all my Favours, her Reckoning for all is not far off. I look'd after him, out of the Window, and he was charmingly dress'd: To be sure, he is a handsome fine Gentleman!—What pity his Heart is not as good as his Appearance! Why can't I hate him?— But don't be uneasy, if you should see this; for it is impossible I should love him; for his Vices all *ugly him over*, as I may say.

My Master sends Word, that he shall not come home to Dinner: I suppose he dines with this Sir *Simon Darnford*. I am much concerned for poor Mr. *Williams*. Mrs. *Jewkes* says, he is confined still, and takes on much. All his Trouble is brought upon him for my sake: This grieves me much. My Master, it seems, will have his Money from him. This is very hard; for it is three fifty Pounds, he gave him, as he thought, as a Salary for three Years that he has been with him. But there was no Agreement between them; and he absolutely depended on my Master's Favour. To be sure, it was the more generous of him to run these Risques for the sake of oppressed Innocence; and I hope he will meet with his Reward in due Time. Alas! for me! I dare not plead for him; that would raise my Oppressor's Jealousy more. And I have not Interest to save myself!

SUNDAY Evening.

Mrs. *Jewkes* has received a Line from my Master. I wonder what it is; but his Chariot is come home without him. But she will tell me nothing; so it is in vain to ask her. I am so fearful of Plots and Tricks, I know not what to do!—Every thing I suspect; for now my Disgrace is avow'd, what can I think!—To be sure the worst will be attempted! I can only pour out my Soul in Prayer to God, for his blessed Protection. But if I must suffer, let me not be long a mournful Survivor!—Only let me not shorten my own Time sinfully!—

This Woman left upon the Table, in the Chamber, this Letter of my Master's to her; and I bolted myself in, till I had transcrib'd it. You'll see how tremblingly by the Lines. I wish poor Mr. *Williams*'s Release at any Rate; but this Letter makes my Heart ake. Yet I have another Day's Reprieve, thank God!

'*Mrs.* JEWKES,

'I have been so press'd on *Williams*'s Affair, that I shall set out this After-noon, in Sir *Simon*'s Chariot, and with Parson *Peters*, who is his Intercessor, for *Stamford*; and shall not be back till to-morrow Evening, if then. As to your Ward, I am thoroughly incensed against her. She has withstood her

Time; and now, would she sign and seal to my Articles, it is too late. I shall discover something, perhaps, by him, and will, on my Return, let her know, that all her insnaring Loveliness shall not save her from the Fate that awaits her. But let her know nothing of this, lest it put her fruitful Mind upon Plots and Artifices. Besure trust her not without another with you at Night, lest she venture the Window in her foolish Rashness: For I shall require her at your Hands.

'Yours, &c.'

I had but just finished taking a Copy of this, and laid the Letter where I had it, and unbolted the Door, when she came up in a great Fright, for fear I should have seen it; but I being in my Closet, and that lying as she left it, she did not mistrust. O, said she, I was afraid you had seen my Master's Letter here, which I carelesly left on the Table. I wish, said I, I had known that. Why sure, said she, if you had, you would not have offer'd to read my Letters. Indeed, said I, I should, at this Time, if it had been in my way—Do, let me see it—Well, said she, I wish poor Mr. *Williams* well off: I understand my Master is gone to make up Matters with him; which is very good. To be sure, added she, he is a very good Gentleman, and very forgiving!—Why, said I, as if I had known nothing of the Matter, how can he make up Matters with him? Is not Mr. *Williams* at *Stamford?* Yes, said she, I believe so; but Parson *Peters* pleads for him, and he is gone with him to *Stamford*, and will not be back to Night: So, we have nothing to do, but to eat our Suppers betimes, and go to-bed. Ay, that's pure, said I; and I shall have good Rest, this Night, I hope. So, said she, you might every Night, but for your own idle Fears. You are afraid of your Friends, when none are near you. Ay, that's true, said I; for I have not one near me.

So have I one more good honest Night before me! What the next may be, I know not; and so I'll try to take in a good deal of Sleep, while I can be easy. And so here I say Good-night, my dear Parents; for I have no more to write about this Night: And tho' his Letter shocks me, yet I will be as brisk as I can, that she mayn't suspect I have seen it.

TUESDAY Night.

For the future, I will always mistrust most when Appearances look fairest. O your poor Daughter, what has she not suffer'd since what I wrote of *Sunday* Night!—My worst Trial, and my fearfullest Danger! O how I shudder to write you an Account of this wicked Interval of Time! For, my dear Parents, will you not be too much frighten'd and affected with my Distress, when I tell you, that his Journey to *Stamford* was all abominable Pretence? for he came home privately, and had well nigh effected all his vile Purposes, and the Ruin of your poor Daughter; and that by such a Plot as I was not in the least apprehensive of: And Oh! you'll hear what a vile and unwomanly Part that wicked Wretch, Mrs. *Jewkes*, acted in it!

I left off with letting you know how much I was pleased, that I had one Night's Reprieve added to my Honesty. But I had less Occasion to rejoice than ever, as you will judge by what I have said already. Take then the dreadful Story as well as I can relate it.

The Maid *Nan* is a little apt to drink, if she can get at Liquor; and Mrs. *Jewkes* happen'd, or design'd, as is too probable, to leave a Bottle of Cherry-brandy in her way, and the Wench drank some of it more than she should; and when she came in to lay the Cloth, Mrs. *Jewkes* perceived it, and fell a rating at her most sadly; for she has too many Faults of her own, to suffer any of the like Sort in any body else, if she can help it; and she bid her get out of her Sight, when we had supp'd, and go to-bed, to sleep off her Liquor, before we came to-bed. And so the poor Maid went muttering up Stairs.

About two Hours after, which was near Eleven o'Clock, Mrs. *Jewkes* and I went up to go to-bed; I pleasing myself with what a charming Night I should have. We lock'd both Doors, and saw poor *Nan*, as I thought, (for Oh! it was my abominable Master, as you shall hear by-and-by) sitting fast asleep, in an Elbow-chair, in a dark Corner of the Room, with her Apron thrown over her Head and Neck. And Mrs. *Jewkes* said, There is that Beast of a Wench fast asleep, instead of being a-bed! I knew, said she, she had taken a fine Dose. I'll wake her, said I. No, don't, said she, let her sleep on; we shall lie better without her. Ay, said I, so we shall, if she don't get Cold.

Said she, I hope you have no Writing to Night. No, reply'd I, I will go to-bed with you, Mrs. *Jewkes*. Said she, I wonder what you can find to write about so much; and am sure you have better Conveniencies of that kind, and more Paper, than I am aware of; and I had intended to romage you, if my Master had not come down; for I 'spy'd a broken Tea-cup with Ink, which gave me a Suspicion; but as he is come, let him look after you, if he will; and if you deceive him, it will be his own Fault.

All this time we were undressing ourselves. And I fetch'd a deep Sigh! What do you sigh so for? said she. I am thinking, Mrs. *Jewkes*, answer'd I, what a sad Life I live, and how hard is my Lot. I am sure the Thief that has robb'd, is much better off than I, 'bating¹ the Guilt; and I should, I think, take it for a Mercy, to be hang'd out of the way, rather than live in these cruel Apprehensions. So, being not sleepy, and in a prattling Vein, I began to give a little History of myself, as I did once before to Mrs. *Jervis*, in this manner.

Here, said I, were my poor honest Parents; they took care to instil good Principles into my Mind, till I was almost twelve Years of Age; and taught me to prefer Goodness and Poverty to the highest Condition of Life; and they confirm'd their Lessons by their own Practice; for they were, of late Years, remarkably poor, and always as remarkably honest, even to a Proverb; for, *as honest as Goodman* ANDREWS, was a Bye-word.[1]

Well then, said I, comes my late dear good Lady, and takes a Fancy to me, and said, she would be the making of me, if I was a good Girl; and she put me to sing, to dance, to play on the Spinnet, in order to divert her melancholy Hours; and also learnt me all manner of fine Needle-work; but still this was her Lesson, *My good* Pamela, *be virtuous, and keep the Men at a Distance*: Well, so I was, I hope, and so I did; and yet, tho' I say it, they all loved me, and respected me; and would do any thing for me, as if I was a Gentlewoman.

But then, what comes next?—Why, it pleased God to take my good Lady; and then comes my Master. And what says he?—Why, in Effect, it is, *Be not virtuous*, Pamela.

So here have I lived above sixteen Years in Virtue and Reputation, and, all at once, when I come to know what is Good and what is Evil, I must renounce all the Good, all the whole sixteen Years Innocence, which, next to God's Grace, I owed chiefly to my Parents and my Lady's good Lessons and Examples, and chuse the Evil; and so, in a Moment's Time, become the vilest of Creatures! And all this, for what I pray? Why truly, for a Pair of Diamond Ear-rings, a Necklace, and a Diamond Ring for my Finger; which would not become me: For a few paltry fine Cloaths; which when I wore, it would make but my former Poverty more ridiculous to every body that saw me; especially when they knew the base Terms I wore them upon. But indeed, I was to have a great Parcel of Guineas beside; I forget how many; for had there been ten times more, they would have been not so much to me, as the honest Six Guineas you trick'd me out of, Mrs. *Jewkes*.

Well, forsooth, but then I was to have I know not how many Pounds a Year for my Life; and my poor Father (there was the Jest of it) was to be the Manager for the abandon'd Prostitute his Daughter: And then (there was the Jest again) my kind, forgiving, virtuous Master, would pardon me all my Misdeeds!

Yes, thank him for nothing, truly. And what, pray, are all these violent Misdeeds?—Why, they are for daring to adhere to the good Lessons that were taught me; and not learning a new one, that would have reversed all my former: For not being contented when I was run away with, in order to ruin me; but contriving, if my poor Wits had been able, to get out of my Danger, and preserve myself honest.

Then was he once jealous of poor *John*, tho' he knew *John* was his own Creature, and helped to deceive me.

Then was he outrageous against poor Parson *Williams*; and him has this good, merciful Master thrown into Gaol; and for what? Why truly, for that, being a Divine, and a good Man, he had the Fear of God before his Eyes, and was willing to forego all his Expectations of Interest, and assist an oppressed poor Creature.

But, to be sure, I must be forward, bold, sawcy, and what not? to dare to run away from certain Ruin, and to try to escape from an unjust Confinement; and I must be married to the Parson, nothing so sure!

He would have had but a poor Catch of me, had I consented; but he and you too know I did not want to marry any body. I only wanted to go to my poor Parents, and to have my own Liberty, and not to be confined to such an unlawful Restraint; and which would not be inflicted upon me, but only that I am a poor, destitute, young Body, and have no Friend that is able to right me.

So, Mrs. *Jewkes*, said I, here is my History in brief. And I am a very unhappy young Creature, to be sure!—And why am I so?—Why, because my Master sees something in my Person that takes his present Fancy; and because I would not be undone.—Why therefore, to chuse, I must, and I shall be undone!—And this is all the Reason that can be given!

She heard me run on all this time, while I was undressing, without any Interruption; and I said, Well, I must go to the two Closets, ever since an Affair of the Closet at the other House, tho' he is so far off. And I had a good mind to wake this poor Maid. No, don't, said she, I charge you. I am very angry with her; and she'll get no Harm there; but if she wakes, she may come to-bed well enough, as long as there is a Candle in the Chimney.

So I looked into the Closets, and kneeled down in my own, as I used to do, to say my Prayers; and this with my under Cloaths in my Hand, all undrest, and passed by the poor sleeping Wench, as I thought, in my Return. But Oh! little did I think, it was my wicked, wicked Master in a Gown and Petticoat of hers, and her Apron over his Face and Shoulders. What Meannesses will not *Lucifer* make his Votaries stoop to, to gain their abominable Ends!

Mrs. *Jewkes*, by this time, was got to-bed, on the further Side, as she used to be; and, to make room for the Maid, when she should awake, I got into Bed, and lay close to her. And I said, Where are the Keys? tho' said I, I am not so much afraid to-night. Here, said the wicked Woman, put your Arm under mine, and you shall find them about my Wrist, as they used to be. So I did; and the abominable Designer held my Hand with her Right-hand, as my Right-arm was under her Left.

In less than a Quarter of an Hour, I said, There's poor *Nan* awake; I hear her stir. Let us go to sleep, said she, and not mind her: She'll come to-bed, when she's quite awake. Poor Soul! said I, I'll warrant she will have the Head-ach finely to-morrow for it. Be silent, said she, and go to sleep; you keep me awake; and I never found you in so talkative a Humour in my Life. Don't chide me, said I; I will say but one thing more: Do you think *Nan* could hear me talk of my Master's Offers? No, no, said she; she was dead asleep. I'm glad of that, said I; because I would not expose my Master to his common Servants; and I knew *you* was no Stranger to his *fine* Articles. Said she, I think they were fine Articles, and you was bewitch'd you did not close in with them: But let us go to sleep. So I was silent; and the pretended *Nan* (O wicked, base, villainous Designer! what a Plot, what an unexpected Plot was this!) seem'd to be awaking; and Mrs. *Jewkes*, abhorred Creature! said, Come, *Nan!*—what are you awake at last? Pr'ythee come to-bed; for Mrs. *Pamela* is in a talking Fit, and won't go to sleep one while.

At that the pretended She came to the Bed-side; and sitting down in a Chair, where the Curtain hid her, began to undress. Said I, Poor Mrs. *Ann*, I warrant your Head achs most sadly! How do you do?—She answer'd not one Word. Said the superlatively wicked Woman, You know I have order'd her not to answer you. And this Plot, to be sure, was laid when she gave her these Orders, the Night before.

I heard her, as I thought, breathe all quick and short: Indeed, said I, Mrs. *Jewkes*, the poor Maid is not well. What ails you, Mrs. *Ann?* And still no Answer was made.

But, I tremble to relate it, the pretended She came into Bed; but quiver'd like an Aspin-leaf; and I, poor Fool that I was! pitied her much.—But well might the barbarous Deceiver tremble at his vile Dissimulation, and base Designs.

What Words shall I find, my dear Mother, (for my Father should not see this shocking Part) to describe the rest, and my Confusion, when the guilty Wretch took my Left-arm, and laid it under his Neck, as the vile Procuress held my Right; and then he clasp'd me round my Waist!

Said I, Is the Wench mad! Why, how now, Confidence? thinking still it had been *Nan*. But he kissed me with frightful Vehemence; and then his Voice broke upon me like a Clap of Thunder. Now, *Pamela*, said he, is the dreadful Time of Reckoning come, that I have threaten'd.—I scream'd out in such a manner, as never any body heard the like. But there was nobody to help me: And both my Hands were secured, as I said. Sure never poor Soul was in such Agonies as I. Wicked Man! said I; wicked, abominable Woman! O God! my God! this *Time*, this *one* Time! deliver me from this Distress! or strike me dead this Moment; and then I scream'd again and again.

Says he, One Word with you, *Pamela*; one Word hear me but; and hitherto you see I offer nothing to you. Is this nothing, said I, to be in Bed here? To hold my Hands between you? I will hear, if you will instantly leave the Bed, and take this villainous Woman from me!

Said she, (O Disgrace of Womankind!) What you do, Sir, do; don't stand dilly-dallying.¹ She cannot exclaim worse than she has done. And she'll be quieter when she knows the worst.

Silence, said he to her; I must say one Word to you, *Pamela*; it is this: You see, now you are in my Power!—You cannot get from me, nor help yourself: Yet have I not offer'd any thing amiss to you. But if you resolve not to comply with my Proposals, I will not lose this Opportunity: If you do, I will yet leave you.

O Sir, said I, leave me, leave me but, and I will do any thing I ought to do.—Swear then to me, said he, that you will accept my Proposals!—And then, (for this was all detestable Grimace) he put his Hand in my Bosom. With Struggling, Fright, Terror, I fainted away quite, and did not come to myself soon; so that they both, from the cold Sweats that I was in, thought me dying—And I remember no more than that, when, with great Difficulty, they brought me to myself, she was sitting on one side of the Bed, with her Cloaths on; and he on the other with his, and in his Gown and Slippers.

Your poor *Pamela* cannot answer for the Liberties taken with her in her deplorable State of Death. And when I saw them there, I sat up in my Bed, without any Regard to what Appearance I made, and nothing about my Neck; and he soothing me, with an Aspect of Pity and Concern, I put my Hand to his Mouth, and said, O tell me, yet tell me not, what I have suffer'd in this Distress! And I talked quite wild,² and knew not what; for, to be sure, I was on the Point of Distraction.

He most solemnly, and with a bitter Imprecation, vow'd, that he had not offer'd the least Indecency; that he was frighten'd at the terrible manner I was taken with the Fit: That he would desist from his Attempt; and begg'd but to see me easy and quiet, and he would leave me directly, and go to his own Bed. O then, said I, take from me this most wicked Woman, this vile Mrs. *Jewkes*, as an Earnest that I may believe you!

And will you, Sir, said the wicked Wretch, for a Fit or two, give up such an Opportunity as this?—I thought you had known the Sex better.—She is now, you see, quite well again!

This I heard; more she might say; but I fainted away once more, at these Words, and at his clasping his Arms about me again. And when I came a little to myself, I saw him sit there, and the Maid *Nan*, holding a Smelling-bottle to my Nose, and no Mrs. *Jewkes*.

He said, taking my Hand, Now will I vow to you, my dear *Pamela*, that I will leave you the Moment I see you better, and pacify'd. Here's *Nan* knows, and will tell you my Concern for you. I vow to God, I have not offer'd any Indecency to you. And since I found Mrs. *Jewkes* so offensive to you, I have sent her to the Maid's Bed, and the Maid shall lie with you to-night. And but promise me that you will compose yourself, and I will leave you. But said I, will not *Nan* also hold my Hand! And will *she* not let you come in again to me?—He said, By Heaven! I will not come in again to-night. *Nan*, undress yourself, go to-bed, and do all you can to comfort the dear Creature: And now, *Pamela*, said he, give me but your Hand, and say you forgive me, and I will leave you to your Repose. I held out my trembling Hand, which he vouchsafed to kiss; and I said, God forgive you, Sir, as you *have been* just in my Distress; and as you *will be* just to what you promise! And he withdrew, with a Countenance of Remorse, as I hoped; and she shut the Doors, and, at my Request, brought the Keys to-bed.

This, O my dear Parents! was a most dreadful Trial. I tremble still to think of it; and dare not recall all the horrid Circumstances of it. I hope, as he assures me, he was not guilty of Indecency; but have Reason to bless God, who, by disabling me in my Faculties, enabled me to preserve my Innocence; and when all my Strength would have signified nothing, magnify'd himself in my Weakness!

I was so weak all Day on *Monday*, that I lay a-bed. My Master shew'd great Tenderness for me; and, I hope, he is really sorry, and that this will be his last Attempt; but he does not say so neither.

He came in the Morning, as soon as he heard the Door open: And I begun to be fearful. He stopt short of the Bed, and said, Rather than give you Apprehensions, I will come no further. I said, Your Honour, Sir, and your Mercy, is all I have to beg. He sat himself on the side of the Bed, and asked kindly how I did?—Begg'd me to be compos'd; said I still look'd a little wildly. And I said, Pray, good Sir, let me not see this infamous Mrs. *Jewkes*; I doubt I cannot bear her Sight. She shan't, said he, come near you all this Day, if you'll promise to compose yourself. Then, Sir, said I, I will try. He pressed my Hand very tenderly, and went out. What a Change does this shew!—O may it be lasting! But, alas! he seems only to have alter'd his Method of Proceeding, but retains, I doubt, his wicked Purpose!

On *Tuesday* about ten o'Clock, when my Master heard I was up, he sent for me down into the Parlour. When I came, he said, Come nearer to me, *Pamela*. I did so, and he took my Hand, and said, You begin to look well again. I am glad of it. You little Slut, how did you frighten me on *Sunday* Night!—Sir, said I, pray name not that Night; and my Eyes overflow'd at the Remembrance, and I turn'd my Head aside.

Said he, Place some little Confidence in me: I know what those charming Eyes mean, and you shall not need to explain yourself: For I do assure you, that as soon as I saw you change, and a cold Sweat bedew your pretty Face, and you fainted away, I quitted the Bed, and Mrs. *Jewkes* did so too. And I put on my Gown, and she fetch'd her Smelling-bottle, and did all we could to restore you; and my Passion for you was all swallow'd up in the Concern I had for your Recovery; for I thought I never saw a Fit so strong and violent in my Life; and fear'd we should not bring you to Life again; for what I saw you in once before was nothing to it. This, said he, might be my Folly, and my Unacquaintedness with what your Sex can shew when they are in Earnest. But this I repeat to you, that your Mind may be intirely comforted.—All I offer'd to you, (and that, I am sure, was innocent) was before you fainted away.

Sir, said I, that was very bad. And it was too plain you had the worst Designs. When, said he, I tell you the Truth in one Instance, you may believe me in the other. I know not, I declare beyond this lovely Bosom, your Sex; but that I did intend what you call the worst, is most certain: And tho' I would not too much alarm you now, I could curse my Weakness and my Folly, which makes me own, that I love you beyond all your Sex, and cannot live without you. But, if I am Master of myself, and my own Resolution, I will not attempt to force you to any thing again. Sir, said I, you may easily keep your Resolution, if you will send me out of your way, to my poor Parents; that is all I beg.

'Tis a Folly to talk of it, said he. You must not, shall not go! And if I could be assur'd you would not attempt it, you should have better Usage, and your Confinement should be made easier to you. But to what End,

Sir, am I to stay, said I? You yourself seem not sure you can keep your own present good Resolutions; and do you think, if I was to stay, when I *could* get away, and be safe, it would not look, as if either I confided too much in my own Strength, or would tempt my Ruin? And as if I was not in earnest to wish myself safe and out of Danger?—And then, how long am I to stay? And to what Purpose? And in what Light must I appear to the World? Would not that censure me, altho' I might be innocent? And you will allow, Sir, that if there be any thing valuable or exemplary in a good Name, or fair Reputation, one must not despise the World's Censure, if one can avoid it.

Well, said he, I sent not for you on this Account, just now. But for two Reasons. The first is, that you promise me, that for a Fortnight to come you will not offer to go away without my express Consent; and this I expect for your own sake, that I may give you a little more Liberty. And the second is, That you will see and forgive Mrs. *Jewkes*; she takes on much, and thinks, that, as all her Fault was her Obedience to me, it would be very hard to sacrifice her, as she calls it, to your Resentment.

As to the first, Sir, said I, it is a hard Injunction, for the Reasons I have mention'd. And as to the second, considering her vile unwomanly Wickedness, and her Endeavours to instigate you more to ruin me, when your returning Goodness seem'd to have some Compassion on me, it is still harder. But to shew my Obedience to your Commands, (for you know, my dear Parents, I might as well make a Merit of my Compliance, when my Refusal would stand me in no stead) I will consent to both; and to every thing else, that you shall be pleas'd to injoin, which I can do with Innocence.

That's my good Girl, said he, and kiss'd me. This is quite prudent, and shews me, that you don't take insolent Advantage of my Favour for you, and will, perhaps, stand you in more stead than you are aware of.

So he rung the Bell, and said, Call down Mrs. *Jewkes*. She came down, and he took my Hand, and put it into hers; and said, Mrs. *Jewkes*, I am oblig'd to you for all your Diligence and Fidelity to me; but *Pamela*, I must own, is not; because the Service I employ'd you in was not so very obliging to her, as I could have wish'd she would have thought it; and you was not to favour her, but obey me. But yet I'll assure you, at the very first Word, she has *once* oblig'd me, by consenting to be Friends with you; and, if she gives me no great Cause, I shall not, perhaps, put you on such disagreeable Service again.—Now, therefore, be you once more Bed-fellows and Board-fellows, as I may say, for some Days longer; and see that *Pamela* sends no Letters nor Messages out of the House, nor keeps a Correspondence unknown to me, especially with that *Williams*; and, as for the rest, shew the dear Girl all the Respect that is due to one I must love, if she will deserve it, as I hope she will yet; and let her be under no unnecessary or harsh Restraints. But your watchful Care is not, however, to cease: And remember that you are not to disoblige me, to oblige her; and that I will not, cannot, yet part with her.

Mrs. *Jewkes* look'd very sullen, and as if she would be glad still to do me a good Turn, if it lay in her Power.

I took Courage then to drop a Word or two for poor Mr. *Williams*; but he was angry with me for it, and said, he could not endure to hear his Name in *my* Mouth; so I was forc'd to have done for that time.

All this time my Papers that I had bury'd under the Rose-bush, lay there still; and I begg'd for Leave to send a Letter to you. So I should, he said, if he might read it first. But this did not answer my Design; and yet I would have sent you such a Letter as he might see, if I had been sure my Danger was over. But that I cannot; for he now seems to take another Method, and what I am more afraid of, because, may-be, he may watch an Opportunity, and join Force with it, on Occasion, when I am least prepar'd: For now, he seems to abound with Kindness, and talks of Love, without Reserve, and makes nothing of allowing himself in the Liberty of kissing me, which he calls innocent; but which I do not like, and especially in the manner he does it; but for a Master to do it at all to a Servant, has Meaning too much in it, not to alarm an honest Body.

WEDNESDAY *Morning.*

I find I am watched and suspected still very close; and I wish I was with you; but that must not be, it seems, this Fortnight. I don't like this Fortnight, and it will be a tedious and a dangerous one to me, I doubt.

My Master just now sent for me down to take a Walk with him in the Garden. But I like him not at all, nor his Ways. For he would have all the way his Arm about my Waist, and said abundance of fond Things to me, enough to make me proud, if his Design had not been apparent. After walking about, he led me into a little Alcove, on the further Part of the Garden; and really made me afraid of myself. For he began to be very teazing, and made me sit on his Knee, and was so often kissing me, that I said, Sir, I don't like to be here at all, I assure you. Indeed you make me afraid!—And what made me the more so, was what he once said to Mrs.

Jewkes, and did not think I heard him, and which, tho' always uppermost with me, I did not mention before, because I did not know how to bring it in, in my Writing.

She, I suppose, had been encouraging him in his Wickedness; for it was before the last dreadful Trial; and I only heard what he answer'd.

Said he, I will try once more; but I have begun wrong. For I see Terror does but add to her Frost; but, she is a charming Girl, and may be thaw'd by Kindness; and I should have melted her by Love, instead of freezing her by Fear.

Is he not a wicked sad Man for this?—To be sure, I blush while I write it. But I trust, that that God, who has deliver'd me from the Paw of the Lion and the Bear;¹ that is, his and Mrs. *Jewkes's* Violences; will also deliver me from this *Philistine*, myself, and my own Infirmities, that I may not defy the Commands of the Living God!—

But, as I was saying, this Expression coming into my Thoughts, I was of Opinion, I could not be too much on my Guard, at all times; more especially when he took such Liberties: For he professed Honour all the Time with his Mouth, while his Actions did not correspond. I begg'd and pray'd he would let me go: And had I not appear'd quite regardless of all he said, and resolv'd not to stay, if I could help it, I know not how far he would have proceeded: For I was forc'd to fall down upon my Knees.

At last he walk'd out with me, still bragging of his Honour, and his Love. Yes, yes, Sir, said I, your Honour is to destroy mine; and your Love is to ruin me, I see it too plainly. But, indeed, I will not walk with you, Sir, said I, any more. Do you know, said he, who you talk to, and where you are?

You may believe I had Reason to think him not so decent as he should be; for I said, As to where I am, Sir, I know it too well, and that I have no Creature to befriend me: And, as to who you are, Sir, let me ask you, what you would have me answer?

Why tell me, said he, what Answer you would make? It will only make you angry, said I; and so I shall fare worse, if possible. I won't be angry, said he. Why then, Sir, said I, you cannot be my late good Lady's Son; for she lov'd me, and taught me Virtue. You cannot then be my Master; for no Master demeans himself so to his poor Servant.

He put his Arm round me, and his other Hand on my Neck; which made me more angry and bold, and he said, What then am I? Why, said I, (struggling from him, and in a great Passion) to be sure you are *Lucifer* himself in the Shape of my Master, or you could not use me thus. These are too great Liberties, said he, in Anger, and I desire that you will not repeat them, for your own sake: For if you have no Decency towards me, I'll have none to you.

I was running from him; and he said, Come back, when I bid you.—So, knowing every Place was alike dangerous to me, and I had nobody to run to, I came back, at his Call, and I held my Hands together, and wept, and said, Pray, Sir, forgive me! No, said he, rather say, Pray, *Lucifer*, forgive me; and now, since you take me for the Devil, how can you expect any Good from me?—How, rather, can you expect any thing but the worst Treatment from me?—You have given me a Character, *Pamela*, and blame me not that I act up to it.

Sir, said I, let me beg you to forgive me. I am really sorry for my Boldness; but indeed you don't use me like a Gentleman; and how can I express my Resentment, if I mince the Matter, while you are so indecent?

Precise Fool, said he, what Indecencies have I offer'd you?—I was bewitch'd I had not gone thro' my Purpose last *Sunday* Night; and then your licentious Tongue had not given the worst Names to little puny Freedoms, that shew my Love and my Folly at the same time. But begone, and learn another Conduct and more Wit, and I will lay aside my foolish Regard for you, and assert myself. Begone, said he, again, with a haughty Air.

Indeed, Sir, said I, I cannot go, till you pardon me, which I beg on my bended Knees. I am truly sorry for my Boldness.—But I see how you go on: You creep by little and little upon me; and now sooth me, and now threaten me; and if I should forbear to shew my Resentment, when you offer Incivilities to me, would not that be to be lost by degrees? Would it not shew that I could bear any thing from you, if I did not express all the Indignation I *could* express, at the first Approaches you make to what I dread? And, have you not as good as avow'd my Ruin?—And have you once made me hope, you will quit your Purposes against me? How then, Sir, can I act, but by shewing my Abhorrence of every Step that makes towards my Undoing? And what is left me but Words? And can these Words be other than such strong ones, as shall shew the Detestation, which, from the Bottom of my Heart, I have for every Attempt upon my Virtue? Judge for me, Sir, and pardon me.

Pardon you, said he, what, when you don't repent?—When you have the Boldness to justify yourself in your Fault? Why don't you say, you never will again offend me? I will endeavour, Sir, said I, always to preserve that Decency towards you which becomes me. But really, Sir, I must beg your Excuse for saying, That when you forget what belongs to Decency in your

Actions, and when Words are all that are left me, to shew my Resentment of such Actions, I will not promise to forbear the strongest Expressions that my distressed Mind shall suggest to me; nor shall your angriest Frowns deter me, when my Honesty is in Question.

What then, said he, do you beg Pardon for? Where is the Promise of Amendment for which I should forgive you? Indeed, Sir, said I, I own that must absolutely depend on your Usage of me: For I will bear any thing you can inflict upon me with Patience, even to the laying down of my Life, to shew my Obedience to you in other Cases; but I cannot be patient, I cannot be passive, when my Virtue is at Stake!—It would be criminal in me, if I was.

He said he never saw such a Fool in his Life! And he walk'd by the Side of me some Yards, without saying a Word, and seem'd vex'd; and, at last walked in, bidding me attend him in the Garden after Dinner. So, having a little Time, I went up, and wrote thus far.

WEDNESDAY Night.

If, my dear Parents, I am not destin'd more surely than ever for Ruin, I have now more Comfort before me, than ever I yet knew. And am either nearer my Happiness or my Misery than ever I was. God protect me from the latter, if it be his blessed Will! I have now such a Scene to open to you, that I know will alarm both your Hopes and your Fears, as it does mine. And this it is.

After my Master had din'd, he took a Turn into the Stables, to look at his Stud of Horses; and, when he came in, he open'd the Parlour-door, where Mrs. *Jewkes* and I sat at Dinner; and, at his Entrance, we both rose up; but he said, Sit still, sit still; and let me see how you eat your Victuals, *Pamela*. O, said Mrs. *Jewkes*, very poorly, Sir, I'll assure you. No, said I, pretty well, Sir, considering. None of your *Considerings!* said he, Pretty-face, and tapp'd me on the Cheek. I blush'd, but was glad he was so good-humour'd; but I could not tell how to sit before him, nor to behave myself. So he said, I know, *Pamela*, you are a nice Carver. My Mother us'd to say so. My Lady, Sir, said I, was very good to me, in every thing, and would always make me do the Honours of her Table for her, when she was with her few select Friends that she lov'd. Cut up, said he, that Chicken. I did so. Now, said he, and took a Knife and Fork, and put a Wing upon my Plate, let me see you eat that. O Sir, said I, I have eat a whole Breast of a Chicken already, and cannot eat so much. But he said, I must eat it for his sake, and he would learn me to eat heartily: So I did eat it; but was much confused at his so kind and unusual Freedom and Condescension. And, good Sirs! you can't imagine how Mrs. *Jewkes* look'd, and star'd, and how respectful she seem'd to me, and call'd me *good Madam!* I'll assure you! urging me to take a little Bit of Tart.

My Master took two or three Turns about the Room, musing and thoughtful, as I had never before seen him; and at last he went out, saying, I am going into the Garden: You know, *Pamela*, what I said to you before Dinner. I rose and curcheed, saying, I would attend his Honour; and he said, Do, good Girl!

Well, said Mrs. *Jewkes*, I see how things will go. O *Madam*, as she call'd me again, I am sure you are to be our Mistress! And then I know what will become of me. Ah! Mrs. *Jewkes*, said I, if I can but keep myself virtuous, 'tis the utmost of my Ambition; and, I hope, no Temptation shall make me otherwise.

Notwithstanding I had no Reason to be pleas'd with his Treatment of me before Dinner, yet I made haste to attend him; and I found him walking by the Side of that Pond, which, for Want of Grace, and thro' a sinful Despondence, had like to have been so fatal to me, and the Sight of which, ever since, has been a Trouble and Reproach to me. And it was by the Side of this Pond, and not far from the Place where I had that dreadful Conflict, that my present Hopes, if I am not to be deceiv'd again, began to dawn, which I presume to flatter myself with being an happy Omen for me, as if God Almighty would shew your poor sinful Daughter, how well I did, to put my Affiance[1] in his Goodness, and not to throw away myself, because my Ruin seem'd inevitable to my short-sighted Apprehension.

So he was pleas'd to say, Well, *Pamela*, I am glad you are come of your own Accord, as I may say: Give me your Hand. I did so; and he look'd at me very steadily, and pressing my Hand all the time, at last said, I will now talk to you in a serious manner.

You have a great deal of Wit, a great deal of Penetration, much beyond your Years; and, as I thought, your Opportunities. You are possess'd of an open, frank and generous Mind; and a Person so lovely, that you excel all your Sex in my Eyes. All these Accomplishments have engag'd my Affections so deeply, that, as I have often said, I cannot live without you; and I would divide with all my Soul, my Estate with you, to make you mine upon my own Terms. These you have absolutely rejected; and that, tho' in sawcy Terms enough, yet, in such a manner, as makes me admire you more. Your pretty Chit-chat to Mrs. *Jewkes*, the last *Sunday* Night, so innocent, and so full of beautiful Simplicity, half disarmed my Resolutions before I approach'd your Bed. And I see you so watchful over your Virtue, that tho' I hop'd to find it otherwise, I cannot but say, my Passion for you is increas'd by it. But now what shall I say further, *Pamela?*—I will make you, tho' a Party, my Adviser in this Matter; tho' not perhaps my definitive Judge.

You know I am not a very abandon'd Profligate: I have hitherto been guilty of no very enormous or vile Actions. This of seizing you, and confining you thus, may, perhaps, be one of the worst, at least to Persons of real Innocence. Had I been utterly given up to my Passions, I should before now have gratify'd them, and not have shewn that Remorse and Compassion for you, which have repriev'd you more than once, when absolutely in my Power; and you are as inviolate a Virgin as you was when you came into my House.

But, what can I do? Consider the Pride of my Condition. I cannot endure the Thought of Marriage, even with a Person of equal or superior Degree to myself; and have declin'd several Proposals of that kind: How then, with the Distance between us, and in the World's Judgment, can I think of making you my Wife?—Yet I must have you; I cannot bear the Thoughts of any other Man supplanting me in your Affections. And the very Apprehension of that, has made me hate the Name of *Williams*, and use him in a manner unworthy of my Temper.

Now, *Pamela*, judge for me; and, since I have told you thus candidly my Mind, and I see yours is big with some important Meaning, by your Eyes, your Blushes, and that sweet Confusion which I behold struggling in your Bosom, tell me with like Openness and Candour, what you think I ought to do, and what you would have me do.——

It is impossible for me to express the Agitations of my Mind on this unexpected Declaration, so contrary to his former Behaviour. His Manner too had something so noble, and so sincere, as I thought; that, alas for me! I found I had Need of all my poor Discretion, to ward off the Blow which this Treatment gave to my most guarded Thoughts. I threw myself at his Feet, for I trembled and could hardly stand; O Sir, said I, spare your poor Servant's Confusion; O spare the poor *Pamela!*—I cannot say what you *ought* to do: But I only beg you will not ruin me; and, if you think me virtuous, if you think me sincerely honest, let me go to my poor Parents. I will vow to you, that I will never suffer myself to be engag'd without your Approbation. As to *my* poor Thoughts, of what you ought to do, I must needs say, that, indeed, I think you ought to regard the World's Opinion, and avoid doing any thing disgraceful to your own Birth and Fortune; and therefore, if you really honour the poor *Pamela* with your Respect, a little Time, Absence, and the Conversation of worthier Persons of my Sex, will effectually enable you to overcome a Regard so unworthy of your Condition: And this, good Sir, is the best Advice I can offer.

Charming Creature, lovely *Pamela*, said he, (with an Ardor, that was never before so agreeable to me) this generous Manner is of a Piece with all the rest of your Conduct. But tell me more explicitly, what you would advise me in the Case.

O Sir, said I, take not Advantage of my Credulity, and these my weak Moments; but, were I the first Lady in the Land, instead of the poor abject *Pamela*, I would, I *could* tell you. But I can say no more.

O my dear Father and Mother! now I know you will indeed be concern'd for me!—For now I am for myself!—And now I begin to be afraid, I know too well the Reason, why all his hard Trials of me, and my black Apprehensions, would not let me hate him.

But be assur'd still, by God's Grace, that I shall do nothing unworthy of your *Pamela*; and if I find that he is still capable of deceiving me, and that this Conduct is only put on to delude me more, I shall think nothing in this World so vile and so odious; and nothing, if he be not the worst of his Kind (as he says, and, I hope, he is not) so desperately guileful as the Heart of Man!

He generously said, I will spare your Confusion, *Pamela*. But I hope, I may promise myself, that you can love me preferably to any other Man; and that no one in the World has had any Share in your Affections; for I am very jealous of what I love, and if I thought you had a secret Whispering in your Soul, that had not yet come up to a Wish, for any other Man breathing, I should not forgive *myself* to persist in my Affection for you; nor *you*, if you did not frankly acquaint me with it.

As I still continued on my Knees, on the Grass Slope by the Pond-side, he sat himself down on the Grass by me, and took me in his Arms, Why hesitates my *Pamela*, said he?—Can you not answer me with Truth, as I wish? If you cannot, speak, and I will forgive you.

O, good Sir, said I, it is not *that*; indeed it is not: But a frightful Word or two that you said to Mrs. *Jewkes*, when you thought I was not in hearing, comes cross my Mind; and makes me dread, that I am in more Danger than ever I was in my Life.

You have never found me a common Liar, said he, (too fearful and foolish *Pamela!*) nor will I answer how long I may hold in my present Mind; for my Pride struggles hard within me, I'll assure you; and if you doubt me, I have no Obligation to your Confidence or Opinion. But at present, I am really sincere in what I say: And I expect you will be so too; and answer directly my Question.

I find Sir, said I, I know not myself; and your Question is of such a Nature, that I only want to tell you what I heard, and to have your kind Answer to it; or else, what I have to say to your Question, may pave the Way to my Ruin, and shew a Weakness that I did not believe was in me.

Well, said he, you may say what you have overheard; for, in not answering me directly, you put my Soul upon the Rack; and half the Trouble I have had with *you*, would have brought to my Arms the finest Lady in *England*.

O Sir, said I, my Virtue is as dear to me, as if I was of the highest Quality; and my Doubts (for which you know I have had too much Reason) have made me troublesome. But now, Sir, I will tell you what I heard, which has given me great Uneasiness.

You talked to Mrs. *Jewkes* of having begun wrong with me, in trying to subdue me with Terror, and of Frost, and such-like;—you remember it well:—and that you would, for the future, change your Conduct, and try to *melt* me, that was your Word, by Kindness.

I fear not, Sir, the Grace of God supporting me, that any Acts of Kindness would make me forget what I owe to my Virtue; but, Sir, I may, I find, be made more miserable by such Acts, than by Terror; because my Nature is too frank and open to make me wish to be ingrateful; and if I should be taught a Lesson I never yet learnt, with what Regret should I descend to the Grave, to think, that I could not hate my Undoer? And, that, at the last great Day, I must stand up as an Accuser of the poor unhappy Soul, that I could wish it in my Power to save!

Exalted Girl, said he, what a Thought is that!—Why now, *Pamela*, you excel your self! You have given me a Hint that will hold me long. But, sweet Creature, said he, tell me what is this Lesson, which you never yet learnt, and which you are so afraid of learning?

If, Sir, said I, you will again generously spare my Confusion, I need not say it: But *this* I will say, in Answer to the Question you seem most solicitous about, That I know not the Man breathing that I would wish to be marry'd to, or that ever I thought of with such a Hope. I had brought my Mind so to love Poverty, that I hop'd for nothing but to return to the best, tho' the poorest, of Parents; and to employ myself in serving God, and comforting them; and you know not, Sir, how you disappointed my Hopes, and my proposed honest Pleasures, when you sent me hither.

Well then, said he, I may promise myself, that neither the Parson, nor any other Man, is any the least secret Motive to your stedfast Refusal of my Offers? Indeed, Sir, said I, you may; and, as you was pleased to ask, I answer, that I have not the least Shadow of a Wish, or Thought, for any Man living.

But, said he; for I am foolishly jealous, and yet it shews my Fondness for you; have you not encourag'd *Williams* to think you will have him? Indeed, Sir, said I, I have not; but the very contrary. And would you not have had him, said he, if you had got away by his Means? I had resolv'd, Sir, said I, in my Mind otherwise; and he knew it, and the poor Man—I charge you, said he, say not a Word in his Favour! You will excite a Whirlwind in my Soul, if you name him with Kindness, and then you'll be borne away with the Tempest.

Sir, said I, I have done!—Nay, said he, but do not have done; let me know the whole. If you have any Regard for him, speak out; for, it would end fearfully for *you*, for *me*, and for *him*, if I found, that you disguis'd any Secret of your Soul from me, in this nice Particular.

Sir, said I, if I have ever given you Cause to think me sincere—Say then, said he, interrupting me, with great Vehemence; and taking both my Hands between his, Say, That you now, in the Presence of God, declare, that you have not any the most hidden Regard for *Williams*, or any other Man.

Sir, said I, I do. As God shall bless me, and preserve my Innocence, I have not. Well, said he, I will believe you, *Pamela*; and in time, perhaps, I may better bear that Man's Name. And, if I am convinc'd that you are not prepossess'd, my Vanity makes me assur'd, that I need not to fear a Place in your Esteem, equal, if not preferable to any Man in *England*. But yet it stings my Pride to the quick, that you was so easily brought, and at such a short Acquaintance, to run away with that College Novice!

O good Sir, said I, may I be heard one Thing, and tho' I bring upon me your highest Indignation, I will tell you, perhaps the unnecessary and imprudent, but yet, the whole Truth.

My Honesty (I am poor and lowly, and am not intitled to call it *Honour*) was in Danger. I saw no Means of securing myself from your avow'd Attempts. You had shew'd you would not stick at little Matters; and what, Sir, could any body have thought of my Sincerity, in preferring that to all other Considerations, if I had not escap'd from these Dangers, if I could have found any way for it?—I am not going to say any thing for him;

but indeed, indeed, Sir, I was the Cause of putting him upon assisting me in my Escape. I got him to acquaint me, what Gentry there were in the Neighbourhood, that I might fly to; and prevail'd upon him;—Don't frown at me, good Sir, for I must tell you the whole Truth!—to apply to one Lady *Jones*; to Lady *Darnford*; and he was so good to apply to Mr. *Peters* the Minister: but they all refus'd me; and then it was he let me know, that there was no honourable Way but Marriage. That I declin'd; and he agreed to assist me for God's sake.

Now, said he, you are going—I boldly put my Hand before his Mouth, hardly knowing the Liberty I took; Pray, Sir, said I, don't be angry; I have just done—I would only say, That rather than have staid to be ruin'd, I would have thrown myself upon the poorest Beggar that ever the World saw, if I thought him honest.—And I hope, when you duly weigh all Matters, you will forgive me, and not think me so bold and so forward as you have been pleas'd to call me.

Well, said he, even in this your last Speech, which, let me tell you, shews more your Honesty of Heart, than your Prudence, you have not overmuch pleas'd me. But I *must* love you; and that vexes me not a little. But tell me, *Pamela*; for now the former Question recurs; Since you so much prize your Honour and your Virtue; since all Attempts against that are so odious to you; and, since I have avowedly made several of these Attempts, do you think it is possible for you to love me *preferably* to any other of my Sex?

Ah! Sir, said I, and here my Doubt recurs, that you may thus graciously use me, to take Advantage of my Credulity.

Still perverse and doubting, said he! Cannot you take me as I am at present; and that, I have told you, is sincere and undesigning, whatever I may be hereafter?—

Ah! Sir, reply'd I, what can I say?——I have already said too much, if this dreadful *Hereafter* should take place. Don't bid me say how well I can—And then, my Face, glowing as the Fire, I, all abash'd, lean'd upon his Shoulder, to hide my Confusion.

He clasp'd me to him with great Ardour, and said, Hide your dear Face in my Bosom, my beloved *Pamela*; your innocent Freedoms charm me!—But then say, How well—what?

If you will be good, said I, to your poor Servant, and spare her, I cannot say too much! But if not, I am doubly undone!—Undone indeed!

Said he, I hope my present Temper will hold; for I tell you frankly, that I have known in this agreeable Hour more sincere Pleasure, than I have experienc'd in all the guilty Tumults that my desiring Soul put me into, in the Hopes of possessing you on my own Terms. And, *Pamela*, you must pray for the Continuance of this Temper; and I hope your Prayers will get the better of my Temptations.

This sweet Goodness overpower'd all my Reserves. I threw myself at his Feet, and embrac'd his Knees: What Pleasure, Sir, you give me, at these gracious Words, is not lent your poor Servant to express!—I shall be too much rewarded for all my Sufferings, if this Goodness hold! God grant it may, for your own Soul's sake, as well as mine. And Oh! how happy should I be, if—

He stopt me, and said, But, my dear Girl, what must we do about the World, and the World's Censure?—Indeed, I cannot marry!

Now was I again struck all of a Heap.[1] However, soon recollecting myself, Sir, said I, I have not the Presumption to hope such an Honour. If I may be permitted to return in Peace and Safety to my poor Parents, to pray for you there; it is all I at present request! This, Sir, after all my Apprehensions and Dangers, will be a great Pleasure to me. And, if I know my own poor Heart, I shall wish you happy in a Lady of suitable Degree: And rejoice most sincerely in every Circumstance that shall make for the Happiness of my late good Lady's most beloved Son!

Well, said he, this Conversation, *Pamela*, is gone farther than I intended it. You need not be afraid, at this rate, of trusting yourself with *me*: But it is I, that ought to be doubtful of myself, when I am with *you!*—But, before I say any thing further on this Subject, I will take my proud Heart to Task; and, till then, let every thing be, as if this Conversation had never pass'd. Only, let me tell you, that the more Confidence you place in me, the more you'll oblige me: But your Doubts will only beget *Cause* of Doubts. And with this ambiguous Saying, he saluted[2] me in a more formal manner, if I may so say, than before, and lent me his Hand, and so we walk'd towards the House, Side-by-side, he seeming very thoughtful and pensive, as if he had already repented him of his Goodness.

What shall I do, what Steps take, if all this be designing!—O the Perplexities of these cruel Doubtings!—To be sure, if he be false, as I may call it, I have gone too far, much too far!—I am ready, on the Apprehension of this, to bite my forward Tongue, (or rather to beat my more forward Heart, that dictated to that poor Machine) for what I have said. But sure, at least, he must be sincere for the *Time!*—He could not be such a practised Dissembler!—If he could, O how desperately wicked is the Heart of Man!—And where could he learn all these barbarous Arts?—If so, it must be native surely to the Sex!—But, silent be my rash Censurings; be hush'd, ye stormy Tumults of my disturbed Mind; for have I not a

Father who is a Man!—A Man who knows no Guile! who would do no Wrong!—who would not deceive or oppress to gain a Kingdom!—How then can I think it is native to the Sex? And I must also hope my good Lady's Son cannot be the *worst* of Men!—If he is, hard the Lot of the excellent Woman that bore him!—But much harder the Hap of your poor *Pamela*, who has fallen into such Hands!—But yet I will trust in God, and hope the best; and so lay down my tired Pen for this Time.

The END of Vol. I.

PAMELA;

OR,

VIRTUE Rewarded.

VOL. II.

The JOURNAL *continued.*

THURSDAY Morning.

Somebody rapp'd at our Chamber-door this Morning soon after it was light: Mrs. *Jewkes* ask'd who it was; my Master said, Open the Door, Mrs. *Jewkes!*—O, said I, for God's sake, Mrs. *Jewkes*, don't. Indeed, said she, but I must; I clung about her. Then, said I, let me slip on my Cloaths first. But he rapp'd again, and she broke from me; and I was frighted out of my Wits, and folded myself in the Bed-cloaths. He enter'd, and said, What, *Pamela*, so fearful, after what pass'd yesterday between us! O Sir, Sir, said I, I fear my Prayers have wanted their wish'd Effect. Pray, good Sir, consider—He sat down on the Bed-side, and interrupted me, No need of your foolish Fears; I shall say but a Word or two, and go away.

After you went to Bed, said he, I had an Invitation to a Ball, which is to be this Night at *Stamford*, on Occasion of a Wedding; and I am going to call on Sir *Simon* and his Lady, and Daughters; for it is a Relation of theirs: So I shall not be at home till *Saturday*. I come therefore to caution *you*, Mrs. *Jewkes*, before *Pamela*, (that she may not wonder at being closer confin'd, than for these three or four Days past) that no body sees her, nor delivers any Letter to her in this Space; for a Person has been seen lurking about, and inquiring after her; and I have been well inform'd, that either Mrs. *Jervis*, or Mr. *Longman*, has wrote a Letter, with a Design of having it convey'd to her: And, said he, you must know, *Pamela*, that I have order'd Mr. *Longman* to give up his Accounts, and have dismiss'd *Jonathan*, and Mrs. *Jervis*, since I have been here; for their Behaviour has been intolerable: and they have made such a Breach between my Sister *Davers* and me, that we shall never, perhaps, make up. Now, *Pamela*, I shall take it kindly in you, if you will confine yourself to your Chamber pretty much for the Time I am absent, and not give Mrs. *Jewkes* Cause of Trouble or Uneasiness; and the rather, as you know she acts by my Orders.

Alas! Sir, said I, I fear all these good Bodies have suffer'd for my sake!—Why, said he, I believe so too; and there never was a Girl of your Innocence, that set a large Family in such Uproar, surely.—But let that pass. You know both of you my Mind, and in part, the Reason of it. I shall only say, that I have had such a Letter from my Sister, that I could not have expected; and, *Pamela*, said he, neither you nor I have Reason to thank her, as you shall know, perhaps, at my Return.—I go in my Coach, Mrs. *Jewkes*, because I take Lady *Darnford*, and Mr. *Peters*'s Niece, and one of Lady *Darnford*'s Daughters; and Sir *Simon* and his other Daughter go in his Chariot; so let all the Gates be fasten'd, and don't take any Airing in either of the two Chariots, nor let any body go to the Gate, without you, Mrs. *Jewkes*. I'll be sure, said she, to obey your Honour.

I will give Mrs. *Jewkes* no Trouble, Sir, said I, and will keep pretty much in my Chamber, and not stir so much as into the Garden, without her; to shew you I will obey in every thing I can. But I begin to fear—Ay, said he, more Plots and Contrivances, don't you?—But I'll assure you, you never had less Reason; and I tell you the Truth; for I am really going to *Stamford*, *this Time*; and upon the Occasion I tell you. And so, *Pamela*, give me your Hand, and one Kiss, and I am gone.

I durst not refuse, and said, God bless you, Sir, where-ever you go!—But I am sorry for what you tell me about your Servants!

He and Mrs. *Jewkes* had a little Talk without the Door; and I heard her say, You may depend, Sir, upon my Care and Vigilance.

He went in his Coach, as he said he should, and very richly dress'd; which looks *like* what he said: But, really, I have had so many Tricks, and Plots, and Surprizes, that I know not what to think. But I mourn for poor Mrs. *Jervis*.—So here is Parson *Williams*; here is poor naughty *John*; here is good Mrs. *Jervis*, and Mr. *Jonathan*, turn'd away for me!—Mr. *Longman* is rich indeed, and so need the less matter it; but I know it will grieve him: And for poor Mr. *Jonathan*, I am sure it will cut that good old Servant to the Heart. Alas for me! What Mischiefs am I the Occasion of?—Or, rather, my Master, whose Actions by me, have made so many of my good kind Friends forfeit his Favour, for my sake!

I am very sad about these things: If he really loved me, methinks he should not be so angry that his Servants loved me too.—I know not what to think!

FRIDAY Night.

I have removed my Papers from under the Rose-bush; for I saw the Gardener begin to dig near that Spot; and I was afraid he would find them. Mrs. *Jewkes* and I were looking yesterday through the Iron Gate that fronted the Elms, and a Gypsey-like Body made up to us, and said; If, Madam, you will give me some broken Victuals, I will tell you both your Fortunes. I said, Let us hear our Fortunes, Mrs. *Jewkes*; but she said, I don't like these sort of People; but we will hear what she'll say to us. I shan't fetch you any Victuals; but I will give you some Pence, said she. But *Nan* coming out, she said, Fetch some Bread, and some of the cold Meat, and you shall have your Fortune told, *Nan*.

This, you'll think, like some of my other Matters, a very trifling thing to write about. But mark the Discovery of a dreadful Plot, which I have made by it. O bless me! what can I think of this naughty, this very naughty Gentleman!—Now will I hate him most heartily. Thus it was:

Mrs. *Jewkes* had no Suspicion of the Woman, the Iron Gate being lock'd, and she of the Outside, and we on the Inside; and so put her Hand thro'. She said, muttering over a Parcel of cramp[1] Words: Why, Madam, you will marry soon, I can tell you. At that she seem'd pleas'd, and said, I am glad to hear that, and shook her fat Sides with laughing. The Woman look'd most earnestly at me all the Time, and as if she had Meaning. Then it came into my Head, from my Master's Caution, that possibly this Woman might be employ'd to try to get a Letter into my Hands; and I was resolved to watch all her Motions. So Mrs. *Jewkes* said, What sort of a Man shall I have, pray?—Why, said she, a Man younger than yourself; and a very good Husband he'll prove.—I am glad of that, said she, and laugh'd again. Come, Madam, let us hear *your* Fortune.

The Woman came to me, and took my Hand, O! said she, I cannot tell your Fortune; your Hand is so white and fine, that I cannot see the Lines: But, said she, and stoop'd, and pulled up a little Tuft of Grass, I have a Way for that; and so rubb'd my Hand with the Mould-part of the Tuft: Now, said she, I can see the Lines.

Mrs. *Jewkes* was very watchful of all her Ways, and took the Tuft, and look'd upon it, lest any thing should be in that. And then the Woman said, Here is the Line of *Jupiter* crossing the Line of Life; and *Mars*—Odd, my pretty Mistress, said she, you had best take care of yourself: For you are hard beset, I'll assure you. You will never be marry'd, I can see; and will

die of your first Child. Out upon thee, Woman! said I, better thou hadst
never come here.

Said Mrs. *Jewkes*, whispering, I don't like this. It looks like a Cheat:
Pray, Mrs. *Pamela*, go in this Moment. So I will, said I; for I have enough
of Fortune-telling. And in I went.

The Woman wanted sadly to tell me more; which made Mrs. *Jewkes*
threaten her, suspecting still the more: And away the Woman went, having
told *Nan* her Fortune, that she would be drown'd.

This thing ran strongly in my Head; and we went an Hour after, to see
if she was lurking about, and Mr. *Colbrand* for our Guard; and looking
thro' the Iron Gate, he spy'd a Man sauntring about the middle of the
Walk; which filled Mrs. *Jewkes* with still more Suspicions. But she said,
Mr. *Colbrand*, you and I will walk towards this Fellow, and see what he
saunters there for: And, *Nan*, do you and Madam stay at the Gate.

So they open'd the Iron Gate, and walked down towards the Man; and,
guessing the Woman, if employ'd, must mean something by the Tuft of
Grass, I cast my Eye that way, whence she pull'd it, and saw more Grass
seemingly pull'd up: then I doubted not something was there for me; so
I walked to it, and standing over it, said to *Nan*, That's a pretty Sort of
a wild Flower that grows yonder, near that Elm, the fifth from us on the
Left; pray pull it for me. Said she, It is a common Weed. Well, said I, but
pull it for me; there are sometimes beautiful Colours in a Weed.

While she went on, I stoop'd, and pull'd up a good Handful of the Grass,
and in it a Bit of Paper, which I put instantly in my Bosom, and dropt the
Grass; and my Heart went pit-a-pat at the odd Adventure. Said I, Let us
go in, Mrs. *Ann*. No, said she, we must stay till Mrs. *Jewkes* comes.

I was all Impatience to read this Paper. And when *Colbrand* and she
return'd, I went in. Said she, Certainly there is some Reason for my Master's
Caution; I can make nothing of this sauntring Fellow; but, to be sure,
there was some Roguery in the Gypsey. Well, said I, if there was, she
lost her Aim, you see! Ay, very true, said she; but that was owing to my
Watchfulness; and you was very good to go away when I spoke to you.

I went up Stairs, and, hasting to my Closet, found the Billet[1] to contain, in a Hand that seem'd disguised, and bad Spelling, the following
Words:

'Twenty Contrivances have been thought of to let you know your Danger;
but all have prov'd in vain. Your Friends hope it is not yet too late to
give you this Caution, if it reaches your Hands. The 'Squire is absolutely
determin'd to ruin you. And because he despairs of any other way, he will
pretend great Love and Kindness to you, and that he will marry you. You

may expect a Parson for this Purpose, in a few Days; but it is a sly artful Fellow of a broken[1] Attorney, that he has hir'd to personate a Minister. The Man has a broad Face, pitted much with the Small-pox, and is a very good Companion. So take care of yourself. Doubt not this Advice. Perhaps you'll have but too much Reason already to confirm you in the Truth of it. From your zealous Well-wisher,

'*Somebody.*'

Now, my dear Father and Mother, what shall we say of this truly diabolical Master! O how shall I find Words to paint my Griefs, and his Deceit! I have as good as confessed I love him; but indeed it was on supposing him good.—This, however, has given him too much Advantage. But now I will break this wicked forward Heart of mine, if it will not be taught to hate him! O what a black, dismal Heart must he have! So here is a Plot to ruin me, and by my own Consent too!—No wonder he did not improve his wicked Opportunities, (which I thought owing to Remorse for his Sin, and Compassion for me) when he had such a Project as this in Reserve!— Here should I have been deluded with the Hopes of a Happiness that my highest Ambition could not have aspired to!—But how dreadful must have been my Lot, when I had found myself an undone Creature, and a guilty Harlot, instead of a lawful Wife? Oh! this is indeed too much, too much for your poor *Pamela* to support! This is the worse, as I hop'd all the Worst was over; and that I had the Pleasure of beholding a reclaimed Gentleman, and not an abandon'd Libertine. What now must your poor Daughter do! Now all her Hopes are dash'd! And if this fails him, then comes, to be sure, my forcible Disgrace! for this shews he will never leave till he has ruin'd me!—O the wretched, wretched *Pamela!*

SATURDAY Noon, One o'Clock.

My Master is come home, and, to be sure, has been where he said. So *once* he has told Truth; and this Matter seems to be gone off without a Plot: No doubt he depends upon his sham, wicked Marriage! He has brought a Gentleman with him to Dinner; and so I have not seen him yet.

Two o'Clock.

I am very sorrowful; and still have greater Reason; for just now, as I was in my Closet, opening the Parcel I had hid under the Rose-bush, to see if it was damag'd by lying so long, Mrs. *Jewkes* came upon me by Surprize, and laid her Hands upon it; for she had been looking thro' the Key-hole, it seems.

I know not what I shall do! For now he will see all my private Thoughts of him, and all my Secrets, as I may say. What a careless Creature I am!—To be sure I deserve to be punish'd.

You know I had the good Luck, by Mr. *Williams*'s means, to send you all my Papers down to *Sunday* Night, the 17th Day of my Imprisonment. But now these Papers contain all my Matters, from that Time, to *Wednesday* the 27th Day of my Distress. And which, as you may now, perhaps, never see, I will briefly mention the Contents to you.

In these Papers, then, are included, An Account of Mrs. *Jewkes*'s Arts, to draw me in to approve of Mr. *Williams*'s Proposal for Marriage; and my refusing to do so; and desiring you not to encourage his Suit to me. Mr. *Williams*'s being wickedly robbed, and a Visit of hers to him; whereby she discover'd all his Secrets. How I was inclined to get off, while she was gone; but was ridiculously prevented by my foolish Fears, &c. My having the Key of the Back-door. Mrs. *Jewkes*'s writing to my Master all the Secrets she had discover'd of Mr. *Williams*; and her Behaviour to me and him upon it. Continuance of my Correspondence with Mr. *Williams* by the Tiles; begun in the Parcel you had. My Reproaches to him for his revealing himself to Mrs. *Jewkes*; and his Letter to me in Answer, threatening to expose my Master, if he deceiv'd him; mentioning in it *John Arnold*'s Correspondence with him; and a Letter which *John* sent, and was intercepted, as it seems. Of the Correspondence being carried on by a Friend of his at *Gainsborough*: Of the Horse he was to provide for me, and one for himself. Of what Mr. *Williams* had own'd to Mrs. *Jewkes*; and of my discouraging his Proposals. Then it contained a pressing Letter of mine to him, urging my Escape before my Master came; with his half-angry Answer to me. Your good Letter to me, my dear Father, sent to me by Mr. *Williams*'s Conveyance; in which you would have me encourage Mr. *Williams*, but leave it to me; and in which, fortunately enough, you take Notice of my being uninclin'd to marry.—My earnest Desire to be with you. The Substance of my Answer to Mr. *Williams*, expressing more Patience, &c. A dreadful Letter of my Master to Mrs. *Jewkes*; which, by Mistake, was directed to me; and one to me, directed by like Mistake, to her; and very free Reflections of mine upon both. The Concern I expressed for Mr. *Williams*'s being taken in, deceived and ruin'd. An Account of Mrs. *Jewkes*'s glorying in her wicked Fidelity.

A sad Description I gave of Monsieur *Colbrand*, a Person he sent down to assist Mrs. *Jewkes* in watching me. My Concern for Mr. *Williams*'s being arrested, and free Reflections on my Master for it. A projected Contrivance of mine, to get away out of the Window, and by the Back-door; and throwing my Petticoat and Handkerchief into the Pond to amuse them, while I got off. An Attempt that had like to have ended very dreadfully for me! My further Concern for Mr. *Williams*'s Ruin on my Account: And lastly, my over-hearing Mrs. *Jewkes* brag of her Contrivance to rob Mr. *Williams*, in order to get at my Papers; which, however, he preserved, and sent safe to you.

These, down to the Execution of my unfortunate Plot, to escape, are, to the best of my Remembrance, the Contents of the Papers, which this merciless Woman seiz'd: For, how badly I came off, and what follow'd, I still have safe, as I hope, sew'd in my Under-coat, about my Hips. In vain were all my Prayers and Tears to her, to get her not to shew them to my Master. For she said, It had now come out, why I affected to be so much alone; and why I was always writing. And she thought herself happy, she said, she had found these; for often and often had she searched every Place she could think of, for Writings, to no Purpose before. And she hoped, she said, there was nothing in them but what any body might see; for, said she, you know, you are all Innocence!—Insolent Creature, said I; I am sure you are all Guilt!—And so you must do your worst; for now I can't help myself; and I see there is no Mercy to be expected from you.

Just now, my Master being coming up, she went to him upon the Stairs, and gave him my Papers. There, Sir, said she; you always said Mrs. *Pamela* was a great Writer; but I never could get at any thing of hers before. He took them, and went down to the Parlour again. And what with the Gypsey Affair, and what with this, I could not think of going down to Dinner; and she told him that too; and so I suppose I shall have him up Stairs, as soon as his Company is gone.

SATURDAY, Six o'Clock,

My Master came up, and, in a pleasanter manner than I expected, said, So, *Pamela*, we have seized, it seems, your treasonable Papers? Treasonable? said I, very sullenly. Ay, said he, I suppose so; for you are a great Plotter; but I have not read them yet.

Then, Sir, said I, very gravely, it will be truly honourable in you not to read them; but give them to me again. Whom, says he, are they written to?—To my Father, Sir, said I; but I suppose you see to whom.—Indeed, return'd he, I have not read three Lines as yet. Then pray, Sir, said I, don't read them; but give them to me again. No, that I won't, said he, till I have read them. Sir, said I, you serv'd me not well in the Letters I used to write formerly; I think it was not worthy your Character to contrive to get them into your Hands, by that false *John Arnold*; for should such a Gentleman as you, mind what your poor Servant writes?—Yes, said he, by all means, mind what such a Servant as *my Pamela* writes.

Your Pamela! thought I. Then the sham Marriage came into my Head; and indeed it has not been out of it, since the Gypsey's Affair.—But, said he, have you any thing in these Papers you would not have me see? To be sure, Sir, said I, there is; for what one writes to one's Father and Mother is not for every body. Nor, said he, am I every body.

Those Letters, added he, that I did see by *John's* Means, were not to your Disadvantage, I'll assure you; for they gave me a very high Opinion of your Wit and Innocence: And if I had not loved you, do you think I would have troubled myself about your Letters?

Alas! Sir, said I, great Pride to me *that!* For they gave you such an Opinion of my Innocence, that you was resolved to ruin me. And what Advantage have they brought me?—Who have been made a Prisoner, and used as I have been, between you and your House-keeper?

Why, *Pamela*, said he, a little serious, why this Behaviour, for my Goodness to you in the Garden?—This is not of a Piece with your Conduct and Softness there, that quite charm'd me in your Favour: And you must not give me Cause to think, that you will be the more insolent, as you find me kinder. Ah! Sir, said I, you know best your own Heart and Designs! But I fear I was too open-hearted then; and that you still keep your Resolution to undo me, and have only changed the Form of your Proceedings.

When I tell you once again, said he, a little sternly, that you cannot oblige me more, than by placing some Confidence in me, I will let you know, that these foolish and perverse Doubts are the worst things you can be guilty of. But, said he, I shall possibly account for the *Cause* of them, in these Papers of yours; for I doubt not you have been sincere to your *Father* and *Mother*, tho' you begin to make *me* suspect you: For I tell you, perverse Girl, that it is impossible you should be thus cold and insensible, after what last passed in the Garden, if you were not prepossessed in some other Person's Favour. And let me add, that if I find it so, it shall be attended with such Effects, as will make every Vein in your Heart bleed.

He was going away in Wrath; and I said, One Word, good Sir, one Word, before you read them, since you *will* read them: Pray make Allowances for all the harsh Reflections that you will find in them, on your own Conduct to me: And remember only, that they were not written for your Sight; and were penn'd by a poor Creature hardly used, and who was in constant Apprehension of receiving from you the worst Treatment that you could inflict upon her.

If that be all, said he, and there be nothing of another Nature, that I cannot forgive, you have no Cause for Uneasiness; for I had as many Instances of your sawcy Reflections upon me in your former Letters, as there were Lines; and yet, you see, I have never upbraided you on that Score; tho', perhaps, I wished you had been more sparing of your Epithets, and your Freedoms of that Sort.

Well, Sir, said I, since you *will*, you *must* read them; and I think I have no Reason to be afraid of being found insincere, or having, in any respect, told you a Falsehood; because, tho' I don't remember all I wrote, yet I know I wrote my Heart; and that is not deceitful. And remember, Sir, another thing, that I always declared I thought myself right to endeavour to make my Escape from this forced and illegal Restraint; and so you must not be angry that I would have done so, if I could.

I'll judge you, never fear, said he, as favourably as you deserve; for you have too powerful a Pleader for you within me. And so went down Stairs.

About nine o'Clock he sent for me down in the Parlour. I went a little fearfully; and he held the Papers in his Hand, and said, Now, *Pamela*, you come upon your Trial. Said I, I hope I have a *just* Judge to hear my Cause. Ay, said he, and you may hope for a *merciful* one too, or else I know not what will become of you.

I expect, continu'd he, that you will answer me directly, and plainly, to every Question I shall ask you.—In the first Place, Here are several Love-letters between you and *Williams*. Love-letters! Sir, said I.—Well, call them what you will, said he, I don't intirely like them, I'll assure you, with all the Allowances you desired me to make for you. Do you find, Sir, said I, that I encouraged his Proposal, or do you not? Why, said he, you discourage his Address in Appearance; but no otherwise than all your cunning Sex do to ours, to make us more eager in pursuing you.

Well, Sir, said I, that is your Comment; but it does not appear so in the Text.[1] Smartly said! says he; where a D---l, gottest thou, at these Years, all this Knowledge; and then thou hast a Memory, as I see by your Papers, that

nothing escapes it. Alas! Sir, said I, what poor Abilities I have, serve only
to make me more miserable!—I have no Pleasure in my Memory, which
impresses things upon me, that I could be glad never *were*, or everlastingly
to *forget*.

Well, said he, so much for that; but where are the Accounts, (since you
have kept so exact a Journal of all that has befallen you) previous to these
here in my Hand? My Father has them, Sir, said I.—By whose Means,
said he?—By Mr. *Williams*'s, said I. Well answered, said he. But cannot
you contrive to get me a Sight of them? That would be pretty, said I. I wish
I could have contrived to have kept those you have from your Sight. Said
he, I must see them, *Pamela*, or I shall never be easy: For I must know how
this Correspondence, between you and *Williams*, begun: And if I can see
them, it shall be better for you, if they answer what these give me Hope
they will.

I can tell you, Sir, very faithfully, said I, what the Beginning was; for I
was bold enough to be the *Beginner*. That won't do, said he; for tho' this
may appear a Punctilio[1] to *you*; to *me* it is of high Importance. Sir, said I,
if you please to let me go to my Father, I will send them to you by any
Messenger you shall send for them. Will you so? said he. But I dare say, if
you will write for them, they will send them to you, without the Trouble
of such a Journey to yourself. And I beg you will.

I think, Sir, said I, as you have seen all my *former* Letters, thro' *John*'s
Baseness, and now *these*, thro' your faithful Housekeeper's officious Watchfulness, you *might* see *all the rest*. But I hope you will not desire it, till I can
see how much my pleasing you in this Particular, will be of Use to myself.

You must trust to my Honour for that. But tell me, *Pamela*, said the sly
Gentleman, since I have seen *these*, Would you have voluntarily shewn me
those, had they been in your Possession?

I was not aware of his Inference, and said, Yes, truly, Sir, I think I
should, if you commanded it. Well, then, *Pamela*, said he, as I am sure you
have found means to continue your Journal, I desire, while the *former Part*
can come, that you will shew me the *succeeding?*—O, Sir, Sir, said I, have
you caught me so!—But indeed you must excuse me there.

Why, said he, tell me truly, Have you not continued your Account till
now? Don't ask me, Sir, said I. But I insist upon your Answer, reply'd
he. Why then, Sir, said I, I will not tell an Untruth; I have.—That's my
good Girl! said he. I love Sincerity at my Heart.—In *another*, Sir, said I,
I presume, you mean!—Well, said he, I'll allow you to be a little witty
upon me; because it is *in you*, and you cannot help it. But you will greatly
oblige me, to shew me, voluntarily, what you have written. I long to see

the Particulars of your Plot, and your Disappointment, where your Papers leave off. For you have so beautiful a manner, that it is partly that, and partly my Love for you, that has made me desirous of reading all you write; tho' a great deal of it is against myself; for which you must expect to suffer a little. And as I have furnished you with the Subject, I have a Title to see the Fruits of your Pen.—Besides, said he, there is such a pretty Air of Romance, as you relate them, in your Plots, and my Plots, that I shall be better directed in what manner to wind up the Catastrophe of the pretty Novel.[1]

If I was your Equal, Sir, said I, I should say this is a very provoking way of jeering at the Misfortunes you have brought upon me.

O, said he, the Liberties you have taken with my Character, in your Letters, set us upon a Par, at least, in that respect. Sir, reply'd I, I could not have taken these Liberties, if you had not given me the Cause: And the *Cause*, Sir, you know, is before the *Effect*.

True, *Pamela*, said he; you chop Logick[2] very prettily. What the Duce do we Men go to School for? If our Wits were equal to Womens, we might spare much Time and Pains in our Education. For Nature learns your Sex, what, in a long Course of Labour and Study, ours can hardly attain to.—But indeed, every Lady is not a *Pamela*.

You delight to banter your poor Servant, said I.

Nay, continued he, I believe I must assume to myself half the Merit of your Wit, too; for the innocent Exercises you have had for it from me, have certainly sharpen'd your Invention.

Sir, said I, could I have been without those *innocent* Exercises, as you are pleased to call them, I should have been glad to have been as dull as a Beetle.[3] But then, *Pamela*, said he, I should not have lov'd you so well. But then, Sir, reply'd I, I should have been safe, easy, and happy.—Ay, may-be so, and may-be not; and the Wife too of some clouterly[4] Plough-boy.

But then, Sir, I should have been content and innocent; and that's better than being a Princess, and not so. And may-be not, said he; for if you had had that pretty Face, some of us keen Fox-hunters should have found you out; and, spite of your romantick Notions, (which then too, perhaps, would not have had such strong Place in your Mind) would have been more happy with the Ploughman's Wife, than I have been with my Mother's *Pamela*. I hope, Sir, said I, God would have given me more Grace.

Well, but, resum'd he, as to these Writings of yours, that follow your fine Plot, I *must* see them. Indeed, Sir, you *must not*, if I can help it. Nothing, said he, pleases me better, than that, in all your Arts, Shifts and Stratagems, you have had a great Regard to Truth; and have, in all your little Pieces of

Deceit, told very few wilful *Fibs*. Now I expect you'll continue this laudable Rule in your Conversation with me.—Let me know then, where you have found Supplies of Pen, Ink, and Paper; when Mrs. *Jewkes* was so vigilant, and gave you but two Sheets at a Time?—Tell me Truth.

Why, Sir, little did I think I should have such Occasion for them; but, when I went away from your House, I begg'd some of each of good Mr. *Longman*, who gave me Plenty. Yes, yes, said he, It must be *good* Mr. *Longman!* All your Confederates are good, every one of them: But such of my Servants as have done their Duty, and obey'd my Orders, are painted out, by you, as black as Devils; nay, so am I too, for that matter.

Sir, said I, I hope you won't be angry; but, saving yourself, do you think they are painted worse than they deserve? or worse than the Parts they acted require?

You say, saving myself, *Pamela*; but is not that Saving a mere Compliment to me, because I am present, and you are in my Hands? Tell me truly.—Good Sir, excuse me; but I fansy I may ask you, Why you should think so, if there was not a little bit of Conscience that told you, there was but too much Reason for it?

He kissed me, and said, I must either do thus, or be angry with you; for you are very sawcy, *Pamela*.—But, with your bewitching Chit-chat, and pretty Impertinence, I will not lose my Question. Where did you hide your Paper, Pens and Ink?

Some, Sir, in one Place, some in another; that I might have some left, if others should be found.—That's a good Girl! said he. I love you for your sweet Veracity. Now tell me where it is you hide your Written-papers, your sawcy Journal?—I must beg your Excuse for that, Sir, said I. But indeed, answer'd he, you will not have it; for I *will* know, and I *will* see them!—This is very hard, Sir, said I; but I must say, you shall not, if I can help it.

We were standing most of this Time; but he then sat down, and took me by both my Hands, and said, Well said, my pretty *Pamela, if you can help it*: But I will not let you help it. Tell me, Are they in your Pocket? No, Sir, said I, my Heart up at my Mouth. Said he, I know you won't tell a downright *Fib* for the World; but for *Equivocation!* no Jesuit ever went beyond you.[1] Answer me then, Are they in *neither* of your Pockets? No, Sir, said I. Are they not, said he, about your Stays? No, Sir, reply'd I; but pray, no more Questions: For ask me ever so much, I will not tell you.

O, said he, I have a way for that. I can do as they do abroad, when the Criminals won't confess; torture them till they do.—But pray, Sir, said I, Is this fair, just or honest? I am no Criminal; and I won't confess.

O, my Girl! said he, many an innocent Person has been put to the Torture, I'll assure you. But let me know where they are, and you shall escape the *Question*,[1] as they call it abroad.

Sir, said I, the Torture is not used in *England*; and I hope you won't bring it up. Admirably said! said the naughty Gentleman.—But I can tell you of as good a Punishment. If a Criminal won't plead with us here in *England*, we *press him* to Death,[2] or till he does plead. And so now, *Pamela*, that is a Punishment shall certainly be yours, if you won't tell without.

Tears stood in my Eyes, and I said, This, Sir, is very cruel and barbarous.—No matter, said he, it is but like your *Lucifer*, you know, in my Shape! And after I have done so many heinous things by you, as *you* think, you have no great Reason to judge so hardly of this; or, at least, it is but of a Piece with the rest.

But, Sir, said I, (dreadfully afraid he had some Notion they were about me) if you *will* be obey'd in this unreasonable Matter; tho' it is sad Tyranny to be sure!—let me go up to them, and read them over again; and you shall see so far as to the End of the sad Story that follows those you have.

I'll see them all, said he, down to this Time, if you have written so far!—Or at least, till within this Week.—Then let me go up to them, said I, and see what I have written, and to what Day to shew them to you; for you won't desire to see every thing. But I will, reply'd he.—But say, *Pamela*, tell me Truth; Are they *above?* I was more affrighted. He saw my Confusion. Tell me Truth, said he. Why, Sir, answer'd I, I have sometimes hid them under the dry Mould in the Garden; sometimes in one Place, sometimes in another; and those you have in your Hand, were several Days under a Rose-bush, in the Garden. Artful Slut! said he; What's this to my Question? Are they not about you?—If, said I, I must pluck them out of my Hiding-place, behind the Wainscot, won't you see me? Still more and more artful! said he.—Is this an Answer to my Question?—I have searched every Place above, and in your Closet, for them, and cannot find them; so I will know where they are. Now, said he, it is my Opinion they are about you; and I never undrest a Girl in my Life; but I will now begin to strip my pretty *Pamela*; and hope I shall not go far, before I find them.

I fell a crying, and said, I will not be used in this manner. Pray, Sir, said I, (for he began to unpin my Handkerchief) consider! Pray, Sir, do!—And pray, said he, do *you* consider. For I will see these Papers. But may-be, said he, they are ty'd about your Knees with your Garters, and stooped. Was ever any thing so vile, and so wicked!—I fell on my Knees, and said, What *can* I do? what *can* I do? If you'll let me go up, I'll fetch them you. Will you, said he, on your Honour, let me see them uncurtail'd, and not offer to make them away; no, not a single Paper?—I will, Sir.—On your Honour? Yes, Sir. And so he let me go up-stairs, crying sadly for Vexation to be so used. Sure nobody was ever so serv'd as I am!

I went to my Closet, and there I sat me down, and could not bear the Thoughts of giving up my Papers. Besides, I must all undress me in a manner to untack them. So I writ thus:

'*SIR*,

'To expostulate with such an arbitrary Gentleman, I know will signify nothing. And most hardly do you use the Power you so wickedly have got over me. I have Heart enough, Sir, to do a Deed that would make you regret using me thus; and I can hardly bear it, and what I am further to undergo. But a superior Consideration with-holds me; thank God, it does!——I will, however, keep my Word, if you insist upon it when you have read this; but, Sir, let me beg you to give me time till to-morrow Morning, that I may just run them over, and see what I put into your Hands against me. And I will then give my Papers to you, without the least Alteration, or adding or diminishing. But I should beg still to be excused, if you please. But if not, spare them to me, but till to-morrow Morning. And this, so hardly am I used, shall be thought a Favour, which I shall be very thankful for.'

I guessed it would not be long before I heard from him. And he accordingly sent up Mrs. *Jewkes* for what I had promised. So I gave her this Note to carry to him. And he sent word, that I must keep my Promise, and he would give me till Morning; but that I must bring them to him without his asking again.

So I took off my Under-coat, and, with great Trouble of Mind, unsew'd them from it. And there is a vast Quantity of it. I will just slightly touch upon the Subject; because I may not, perhaps, get them again for you to see.

They begin with an Account of my attempting to get away, out of the Window, first, and then throwing my Petticoat and Handkerchief into the Pond. How sadly I was disappointed; the Lock of the Back-door being changed. How, in trying to climb over the Door, I tumbled down, and was piteously bruised; the Bricks giving way, and tumbling upon me. How, finding I could not get off, and dreading the hard Usage I should receive, I was so wicked to be tempted to throw myself into the Water. My sad

Reflections upon this Matter. How Mrs. *Jewkes* used me on this Occasion, when she found me. How my Master had like to have been drown'd in Hunting; and my Concern for his Danger, notwithstanding his Usage of me. Mrs *Jewkes*'s wicked Reports to frighten me, that I was to be marry'd to an ugly *Swiss*; who was to sell me on the Wedding-day to my Master. Her vile way of talking to me, like a *London* Prostitute. My Apprehensions on seeing Preparations made for my Master's coming. Their causless Fears, that I was trying to get away again, when I had no Thought of it; and my bad Usage upon it. My Master's dreadful Arrival; and his hard, very hard Treatment of me; and Mrs. *Jewkes*'s insulting of me. His Jealousy of Mr. *Williams* and me. How Mrs. *Jewkes* vilely instigated him to Wickedness. And down to here, I put into one Parcel, hoping that would content him. But for fear it should not, I put into another Parcel the following, *viz.*

A Copy of his Proposals to me, of a great Parcel of Gold, and fine Cloaths and Rings, and an Estate of I can't tell what a Year; and 50 *l.* a Year for the Life of both of you, my dear Parents, to be his Mistress; with an Insinuation, that, may-be, he would marry me at a Year's End. All sadly vile; with Threatnings, if I did not comply, that he would ruin me, without allowing me any thing. A Copy of my Answer, refusing all with just Abhorrence. But begging at last his Goodness to me, and Mercy on me, in the most moving manner I could think of. An Account of his angry Behaviour, and Mrs. *Jewkes*'s wicked Advice hereupon. His trying to get me to his Chamber; and my Refusal to go. A deal of Stuff and Chit-chat between me and the odious Mrs. *Jewkes*; in which she was very wicked, and very insulting. Two Notes I wrote, as if to be carry'd to Church, to pray for his reclaiming, and my Safety; which Mrs. *Jewkes* seiz'd, and officiously shew'd him. A Confession of mine, that notwithstanding his bad Usage, I could not hate him. My Concern for Mr. *Williams*. A horrid Contrivance of my Master's to ruin me; being in my Room, disguised in Cloaths of the Maid's, who lay with me and Mrs. *Jewkes*. How narrowly I escaped, (it makes my Heart ake to think of it still!) by falling into Fits. Mrs. *Jewkes*'s detestable Part in this sad Affair. How he seem'd mov'd at my Danger, and forbore his abominable Designs; and assur'd me he had offer'd no Indecency. How ill I was for a Day or two after; and how kind he seem'd. How he made me forgive Mrs. *Jewkes*. How, after this, and great Kindness pretended, he made rude Offers to me in the Garden, which I escaped. How I resented them. Then I had written how kind and how good he behav'd himself to me; and how he praised me, and gave me great Hopes of his being good at last. Of the too tender Impression this made upon me; and how I began to be afraid of my own Weakness and Consideration for him, tho' he had used me so ill. How sadly jealous he was of Mr. *Williams*; and how I, as I justly could, clear'd myself as to his Doubts on that Score. How, just when he had raised me up to the highest Hope of his Goodness, he dash'd me sadly again, and went off more coldly. My free Reflections upon this trying Occasion.

This brought Matters down from *Thursday* the 20th Day of my Imprisonment, to *Wednesday* the 41st.

And there I was resolv'd to end, let what would come; for there is only *Thursday*, *Friday* and *Saturday*, to give an Account of; and *Thursday* he set out to a Ball at *Stamford*; and *Friday* was the Gypsey Story, and this is *Saturday*, his Return from *Stamford*. And, truly, I shall have but little Heart to write, if he is to see all.

So these two Parcels of Papers I have got ready for him against to-morrow Morning. To be sure I have always used him very freely in my Writings, and shew'd him no Mercy; but yet he must thank himself for it; for I have only writ Truth; and I wish he had deserv'd a better Character at my hands, as well for his own sake as mine—So, tho' I don't know whether ever you'll see what I write, I must say, that I will go to-bed, with remembring you in my Prayers, as I always do, and as I know you do me: And so God bless you. Good Night.

SUNDAY Morning.

I remember what he said, of not being obliged to ask again for my Papers; and what I was forced to do, and could not help it, I thought I might as well do, in such a manner as might shew I would not disoblige on purpose. Tho' I stomach'd this matter very heavily too. I had therefore got in Readiness my two Parcels; and he not going to Church in the Morning, bid Mrs. *Jewkes* tell me, he was gone into the Garden.

I knew that was for me to go to him; and so I went. For how can I help being at his Beck? which grieves me not a little, tho' he is my Master, as I may say; for I am so wholly in his Power, that it would do me no good to incense him; and if I refused to obey him in little Matters, my Refusal in greater would have the less Weight. So I went down to the Garden; but as he walked in one Walk, I took another; that I might not seem too forward neither.

He soon 'spy'd me, and said, Do you expect to be courted to come to me? Sir, said I, and cross'd the Walk to attend him, I did not know but I should interrupt you in your Meditations this good Day.

Was that the Case, said he, truly, and from your Heart? Why, Sir, said I, I don't doubt but you have very good Thoughts sometimes: Tho' not towards me!—I wish, said he, I could avoid thinking so well of you, as I do. But where are the Papers?—I dare say, you had them about you yesterday; for you say in those I have, that you will bury your Writings in the Garden, for fear you should be *search'd*, if you did not escape. This, added he, gave me a glorious Pretence to search you; and I have been vexing myself all Night, that I did not strip you, Garment by Garment, till I had found them. O fie, Sir, said I; let me not be scar'd, with hearing that you had such a Thought in earnest.

Well, said he, I hope you have not now the Papers to give me; for I had rather find them myself, I'll assure you.

I did not like this way of Talk at all; and, thinking it best, not to dwell upon it, I said, Well, but, Sir, you will excuse me, I hope, giving up my Papers.

Don't trifle with me, said he; Where are they?—I think I was very good to you last Night, to humour you as I did. If you have either added or diminish'd, and have not strictly kept your Promise, woe be to you! Indeed, Sir, said I, I have neither added nor diminish'd. But here is the Parcel, that goes on with my sad Attempt to escape, and the terrible Consequences it had like to have been follow'd with. And it goes down to the naughty Articles you sent me. And, as you know all that has happen'd since, I hope these will satisfy you.

He was going to speak; but I said, to drive him from thinking of any more; And I must beg you, Sir, to read the Matter favourably, if I have exceeded in any Liberties of my Pen.

I think, said he, half-smiling, you may wonder at my Patience, that I can be so easy to read myself abus'd as I am by such a saucy Slut.—Sir, said I, I have wonder'd you should be so desirous to see my bold Stuff; and for that very Reason, I have thought it a very *good* or a very bad *Sign*. What, said he, is your *good* Sign?—That it may not have an unkind Effect upon your Temper, at last, in my Favour, when you see me so sincere. Your *bad* Sign? Why, that if you can read my Reflections and Observations upon your Treatment of me, with Tranquillity, and not be mov'd, it is a Sign of a very cruel and determin'd Heart. Now, pray Sir, don't be angry at my Boldness, in telling you so freely my Thoughts. You may, perhaps, said he, be least mistaken when you think of your bad Sign: God forbid! said I.

So I took out my Papers; and said, Here, Sir, they are. But, if you please to return them, without breaking the Seal, it will be very generous: And I will take it for a great Favour, and a good Omen.

He broke the Seal instantly, and open'd them. So much for your Omen, said he. I am sorry for it, said I; and was walking away. Whither now, said he? Sir, I was going in, that you might have Time to read them, if you thought fit. He put them into his Pocket, and said, You have more than these. Yes, Sir; but all that they contain you know, as well as I.—But I don't know, said he, the Light you put Things in; and so give them me, if you have not a Mind to be search'd.

Sir, said I, I can't stay, if you won't forbear that ugly Word.—Give me then no Reason for it. Where are the other Papers? Why then, unkind Sir, if it must be so, here they are. And so I gave him out of my Pocket the second Parcel, seal'd up, as the former, with this Superscription; *From the naughty Articles, down, thro' sad Attempts, to* Thursday *the 42d Day of my Imprisonment.* This is last *Thursday,* is it?—Yes, Sir; but now you *will* see what I write, I will find some other way to employ my Time: For I can neither write so free, nor with any Face, what must be for your Perusal, and not for those I intended to divert with my melancholy Stories.

Yes, said he, I would have you continue your Penmanship by all means; and I assure you, in the Mind I am in, I will not ask you for any after these; except any thing very extraordinary occurs. And I have, added he, another thing to tell you, That if you send for those from your Father, and let me read them, I may very probably give them all back again to you. And so I desire you will do it.

This a little encourages me to continue my Scribbling; but for fear of the worst, I will, when they come to any Bulk, contrive some way to hide them, if I can, that I may protest I have them not about me, which before I could not say of a Truth; and that made him so resolutely bent to try to find them upon me; for which I might have suffer'd frightful Indecencies.

He led me then to the Side of the Pond; and sitting down on the Slope, made me sit by him. Come, said he, this being the Scene of Part of your Project, and where you so artfully threw in some of your Cloaths, I will just look upon that Part of your Relation. Sir, said I, let me then walk about, at a little Distance, for I cannot bear the Thought of it. Don't go far, said he.

When he came, as I suppose, to the Place where I mention'd the Bricks falling upon me, he got up, and walk'd to the Door, and look'd upon the broken Part of the Wall; for it had not been mended; and came back, reading on to himself, towards me; and took my Hand, and put it under his Arm.

Why this, said he, my Girl, is a very moving Tale. It was a very desperate Attempt, and had you got out, you might have been in great Danger; for you had a very bad and lonely Way; and I had taken such Measures, that let you have been where you would, I would have had you.

You may see, Sir, said I, what I ventur'd rather than be ruin'd; and you will be so good as hence to judge of the Sincerity of my Professions, that my Honesty is dearer to me than my Life. Romantick Girl! said he, and read on.

He was very serious at my Reflections, on what God enabled me to escape. And when he came to my Reasonings, about throwing myself into the Water, he said, Walk gently before; and seem'd so mov'd, that he turn'd away his Face from me; and I bless'd this good Sign, and began not so much to repent at his seeing this mournful Part of my Story.

He put the Papers in his Pocket, when he had read my Reflections, and Thanks for escaping from *myself*; and he said, taking me about the Waist, O my dear Girl! you have touch'd me sensibly with your mournful Relation, and your sweet Reflections upon it. I should truly have been very miserable, had it taken Effect. I see you have been us'd too roughly; and it is a Mercy you stood Proof in that fatal Moment.

Then he most kindly folded me in his Arms; Let us, say I too, my *Pamela*, walk from this accursed Piece of Water; for I shall not, with Pleasure, look upon it again, to think how near it was to have been fatal to my Fair-one. I thought, said he, of terrifying you to my Will, since I could not move you by Love; and Mrs. *Jewkes* too well obey'd me, when the Terrors of your Return, after your Disappointment, were so great, that you had hardly Courage to stand them; but had like to have made so fatal a Choice, to escape the Treatment you apprehended.

O Sir, said I, I have Reason, I am sure, to bless my dear Parents, and my good Lady, your Mother, for giving me something of a religious Education; for, but for that, and God's Grace, I should more than upon one Occasion, have attempted, at least, a desperate Act: And I the less wonder how poor Creatures, who have not the Fear of God before their Eyes, and give way to Despondency, cast themselves into Perdition.

Come, kiss me, said he, and tell me you forgive me for rushing you into so much Danger and Distress. If my Mind hold, and I can see those former Papers of yours, and that these in my Pocket give me no Cause to alter my Opinion, I will endeavour to defy the World, and the World's Censures, and make my *Pamela* Amends, if it be in the Power of my whole Life, for all the Hardships I have inflicted upon her.

All this look'd well; but you shall see how strangely it was all turn'd. For this Sham-marriage then came into my Mind again; and I said, Your poor Servant is far unworthy of this great Honour; for what will it be, but to create Envy to herself, and Discredit to you? Therefore, Sir, permit me to return to my poor Parents, and that is all I have to ask.

He was in a fearful Passion then. And is it thus, said he, in my fond conceding Moments, that I am to be despis'd, and thus answer'd?—Precise, perverse, unseasonable *Pamela*, begone from my Sight, and know as well how to behave in a hopeful Prospect, as in a distressful State; and then, and not till then, shalt thou attract the Shadow of my Notice.

I was startled, and going to speak: But he stampt with his Foot, and said, Begone, I tell you. I cannot bear this stupid romantick Folly.

One Word, said I; but one Word, I beseech you, Sir.

He turn'd from me in great Wrath, and took down another Alley, and so I went in with a very heavy Heart; and fear I was too unseasonable, just at a Time, when he was so condescending: But if it was a Piece of Art of his Side, as I apprehended, to introduce the Sham-wedding, (and to be sure he is very full of Stratagem and Art) I think I was not so much to blame.

So I went up to my Closet; and wrote thus far, while he walk'd about till Dinner was ready; and he is now sat down to it, as I hear by Mrs. *Jewkes*, very sullen, thoughtful, and out of Humour; and she asks what I have done to him?—Now again, I dread to see him!—When will my Fears be over?—

Three o' Clock.

Well, he continues exceeding wroth. He has order'd his travelling Chariot to be got ready, with all Speed. What is to come next, I wonder!—

Sure I did not say *so much!* But see the Lordliness of a high Condition!—A poor Body must not put in a Word when they take it into their Heads to be angry! What a fine Time a Person of unequal Condition would have of it, if even they were to marry such an one!—His poor dear Mother spoil'd him at first.[1] Nobody must speak to him or contradict him, as I have heard, when he was a Child, and so he has not been us'd to be controul'd, and cannot bear the least Thing that crosses his violent Will. This is one of the Blessings of a high Condition! Much good may do them with their Pride of Birth, and Pride of Fortune, say I!—All that it serves for, as far as I can see, is to multiply their Disquiets, and every body's else that has to do with them.

So, so! where will this end!—Mrs. *Jewkes* has been with me from him, and she says, I must get me out of the House this Moment! Well, said I, but where am I to be carry'd next? Why, home, said she, to your Father and Mother. And, can it be, said I!—No, no, I doubt I shall not be so happy as that!—To be sure, some bad Design is on foot again! To be sure it is!—Sure, sure, said I, Mrs. *Jewkes*, he has not found out some other House-keeper worse than you! She was very angry, you may well think. But I know she can't be made worse than she is.

She came up again. Are you ready? said she. Bless me, said I, you are very hasty: I have heard of this not a Quarter of an Hour ago. But I shall be soon ready; for I have but little to take with me and no kind Friends in this House to take Leave of, to delay me. Yet, like a Fool, I can't help crying. Pray, said I, just step down, and ask, if I may not have my Papers?

So, I am quite ready now, against she comes up with an Answer; and so I will put up these few Writings in my Bosom, that I have left.

I don't know what to think—nor how to judge; but I shall ne'er believe I am with you till I am on my Knees before you, begging both your Blessings. Yet I am sorry he is so angry with me! I thought I did not say so much.

There is, I see, the Chariot drawn out, the Horses to, the grim *Colbrand* going to get a Horse-back. What will be the End of all this!

MONDAY.

Well, where this will end I cannot say. But here I am, at a little poor Village, almost such an one as yours; I shall learn the Name of it by-and-by. And *Robin* assures me he has Orders to carry me to you, my dear Father and Mother. God send he may say Truth, and not deceive me again. But having nothing else to do, and I am sure I shall not sleep a Wink to-night, if I was to go to bed, I will write my Time away, and take up my Story where I left off, on *Sunday* Afternoon.

Mrs. *Jewkes*, came up to me, with this Answer about my Papers. My Master says, he will not read them yet, lest he should be mov'd by any thing in them to alter his Resolution. But, if he shall think it worth while to read them, he will send them to you afterwards to your Father's. But, said she, here are your Guineas that I borrow'd: For all is over now, I find, with you.

She saw me cry; and said, Do you repent?—Of what, said I?—Nay, I can't tell, said she; but to be sure he has had a Taste of your satirical Flings,

or he would not be so angry. Oh! said she, and held up her Hand, Thou
hast a Spirit!—but I hope it will now be brought down.—I hope so too,
said I.—

Well, added I, I am ready. She lifted up the Window, and said, I'll
call *Robin* to take your Portmanteau: Bag and Baggage,¹ said she, I'm glad
you're going! I have no Words, said I, to throw away upon *you*, Mrs. *Jewkes*;
but, making her a very low Curchee, I most heartily thank you for all your
virtuous Civilities to me. And so, adieu; for I'll have no Portmanteau, I'll
assure you, nor any thing but these few Things that I brought with me in
my Handkerchief, besides what I have on. For I had all this Time worn my
own bought Cloaths, tho' my Master would have had it otherwise often;
but I had put up Paper, Ink and Pens, however.

So down I went, and as I went by the Parlour, she stept in, and said, Sir,
you have nothing to say to the Girl before she goes? I heard him say, tho'
I did not see him, Who bid you say *the Girl*, Mrs. *Jewkes*, in that Manner?
She has offended only me!

I beg your Honour's Pardon, said the Wretch; but if I was your Honour,
she should not, for all the Trouble she has cost you, go away scot-free. No
more of this, as *I told you before*, said he: What! when I have such Proof,
that her Virtue is all her Pride, shall I rob her of that?—No, said he, let
her go, perverse and foolish as she is; but she *deserves* to go honest, and she
shall go so!

I was so transported with this unexpected Goodness, that I open'd the
Door before I knew what I did; and I said, falling on my Knees at the Door,
with my Hands folded and lifted up, O thank you, thank your Honour a
Million of Times!—May God bless you for this Instance of your Goodness
to me! I will pray for you as long as I live, and so shall my dear Father
and Mother. And, Mrs. *Jewkes*, said I, I will pray for *you* too, poor wicked
Wretch that you are!

He turn'd from me, and went into his Closet, and shut the Door. He
need not have done so; for I would not have gone nearer to him!

Surely I did not say so much to incur all this Displeasure!

I think I was loth to leave the House. Can you believe it?—What could be
the Matter with me, I wonder!—I felt something so strange, and my Heart
was so lumpish!—I wonder what ail'd me!—But this was so *unexpected!*—I
believe that was all!—Yet I am very strange still. Surely, surely, I cannot be
like the old murmuring *Israelites*,² to long after the Onions and Garlick of
Egypt, when they had suffer'd there such heavy Bondage?—I'll take thee,
O lumpish, contradictory, ungovernable Heart, to severe Task for this thy
strange Impulse, when I get to my dear Father's and Mother's; and if I

find any thing in thee that should not be, depend upon it, thou shalt be humbled, if strict Abstinence, Prayer and Mortification will do it!

But yet, after all, this last Goodness of his has touched me too sensibly. I wish I had not heard it, almost; and yet methinks I am glad I did; for I should rejoice to think the best of him, for his own sake.

Well, and so I went to the Chariot, the same that brought me down. So, Mr. *Robert*, said I, here I am again! a pure Sporting-piece for the Great! a mere Tennis-ball of Fortune!¹ You have your Orders, I hope! Yes, Madam, said he. Pray now, said I, don't Madam me, nor stand with your Hat off to such a one as I. Had not my Master, said he, order'd me not to be wanting in Respects to you, I would have shewn you all I could. Well, said I, with my Heart full, That's very kind, Mr. *Robert.*

Mr. *Colbrand*, mounted on Horseback, with Pistols before him, came up to me, as soon as I got in, with his Hat off too. What, Monsieur, said I, are *you* to go with me?—Part of the Way, he said, to see you safe! I *hope* that's kind too in you, Mr. *Colbrand*, said I.

I had nobody to wave my Handkerchief to now, nor to take Leave of; and so I resign'd myself to my Contemplations, with this strange wayward Heart of mine, that I never found so ungovernable and awkward before.

So away drove the Chariot! And when I had got out of the Elm-walk, and into the great Road, I could hardly think but I was in a Dream all the Time. A few Hours before in my Master's Arms almost, with twenty kind Things said to me, and a generous Concern for the Misfortunes he had brought upon me; and only by one rash half Word exasperated against me, and turn'd out of Doors, at an Hour's Warning; and all his Kindness changed to Hate! And I now, from Three o'Clock to Five, several Miles off.—But if I am going to you, all will be well again, I hope!

Lack-a-day, what strange Creatures are Men! Gentlemen, I should say rather! For, my dear deserving good Mother, tho' Poverty be both your Lots, has had a better Hap; and you are, and have always been, blest in one another!—Yet this pleases me too, he was so good, he would not let Mrs. *Jewkes* speak ill of me; and scorn'd to take her odious unwomanly Advice. O what a black Heart has this poor Wretch! So I need not rail against Men so much; for my Master, bad as I have thought him, is not half so bad as this Woman!—To be sure she must be an Atheist! Do you think she is not?——

We could not reach further than this little poor Place, and sad Alehouse, rather than Inn; for it began to be dark, and *Robin* did not make so much

Haste as he might have done: And he was forc'd to make hard Shift for his Horses. Mr. *Colbrand* and *Robert* too are very civil. I see he has got my Portmanteau lash'd behind the Coach. I did not desire it; but I shall not come quite empty. A thorough Riddance of me, I see!—Bag and Baggage! as Mrs. *Jewkes* says. Well, my Story surely would furnish out a surprizing kind of Novel, if it was to be well told.

Mr. *Robert* came up to me, just now, and begg'd me to eat something. I thank'd him; but said I could not eat. I bid him ask Mr. *Colbrand* to walk up; and he came; but neither of them would sit, nor put their Hats on. What Mockado[1] is this to such a poor Soul as I! I ask'd them, if they were at Liberty to tell me the Truth of what they were to do with me? if not, I would not desire it.—They both said, *Robin* was order'd to carry me to my Father's. And Mr. *Colbrand* was to leave me within ten Miles, and then strike off for the other House, and wait till my Master arriv'd there. They both spoke so solemnly, that I cannot but believe them.

But when *Robin* went down, the other said, he had a Letter to give me next Day, at Noon, when we baited, as we were to do, at Mrs. *Jewkes's* Relations.—May I not, said I, beg the Favour to see it to-night? He seem'd so loth to deny me; that I have Hopes, I shall prevail on him by-and-by.

Well, my dear Father and Mother, I have, on great Promises of Secrecy, and making no Use of it, got the Letter. I will try if I can open it, without breaking the Seal, and will take a Copy of it, by-and-by: For *Robin* is in and out; there being hardly any Room in this little House for one to be long alone. Well, this is the Letter.

'When these Lines are deliver'd to you, you will be far on your Way to your Father and Mother, where you have so long desired to be. And, I hope, I shall forbear thinking of you with the least Shadow of that Fondness my foolish Heart had entertain'd for you. I bear you, however, no Ill-will; but the End of my detaining you being over, I would not that you should tarry with me an Hour more than needed, after the ungenerous Preference you gave against me, at a Time that I was inclined to pass over all other Considerations, for an honourable Address to you; for well I found the Tables intirely turn'd upon me, and that I was in far more Danger from *you* than you was from *me*; for I was just upon resolving to defy all the Censures of the World, and to make you my Wife.

'I will acknowledge another Truth; That had I not parted with you as I did, but permitted you to stay till I had read your Journal, reflecting, as I doubt not I shall find it, and till I had heard your bewitching Pleas in your Behalf, I fear'd I could not trust myself with my own Resolution. And this is the Reason, I frankly own, that I have determin'd not to see you, nor hear you speak; for, well I know my Weakness in your Favour.

'But I will get the better of this fond Folly. Nay, I hope I have already done it, since it was likely to cost me so dear. And I write this to tell you, that I wish you well with all my Heart, tho' you have spread such Mischiefs thro' my Family.——And yet, I cannot but say, that I could wish you would not think of marrying in haste; and particularly that you would not have this cursed *Williams*.—But what is all this to me now?—— Only, my Weakness makes me say, That as I had already look'd upon you as mine; and you have so soon got rid of your first Husband, so you will not refuse, to my Memory, the Decency that every common Person observes, to pay a Twelve-month's Compliment, tho' but a mere Compliment, to my Ashes.

'Your Papers shall be faithfully return'd you, and I have paid so dear for my Curiosity in the Affection they have rivetted upon me for you, that you would look upon yourself amply reveng'd, if you knew what they have cost me.

'I thought of writing but a few Lines; but I have run into Length. I will now try to recollect my scatter'd Thoughts, and resume my Reason, and shall find Trouble enough to replace my Affairs, and my own Family; and to supply the Chasms you have made in it: For, let me tell you, tho' I can forgive you, I never can my Sister, nor my Domestics; for my Vengeance must be wreak'd somewhere.

'I doubt not your Prudence in forbearing to expose me any more than is necessary for you own Justification; and for *that*, I will suffer myself to be accused by you, and will also accuse myself, if it be needful. For I am, and will ever be,

'*Your affectionate Well-wisher.*'

This Letter, when I expected some new Plot, has affected me more than any thing of that Sort could have done. For here is plainly his great Value for me confess'd, and his rigorous Behaviour accounted for in such a Manner, as tortures me much. And all this wicked Gypsey Story is, as it seems, a Forgery upon us both, and has quite ruin'd me! For, Oh! my dear Parents, forgive me! but I found to my Grief before, that my Heart was too partial in his Favour; but *now*, with so much Openness, so much Affection, nay, so much *Honour* too, (which was all I had before doubted, and kept me on the Reserve) I am quite overcome. This was a Happiness, however, I had no Reason to expect. But to be sure, I must own to you, that I shall never be able to think of any body in the World but him!—Presumption, you will say; and so it is: But Love is not a voluntier Thing:—*Love*, did I say!—But, come, I hope not!—At least it is not, I hope, gone so far, as to make me *very* uneasy; for I know not *how* it came, nor when it begun; but creep, creep it has, like a Thief upon me; and before I knew what was the Matter, it look'd like Love.

I wish, since it is too late, and my Lot determin'd, that I had not had this Letter; nor heard him take my Part to that vile Woman; for then I should have bless'd myself, in having escap'd so happily his designing Arts upon my Virtue; but *now*, my poor Mind is all topsy-turvy'd, and I have made an Escape, to be more a Prisoner!

But, I hope, since thus it is, that all will be for the best; and I shall, with your prudent Advice, and pious Prayers, be able to overcome this Weakness.—But, to be sure, my dear Sir, I will keep a longer Time than a Twelve-month, as a true Widow, for a Compliment, and *more* than a Compliment, to your Ashes!—O the dear Word!—How kind, how moving, how affectionate is that Word! O why was I not a Duchess, to shew my Gratitude for it? but must labour under the Weight of an Obligation, even had this Happiness befallen me, that would have press'd me to Death, and which I never could return by a whole Life of faithful Love, and chearful Obedience.

O forgive your poor Daughter!—I am sorry to find this Trial so sore upon me; and that all the Weakness of my weak Sex, and tender Years, who never before knew what it was to be so touch'd, is rais'd against me, and too mighty to be withstood by me.—But Time, Prayer, and Resignation to God's Will, and the Benefits of your good Lessons and Examples, I hope, will enable me to get over this so heavy a Trial.—O my treacherous, treacherous Heart! to serve me thus! And give no Notice to me of the Mischiefs thou wast about to bring upon me! But thus foolishly to give thyself up to the proud Invader, without ever consulting thy poor Mistress in the least! But thy Punishment will be the *first* and the *greatest*; and well deservest thou to smart, O perfidious Traitor, for giving up so weakly, thy *whole Self*, before a Summons came, and to one too, who had us'd me so hardly! And when, likewise, thou hadst so well maintain'd thy Post against the most violent and avowed, and therefore, as I thought, more dangerous Attacks.

After all, I must either not shew you this my Weakness, or tear it out of my Writing.—*Memorandum*, to consider of this, when I get home.

MONDAY Morning Eleven o'Clock.

We are just come in here, to the Relations of Mrs. *Jewkes*. The first Compliment I had, was, in a very impudent manner, How I liked the

'Squire?—I could not help saying, Bold, forward Woman! Is it for you, who keep an Inn, to treat Passengers at this Rate? She was but in jest, she said, and begg'd Pardon: And she came, and begg'd Excuse again, very submissively, after *Robin* and Mr. *Colbrand* had talk'd to her a little.

The latter here, in great Form, gave me, before *Robin*, the Letter, which I had given him back for that purpose. And I retir'd, as if to read it; and so I did; for I think I can't read it too often; tho', for my Peace of Mind sake, I might better try to forget it. I am sorry, methinks, I cannot bring you back a sound Heart; but indeed it is an honest one, as to any body but me; for it has deceived nobody else: Wicked thing as it is!

More and more surprizing Things still!—
Just as I had sat down, to try to eat a bit of Victuals, to get ready to pursue my Journey, came in Mr. *Colbrand*, in a mighty Hurry. O Madam! Madam! said he, Here be de Groom from de 'Squire *B.* all over in a Lather, Man and Horse! O how my Heart went pit-a-pat!—What now, thought I, is to come next! He went out, and presently return'd with a Letter for me, and another, inclosed, for Mr. *Colbrand.* This seem'd odd, and put me all in a Trembling. So I shut the Door; and, never, sure, was the like known! found the following agreeable Contents.

'In vain, my *Pamela*, do I find it to struggle against my Affection for you. I must needs, after you were gone, venture to entertain myself with your Journal. When I found Mrs. *Jewkes*'s bad Usage of you, after your dreadful Temptations and Hurts; and particularly your generous Concern for me, on hearing how narrowly I escaped drowning (tho' my Death would have been your Freedom, and I had made it your Interest to wish it); and your most agreeable Confession in another Place, that notwithstanding all my hard Usage of you, you could not *hate* me; and that expressed in so sweet, so soft, and so innocent a manner, that I flatter myself you may be brought to *love* me, (together with the other Parts of your admirable Journal) I began to repent my parting with you. But, God is my Witness, for no unlawful End, as you would call it; but the very contrary. And the rather, as all this was improv'd in your Favour, by your Behaviour at leaving my House: For, Oh! that melodious Voice praying for me at your Departure, and thanking me for my Rebuke to Mrs. *Jewkes*, still hangs upon my Ears, and quavers upon my Memory. And tho' I went to-bed, I could not rest; but about Two got up, and made *Thomas* get one of the best Horses ready, in order to set out to overtake you, while I sat down to write this to you.

'Now, my dear *Pamela*, let me beg of you, on the Receipt of this, to order *Robin* to drive you back again to my House. I would have set out myself, for the Pleasure of bearing you Company back in the Chariot; but am really indisposed: I believe, with Vexation that I should part thus with my Soul's Delight, as I now find you are, and must be, in spight of the Pride of my own Heart.

'You cannot imagine the Obligation your Return will lay me under to your Goodness; and yet, if you will not so far favour me, you shall be under no Restraint, as you will see by my Letter inclosed to *Colbrand*; which I have not sealed, that you may read it. But spare me, my dearest Girl, the Confusion of following you to your Father's; which I must do, if you persist to go on; for I find I cannot live a Day without you.

'If you are the generous *Pamela* I imagine you to be, (for hitherto you have been all Goodness, where it has not been merited) let me see, by this new Instance, the further Excellency of your Disposition; let me see you can forgive the Man who loves you more than himself; let me see by it, that you are not prepossess'd in any other Person's Favour: And one Instance more I would beg, and then I am all Gratitude; and that is, That you would dispatch Monsieur *Colbrand* with a Letter to your Father, assuring him, that all will end happily; and that he will send to you, at my House, the Letters you found means, by *Williams's* Conveyance, to send him: And when I have all my proud, and, perhaps, punctilious Doubts answer'd, I shall have nothing to do, but to make you happy, and be so my self. For I must be

'*Yours, and only Yours.*'

'*Monday* Morn. near
  'three o'Clock.'

O my exulting Heart! how it throbs in my Bosom, as if it would reproach me for so lately upbraiding it for giving way to the Love of so dear a Gentleman!—But, take care thou art not too credulous neither, O fond Believer! Things that we wish, are apt to gain a too ready Credence with us. This sham Marriage is not yet clear'd up; Mrs. *Jewkes*, the vile Mrs. *Jewkes!* may yet instigate the Mind of this Master: His Pride of Heart, and Pride of Condition, may again take place; and a Man that could, in so little a Space, first love me, then hate me, then banish me his House, and send me away disgracefully; and now send for me again, in such affectionate Terms; may still waver, may still deceive thee. Therefore will I not acquit thee yet, O credulous, fluttering, throbbing Mischief! that art so ready to believe what thou wishest: And I charge thee to keep better Guard than thou hast lately done, and lead me not to follow too implicitly thy flattering and desirable Impulses. Thus foolishly dialogu'd I with my Heart; and yet all the time this Heart is *Pamela*.

I open'd the Letter to Monsieur *Colbrand*; which was in these Words:

'Monsieur,

'I am sure you'll excuse the Trouble I give you. I have, for good Reasons, changed my Mind; and I have besought it as a Favour, that Mrs. *Andrews* will return to me the Moment *Tom* reaches you. I hope, for the Reasons I have given her, she will have the Goodness to oblige me. But if not, you are to order *Robin* to pursue his Directions, and set her down at her Father's Door. If she *will* oblige me in her Return, perhaps she'll give you a Letter to her Father, for some Papers to be deliver'd to you for her. Which you'll be so good, in that Case, to bring to her *here*. But if she will *not* give you such a Letter, you'll return with her to me, if she pleases to favour me so far; and that with all Expedition, that her Health and Safety will permit; for I am pretty much indisposed; but hope it will be but slight, and soon go off. I am

'Yours, &c.

'On second Thoughts, let *Tom* go forward with Mrs. *Andrews*'s Letter, if she pleases to give one, and you return with her, for her Safety.'

Now this is a dear generous Manner of treating me. O how I love to be generously used!—Now, my dear Parents, I wish I could consult you for your Opinions, how I should act. Should I go back, or should I not?—I doubt he has got too great Hold in my Heart, for me to be easy presently, if I should refuse: And yet this Gypsey Information makes me fearful.

Well, I will, I think, trust in his Generosity! Yet is it not too great a Trust?—especially considering how I have been used!—But then that was while he vow'd his bad Designs; and now he gives great Hope of his good ones. And I *may* be the means of making many happy, as well as myself, by placing a generous Confidence in him.

And then, I think, he might have sent to *Colbrand*, and to *Robin*, to carry me back, whether I would or not. And how different is his Behaviour to that? And would it not look as if I am *prepossess'd*, as he calls it, if I don't oblige him; and as if it was a silly female Piece of Pride to make him follow me to my Father's; and as if I would use him hardly in *my* Turn, for his having used me ill in *his?* Upon the whole, I resolved to obey him; and if he uses me ill afterwards, double will be his ungenerous Guilt!—Tho' hard will be my Lot, to have my Credulity so justly blameable as it will then seem. For, to be sure, the World, the wise World, that never is wrong itself, judges always by Events. And if he should use me ill, then I shall be blamed for trusting him: If well, O then I did right, to be sure!—But how would my Censurers act in my Case, before the Event justifies or condemns the Action, is the Question?

Then I have no Notion of obliging by Halves; but of doing things with a Grace, as one may say, where they *are* to be done; and so I wrote the desir'd Letter to you, assuring you, that I had before me happier Prospects than ever I yet had; and hoped all would end well. And that I begg'd you would send me, by Mr. *Thomas*, my Master's Groom, the Bearer of it, those Papers, which I had sent you by Mr. *Williams's* Conveyance: For that they imported me much, for clearing up a Point in my Conduct, that my Master was desirous to know, before he resolved to favour me, as he had intended.—But you will have that Letter, before you can have this; for I would not send you this without the preceding; which now is in my Master's Hands.

And so, having given the Letter to Mr. *Thomas*, for him to carry to you, when he had baited and rested, after his great Fatigue, I sent for Monsieur *Colbrand* and *Robin*; and gave to the former his Letter; and when he had read it, I said, You see how things stand. I am resolved to return to our Master; and as he is not so well as were to be wished, the more Haste you make, the better: And don't mind my Fatigue; but consider only yourselves, and the Horses. *Robin*, who guess'd the matter, by his Conversation with *Thomas*, (as I suppose) said, God bless you, Madam, and reward you, as your Obligingness to my good Master deserves; and may we all live to see you triumph over Mrs. *Jewkes*.

I wonder'd to hear him say so; for I was always careful of exposing my Master, or even that naughty Woman, before the common Servants. But yet I question whether *Robin* would have said this, if he had not guessed, by *Thomas's* Message, and my resolving to return, that I might stand well with his Master. So selfish are the Hearts of poor Mortals, that they are ready to change as Favour goes!

So they were not long getting ready; and I am just setting out, back again; and I hope in God, shall have no Reason to repent it.

Robin put on very vehemently; and when we came to the little Town, where we lay on *Sunday* Night, he gave his Horses a Bait; and said, he would push for his Master's that Night, as it would be Moon-light, if I should not be too much fatigu'd; because there was no Place between that and the Town adjacent to his Master's, fit to put up for the Night. But Monsieur *Colbrand*'s Horse beginning to give way, made a Doubt between them: Wherefore I said (hating to lie on the Road) If it could be done, I should bear it well enough, I hoped; and that Monsieur *Colbrand* might leave his Horse, when it fail'd, at some House, and come into the Chariot. This pleased them both; and about twelve Miles short, he left the Horse, and took off his Spurs and Holsters, &c. and, with Abundance of ceremonial Excuses, came into the Chariot; and I sat the easier for it; for my Bones ached sadly with the Jolting, and so many Miles travelling in so few Hours, as I had done, from *Sunday* Night, Five o'Clock. But, for all this, it was Eleven o'Clock at Night when we came to the Village adjacent to my Master's; and the Horses began to be very much tired, and *Robin* too; but I said, It would be pity to put up only three Miles short of the House.

So about One we reach'd the Gate; but every body was a-bed. But one of the Helpers got the Keys from Mrs. *Jewkes*, and open'd the Gates; and the Horses could hardly crawl into the Stables. And I, when I went to get out of the Chariot, fell down, and thought I had lost the Use of my Limbs.

Mrs. *Jewkes* came down, with her Cloaths huddled on, and lifted up her Hands and Eyes, at my Return. But shew'd more Care of the Horses than of me. By that time the two Maids came; and I made shift to creep in as well as I could.

It seems my poor Master was very ill indeed, and had been upon the Bed most part of the Day; and *Abraham* (who succeeded *John*) sat up with him. And he was got into a fine Sleep, and heard not the Coach come in, nor the Noise we made; for his Chamber lay towards the Garden, on the other Side the House. Mrs. *Jewkes* said, He had a feverish Complaint, and had been blooded; and, very prudently, order'd *Abraham*, when he awaked, not to tell him I was come, for fear of surprizing him, and augmenting his Fever; nor, indeed, to say any thing of me, till she herself broke it to him in the Morning, as she should see how he was.

So I went to-bed with Mrs. *Jewkes*, after she had caused me to drink almost half a Pint of burnt Wine,[1] made very rich and cordial, with Spices; which I found very refreshing, and set me into a Sleep I little hoped for.

TUESDAY *Morning.*

Getting up pretty early, I have written thus far, while Mrs. *Jewkes* lies snoring in bed, fetching-up[2] her last Night's Disturbance. I long for her Rising, to know how my poor Master does. 'Tis well for her she can sleep so purely. No Love, but for herself, will ever break her Rest, I am sure. I am deadly sore all over, as if I had been soundly beaten. Yet I did not think I could have liv'd under such Fatigue.

Mrs. *Jewkes*, as soon as she got up, went to know how my Master did, and he had had a good Night; and having drank plentifully of Sack-whey,[1] had sweated much; so that his Fever had abated considerably. She said to him, that he must not be surprized, and she would tell him News. He asked, What? and she said, I was come. He raised himself up in his Bed; Can it be? said he:—What, already!—She told him, I came last Night. Monsieur *Colbrand* coming to inquire of his Health, he order'd him to draw near him, and was infinitely pleased with the Account he gave him of the Journey; my Readiness to come back, and my Willingness to reach home that Night. And he said, Why, these tender Fair-ones, I think, bear Fatigue better than us Men. But she is very good, to give me such an Instance of her Readiness to oblige me. Pray, Mrs. *Jewkes*, said he, take great Care of her Health; and let her lie a-bed all Day. She told him, I had been up these two Hours. Ask her, said he, if she will be so good as to pay me a Visit; if she won't, I'll rise, and go to her. Indeed, Sir, said she, you must lie still; and I'll go to her. But don't urge her too much, said he, if she be unwilling.

She came to me, and told me all the above; and I said, I would most willingly wait upon him. For indeed I longed to see him, and was much grieved he was so ill.—So I went down with her. Will she come? said he, as I enter'd the Room. Yes, Sir, said she; and she said, at the first Word, Most willingly. Sweet Excellence! said he.

As soon as he saw me, he said, O my beloved *Pamela!* you have made me quite well. I'm concern'd to return my Acknowledgments to you in so unfit a Place and Manner; but will you give me your Hand? I did, and he kissed it with great Eagerness. Sir, said I, you do me too much Honour!—I am sorry you are ill.—I can't be ill, said he, while you are with me. I am well already.

Well, said he, and kissed my Hand again, you shall not repent this Goodness. My Heart is too full of it, to express myself as I ought. But I am sorry you have had such a fatiguing Time of it.—Life is no Life without you! If you had refused me, and yet I had hardly Hopes you would oblige me, I should have had a severe Fit of it, I believe; for I was taken very oddly, and knew not what to make of myself: But now I shall be well instantly. You need not, Mrs. *Jewkes*, added he, send for the Doctor from *Stamford*, as we talked Yesterday; for this lovely Creature is my Doctor, as her Absence was my Disease.

He begg'd me to sit down by his Bed-side, and asked me, If I had obliged him with sending for my former Pacquet? I said, I had, and hoped it would be brought. He said, It was doubly kind.

I would not stay long, because of disturbing him. And he got up in the Afternoon, and desir'd my Company; and seem'd quite pleas'd, easy, and much better. He said, Mrs. *Jewkes*, after this Instance of my good *Pamela's* Obligingness in her Return, I am sure we ought to leave her intirely at her own Liberty; and pray, if she pleases to take a Turn in the Chariot, or in the Garden, or to the Town, or where-ever she will, she must be left at Liberty, and asked no Questions; and do you do all in your Power to oblige her. She said, she would, to be sure.

He took my Hand, and said, One thing I will tell you, *Pamela*, because I know you will be glad to hear it, and yet not care to ask me, I have taken *Williams's* Bond for the Money; for how the poor Man had behaved, I can't tell; but he could get no Bail; and if I have no fresh Reason given me, perhaps I shall not exact the Payment; and he has been some time at Liberty; and now follows his School; but, methinks, I could wish you would not see him at present.

Sir, said I, I will not do any thing to disoblige you wilfully; and I am glad he is at Liberty, because I was the Occasion of his Misfortunes. I durst say no more, tho' I wanted to plead for the poor Gentleman; which, in Gratitude, I thought I ought, when I could do him Service. I said, I am sorry, Sir, Lady *Davers*, who loves you so well, should have incurr'd your Displeasure, and there should be any Variance between your Honour and her. I hope it was not on my Account. He took out of his Waistcoat Pocket, as he sat in his Gown, his Letter-case, and said, Here, *Pamela*, read that when you go up Stairs, and let me have your Thoughts upon it; and that will let you into the Affair. He said, he was very heavy of a sudden, and would lie down, and indulge for that Day; and if he was better in the Morning, would take an Airing in the Chariot. And so I took my Leave for the present, and went up to my Closet, and read the Letter he was pleased to put into my Hands; and which is as follows:

'*Brother*,

'I am very uneasy at what I hear of you; and must write, whether it please you or not, my *full* Mind. I have had some People with me, desiring me to interpose with you; and they have a greater Regard for your Honour, than, I am sorry to say it, you have yourself. Could I think that a Brother of mine would so meanly run away with my late dear Mother's Waiting-maid, and keep her a Prisoner from all her Friends, and to the Disgrace of your own. But I thought, when you would not let the Wench come to me on my Mother's Death, that you meant no good.—I blush for you, I'll assure you. The Girl was an innocent, good Girl; but I suppose that's over with her now, or soon will. What can you mean by this, let me ask you? Either you will have her for a kept Mistress, or for a Wife. If the former; there are enough to be had, without ruining a poor Wench that my Mother lov'd, and who really was a very good Girl; and of *this* you may be asham'd. As to the *other*, I dare say, you don't think of it; but if you *should*, you would be utterly inexcusable. Consider, Brother, that ours is no up-start Family; but is as ancient as the best in the Kingdom; and, for several Hundreds of Years, it has never been known that the Heirs of it have disgraced themselves by unequal Matches: And you know you have been sought to by some of the first Families in the Nation, for your Alliance. It might be well enough, if you were descended of a Family of Yesterday, or but a Remove or two from the Dirt you seem so fond of. But, let me tell you, that I, and all mine, will renounce you for ever, if you can descend so meanly; and I shall be ashamed to be called your Sister. A handsome Gentleman as you are in your Person; so happy in the Gifts of your Mind, that every body courts your Company; and possess'd of such a noble and clear Estate; and very rich in Money besides, left you by the best of Fathers and Mothers, with such ancient Blood in your Veins, untainted! for *you* to throw away yourself thus, is intolerable; and it would be very wicked in you to ruin the Wench too. So that I beg you will restore her to her Parents, and give her 100 *l.* or so, to make her happy in some honest Fellow of her own Degree; and that will be doing something, and will also oblige and pacify

'*Your much grieved Sister.*

'If I have written too sharply, consider it is my Love to you, and the Shame you are bringing upon yourself; and I wish this may have the Effect upon you intended by your very loving Sister.'

    This is a sad Letter, my dear Father and Mother; and one may see how poor People are despised by the Proud and the Rich; and yet we were all on a foot originally: And many of these Gentlefolks, that brag of their ancient Blood, would be glad to have it as wholsome, and as really untainted, as ours!—Surely these proud People never think what a short Stage Life is; and that, with all their Vanity, a Time is coming, when they shall be obliged to submit to be on a Level with us; and true said the Philosopher,[1] when he looked upon the Skull of a King, and that of a poor Man, that he saw no Difference between them. Besides, do they not know, that the richest of Princes, and the poorest of Beggars, are to have one great and tremendous Judge, at the last Day; who will not distinguish between them, according to their Qualities in Life?—But, on the contrary, may make their Condemnations the greater, as their neglected Opportunities were the greater? Poor Souls! how I pity their Pride!—O keep me, gracious God! from *their* high Condition, if my Mind shall ever be tainted with their Vice! or polluted with so cruel and inconsiderate a Contempt of the humble Estate which they behold with so much Scorn!

But besides, how do these Gentry know, that supposing they could trace back their Ancestry, for one, two, three, or even five hundred Years, that then the original Stems of these poor Families, tho' they have not kept such elaborate Records of their Good-for-nothingness, as it often proves, were not still deeper rooted?—And how can they be assured, that one hundred Years hence or two, some of those now despised upstart Families, may not revel in their Estates, while their Descendants may be reduced to the other's Dunghils?—And, perhaps, such is the Vanity, as well as Changeableness of human Estates, in *their* Turns set up for Pride of Family, and despise the others!

These Reflections occurr'd to my Thoughts, made serious by my Master's Indisposition, and this proud Letter, of the *lowly* Lady *Davers*, against the *high-minded* Pamela. *Lowly*, I say, because she could *stoop* to such vain *Pride*; and *high-minded I*, because I hope I am too *proud* ever to do the like!—But, after all, poor Wretches that we be! we scarce know what we *are*, much less what we *shall be!*—But, once more, pray I, to be kept from the sinful Pride of a high Estate!

On this Occasion I recall the following Lines, which I have read; where the Poet[1] argues in a much better manner.

> ---------*Wise Providence*
> *Does various Parts for various Minds dispense;*
> *The* meanest Slaves, *or those who* hedge *and* ditch,
> *Are useful, by their Sweat, to feed the* Rich.
> *The* Rich, *in due Return, impart their Store;*
> *Which comfortably feeds the lab'ring* Poor.
> *Nor let the* Rich *the* lowest Slave *disdain,*
> *He's* equally *a* Link *of Nature's* Chain;
> *Labours to the* same End, *joins in* one View;
> *And* both alike *the* Will divine *pursue:*
> *And, at the last, are levell'd,* King *and* Slave,
> *Without Distinction, in the silent Grave.*

WEDNESDAY Morning.

My Master sent me a Message just now, that he was so much better, that he would take a Turn after Breakfast, in the Chariot, and would have me give him my Company! I hope I shall know how to be humble, and comport myself as I should do under all these Favours.

Mrs. *Jewkes* is one of the most obliging Creatures in the World; and I have such Respects shewn me by every one, as if I was as great as Lady *Davers.*—But now, if this should all end in the Sham-marriage!—It cannot be, I hope. Yet the Pride of Greatness and Ancestry, and such-like, is so strongly set out in Lady *Davers*'s Letter, that I cannot flatter myself to be so happy as all these desirable Appearances make for me. Should I be *now* deceived, I should be worse off than ever. But I shall see what Light this new Honour will procure me!—So I'll get ready. But I won't, I think, change my Garb. Should I do it, it would look as if I would be nearer on a Level with him: And yet, should I not, it may be thought a Disgrace to him; but I will, I think, open the Portmanteau, and, for the first time, since I came hither, put on my best Silk Night-gown. But then that will be making myself a sort of Right to the Cloaths I had renounced; and I am not yet quite sure I shall have no other Crosses to encounter. So I will go as I am; for tho' ordinary, I am as clean as a Penny, tho' I say it. So I'll e'en go as I am, except he orders otherwise. Yet Mrs. *Jewkes* says, I ought to dress as fine as I can!—But I say, I think not. As my Master is up, and at Breakfast, I will venture down to ask him how he will have me be.—

Well, he is kinder and kinder, and, thank God, purely recover'd!—How charmingly he looks, to what he did Yesterday! Blessed be God for it!

He arose and came to me, and took me by the Hand, and would set me down by him; and he said, My charming Girl seem'd going to speak. What would you say?—Sir, said I, (a little asham'd) I think it is too great an Honour to go into the Chariot with you! No, my dear *Pamela*, said he; the *Pleasure* of your Company will be greater than the *Honour* of mine; and so say no more on that Head.

But, Sir, said I, I shall disgrace you to go thus. You will grace a Prince, my Fair-one, said the good kind, kind Gentleman! in that Dress, or any you shall chuse. And you look so pretty, that if you shall not catch Cold, in that round-ear'd Cap, you shall go just as you are. But, Sir, said I, then you'll be pleased to go a By-way, that it mayn't be seen you do so much Honour to your Servant. O my good Girl, said he, I doubt you are afraid of yourself being talk'd of, more than me. For I hope, by degrees, to take off the World's Wonder, and teach them to expect what is to follow, as a Due to my *Pamela*.

O the dear good Man! There's for you, my dear Father and Mother!—Did I not do well now to come back!—O could I get rid of my Fears of this Sham-marriage, (for all this is not yet inconsistent with that frightful Scheme) I should be too happy!

So I came up, with great Pleasure, for my Gloves; and now wait his kind Commands. Dear, dear Sir! said I to myself, as if I was speaking to him, for *God's* sake let me have no more Trials and Reverses; for I could not bear it now, I verily think!

At last the welcome Message came, that my Master was ready; and so I went down as fast as I could; and he, before all the Servants, handed me in, as if I was a Lady; and then came in himself. Mrs. *Jewkes* begg'd he would take care he did not catch Cold, as he had been ill. And I had the Pride to hear his new Coachman say, to one of his Fellow-servants, They are a charming Pair, I am sure! 'tis pity they should be parted!—O my dear Father and Mother! I fear your Girl will grow as proud as any thing! And especially you will think I have Reason to guard against it, when you read the kind Particulars I am going to relate.

He order'd Dinner to be ready by Two; and *Abraham*, who succeeds *John*, went behind the Coach. He bid *Robin* drive gently, and told me, he wanted to talk to me about his Sister *Davers*, and other Matters. Indeed, at first setting out, he kissed me a little too often, that he did; and I was afraid of *Robin's* looking back, thro' the Fore-glass, and People seeing us as they passed; but he was exceedingly kind to me, in his Words, as well. At last, he said,

You have, I doubt not, read, over and over, my Sister's sawcy Letter; and find, as I told you, that you are no more obliged to her than I am. You see she intimates that some People had been with her; and who should they be but the officious Mrs. *Jervis*, and Mr. *Longman*, and *Jonathan!* And so that has made me take the Measures I did in dismissing them my Service.—I see, said he, you are going to speak on their Behalfs; but your Time is not come to do that, if ever I shall permit it.

My Sister, says he, I have been beforehand with; for I have renounced her. I am sure I have been a kind Brother to her; and gave her to the Value of 3000 *l.* more than her Share came to by my Father's Will, when I enter'd upon my Estate. And the Woman, surely, was beside herself with Passion and Insolence, when she wrote me such a Letter; for well she knew I would not bear it. But you must know, *Pamela*, that she is much incensed, that I will give no Ear to a Proposal of hers, of a Daughter of my

Lord ------ who, said he, neither in Person or Mind, or Acquirements, even with all her Opportunities, is to be named in a Day with my *Pamela*. But yet you see the Plea, my Girl, which I made to you before, of this Pride of Condition, and the World's Censure, which, I own, sticks a little too close with me still. For a Woman shines not forth to the Publick as a Man; and the World sees not your Excellencies and Perfections: If it did, I should intirely stand acquitted by the severest Censurers. But it will be taken in the Lump; that here is Mr. *B-----*, with such and such an Estate, has married his Mother's Waiting-maid; not considering there is not a Lady in the Kingdom that can outdo her, or better support the Condition to which she will be raised, if I should marry her. And, said he, putting his Arm round me, and again kissing me, I pity my dear Girl too, for *her* Part in this Censure; for, here will she have to combat the Pride and Slights of the neighbouring Gentry all around us. Sister *Davers*, you see, will never be reconciled to you. The other Ladies will not visit you; and you will, with a Merit transcending them all, be treated as if unworthy their Notice. Should I now marry my *Pamela*, how will my Girl relish all this? Won't these be cutting things to my Fair-one? For, as to me, I shall have nothing to do, but, with a good Estate in Possession, to brazen out the Matter, of my former Jokes on this Subject, with my Companions of the Chace, the Green, and the Assemblée;[1] stand their rude Jests for once or twice, and my Fortune will create me always Respect enough, I warrant you. But, I say, what will my poor Girl do, as to her Part, with her own Sex? For some Company you must keep. My Station will not admit it to be with my common Servants; and the Ladies will fly your Acquaintance; and still, tho' my Wife, will treat you as my Mother's Waiting-maid.—What says my Girl to this?

You may well guess, my dear Father and Mother, how transporting these kind, these generous and condescending Sentiments were to me!—I thought I had the Harmony of the Spheres all around me; and every Word that dropt from his Lips, was as sweet as the Honey of *Hybla*[2] to me.—Oh! Sir, said I, how inexpressibly kind and good is all this! Your poor Servant has a much greater Struggle than this to go thro', a more knotty Difficulty to overcome.

What is that? said he, a little impatiently: I will not forgive your Doubts now!—No, Sir, said I, I cannot doubt; but it is, how I shall *support*, how I shall *deserve*, your Goodness to me!—Dear Girl! said he, and hugg'd me to his Breast, I was afraid you would have made me angry again; but that I would not be; because I see you have a grateful Heart; and this your kind and chearful Return, after such cruel Usage as you had experienced in my

House, enough to make you detest the Place, has made me resolve to bear any thing in you, but Doubts of my Honour, at a Time when I am pouring out my Soul, with a true and affectionate Ardour, before you.

But, good Sir, said I, my greatest Concern will be for the rude Jests you will have to encounter with yourself, for thus stooping beneath yourself. For as to me, considering my lowly Estate, and little Merit, even the Slights and Reflections of the Ladies will be an Honour to me: And I shall have the Pride to place more than half their Ill-will, to their Envy at my Happiness. And if I can, by the most chearful Duty, and resigned Obedience, have the Pleasure to be agreeable to you, I shall think myself but too happy, let the World say what it will.

He said, You are very good, my dearest Girl: But how will you bestow your Time, when you will have no Visits to receive or pay? No Parties of Pleasure to join in? No Card-tables to employ your Winter Evenings, and even, as the Taste is, half the Day, Summer and Winter? And you have often play'd with my Mother too, and so know how to perform a Part there, as well as in the other Diversions: And I'll assure you, my Girl, I shall not desire you to live without such Amusements, as my Wife might expect, were I to marry a Lady of the first Quality.

O, Sir, said I, you are all Goodness! How shall I bear it!—But do you think, Sir, in such a Family as yours, a Person, whom you shall honour with the Name of Mistress of it, will not find useful Employments for her Time, without looking abroad for any others?

In the first Place, Sir, if you will give me Leave, I will myself look into such Parts of the Family Oeconomy, as may not be beneath the Rank to which I shall have the Favour of being exalted, if any such there can be; and this, I hope, without incurring the Ill-will of any *honest* Servant.

Then, Sir, I will ease you of as much of your Family Accounts, as I possibly can, when I have convinced you, that I am to be trusted with them; and, you know, Sir, my late good Lady made me her Treasurer, her Almoner, and every thing.

Then, Sir, if I must needs be visiting or visited, and the Ladies won't honour me so much, or even if they *would* now-and-then, I will receive and pay Visits, if your Goodness will allow me so to do, to the sick Poor in the Neighbourhood around you; and administer to their Wants and Necessities, in such small Matters, as may not be hurtful to your Estate, but comfortable to them; and intail upon you their Blessings, and their Prayers for your dear Health and Welfare.

Then I will assist your Housekeeper, as I used to do, in the making Jellies, Comfits, Sweetmeats, Marmalades, Cordials; and to pot, and candy, and preserve, for the Uses of the Family. And to make myself all the fine Linen of it, for yourself and me.

Then, Sir, if you will sometimes indulge me with your Company, I will take an Airing in your Chariot now-and-then: And when you shall return home from your Diversions on the Green, or from the Chace, or where-ever you shall please to go, I shall have the Pleasure of receiving you with Duty, and a chearful Delight; and, in your Absence, count the Moments till you return; and you will, may-be, fill up the sweetest Part of my Time, with your agreeable Conversation, for an Hour or two now-and-then; and be indulgent to the impertinent Over-flowings of my grateful Heart, for all your Goodness to me.

The Breakfasting-time, the Preparation for Dinner, and sometimes to entertain your chosen Friends, and the Company you shall bring home with you, Gentlemen, if not Ladies, and the Supperings, will fill up a great Part of the Day, in a very necessary manner.

And, may-be, Sir, now and then a good-humour'd Lady will drop in; and, I hope, if they do, I shall so behave myself, as not to *add* to the Disgrace you will have brought upon yourself; for indeed, I will be very circumspect, and try to be as discreet as I can; and as humble too, as shall be consistent with your Honour.

Cards, 'tis true, I can play at, in all the usual Games, that our Sex indulge in; but this I am not fond of, and shall never desire to use them, but as it may encourage such Ladies, as you may wish to see, not to abandon your House for want of an Amusement they are used to.

Musick, which my good Lady taught me, will fill up some Intervals, if I should have any.

And then, Sir, you know, I love Reading, and Scribbling; and tho' all the latter will be employ'd in the Family Accounts, between the Servants and me, and me and your good Self; yet Reading is a Pleasure to me, that I shall be unwilling to give up, at proper times, for the best Company in the World, except yours. And, O Sir! that will help to polish my Mind, and make me worthier of your Company and Conversation; and, with the Explanations you will give me, of what I shall not understand, will be a sweet Employment, and Improvement too.

But one thing, Sir, I ought not to forget, because it is the chief; my Duty to God, will, I hope, always employ some good Portion of my Time, with Thanks for his superlative Goodness to me; and to pray for *you* and *myself*: For *you*, Sir, for a Blessing on you, for your great Goodness to such an unworthy Creature: For *myself*, that I may be enabled to dis-charge my Duty to you, and be found grateful for all the Blessings I shall receive at the Hands of Providence, by means of your Generosity and Condescension.

With all this, Sir, said I, can you think I shall be at a Loss to pass my Time? But, as I know, that every Slight to me, if I come to be so happy, will be, in some measure, a Slight to you, I will beg of you, Sir, not to let me go very fine in Dress; but appear only so, as that you may not be ashamed of it, after the Honour I shall have of being called by your worthy Name: For well I know, Sir, that nothing so much excites the Envy of my own Sex, as seeing a Person set above them in Appearance, and in Dress. And that would bring down upon me an hundred *sawcy Things*, and *low-born Brats*, and I can't tell what!

There I stopt; for I had prattled a great deal; and he said, clasping me to him, Why stops my dear *Pamela?*—Why does she not proceed? I could dwell upon your Words all the Day long; and you shall be the Directress of your own Pleasures, and your own Time, so sweetly do you chuse to employ it: And thus shall I find some of my own bad Actions aton'd for by your exemplary Goodness, and God will bless me for your sake!

O, said he, what Pleasure you give me in this sweet Foretaste of my Happiness! I will now defy the sawcy, busy Censurers of the World, and bid them know your Excellence, and my Happiness, before they, with unhallow'd Lips, presume to judge of my Actions, and your Merit!— And, let me tell you, my *Pamela*, that I can add my Hopes of a still more pleasing Amusement; and what your bashful Modesty would not permit you to hint; and which I will no otherwise touch upon, lest it should seem, to your Nicety, to detract from the present Purity of my good Intentions, than to say, I hope to have superadded to all these, such an Employment, as will give me a View of perpetuating my happy Prospects, and my Family at the same time; of which I am almost the only Male.

I blushed, I believe, yet could not be displeased at the decent and charming manner with which he insinuated this distant Hope: And Oh! judge for me, how my Heart was affected with all these things!

He was pleased to add another charming Reflection, which shew'd me the noble Sincerity of his kind Professions. I do own to you, my *Pamela*, said he, that I love you with a purer Flame than ever I knew in my whole Life! A Flame, to which I was a Stranger, and which commenced for you in the Garden; tho' you, unkindly, by your unseasonable Doubts, nipp'd the opening Bud, while it was too tender to bear the cold Blasts of Slight or Negligence. And I know more sincere Joy and Satisfaction in this sweet Hour's Conversation with you, than all the guilty Tumults of my former

Passion ever did, or (had even my Attempts succeeded) ever could have afforded me.

O, Sir, said I, expect not Words, from your poor Servant, equal to these most generous Professions. Both the Means, and the Will, I now see, are given to you, to lay me under an everlasting Obligation! How happy shall I be, if, tho' I cannot be worthy of all this Goodness and Condescension, I can prove myself not intirely unworthy of it! But I can only answer for a grateful Heart; and if ever I give you Cause wilfully, (and you will generously allow for *involuntary* Imperfections) to be disgusted with me, may I be an Out-cast from your House and Favour, and as much repudiated, as if the Law had divorced me from you!

But, Sir, continued I, tho' I was so unseasonable as I was in the Garden, you would, I flatter myself, had you then heard me, have pardon'd my Imprudence, and own'd I had some Cause to fear, and to wish to be with my poor Father and Mother; and this I the rather say, that you should not think me capable of returning Insolence for your Goodness; or appearing foolishly ungrateful to you, when you was so kind to me.

Indeed, *Pamela*, said he, you gave me great Uneasiness; for I love you too well not to be jealous of the least Appearance of your Indifference to me, or Preference of any other Person, not excepting your Parents themselves. This made me resolve not to hear you; for I had not got over my Reluctance to Marriage; and a little Weight, you know, turns the Scale, when it hangs in an equal Balance. But yet, you see, that tho' I could part with you, while my Anger held, yet the Regard I had then newly profess'd for your Virtue, made me resolve not to offer to violate it; and you have seen likewise, that the painful Struggle I underwent when I began to reflect, and to read your moving Journal, between my Desire to recal you, and my Doubt, that you would return, (tho' yet I resolved not to force you to it) had like to have cost me a severe Illness: But your kind and chearful Return has dispelled all my Fears, and given me Hope, that I am not indifferent to you; and you see how your Presence has chas'd away my Illness.

I bless God for it, said I; but since you are so good as to encourage me, and will not despise my Weakness, I will acknowledge, that I suffer'd more than I could have imagined, till I experienced it, in being banish'd your Presence in so much Anger; and the more still was I affected, when you answer'd so generously, the wicked Mrs. *Jewkes* in my Favour, at my leaving your House: For this, Sir, awaken'd all my Reverence for you; and you saw I could not forbear, not knowing what I did, to break boldly in upon you, and acknowledge your Goodness on my Knees. 'Tis true, my dear *Pamela*, said he, we have sufficiently tortur'd one another; and the only Comfort that can result from it, will be, reflecting upon the Matter coolly and with Pleasure, when all these Storms are overblown, (as I hope they now are) and we sit together secur'd in each other's good Opinion, recounting the uncommon Gradations, by which we have ascended to the Summit of that Felicity, which I hope we shall shortly arrive at.

Mean-time, said the good Gentleman, let me hear what my dear Girl would have said in her Justification, could I have trusted myself with her, as to her Fears, and the Reason of her wishing herself from me, at a Time that I had begun to shew my Fondness for her, in a manner that I thought would have been agreeable to her and Virtue.

I pulled out of my Pocket the Gypsey Letter; but I said, before I shew'd it to him, I have this Letter, Sir, to shew you, as what, I believe you will allow, must have given me the greatest Disturbance: But first, as I know not who is the Writer, and it seems to be in a disguis'd Hand, I would beg it as a Favour, that if you guess who it is, which I cannot, it may not turn to their Prejudice, because it was written very probably with no other View than to serve me.

He took it, and read it. And it being signed *Somebody*, he said, Yes, this is indeed from *Somebody*; and, disguis'd as the Hand is, I know the Writer: Don't you see by the Setness of some of these Letters, and a little Secretary[1] Cut here and there, especially in that *c*, and that *r*, that it is the Hand of a Person bred in the Law-way? Why, *Pamela*, said he, 'tis old *Longman*'s Hand. An officious Rascal as he is!—But I have done with him! O Sir, said I, it would be too insolent in me to offer (so much am I myself overwhelm'd with your Goodness) to defend any body that you are angry with; yet, Sir, so far as they have incurr'd your Displeasure for my sake, and for no other Want of Duty or Respect, I could wish—But I dare not say more.——

But, said he, as to the Letter, and the Information it contains:—Let me know, *Pamela*, when you receiv'd this? On the *Friday*, Sir, said I, that you was gone to the Wedding at *Stamford*.—How could it be convey'd to you, said he, unknown to Mrs. *Jewkes*, when I gave her such a strict Charge to attend you, and you yourself promis'd me, you would not throw yourself in the Way of such Intelligence! For, said he, when I went to *Stamford*, I knew from a private Intimation given me, that there would be an Attempt made to see you, or give you a Letter, by somebody, if not to get you away; but was not certain from what Quarter, whether from my Sister *Davers*, Mrs. *Jervis*, Mr. *Longman*, or *John Arnold*, or your Father; and as I was then but struggling with myself, whether to give way to my honourable Inclinations, or to free you, and let you go to your Father, that I might avoid the Danger I found myself in of the former (for I had absolutely resolved never to wound again even your Ears with any Proposals of a contrary Nature); that was the Reason I desir'd you to permit Mrs. *Jewkes*, to be so much on her Guard till I came back, when I thought I should have decided this disputed Point within myself, between my Pride and my Inclinations.

This, good Sir, said I, accounts well to me, for your Conduct in that Case, and for what you said to me and Mrs. *Jewkes* on that Occasion; and I see more and more how much I may depend upon your Honour and Goodness to me.—But I will tell you all the Truth. And then I recounted to him the whole Affair of the Gypsey, and how the Letter was put among the loose Grass, &c. And he said, The Man who thinks a thousand Dragons sufficient to watch a Woman, when her Inclination takes a contrary Bent, will find all too little; and she will engage the Stones in the Street, or the Grass in the Field, to act for her, and help on her Correspondence. If the Mind, said he, be not engag'd, I see there is hardly any Confinement sufficient for the Body; and you have told me a very pretty Story; and, as you never gave me any Reason to question your Veracity, even in your severest Trials, I make no doubt of the Truth of what you have now mentioned. And I will in my Turn give you such a Proof of mine, that you shall find it carry Conviction with it.

You must know then, my *Pamela*, that I had actually form'd such a Project, so well inform'd was this old rascally *Somebody*; and the Time was fix'd, for the very Person describ'd in this Letter, to be here; and I had thought he should have read some Part of the Ceremony (as little as was possible, to deceive you) in my Chamber; and so I hop'd to have you mine upon Terms that then would have been much more agreeable to me than real Matrimony. And I did not in Haste intend you the Mortification of being undeceiv'd; so that we might have liv'd for Years, perhaps, very lovingly together; and I had, at the same time been at Liberty to confirm or abrogate it, as I pleas'd.

O Sir, said I, I am out of Breath with the Thoughts of my Danger. But what good Angel prevented this deep-laid Design to be executed?

Why, *your* good Angel, *Pamela*, said he; for when I began to consider that it would have made you miserable, and me not happy; that if you should have a dear little one, it would be out of my own Power to legitimate it, if I should wish it to inherit my Estate; and that, as I am almost the last of my Family, and most of what I possess must descend to a strange Line, and disagreeable and unworthy Persons; notwithstanding that I might, in this Case, have Issue of my own Body: When I further consider'd your untainted Virtue, what Dangers and Trials you had undergone, by my Means, and what a world of Troubles I had involv'd you in, only because you were beautiful and virtuous, which had excited all my Passion for you; and reflected also upon your try'd Prudence and Truth, I, tho' I doubted not effecting this my last Plot, resolv'd to overcome myself; and however I might suffer in struggling with my Affection for you, to part with you, rather than to betray you under so black a Veil. Besides, said he, I remember'd how much I had exclaim'd against and censur'd an Action of this kind, that had been attributed to one of the first Men of the Law,[1] and of the Kingdom, as he afterwards became; and that it was but treading in a Path that another had mark'd out for me; and, as I was assur'd, with no great Satisfaction to himself, when he came to reflect; my foolish Pride was a little piqu'd with this, because I lov'd to be, if I was out of the way,[2] my own Original, as I may call it: On all these Considerations it was, that I rejected this Project, and sent Word to the Person, that I had better consider'd of the Matter, and would not have him come, till he heard farther from me: And, in this Suspense, I suppose, some of your Confederates, *Pamela*, (for we have been a Couple of Plotters, tho' your Virtue and Merit have engag'd you faithful Friends and Partisans, which my Money and Promises could hardly do) one way or other got Knowledge of it, and gave you this Notice; but perhaps, it would have come too late, had not your white Angel got the better of my black one, and inspir'd me with Resolutions to abandon the Project just as it was to be put in Execution. But yet I own, that, from these Appearances, you was but too well justify'd in your Fears, on this odd way of coming at this Intelligence; and I have only one thing to blame you for, that tho' I was resolv'd not to hear you in your own Defence, yet, as you have so ready a Talent at your Pen, you might have clear'd your Part of this Matter up to me by a Line or two; and when I had known what seeming good Grounds you had for pouring cold Water on a young Flame, that was just then rising to an honourable Expansion, I should not have imputed it, as I was apt to do, to unseasonable Insult for my Tenderness to you on one hand; to perverse Nicety on the other; or to, what I was most alarm'd by, and concern'd for, Prepossession for some other Person. And this would have sav'd us both much Fatigue, I of Mind, you of Body.

And indeed, Sir, said I, of *Mind* too; and I could not better manifest this, than by the Chearfulness with which I obey'd your Recalling me to your Presence.

Ay, that my dear *Pamela*, said he, and clasp'd me in his Arms, was the kind, the inexpressibly kind Action that has rivetted my Affections to you, and gives me to pour out, in this free and unreserv'd manner, my whole Soul in your Bosom.

I said, I had the less Merit in this my Return, because I was driven by an irresistible Impulse to it, and could not help it if I would.

This, said he, (and honour'd me, by kissing my Hand) is engaging indeed, if I may hope that my *Pamela's* gentle Inclination for her Persecutor, was the strongest Motive to her Return; and I so much value a voluntier Love, in the Person I would wish for my Wife, that I would have even Prudence and Interest, hardly nam'd, in Comparison with it. And can you return me sincerely the honest Compliment I now make you, that as in the Act that I hope shall soon unite us together, it is impossible that I should have any View to my Interest; and, that Love, true Love, is the *only* Motive by which I am directed; that, were I not what I am, you could give me the Preference to any other Person in the World that you know, notwithstanding all that has pass'd between us? Why, said I, should your so much obliged *Pamela* refuse to answer this kind Question? Cruel, as I have thought you, and dangerous your Views to my Honesty; You, Sir, are the only Person living that ever was more than indifferent to me; and before I knew this was what I blush now to call it, I could not hate you, or wish you ill, tho' from my Soul, the Attempts you made, were shocking and most distasteful to me.

I am satisfy'd, my *Pamela*, said he; nor do I want to see those Papers that you have kindly written for to your Father; tho' I still wish to see them too, for the sake of the sweet manner in which you write your Sentiments; and to have before me the whole Series of your Sufferings, that I may know whether all my future Kindness is able to recompense you for them.

In this manner, my dear Father and Mother, did your happy Daughter find herself bless'd by her generous Master! An ample Recompence for all her Sufferings, did I think this sweet Conversation only. A hundred tender Things he express'd besides, that tho' they never can escape my Memory, yet would be too tedious to write down. Oh how I bless'd God, and, I hope, ever shall, for all his gracious Favours to his unworthy Handmaid! What a happy Change is this. And who knows but my kind, my generous Master may put it in my Power, when he shall see me not quite unworthy of it, to be a Means, without injuring him, to dispense around me, to many Persons, the happy Influences of the Condition to which I shall be, by his kind Favour, exalted? Doubly blest shall I be, in particular, if I can return the hundredth Part of the Obligations I owe to such honest good

Parents, to whose pious Instructions and Examples, under God, I owe all my present Happiness and future Prospects.—O the Joy that fills my Mind on these proud Hopes! on these delightful Prospects!—It is too mighty for me; and I must sit down to ponder all these Things, and to admire and bless the Goodness of that Providence, which has, thro' so many intricate Mazes, made me tread the Paths of Innocence, and so amply rewarded me, for what it has itself enabled me do! All Glory to God alone be ever given for it, by your poor enraptur'd Daughter!——

I will now continue my most pleasing Relation.

As the Chariot was returning home from this sweet Airing, he said, From all that has pass'd between us, in this pleasing Turn, my *Pamela* will see, and will believe, that the Trials to her Virtue are all over from me: But perhaps, there will be some few yet to come to her Patience and Humility. For I have, at the earnest Importunity of Lady *Darnford*, and her Daughters, promised them a Sight of my beloved Girl: And so I intend to have their whole Family, and Lady *Jones*, and Mrs. *Peters*'s Family, to dine with me once in a few Days. And as I believe you would hardly chuse at present to grace the Table on the Occasion, till you can do it in your own Right, I would be glad you will not refuse coming down to us, if I desire it; for I would preface our Nuptials, said the dear Gentleman! O what a sweet Word was that!—with the good Opinion of these Gentry of your Merits, and to see you, and your sweet Manner, will be enough for that Purpose; and so, by degrees, prepare my Neighbours for what is to follow: And they already have your Character from me, and are dispos'd to admire you.

Sir, said I, after all that has pass'd, I should be unworthy if I could not say, that I *can* have no Will but yours; and however awkwardly I shall behave in such Company, weigh'd down with the Sense of your Obligations, on one Side, and my own Unworthiness, with their Observations, on the other, I will not scruple to obey you.

I am oblig'd to you, *Pamela*, said he; and pray be only dress'd as you are; for, as they know your Condition, and I have told them the Story of your present Dress, and how you came by it, one of the young Ladies begs it as a Favour, that they may see you just as you are: And I am the rather pleas'd it should be so, because they will perceive you owe nothing to Dress, and make a much better Figure with your own native Stock of Loveliness, than the greatest Ladies do in the most splendid Attire, and stuck out with the most glittering Jewels.

O Sir, said I, your Goodness beholds your poor Servant in a Light greatly beyond her Merit! But it must not be expected that others, Ladies especially, will look at me with your favourable Eyes: But, nevertheless, I should be best pleas'd to wear always this humble Garb, till you, for your own sake, shall order it otherwise: For, oh! Sir, said I, I hope it will be always my Pride to glory most in your Goodness; and it will be a Pleasure to me to shew every one, that, with respect to my Happiness in this Life, I am intirely the Work of your Bounty; and to let the World see from what a lowly Original you have rais'd me to Honours, that the greatest Ladies would rejoice in.

Admirable *Pamela*, said he, excellent Girl!——Surely thy Sentiments are superior to those of all thy Sex!—I might have *addressed* a hundred fine Ladies; but never, surely, could have had Reason to *admire* one as I do you.

As, my dear Father and Mother, I repeat these generous Sayings, only as they are the Effect of my Master's Goodness, and am far from presuming to think I deserve one of them; so I hope you will not attribute it to my Vanity; for, I do assure you, I think I ought rather to be more *humble*, as I am more *oblig'd*: For it must be always a Sign of a poor Condition to receive Obligations one cannot repay; as it is of a rich Mind, when it can confer them, without expecting or *needing* a Return. It is, on one side, the State of the human Creature compar'd, on the other, to the Creator; and so, with due Deference, may be said to be God-like, and that is the highest that can be said.

The Chariot brought us home at near the Hour of Two, and, blessed be God, my Master is pure and well, and chearful; and that makes me hope he does not repent him of his Goodness. He handed me out of the Chariot, and to the Parlour, with the same Goodness, that he shew'd when he put me in it, before several of the Servants. Mrs. *Jewkes* came to inquire how he did. Quite well, Mrs. *Jewkes*, said he, quite well; I thank God, and this good Girl, for it!—I am glad of it, said she; but I hope you are not the worse for my Care, and my Doctoring you!—No, but the better Mrs. *Jewkes*, said he, you have much oblig'd me by both.

Then he said, Mrs. *Jewkes*, you and I have used this good Girl very hardly—I was afraid, Sir, said she, I should be the Subject of her Complaints.—I assure you, said he, she has not open'd her Lips about you. We have had quite a different Subject to talk of; and I hope she will forgive us both: you especially, she must; because you have done nothing but by my Orders. But I only mean, that the necessary Consequence of those Orders has been very grievous to my *Pamela*: And now comes our Part to make her Amends, if we can.

Sir, said she, I always said to Madam, (as she call'd me) that you was very good, and very forgiving. No, said he, I have been stark naught, and it is she, I hope, will be very forgiving. But all this Preamble is to tell you, Mrs. *Jewkes*, that now I desire you'll study to oblige her, as much as (to obey me) you was forc'd to disoblige her before. And you'll remember, that in every thing she is to be her own Mistress.

Yes, said she, and mine too, I suppose, Sir? Ay, said the generous Gentleman, I believe it will be so in a little Time.—Then, said she, I know how it will go with me! And so put her Handkerchief to her Eyes.—*Pamela*, said my Master, comfort poor Mrs. *Jewkes*.

This was very generous, already to seem to put her in my Power; and I took her by the Hand, and said, I shall never take upon myself, Mrs. *Jewkes*, to make a bad Use of any Opportunities that may be put into my Hands, by my generous Master; nor shall I ever wish to do you Prejudice, if I might: For I shall consider, that what you have done, was in Obedience to a Will which it will become me also to submit to; and so, tho' we shall be acted very differently as to the Effects, yet as these Effects proceed from one Cause, it shall be always reverenced by me.

See there, Mrs. *Jewkes*, said my Master, we are both in generous Hands; and indeed, if she did not pardon you, I should think she but half forgave me, because you acted by my Instructions.—Well, said she, God bless you both together, since it must be so; and I will double my Diligence to oblige my Lady, as I find she will soon be.

O my dear Father and Mother, now pray for me on another Score! for fear I should grow too proud, and be giddy and foolish with all these promising Things, so soothing to the Vanity of my Years and Sex. But even to this Hour can I pray, that God would remove from me all these delightful Prospects, if they should so corrupt my Mind, as to make me proud, and vain, and not acknowledge, with thankful Humility, the blessed Providence which has so visibly conducted me thro' the dangerous Paths I have trod, to this happy Moment.

My Master was pleas'd to say, that he thought I might as well dine with him, as he was alone. But, I said, I begg'd he would excuse me, for fear so much Excess of Goodness and Condescension, all at once, should turn my Head; and that he would by slower Degrees bring on my Happiness, lest I should not know how to bear it.

Persons that doubt themselves, said he, seldom do amiss. And if there was any Fear of what you say, you could not have had it in your Thoughts: For none but the Presumptuous, the Conceited, and the Thoughtless, err capitally. But nevertheless, said he, I have such an Opinion of your Prudence, that I shall generally think what you do right, because it is you that do it.

Sir, said I, your kind Expressions shall not be thrown away upon me, if I can help it; for they will task me, with the Care of endeavouring to deserve your good Opinion, and your Approbation, as the best Rule of my Conduct.

Being then about to go up Stairs, Permit me, Sir, said I, (looking about me, with some Confusion, to see nobody was there) thus on my Knees to thank you, as I often wanted to do in the Chariot, for all your Goodness to me, which shall never, I hope, be cast away upon me. And so I had the Boldness to kiss his Hand.

I wonder, since how I came to be so forward; but what could I do?—My poor grateful Heart was like a too full River, which overflows its Banks; and it carry'd away my Fear and my Shame-facedness, as that does all before it, on the Surface of the Waters!

He clasp'd me in his Arms, with Transport, and condescendingly kneel'd by me, and kissing me, said, O my dear obliging good Girl, on my Knee, as you on yours, I vow to you everlasting Truth and Fidelity; and may God but bless us both with half the Pleasures that seem to lie before us, and we shall have no Reason to envy the Felicity of the greatest Princes! O Sir, said I, how shall I support so much Goodness!—I am poor, indeed, in *every thing*, compar'd to you! And how far, very far, do you, in every generous Way, leave me behind you!

He rais'd me, and as I bent towards the Door, led me to the Stairs Foot, and saluting me there again, I went up to my Closet, and threw myself on my Knees in Raptures of Joy, and bless'd that gracious God, who had thus chang'd my Distress to Happiness, and so abundantly rewarded me for all the Sufferings I had pass'd thro'.—And Oh! how light, how very light, do all those Sufferings *now* appear, which *then* my repining Mind made so formidable to me!—Hence, in every State of Life, and in all the Changes and Chances of it, for the future, will I trust in Providence, who knows what is best for us, and frequently turns the very Evils we most dread, to be the Causes of our Happiness, and of our Deliverance from greater!—My Experiences, young as I am, as to this great Point of Reliance in God, are strong, tho' my Judgment in general may be weak and unformed; but you'll excuse these Reflections, because they are your beloved Daughter's; and, so far as they are not amiss, derive themselves from the Benefit of yours and my late good Lady's Examples and Instructions.

I have wrote a vast deal in a little Time. And shall only say, to conclude this delightful *Wednesday*, That in the Afternoon my good Master was so well, that he rode out on Horseback, and came home about Nine at Night; and then came up to me, and seeing me with Pen and Ink before me in my Closet, said, I come only to tell you I am very well, my *Pamela*, and, as I have a Letter or two to write, I will leave you to proceed in yours, as I suppose that was your Employment; (for I had put by my Paper at his coming up) and so he saluted me, bid me Good-night, and went down; and I finish'd down to this Place before I went to-bed. Mrs. *Jewkes* told me, if it was more agreeable to me, she would lie in another Room; but I said, No thank you, Mrs. *Jewkes*; pray let me have your Company. And she made me a fine Curchee, and thank'd me.—How Times are alter'd!

THURSDAY.

This Morning my Master came up to me, and talk'd with me on various Subjects for a good while together in the most kind manner. Among other Things, he ask'd me, if I chose to order any new Cloaths against my Marriage (O how my Heart flutters when he mentions this Subject so freely!) I said, I left every thing to his good Pleasure, only repeating my Request, for the Reasons afore-given, that I might not be too fine.

He said, I think, my Dear, it shall be very private: I hope you are not afraid of a Sham-marriage; and pray get the Service by Heart, that you may see nothing is omitted. I glow'd between Shame and Delight. O how I felt my Cheeks burn!

I said I fear'd nothing, I apprehended nothing, but my own Unworthiness. Said he, I think it shall be done within these Fourteen Days, from this Day, at this House. O how I trembled; but not with Grief, you may believe!—What says my Girl? Have you to object against any Day of the next Fourteen? because my Affairs require me to go to my other House, and I think not to stir from this, till I am happy in you?

I have no Will but yours, said I, (all glowing like the Fire, as I could feel:) But, Sir, did you say in the *House?* Ay, said he; for I care not how privately it be done; and it must be very publick if we go to Church. It is a *Holy Rite*, Sir, said I, and would be better, methinks, in a *Holy Place*.

I see, (said he, most kindly) my lovely Maid's Confusion; and your trembling Tenderness shews, I ought to oblige you all I may. Therefore, I will order my own little Chapel, which has not been us'd for two Generations, for any thing but a Lumber-room, because our Family seldom resided here long together, to be clear'd and clean'd, and got ready for the Ceremony, if you dislike your own Chamber, or mine.

Sir, said I, that will be better than the Chamber; and I hope it will never be lumber'd again, but kept to the Use, for which, as I *presume*, it has been consecrated. O yes, said he, it has been consecrated, and that many Ages ago, in my Great Great-grandfather's Time, who built that and the good old House together.

But now, my good Girl, if I do not too much add to your sweet Confusion, shall it be in the first Seven Days, or the second, of this Fortnight? I look'd down, quite out of Countenance. Tell me, said he?

In the Second, if you please, Sir, said I.—As *you* please, said he, most kindly; but I should thank you, *Pamela*, if you chuse the first. I'd *rather*, Sir, if you please, said I, have the second. Well, said he, be it so; but don't defer it to the last Day of the Fourteen.

Pray, Sir, said I, since you embolden me to talk on this important Subject, may I not send my dear Father and Mother word of my Happiness?—Yes, you may, said he; but charge them to keep it secret, till you or I direct the contrary. And I told you I would see no more of your Papers; but I meant, I would not without your Consent: But if you will shew them to me, (and now I have no other Motive for my Curiosity, but the Pleasure I take in reading what you write) I shall acknowledge it as a Favour.

If, Sir, said I, you will be pleas'd to let me write over again one Sheet, I will, tho' I had rely'd upon your Word, and not wrote them for your Perusal. What is that, said he? tho' I cannot consent to it beforehand: For I more desire to see them, because they are your true Sentiments at *the Time*, and because they were *not* written for my Perusal. Sir, said I, What I am loth you should see, are very severe Reflections on the Letter I receiv'd by the Gypsey, when I apprehended your Design of the Sham-marriage; tho' there are other things I would not have you see; but that is the worst. It can't be worse, said he, my dear Sauce-box, than I have seen already; and, I will allow your treating me in ever so black a Manner on that Occasion, because it must have a very black Appearance to you.—Well, Sir, said I, I think I will obey you, before Night. But don't alter a Word, said he. I won't, Sir, reply'd I, since you order it.

While we were talking, Mrs. *Jewkes* came up, and said *Thomas* was return'd. O, said my Master, let him bring up the Papers. For he hop'd, and so did I, that you had sent them by him. But it was a great Balk, when he came up and said, Sir, Mr. *Andrews* did not care to deliver them; and would have it, that his Daughter was forc'd to write that Letter to him: And indeed, Sir, said he, the old Gentleman took on sadly, and would have it that his Daughter was undone, or else, he said, she would not have turn'd back, when on her Way, (as I told him she did, said *Thomas*) instead of coming to them. I began to be afraid now that all would be bad for me again.

Well, *Tom*, said he, don't mince the Matter. Tell me, before Mrs. *Andrews*, what they said. Why, Sir, both he and Goody *Andrews*, after they had conferr'd together upon *your* Letter, Madam, came out, weeping bitterly, that griev'd my very Heart; and they said, Now all was over with their poor Daughter; and either she had wrote that Letter by Compulsion, or had yielded to your Honour, so they said, and was, or would be ruin'd!

My Master seem'd vex'd, as I fear'd. And I said, Pray, Sir, be so good to excuse the Fears of my honest Parents! They cannot know your Goodness to me.

And so, (said he, without answering me,) they refus'd to deliver the Papers? Yes, and please your Honour, said *Thomas*, tho' I told them, that you, Madam, of your own Accord, on a Letter I had brought you, very chearfully wrote what I carry'd. But the old Gentleman, said, Why, Wife, there are in these Papers twenty Things nobody should see but ourselves, and especially not the 'Squire. O the poor Girl has had so many Stratagems to contend with, that now, at last, she has met with one that has been too hard for her. And can it be possible for us to account for her setting out to come to us, in such Post-haste, and when she had got above Half-way, to send us this Letter, and to go back again of her own Accord, as you say; when we know that all her Delight would have been to come to us, and to escape from the Perils she has been so long contending with? And then, and please your Honour, he said, he could not bear this; for his Daughter was ruin'd, to be sure, before now. And so, said he, the good old Couple sat themselves down, and Hand-in-hand, leaning upon each other's Shoulder, did nothing but lament.—I was, said he, piteously griev'd; but all I could say could not comfort them; nor would they give me the Papers; tho' I told them I should deliver them only to Mrs. *Andrews* herself. And so, and please your Honour, I was forced to come away without them.

My good Master saw me all bath'd in Tears at this Description of your Distress and Fears for me, and he said, I would not have you take on so. I am not angry with your Father in the main; he is a good Man; and I would have you write out of Hand, and it shall be sent by the Post, to Mr. *Atkins*, who lives within two Miles of your Father, and I'll inclose it in a Cover of mine, in which I'll desire Mr. *Atkins*, the Moment it comes to his Hand, to convey it safely to your Father or Mother: And say nothing of their sending the Papers, that it may not make them uneasy; for I want not now to see them on any other Score than that of mere Curiosity; and that will do at any Time. And so saying, he saluted me, before *Thomas*, and with his own Handkerchief wip'd my Eyes; and said to *Thomas*, The good old Folks are not to be blam'd in the main. They don't know my honourable Intentions by their dear Daughter: Who, *Tom*, will, in a little Time, be your Mistress; tho' I shall keep the Matter private some Days, and would not have it spoken of by my Servants out of my House.

Thomas said, God bless your Honour. You know best. And I said, O Sir, you are all Goodness!—How kind is this, to forgive the Disappointment, instead of being angry, as I fear'd you would. *Thomas* then withdrew. And my Master said, I need not remind you of writing out of Hand, to make the good Folks easy: And I will leave you to yourself for that Purpose; only send me down such of your Papers, as you are willing I should see, with which I shall entertain myself for an Hour or two. But one Thing, added he, I forgot to tell you, the neighbouring Gentry I mentioned, will be here to-morrow to dine with me; and I have order'd Mrs. *Jewkes* to prepare for them. And *must I*, Sir, said I, be shewn to them? O yes, said he, that's the chief Reason of their coming. And you'll see no body equal to yourself; don't be concern'd.

I open'd my Papers, as soon as my Master had left me, and laid out those beginning on the *Thursday* Morning he set out for *Stamford*, with the Morning Visit he made me before I was up, and the Injunctions of Watchfulness, &c. to Mrs. *Jewkes*; the next Day's Gypsey Affair, and my Reflections, in which I call'd him *truly diabolical*, and was otherwise very severe, on the strong Appearances the Matter had then against him. His Return on *Saturday*, with the Dread he put me in, on the offering to search me for my Papers which followed those he had got by Mrs. *Jewkes*'s Means. My being forc'd to give them up. His Carriage to me after he had read them; and Questions to me. His great Kindness to me on seeing the Dangers I had escap'd, and the Troubles I had undergone. And how I unseasonably, in the midst of his Goodness, express'd my Desire of being sent to you, having the Intelligence of a Sham-marriage, from the Gypsey, in my Thoughts. How this inrag'd him, and made him turn me that very *Sunday* out of his House, and send me on my Way to you. The Particulars of my Journey, and my Grief at parting with him; and my free Acknowledgments to you, that I found, unknown to myself, I had begun to love him, and could not help it. His sending after me, to beg my Return; but yet generously leaving me at my Liberty, when he might have forc'd me to return whether I was willing or not. My Resolution to oblige him, and fatiguing Journey back. My Concern for his Illness on my Return. His kind Reception of me, and shewing me his Sister *Davers*'s angry Letter, against his Behaviour to me, desiring him to set me free, and threatening to renounce him as a Brother if he should degrade himself by marrying me. My serious Reflections on this Letter, *&c.* (all which, I hope, with the others, you will shortly see) and this carry'd Matters down to *Tuesday* Night last.

All that follow'd was so kind of his Side, being our Chariot Conference, as above, on *Wednesday* Morning, and how good he has been ever since, that I thought I would go no farther; for I was a little asham'd to be so very open on that tender and most grateful Subject; tho' his great Goodness to me deserves all the Acknowledgments I can possibly make.

And when I had look'd these out, I carried them down myself into the Parlour to him, and said, putting them into his Hands, Your Allowances, good Sir, as heretofore; and if I have been too open and free in my Reflections or Declarations; let my Fears on one Side, and my Sincerity on the other, be my Excuse. You are very obliging, my good Girl, said he. You have nothing to apprehend from my Thoughts, any more than from my Actions.

So I went up, and wrote the Letter to you, briefly acquainting you with my present Happiness, and my Master's Goodness, and expressing that Gratitude of Heart, which I owe to the kindest Gentleman in the World, and assuring you, that I should soon have the Pleasure of sending back to you, not only those Papers, but all that succeeded them to this Time, as I know you delight to amuse yourself in your Leisure Hours with my Scribble; and I said, carrying it down to my Master, before I seal'd it, Will you please, Sir, to take the Trouble of reading what I write to my dear Parents? Thank you *Pamela*, said he, and set me on his Knee, while he read it, and seem'd much pleas'd with it, and giving it me again, you are very happy, said he, my beloved Girl, in your Style and Expressions: And the affectionate Things you say of me, are inexpressibly obliging; and again, with this Kiss, said he, do I confirm for Truth all that you have promis'd for my Intentions in this Letter.—O what Halcyon Days are these? God continue them!—A Change now, would kill me quite.

He went out in his Chariot in the Afternoon; and in the Evening return'd, and sent me Word, he would be glad of my Company for a little Walk in the Garden; and down I went that very Moment.

He came to meet me. So, said he, how does my dear Girl do now?—Who do you think I have seen since I have been out?—I don't know, Sir, said I. Why, said he, there is a Turning in the Road, about five Miles off, that goes round a Meadow, that has a pleasant Foot-way, by the Side of a little Brook, and a double Row of Limes on each Side, where now and then the Gentry in the Neighbourhood, walk, and angle, and divert themselves—I'll shew it you next Opportunity—And I stept out of my Chariot, to walk cross this Meadow, and bid *Robin* meet me with it on the further Part of it. And who should I 'spy there, walking, with a Book in his Hand, reading, but your humble Servant Mr. *Williams?*—Don't blush, *Pamela*, said he— As his Back was to me, I thought I would speak to the Man, and before he saw me, I said, How do you, old Acquaintance? (for, said he, you know we were of one College for a Twelvemonth). I thought the Man would have jump'd into the Brook, he gave such a Start at hearing my Voice, and seeing me.

Poor Man! said I. Ay, said he, but not too much of your poor Man, in that soft Accent, neither, *Pamela.*—Said I, I am sorry my Voice is so startling to you, Mr. *Williams.* What are you reading? Sir, said he, and stammer'd with the Surprize, It is the *French Telemachus;*[1] for I am about perfecting myself, if I can, in the *French* Tongue.—Thought I, I had rather so, than perfecting my *Pamela* in it.—You do well, reply'd I.—Don't you think that yonder Cloud may give us a small Shower? and it did a little begin to wet.—He said, he believ'd not much.

If, said I, you are for the Village, I'll give you a Cast;[2] for I shall call at Sir *Simon*'s, in my Return from the little Round I am taking. He ask'd me If it was not too great a Favour?—No, said I, don't talk of that; let us walk to the further Opening there, and we shall meet my Chariot.

So, *Pamela*, continued my Master, we fell into Conversation, as we walk'd. He said, he was very sorry he had incurr'd my Displeasure; and the more, as he had been told, by Lady *Jones*, who had it from Sir *Simon*'s Family, that I had a more honourable View than at first was apprehended. I said, We Fellows of Fortune, Mr. *Williams*, take sometimes a little more Liberty with the World than we ought to do; wantoning, very probably, as you contemplative Folks would say, in the Sun-beams of a dangerous Affluence, and cannot think of confining ourselves to the common Paths, tho' the safest and most eligible, after all. And you may believe I could not very well like to be supplanted in a View that lay next my Heart; and that by an old Acquaintance, whose Good, before this Affair, I was studious to promote.

I would only say, Sir, said he, that my *first* Motive was intirely such as became my Function: And, very politely, said my Master, he added, And I am very sure, that however inexcusable I might seem in the *Progress* of the Matter, yourself, Sir, would have been sorry to have it said, you had cast your Thoughts on a Person, that nobody could have wish'd for but yourself.

Well, Mr. *Williams*, said I, I see you are a Man of Gallantry as well as Religion: But what I took most amiss was, that, if you thought me doing a wrong Thing, you did not expostulate with me, as your Function might allow you, upon it; but immediately determin'd to counterplot me, and to turn as much an Intriguer for a Parson, as I was for a Laick, and attempt to secure to yourself a Prize, you would have robb'd me of, and that from my own House. But the Matter is at an End, and I retain not any Malice upon it, tho' you did not *know*, but I should, at last, do honourably by her, as I actually intend.

I am sorry for myself, Sir, said he, that I should so unhappily incur your Displeasure; but I rejoice for her sake in your honourable Intentions: Give me Leave only to say, That if you make Mrs. *Andrews* your Lady, she will do Credit to your Choice with every body that sees her, or comes to know her; and for Person and Mind both, you may challenge the County.

In this manner, said my Master, did the Parson and I confabulate; and I set him down at his Lodgings in the Village. But he kept your Secret, *Pamela*, and would not own, that you gave Encouragement to his Address as to Matrimony.

Indeed, Sir, said I, he could not say that I did; and I hope you believe me. I do, I do, said he; but 'tis still my Opinion, that if, when I saw Plots set up against my Plots, I had not, as I had, discover'd the Parson, it might have gone to a Length that would have put our present Situation out of both our Powers.

Sir, said I, when you consider that my utmost Presumption could not make me hope for the Honour you now seem to design me; that therefore, I had no Prospect before me but Dishonour; and was so hardly us'd into the Bargain, I should have seem'd very little in Earnest in my Professions of Honesty, if I had not endeavour'd to get away: But yet I resolv'd not to think of Marriage; for I never saw the Man I could love, till your Goodness embolden'd me to look up to you.

I should, my dear *Pamela*, said he, make a very ill Compliment to my Vanity, if I did not believe you; tho' at the same time, Justice calls upon me to own, that it is, all Things consider'd, beyond my Merit.

There was a sweet noble Expression for your poor Daughter, my dear Father and Mother!—And from my Master too!

I was glad to hear this Account of the Interview between Mr. *Williams* and himself; but I dar'd not to say so. I hope in Time he will be re-instated in his good Graces.

He was so good as to tell me, he had given Orders for the Chapel to be clear'd. O how I look forward with inward Joy, yet with Fear and Trembling!

FRIDAY.

About Twelve o'Clock came Sir *Simon*, and his Lady and two Daughters, and Lady *Jones*, and a Sister-in-law of hers, and Mr. *Peters*, and his Spouse and Niece. Mrs. *Jewkes*, who is more and more obliging, was much concern'd I was not dress'd in some of my best Cloaths, and made me many Compliments.

They all went into the Garden for a Walk, before Dinner, and, I understood, were so impatient to see me, that my Master took them into the largest Alcove, after they had walk'd two or three Turns, and stept himself to me. Come, my *Pamela*, said he, the Ladies can't be satisfy'd without seeing you, and I desire you'll come. I said, I was asham'd; but I would obey him. Said he, The two young Ladies are dress'd out in their best Attire; but they make not such an Appearance as my charming Girl in this ordinary Garb.—Sir, said I, shan't I follow you there? for I can't bear you should do me so much Honour. Well, said he, I'll go before you. And he bid Mrs. *Jewkes* bring a Bottle or two of Sack, and some Cake. So he went down to them.

This Alcove fronts the longest Gravel Walk in the Garden, so that they saw me all the Way I came, for a good Way; and my Master told me afterwards, with Pleasure, all they said of me.

Will you forgive the little vain Slut your Daughter, if I tell you all, as he was pleas'd to tell me? He said, 'spying me first, Look there, Ladies, comes my pretty Rustick!—They all, I saw, which dash'd me, stood at the Windows and in the Door-way, looking full at me.

My Master told me, that Lady *Jones* said, She is a charming Creature, I see that, at this Distance. And Sir *Simon*, it seems, who has been a sad Rake in his younger Days, swore he never saw so easy an Air, so fine a Shape, and so graceful a Presence.—The Lady *Darnford* said, I was a sweet Girl. And Mrs. *Peters* said very handsome Things. Even the Parson said,

I should be the Pride of the County. O dear Sirs! all this was owing to the Light my good Master's Favour plac'd me in, which made me shine out in their Eyes beyond my Deserts. He said the young Ladies blush'd, and envy'd me.

When I came near, he saw me dash'd and confus'd, and was so good to meet me, Give me your Hand, said he, my good Girl, you walk too fast (for indeed I wanted to be out of their gazing). I did so, with a Curchee, and he led me up the Steps of the Alcove, and in a most Gentleman-like Manner presented me to the Ladies, and they all saluted me, and said, They hop'd to be better acquainted with me: and Lady *Darnford* was pleas'd to say, I should be the Flower of their Neighbourhood. Sir *Simon* said, Good Neighbour, by your Leave, and saluting me, added, Now will I say, that I have kiss'd the loveliest Maiden in *England*. But for all this, methought I ow'd him a Grudge for a Tell-tale, tho' all had turn'd out so happily. Mr. *Peters* very gravely follow'd his Example, and said, like a Bishop, God bless you, fair Excellence. Said Lady *Jones*, Pray, dear Madam, sit down by me. And they all sat down; but I said, I would stand, if they pleas'd. No, *Pamela*, said my Master, Pray sit down with these good Ladies, my Neighbours:—They will indulge it to you, for *my* sake, till they know you better; and for *your own*, when they are acquainted with you. Sir, said I, I shall be proud to deserve their Indulgence.

They all so gaz'd at me, that I could not look up; for I think it is one of the Distinctions of Persons of Condition, and well-bred People, to put bashful Bodies out of Countenance. Well, Sir *Simon*, said my Master, what say you now to my pretty Rustick?—He swore a great Oath, that he should better know what to say to me if he was as young as himself. Lady *Darnford* said, You will never leave, Sir *Simon*.

Said my Master, You are a little confus'd, my good Girl, and out of Breath; but I have told all my kind Neighbours here a good deal of your Story, and your Excellence. Yes, said Lady *Darnford*, my dear Neighbour, as I will call you; we that are here present have all heard of your uncommon Story. Madam, said I, you have then heard what must make your kind Allowance for me very necessary. No, said Mrs. *Peters*, we have heard what will always make you valued as an Honour to our Sex, and as a worthy Pattern for all the young Ladies in the County. You are very good, Madam, said I, to make me able to look up, and be thankful for the Honour you are all pleas'd to do me.

Mrs. *Jewkes* came in with the Canary, brought by *Nan*, to the Alcove, and some Cake on a Silver Salver; and I said, Mrs. *Jewkes*, let me be your Assistant; I will serve the Ladies with the Cake. And so I took the Salver, and went round to the good Company with it, ending with my Master. The Lady *Jones* said, she never was serv'd with such a Grace, and it was giving me too much Trouble. O Madam, said I, I hope my good Master's Favour will never make me forget that it is my Duty to wait upon his Friends.—*Master*, sweet one, said Sir *Simon*, I hope you won't always call the 'Squire by that Name, for fear it should become a Fashion for all our Ladies to do the like thro' the County. I, Sir, said I, shall have many Reasons to continue this Style, which cannot affect your good Ladies.

Sir *Simon*, said Lady *Jones*, you are very arch upon us; but I see very well, that it will be the Interest of all the Gentlemen, to bring their Ladies into an Intimacy with one that can give them such a good Example. I am sure then, Madam, said I, it must be after I have been polish'd and improv'd by the Honour of such an Example as yours.

They all were very good and affable, and the young Lady *Darnford*, who had wish'd to see me in this Dress, said, I beg your Pardon, dear Miss, as she call'd me; but I had heard how sweetly this Garb became you, and was told the History of it; and I begg'd it as a Favour that you might oblige us with your Appearance in it. I am much oblig'd to your Ladyship, said I, that your kind Prescription was so agreeable to my Choice. Why, said she, *was* it your Choice then?—I am glad of that: Tho' I am sure your Person must *give* and not *take* Ornament from any Dress.

You are very kind, Madam, said I: But there will be the less Reason to fear I should forget the high Obligations I shall have to the kindest of Gentlemen, when I can delight to shew the humble Degree from which his Goodness has rais'd me.—My dear *Pamela*, said my Master, if you proceed at this Rate, I must insist upon your first Seven Days. You know what I mean. Sir, said I, you are all Goodness!

They drank a Glass of Sack each, and Sir *Simon* would make me do so; saying, It is a Reflection, Madam, upon all the Ladies, if you don't do as they do. No, Sir *Simon*, said I, that can't be, because the Ladies Journey hither makes a Glass of Canary a proper Cordial for them. But I won't refuse; because I will do myself the Honour of drinking good Health to you, and all this worthy Company.

Said good Lady *Darnford*, to my Master, I hope, Sir, we shall have Mrs. *Andrews*'s Company at Table. He said, very obligingly, Madam, it is her Time now: and I will leave it to her Choice. If my good Ladies, then, will forgive me, Sir, said I, I had rather be excused. They all said, I must not be excused. I begg'd I might. Your Reason for it, my dear *Pamela*, said my Master? as the Ladies request it, I wish you would oblige them. Sir, reply'd I, your Goodness will make me, every Day, worthier of the Honour the

Ladies do me; and when I can persuade myself that I am more worthy of it than at present, I shall with great Joy embrace all the Opportunities they will be pleased to give me.

Mrs. *Peters* whisper'd Lady *Jones*, as my Master told me afterwards; Did you ever see such Excellence, such Prudence, and Discretion? Never in my Life, said the other good Lady. She will adorn, she was pleas'd to say, her Distinction. Ay, said Mrs. *Peters*, she would adorn any Station in Life.

My good Master was highly delighted, generous Gentleman as he is! with the favourable Opinion of the Ladies; and I took the more Pleasure in it, because their Favour seem'd to lessen the Disgrace of his stooping so much beneath him.

Lady *Darnford* said, We will not oppress you; tho' we could almost blame your too punctilious Exactness; but if we excuse Mrs. *Andrews* at Dinner, we must insist upon her Company at the Card-table, and at a Dish of Tea: For we intend to pass the whole Day with you, Sir, as we told you. What say you to that, *Pamela*, said my Master? Sir, reply'd I, whatever you and the Ladies please, I will chearfully do. They said I was very obliging. But Sir *Simon* rapt out an Oath, and said, that *they* might dine together if they would; but *he* would dine with me, and nobody else. For, said he, I say, 'Squire, as Parson *Williams* said, (by which I found my Master had told them the Story) you must not think you have chosen one that nobody can like but yourself.

The young Ladies said, If I pleas'd, they would take a Turn about the Garden with me. I answer'd I would very gladly attend them; and so we three, and Lady *Jones*'s Sister-in-law, and Mr. *Peters*'s Niece, walk'd together. They were very affable, kind and obliging; and we soon enter'd into a good deal of Familiarity; and I found Miss *Darnford* a very agreeable Person. Her Sister was a little more on the Reserve; and I afterwards heard, that, about a Year before, she should fain have had my Master make his Addresses to her; but tho' Sir *Simon* is reckon'd rich, she was not thought a sufficient Fortune for him. And now, to have him look down so low as me, must be a sort of Mortification to a poor young Lady!—and I pity'd her—Indeed I did!—I wish all young Persons of my Sex could be as happy as I am likely to be.

My Master told me afterwards, that I left the other Ladies, and Sir *Simon* and Mr. *Peters*, full of my Praises; so that they could hardly talk of any thing else: one launching out upon my Complexion, another upon my Eyes, my Hand, and, in short, for you'll think me sadly proud, upon my whole Person, and Behaviour; and they all magnify'd my Readiness and

Obligingness in my Answers, and the like: And I was glad of it, as I said, for my good Master's sake, who seem'd quite pleas'd and rejoic'd. God bless him, for his Goodness to me!

Dinner not being ready, the young Ladies propos'd a Tune upon the Spinnet. I said, I believ'd it was not in Tune. They said, they knew it was but a few Months ago. If it is, said I, I wish I had known it; tho' indeed, Ladies, added I, since you know my Story, I must own, that my Mind has not been long in Tune, to make use of it. So they would make me play upon it, and sing to it; which I did, a Song my dear good Lady had learn'd me, and us'd to be pleas'd with, and which she brought with her from *Bath*. And the Ladies were much taken with the Song, and were so kind as to approve my Performance: And Miss *Darnford* was pleas'd to compliment me, that I had all the Accomplishments of my Sex. I said, I had had a good Lady, in my Master's Mother, who had spar'd no Pains nor Cost to improve me. She said, she wish'd the 'Squire could be prevail'd upon to give a Ball on an approaching happy Occasion, that we might have a Dancing-match, *&c.*—But I can't say I do; tho' I did not say so; for these Occasions I think are too solemn for the *Principals*, at least of our Sex, to take Part in, especially if they have the same Thoughts of the Solemnity that I have: For indeed, tho' I am in such an enviable Prospect of Happiness, I must own to you, my dear Parents, that I have something very awful upon my Mind, when I think of the Matter, and shall more and more, as it draws nearer and nearer. This is the Song.

I.

Go, happy Paper, *gently steal,*
And underneath her Pillow *lie;*
There, in soft Dreams, *my* LOVE *reveal,*
That LOVE *which I must still conceal,*
And, wrapt in awful Silence, *die.*

II.

Should Flames *be doom'd thy hapless Fate,*
To Atoms THOU *would'st quickly turn,*
MY Pains *may bear a longer Date;*
For should I live, *and should she* hate,
In endless *Torments I should* burn.

III.

Tell fair AURELIA, *she has Charms,*
Might in a Hermit *stir Desire.*

T' attain the Heav'n that's in her Arms,
I'd quit the World's *alluring Harms,*
And to a Cell, *content, retire.*

IV.

Of all that pleas'd my ravish'd Eye
Her Beauty *should supply the Place;*
Bold Raphael's *Strokes, and* Titian's Dye,
Should but in vain presume to vye
With her inimitable Face.

V.

No more I'd wish for Phœbus' Rays,
To gild the Object of my Sight;
Much less the Taper's *fainter Blaze;*
Her Eyes *should measure out my* Days;
And when she slept, it should be Night.[1]

About four o'Clock. My Master just came up to me, and said, If you should see Mr. *Williams* below, do you think, *Pamela*, you should not be surpriz'd?—No, Sir, said I, I hope not. Why should I? Expect, said he, a Stranger then, when you come down to us in the Parlour; for the Ladies are preparing themselves for the Card-table, and they insist upon your Company—You have a mind, Sir, said I, I believe, to try all my Courage. Why, said he, does it want Courage to see him? No, Sir, said I, not at all. But I was grievously dash'd to see all those strange Ladies and Gentlemen; and now to see Mr. *Williams* before them, as some of them refus'd his Application for me, when I wanted to get away, it will a little shock me, to see them smile, in recollecting what has pass'd of that kind. Well, said he, guard your Heart against Surprizes, tho' you shall see, when you come down, a Man that I can allow you to love dearly; tho' hardly preferably to me.

This surprizes me much. I am afraid he begins to be jealous of me. What will become of me, (for he look'd very seriously) if any Turn should happen now!—My Heart akes! I know not what's the Matter. But I will go down as brisk as I can, that nothing may be imputed to me. Yet I wish this Mr. *Williams* had not been there now when they are all there; because of their Fleers at him and me. Otherwise I should be glad to see the poor Gentleman; for indeed I think him a good Man, and he has suffer'd for my sake.

So, I am sent for down to Cards. I'll go; but wish I may continue their good Opinions of me: For I shall be very awkward. My Master, by his serious Question, and bidding me guard my Heart against Surprizes, tho' I should see, when I came down, a Man he can allow me to love dearly, tho' hardly better than he, has quite alarm'd me, and made me sad!—I hope he loves me!—But whether he does or not, I am in for it now, over Head and Ears, I doubt, and can't help loving him; 'tis a Folly to deny it. But to be sure I cannot love any Man preferably to him. I shall soon know what he means.

Now, my dear Mother, must I write to you. Well might my good Master say so mysteriously as he did, about guarding my Heart against Surprizes. I never was so surpriz'd in my Life; and never could see a Man I lov'd so dearly!—O my dear Mother, it was my dear, dear Father, and not Mr. *Williams*, that was below ready to receive and to bless your Daughter; and both my Master and he enjoin me to write how the whole Matter was, and what my Thoughts were on this joyful Occasion.

I will take the Matter from the Beginning, that God directed his Feet to this House, to this Time, as I have had it from Mrs. *Jewkes*, from my Master, my Father, the Ladies, and my own Heart and Conduct, as far as I know of both; because they command it, and you will be pleased with my Relation; and so, as you know how I came by the Connection, will make one uniform Relation of it.

It seems then, that my dear Father and you were so uneasy to know the Truth of the Story that *Thomas* had told you, and fearing I was betrayed, and quite undone, that he got Leave of Absence, and set out the Day after *Thomas* was there; and so, on *Friday* Morning, he got to the neighbouring Town; and there he heard, that the Gentry in the Neighbourhood were at my Master's, at a great Entertainment. He put on a clean Shirt and Neckcloth, that he brought in his Pocket, at an Alehouse there, and got shav'd; and so, after he had eat some Bread and Cheese, and drank a Can of Ale, he set out for my Master's House, with a heavy Heart, dreading for me, and in much fear of being brow-beaten. He had, it seems, asked, at the Alehouse, what Family the 'Squire had down here, in hopes to hear something of me; and they said, A House-keeper, two Maids, and, at present, two Coachmen, and two Grooms, a Footman, and a Helper. Was that all? he said. They told him, There was a young Creature there, belike, who *was*, or *was to be*, his Mistress, or somewhat of that Nature; but had been his Mother's Waiting-maid. This, he said, grieved his Heart, and made out what he fear'd.

So he went on, and, about Three o'Clock in the Afternoon, came to the Gate; and ringing there, Sir *Simon*'s Coachman went to the Iron-gate; and he ask'd for the Housekeeper; tho' from what I had wrote, in his Heart, he could not abide her. She sent for him in, little thinking who he was, and ask'd him, in the little Hall, what his Business with her was?—Only, Madam, said he, whether I cannot speak one Word with the 'Squire? No, Friend, said she; he is engaged with several Gentlemen and Ladies. Said he, I have Business with his Honour, of greater Consequence to me than either Life or Death; and Tears stood in his Eyes.

At that she went into the great Parlour, where my Master was talking very pleasantly with the Ladies; and she said, Sir, here is a good tight old Man, that wants to see you on Business of Life and Death, he says, and is very earnest. Ay, said he, Who can that be!—Let him stay in the little Hall, and I'll come to him presently. They all seem'd to stare; and Sir *Simon* said, No more nor less, I dare say, my good Friend, but a Bastard Child. If it is, said Lady *Jones*, bring it in to us. I will, said he.

Mrs. *Jewkes* tells me, my Master was much surpriz'd, when he saw who it was; and she much more, when my dear Father said,—Good God! give me Patience! but, as great as you are, Sir, I must ask for my Child! And burst out into Tears. O what Trouble have I given you both! My Master said, taking him by the Hand, Don't be uneasy, Goodman *Andrews*, your Daughter is in the way to be happy!

This alarm'd my dear Father, and he said, What! then is she dying? And trembled he could scarce stand. My Master made him sit down, and sat down by him, and said, No, God be praised! she is very well; and pray be comforted; I cannot bear to see you thus apprehensive; but she has wrote you a Letter to assure you, that she has Reason to be well satisfied and happy.

Ah! Sir, said he, you told me once she was in *London*, waiting on a Bishop's Lady, when all the time she was a severe Prisoner here.—Well, that's all over now, Goodman *Andrews*, said my Master: but the Times are alter'd; for now the sweet Girl has taken me Prisoner; and, in a few Days, I shall put on the pleasantest Fetters that ever Man wore.

O, Sir, said he, you are too pleasant for my Griefs. My Heart's almost broke. But may I not see my poor Child? You shall presently, said he; for she is coming down to us; and since you won't believe me, I hope you will her.

I will ask you, good Sir, said he, but one Question till then, that I may know how to look upon her when I see her. Is she honest? Is she virtuous?—As the new-born Babe, Mr. *Andrews*, said my good Master; and, in twelve Days time, I hope, will be my Wife!—

O flatter me not, good your Honour, said he: It cannot be! it cannot be!—I fear you have deluded her with strange Hopes; and would make me believe Impossibilities!—Mrs. *Jewkes*, said he, do you tell my dear *Pamela*'s good Father, when I go out, all you know concerning me, and your Mistress that is to be. Mean time, make much of him, and set out what you have; and make him drink a Glass of Wine he likes best. If this be Wine, added he, fill me a Bumper.

She did so; and he took my Father by the Hand, and said, Believe me, good Man, and be easy; for I can't bear to see you tortur'd in this cruel Suspense: Your dear Daughter is the beloved of my Soul. I am glad you are come! For you'll see us all in the same Story. And here's your Dame's Health; and God bless you both, for being the happy Means of procuring for me so great a Blessing! And so he drank a Bumper to this most obliging Health.

What do I hear! it cannot surely be! said my Father. And your Honour is too good, I hope, to mock a poor old Man!—This ugly Story, Sir, of the Bishop, runs in my Head!—But you say, I shall see my dear Child!—And I shall see her honest!—If not, poor as I am, I would not own her!

My Master bid Mrs. *Jewkes* not let me know yet, that my Father was come, and went to the Company, and said, I have been agreeably surpriz'd. Here is honest old Goodman *Andrews* come full of Grief, to see his Daughter; for he fears she is seduced; and tells me, good honest Man, that, poor as he is, he will not own her, if she be not virtuous. O, said they all, with one Voice almost, dear Sir! shall we not see the good old Man you have so praised for his plain good Sense and honest Heart? If, said he, I thought *Pamela* would not be too much affected with the Surprize, I would make you all witness to their first Interview; for never did Daughter love a Father, or a Father a Daughter, as they two do one another. Miss *Darnford*, and all the Ladies, and the Gentlemen too, begg'd it might be so. But was not this very cruel, my dear Mother? For well might they think I should not support myself in such an agreeable Surprize.

He said, kindly, I have but one Fear, that the dear Girl may be too much affected. O, said Lady *Darnford*, we'll all help to keep up her Spirits. Says he, I'll go up and prepare her; but won't tell her of it. So he came up to me, as I have said, and amus'd me about Mr. *Williams*, to half prepare me for some Surprize; tho' that could not have been any thing to this. And he left me, as I said, in that Suspense, at his mystical Words, saying, he would send to me, when they were going to Cards.

My Master went from me to my Father, and asked if he had eaten any thing. No, said Mrs. *Jewkes*; the good Man's Heart's so full, he cannot eat, nor do any thing, till he has seen his dear Daughter. That shall soon be, said my Master. I will have you come in with me; for she is going to sit down with my Guests, to a Game at Quadrille;[1] and I will send for her down. O, Sir, said my Father, don't, don't let me; I am not fit to appear before your Guests; let me see my Daughter by myself, I beseech you. Said he, They all know your honest Character, Goodman *Andrews*, and long to see you, for *Pamela*'s sake.

So he took my Father by the Hand, and led him in, against his Will, to the Company. They were all very good. My Master kindly said, Ladies and Gentlemen, I present to you one of the honestest Men in *England*; my good *Pamela*'s Father. Mr. *Peters* went to him, and took him by the Hand, and said, We are all glad to see you, Sir; you are the happiest Man in the World in a Daughter, that we never saw before to Day; but cannot enough admire her.

Said my Master, This Gentleman, Goodman *Andrews*, is the Minister of the Parish; but is not young enough for Mr. *Williams*. This cutting Joke, my poor Father said, made him fear, for a Moment, that all was a Jest.—Sir *Simon* also took him by the Hand, and said, Ay, you have a sweet Daughter, Honesty; we are all in Love with her. And the Ladies came, and said very fine things: Lady *Darnford* particularly, That he might think himself the happiest Man in *England*, in such a Daughter. If, and please you, Madam, said he, she be but vertuous, 'tis all in all: For all the rest is Accident. But, I doubt, his Honour has been too much upon the Joke with me. No, said Mrs. *Peters*, we are all Witness that he intends very honourably by her.—It is some Comfort, said he, and wiped his Eyes, that such good Ladies say so!—But I wish I could see her.

They would have had him sit down by them, but he would only sit behind the Door, in the Corner of the Room, so that one could not soon see him, as one came in; because the Door open'd against him, and hid him almost. The Ladies all sat down; and my Master said, Desire Mrs. *Jewkes* to step up; and tell Mrs. *Andrews* the Ladies wait for her. So down I came.

Miss *Darnford* rose, and met me at the Door, and said, Well, Miss, we long'd for your Company. I did not see my dear Father; and, it seems, his Heart was too full to speak; and he got up, and sat down three or four times successively, unable to come to me, or to say any thing. The Ladies looked that way; but I would not, supposing it was Mr. *Williams*. And they made me sit down between Lady *Darnford* and Lady *Jones*; and asked me, what we should play at? I said, At what your Ladyships please. I wonder'd to see them smile, and look upon me, and to that Corner of the Room; but I was afraid of looking that way, for fear of seeing Mr. *Williams*; tho' my Face was that way too, and the Table before me.

Said my Master, Did you send your Letter away to the Post-house, my good Girl, for your Father? To be sure, Sir, said I, I did not forget that. I took the Liberty to desire Mr. *Thomas* to carry it. What, said he, I wonder, will the good old Couple say to it? O Sir, said I, your Goodness will be a Cordial to their dear honest Hearts! At that, my dear Father, not able to contain himself, nor yet to stir from the Place, gush'd out into a Flood of Tears, which he, good Soul! had been struggling with, it seems; and cry'd out, O my dear Child!

I knew the Voice, and lifting up my Eyes, and seeing my Father, gave a Spring, overturn'd the Table, without Regard to the Company, and threw myself at his Feet, O my Father! my Father! said I, can it be!—Is it you? Yes, it is! It is! O bless your happy—Daughter! I would have said, and down I sunk.

My Master, seem'd concern'd.—I fear'd, said he, that the Surprize would be too much for her Spirits; and all the Ladies run to me, and made me drink a Glass of Water; and I found myself incircled in the Arms of my dearest Father.—O tell me, said I, every thing! How long have you been here? When did you come? How does my honour'd Mother? and half a dozen Questions more, before he could answer one.

They permitted me to retire, with my Father; and then I pour'd forth all my Vows, and Thanksgivings to God for this additional Blessing; and confirm'd all my Master's Goodness to his scarce-believing Amazement. And we kneeled together, blessing God, and blessing one another, for several ecstatick Minutes; and my Master coming in soon after, my dear Father said, O Sir, what a Change is this! May God reward you! may God bless you in this World and the next!

May God bless us all! said he. But how does my sweet Girl! I have been in Pain for you!—I am sorry I did not apprize you before hand.

O Sir, said I, it was You! and all you do must be good.—But this was a Blessing so unexpected!

Well, said he, you have given Pain to all the Company. They will be glad to see you, when you can; for you have spoiled all their Diversion: And yet painfully delighted them at the same time. Mr. *Andrews*, said he, you make this House your own; and the longer you stay, the more welcome you'll be. After you have a little compos'd yourself, my dear Girl, step in to us again. I am glad to see you so well so soon. And so he left us.

See you, my dear Father, said I, what Goodness there is in this once naughty Master! O pray for him! and pray for me, that I may deserve it!

How long has this happy Change been wrought, said he, my dear Child!—O, said I, several happy Days!—I have wrote down every thing; and you'll see, from the Depth of Misery, what God has done for your happy Daughter!

Blessed be his Name! said he. But do you say he will marry you! Can it be, that such a brave Gentleman will make a Lady of the Child of such a poor Man as I? O the Goodness of God! How will your poor dear Mother be able to support these happy Tidings? I will set out to-morrow, to acquaint her with it. For I am but half happy till the dear good Woman shares it with me!—To be sure, my dear Child, we ought to go into some far Country, to hide ourselves, that we may not disgrace you by our Poverty!

O my dear Father, said I, now you are unkind for the first Time. Your Poverty has been my Glory, and my Riches; and I have nothing to brag of, but that I ever thought it an Honour to me, rather than a Disgrace; because you were always so honest, that your Child might well boast of such a Parentage!

In this manner, my dear Mother, did we pass the happy Moments, till Miss *Darnford* came to me, and said, How do you do, dear Miss? I rejoice to see you well! Pray let us have your Company. And, said she, taking my Father's Hand, and yours too, good Mr. *Andrews*.

This was very obliging, I told her; and we went to the great Parlour; and my Master took my Father by the Hand, and made him sit down by him, and drink a Glass of Wine with him. Mean time, I made my Excuses to the Ladies, as well as I could; which they readily granted me. But Sir *Simon*, after his comical manner, put his Hands on my Shoulders, Let me see, let me see, said he, where your Wings grow; for I never saw any body fly like you?—Why, said he, you have broke Lady *Jones*'s Shins with the Table. Shew her else, Madam.

His Pleasantry made them laugh. And I said, I was very sorry for my Extravagancy: And if it had not been my Master's Doings, I should have said, it was a Fault to permit me to be so surprized, and put out of myself, before such good Company. They said, All was very excusable; and they were glad I suffer'd no more by it. They were so kind, as to excuse me at Cards, and play'd by themselves; and I went, by my Master's Command, and sat on the other Side, in the happiest Place I ever was blest with, between two of the dearest Men in the World to me, and each holding one of my Hands;—my Father, every now-and-then, with Tears in his Eyes, blessing God, and saying, Could I ever have hoped this!

I asked him, if he had been so kind as to bring the Papers with him? He said he had, and looked at me, as who should say, Must I give them to you now?—I said, Be pleased to let me have them. He pulled them from his Pocket; and I stood up, and, with my best Duty, gave them into my Master's Hands. He said, Thank you, *Pamela.* Your Father shall take all with him, to see what a sad Fellow I have been, as well as the present happier Alteration. But I must have them all again, for the Writer's sake.

The Ladies and Gentlemen would make me govern the Tea-table, whatever I could do; and *Abraham* attended me, to serve the Company. My Master and my Father sat together, and drank a Glass or two of Wine instead of Tea; and Sir *Simon* jok'd with my Master, and said, I warrant you would not be such a Woman's Man, as to drink Tea, for ever so much, with the Ladies. But your Time's coming, and, I doubt not, you'll be made as conformable as I.

My Master was very urgent with them to stay Supper; and, at last, they comply'd, on Condition that I would grace the Table, as they were pleased to call it. I begg'd to be excus'd. My Master said, Don't be excus'd, *Pamela,* since the Ladies desire it. And besides, said he, we won't part with your Father; and so you may as well stay with us.

I was in hope my Father and I might sup by ourselves, or only with Mrs. *Jewkes.* And Miss *Darnford,* who is a most obliging young Lady, said, We will not part with you; indeed we won't.

When Supper was brought in, Lady *Darnford* took me by the Hand, and said to my Master, Sir, by your Leave; and would have plac'd me at the Upper-end of the Table. Pray, pray, Madam, said I, excuse me, I cannot do it, indeed I cannot. *Pamela,* said my Master, to the great Delight of my good Father, as I could see by his Looks, Oblige Lady *Darnford,* since she desires it. It is but a little before your Time, you know.

Dear, good Sir, said I, pray don't command it! Let me sit by my Father, pray! Why, said Sir *Simon,* here's ado indeed; Sit down at the Upper-end, as you should do! and your Father shall sit by you there. This put my dear Father upon Difficulties. And my Master said, Come, I'll place you all: And so put Lady *Darnford* at the Upper-end, Lady *Jones* at her Right-hand, and Mrs. *Peters* on the other; and he placed me between the two young Ladies; but very genteely put Miss *Darnford* below her younger Sister; saying, Come, Miss, I put you here, because you shall hedge in this little Cuckow; for I take notice, with Pleasure, of your Goodness to her; and besides, all you very young Ladies should sit together. This seem'd to please both Sisters; for had the youngest Miss been put there, it might have piqu'd her, as matters had been formerly, to be placed below me; whereas Miss *Darnford* giving Place to her younger Sister, made it less odd she should to me; especially with that handsome Turn of the dear Man, as if I was a Cuckow, and to be hedg'd in.

My Master kindly said, Come, Mr. *Andrews*, you and I will sit together. And so took his Place at the Bottom of the Table, and set my Father on his Right-hand; and Sir *Simon* would sit on his Left. For, said he, Parson, I think the Petticoats should sit together; and so do you sit down by that Lady (his Sister). A boiled Turkey standing by me, my Master said, Cut up that Turkey, *Pamela*, if it be not too strong Work for you, that Lady *Darnford* may not have too much Trouble. So I carv'd it in a Trice, and helped the Ladies. Miss *Darnford* said, I would give something to be so dextrous a Carver. O Miss, said I, my late good Lady would always make me do these things, when she entertained her Female Friends; as she used to do on particular Days.

Ay, said my Master, I remember my poor Mother would often say, if I, or any body at Table, happen'd to be a little out in Carving, I'll send up for my *Pamela*, to shew you how to carve. Said Lady *Jones*, Mrs. *Andrews* has every Accomplishment of her Sex. She is quite wonderful for her Years. Miss *Darnford* said, And I can tell you, Madam, that she plays sweetly upon the Spinnet, and sings as sweetly to it; for she has a fine Voice. Foolish, said Sir *Simon*, who, that hears her speak, knows not that? and who, that sees her Fingers, believes not that they were made to touch any Key?[1] O, Parson! said he, 'tis well you're by, or I should have had a Blush from the Ladies. I hope not, Sir *Simon*, said Lady *Jones*; for a Gentleman of your Politeness, would not say any thing that would make Ladies blush.—No, no, said he, for the World: But if I had, it would have been as the Poet says,

They blush, because they understand.[2]

When the Company went away, Lady *Darnford*, Lady *Jones*, and Mrs. *Peters*, severally invited my Master, and me with him, to their Houses; and begg'd he would permit me, at least, to come before we left these Parts. And they said, We hope, when the happy Knot is ty'd, you will induce the 'Squire to reside more among us. We were always glad, said Lady *Darnford*, when he was here; but now shall have double Reason. O what grateful things were these to the Ears of my good Father!

When the Company was gone, my Master ask'd my Father, if he smoak'd; he said, No. He made us both sit down by him; and he said,

I have been telling this sweet Girl, that, in Fourteen Days, and two of them are gone, she must fix on one, to make me happy: And have left it to her to chuse either one of the first or the last Seven. My Father held up his Hands and Eyes; God bless your Honour, said he, is all I can say! Now, *Pamela*, said my Master, taking my Hand, don't let a little wrong-timed Bashfulness take place, without any other Reason, because I should be glad to go to *Bedfordshire* as soon as I could; and I would not return till I carry my Servants there a Mistress, who should assist me to repair the Mischiefs she has made in it.

I could not look up for Confusion. And my Father said, My dear Child, I need not, I am sure, prompt your Obedience in whatever will most oblige so good a Master. What says my *Pamela?* said my Master. She does not use to be at a Loss for Expression. Sir, said I, were I too sudden, it would look as if I doubted whether you would hold in your Mind, and was not willing to give you Time for Reflection. But otherwise, to be sure, I ought to resign myself implicitly to your Will.

Said he, I want not Time for Reflection. For I have often told you, and that long ago, I could not live without you. And my Pride of Condition made me both tempt and terrify you to other Terms; but your Virtue was Proof against all Temptation, and was not to be aw'd by Terrors: Wherefore, as I could not conquer my Passion for you, I corrected myself, and resolved, since you would not be mine upon my Terms, you should upon your own: And now I desire you not on any other, I assure you. And, I think, the sooner it is done, the better. What say you, Mr. *Andrews?* Sir, said he, there is so much Goodness of your Side, and, blessed be God! so much Prudence of my Daughter's, that I must be quite silent. But when it is done, I and my poor Wife, shall have nothing to do, but to pray for you both, and to look back with Wonder and Joy, on the Ways of Providence.

This, said my Master, is *Friday* Night; and suppose, my Girl, it be next *Monday, Tuesday, Wednesday,* or *Thursday* Morning?—Say, my *Pamela.*

Will you, Sir, said I, excuse me till to-morrow for an Answer?—I will, said he. And he touch'd the Bell, and called for Mrs. *Jewkes.* Where, said he, does Mr. *Andrews* lie to-night? You'll take care of him: He's a very good Man; and will bring a Blessing upon every House he sets his Foot in.

My dear Father wept for Joy; and I could not refrain keeping him Company. And my Master saluting me, bid us Good-night, and retir'd. And I waited upon my dear Father, and was so full of Prattle, of my Master's Goodness, and my future Prospects, that I believed afterwards I was turned all into Tongue. But he indulged me, and was transported with Joy; and went to-bed, and dreamt of nothing but *Jacob*'s Ladder,[1] and Angels ascending and descending, to bless him, and his Daughter.

SATURDAY.

I rose up early in the Morning; but found my Father was up before me, and was gone to walk in the Garden. I went to him: And with what Delight, with what Thankfulness, did we go over every Scene of it, that had before been so dreadful to me! The Fish-Pond, the Back-door, and every Place: O what Reason had we for Thankfulness and Gratitude!

About Seven o'Clock, my good Master join'd us, in his Morning-gown and Slippers; and looking a little heavy, I said, Sir, I fear you had not good Rest last Night. That is your Fault, *Pamela*, said he: After I went from you, I must needs look into your Papers, and could not leave them till I had read them thro'; and so 'twas Three o'Clock before I went to sleep. I wish, Sir, said I, you had had better Entertainment. The worst Part of it, said he, was what I had brought upon myself; and you have not spar'd me. Sir, said I—He interrupting me, said, Well, I forgive you. You had too much Reason for it. But I find, plain enough, that if you had got away, you would soon have been *Williams*'s Wife: And I can't see how it could well have been otherwise. Indeed, Sir, said I, I had no Notion of it, or of being any body's. I believe so, said he; but it must have come on as a Thing of Course; and I see your Father was for it. Sir, said he, I little thought of the Honour your Goodness would confer upon her; and I thought that would be a Match above what we could do for her, a great deal. But when I found she was not for it, I resolved not to urge her; but leave all to God's Grace, and her own Prudence.

I see, said he, all was sincere, honest, and open; and I speak of it, if it had been done, as a thing that could hardly well be avoided; and I am quite satisfied. But, said he, I must observe, as I have an hundred times, with Admiration, what a prodigious Memory, and easy and happy Manner of Narration this excellent Girl has! And tho' she is full of her pretty Tricks and Artifices, to escape the Snares I had laid for her, yet all is innocent, lovely, and uniformly beautiful. You are exceedingly happy in a Daughter; and, I hope, I shall be so in a Wife.—Or, said my Father, may she not have that Honour!—I fear it not, said he; and hope I shall deserve it of her.

But, *Pamela*, said my Master, I am sorry to find, in some Parts of your Journal, that Mrs. *Jewkes* carry'd her Orders a little too far. And I the more take Notice of it, because you have not complain'd to me of her Behaviour, as she might have expected for some Parts of it. Tho' a good deal was occasion'd by my strict Orders.—But she had the Insolence to strike my Girl! I find. Sir, said I, I was a little provoking, I believe; but as we forgave one another, I was the less intitled to complain of her.

Well, said he, you are very good; but if you have any particular Resentment, I will indulge it so far, as that she shall hereafter have nothing to do where you are. Sir, said I, you are so kind, that I ought to forgive every body; and when I see that God has brought about my Happiness by the very Means that I thought then my great Grievance; I ought to bless those Means, and forgive all that was disagreeable to me at the time, for the great Good that has issued from it.—That, said he, and kissed me, is sweetly consider'd! and it shall be my Part to make you Amends for what you have suffer'd, that you may still think lighter of the one, and have Cause to rejoice in the other.

My dear Father's Heart was full; and he said, with his Hands folded, and lifted up, Pray, Sir, let me go,—let me go,—to my dear Wife! and tell her all these blessed things, while my Heart holds! for it is ready to burst with Joy! Good Man! said my Master,—I love to hear this honest Heart of yours speaking at your Lips. I injoin you, *Pamela*, to continue your Relation, as you have Opportunity; and tho' your Father be here, write to your Mother, that this wondrous Story be perfect, and we, your Friends, may read and admire you more and more. Ay, pray, pray do, my dear Child, said my Father. And this is the Reason that I write on, my dear Mother, when I thought not to do it, because my Father could tell you all that passed while he was here.

My Master took notice of my Psalm, and was pleas'd to commend it; and said, That I had very charitably turn'd the last Verses, which, in the Original, was full of heavy Curses, to a Wish, that shew'd I was not of an implacable Disposition; tho' my then Usage might have excused it, if I had. But, said he, I think you shall sing it to me to-morrow.

After we have breakfasted, added he, if you have no Objection, *Pamela*, we'll take an Airing together; and it shall be in the Coach, because we'll have your Father's Company. He would have excus'd himself; but my Master would have it so. But he was much ashamed, because he was not in a Dress for my Master's Company.

My Master would make us both breakfast with him, on Chocolate; and he said, I would have you, *Pamela*, begin to dress as you used to do; for now, at least, you may call your *two other Bundles* your own; and if you want any thing against the approaching Occasion, private, as I design it,

I'll send to *Lincoln* for it, by a special Messenger. I said, My good Lady's Bounty, and his own, had set me much above my Degree, and I had very good things of all Sorts; and I did not desire any other, because I would not excite the Censure of the Ladies. That would be a different thing, he was pleased to say, when he publickly own'd his Nuptials, after we came to the other House. But at present, if I was satisfied, he would not make Words with me.

I hope, Mr. *Andrews*, said he to my Father, you'll not leave us till you see the Affair over, and then you'll be *sure* I mean honourably; and besides, *Pamela* will be induced to set the Day sooner. O Sir, said he, I bless God, I have no Reason to doubt your meaning honourably; and I hope you'll excuse me, if I set out on *Monday* Morning, very early, to my dear Wife, and make her as happy as I am.

Why, *Pamela*, said my good Master, may it not be perform'd on *Tuesday*, and then your Father, may-be, will stay?—I should have been glad to have had it to-morrow, added he; but I have sent Monsieur *Colbrand* for a Licence, that you may have no Scruple unanswer'd; and he can't very well be back before to-morrow Night, or *Monday* Morning.

This was most agreeable News. I said, Sir, I know my dear Father will want to be at home. And as you was so good to give me a Fortnight from last *Thursday*, I should be glad you'll be pleased to indulge me with some Day in the second Seven. Well, said he, I will not be too urgent; but the sooner you fix, the better. Mr. *Andrews*, we must leave something to these *Jephtha*'s Daughters,[1] in these Cases, he was pleased to say: I suppose the little bashful Folly, which, in the happiest Circumstances, may give a kind of Regret to quit the Maiden State, and an Aukwardness at the Entrance of a new one, is a Reason with *Pamela*; and so she shall name her Day. Sir, said he, you are all Goodness.

I went up soon after, and new dress'd myself, taking Possession, in a happy Moment, I hope, of my *two Bundles*, as my good Master was pleased to call them, (alluding to my former Division of those good things my Lady and himself bestow'd upon me) and so put on fine Linen, silk Shoes, and fine white Cotton Stockens, a fine quilted Coat, a delicate green mantua[2] silk Gown and Coat; a *French* Necklace, and a lac'd Head, and Handkerchief, and clean Gloves; and taking my Fan in my Hand, I, like a little proud Hussy, looked in the Glass, and thought myself a Gentlewoman once more; but I forgot not to thank God, for being able to put on this Dress with so much Comfort.

Mrs. *Jewkes* would help to dress me, and complimented me highly, saying, among other things, that now I looked like her Lady indeed! And as, she said, the little Chapel was ready, and Divine Service would be read in it to-morrow, she wished the happy Knot might then be ty'd. Said she, Have you not seen the Chapel, Madam, since it has been cleaned out?— No, said I; but are we to have Service in it to-morrow, do you say?—I am glad of that; for I have been a sad Heathen lately, sore against my Will!—But who is to officiate?—Somebody, reply'd she, Mr. *Peters* will send. You tell me very good News, said I, Mrs. *Jewkes.* I hope it will never be a Lumber-room again.—Ay, said she, I can tell you more good News; for the two Miss *Darnford*'s, and Lady *Jones*, are to be here at the Opening of it; and will stay and dine with you. My Master, said I, has not told me that. You must alter your Stile, Madam, said she. It must not be *Master*, now, sure!—O, return'd I, that is a Language I shall never forget. He shall always be my Master; and I shall think myself more and more his Servant.

My poor Father did not know I went up to dress myself; and he said, his Heart misgave him, when he saw me first, for fear I was made a Fool of, and that here was some fine Lady that was to be my Master's true Wife. And he stood in Admiration, and said, O, my dear Child, how well will you become your happy Condition! Why you look like a Lady already!—I hope, my dear Father, said I, and boldly kissed him, I shall always be your dutiful Daughter, whatever my Condition be.

My Master sent me word he was ready; and when he saw me, said, Dress as you will, *Pamela*, you're a charming Girl; and so handed me to the Coach, and would make my Father and me sit both on the Fore-side; and sat backwards, over-against[1] me; and bid the Coachman drive to the Meadow; that is, where he once met Mr. *Williams.*

The Conversation was most agreeable to me, and to my dear Father, as we went; and he more and more exceeded in Goodness and Generosity; and, while I was gone up to dress, he had presented my Father with twenty Guineas; desiring him to buy himself and my Mother such Apparel, as they should think proper; and lay it all out: But I knew not this till after that we came home; my Father having no Opportunity to tell me of it.

He was pleased to tell me of the Chapel being got in tolerable Order; and said, it look'd very well; and against he came down next, it should be all new white-wash'd, and painted, and lin'd; and a new Pulpit-cloth, Cushion, Desk, &c. and that it should always be kept in order for the future. He told me, the two Miss *Darnford*'s, and Lady *Jones*, would dine with him on *Sunday*; And with their Servants and mine, said he, we shall make a tolerable little Congregation. And, added he, have I not well contriv'd, to shew you, that the Chapel is really a little House of God, and has been consecrated, before we solemnize our Nuptials in it?—O, Sir, reply'd I, your Goodness to me is inexpressible! Mr. *Peters*, said he, offer'd to come and officiate in it; but would not stay to dine with me, because he has Company at his own House; and so I intend that Divine Service shall be perform'd in it, by one to whom I shall make some yearly Allowance, as a sort of Chaplain.—You look serious, *Pamela*, added he; I know you think of your Friend *Williams*. Indeed, Sir, said I, if you won't be angry, I did. Poor Man! I am sorry I have been the Cause of his disobliging you.

When we came to the Meadow, where the Gentry have their Walk sometimes, the Coach stopt, and my Master alighted, and led me to the Brook-side; and it is a very pretty Summer Walk. He asked my Father, if he chose to walk out, or go on in the Coach, to the further End. He, poor Man, chose to go in the Coach, for fear, he said, any Gentry should be walking there; and he told me, he was most of the way upon his Knees, in the Coach, thanking God for his gracious Mercies and Goodness; and begging a Blessing upon my good Master and me.

I was quite astonish'd, when we came into the shady Walk, to see Mr. *Williams* there. See there, said my Master, there's poor *Williams*, taking his solitary Walk again, with his Book. And it seems, it was so contriv'd; for Mr. *Peters* had been, as I since find, desir'd to tell him, to be in that Walk at such an Hour in the Morning.

So, old Acquaintance, said my Master, again have I met you in this Place? What Book are you now reading? He said, It was *Boileau*'s *Lutrin*.[1] Said my Master, You see I have brought with me my little Fugitive, that would have been: While you are perfecting yourself in *French*, I am trying to learn *English*; and hope soon to be Master of it.

Mine, Sir, said he, is a very beautiful Piece of *French*: But your *English* has no Equal.

You are very polite, Mr. *Williams*, said my Master. And he that does not think as you do, deserves no Share in her. Why, *Pamela*, added he, very generously, why so strange, where you have once been so familiar? I do assure you both, that I mean not, by this Interview, to insult Mr. *Williams*, or confuse you. Then I said, Mr. *Williams*, I am very glad to see you well; and tho' the generous Favour of my good Master has happily changed the Scene, since you and I last saw one another, I am nevertheless very glad of an Opportunity to acknowledge, with Gratitude, your good Intentions, not so much to serve me, as *me*, but as a Person that then had great Reason to believe herself in Distress. And, I hope, Sir, added I, to my Master, your Goodness will permit me to say this.

You, *Pamela*, said he, may make what Acknowledgments you please to Mr. *Williams*'s good Intentions; and I would have you speak as you think; but I do not apprehend myself to be quite so much oblig'd to those Intentions.

Sir, said Mr. *Williams*, I beg leave to say, I knew well, that, by Education, you was no Libertine; nor had I Reason to think you so by Inclination; and when you came to reflect, I hoped you would not be displeased with me. And this was no small Motive to me, at first, to do as I did.

Ay, but, Mr. *Williams*, said my Master, could you think, that I should have had Reason to thank you, if, above all her Sex, I loved one Person, and you had robbed me of her, and marry'd her yourself?—And then, said he, you are to consider, that she was of long Acquaintance with me, and a quite new one to you; that I had sent her down to my own House, for better securing her; and that you, who had Access to my House, could not effect your Purpose, without being guilty, in some sort, of a Breach of the Laws of Hospitality and Friendship. As to my Designs upon her, I own they had not the best Appearance; but still I was not answerable to Mr. *Williams* on that Score; much less could you be excus'd, to invade a Property so very dear to me, and to endeavour to gain an Interest in her Affections, tho' you could not be certain, that Matters would not turn out as they have actually done.

I own, said he, that some Parts of my Conduct seem exceptionable, as you state it. But, Sir, I am but a young Man. I meant no Harm. I had no Interest, I am sure, to incur your Displeasure; and when you think of every thing, and the inimitable Graces of Person, and Perfections of Mind, that adorn this excellent Lady, (so he called me) you will, perhaps, find your Generosity allow something as an Extenuation of a Fault, which your Anger would not permit as an Excuse.

I have done, said my Master; nor did I meet you here to be angry with you. *Pamela* knew not that she should see you; and now you are both present, I would ask you, Mr. *Williams*, If, now you know my honourable Designs towards this good Girl, you can really be *almost*, I will not say *quite*, as well pleased with the Friendship of my Wife, as you could be with the Favour of Mrs. *Andrews?*

Sir, said he, I will answer you truly. I think I could have preferr'd, with her, any Condition that could have befallen me, had I consider'd only *myself.* But, Sir, I was very far from having any Encouragement to expect her *Favour*; and I had much more Reason to believe, that if she could have hoped for your Goodness, her Heart was too much pre-engaged, to think of any body else. And give me Leave further to say, Sir, That tho' I tell you sincerely my Thoughts, were I only to consider *myself*; yet when I consider *her Good*, and *her Merit*, I should be highly ungenerous, were it put to my *Choice*, if I could not wish her in a Condition so much superior to what I could do for her, and so very answerable to her Merit.

Pamela, said my Master, *you* are obliged to Mr. *Williams*, and ought to thank him: He has distinguished well. But as for *me*, who had like to have lost you by his means, I am glad the Matter was not left to his *Choice*. Mr. *Williams*, said he, I give you *Pamela*'s Hand, because I know it will be pleasing to her, in Token of her Friendship and Esteem for you; and I give you mine, that I will not be your Enemy. But yet I must say, that I think I owe this proper Manner of your Thinking more to your Disappointment, than to the Generosity you talk of.

Mr. *Williams* kissed my Hand, as my Master gave it him; and my Master said, Sir, you will go home and dine with me, and I'll shew you my little Chapel; and do you, *Pamela*, look upon yourself at Liberty to number Mr. *Williams* in the List of your Friends.

How generous, how noble was this! Mr. *Williams* (and so had I) had Tears of Pleasure in his Eyes. I was silent; but Mr. *Williams* said, Sir, I shall be taught, by your Generosity, to think myself inexcusably wrong, in every Step I took, that could give you Offence; and my future Life shall shew my respectful Gratitude.

We walked on till we came to the Coach, where was my dear Father. *Pamela*, said my Master, tell Mr. *Williams* who that good Man is. O, Mr. *Williams!* said I, it is my dear Father; And, my Master was pleased to say, one of the honestest Men in *England*. *Pamela* owes every thing that she is to be, as well as her Being, to him; for, I think, she would not have brought me to this, nor made so great Resistance, but for the good Lessons, and religious Education she imbib'd from him.

Mr. *Williams* said, taking my Father's Hand, You see, good Mr. *Andrews*, with inexpressible Pleasure, the Fruits of your pious Care; and now are in a way, with your beloved Daughter, to reap the happy Effects of it.—I am overcome, said my dear Father, with his Honour's Goodness. But I can only say, I bless *God*, and bless *him*.

Mr. *Williams* and I being nearer the Coach than my Master; and he offering to draw back, to give way to him, he kindly said, Pray, Mr. *Williams*, oblige *Pamela* with your Hand; and step in yourself. He bow'd, and took my Hand, and my Master made him step in, and sit next me, all that ever he could do, and sat himself over-against him, next my Father, who sat against me.

And he said, Mr. *Andrews*, I told you Yesterday, that the Divine you saw, was *not* Mr. *Williams*; I now tell you, this Gentleman *is*: And tho' I have been telling him, I think not *myself* obliged to his Intentions; yet I will own, that *Pamela* and *you* are; and tho' I won't promise to love him, I would have you.

Sir, said Mr. *Williams*, you have a way of overcoming, that hardly all my Reading affords an Instance of the like; and it is the more noble, as it is on this Side, as I presume, the happy Ceremony; which, great as your Fortune is, will lay you under an Obligation to so much Virtue and Beauty, when she becomes yours; for you will then have a Treasure that Princes might envy.

Said my generous Master, (God bless him!) Mr. *Williams*, it is impossible that you and I should long live at Variance, when our Sentiments agree so well together, on Subjects the most material.

I was quite confused; and my Master seeing it, took my Hand, and said, Look up, my good Girl! and collect yourself.—Don't injure Mr. *Williams* and me so much, as to think we are capping Compliments, as we used to do Verses,[1] at School. I dare answer for us both, that we say not a Syllable we don't think.

O, Sir, said I, how unequal am I to all this Goodness! Every Moment that passes, adds to the Weight of the Obligations you oppress me with.

Think not too much of that, said he, most generously. Mr. *Williams*'s Compliments to you have great Advantage of mine: For, tho' equally sincere, I have a great deal to say, and to do, to compensate the Sufferings I have made you undergo; and, at last, must sit down dissatisfied, because those will never be aton'd by all I can do for you.

He saw my dear Father quite unable to support these affecting Instances of his Goodness; and he let go my Hand, and took his, and said, seeing his Tears, I wonder not, my dear *Pamela*'s Father, that your honest Heart springs thus to your Eyes, to see all her Trials at an End. I will not pretend to say, that I had formerly either Power or Will to act thus. But since I began to resolve on the Change you see, I have reap'd so much Pleasure in it, that my own *Interest* will keep me steady. For, till within these few Days, I knew not what it was to be happy.

Poor Mr. *Williams*, with Tears of Joy in his Eyes, said; How happily, Sir, have you been touched by the Divine Grace, before you have been hurried into the Commission of Sins, that the deepest Penitence could hardly have aton'd for!—God has enabled you to stop short of the Evil; and you have nothing to do, but to rejoice in the Good, which now will be doubly so, because you can receive it without the least inward Reproach.

You do well, said he, to remind me, that I owe all this to the Grace of God. I bless Him for it; and I thank this good Man for his excellent Lessons. I thank his dear Daughter for following them: And, I hope, from *her* good Example, and *your* Friendship, Mr. *Williams*, in time, to be half as good as my Tutoress. And that, said he, I believe you'll own, will make me, without Disparagement to any Gentleman, the best Fox-hunter in *England.*—Mr. *Williams* was going to speak: And he said, You put on so grave a Look, Mr. *Williams*, that, I believe, what I have said, with you practical good Folks, is liable to Exception: But I see we were become quite grave; and we must not be too serious neither.

What a happy Creature, my dear Mother, is your *Pamela!*—O may my thankful Heart, and the good Use I may be enabled to make of the Blessings before me, be a Means to continue this delightful Prospect to a long Date, for the sake of the dear good Gentleman, who thus becomes the happy Instrument, in the Hands of Providence, to bless all he smiles upon! To be sure, I shall never enough acknowledge the Value he is pleased to express for my Unworthiness, in that he has prevented[1] my Wishes, and, unask'd, sought the Occasion of being reconciled to a good Man, who, for my sake, had incurred his Displeasure; and whose Name he could not, a few Days before, permit to pass thro' my Lips: But see the wonderful Ways of Providence! The very things that I most dreaded his seeing or knowing, the Contents of my Papers, have, as I hope, satisfy'd all his Scruples, and been a Means to promote my Happiness.

Henceforth let not us poor short-sighted Mortals pretend to rely on our own Wisdom; or vainly think, that we are absolutely to direct for ourselves. I have abundant Reason, I am sure, to say, that when I was most disappointed, I was nearer my Happiness. For, had I made my Escape, which was so often my chief Point of View, and what I had placed my Heart upon, I had escaped the Blessings now before me, and fallen, perhaps headlong, into the Miseries I would have avoided! And yet, after all, it was necessary I should take the Steps I did, to bring on this wonderful Turn! O the unsearchable Wisdom of God![2]—And how much ought I to adore the Divine Goodness, and humble myself, who am made a poor Instrument, as, I hope, not only to magnify his Graciousness to this fine Gentleman and myself; but to dispense Benefits to others? Which God of his Mercy grant!

In the agreeable manner I have mentioned, did we pass the Time in our second happy Tour; and I thought Mrs. *Jewkes* would have sunk into the Ground, when she saw Mr. *Williams* brought in the Coach with us, and treated so kindly. We dined together in a most pleasant, and easy, and frank manner; and I found I needed not, from my Master's Generosity, to be under any Restraint, as to my Conduct to this good Clergyman; for he, so often as he fansy'd I was reserv'd, mov'd me to be free with him, and to him; and several times called upon me to help my Father and Mr. *Williams*; and seem'd to take great Delight in seeing me carve and help round, as indeed he does in every thing I do.

After Dinner we went and looked into the Chapel; which is a very pretty one, and very decent; and when finish'd, as he designs it, against his next coming down, will be a very pretty Place.

My Heart, my dear Mother, when I first sat my Foot in it, throbb'd a good deal, with awful Joy, at the Thoughts of the Solemnity, which, I hope, will be, in a few Days, performed here. And when I came up towards the little pretty Altar-piece, while they were looking at a Communion-picture, and saying it was prettily done, I gently stept into a Corner, out of Sight, and poured out my Soul to God, on my Knees, in Thankfulness and Supplication, that, after having been so long absent from Divine Service, the first time that I enter'd into a House dedicated to His Honour, should be with such blessed Prospects before me; and begging of God to continue me humble, and to make me not unworthy of his Mercies; and that he would be pleased to bless the *next* Author of it, my good Master.

I heard my Master say, Where's *Pamela?* And so I broke off sooner than I would, and went up to him.

He said, Mr. *Williams*, I hope I have not so offended you, by my Conduct past, (for really it is what I ought to be ashamed of) as that you will refuse to officiate, and to give us your Instructions here to-morrow. Mr. *Peters* was so kind, for the first time, to offer it; but I know it would be inconvenient for him; and besides, I was willing to make this Request to you an Introduction to our Reconciliation.

Sir, said he, most willingly, and most gratefully will I obey you. Tho', if you expect a Discourse, I am wholly unprepar'd for the Occasion. I would not have it, reply'd he, pointed to any particular Occasion; but if you have one upon the Text,—*There is more Joy in Heaven over one Sinner that repenteth, than over Ninety-nine just Persons that need not Repentance*;[1] and if it makes me not such a sad Fellow as to be pointed at by mine and the Ladies Servants we shall have here, I shall be well content. 'Tis a general Subject, added he, makes me speak of that; but any one you please will do; for you cannot make a bad Choice, I am sure.

Sir, said he, I have one upon that Text; but I am ready to think, that a Thanksgiving one, which I made on a great Mercy to myself, if I may be permitted to make my own Acknowledgments of your Favour the Subject of a Discourse, will be suitable to my grateful Sentiments. It is on the Text,—*Now lettest thou thy Servant depart in Peace; for my Eyes have seen thy Salvation.*[1]

That Text, said I, will be a very suitable one for me. Not so, *Pamela*, said my Master; because I don't let you *depart* in *Peace*; but I hope you will *stay here* with *Content*.

O but, Sir, said I, I have seen *God's Salvation!*—I am sure, added I, if any body ever had Reason, I have, to say, with the blessed Virgin, *My Soul doth magnify the Lord*; for *he hath regarded the low Estate of his Handmaiden,—and exalted one of low Degree.*[2]

Said my good Father, I am sure, if there were Time for it, the Book of *Ruth*[3] would afford a fine Subject for the Honour done my dear Child.

Why, good Mr. *Andrews*, said my Master, should you say so?—I know that Story, and Mr. *Williams* will confirm what I say, that my good Girl here will confer at least as much Honour as she will receive.

Sir, said I, you are inexpressibly generous; but I shall never think so. Why, my *Pamela*, said he, that's another thing: It will be best for me to think you will; and it will be kind in you to think you shan't; and then we shall have always an excellent Rule to regulate our Conduct by to one another.

Was not this finely, nobly, wisely said, my dear Mother?——O what a blessed thing it is to be match'd to a Man of Sense and Generosity!—How edifying!—How!——But what shall I say!—I am at a Loss for Words.

Mr. *Williams* said, When we came out of the little Chapel, he would go home, and look over his Discourses, for one for the next Day. My Master said, I have one thing to say, before you go.—When my Jealousy, on Account of this good Girl, put me upon such a vindictive Conduct to you, you know I took a Bond for the Money I had caused you to be troubled for: I really am ashamed of the Matter; because I never intended, when I presented it to you, to have it again, you may be sure: But I knew not what might happen between you and her, nor how far Matters might have gone between you; and so I was willing to have that in Awe over you. And, I think, it is no extraordinary Present, therefore, to give you up your Bond again, cancell'd. And so he took it from his Pocket, and gave it him. I think, added he, all the Charges attending it, and the Trouble you had, were defray'd by my Attorney: I order'd that they should. They were, Sir, said he; and Ten thousand Thanks to you for this Goodness, and the kind manner in which you do it!—If you *will* go, Mr. *Williams*, said he, shall my Chariot carry you home? No, Sir, answer'd he, I thank you. My Time will be so well employ'd all the way in thinking of your Favours, that I chuse to meditate upon them, as I walk home.

My dear Father was very uneasy about his Habit, for appearing at Chapel next Day, because of Miss *Darnfords*, and the Servants, for fear, poor Man, he should disgrace my Master; and he told me, when he was mentioning this, my Master's kind Present of Twenty Guineas for Cloaths, for you both; which made my Heart truly joyful. But Oh! to be sure, I never can deserve the hundredth Part of his Goodness!—It is almost a hard thing to lie under the Weight of such deep Obligations on one side; and such a Sense of one's own Unworthiness of the other!—O! what a Godlike Power is that of doing Good!—I envy the Rich and the Great for nothing else!

My Master coming to us just then, I said, Oh! Sir, will your Bounty know no Limits! My dear Father has told me what you have given him!—A Trifle, *Pamela*, said he; a little Earnest only of my Kindness.—Say no more of it. But did I not hear the good Man expressing some sort of Concern for somewhat? Hide nothing from me, *Pamela*. Only, Sir, said I, he knew not how to absent himself from Divine Service, and yet is afraid of disgracing you by appearing.

Fie, Mr. *Andrews*, said he, I thought you knew that the outward Appearance was nothing. I wish I had as good a Habit inwardly, as you have. But I'll tell you, *Pamela*, your Father is not much thinner than I am, nor much shorter; he and I will walk up together to my Wardrobe; tho' it is not so well stor'd here, as in *Bedfordshire*.

And so, said he, pleasantly, Don't you pretend to come near us, till I call you; for you must not yet see how Men dress and undress themselves. O, Sir, said my Father, I beg to be excused. I am sorry you are told. So am not I, said my Master: Pray come along with me.

He carry'd him up Stairs, and shew'd him several Suits; and would have had him take his Choice. My poor Father was quite confounded: For my Master saw not any he thought too good, and my Father none that he thought bad enough. And my good Master, at last, (he fixing his Eye upon a fine Drab,[1] which he thought looked the plainest) would help him to try the Coat and Waistcoat on himself; and indeed, one would not have thought it, because my Master is taller, and rather plumper, as I thought; but, as I saw afterwards, they fitted him very well: And being plain, and lined with the same Colour, and made for travelling in a Coach, pleased my poor Father much. He gave him the whole Suit, and calling up Mrs. *Jewkes*, said, Let these Cloaths be well aired against to-morrow Morning. Mr. *Andrews* brought only with him his common Apparel, not thinking to stay *Sunday* with us. And pray see for some of my Stockens; and whether none of my Shoes will fit him; and see also for some of my Linen; for we have put the good Man quite out of his Course, by keeping him *Sunday* over. He was then pleased to give him the silver Buckles out of his own Shoes. So, my good Mother, you must expect to see my dear Father a great Beau. Wig, said my Master, he wants none; for his own venerable white Locks are better than all the Perukes in *England.*—But I am sure I have Hats enow somewhere. I'll take care of every thing, Sir, said Mrs. *Jewkes.*—And my poor Father, when he came to me, could not refrain Tears. I know not how, said he, to comport myself under these great Favours. O my Child, it is all owing to God's Goodness, and your Virtue.

SUNDAY.

This blessed Day all the Family seem'd to take Delight to equip themselves for the Celebration of the Sabbath, in the little Chapel; and Lady *Jones* and Mr. *Williams* came in her Chariot, and the two Miss *Darnfords*, in their own; with each a Footman, besides the Coachman. And we breakfasted together, in a most agreeable manner. My dear Father appeared quite spruce and neat, and was greatly caressed by the three Ladies. As we were at Breakfast, my Master told Mr. *Williams*, we must let the Psalms alone, he doubted, for want of a Clerk; but Mr. *Williams* said, No, nothing should be wanting that he could supply. My Father said, If it might be permitted him, he would, as well as he was able, perform that Office; for it was always what he had taken Delight in. And as I know he had learnt Psalmody formerly, in his Youth, and had constantly practised it in private, at home, of *Sunday* Evenings, (as well as endeavour'd to teach it in the little School he so unsuccessfully set up, at the Beginning of his Misfortunes, before he took to hard Labour) I was in no Pain for his undertaking it in this little Congregation. They seemed much pleased with this; and so we went to Chapel, and made a pretty tolerable Appearance; Mrs. *Jewkes*, and all the Servants attending, but the Cook; and I never saw Divine Service perform'd with more Solemnity, nor assisted at with greater Devotion and Decency; my Master, Lady *Jones*, and the two Misses, setting a lovely Example.

My good Father perform'd his Part with great Applause, making the
Responses as if he had been a practised Parish Clerk; and giving the[a] xxiii[d]
Psalm, which consisting of but three Staves,[1] we had it all; and he read the
Line, and began the Tune with a Heart so intirely affected with the Duty,
that he went thro' it distinctly, calmly, and fervently at the same time; so
that Lady *Jones* whisper'd me, That good Men were fit for all Companies,
and present to every laudable Occasion: And Miss *Darnford* said, God
bless the dear good Man!—You must think how I rejoiced in my Mind!

I know, my dear Mother, you can say most of the shorter Psalms by
Heart; so I need not transcribe it, especially as your chief Treasure is a
Bible; and a worthy Treasure it is. I know nobody makes more or better
Use of it.

Mr. *Williams* gave us an excellent Discourse on Liberality and Generosity, and the Blessing attending the right Use of Riches, from the xi[th]
Chapter of *Proverbs*, ver. 24, 25. *There is that scattereth, and yet increaseth;
and there is that withholdeth more than is meet; but it tendeth to Poverty. The
liberal Soul shall be made fat: and he that watereth, shall be watered also himself.*
And he treated the Subject in so handsome a manner, that my Master's
Delicacy, who, at first, was afraid of some personal Compliments, was not

---

[a] *The Lord is only my Support,*
   And he that doth me feed:
 How can I then lack any thing,
   Whereof I stand in need?
 In Pastures green he feedeth me,
   Where I do safely lie;
 And after leads me to the Streams,
   Which run most pleasantly.

 And when I find myself near lost,
   Then home he doth me take;
 Conducting me in his right Path,
   E'en for his own Name's sake.
 And tho' I were e'en at Death's Door,
   Yet would I fear no Ill:
 For both thy Rod, and Shepherd's Crook,
   Afford me Comfort still.

 Thou hast my Table richly spread
   In Presence of my Foe.
 Thou hast my Head with Balm refresh'd;
   My Cup doth overflow.
 And finally, while Breath doth last,
   Thy Grace shall me defend:
 And in the House of God will I
   My Life for ever spend.

offended, he judiciously keeping to Generals; and it was an elegant and sensible Discourse, as my Master said.

My Father was, as in the Clerk's Place, just under the Desk; and Lady *Jones* beckon'd her Footman, and whisper'd him to beg him to favour us with another Psalm, when the Sermon was ended, he, thinking as he said afterwards, that the former was rather of the longest, chose the shortest in the Book; which, you know, is the cxvii[th].[a]

My Master thanked Mr. *Williams* for his excellent Discourse, and so did the Ladies; as also I did, most heartily, and he was pleased to take my dear Father by the Hand, as Mr. *Williams* also did, and thanked him. The Ladies also made him their kind Compliments; and the Servants all looked upon him with Countenances of Respect and Pleasure.

At Dinner, do what I could, I was forced to take the Upper-end of the Table; and my Master sat at the Lower-end, between Mr. *Williams* and my Father. And he said, *Pamela*, you are so dextrous, that I think you may help the Ladies yourself; and I will help my two good Friends. I should have told you tho', that I dressed myself in a flower'd Satten, that was my Lady's, and look'd quite fresh and good, and which was given me at first by my Master; and the Ladies, who had not seen me out of my Homespun before, made me abundance of fine Compliments, as soon as they saw me first.

Talking of the Psalms, just after Dinner, my Master was very naughty, if I may so say: For he said to my Father, Mr. *Andrews*, I think, in the Afternoon, as we shall have only Prayers, we may have one longer Psalm; and what think you of the cxxxvii[th]?—O good Sir! said I, pray, pray, not a Word more!—Say what you will, *Pamela*, said he, you shall sing it to us, according to your own Version, before these good Ladies go away. My Father smil'd, but was half concern'd for me; and said, Will it bear, and please your Honour?—O ay, said he, never fear it; so long as Mrs. *Jewkes* is not in the Hearing.

This excited all the Ladies Curiosity; and Lady *Jones* said, She should be loth to desire to hear any thing that would concern me; but should be glad I would give Leave for it. Indeed, Madam, said I, I must beg you

---

a   *O All ye Nations of the World,*
      Praise ye the Lord always:
    And all ye People ev'ry-where
        Set forth his noble Praise.
    For great his Kindness is to us;
        His Truth doth not decay:
    Wherefore praise ye the Lord our God;
        Praise ye the Lord alway.

won't insist upon it. I cannot bear it.—You shall see it indeed, Ladies, said
my Master; and pray, *Pamela*, not always as you please, neither.—Then,
pray, Sir, said I, not in my hearing, I hope.—Sure, *Pamela*, return'd he,
you would not write what is not fit to be heard!—But, Sir, said I, there are
particular Cases, Times, and Occasions, that may make a thing passable at
one time, that would not be tolerable at another. O, said he, let me judge
of that, as well as you, *Pamela.* These Ladies know a good Part of your
Story; and, let me tell you, what they know is more to your Credit than
mine; so that if I have no Averseness to reviving the Occasion, you may
very well bear it. Said he, I will put you out of your Pain, *Pamela*; I believe
I put it in my Pocket on purpose.

I stood up, and said, Indeed, Sir, I can't bear it! I hope you'll allow me to
leave the Room a Minute, if you will read it. Indeed, but I won't, answer'd
he. Lady *Jones* said, Pray, good Sir, don't let us hear it, if Mrs. *Andrews* be
so unwilling. Well, *Pamela*, said my Master, I will put it to your Choice,
whether I shall read it now, or you will sing it by-and-by. That's very hard,
Sir, said I. It must be one, I assure you, said he. Why then, Sir, reply'd I,
you must do as you please; for I cannot sing it.

Well, then, said my Master, I find I must read it; and yet, added he,
after all, I had as well let it alone; for it is no great Reputation to myself.
O then, said Miss *Darnford*, pray let us hear it to chuse.

Why then, proceeded he, the Case was this: *Pamela*, I find, when she
was in the Time of her Confinement, (that is, added he, when she was
taken Prisoner, in order to make me one; for that is the Upshot of the
Matter) in the Journal she kept, which was intended for nobody's Perusal
but her Parents, tells them, That she was importuned, one *Sunday*, by
Mrs. *Jewkes*, to sing a Psalm; but her Spirits not permitting, she declin'd
it: But after Mrs. *Jewkes* was gone down, she says, she recollected, that the
cxxxvii[th] Psalm was applicable to her own Case; Mrs. *Jewkes* having often,
on other Days, in vain, besought her to sing a Song. That thereupon she
turn'd it more to her own supposed Case; and believing Mrs. *Jewkes* had a
Design against her Honour, and looking upon her as her Gaoler, she thus
gives her Version of this Psalm. But pray, Mr. *Williams*, do you read one
Verse of the common Translation,[1] and I will read one of *Pamela*'s. Then
Mr. *Williams* pulling out his little Pocket Common-prayer Book, read the
first two Stanzas.

I.

When we did sit in Babylon,
The Rivers round about:

Then in Remembrance of Sion,
The Tears for Grief burst out.

II.

We hang'd our Harps and Instruments
The Willow-trees upon:
For in that Place Men, for that Use,
Had planted many a one.

My Master then read:

I.

When sad, I sat in B----n-hall,
All watched round about;
And thought of every absent Friend,
The Tears for Grief burst out.

II.

My Joys, and Hopes, all overthrown,
My Heart-strings almost broke:
Unfit my Mind for Melody,
Much more to bear a Joke.

The Ladies said, It was very pretty; and Miss *Darnford*, That somebody else had well observ'd, that I had need to be less concerned than themselves.

I knew, said my Master, I should get no Credit by shewing this. But let us read on, Mr. *Williams*. So Mr. *Williams* read;

III.

Then they, to whom we Pris'ners were,
Said to us tauntingly;
Now let us hear your Hebrew *Songs,*
And pleasant Melody.

Now this, said my Master, is very near: And read;

III.

Then she, to whom I Pris'ner was,
Said to me tauntingly;
Now chear your Heart, and sing a Song,
And tune your Mind to Joy.

Mighty sweet, said Mr. *Williams.* But let us see how the next Verse is turn'd. It is this:

IV.

Alas! said we, who can once frame
His heavy Heart to sing
The Praises of our loving God,
Thus under a strange King?

Why, said my Master, it is turn'd with beautiful Simplicity, thus:

IV.

Alas! said I, how can I frame
My heavy Heart to sing,
Or tune my Mind, while thus inthrall'd
By such a wicked Thing!

Very pretty, said Mr. *Williams.* Lady *Jones* said, O dear, Madam, can you wish that we should be depriv'd of this new Instance of your Genius and Accomplishments?

O! said my dear Father, you will make my good Child proud. No, said my Master, very generously, *Pamela* can't be proud. For no one is proud to hear themselves prais'd, but those who are not us'd to it.—But proceed, Mr. *Williams.* He read;

V.

But yet, if I Jerusalem
Out of my Heart let slide;
Then let my Fingers quite forget
The warbling Harp to guide.

Well, now, said my Master, for *Pamela's* Version!

V.

But yet, if from my Innocence
I, ev'n in Thought, should slide;
Then let my Fingers quite forget
The sweet Spinnet to guide.

Mr. *Williams* read;

VI.

And let my Tongue within my Mouth,
Be ty'd for ever fast,

> *If I rejoice before I see*
> *Thy full Deliv'rance past.*

This also, said my Master, is very near.

VI.

> *And let my Tongue, within my Mouth,*
> *Be lock'd for ever fast,*
> *If I rejoice before I see*
> *My full Deliv'rance past.*

Now, good Sir, said I, oblige me; don't read any further: Pray don't! O pray, Madam, said Mr. *Williams*, let me beg to have the rest read; for I long to know who you make the Sons of *Edom*, and how you turn the Psalmist's Execrations against the insulting *Babylonians*.[1]

Well, Mr. *Williams*, reply'd I, you should not have said so. O, said my Master, that is one of the best things of all. Poor Mrs. *Jewkes* stands for *Edom*'s Sons; and we must not lose this, because I think it one of my *Pamela*'s Excellencies, that tho' thus oppress'd, she prays for no Harm upon the Oppressor. Read, Mr. *Williams*, the next Stanza. So he read;

VII.

> *Therefore, O Lord, remember now*
> *The cursed Noise and Cry,*
> *That* Edom's *Sons against us made,*
> *When they rais'd our City.*

VIII.

> *Remember, Lord, their cruel Words,*
> *When, with a mighty Sound,*
> *They cried, Down, yea, down with it,*
> *Unto the very Ground.*

Well, said my Master, here seems, in what I am going to read, a little bit of a Curse indeed; but I think it makes no ill Figure in the Comparison.

VII.

> *And thou, Almighty! recompense*
> *The Evils I endure,*
> *From those who seek my sad Disgrace,*
> *So causeless! to procure.*

And now, said he, for *Edom*'s Sons! Tho' a little severe in the Imputation.

VIII.

Remember, Lord, this Mrs. Jewkes,
When with a mighty Sound,
She cries, Down with her Chastity,
Down to the very Ground!

Sure, Sir, said I, this might have been spar'd! But the Ladies and Mr. *Williams* said, No, by no means! And I see the poor wicked Woman has no Favourers among them.

Now, said my Master, read the Psalmist's heavy Curses: And Mr. *Williams* read;

IX.

Ev'n so shalt thou, O Babylon!
At length to Dust be brought:
And happy shall that Man be call'd,
That our Revenge hath wrought.

X.

Yea, blessed shall that Man be call'd,
That takes thy little ones,
And dasheth them in pieces small
Against the very Stones.

Thus, said he, very kindly, has *my Pamela* turn'd these Lines.

IX.

Ev'n so shalt thou, O wicked one,
At length to Shame be brought:
And happy shall all those be call'd,
That my Deliv'rance wrought.

X.

Yea, blessed shall the Man be call'd,
That shames thee of thy Evil,
And saves me from thy vile Attempts,
And thee, too, from the D---l.

I fansy this blessed Man, said my Master, smiling, was, at that time, hoped to be you, Mr. *Williams*, if the Truth was known. Sir, said he, whoever it was intended for then, it can be nobody but your good Self now.

I could hardly hold up my Head for the Praises the kind Ladies were pleased to heap upon me. I am sure, by this, they are very partial in my Favour; all because my Master is so good to me, and loves to hear me praised; for I see no such Excellence in these Lines, as they would make me believe, besides what is borrow'd from the *Psalmist.*

We all, as before, and the Cook-maid too, attended the Prayers of the Church in the Afternoon; and my dear Father concluded with the following Stanzas of the cxlv[th] Psalm; suitably magnifying the holy Name of God for all his Mercies; but did not observe altogether the Method in which they stand; which was the less necessary, he thought, as he gave out the Lines.

> *The Lord is just in all his ways;*
> *His Works are holy all:*
> *And he is near all those that do*
> *In Truth upon him call.*
>
> *He the Desires of all of them*
> *That fear him, will fulfil,*
> *And he will hear them when they cry,*
> *And save them all he will.*
>
> *The Eyes of all do wait on thee;*
> *Thou dost them all relieve:*
> *And thou to each sufficing Food,*
> *In Season due, dost give.*
>
> *Thou openest thy plenteous Hand,*
> *And bounteously dost fill*
> *All things whatever that do live,*
> *With Gifts of thy Good-will.*
>
> *My thankful Mouth shall gladly speak*
> *The Praises of the Lord:*
> *All Flesh to praise his holy Name,*
> *For ever shall accord.*

We walked in the Garden till Tea was ready; and as we went by the Back-door, my Master said to me, *Of all the Flowers in the Garden, the Sun-flower is the fairest!*—O, Sir, said I, let that be now forgot! Mr. *Williams* heard him say so, and seem'd a little out of Countenance: Whereupon my Master said, I mean not to make you serious, Mr. *Williams*; but we see how strangely things are brought about. I see other Scenes hereabouts, that, in my *Pamela's* Dangers, give me more Cause of Concern, than any thing you ever did, should give you. Sir, said he, you are very generous.

My Master and Mr. *Williams* afterwards walked together, for a Quarter of an Hour, and talked about general things, and some scholastick Subjects, and joined us, very well pleased with one another's Conversation.

Lady *Jones* said, putting herself on one side of me, as my Master was of the other, But pray, Sir, when is the happy Time to be? We want it over, that we may have you with us, as long afterwards as you can. Said my Master, I would have it to-morrow or next Day, at farthest, if *Pamela* will: For I have sent for a Licence, and the Messenger will be here to-night, or early in the Morning, I hope. But, added he, pray, *Pamela*, do not take beyond *Thursday.* She was pleased to say, Sure it will not be delay'd by you, Madam, more than needs!—Well, said he, now *you* are on my Side, I will leave you with her, to settle it: And, I hope, she will not let little bashful Niceties be important with her; and so he joined the two Misses.

Lady *Jones* told me, I was to blame, she would take upon her to say, if I delay'd it a Moment; because she understood Lady *Davers* was very uneasy at the Prospect that it would be so; and if any thing should happen, it would be a sad thing!—Madam, said I, when he was pleased to mention it to me first, he said it should be in fourteen Days; and afterwards, ask'd me if I would have it in the first or the second Seven. I answer'd,—for how could I do otherwise? In the second: He desir'd it might not be the last Day of the second Seven. Now, Madam, said I, as he was *then* pleased to speak his Mind, no doubt, I would not for any thing seem too forward.

Well, but, said she, as he now urges you in so genteel and gentlemanly a manner for a shorter Day, I think, if I was in your place, I would agree to it. She saw me hesitate and blush, and said, Well, you know best; but I say only what I would do. I said, I would consider of it; and if I saw he was very earnest, to be sure I should think I ought to oblige him.

Miss *Darnfords* were begging to be at the Wedding, and to have a Ball: And they said, Pray, Mrs. *Andrews*, second our Requests, and we shall be greatly obliged to you. Indeed, Ladies, said I, I cannot promise that, if I might. Why so? said they.—Because, answer'd I,—I know not what! But, I think, one may, with Pleasure, celebrate an *Anniversary* of one's Nuptials; but the *Day itself*—Indeed, Ladies, I think it is too solemn a Business, for the *Parties* of our Sex, to be very gay upon! It is a quite serious and awful Affair: And I am sure, in your own Cases, you would be of my Mind. Why then, said Miss *Darnford*, the more need one has to be as light-hearted and merry as one can.

I told you, said my Master, what sort of an Answer you'd have from *Pamela*. The younger Miss said, She never heard of such grave Folks in her Life, on such an Occasion! Why, Sir, said she, I hope you'll sing Psalms all Day, and Miss will fast and pray! Such Sackcloth and Ashes Doings, for a Wedding, did I never hear of!—She spoke a little spitefully, I thought; and I return'd no Answer. I shall have enough to do, I reckon, in a-while, if I am to answer every one that will envy me!

We went in to Tea, and all the Ladies could prevail upon my Master for, was a Dancing-match before he left this Country; but Miss *Darnford* said, It should then be at their House; for, truly, if she might not be at the Wedding, she would be affronted, and come no more hither, till we had been there.

When they were gone, my Master would have had my Father stay till the Affair was over; but he begg'd he might set out as soon as it was light in the Morning; for, he said, my Mother would be doubly uneasy at his Stay; and he burned with Impatience, to let her know all the happy things that had befallen her Daughter. When my Master found him so desirous to go, he called Mr. *Thomas*, and order'd him to get a particular Bay-horse ready betimes in the Morning, for my Father, and a Portmanteau, to put his Things in; and to attend him a Day's Journey; And if, said he, Mr. *Andrews* chuses it, see him safe to his own Home. And, added he, as that Horse will serve you, Mr. *Andrews*, to ride backwards and forwards, to see us when we go to *Bedfordshire*, I make you a Present of it, with the Accoutrements. And seeing my Father going to speak, he added, I won't be said Nay. O how good was this!

He also said a great many kind things at Supper-time, and gave him all the Papers he had of mine; but desir'd, when he and my Mother had read them, that he would return them to him again. And then he said, So affectionate a Father and Daughter may, perhaps, be glad to be alone together; therefore, remember me to your good Wife, and tell her, it will not be long, I hope, before I see you together, on a Visit to your Daughter, at my other House; and so I wish you Good-night, and a good Journey, if you go before I see you; and then he shook Hands, and left my dear Father almost unable to speak, thro' the Sense of his Favours and Goodness.

You may believe, my dear Mother, how loth I was to part with my good Father; and he was also unwilling to part with me; but he was so impatient to see you, and tell you the blessed Tidings, with which his Heart overflow'd, that I could hardly wish to detain him.

Mrs. *Jewkes* brought two Bottles of Cherry-brandy, and two Bottles of Cinamon-water, and some Cake; and they were put up in the Portmanteau, with my Father's newly presented Cloaths; for he said, he would not, for any thing, be seen in them in his Neighbourhood, till I was actually known, by every body, to be marry'd; nor would he lay out any part of the twenty Guineas till then neither, for fear of Reflections; and then he would consult me as to what he should buy. Well, said I, as you please, my dear Father; and I hope now we shall often have the Pleasure of hearing from one another, without needing any Art or Contrivances.

He said, he would go to-bed betimes, that he might be up as soon as it was light; and so he took Leave of me, and said he would not love me, if I got up in the Morning to see him go; which would but make us more loth to part, and grieve us both all Day.

Mr. *Thomas* brought him a Pair of Boots, and told him, he would call him up at peep of Day, and put up every thing over Night; and so I received his Blessing and his Prayers, and his kind Promises of procuring the same from you, my dear Mother, and went up to my Closet with a heavy Heart, and yet a half pleased one, if I may so say; for that, as he must go, he was going to the best of Wives, and with the best of Tidings. But I begg'd he would not work so hard as he had done; for I was sure my Master would not have given him twenty Guineas for Cloaths, if he had not designed to do something else for him; and that he should be the less concern'd at receiving Benefits from my good Master, because he, who had so many Persons to employ in his large Possessions, could make him serviceable, to an equivalent Degree, without hurting any body else.

He promised me fair; and pray, dear Mother, see he performs. I hope my Master will not see this. For I will not send it you, at present, till I can send you the best of News; and the rather, as my dear Father can supply the greatest Part of what I have written, since the Papers he carries you, by his own Observation. So, God bless you both! Good-night! And send my Father a safe Journey, and a happy Meeting to you both!

MONDAY.

M. *Colbrand* being return'd, my Master came up to me to my Closet, and brought me the Licence. O how my Heart flutter'd at the Sight of it! Now, *Pamela*, said he, tell me, If you can oblige me with the Day. Your Word is all that's wanting! I made bold to kiss his dear Hand; and tho' unable to look up, said,—I know not what to say, Sir, to all your Goodness! I would not, for any Consideration, that you should believe me capable of receiving negligently an Honour, that all the Duty of a long Life, were it to be lent me, will not be sufficient to enable me to be grateful for. I ought to resign myself, in every thing I may or can, implicitly to your Will. But—But what? said he, with a kind Impatience!—Why, Sir, said I, when from last *Thursday* you mention'd Fourteen Days, I had Reason to think that Term your Choice; and my Heart is so wholly yours, that I am afraid of nothing, but that I may be forwarder than you wish. Impossible, my dear Creature, said he, and folded me in his Arms; impossible! If this be all, it shall be set about this Moment, and this happy Day shall make you mine!—I'll send away instantly, said the dear Gentleman, and was going.

I said, No, pray, Sir, pray, Sir, hear me!—Indeed it cannot be to-day!—Cannot! said he.—No, indeed, Sir! said I.—And was ready to sink to see his generous Impatience! Why flatter'd you then, my fond Heart, said he, with the Hope that it might!—Sir, said I, I will tell you what I had thought, if you'll vouchsafe me your Attention. Do then, said he!

I have, Sir, proceeded I, a great Desire, that whenever the Day is, it may be of a *Thursday*:[1] Of a *Thursday* my dear Father and Mother were marry'd, and tho' poor, they are a very happy Pair.—Of a *Thursday* your poor *Pamela* was born: Of a *Thursday* my dear good Lady took me from my Parents into her Protection: Of a *Thursday*, Sir, you caus'd me to be carry'd away to this Place, to which I now, by God's Goodness and your Favour, owe so amazingly all my present Prospects; and of a *Thursday* it was, you nam'd to me that Fourteen Days from that, you would confirm my Happiness. Now, Sir, if you please to indulge my superstitious Folly, you will greatly oblige me: I was sorry, Sir, for this Reason, when you bid me not defer till the last Day of the Fourteen, that *Thursday* in next Week was that last Day.

This, *Pamela*, is a little superstitious, I must needs say; and I think you should begin now to make another Day in the Week a happy one; as for Example, On a *Monday*, may you say, my Father and Mother concluded to be marry'd on the *Thursday* following. Of a *Monday*, so many Years ago, my Mother was preparing all her Matters, to be brought to-bed on the *Thursday* following. Of a *Monday*, several Weeks ago, it was that you had but two Days more to stay, till you was carry'd away on *Thursday*. On a *Monday*, I myself, said he, well remember, it was, that I wrote you the Letter, that prevail'd on you so kindly to return to me; and, on the same Day, you *did* return to my House here; which I hope, my Girl, will be as propitious an Æra as any you have nam'd: And now, lastly, will you say, which will crown the Work; And, on a *Monday* I was marry'd.—Come, come, my Dear, added he, *Thursday* has reign'd long enough o' Conscience; let us now set *Monday* in its Place, or at least on an Equality with it, since you see it has a very good Title, and as we now stand in the Week before us, claims Priority; and then, I hope, we shall make *Tuesday, Wednesday, Friday, Saturday* and *Sunday*, as happy Days, as *Monday* and *Thursday*; and so, by God's Blessing, move round as the Days move, in a delightful Circle, till we are at a Loss what Day to prefer to the rest.

O how charmingly was this said!—And how sweetly kind!

Indeed, Sir, said I, you rally my Folly very agreeably; but don't let a little Matter stand in the way, when you are so generously obliging in greater! Indeed I like *Thursday* best, if I may chuse.

Well then, said he, if you can say, you have a better Reason than this, I will oblige you; else I'll send away for the Parson this Moment!

And so, I protest, he was going!—Dear Sirs, how I trembled!—Stay, stay, Sir, said I: We have a great deal to say first; I have a deal of silly Prate to trouble you with!—Well, say then, in a Minute, reply'd he, the most material; for all we have to say may be talk'd of while the Parson is coming!—O but indeed, and indeed, said I, it cannot be to-day!—Well then, shall it be to-morrow? said he.—Why, Sir, if it must not be of a *Thursday*, you have given so many pleasant Distinctions for a *Monday*, that let it then be next *Monday*!—What! a Week still? said he. Sir, answer'd I, if you please; for *that* will be, as you injoin'd, within the second Seven Days. Why, Girl, said he, 'twill be Seven Months till next *Monday*. Let it, said he, if not to-morrow, be on *Wednesday*; I protest I will stay no longer.

Then, Sir, return'd I, please to defer it, however, for one Day more, and it will be my beloved *Thursday!* If I consent to defer it till then, may I hope, my *Pamela*, said he, that next *Thursday* shall certainly be the happy Day?—*Yes, Sir*, said I; and I am sure I look'd very foolishly!

And yet, my dear Father and Mother, why should I, with such a fine Gentleman! And whom I so dearly love! And so much to my Honour too? But there is something greatly awful upon my Mind, in the solemn Circumstance, and a Change of Condition never to be recall'd, tho' all the Prospects are so desirable. And I can but wonder, at the thoughtless Precipitancy with which most young Folks run into this important Change of Life!

So now, my dear Parents, have I been brought to fix so near a Day as next *Thursday*; and this is *Monday*. O dear, it makes one out of Breath almost to think of it. This, tho', was a great Cut-off; a whole Week out of ten Days. I hope I am not too forward! I'm sure, if it obliges my dear Master, I am justify'd; for he deserves all things of me, in my poor Power.

After this, he rode out on Horse-back, attended by *Abraham*, and did not return till Night. How by degrees, Things steal upon one! I thought even this small Absence tedious, and the more as we expected him home to Dinner.—I wish I may not be too fond, and make him indifferent: But yet, my dear Father and Mother, you were always fond of one another, and never indifferent, let the World run as it would.—

When he returned, he said, he had had a pleasant Ride, and was led out to a greater Distance than he intended. At Supper he told me, that he had a great mind Mr. *Williams* should marry us; because, he said, it should shew a thorough Reconciliation of his Part: But, said he, most generously, I am apprehensive on what passed between you, that the poor Man will take it hardly, and as a sort of Insult, which I am not capable of. What says my Girl?—Do you think he would? I hope not, Sir, said I: For, as to what he may think, I can't answer; but as to any Reason for his Thoughts, I could. But indeed, Sir, said I, you have been already so generous, that he cannot, I think, mistake your Goodness.

He then spoke with some Resentment of Lady *Davers*'s Behaviour, and I ask'd, If any thing new had occurr'd? Yes, said he; I have had a Letter deliver'd me from her impertinent Husband, professedly at her Instigation, that amounted to little less than a Piece of insolent Bravery, on supposing I was about to marry you. I was so provok'd, added he, that after I had read it, I tore it into a hundred Pieces, and scatter'd them in the Air, and bid the Man who brought it, let his Master know what I had done with his Letter; and so would not permit him to speak to me, as he would fain have done.—I think the Fellow talk'd somewhat of his Lady coming hither; but she shall not set her Foot within my Doors; and I suppose this Treatment will hinder her.

I was much concern'd at this: And he said, Had I an hundred Sisters, *Pamela*, their Opposition should have no Weight with me; and I did not intend you should know it; but you can't but expect a little Difficulty from the Pride of my Sister, who have suffer'd so much from that of her Brother; and we are too nearly ally'd in Mind as well as Blood, I find.—But this is not her Business. And if she would have made it so, she should have done it with more *Decency*. Little Occasion had *she* to boast of her Birth, that knows not what belongs to good Manners.

I said, I am very sorry, Sir, to be the unhappy Occasion of a Misunderstanding between so good a Brother, and so worthy a Sister. Don't say so, *Pamela*, because this is an indispensable Consequence of the happy Prospect before us. Only, bear it well yourself, because she is my Sister, and leave it to me to make her sensible of her own Rashness.

If, Sir, said I, the most lowly Behaviour, and humble Deportment, and in every thing shewing a dutiful Regard to good Lady *Davers*, will have any Weight with her Ladyship, assure yourself of all in my Power to mollify her. No, *Pamela*, return'd he, don't imagine, when you are my Wife, I will suffer you to do any thing unworthy of that Character. I know the Duty of a Husband, and will protect your Gentleness to the utmost, as if you were a Princess by Descent.

You are inexpressibly good, Sir, said I; but I am far from taking a gentle Disposition, to shew a Meanness of Spirit: And this is a Trial I ought to expect; and well I may bear it, that have so many Benefits to set against it, which all spring from the same Cause.

Well, said he, all the Matter shall be this: We will talk of our Marriage as a Thing to be done next Week. I find I have Spies upon me where-ever I go, and whatever I do. But now, I am on *so* laudable a Pursuit, that I value them not, nor their Employers. I have already order'd my Servants to communicate with nobody for ten or twelve Days to come. And Mrs. *Jewkes* tells me, every one names *Thursday* come Sev'nnight for our Nuptials. So I will get Mr. *Peters*, who wants to see my little Chapel, to assist Mr. *Williams*, under the Notion of breakfasting with me, next *Thursday* Morning, since you won't have it sooner; and there will want nobody else; and I will beg of Mr. *Peters* to keep it private, even from his own Family, for a few Days. Has my Girl any Objection?

O Sir, answer'd I, you are so generous in all your Ways, I can have no Objections!—But I hope Lady *Davers* and you will not proceed to irreconcileable Lengths; and when her Ladyship comes to see you, and to tarry with you, two or three Weeks, as she us'd to do, I will keep close up,[1] so as not to disgust her with my Sight. Well, *Pamela*, said he, we will talk of that afterwards. You must do then as I shall think fit: And I shall be able to judge what both you and I ought to do. But what still aggravates the Matter is, that she should instigate the titled Ape her Husband to write to me, after she had so little succeeded herself. I wish I had kept his Letter, that I might shew you how a Man that *acts* generally like a Fool, can take upon him to *write* like a Lord. But, I suppose it is of my Sister's Penning, and he, poor Man, is the humble Copier.

TUESDAY.

Mr. *Thomas* is return'd from you, my dear Father, with the good News of your Health, and continuing your Journey to my dear Mother, where I hope to hear soon you are arriv'd. My Master has just now been making me play upon the Spinnet, and singing to it; and was pleas'd to commend me for both. But he does so for every thing I do, so partial does his Goodness make him to me.

One o'Clock.

We are just return'd from an Airing in the Chariot; and I have been delighted with his Conversation upon *English* Authors, Poets particularly. He entertain'd me also with a Description of some of the Curiosities he had seen in *Italy* and *France*, when he made what the polite World call the grand Tour.[1] He said, he wanted to be at his other Seat; for he knew not well how to employ himself here, having not purpos'd to stay half the Time: And when I get there, *Pamela*, said he, you will hardly be troubled with so much of my Company, after we are settled; for I have a great many things to adjust; and I must go to *London*: For I have Accounts that have run longer than ordinary with my Banker there. And I don't know, added he, but the ensuing Winter, I may give you a little Taste of the Diversions of the Town for a Month or so. I said, his Will and Pleasure should determine mine; and I never would, as near as I could, have a Desire after those, or any other Things that were not in his own Choice.

He was pleas'd to say, I make no doubt I shall be very happy in you; and hope you will be so in me: For, said he, I have no very enormous Vices to gratify; tho' I pretend not to the greatest Purity neither, my Girl. Sir, said I, if you can account to your own Mind, I shall always be easy in whatever you do. But our greatest Happiness here, Sir, continued I, is of very short Duration; and this Life, where longest, is a poor transitory Stage; and I hope we shall be so happy as to be enabled to look forward, with Comfort, to one other, where our Pleasures will be everlasting.

You say well, *Pamela*, and I shall, by degrees, be more habituated to this way of thinking, as I more and more converse with you; but at present, you must not be over serious with me, all at once. Tho' I charge you, never forbear to mingle your sweet Divinity in our Conversation, whenever it can be brought in *à-propos*, and with such a Chearfulness of Temper, as shall not throw a gloomy Cloud over our innocent Enjoyments.

I was abash'd at this, and silent, fearing I had offended; but he said, If you attend rightly to what I said, I need not tell you again, *Pamela*, not to be discourag'd from suggesting to me, on every proper Occasion, the pious Impulses of your own amiable Mind. Sir, said I, you will be always indulgent, I make no doubt, to my Imperfections, so long as I mean well.

My Master made me dine with him, and would eat nothing but what I help'd him to; and my Heart is, every Hour, more and more inlarg'd with his Goodness and Condescension. But still, what ails me, I wonder! a strange sort of Weight hangs upon my Mind, as *Thursday* draws on, which makes me often sigh involuntarily, and damps, at times, the Pleasures of my delightful Prospects!—I hope this is not ominous; but only the foolish Weakness of an over-thoughtful Mind, on an Occasion the most solemn and important of one's Life, next to the last Scene, which shuts up all.

I could be very serious! But I will commit all my Ways to that blessed Providence, which hitherto has so wonderfully conducted me, thro' real Evils, to this hopeful Situation.

I only fear, and, sure, I have great Reason, that I shall be too unworthy, to hold the Affections of so dear a Gentleman!—God teach me Humility, and to know my own Demerit! And this will be, next to his Grace, my surest Guard, in the State of Life to which I am most unworthily going to be exalted. And don't cease your Prayers for me, my dear Parents; for, perhaps, this new Condition may be subject to still worse Hazards than those I have escap'd; as would be the Case, were Conceitedness, Vanity, and Pride, to take hold of my frail Heart! and if I was, for my Sins, to be left to my own Conduct, a frail Ship in a tempestuous Ocean, without Ballast, or other Pilot than my own inconsiderate Will. But my Master said, on another Occasion, that those who doubted most, always erred least; and, I hope, I shall always doubt my own Strength, my own Worthiness!

I will not trouble you with twenty sweet agreeable things, that pass'd in Conversation with my excellent Benefactor; nor with the Civilities of Mr. *Colbrand*, Mrs. *Jewkes*, and all the Servants, who seem to be highly pleas'd with me, and with my Conduct to them: And, as my Master, hitherto, finds no Fault that I go too low, nor they that I carry it too high, I hope I shall continue to have every body's Good-will. But yet, will I not seek to gain any one's by little Meannesses or Debasements; but aim at an uniform and regular Conduct, willing to conceal *involuntary* Errors, as I would have my own forgiven, and not too industrious to discover *real* ones, or to hide such, if any such should appear, as might encourage bad Hearts, or unclean Hands, in material Cases, where my Master should receive Damage, or where the Morals of the Transgressors should appear wilfully and habitually corrupt. In short, I will endeavour, as much as I can, that a good Servant shall in me find a kind Encourager; an indifferent one be made better, by inspiring them with a laudable Emulation; and a bad one, if not too bad in Nature, and quite irreclaimable, reform'd by Kindness, Expostulation, and even proper Menaces, if necessary, but most by a good Example. All this, if God pleases.

WEDNESDAY.

Now, my dear Parents, I have but this *one* Day, between me and the most solemn Rite that can be perform'd. My Heart cannot yet shake off this heavy Weight. Sure I am ingrateful to God's Goodness, and the Favour of the best of Benefactors!—Yet I hope I am not!—For at times, my Mind is all Exultation, with the Prospect of what Good to-morrow's happy Solemnity may possibly, by Leave of my generous Master, put it in my Power to do. O how shall I find Words to express, as I ought, my Thankfulness, for all the Mercies before me!—

WEDNESDAY Evening.

My dear Master is all Love and Tenderness! He sees my Weakness, and he generously pities and comforts me! I begg'd to be excus'd Supper; but he brought me down himself from my Closet; and plac'd me by him, bidding *Abraham* not wait. I could not eat, and yet I try'd, for fear he should be angry. He kindly forbore to hint any thing of the dreadful, yet delightful to-morrow! and put, now-and-then, a little Bit on my Plate, and guided it to my Mouth. I was concern'd to receive his Goodness with so ill a Grace. Well, said he, if you won't eat with me, drink at least, with me: I drank two Glasses by his Over-persuasions, and said, I am really asham'd of myself. Why, indeed, said he, my dear Girl, I am not a very dreadful Enemy, I hope! I cannot bear any thing that is the least concerning to you. Oh! Sir, said I, all is owing to the Sense I have of my own Unworthiness!—To be sure, it cannot be any thing else.

He rung for the Things to be taken away! And then reach'd a Chair, and sat down by me, and put his kind Arms about me, and said the most generous and affecting Things that ever dropt from the Honey-flowing Mouth of Love! All I have not time to repeat. Some I will; and oh! indulge your foolish Daughter, who troubles you with her weak Nonsense; because what she has to say, is so affecting to her; and because, if she went to-bed, instead of scribbling, she cannot sleep.

This sweet Confusion and Thoughtfulness in my beloved *Pamela*, said the kind Man, on the near Prospect of our happy Union, when I hope all Doubts are clear'd up, and nothing of Dishonour is apprehended, shew me most abundantly, what a Wretch I was to attempt such Purity with a worse Intention!—No wonder, that one so virtuous, should find herself deserted of Life itself, on a Violence so dreadful to her Honour, and refuge herself in the Shadow of Death.—But now, my dearest *Pamela*, that you have seen a Purity on my Side, as nearly imitating your own, as our Sex can shew to yours; and that I have, all the Day long, suppress'd even the least Intimation of the coming Day, that I might not alarm your tender Mind; why all this Concern, why all this affecting, yet sweet Confusion! You have a generous Friend, my dear Girl, in me! a Protector now, not a Violator of your Innocence! Why then, once more I ask, this strange Perplexity, this sweet Confusion?

O Sir, said I, and hid my Face in his Arms! expect not Reason from a foolish Creature! You should have still indulg'd me in my Closet!—I am ready to beat myself for this ungrateful Return to your Goodness. But I know not what!—I am, to be sure, a silly Creature. O had you but suffer'd me to stay by myself above, I should have made myself asham'd of so culpable a Behaviour!—But Goodness added to Goodness every Moment, and the Sense of my own Unworthiness, quite confound me!

Now, said the generous Man, will I, tho' reluctantly, make a Proposal to my sweet Girl.—If I have been too pressing for the Day: If another Day will still be more obliging: If you have Fears that will not then be, you shall say but the Word, and I'll submit. Yes, tho' I have, my *Pamela*, for these three Days past, thought every tedious Hour a Day, till *Thursday* comes, if you earnestly desire it, I will postpone it. Say, my dear Girl, freely say; but accept not my Proposal, without great Reason; which yet I will not ask for.

Sir, said I, I can expect nothing but superlative Goodness, I have now been so long us'd to it from you. This is a most generous Instance of it; but, I fear—yes, I fear, it will be but too much the same thing, some Days hence, when the happy, yet, Fool that I am! dreaded Time, shall be equally near!—

Kind, lovely Charmer, said he, now do I see you are to be trusted with Power, from the generous Use you make of it!—Not one offensive Word, or Look from me, shall wound your nicest Thoughts; but pray try to subdue this Over-scrupulousness, and unseasonable Timidity. I persuade myself you will if you can!

Indeed, Sir, I will, said I; for I am quite asham'd of myself, with all these lovely Prospects before me!—The Honours you do me, the Kindness you shew me! I cannot forgive myself! For oh! if I know the least of this idle foolish Heart of mine, it has not a misgiving Thought of your Goodness, and I should abhor it, if it were capable of the least Affectation.—But, dear good Sir, leave me a little to myself, and I will take myself to severer Task than your Goodness will let *you* do! And I will present my Heart before you, a worthier Offering to you, than at present its wayward Follies will let it seem to be.—But one thing is, one has no kind Friend of one's own Sex, to communicate one's foolish Thoughts to, and to be strengthen'd by their Comfortings!—But I am left to myself, and oh! what a weak silly Thing I am!—

He kindly withdrew, to give me Time to recollect myself, and in about half an Hour return'd. And then, that he might not begin at once upon the Subject, and say at the same time something agreeable to me, said, Your Father and Mother have had a great deal of Talk by this Time, about you, *Pamela*. O, Sir, return'd I, your Goodness has made them quite happy. But I can't help being concern'd about Lady *Davers*.

He said, I am vex'd I did not hear the Footman out; because it runs in my Head, he talk'd somewhat about her coming hither. She will meet with but an indifferent Reception from me, without she comes resolv'd to behave better than she writes.

Pray, Sir, said I, be pleas'd to bear with my good Lady, for two Reasons. What are they, said he? Why first, Sir, answer'd I, Because she is your Sister, and, to be sure, may very well think, what all the World will, that you have much demean'd yourself in making me happy. And next, Because, if her Ladyship finds you out of Temper with her, it will still aggravate her more against me; and every time that any warm Words you may use between you, come into her Mind, she will disdain me more.

Don't concern yourself about it, said he; for we have more proud Ladies than she in our t'other Neighbourhood, who perhaps, have still less Reason to be punctilious about their Descent, and yet will form themselves upon her Example, and say, Why, his own Sister will not forgive him, nor visit him! And so, if I can subdue her Spirit, which is more than her Husband ever could, or indeed any body else, it is a great Point gain'd: And, if she gives me Reason, I'll try for it, I assure you.

Well, but my dear Girl, continu'd he, since the Subject is so important, may I not say one Word about to-morrow?—Sir, said I, I hope I shall be less a Fool: I have talk'd as harshly to my Heart, as Lady *Davers* can do, and the naughty Thing suggests to me a better and more grateful Behaviour.

He smil'd, and kissing me, said, I took Notice, *Pamela*, of what you observ'd, that you have none of your own Sex with you: I think it is a little hard upon you; and I should have lik'd you should have had Miss *Darnford*; but then her Sister must have been ask'd; and I might as well make a publick Wedding; which, you know, would have requir'd Cloaths, and other Preparations. Besides, added he, a foolish Proposal was once made me of that second Sister, who has two or three thousand Pounds more than the other, left her by a Godmother, and she can't help being a little piqu'd; tho', said he, it was a Proposal they could not expect should succeed; for there is nothing in her Person nor Mind; and her Fortune, as that must have been the only Inducement, would not do by any means; and so I discourag'd it at once.

I am thinking, Sir, said I, of another mortifying Thing too; That were you to marry a Lady of Birth and Fortune, answerable to your own, all the Eve to the Day, would be taken up in reading, signing and sealing of Settlements, and Portion, and such-like. But now the poor *Pamela* brings you nothing at all! And the very Cloaths she wears, so very low is she, are intirely the Effects of your Bounty, and that of your good Mother! This makes me a little sad!—For, alas! Sir, I am so much oppressed by your Favours, and the Sense of the Obligations I owe you, that I cannot look up with the Confidence that I otherwise should, on this awful Occasion.

There is, my dear *Pamela*, said he, where the Power is wanting, as much Generosity in the Will as in the Action. To all that know your Story and your Merit, it will appear, that I cannot recompense you for what I have made you suffer. You have had too many hard Struggles and Exercises; and have nobly overcome; and who shall grudge you the Reward of the hard-bought Victory?—This Affair is so much the Act of my own Will, that I glory in being capable of distinguishing so much Excellence; and my Fortune is the more pleasurable to me, as it gives me Hope that I may make you some Part of Satisfaction for what you have undergone.

This, Sir, said I, is all Goodness, unmerited on my Side; and makes my Obligations the greater! I can only wish for more Worthiness!—But how poor is it to offer nothing but Words for such generous Deeds!—And to say, I *wish!*—For what is a Wish, but the acknowledg'd want of Power to oblige! And a Demonstration of one's Poverty, in every thing but *Will?*

And that, my dear Girl, said he, is every thing! 'Tis All I want! 'Tis All that God himself requires of us; for where there is a *Will*, the Actions must be govern'd by it, or it cannot be called a Will: But no more of these little Doubts, tho' they are the natural Impulses of a generous and grateful Heart. I want not to be employ'd in Settlements: That is for those to regard, who make Convenience and Fortune the prime Considerations. I have Possessions ample enough for us both; and you deserve to share them with me; and you shall do it, with as little Reserve, as if you had brought me what the World reckons an Equivalent: For, as to my own Opinion, you bring me what is infinitely more valuable, an experienc'd Truth, a well-try'd Virtue, and a Wit and Behaviour more than equal to the Station you will be placed in: To say nothing of this sweet Person, that itself might captivate a Monarch; and of the Meekness of a Temper, and Sweetness of Disposition, which make you superior to all the Women I ever saw.

Thus kind and soothing, and honourably affectionate was the dear Gentleman, to the unworthy, doubting, yet assured *Pamela*; and thus patiently did he indulge, and generously pardon, my impertinent Weakness. He offer'd to go himself to Lady *Jones*, in the Morning, and reveal the Matter to her, and desire her Secrecy and Presence; but I said, That would disoblige the young Lady *Darnfords*. No, Sir, said I, I will cast myself upon your generous Kindness; for why should I fear the kind Protector of my Weakness, and the Guide and Director of my future Steps?

You cannot, said he, forgive Mrs. *Jewkes*; for she must know it; and suffer her to be with you? Yes, Sir, said I, I can: She is very civil to me now: And her former Wickedness I will forgive, for the sake of the happy Fruits that have attended it; and because *you* mention her.

Well, said he, I will call her in, if you please!—As you please, Sir, said I. And he rung for her; and when she came in, he said, Mrs. *Jewkes*, I am going to intrust you with a Secret. Sir, answer'd she, I will be sure to keep it as such. Why, said he, we intend to-morrow, privately as possible, for our Wedding-day; and Mr. *Peters* and Mr. *Williams* are to be here, as to Breakfast with me, and to shew Mr. *Peters* my little Chapel. As soon as the Ceremony is over, we will take a little Airing in the Chariot, as we have done at other times; and so it will not be wonder'd that we are dress'd. And the two Parsons have promis'd Secrecy, and will go home. I believe you can't well avoid letting one of the Maids into the Secret; but that I leave to you.

Sir, reply'd she, we all concluded it would be in a few Days; and I doubt it won't be long a Secret. No, said he, I don't desire it should; but you know we are not provided for a publick Wedding, and I shall declare it when we go to *Bedfordshire*, which won't be long. But the Men, who lie in the Out-houses, need not know it; for, by some means or other, my Sister *Davers* knows all that passes.

Do you know, Sir, said she, that her Ladyship intends to be down here with you, in a few Days? Her Servant told me so, who brought you the Letter you was angry at. I hope, said he, we shall be set out for t'other House first; and shall be pleased she loses her Labour. Sir, continu'd she, her Ladyship proposes to be here time enough to hinder your Nuptials; which she, as well as we did, takes will be the Latter-end of next Week. Well, said he, let her come; but yet I desire not to see her.

Mrs. *Jewkes* said to me, Give me Leave, Madam, to wish you all manner of Happiness. But I am afraid I have too well obey'd his Honour, to be forgiven by you. Indeed, Mrs. *Jewkes*, return'd I, you will be more your own Enemy than I will be. I will look all forward: And shall not presume, so much as by a Whisper, to set my good Master against any one he pleases to approve of. And, as to his old Servants, I shall always value them, and never offer to dictate to his Choice, or influence it by my own Caprices.

Mrs. *Jewkes*, said my Master, you find you have no Cause to apprehend any thing. My *Pamela* is very placable; and as we have both been Sinners together, we must be both included in one Act of Grace.

Such an Example of Condescension, as I have before me, Mrs. *Jewkes*, said I, may make you very easy; for I must be highly unworthy, if I did not forego all my little Resentments, if I had any, for the sake of so much Goodness to myself.

You are very kind, Madam, said she; and you may depend upon it, I will atone for all my Faults, by my future Duty and Respect to you, as well as to my Master.

That's well said on both sides, said he; but, Mrs. *Jewkes*, to assure you that my good Girl here has no Malice, she chuses you to attend her in the Morning, at the Ceremony, and you must keep up her Spirits.—I shall, reply'd she, be very proud of the Honour: But I cannot, Madam, but wonder to see you so very low-spirited, as you have been these two or three Days past, with so much Happiness before you.

Why, Mrs. *Jewkes*, answer'd I, there can be but one Reason given; and that is, that I am a sad Fool!—But, indeed, I am not ingrateful neither; nor would I put on a foolish Affectation: But my Heart, at times, sinks within me; I know not why, except at my own Unworthiness, and because the Honour done me is too high for me to support myself under, as I should do. It is an Honour, Mrs. *Jewkes*, added I, I was not born to; and no wonder then, I behave so aukwardly. She made me a fine Compliment upon it, and withdrew, repeating her Promises of Care, Secrecy, &c.

He parted with me, with infinite Tenderness; and I came up, and set to writing, to amuse my Thoughts, and wrote thus far. And Mrs. *Jewkes* being come up, and it being past Twelve, I will go to-bed; but not one Wink, I fear, shall I get this Night!—I could beat myself for Anger. Sure there is nothing ominous in this strange Folly!—But I suppose all young Maidens are the same, so near so great a Change of Condition, tho' they carry it off more discreetly than I.

THURSDAY, Six o'Clock in the Morning.

I might as well have not gone to-bed last Night, for what Sleep I had. Mrs. *Jewkes* often was talking to me, and said several things that would have been well enough from any body else of our Sex; but the poor Woman has so little Purity of Heart, that it is all *Say* from her, and goes no further than my Ears.

I fancy my Master has not slept much neither; for I heard him up, and walking about his Chamber, ever since Break of Day. To be sure, poor Gentleman, he must have some Concern, as well as I; for here he is going to marry a poor foolish unworthy Girl, brought up on the Charity, as one may say, (at least, Bounty) of his worthy Family! And this foolish Girl must be, to all Intents and Purposes, after Twelve o'Clock this Day, as much his Wife, as if he were to marry a Dutchess!—And here he must stand the Shocks of common Reflection; The great 'Squire *B.* has done finely! he has marry'd his poor Servant *Wench!* will some say. The Ridicule and rude Jests of his Equals, and Companions too, he must stand: And the Disdain of his Relations, and Indignation of Lady *Davers,* his lofty Sister!—Dear good Gentleman! he will have enough to do, to be sure!—O how shall I merit all these things at his Hands! I can only do the best I can; and pray to God to reward him, and to resolve to love him with a pure Heart, and serve him with a sincere Obedience. I hope the dear Gentleman will continue to love me for this; for, alas! I have nothing else to offer! But, as I can hardly expect so great a Blessing, if I can be secure from his Contempt, I shall not be unfortunate; and must bear his Indifference, if his rich Friends should inspire him with it, and proceed with doing my Duty with Chearfulness.

Half an Hour past Eight o'Clock.

My good dear Master, my kind Friend, my generous Benefactor, my worthy Protector, and, Oh! all the good Words in one, my affectionate Husband, that is so soon to be, (be curbed in, my proud Heart, know thyself, and be conscious of thy Unworthiness!—) has just left me, with the kindest, tenderest Expressions, and gentlest Behaviour that ever blest a happy Maiden. He approached me with a sort of reined-in Rapture. My *Pamela!* said he, May I just ask after your Employment! Don't let me chide my dear Girl this Day, however. The two Parsons will be here to Breakfast with us at Nine; and yet you are not a bit dress'd! Why this Absence of Mind, and sweet Irresolution!

Why, indeed, Sir, said I! I will set about a Reformation this Instant! He saw the Common-prayer Book lying in the Window. I hope, said he, my lovely Maiden has been conning[1] the Lesson she is by-and-by to repeat. Have you not, *Pamela?* and clasped his Arms about me, and kissed me. Indeed, Sir, said I, I have been reading over the solemn Service?—And what thinks my Fairest, for so he called me, of it?—O Sir, 'tis very awful, and makes one shudder to reflect upon it!—No wonder, said he, it should affect my sweet *Pamela*: I have been looking into it this Morning, and I can't say, but I think it a solemn, but very suitable Service. But this I tell my dear Love, continu'd he, and again clasped me to him, There is not a Tittle in it, that I cannot joyfully subscribe to: And that, my dear *Pamela*, should make you easy, and join chearfully in it with me. I kissed his dear Hand; O my generous, kind Protector, said I, how gracious is it to confirm thus the doubting Mind of your poor Servant! which apprehends nothing so much as her own Unworthiness of the Honour and Blessing that await her!—He was pleased to say, I know well, my dearest Creature, that, according to the Liberties we People of Fortune generally give ourselves, I have promised a great deal, when I say so. But I would not have said it, if, deliberately, I could not with all my Heart. So, banish from your Mind all Doubts and Difficulties; let a generous Confidence in me take place; and let me see it does, by your Chearfulness, in this Day's solemn Business; and then I will love you for ever!

May God Almighty, Sir, said I, reward all your Goodness to me!—That is all I can say. But, Oh! how kind it is in you, to supply the want of the Presence and Comfortings of a dear Mother; of a loving Sister, or of the kind Companions of my own Sex, which most Maidens have, to sooth their Anxieties on the so near Approach of so awful a Solemnity!—You, Sir, are All these tender Relations in One to me! Your Condescensions and Kindness shall, if possible, embolden me to look up to you without that sweet Terror, that must confuse poor bashful Maidens, on such an Occasion, when they are surrender'd up to a more doubtful Happiness, and to half strange Men; whose good Faith, and good Usage of them, must be less experienced, and is all involv'd in the dark Bosom of Futurity,[1] and only to be proved by the Event.

This, my dear *Pamela*, said he, is most kindly said!—It shews me, that you enter gratefully into my Intention. For I would, by my Conduct, supply all these dear Relations to you; and I voluntarily promise, from my Heart, to you, what I think I could not with such assured Resolutions of Performance, to the highest-born Lady in the Kingdom. For, let me tell my sweet Girl, that, after having been long tost by the boisterous Winds of a more culpable Passion, I have now conquer'd it, and am not so much the Victim of your Love, all charming as you are, as of your Virtue; and therefore I may more boldly promise for myself, having so stable a Foundation for my Affection; which, should this outward Beauty fail, will increase with your Virtue, and shine forth the brighter, as that is more illustriously display'd, by the augmented Opportunities which the Condition you are now entering into, will afford you.—O the dear charming Man! how nobly, and encouragingly kind was all this!

I could not suitably express myself, and he said, I see my Girl is at a Loss for Words! I doubt not your kind Acceptance of my Declarations. And when I have acted too much the Part of a Libertine formerly, for you to look back without some Anxiety, I ought not, being now happily convicted, to say less.—But why loses my dear Girl her Time? I will now only add, that I hope for many happy Years to make good, by my Conduct, what so willingly flows from my Lips.

He kissed me again, and said, But, whatever you do, *Pamela*, be chearful; for else, may-be, of the small Company we shall have, some one, not knowing how to account for your too nice Modesty, may think there is *some other* Person in the World, whose Addresses would be still more agreeable to you.

This he said with an Air of Sweetness and Pleasantry; but it alarm'd me exceedingly, and made me resolve to appear as calm and chearful as possible. For this was indeed a most affecting Expression, and enough to make me, if any thing can, behave as I ought, and to force my idle Fears to give way to Hopes, so much better grounded.—And I began almost, on this Occasion, to wish Mr. *Williams* were not to marry me, lest I should behave like a Fool; and so be liable to an Imputation, which I should be most unworthy if I deserved.

So I set about dressing me instantly; and he sent Mrs. *Jewkes* to assist me. But I am never long a Dressing, when I set about it; and my Master has now given me a Hint, that will, for half an Hour more, at least, keep my Spirits in a brisk Circulation. Yet it concerns me a little too, lest he should have any, the least Shadow of a Doubt, that I am not, Mind and Person, intirely his. And so being now ready, and not called to Breakfast, I sat down and writ thus far. I might have mention'd, that I dress'd myself in a rich white Sattin Night-gown, that had been my good Lady's, and my best Headcloths, &c. I have got such a Knack of writing, that, when I am by myself, I cannot sit without a Pen in my Hand.—But I am now called to Breakfast. I suppose the Gentlemen are come!—Now, Courage, *Pamela*; Remember thou art upon thy good Behaviour:—Fie upon it! my Heart begins to flutter again!—Foolish Heart! lie still! Never, sure, was any Maiden's perverse Heart under so little Command as mine!—It gave itself away, at first, without my Leave; it has been, for Weeks, pressing me with its Wishes; and yet now, when it should be happy itself, and make me so, it is throb, throb, throb,[1] like a little Fool; and filling me with such unseasonable Misgivings, as abate the rising Comforts of all my better Prospects!

THURSDAY, near Three o-Clock.

I thought I should have found no Time nor Heart to write again this Day. But here are three Gentlemen come, unexpectedly, to dine with my Master; and so I shall not appear. He has done all he could, civilly, to send them away; but they will stay, tho', I believe, he had rather they would not. And so I have nothing to do but to write till I go to Dinner myself with Mrs. *Jewkes*: For my Master was not prepared for this Company; and it will be a little latish to-day. So I will begin with my happy Story where I left off.

When I came down to Breakfast, Mr. *Peters* and Mr. *Williams* were both there. And as soon as my Master heard me coming down, he met me at the Door, and led me in with great Tenderness. He had kindly spoke to them, as he told me afterwards, to mention no more of the Matter to me, than needs must. I paid my Respects to them, I believe, a little aukwardly, and was almost out of Breath; but said, I had come down a little too fast.

When *Abraham* came in to wait, my Master said, (that the Servants should not mistrust) 'Tis well, Gentlemen, you came as you did: For my good Girl and I were going to take an Airing till Dinner-time. I hope you'll stay and dine with me. Sir, said Mr. *Peters*, we won't hinder you; I only came, having a little Time upon my Hands, to see your Chapel; but must be at home at Dinner; and Mr. *Williams* will dine with me. Well then, said my Master, we will pursue our Intention, and ride out for an Hour or two, as soon as I have shewed Mr. *Peters* my little Chapel. Will you, *Pamela*, after Breakfast, walk with us to it? If——if, said I, and had like to have stammer'd, foolish that I was! *if* you please, Sir. I could look none of them in the Face! *Abraham* looking at me; Why, Child, said my Master, you have hardly recover'd your Fright yet: How came your Foot to slip? 'Tis well you did not hurt yourself. Said Mr. *Peters*, improving the Hint, You han't sprain'd your Ankle, Madam, I hope? No, Sir, said I, I believe not! But 'tis a little *painful* to me. And so it was; for I meant my Foolishness!—— *Abraham*, said my Master, bid *Robin* put the Horses to the Coach, instead of the Chariot; and if these Gentlemen *will* go, we can set them down. No matter, Sir, said Mr. *Peters*, I had as lieve walk, if Mr. *Williams* chuses it. Well then, said my Master, let it be the Chariot, as I told him.

I could eat nothing, tho' I attempted it; and my Hand shook so, I spilled some of my Chocolate, and so put it down again; and they were all very good, and looked another way. My Master said, when *Abraham* was out,

I have a quite plain Ring here, Mr. *Peters*. And I hope the Ceremony will dignify the Ring; and that I shall give my Girl Reason to think it, for that Cause, the most valuable one that can be presented her. Mr. *Peters* said, he was sure I should set more by it, than the richest Diamond in the World.

I had bid Mrs. *Jewkes* not to dress herself, lest she should give Cause of Mistrust; and she took my Advice.

When Breakfast was over, my Master said, before *Abraham*, Well, Gentlemen, we will step into the Chapel; and you must give me your Advice, as to the Alterations I design. I am in the more Haste, because the Survey you are going to take of it, for the Alterations, will take up a little time; and we shall have but a small Space between that and Dinner, for the Tour I design to make.—*Pamela*, you'll give us your Opinion, won't you? Yes, Sir, said I; I'll come after you.

So they went out, and I sat down in the Chair again, and fanned myself; I am sick at Heart, said I, I think, Mrs. *Jewkes*. Said she, Shall I fetch you a little Cordial?—No, said I, I am a sad Fool! I want Spirits, that's all. She took her Smelling-bottle, and would have given it me; but I said, Keep it in your Hand; may-be, I may want it; but I hope not.

She gave me very good Words; and begg'd me to go: And I got up, but my Knees beat so against one another, I was forced to sit down again. But, at last, I held by her Arm, and passing by *Abraham*, I said, This ugly Slip, coming down Stairs, has made me limp, tho'; so I must hold by you. Do you know, said I, what Alterations there are to be in the Chapel, that we must all give our Opinions of them?

Nan, she told me, was let into the Secret; and she had order'd her to stay at the Chapel Door, to see that nobody came in. My dear Master came to me, at entering the Chapel, and took my Hand, and led me up to the Altar. Remember, my dear Girl, whisper'd he, and be chearful. I am, I will, Sir, said I; but I hardly knew what I said; and so you may believe, when I said to Mrs. *Jewkes*, Don't leave me; pray, Mrs. *Jewkes*, don't leave me; as if I had all Confidence in her, and none where it was most due. So she kept close to me. God forgive me! but I never was so absent in my Life, as at first: Even till Mr. *Williams* had gone on in the Service, so far as to the awful Words about *requiring us, as we should answer at the dreadful Day of Judgment*; and then the solemn Words,[1] and my Master's whispering, Mind this, my Dear, made me start. Said he, still whispering, Know *you* any Impediment? I blush'd, and said, softly, None, Sir, but my great Unworthiness.

Then follow'd the sweet Words, *Wilt thou have this Woman to thy wedded Wife*, &c. and I began to take Heart a little, when my dearest Master answer'd, audibly, to this Question, *I will*. But I could only make a Curchee, when they asked me; tho', I am sure, my Heart was readier than my Speech, and answer'd to every Article of *obey, serve, love* and *honour*.

Mr. *Peters* gave me away, and I said after Mr. *Williams*, as well as I could, as my dear Master did, with a much better Grace, the Words of Betrothment; and the Ceremony of the Ring passing next, I received the dear Favour at his worthy Hands, with a most grateful Heart; and he was pleased to say afterwards, in the Chariot, that when he had done saying, *With this Ring I thee wed*, &c. I made a Curchee,[1] and said, Thank you, Sir. May-be, I did; for, I am sure, it was a most grateful Part of the Service; and my Heart was overwhelm'd with his Goodness, and the tender Grace wherewith he perform'd it. I was very glad, that the next Part was the Prayer, and Kneeling; for I trembled so, I could hardly stand, betwixt Fear and Delight.

The joining of our Hands afterwards, the Declaration of our being marry'd to the few Witnesses present; for, reckoning *Nan*, whose Curiosity would not let her stay at the Door, they were but Mr. *Peters*, Mrs. *Jewkes*, and she; the Blessing, the Psalm, and the subsequent Prayers, and the concluding Exhortation, were so many beautiful, welcome and lovely Parts of this divine Office, that my Heart began to be delighted with them, and my Spirits to be a little freer.

And thus, my dearest, dear Parents, is your happy, happy, thrice happy *Pamela*, at last, marry'd; and to who?—Why, to her beloved, gracious Master! the Lord of her Wishes!—And thus the dear, once naughty Assailer of her Innocence, by a blessed Turn of Providence, is become the kind, the generous Protector and Rewarder of it. God be evermore blessed and praised! and make me not wholly unworthy of such a transcendent Honour!—And bless and reward the dear, dear good Gentleman, who has thus exalted his unworthy Servant, and given her a Place, which the greatest Ladies would think themselves happy in!

My Master saluted me most ardently, and said, God give you, my dear Love, as much Joy on this Occasion, as I have. And he presented me to Mr. *Peters*, who saluted me; and said, You may excuse me, dear Madam; for I gave you away, and you are my Daughter. And Mr. *Williams* modestly withdrawing a little way; Mr. *Williams*, said my Master, pray accept my Thanks, and wish your *Sister* Joy. So he saluted me too; and said, Most heartily, Madam, I do. And I will say, that to see so much Innocence and Virtue, so eminently rewarded, is one of the greatest Pleasures I have ever known. This my Master took very kindly.

Mrs. *Jewkes* would have kissed my Hand at the Chapel Door; but I put my Arms about her Neck, for I had got a new Recruit of Spirits just then, and kissed her; and said, Thank you, Mrs. *Jewkes*, for accompanying me. I have behav'd sadly. No, Madam, said she, pretty well, pretty well! While the Gentlemen were talking, I dropt down on my Knees in a Corner, and once more blessed God for this so signal a Mercy; and Mr. *Peters* afterwards walked out with me; and Mr. *Williams* and my Master talked together, and came out after us.

Mr. *Peters*, when we came into the Parlour, said, I once more, Madam, must wish you Joy of this happy Occasion. I wish every Day may add to your Comforts; and may you very long rejoice in one another; for you are the loveliest Couple I ever saw join'd. I told him, I was infinitely oblig'd to his kind Opinion, and good Wishes; and hoped my future Conduct would not make me unworthy of them.

My good Benefactor came in with Mr. *Williams*: So, my dear Life, said he, How do you do? A little more compos'd, I hope!—Well, you see this is not so dreadful an Affair as you apprehended. Sir, said Mr. *Peters*, very kindly, 'tis a very solemn Circumstance, and I love to see it so reverently and awfully enter'd upon. It is a most excellent Sign; for the most thoughtful Beginnings make the most prudent Proceedings. Mrs. *Jewkes*, of her own accord, came in with a large silver Tumbler, filled with Sack, and a Toast, and Nutmeg, and Sugar;[1] and my Master said, That's well thought of, Mrs. *Jewkes*; for we have made but sorry Breakfastings. And he would make me take some of the Toast; as they all did, and drank pretty heartily: And I drank a little, and it chear'd my Heart, I thought, for an Hour after.

My Master took a fine Diamond Ring from his Finger, and presented it to Mr. *Peters*; who receiv'd it very kindly. And to Mr. *Williams* he said, My old Acquaintance, I have reserv'd for you, against a Variety of Sollicitations, the Living I always design'd for you; and I beg you'll prepare to take Possession of it; and as the doing it may be attended with some Expence, pray accept of this towards it; and so he gave him (as he told me afterwards it was) a Bank Note of 50 *l.*

So did this generous good Gentleman bless us all, and me in particular; for whose sake he was as bounteous as if he had marry'd one of the noblest Fortunes.

So he took his Leave of the Gentlemen, recommending Secrecy again, for a few Days, and they left him; and none of the Servants suspected any thing, as Mrs. *Jewkes* believes. And then I threw myself at his Feet, blessing God, and blessing him for his Goodness, and he overwhelm'd me with Kindness; calling me his sweet Bride, and twenty lovely Epithets, that swell my grateful Heart beyond the Power of Utterance.

He afterwards led me to the Chariot; and we took a delightful Tour round the neighbouring Villages; and he did all he could, to dissipate those still perverse Anxieties that dwell upon my Mind, and, do what I can, spread too thoughtful an Air, as he tells me, over my Countenance.

We came home again by half an Hour after One; and he was pleasing himself with thinking, not to be an Hour out of my Company this blessed Day, that (as he was so good as to say) he might inspire me with a Familiarity that should improve my Confidence in him, when he was told, that a Footman of Sir *Charles Hargrave* had been here, to let him know, that his Master, and two other Gentlemen, were on the Road to take a Dinner with him, in their Way to *Nottingham*.

He was heartily vex'd at this, and said to me, He should have been glad of their Companies at any other Time; but that it was a barbarous Intrusion now; and he wish'd they had been told he would not be at home at Dinner: And besides, said he, they are horrid Drinkers, and I shan't be able to get them away to Night, perhaps; for they have nothing to do, but travel round the Country, and beat up[1] their Friends Quarters all the Way; and 'tis all one to them, whether they stay a Night, or a Month, at a Place. But, added he, I'll find some way, if I can, to turn them off, after Dinner.—Confound them, said he, in a violent Pet, that they should come this Day, of all the Days in the Year!

We had hardly alighted, and got in, before they came; three mad Rakes they seem'd to be, as I looked out of the Window, setting up a Hunting-note, as soon as they came to the Gate, that made the Court-yard echo again, and smacking their Whips in Concert.

So I went up to my Chamber, and saw (what made my Heart throb) Mrs. *Jewkes's* officious Pains to put the Room in Order for a Guest, that however welcome, as now my Duty teaches me to say, is yet dreadful to me to think of. So I refuged myself in my Closet, and had recourse to Pen and Ink, for my Amusement, and to divert my Anxiety of Mind.—If one's Heart is so sad, and one's Apprehensions so great, where one so extremely loves, and is so extremely obliged; What must be the Case of those poor Maidens, who are forced, for sordid Views, by their tyrannical Parents, or Guardians, to marry the Man they almost hate, and, perhaps, to the Loss of the Man they most love? O that is a sad thing indeed!—And what have not such cruel Parents to answer for? and what do not such poor innocent Victims suffer?—But, blessed be God, this Lot is far from being mine!

My good Master, for I cannot yet have the Presumption to call him by a more tender Epithet, came up to me; and said, Well, I just came to ask my dear Bride! (O the charming, charming Word!) how she does? I see you are writing, my Dear, said he. These confounded Rakes are half mad, I think, and will make me so! However, said he, I have order'd my Chariot to be got ready, as if I was under an Engagement five Miles off, and will set them out of the House, if possible; and then ride round, and come back, as soon as I can get rid of them. I find, said he, Lady *Davers* is full of our Affairs. She has taken great Freedoms with me before Sir *Charles*; and they have all been at me, without Mercy; and I was forced to be very serious with them, or else they would have come up to have seen you, as I would not call you down.—He kissed me, and said, I shall quarrel with them, if I can't get them away; for I have lost two or three precious Hours with my Soul's Delight; and so he went down.

Mrs. *Jewkes* ask'd me to walk down to Dinner in the little Parlour. I went down, and she was so complaisant as to offer to wait upon me at Table; and would not be persuaded, without Difficulty, to sit down with me. But I insisted she should; For, said I, it would be very extraordinary if one should so soon go into such Distance, Mrs. *Jewkes!*——Whatever the Station of our good Master may require of me, added I, I hope I shall always conduct myself in such a manner, that Pride and Insolence shall bear no Part in my Character. You are very good, Madam, said she; but I will always know my Duty to my Master's Lady.—Why then, reply'd I, if I must take State upon me so early, Mrs. *Jewkes*, let me exact from you what you call your Duty; and sit down with me when I desire you. This prevailed upon her; and I made shift to eat a bit of Apple-pie, and a little Custard; but I had no Appetite to any thing else.

My good Master came in again, and said, Well, thank my Stars! these Rakes are going now; but I must set out with them; and I chuse my Chariot; for if I took Horse, I should have Difficulty to part with them; for they are like a Snow-ball, and intend to gather Company as they go, to make a merry Tour of it for some Days together. We both got up, when he came in; Fie, *Pamela*, said he! why this Ceremony now?—Sit still, Mrs. *Jewkes!*—Nay, Sir, said she, I was loth to sit down, but my Lady would have me!—She is very right, Mrs. *Jewkes*, said my Master, and tapp'd me on the Cheek; for we are not yet half marry'd; and so she is not above half your Lady yet!—Don't look so down, don't be so silent, my Dearest, said he; why, you hardly spoke twenty Words to me all the time we were out together. Something I will allow for your bashful Sweetness; but not too much.—Mrs. *Jewkes*, have you no pleasant Tales to tell my *Pamela*, to make her smile, till I return?—Yes, Sir, said she, I could tell twenty pleasant Stories; but my Lady is too nice to hear them; and yet, I hope, I should not be shocking neither. Ah! poor Woman! thought I; thy chastest Stories will make a modest Person blush, if I know thee; and I desire to hear none of them. My Master said, Tell her one of the shortest you have, in my Hearing. Why, Sir, said she, I knew a bashful young Lady, as Madam may be, marry'd to ----- Dear Mrs. *Jewkes*, interrupted I, no more of your

Story, I beseech you! I don't like the Beginning of it. Go on, Mrs. *Jewkes*, said my Master. No, pray, Sir, don't require it, said I; pray don't. Well, said he, then we'll have it another time, Mrs. *Jewkes*.

And so *Abraham* coming to tell him, the Gentlemen were going, and his Chariot was ready; Thank God, said he; and went to them, and sat out with them. I took a Turn in the Garden, with Mrs. *Jewkes*, after they were gone: And having walked a-while, I said, I should be glad of her Company down the Elm-walk, to meet the Chariot: For, Oh! I know not how to look up at him, when he is with me; nor how to bear his Absence, when I have Reason to expect him! What a strange Contradiction there is in this unaccountable Passion!

What a different Aspect every thing in and about this House bears now, to my thinking, to what it once had! The Garden, the Pond, the Alcove, the Elm-walk. But, Oh! my Prison is become my Palace; and no wonder every thing wears another Face! We sat down upon the broad Style, leading towards the Road, and Mrs. *Jewkes* was quite another Person to me, to what she was the last time I sat there!

At last my best Beloved return'd, and alighted there. What, my *Pamela!* (said he, and kissed me) brings you this way? I hope, to meet me?—Yes, Sir, said I. That's kind, indeed, said he; but why that averted Eye?—that down-cast Countenance, as if you was afraid of me? You must not think so, Sir, said I. Revive my Heart then, said he, with a more chearful Aspect; and let that over-anxious Sollicitude which appears in the charmingest Face in the World, be chased from it.—Have you, my dear Girl, any Fears that I can dissipate; any Doubts that I can obviate; any Hopes that I can encourage; any Request that I can gratify? Speak, my dear *Pamela*; and if I have Power, *but* speak, and to purchase one Smile, it shall be done!

I cannot, Sir, said I, have any Fears, any Doubts, but that I shall never be able to deserve all your Goodness. I have no Hopes, but that my future Conduct may be agreeable to you, and my determined Duty well accepted. Nor have I any Request to make, but that you will forgive all my Imperfections; and, among the rest, this foolish Weakness, that makes me seem to you, after all the generous Things that have passed, to want this further Condescension, and these kind Assurances. But, indeed, Sir, I am oppress'd by your Bounty; my Spirits sink under the Weight of it; and the Oppression is still the greater, as I see not how, possibly, in my whole future Life, by all I can do, to merit the least of your Favours.

I know your grateful Heart, said he, but remember, my Dear, what the Lawyers tell us, That Marriage is the highest Consideration which the Law knows. And this, my sweet Bride, has made you mine, and me yours; and you have the best Claim in the World to share my Fortune with me. But, set that Consideration aside, what is the Obligation you have to me? Your Mind is pure as that of an Angel, and as much transcends mine. Your Wit and your Judgment, to make you no Compliment, are more than equal to mine: You have all the Graces that Education can give a Woman; improv'd by a Genius which makes those Graces natural to you. You have a Sweetness of Temper, and a noble Sincerity, beyond all Compare; and in the Beauty of your Person, you excel all the Ladies I ever saw. Where then, my Dearest, is the Obligation, if not on my side to you?—But to avoid these Comparisons, let us talk of nothing henceforth but Equality; for if you will set the Riches of your Mind, and your unblemished Virtue, against my Fortune, (which is but an accidental Good, as I may call it, and all I have to boast of) the Condescension will be yours; and I shall not think I can possibly deserve you, till, after your sweet Example, my future Life shall become nearly as blameless as yours.

O Sir, said I, what Comfort do you give me, that, instead of my being in Danger of being insnared by the high Condition to which your Goodness has exalted me, you make me hope, that I shall be confirm'd and improv'd by you; and that we may have a Prospect of perpetuating each other's Happiness, till Time shall be no more!—But, Sir, I will not, as you once caution'd me, be too serious. I will resolve, with these sweet Encouragements, to be, in every thing, what you would have me be! And I hope I shall, more and more, shew you that I have no Will but yours. He kissed me very tenderly, and thanked me for this kind Assurance, as he called it. And so we enter'd the House, Mrs. *Jewkes* having left us as soon as my Master alighted.

Eight o'Clock at Night.

Now these sweet Assurances, my dear Father and Mother, you will say, must be very Consolatory to me, and voluntierly on his Side, all that could be wish'd for on mine; and I was resolved, if possible, to subdue my idle Fears and Apprehensions.

Ten o'Clock at Night.

As we sat at Supper, he was generously kind to me, as well in his Actions as Expressions. He took notice, in the most delicate manner, of my Endeavour to conquer my Foibles, and said, I see, with Pleasure, my dear Girl strives to comport herself in a manner suitable to my Wishes: I see even thro' the sweet tender Struggles of your over-nice Modesty, how much I owe to your

Desire of obliging me. As I have once told you, that I am the Conquest more of your Virtue than your Beauty; so, not one alarming Word or Look shall my beloved *Pamela* hear or see, to give her Reason to suspect the Truth of what I aver. You may the rather believe me, continued he, as you may see the Pain I have to behold any thing that concerns you, even tho' your Concern be causeless. And yet I will indulge my dear Girl's bashful Weakness so far, as to own that so pure a Mind may suffer from Apprehension, on so important a Change as this; and I can therefore be only displeased with such Part of your Conduct, as may make your Sufferings greater than my own; when I am resolved, thro' every Stage of my future Life, in all Events, to study to make them less.

After Supper, of which, with all his sweet Persuasions, I could hardly taste, he made me drink two Glasses of Champaign, and afterwards a Glass of Sack; which he kindly forced upon me, by naming your Healths: And as the Time of retiring drew on, he took notice, but in a very delicate manner, how my Colour went and came; and how foolishly I trembled. Nobody, surely, in such delightful Circumstances, ever behav'd so silly!—And he said, My dearest Girl, I fear you have had too much of my Company for so many Hours together; and would better recollect yourself, if you retir'd for half an Hour to your Closet.

I wished for this, but durst not say so much, lest he should be angry; for, as the Hours grew on, I found my Apprehensions increase, and my silly Heart was the unquieter, every time I could lift up my Eyes to his dear Face; so sweetly terrible did he appear to my Apprehensions. I said, You are all Goodness, dear Sir; and I boldly kissed his dear Hand, and pressed it to my Lips, with both mine. And he saluting me very fervently, gave me his Hand, seeing me hardly able to stand, and led me to my Chamber-door, and then most generously withdrew.

I went to my Closet; and the first thing I did, on my Knees, again thanked God for the Blessing of the Day; and besought his Divine Goodness to conduct my future Life in such a manner, as should make me a happy Instrument of his Glory. After this, being now left to my own Recollection, I grew a little more assured and lightsome; and the Pen and my Paper being before me, I amused myself with writing thus far.

Eleven o'Clock Thursday *Night.*

Mrs. *Jewkes* being come up with a Message, desiring to know, whether her Master may attend upon me in my *Closet*; and hinting to me, that, however, she believed, he did not expect to find me *there*, I have sent Word, that I beg he would indulge me one Quarter of an Hour.—So, committing myself to the Mercies of the Almighty, who has led me thro' so many strange Scenes of Terror and Affrightment, to this happy, yet awful Moment, I will wish you, my dear Parents, a good Night; and tho' you will not see this in time, yet I know I have your hourly Prayers; and therefore cannot fail of them now. So, Good-night, Good-night! God bless you, and God bless me. *Amen, Amen*, if it be his blessed Will, subscribes

Your ever dutiful Daughter!

FRIDAY Evening.

O how this dear, excellent Man indulges me in every thing! Every Hour he makes me happier, by his sweet Condescension, than the former. He pities my Weakness of Mind, allows for all my little Foibles, endeavours to dissipate my Fears; his Words are so pure, his Ideas so chaste, and his whole Behaviour so sweetly decent, that never, surely, was so happy a Creature as your *Pamela!* I never could have hoped such a Husband could have fallen to my Lot! And much less, that a Gentleman, who had allow'd himself in Attempts, that now I will endeavour to forget for ever, should have behav'd with so very delicate and unexceptionable a Demeanour. No light, frothy Jests drop from his Lips; no alarming Railleries; no offensive Expressions, nor insulting Airs, reproach or wound the Ears of your happy, thrice happy Daughter. In short, he says every thing that may embolden me to look up, with Pleasure, upon the generous Author of my Happiness.

At Breakfast, when I knew not how to see him, he embolden'd me by talking of *you*, my dear Parents; a Subject, he generously knew, I could talk of: And gave me Assurances, that he would make you both happy. He said, he would have me send you a Letter, to acquaint you with my Nuptials; and, as he could make Business that way, *Thomas* should carry it purposely, as to-morrow. Nor will I, said he, my dear *Pamela*, desire to see your Writings, because I told you I would not; for now will I, in every thing, religiously keep my Word with my dear Spouse (O the dear delightful Word!); and you may send all your Papers to them, from those they have, down to this happy Moment; only let me beg they will preserve them, and let me have them when they have read them, as also those I have not seen; which, however, I desire not to see till then; but then shall take it for a Favour, if you will grant it.

It will be my Pleasure, as well as my Duty, Sir, said I, to obey you in every thing. And I will write up to the Conclusion of this Day, that they may see how happy you have made me.

I know you will both join with me to bless God for his wonderful Mercies and Goodness to you, as well as to me: For he was pleased to ask me particularly after your Circumstances, and said, he had taken notice that I had hinted, in some of my first Letters, that you ow'd Money in the World; and he gave me Fifty Guineas, and bid me send them to you in my Pacquet, to pay your Debts, as far as they would go; and that you would quit your present Business, and put yourself, and my dear Mother, into a creditable Appearance; and he would find a better Place of Abode for you than that you had, when he returned to *Bedfordshire*. O how shall I bear all these exceeding great and generous Favours!—I send them, wrapt up, Five Guineas in a Parcel, in double Papers.

To me he gave no less than One hundred Guineas more; and said, I would have you, my Dear, give Mrs. *Jewkes*, when you go away from hence, what you think fit, out of these, as from yourself!—Nay, good dear Sir, said I, let that be what you please. Give her then, said he, Twenty Guineas, as a Compliment on your Nuptials. Give *Colbrand* Ten Guineas: Give the two Coachmen, Five Guineas each; to the two Maids at this House, Five Guineas each: Give *Abraham* Five Guineas: Give *Thomas* Five Guineas; and give the Gardeners, Grooms and Helpers, Twenty Guineas among them. And when, said he, I return with you to the other House, I will make you a suitable Present, to buy you such Ornaments as are fit for my beloved Wife to appear in. For now, my *Pamela*, continu'd he, you are not to mind, as you once proposed, what other Ladies will say; but to appear as my Wife ought to do. Else it will look as if what you thought of, as a Means to avoid the Envy of others of your Sex, was a wilful Slight in me, which, I hope, I never shall be guilty of; and I will shew the World, that I value you as I ought, and as if I had marry'd the first Fortune in the Kingdom: And why should it not be so? When I know none of the first Quality that matches you in Excellence?

He saw I was at a Loss for Words, and said, I see, my dearest Bride! my Spouse! my Wife! my *Pamela!* your grateful Confusion. And kissing me, as I was going to speak, I will stop your dear Mouth, said he: You shall not so much as thank me; for when I have done ten times more than this, I shall but poorly express my Love for so much Beauty of Mind, and Loveliness of Person; which thus, said he, and clasped me to his generous Bosom, I can proudly now call my own!—O how can I think of any thing, but returned Love, Joy and Gratitude!

And thus generously did he banish from my Mind those painful Reflections, and bashful Apprehensions, that made me dread to see him, for the first time this Day, when I was called to attend him at Breakfast, and made me all Ease, Composure and Tranquillity.

He then, thinking I seem'd somewhat thoughtful, proposed a little Turn in the Chariot, till Dinner-time; and this was another sweet Relief to me; and he diverted me with twenty agreeable Relations, of what Observations he had made in his Travels; and gave me the Characters of the Ladies and Gentlemen in his other Neighbourhood; telling me whose Acquaintance he would have me most cultivate; and when I mention'd Lady *Davers*, with Apprehension, he said, To be sure I love my Sister dearly, notwithstanding her violent Spirit; and I know she loves me; and I can allow a little for her Pride, because I know what once my own was; and because she knows not my *Pamela*, and her Excellencies, as I do. But you must not, my Dear, forget what belongs to your Character, as my Wife, nor meanly stoop to her; tho' I know you will chuse, by Softness, to try to move her to a proper Behaviour. But it shall be my Part to see that you do not yield too much.

However, continued he, as I would not publickly declare my Marriage here, I hope she won't come near us till we are in *Bedfordshire*; and then, when she knows we are marry'd, she will keep away, if she is not willing to be reconcil'd; for she dare not, surely, come to quarrel with me, when she knows it is done; for that would have an hateful and wicked Appearance, as if she would try to make Differences between Man and Wife.—But we will have no more of this Subject, nor talk of any thing, added he, that shall give Concern to my Dearest. And so he changed the Talk to a more pleasing Subject, and said the kindest and most soothing things in the World.

When we came home, which was about Dinner-time, he was the same obliging, sweet Gentleman; And, in short, is studious to shew, on every Occasion, his generous Affection to me. And, after Dinner, he told me, he had already wrote to his Draper, in Town, to provide him new Liveries; and to his late Mother's Mercer, to send him down Patterns of the most fashionable Silks, for my Choice. I told him, I was unable to express my Gratitude for his Favours and Generosity; and as he knew best what befitted his own Rank and Condition, I would wholly remit myself to his good Pleasure; but, by all his repeated Bounties to me, of so extraordinary a Nature, I could not but look forward with Awe, upon the Condition to which he had exalted me; and now I feared I should hardly be able to act up to it in such a manner as should justify the Choice he had condescended to make. But that, I hoped, I should have not only his generous Allowance for my Imperfections, which I could only assure him should not be wilful ones, but his kind Instructions; and that as often as he observ'd any Part of my Conduct such as he would have alter'd, and could not intirely approve, that he would let me know it; and I would think his Reproofs of beginning Faults the kindest and most affectionate things in the World; because they would keep me from committing greater; and be a Means to continue to me the Blessing of his good Opinion.

He answer'd me in the kindest manner; and assured me, That nothing should ever lie upon his Mind which he would not reveal, and give me an Opportunity either of convincing him, or being convinced myself.

He then asked me, When I should be willing to go to the *Bedfordshire* House? I said, Whenever he pleased. Said he, We will come down hither again before the Winter, if you please, in order to cultivate the Acquaintance you have begun with Lady *Jones*, and Sir *Simon*'s Family; and, if it please God to spare us to one another, in the Winter I will give you, as I promised, for two or three Months, my Company in *London*. And, I think, added he, if my Dear pleases, we will set out next Week, about *Tuesday*, for t'other House. I can have no Objection, Sir, said I, to any thing you propose; but how will you avoid Miss *Darnford*'s Sollicitation for an Evening, to dance? Why, said he, we can make *Monday* Evening do for that Purpose, if they won't excuse us. But, if you please, said he, I will invite Lady *Jones*, Mr. *Peters* and his Family, and Sir *Simon* and his Family, to my little Chapel, on *Sunday* Morning, and to stay Dinner with me; and then I will declare my Marriage to them, because my dear Life shall not leave this Country, with the least Reason for a Possibility of any body's doubting that it is so. Oh! how good this was!—But, indeed, his Conduct is all of a Piece, noble, kind, and considerate! What a happy Creature, by God's Goodness, am I!—And then, may-be, said he, they will excuse us till we return into this County again, as to the Ball. Is there any thing, added he, that my beloved *Pamela* has still to wish? if you have, freely speak.

Hitherto, my dearest Sir, reply'd I, you have not only prevented my Wishes, but my Hopes, and even my Thoughts. And yet I must own, since your kind Command of speaking my Mind, seems to shew that you expect from me, I should say something, that I have only one or two things to wish more, and then I shall be too happy. Say, said he, what they are? Sir, proceeded I, I am, indeed, ashamed to ask any thing, lest it should not be agreeable to you; and lest it should look as if I was taking Advantage of your kind Condescensions to me, and knew not when to be satisfy'd!

I will only tell you, *Pamela*, said he, that you are not to imagine, that these things which I have done, in hopes of obliging you, are the sudden

Impulses of a *new* Passion for you. But, if I can answer for my own Mind, they proceed from a regular and uniform Desire of obliging you; which, I hope, will last as long as your Merit lasts; and that, I make no doubt, will be as long as I live; and I can the rather answer for this, because I really find so much Delight in myself in my present way of Thinking and Acting, as infinitely over-pays me; and which, for that Reason, I am likely to continue for *both* our sakes. My beloved *Wife*, therefore, said he, for, methinks, I am grown fond of a Name I once despised, may venture to speak her Mind; and I will promise, that, so far as it is agreeable to me, and I chearfully can, I will comply; and you will not insist upon it, if that cannot be the Case.

To be sure, Sir, said I, I ought not, neither will I. And now you embolden me to become an humble Petitioner; and that, as I ought, upon my Knees, for the reinstating such of your Servants, as I have been the unhappy Occasion of their disobliging you. He raised me up, and said, My beloved *Pamela* has too often been in this suppliant Posture to me, to permit it any more. Rise, my Fairest, and let me know whom, in particular, you would reinstate; and he kindly held me in his Arms, and pressed me to his beloved Bosom. Mrs. *Jervis*, Sir, said I, in the first place; for she is a good Woman; and the Misfortunes she has had in the World, make your Displeasure most heavy to her.

Well, said he, who next? Mr. *Longman*, Sir, said I; and, I am sure, kind as they have been to me, yet would I not ask it, if I could not vouch for their Integrity, and if I did not think it was my dear Master's Interest to have such good Servants.

Have you any thing further? said he.—Sir, said I, your good old Butler, who has so long been in your Family, before the Day of your happy Birth; I would, if I might, become an Advocate for!

Well, said he, I have only to say, That had not Mr. *Longman*, and Mrs. *Jervis*, and *Jonathan* too, joined in a Body, in a bold Appeal to Lady *Davers*, which has given her the insolent Handle she has taken to intermeddle in my Affairs, I could easily have forgiven all the rest of their Conduct; tho' they have given their Tongues no little Licence about me; but I could have forgiven them, because I desire every body to love you; and it is with Pride that I observe the Opinion and Love of them, and every body else that knows you, justify my own.—But yet, I will forgive even this, because my *Pamela* desires it; and I will send a Letter myself, to tell *Longman* what he owes to your Interposition, if the Estate he has made in my Family, does not set him above the Acceptance of it. And, as to Mrs. *Jervis*, do you, my Dear, write a Letter to her, and give her your Commands, instantly, on the Receipt of it, to go and take Possession of her former Charge; for now, my dearest Girl, she will be more immediately your Servant; and I know you love her so well, that you'll go thither with the more Pleasure, to find her there.—But don't think, added he, that all this Compliance is to be for nothing. Ah! Sir, said I, tell me but what I can do, poor as I am in Power, but rich in Will; and I will not hesitate one Moment. Why then, said he, of your own Accord, reward me for my chearful Compliance, with one sweet Kiss.—I instantly said, Thus then, dear Sir, will I obey; and, Oh! you have the sweetest and most generous way in the World, to make that a Condition, which gives me double Honour, and adds to my Obligations. And so I clasped my Arms about his Neck, and was not ashamed to kiss him once, and twice, and three times, once for every forgiven Person.

Now, my dearest *Pamela*, said he, what other things have you to ask? Mr. *Williams* is already taken Care of; and, I hope, will be happy.—Have you nothing to say for *John Arnold?*

Why, dear Sir, said I, you have seen the poor Fellow's Penitence in my Letters.—Yes, my Dear, so I have; but that is his Penitence for his having serv'd me, against you; and, I think, when he would have betray'd me afterwards, he deserves nothing to be said or done for him by either.

But, dear Sir, said I, this is a Day of Jubilee; and the less he deserves, poor Fellow, the more will be your Goodness. And let me add one Word; That as he was divided in his Inclinations between his Duty to you, and good Wishes to me, and knew not how to distinguish between the one and the other, when he finds us so happily united by your great Goodness to me, he will have no more Puzzles in his Duty; for he has not failed in any other Part of it; but, I hope, will serve you faithfully for the future.

Well then, suppose I put Mrs. *Jewkes* in a good way of Business, in some Inn, and give her *John* for a Husband? And then your Gypsey Story will be made out, that she will have a Husband younger than herself.

You are all Goodness, Sir, said I. I can freely forgive poor Mrs. *Jewkes*, and wish her happy. But permit me, Sir, to ask, Would not this look like a very heavy Punishment to poor *John?*—And as if you could not forgive him, when you are so generous to every body else?

He smiled, and said, O my *Pamela*, this for a forgiving Spirit, is very severe upon poor *Jewkes*: But I shall never, by the Grace of God, have any more such trying Services to put him or the rest upon; and if *you* can forgive him, I think *I* may; and so *John* shall be at your Disposal. And now let me know, what my *Pamela* has further to wish?

O my dearest Sir, said I, not one single Wish more has your grateful *Pamela*. My Heart is overwhelm'd with your Goodness! Forgive these

Tears of Joy, added I!—You have left me nothing to pray for, but that God will bless you with Life, and Health, and Honour, and continue to me the Blessing of your Esteem; and I shall then be the happiest Creature in the World.

He clasped me in his Arms, and said, You cannot, my dear Life, be so happy in me, as I am in you. O how heartily I despise all my former Pursuits and headstrong Appetites! what Joys, what true Joys, flow from virtuous Love! Joys which the narrow Soul of the Libertine cannot take in, nor his Thought conceive!——And which I myself, whilst a Libertine, had not the least Notion of!

But, said he, I expected, my dear Spouse, my *Pamela*, had something to ask for herself: But since all her own Good is absorbed in the Delight her generous Heart takes in promoting that of others, it shall be my Delight to prevent her Wishes, and to study to make her Care for herself unnecessary, by my anticipating Kindness.

In this manner, my dear Parents, is your happy Daughter blessed in a Husband! O how my exulting Heart leaps at the dear, dear Word!—And I have nothing to do, but to be humble, and to look up with Gratitude to the all-gracious Dispenser of these Blessings!

So, with a thousand Thanks, I afterwards retired to my Closet, to write you thus far. And having compleated what I purpose for this Pacquet, and put up the kind, obliging Present, I have nothing more to say, but that I hope soon to see you both, and receive your Blessings on this happy, thrice happy Occasion. And so, hoping for your Prayers, that I may preserve an humble and upright Mind to my gracious God, a dutiful Gratitude to my dear Master and Husband,—that I may long rejoice in the Continuance of these Blessings and Favours, and that I may preserve, at the same time, an obliging Deportment to every one else, I conclude myself,

Your ever dutiful and most happy Daughter,
PAMELA B-----.

O think it not my Pride, my dear Parents, that sets me on glorying in my Change of Name. Yours will be always dear to me, and what I shall never be ashamed of, I am sure! But yet—For such a Husband!—What shall I say, since Words are too faint to express my Gratitude and my Joy!

I have taken Copies of my Master's Letter to Mr. *Longman*, and mine to Mrs. *Jervis*, which I will send with the further Occurrences when I go to the other dear House, or give you when I see you, as I now hope soon to do.

SATURDAY Morning, the Third of my happy Nuptials.

I must still write on, till I come to be settled in the Duty of the Station to which I am so generously exalted, and to let you participate with me the transporting Pleasures that arise from my new Condition, and the Favours that are hourly heaped upon me by the best of Husbands. When I had got my Pacquet for you finish'd, I then set about writing, as he had kindly directed me, to Mrs. *Jervis*; and had no Difficulty till I came to sign my Name; and so I brought it down with me, when I was called to Supper, unsigned.

My good Master, I hardly have yet the Courage to call him freely by a tenderer Name, had been writing to Mr. *Longman*; and he said, pleasantly, See here, my Dearest, what I have written to your *Somebody*. I read as follows:

'Mr. LONGMAN,

'I have the Pleasure to acquaint you, that last *Thursday* I was marry'd to my beloved *Pamela*. I have had Reason to be disobliged with you, and Mrs. *Jervis* and *Jonathan*, not for your Kindness to, and Regard for my dear Spouse, that now is, but for the manner in which you appealed to my Sister *Davers*; which has made a very wide Breach between her and me. But as it was one of her first Requests, that I would overlook what had past, and reinstate you all in your former Charges, I think myself obliged, without the least Hesitation, to comply with it. So, if you please, you may enter again upon an Office which you have always executed with unquestionable Integrity, and to the Satisfaction of

'Yours, &c.

'*Friday Afternoon.*

'I shall set out next *Tuesday* or *Wednesday*, God willing, for *Bedfordshire*; and desire to find *Jonathan*, as well as you, in your former Offices; in which, I dare say, you'll have the more Pleasure, as you have such an early Instance of the Sentiments of my dear Wife, from whose Goodness you may expect every agreeable thing. She writes herself to Mrs. *Jervis.*'

I thanked him most gratefully for his Goodness, and afterwards took the above Copy of it. And shew'd him my Letter to Mrs. *Jervis*, as follows:

'My dear Mrs. JERVIS,

'I have joyful Tidings to communicate to you. For Yesterday I was happily marry'd to the best of Gentlemen, yours and my beloved Master. I have only now to tell you, that I am inexpressibly happy: That my generous Benefactor denies me nothing, and even anticipates my Wishes. You may be sure I could not forget my dear Mrs. *Jervis*; and I made it my Request, and had it granted, as soon as asked, that you might return to the kind Charge, which you executed with so much Advantage to our Master's Interest, and so much Pleasure to all under your Direction. All the Power that is put into my Hands, by the most generous of Gentlemen, shall be exerted to make every thing easy and agreeable to you; and as I shall soon have the Honour of attending my beloved Spouse to *Bedfordshire*, it will be a very considerable Addition to my Delights, and to my unspeakable Obligations to the best of Men, to see my dear Mrs. *Jervis*, and to be received by her with that Pleasure, which I promise myself from her Affection. For I am, my dear good Friend, and always will be,

> '*Yours, very affectionately and gratefully*,
> 'PAMELA -------.'

He read this Letter, and said, 'Tis Yours, my Dear, and must be good: But don't you put your Name to it? Sir, said I, your Goodness has given me a Right to a very honourable one: But as this is the first Occasion of this kind, except that to my dear Father and Mother, I think I ought to shew it you unsign'd, that I may not seem over-forward to take Advantage of the Honour you have done me.

However sweetly humble and requisite, said he, this may appear to my dear *Pamela*'s Niceness, it befits me to tell you, that I am, every Moment, more and more pleased with the Right you have to my Name: And, my dear Life, added he, I have only to wish I may be half as worthy as you are of the happy Knot so lately knit. He then took a Pen himself, and wrote after *Pamela*, his most worthy Surname; and I under-wrote thus: "O rejoice with me, my dear Mrs. *Jervis*, that I am enabled, by God's Graciousness, and my dear Master's Goodness, thus to write myself."

These Letters, and the Pacquet to you, were sent away by Mr. *Thomas* early this Morning.

My dearest Master is just gone to take a Ride out, and intends to call upon the Lady *Jones*, Mr. *Peters*, and Sir *Simon Darnford*, to invite them to Chapel and Dinner to-morrow; and says, he chuses to do it himself, because the Time is so short, they will, perhaps, deny a Servant.

I forgot to mention, that Mr. *Williams* was here Yesterday, to ask Leave to go to see his new Living, and to provide for taking Possession of it; and seem'd so pleased with my Master's Kindness and Fondness for me, as well as his generous Deportment to himself, that he left us in such a

Disposition, as shew'd him quite happy. I am very glad of it; for it would rejoice me to be an humble Means of making all Mankind so: And Oh! what Returns ought I not to make to the Divine Goodness! and how ought I to strive to diffuse the Blessings I experience, to all in my Knowledge!— For else, what is it for such a Worm as I to be exalted! What is my *single* Happiness, if I suffer it, Niggard-like, to extend no further than myself?— But then, *indeed*, do God Almighty's Creatures act worthy of the Blessings they receive, when they make, or endeavour to make, the whole Creation, so far as is in the Circle of their Power, happy!

Great and good God! as thou hast enlarged my Opportunities, enlarge also my Will, and make me delight in dispensing to others, a Portion of that Happiness which I have myself so plentifully receiv'd at the Hands of thy gracious Providence! Then shall I not be useless in my Generation!— Then shall I not stand a single Mark of God's Goodness to a poor worthless Creature, that in herself is of so poor Account in the Scale of Beings,[1] a mere Cypher[2] on the wrong Side of a Figure; but shall be placed on the right Side; and, tho' nothing worth in myself, shall give Signification by my Place, and multiply the Blessings I owe to God's Goodness, who has distinguish'd me by so fair a Lot!

This, as I conceive, is the indispensable Duty of a high Condition; and how great must be the Condemnation of poor Creatures, at the great Day of Account, when they shall be asked, What Uses they have made of the Opportunity put into their Hands? and are able only to say, We have lived but to ourselves. We have circumscribed all the Power thou hast given us into one narrow, selfish Circle: We have heaped up Treasures for those who came after us, tho' we know not whether they will not make a still worse Use of them than we ourselves did. And how can such poor selfish Pleaders expect any other Sentence, than the dreadful, *Depart, ye Cursed!*[3]

But sure, my dear Father and Mother, such Persons can have no Notion of the exalted Pleasures that flow from doing Good, were there to be no After-account at all!

There is something so satisfactory and pleasing to Reflection, on the being able to administer Comfort and Relief to those who stand in need of it, as infinitely rewards the beneficent Mind. And how often have I experienced this in my good Lady's time; tho' but the second-hand Dispenser of her Benefits to the Poor and Sickly, when she made me her Almoner!—How have I been affected with the Blessings which the Miserable have heaped upon her for her Goodness, and upon me for being but the humble Conveyer of her Bounty to them!—And how delighted have I been, when the moving Reports I have made of a particular Distress, has augmented my good Lady's first Intentions in its Relief!

This I recall, with Pleasure, because it is now, by God's Goodness, become my Part to do those good things she was wont to do: And Oh! let me watch myself, that my prosperous State do not make me forget to look up with due Thankfulness, to the Providence which has intrusted me with the Power, that so I may not incur a terrible Woe by the Abuse or the Neglect of it!

Forgive me these Reflections,[1] my dear Parents, and let me have your Prayers, that I may not find my present Happiness a Snare to me; but that I may consider, that more and more will be expected from me, in Proportion to the Power given me; and that I may not so unworthily act as if I believ'd I ought to set up my Rest in my *mean Self*, and think nothing further to be done, with the Opportunities put into my Hand, by the Divine Favour, and the best of Men![2]

SATURDAY, Seven o'Clock in the Evening.

My Master return'd home to Dinner, in Compliment to me, tho' much press'd to dine with Lady *Jones*, as he was also by Sir *Simon*, to dine with him. But Mr. *Peters* could not conveniently provide a Preacher for his own Church to-morrow Morning, at so short a Notice; Mr. *Williams* being gone, as I said, to his new Living; but believed he could for the Afternoon; and so he promised to give his Company to Dinner, and to read Afternoon Service; and this made my Master invite all the rest, as well as him, to Dinner, and not to Church; and made them promise to come; and told Mr. *Peters*, he would send his Coach for him and his Family.

Miss *Darnford* told him, pleasantly, she would not come, unless he would promise her to be at his Wedding; by which, I find, Mr. *Peters* has kept the Secret, as my Master desired.

He was pleased to give me an Airing after Dinner in the Chariot, and renew'd his kind Assurances to me, and, if possible, is kinder than ever. This is sweetly comfortable to me; because it shews me, he does not repent of his Condescensions to me; and it encourages me to look up to him with more Satisfaction of Mind, and less Doubtfulness.

I begg'd Leave to send a Guinea to a poor Body in the Town, that I heard, by Mrs. *Jewkes*, lay very ill, and was very destitute. He said, Send two, my Dear, if you please. Said I, Sir, I will never do any thing of this kind without letting you know what I do. He most generously answer'd, I shall then, perhaps, have you do less Good than you would otherwise do, from a Doubt of me; tho', I hope, your Discretion, and my own Temper, which is not avaricious, will make such Doubt causeless.

Now, my Dear, continued he, I'll tell you how we will order this Point, to avoid even the Shadow of Uneasiness on one side, or Doubt on the other.

As to your Father and Mother, in the first Place, they shall be quite out of the Question; for I have already determined in my Mind about them; and it is thus: They shall go down, if they and you think well of it, to my little *Kentish* Estate; which I once mentioned to you in such a manner, as made you reject it with a Nobleness of Mind, that gave me Pain then, but Pleasure since. There is a pretty little Farm and House, untenanted, upon that Estate, and tolerably stock'd, and I will further stock it for them; for such industrious Folks won't know how to live without some Employment; and it shall be their's for both their Lives, without paying any Rent; and I will allow them 50 *l. per Annum* besides, that they may keep up the Stock, and be kind to any other of your Relations, without being beholden to you or me, for small matters; and for greater, where needful, you shall always have it in your Power to accommodate them; for I shall never question your Prudence. And we will, so long as God spares our Lives, go down once a Year to see them, and they shall come up as often as they please, it cannot be too often, to see us; for I mean not this, my Dear, to send them from us.—Before I proceed, Does my *Pamela* like this?

O, Sir, said I, either I have not Words, or else the *English* Tongue affords them not, to express sufficiently my Gratitude. Learn me, dear Sir, continued I, and pressed his dear Hands to my Lips, learn me some other Language, if there be any, that abounds with more grateful Terms, that I may not thus be choaked with Meanings, for which I can find no adequate Utterance.

My Charmer! says he, your Language is all wonderful, as your Sentiments; and you most abound when you seem most to want!—All that I wish, is, to find my Proposals agreeable to you; and if my *first* are not, my *second* shall be, if I can but know what you wish.

Did I say too much, my dearest Parents, when I said, he was, if possible, kinder and kinder!—O the blessed Man! How my Heart is overwhelm'd with his Goodness!

Well, said he, my Dearest, let me desire you to mention this to them, and see if they approve it. But if it be your Choice, and theirs, to have them nearer to you, or even under the Roof with you, I will freely consent to it.

O no, Sir, said I (and I fear almost sinn'd in my grateful Flight) I am sure they would not chuse that; they could not, perhaps, serve God so well, if they were to live with you; for, so constantly seeing the Hand that blesses them, they would, may-be, as must be my Care to avoid, be tempted to look no further in their Gratitude, than to the dear Dispenser of such innumerable Benefits!

Excellent Creature! said he, my Beloved wants no Language, nor Sentiment neither! and her charming Thoughts, so sweetly express'd, would grace any Language; and this is a Blessing almost peculiar to my Fairest.—Your so kind Acceptance, my *Pamela*, added he, repays the Benefit, with Interest, and leaves me under Obligation to your Goodness.

But now, my Dearest, I will tell you what we will do, with regard to Points of your own private Charity; for, far be it from me, to put under that Name the Subject we have been mentioning: Because that, and more than that, is *Duty*, to Persons so worthy, and so nearly related to my *Pamela*, and, as such, to myself.—O how the sweet Man out-does me in Thoughts, Words, Power, and every thing!

And this, said he, lies in very small Compass; for I will allow you Two hundred Pounds a Year, which *Longman* shall constantly pay you, at Fifty Pounds a Quarter, for your own Use, and of which I expect no Account; to commence from the Day you enter into my other House; I mean, said he, that the first Fifty Pounds shall then be due; because you shall have something to begin with. And, added the dear generous Man, if this be pleasing to you, let it, since you say you want Words, signify it by such a sweet Kiss as you gave me Yesterday. I hesitated not a Moment to comply with these obliging Terms, and threw my Arms about his dear Neck, tho' in the Chariot, and blessed his Goodness to me. But indeed, Sir, said I, I cannot bear this generous Treatment. He was pleased to say, Don't be uneasy, my Dear, about these Trifles; God has bless'd me with a very good Estate, and all of it in a prosperous Condition, and well tenanted. I lay up Money every Year, and have besides, large Sums in Government and other Securities; so that you will find, what I have hitherto promised, is very short of that Proportion of my Substance, which, as my dearest Wife, you have a Right to.

In this sweet manner did we pass the Time till Evening, when the Chariot brought us home; and then our Supper succeeded in the same agreeable manner. And thus, in a rapturous Circle, the Time moves on; every Hour bringing with it something more delightful than the past!— Sure nobody was ever so blest as I!

SUNDAY, the Fourth Day of my Happiness.

Not going to Chapel this Morning, the Reason of which I told you, I bestowed the Time, from the Hour of my Beloved's rising, to Breakfast, in Prayer and Thanksgiving, in my Closet; and now I begin to be quite easy, chearful and free in my Spirits; and the rather, as I find myself encouraged by the Tranquility, Serenity, and pleasing Vivacity in the Temper and Behaviour of my beloved Spouse; who thereby shews he does not repent of his Goodness to me.

I attended him to Breakfast, and drank my Chocolate with great Pleasure, and eat two Bits of Toast; and he seemed quite pleased with me, and said, Now does my Dearest begin to look upon me with an Air of Serenity and Satisfaction: It shall be always, added he, my Delight to give you Occasion for this sweet becoming Aspect of Confidence and Pleasure in me.—My Heart, dear Sir, said I, is quite easy, and has lost all its foolish Tumults, which combating with my Gratitude, gave an ingrateful Appearance to my Behaviour: But now your Goodness, Sir, has enabled it to get the better of its uneasy Apprehensions, and my Heart is all of one Piece, and devoted to you, and grateful Tranquillity. And could I be so happy as to see you and my good Lady *Davers* reconciled, I have nothing in this World to wish for more, but the Continuance of your Favour. He said, I wish this Reconciliation, my Dearest, as well as you; and I do assure you, more for your sake than my own: And if she would behave tolerably, I would make the Terms easier to her for that Reason.

He said, I will lay down one Rule for you, my *Pamela*, to observe in your Dress; and I will tell you every thing I like or dislike, as it occurs to me; and I would have you do the same, on your Part, that nothing may lie upon either of our Minds that shall occasion the least Reservedness.

I have often observed, in marry'd Folks, that, in a little while, the Lady grows careless in her Dress; which, to me, looks as if she would take no Pains to secure the Affection she had gained, and shews a Slight to her Husband, that she had not to her Lover: Now, you must know, this has always given me great Offence; and I should not forgive it, even in my *Pamela*; tho' she would have this Excuse for herself, that thousands could not make, That she looks lovely in every thing. So, my Dear, I shall expect of you always, to be dress'd by Dinner-time, except something extraordinary happens; and this, whether you are to go abroad, or stay at home. For this, my Love, will continue to you that sweet Ease in your Dress and Behaviour, which you are so happy a Mistress of; and whoever I bring home with me to my Table, you will be in Readiness to receive them; and will not want to make those foolish Apologies, to unexpected Visitors, that carry with them a Reflection on the Conduct of those who make them; and besides, will convince me, that you think yourself obliged to appear as graceful to your Husband, as you would to Persons less familiar to your Sight.

This, dear Sir, said I, is a most obliging Injunction; and I most heartily thank you for it, and will always take care to obey it.—Why, my Dear, said he, you may better do this than half your Sex: Because they too generally act in such a manner, as if they seem'd to think it the Privilege of Birth and Fortune, to turn Day into Night, and Night into Day, and are seldom stirring till 'tis time to sit down to Dinner; and so all the good old Family Rules are revers'd; for they breakfast when they should dine; dine, when they should sup; and sup, when they should go to-bed; and, by the Help of dear Quadrille, sometimes go to-bed when they should rise.—In any thing but these, my Dear, continued he, I expect you to be a Lady. And my good Mother was one of this old-fashion'd Cut, tho', in all other respects, as worthy a Lady as any in the Kingdom. And so you have not been used to the new Way, and may the easier practise the other.

Dear Sir, said I, pray give me more of your sweet Injunctions. Why then, continued he, I shall, in the usual Course, and generally, if not hinder'd by Company, like to go to-bed with my Dearest, by Eleven; and if I don't, shan't hinder you. I ordinarily now rise by Six, in Summer. I will allow you to lie half an Hour after me, or so.

Then you'll have some time at your own Dispose, till you give me your Company to breakfast; which may be always so, as that we may have done at a little after Nine.

Then will you have several Hours, again, at your Disposal, till Two o'Clock, when I shall like to sit down at Table.

You will then have several useful Hours more to employ yourself in, as you shall best like; and I would generally go to Supper by Eight; and when we are resolved to stick to these old-fashion'd Rules, as near as we can, we shall make our Visitors conform to them too, and expect them from us, and suit themselves accordingly: For I have always observ'd, that it is in every one's Power to prescribe Rules to himself. It is only standing a few ridiculous Jests at first, and that too from such, generally, as are not the most worthy to be minded; and, after a while, they will say, It signifies nothing to ask him: He will have his own Way. There is no putting him out of his Byass. He is a regular Piece of Clockwork, will they joke, and all that: And why, my Dear, should we not be so? For Man is as frail a

Piece of Machinery, as any Clockwork whatever; and, by Irregularity, is as subject to be disorder'd.

Then, my Dear, continued the charming Man, when they see they are received, at my Times, with an open Countenance and chearful Heart; when they see Plenty and Variety at my Board, and meet a kind and hearty Welcome from us both, they will not offer to break in upon my Conditions, nor grudge me my regular Hours: And as most of these People have nothing to do, except to rise in a Morning, they may as well come to Breakfast with us, at half an Hour after Eight, in Summer, as at Ten or Eleven. To Dinner at Two, as at Four, Five, or Six; and to Supper at Eight, as at Ten or Eleven. And then our Servants too will know, generally, the Times of their Business, and the Hours of their Leisure or Recess; and we, as well as they, shall reap the Benefit of this Regularity. And who knows, my Dear, but we may revive the good old Fashion in our Neighbourhood, by this means?—At least, it will be doing our own Parts towards it; and answering the good Lesson I learned at School, *Every one mend one.*[1] And the worst that will happen will be, that when some of my Brother Rakes, such as those we were broke in upon, so unwelcomly, last *Thursday,* are got out of the Way, if that can ever be, and fall to considering whom they shall go to dine with in their Rambles, they will only say, We must not go to him; for his Dinner-time is over; and so they'll reserve me for another time, when they happen to suit it better; or, perhaps, they will take a Supper and a Bed with me instead of it.

Now, my Dearest, continued the kind Man, you see here are more of my Injunctions, as you call them; and tho' I will not be so set, as to quarrel if they are not always exactly comply'd with; yet, as I know you won't think them unreasonable, I shall be glad they may as often as they can; and you will give your Orders accordingly, to *your* Mrs. *Jervis,* who is a good Woman, and will take Pleasure in obeying you.

O dearest, dear Sir, said I, have you no more of your sweet Injunctions to honour me with? They oblige and improve me at the same time!—What a happy Lot is mine!—God Almighty reward your Goodness to me!

Why, let me see, my Dearest, said he.—But I think of no more at present. For it would be needless to say, how much I value you for your Sweetness of Temper, and that open Chearfulness of Countenance which adorns you, when nothing has given my Fairest Apprehensions for her Virtue: A Sweetness, and a Chearfulness, that prepossesses in your Favour, at first Sight, the Mind of every one that beholds you.—I need not, I hope, say, that I would have you diligently preserve this sweet Appearance: Let no thwarting Accident, no cross Fortune, (for we must not expect to be exempt from such, happy as we now are in each other!) deprive this sweet Face of this its principal Grace: And when any thing unpleasing happens, in a quarter of an Hour, at farthest, begin to mistrust yourself, and apply to your Glass; and if you see a Gloom arising, or arisen, banish it instantly, smooth your dear Countenance, resume your former Composure; and then, my Dearest, whose Heart must always be seen in her Face, and cannot be a Hypocrite, will find this a means to smooth her Passions also; and if the Occasion be too strong for so sudden a Conquest, she will know how to do it more effectually, by repairing to her Closet, and begging that gracious Assistance, which has never yet failed her: And so shall I, my Dear, who, as you once, but too justly, observ'd, have been too much indulged by my good Mother, have an Example from you, as well as a Pleasure in you which will hardly ever be palled.

One thing, continued he, I have frequently observed, at the Houses of other Gentlemen, That when we have unexpectedly visited, or broke in upon the Family Order, laid down by their Ladies; and especially if any of us have lain under the Suspicion of having occasionally seduced our marry'd Companion into bad Hours, or given indifferent Examples, the poor Gentleman has been oddly affected at our coming; tho' the good Breeding of the Lady has made her just keep up Appearances. He has looked so conscious; has been so afraid, as it were, to disoblige; has made so many Excuses for some of us, before we have been accused, as has always shewn me how unwelcome we have been; and how much he is obliged to compound with his Lady for a tolerable Reception of us; and, perhaps, she too, in Proportion to the honest Man's Concern to court her Smiles, has been more reserv'd, stiff and formal; and has behav'd with an Indifference, and Slight, that has often made me wish myself out of *her* House; for too plainly have I seen, that it was not *his*.

This, my Dear, you will judge by my Description, has afforded me Subject for Animadversion upon the marry'd Life; for a Man may not (tho', in the main, he is willing to flatter himself, that he is Master of his House, and will assert himself upon great Occasions, when his Prerogative is strongly invaded) be always willing to contend; and such Women as those I have described, are always ready to take the Field, and are worse Enemies than the old *Parthians*,[1] who annoy most, when they seem to retreat; and never fail to return to the Charge again, and carry on the offensive War, till they have tired out Resistance, and made the Husband willing, like a vanquish'd Enemy, to compound for small Matters, in order to preserve something. At least, the poor Man does not care to let his Friends see his Case, and so will not provoke a Fire to break out, that, he sees, (and so do his Friends too) the meek Lady has much ado to smother; and which, very possibly, burns with a most comfortable Ardour, after we are gone.

You smile, my *Pamela*, said he, at this whimsical Picture; and I am sure, I never shall have Reason to include you in these disagreeable Out-lines; but yet I will say, that I expect from you, whoever comes to my House, that you accustom yourself to one even, uniform Complaisance: That no Frown take place on your Brow: That however ill or well provided we may be for their Reception, you shew no Flutter or Discomposure: That whoever you may have in your Company at the Time, you signify not, by the least reserved Look, that the Stranger is come upon you unseasonably, or at a Time you wished not. But be facetious, kind, obliging to all; and if to any one more than another, to such as have the least Reason to expect it from you, or who are most inferior at the Table; for thus will you, my *Pamela*, chear the doubting Mind, quiet the uneasy Heart, and diffuse Ease, Pleasure, and Tranquillity around my Board.

And be sure, my Dear, continued he, let no little Accidents ruffle your Temper. I shall never forget once, that I was at Lady *Arthur*'s; and a Footman happen'd to stumble, and let fall a fine China Dish, and broke it all to pieces: It was grievous to see the Uneasiness it gave the poor Lady. And she was so sincere in it, that she suffer'd it to spread all over the Company, and it was a pretty large one too; and not a Person in it, but turn'd either her Consoler, or fell into Stories of the like Misfortunes; and so we all became, for the rest of the Evening, nothing but blundering Footmen, and careless Servants, or were turn'd into broken Jars, Plates, Glasses, Tea-cups, and such-like brittle Substances. And it affected me so much, that when I came home, I went to-bed, and dreamt, that *Robin*, with the Handle of his Whip, broke the Fore-glass of my Chariot; and I was so sollicitous, methought, to keep the good Lady in Countenance for *her* Anger, that I broke his Head in Revenge, and stabb'd one of my Coach-horses. And all the Comfort I had when it was done, methought, was, that I had not exposed myself before Company; and there were no Sufferers but guilty *Robin*, and one innocent Coach-horse; for when my Hand was in, I might as reasonably have killed the other three.

I was exceedingly diverted with these facetious Hints, and the pleasant manner in which he gave them; and I promis'd to improve by the excellent Lessons contain'd in them.

I then went up and dressed myself, as like a Bride as I could, in my best Cloaths, and, on Enquiry, finding my dearest Master was gone to walk in the Garden, I went to find him out. He was reading in the little Alcove; and I said, Sir, am I licens'd to intrude upon you, without your Commands?—No, my Dear, said he, because you cannot *intrude.* I am so wholly yours, that where-ever I am, you have not only a Right to join me; but you do me a very acceptable Favour at the same time.

I have, Sir, said I, obey'd your first kind Injunction, as to dressing myself before Dinner; but, may-be, you are busy, Sir? He put up the Paper he was reading, and said, I can have no Business or Pleasure of equal Value to your Company, my Dear. What was you going to say?—Only, Sir, to know, if you have any more kind Injunctions to give me?—I could hear you talk a whole Day together.—You are very obliging, *Pamela*, said he; but you are so perfectly what I wish, that I might have spar'd those I gave you; but I was willing you should have a Taste of my Freedom with you, to put you upon the like with me. For I am confident there can be no Friendship lasting without Freedom, and without communicating to one another even the little Caprices, if my *Pamela* can have any such, which may be most affecting to us.

Now, my Dear, said he, be so kind to find some Fault with me, and tell me what you would wish me to do, to appear more agreeable to you. O, Sir, said I, and I could have kissed him, but for Shame, (To be sure I shall grow a sad fond Hussy!) I have not one single thing to wish for; no, not one!—He saluted me very kindly, and said, he should be sorry if I had, and forbore to speak it. Do you think, my dear Sir, said I, that your *Pamela* has no Conscience? Do you think, that because you so kindly oblige her, and delight in obliging her, that she must rack her Invention for Trials of your Goodness, and knows not when she is happy!—O my dearest Sir, added I, less than one half of the Favours you have so generously conferred upon me, would have exceeded my utmost Wishes!

My dear Angel, said he, and kissed me again, I shall be troublesome to you with my Kisses, if you continue thus sweetly obliging, in your Actions and Expressions. O Sir, said I, I have been thinking, as I was dressing myself, what an excellent Example you have given me of the Lessons you teach me. For here, Sir, you are most charmingly dress'd yourself, as you have commanded me, before Dinner.

Then, Sir, when you command me, at your Table, to chear the doubting Mind, and comfort the uneasy Heart, and to behave most kindly to those who have least Reason to expect it, and are most inferior; how sweetly, in every Instance that could possibly occur, have you done this yourself, by your poor, unworthy *Pamela*, till you have diffused, in your own dear Words, Ease, Pleasure and Tranquillity around my glad Heart.

Then again, Sir, when you bid me not be disturbed by little Accidents, or by Strangers coming in upon me unexpectedly, how noble an Instance did you give me of this; when, on our dear Wedding day, the coming of Sir *Charles Hargrave*, and the other two Gentlemen, (for which you was quite unprovided, and hinder'd our Happiness of dining together on that chosen Day) did not so disturb you, but that you entertained the Gentlemen pleasantly, and parted with them civilly and kindly!—What charming Instances are these, I have been recollecting with Pleasure, of your pursuing the Doctrine you deliver!

My Dear, said he, these Observations are very kind in you, and much to my Advantage: But if I do not always, (for I fear these were too much Accidents) so well pursue the Doctrines I lay down, my *Pamela* must not expect that my Imperfections will be a Plea for her Non-observance of my Lessons, as you call them; for, I doubt, I shall never be half so perfect as you; and so I cannot permit you to fall back in your Goodness, tho' I may find myself unable to advance, as I ought, in my Duty.

I hope, Sir, said I, by God's Grace, I never shall. I believe it, said he; but I only mention this, knowing my own Defects, lest my future Lessons should not be so well warranted by my Practice, as in the Instances you have kindly recollected.

He was pleased to take Notice of my Dress, and spanning my Waste with his Hands,[1] said, What a sweet Shape is here! It would make one regret to lose it; and yet, my beloved *Pamela*, I shall think nothing but that Loss wanting, to complete my Happiness!—I put my bold Hand before his Mouth, and said, Hush, hush! O fie, Sir!—The freest thing you have ever yet said, since I have been yours!—He kissed my Hand, and said, Such an innocent Wish, my Dearest, may be permitted me, because it is the End of the Institution.—But say, Would such a Case be unwelcome to my *Pamela?*—I will say, Sir, said I, and hid my blushing Face on his Bosom, that your Wishes, in every thing, shall be mine; but pray, Sir, say no more!—He kindly saluted me, and thanked me, and changed the Subject.—I was not too free, I hope!

Thus we talked, till we heard the Coaches; and then he said, Stay here, in the Garden, my Dear, and I'll bring the Company to you. And when he was gone, I passing by the Back-door, kneeled down against it, and blessed God for not permitting my then so much desired Escape. I went to the Pond, and kneeled down on the mossy Bank, and again blessed God there, for his Mercy in my Escape from myself, my then worst Enemy, tho' I thought I had none but Enemies, and no Friend near me. And so I ought to do in almost every Step of this Garden, and every Room in this

House!—And I was bending my Steps to the dear little Chapel to make my Acknowledgment there; but I saw the Company coming towards me.

Miss *Darnford* said, So, Miss! how do you do now? O, you look so easy, so sweetly, so pleased, that I know you'll let me dance at your Wedding; for I shall long to be there. Lady *Jones* was pleased to say, I look'd like an Angel. And Mrs. *Peters* said, I improved upon them every time they saw me. Lady *Darnford* was also pleased to make me a fine Compliment, and said, I looked freer and easier every time she saw me. Dear-heart! I wish, thinks I, you would spare these Compliments; for I shall have some Joke, I doubt, passed upon me by-and-by, that will make me suffer for all these fine things.

Mr. *Peters* said, softly, God bless you, dear *Daughter!*—But not so much as my Wife knows it.—Sir *Simon* came in last, and took me by the Hand, and said, 'Squire *B.* by your Leave. And kissed my Hand five or six times, as if he was mad; and held it with both his, and made a very free Jest, by way of Compliment, in his Way. Well, I think a *young Rake* is hardly tolerable; but an *old Rake*, and an *old Beau*, are two very sad Things!—And all this before Daughters Women-grown!—I whisper'd my Dearest, a little after, and said, I fear I shall suffer much from Sir *Simon's* rude jokes, by-and-by, when you reveal the Matter!—'Tis his way, my Dear, said he; you must now grow above these things.—Miss *Nanny Darnford* said to me, with a sort of half-grave, ironical Air,—Well, Miss, if I may judge by your easy Deportment now, to what it was when I last saw you, I hope you will let my Sister, if you won't me, see the happy Knot ty'd! For she is quite wild about it.—I curcheed, and only said, You are all very good to me, Ladies.—Mr. *Peters's* Niece said, Well, Miss, I hope, before we part, we shall be told the happy Day. My good Master heard her, and said, You shall, you shall, Madam!—That's pure! said Miss *Darnford.*

He took me aside, and said, softly, Shall I lead them to the Alcove, and tell them there, or stay till we go in to Dinner?—Neither, Sir, I think, said I; I fear I shan't stand it.—Nay, said he, they must know it; I would not have invited them else.—Why then, Sir, said I, let it alone till they are going away.—Then, reply'd he, you must pull off your Ring. No, no, Sir, said I, that I must not.—Well, said he, do you tell Miss *Darnford* of it yourself.—Indeed, Sir, answer'd I, I cannot.

Mrs. *Jewkes* came officiously[1] to ask my Master, just then, if she should bring a Glass of Rhenish[2] and Sugar before Dinner for the Gentlemen and Ladies; and he said, That's well thought of; bring it, Mrs. *Jewkes.*

And she came, with *Nan* attending her, with two Bottles and Glasses, and a Salver; and must needs, making a low Curchee, offer first to me, saying, Will your Ladyship begin? I colour'd like Scarlet, and said, No;—my Master, to be sure!

But they all took the Hint; and Miss *Darnford* said, I'll be hang'd if they have not stole a Wedding. Said Mrs. *Peters*, It must be certainly so! Ah! Mr. *Peters*.

I'll assure you, said he, I have not marry'd them. Where were you, said she, and Mr. *Williams*, last *Thursday* Morning? Said Sir *Simon*, Let me alone, let me alone; if any thing has been stolen, I'll find it out; I'm a Justice of the Peace, you know. And so he took me by the Hand, and said, Come, Madam, answer me, by the Oath you have taken; Are you marry'd or not?

My Master smiled to see me look so like a Fool; and I said, Pray, Sir *Simon!*—Ay, ay, said he, I thought you did not look so smirking upon us for nothing.—Well then, *Pamela*, said my Master, since your Blushes discover you, don't be ashamed, but confess the Truth!

Now, said Miss *Darnford*, I am quite angry. And said Lady *Darnford*, I am quite pleas'd; let me give you Joy, dear Madam, if it be so. And so they all said, and saluted me round.—I was vexed it was before Mrs. *Jewkes*; for she shook her fat Sides, and seem'd highly pleas'd to be a Means of discovering it.

Nobody, said my Master, wishes me Joy. No, said Lady *Jones*, very obligingly, nobody need; for with such a peerless Spouse, you want no good Wishes!—And he saluted them; and when he came last to me, said, before them all, Now, my sweet Bride, my *Pamela*, let me conclude with you; for here I began to love, and here I desire to end loving, but not till my Life ends.

This was sweetly said, and taken great Notice of; and it was doing Credit to his own generous Choice, and vastly more than I merited.

But I was forced to stand a many more Jokes afterwards. For Sir *Simon* said, several times, Come, come, Madam, now you are become one of us, I shall be a little less scrupulous than I have been, I'll assure you.

When we came in to Dinner, I made no Difficulty of what all offer'd me, the Upper-end of the Table; and perform'd the Honours of it with pretty tolerable Presence of Mind, considering. And, with much ado, my good Benefactor promising to be down again before Winter, we got off the Ball; but appointed *Tuesday* Evening, at Lady *Darnford*'s, to take Leave of all this good Company, who promised to be there, my Master designing to set out on *Wednesday* Morning for *Bedfordshire*.

We had Prayers in the little Chapel, in the Afternoon; but they all wished for the good Clerk again, with great Encomiums upon you, my dear Father; and the Company staid Supper also, and departed exceeding well satisfied, and with abundance of Wishes for the Continuance of our mutual Happiness; and my Master desired Mr. *Peters* to answer for him to the Ringers, at the Town,[1] if they should hear of it, till our Return into this Country, and that then he would be bountiful to them; because he would not publickly declare it till he had first done so in *Bedfordshire*.

MONDAY, *the fifth Day.*

I have had very little of my dear Friend's Company this Day; for he only staid Breakfast with me, and rid out to see a sick Gentleman about eighteen Miles off, who begg'd (by a Man and Horse on purpose) to speak with him, believing he should not recover, and upon Part of whose Estate my Master has a Mortgage. He said, My Dearest, I shall be very uneasy, if I am oblig'd to tarry all Night from you; but, lest you should be alarm'd, if I don't come home by Ten, don't expect me: For poor Mr. *Carlton* and I have pretty large Concerns together, and if he should be very ill, and would be comforted by my Presence, (as I know he loves me, and his Family will be more in my Power if he dies, than I wish for) Charity will not let me refuse.

It is now Ten o'Clock at Night, and I fear he will not return. I fear for the sake of his poor sick Friend, who I doubt is worse. Tho' I know not the Gentleman, I am sorry for his own sake, for his Family's sake, and for my dear Master's sake, who by his kind Expressions I find loves him: And methinks I should be sorry any Grief should touch his generous Heart; tho' yet, there is no living in this World, without too many Occasions for Concern, even in the most prosperous State. And it is fit it should be so; or else, poor Wretches as we are! we should look no further, but be like sensual Travellers on a Journey homeward, who, meeting with good Entertainment at some Inn on the Way, put up their Rest there, and never think of pursuing their Journey to their proper Home.—This, I remember, was often a Reflection of my good Lady's, to whom I owe it.

Eleven o' Clock.

Mrs. *Jewkes* has been with me, and ask'd if I will have her for a Bedfellow in want of a better? I said, I thank'd her; but I would see how it was to lie by myself one Night.

I might have mention'd, that I made Mrs. *Jewkes* dine and sup with me, and she was much pleas'd with it, and my Behaviour to her. And I could see by her Manner, that she was a little struck inwardly at some of her former Conduct to me. But, poor Wretch, it is, I much fear, because I am what I am; for she has otherwise very little Remorse, I doubt.—Her Talk and Actions are intirely different from what they us'd to be, quite circumspect and decent; and I should have thought her virtuous, and even pious, had I never known her in another Light.

By this, we may see, my dear Father and Mother, of what Force Example is; and what is in the Power of the Heads of Families to do: And this shews, that evil Examples, in Superiors, are doubly pernicious, and doubly culpable, because such Persons are bad *themselves*, and not only do no *Good*, but much *Harm*, to *others*; and the Condemnation of such must, to be sure, be so much the greater!—And how much the greater still must my Condemnation be, who have had such a religious Education under you, and been so well nurtur'd by my good Lady, if I should forget, with all these Mercies heap'd upon me, what belongs to the Station God has preferr'd me to!—Oh how I long to be doing some Good! For all that is past yet, is my dear, dear Master's; God bless him! and return him safe to my Wishes; for methinks already 'tis a Week since I saw him! If my Love would not be troublesome and impertinent, I should be nothing else; for I have a true grateful Spirit, and I had Need to have such a one; for I am poor in every thing but Will.

TUESDAY Morning, Eleven o' Clock.

My dear, dear—Master (I'm sure I should still say; but I will learn to rise to a softer Epithet, now-and-then) is not yet come. I hope he is safe and well!—So Mrs. *Jewkes* and I went to Breakfast. But I can do nothing but talk and think of him, and all his Kindness to me, and to you, which is still me, more intimately!—I have just receiv'd a Letter from him, which he wrote Over-night, as I find by it, and sent early the next Morning. This is a Copy of it.

To Mrs. ANDREWS.

'My dearest PAMELA,   *Monday Night.*

'I hope my not coming home this Night will not frighten you. You may believe I can't help it. My poor Friend is so very ill, that I doubt he can't recover. His Desires to have me stay with him are so strong, that I shall sit up all Night with him, as it is now near One o' Clock in the Morning; for he can't bear me out of his Sight: And I have made him and his distress'd Wife and Children so easy, in the kindest Assurances I could give him, of my Consideration for him and them, that I am look'd upon (as the poor disconsolate Widow, as she, I doubt, will soon be, tells me) as their good Angel. I could have wish'd we had not engag'd to the good Neighbourhood at Sir *Simon*'s for to-morrow Night; but I am so desirous to set out on *Wednesday* for the other House, that, as well as in Return for the Civilities of so many good Friends, who will be there on Purpose, I would not put it off. What I beg of you, therefore, my Dear, is, that you would go in the Chariot to Sir *Simon*'s, the sooner in the Day the better, because you will be diverted with the Company, who all so much admire you; and I hope to join you there by your Tea-time in the Afternoon, which will be better than going home, and returning with you, as it will be six Miles Difference to me; and I know the good Company will excuse my Dress, on the Occasion. I count every Hour of this little Absence for a Day; for I am, with the utmost Sincerity,

'My dearest Love,
'For ever Yours, &c.

'If you could go to dine with them, it will be a Freedom that would be very pleasing to them, and the more, as they don't expect it.'

I began to have a little Concern, lest his Fatigue should be too great, and for the poor sick Gentleman and Family; but told Mrs. *Jewkes*, that the least Intimation of his Choice should be a Command to me, and so I would go to Dinner there; and order'd the Chariot to be got ready to carry me: when a Messenger came up, just as I was dress'd, to tell her, she must come down immediately. I see at the Window, that Visitors are come; for there is a Chariot and six Horses, the Company gone out of it, and three Footmen on Horseback; and I think the Chariot has Coronets. Who can it be, I wonder?—But here I will stop, for I suppose I shall soon know.

Good-sirs! how unlucky this is! What shall I do?—Here is Lady *Davers* come; her ownself! And my kind Protector a great, great many Miles off.—Mrs. *Jewkes* out of Breath comes and tells me this, and says she is inquiring for my Master and me. She ask'd her, it seems, naughty Lady as she is, if I was *whor'd* yet! There's a Word for a Lady's Mouth!—Mrs. *Jewkes* says, she knew not what to answer. And my Lady said, She is not marry'd, I hope? And, said she, I said, No; because you have not own'd it yet publickly. My Lady said, That was well enough. Said I, I will run away, Mrs. *Jewkes*; and let the Chariot go to the Bottom of the Elm-walk, and I will steal out of the Door unperceiv'd.—But, said she, she is inquiring for you, Madam, and I said you was within, but going out; and she said, she would see you presently, as soon as she could have Patience. What did she call me, said I? *The Creature*, Madam: *I will see the Creature*, said she, *as soon as I can have Patience.* Ay, but, said I, *the Creature* won't let her, if she can help it.

Pray, Mrs. *Jewkes* favour my Escape for this once, for I am sadly frighted.—Said she, I'll bid the Chariot go down as you order, and wait till you come; and I'll step down, and shut the Hall-door, that you may pass down unobserv'd; for she sits cooling herself in the Parlour over-against the Stair-case. That's a good Mrs. *Jewkes!* said I: But who has she with her? Her Woman, said she, and her Nephew; but he is on Horseback, and is gone into the Stables; and they have three Footmen.—And I wish, said I, they were all *three* hundred Miles off!—What shall I do!—So I wrote thus far, and wait impatiently to hear the Coast is clear.—

Mrs. *Jewkes* tells me, I must come down, or she will come up. What does she call me now? said I. *Wench*, Madam. *Bid the Wench come down to me.* And her Nephew, and her Woman are with her.

Said I, I can't go, and that's enough!—You might contrive it that I might get out, if you would.—Indeed, Madam, said she, I cannot; for I went to shut the Door, and she bid me let it stand open; and there she sits over-against the Stair-case. Then, said I, I'll get out of the Window, I think!—(and fann'd myself) for I am sadly frighted. Laud, Madam, said she, I wonder you so much disturb yourself!—You're on the right Side the Hedge,¹ I'm sure; and I would not be so discompos'd for any body. Ay, said I, but who can help Constitution? I dare say you would no more be so discompos'd, than I can help it.—Said she, Indeed, Madam, if it was to me, I would put on an Air as Mistress of the House, as you are, and go and salute her Ladyship, and bid her welcome. Ay, ay, reply'd I, fine Talking!—But how unlucky this is, your good Master is not at home!

What Answer shall I give her, said she, to her desiring to see you?—Tell her, said I, I am sick a-bed; I'm dying,² and must not be disturb'd; I'm gone out,—or any thing!

But her Woman came up to me, just as I had utter'd this, and said, How do you do, Mrs. *Pamela?* My Lady desires to speak with you. So I must go.—Sure she won't beat me!—Oh that my dear Protector was at home!

Well, now I will tell you all that happen'd in this frightful Interview.—And very bad it was.

I went down, dress'd as I was, and my Gloves on, and my Fan in my Hand, to be just ready to get into the Chariot, when I could get away; and I thought all my trembling Fits had been over now; but I was mistaken, for I trembled sadly. Yet resolv'd to put on as good an Air as I could.

So I went to the Parlour, and said, making a very low Curchee, Your Servant, my good Lady! And your Servant again, said she, *my Lady*, for I think you are dress'd out like one.

A charming Girl tho', said her rakish Nephew, and swore a great Oath; dear Aunt, forgive me, but I must kiss her, and was coming to me. And I said, Forbear, uncivil Gentleman! I won't be us'd freely. *Jackey*, said my Lady, sit down, and don't touch the Creature!—She's proud enough already. There's a great Difference in her Air, I'll assure you, since I saw her last.

Well, Child, said she, sneeringly, how dost find thyself?—Thou'rt mightily come on of late!—I hear strange Reports about thee!—Thou'rt almost got into Fool's Paradise,[1] I doubt!—And wilt find thyself terribly mistaken in a little while, if thou thinkest my Brother will disgrace his Family to humour thy Baby-face!

I see, said I, sadly vex'd, (her Woman and Nephew smiling by) your Ladyship has no very important Commands for me, and I beg Leave to withdraw. *Beck*, said she, to her Woman, shut the Door; my young Lady and I must not have done so soon.

Where's your well-manner'd Deceiver gone, Child? says she.—Said I, When your Ladyship is pleas'd to speak intelligibly, I shall know how to answer.

Well, but my dear Child, said she in Drollery, don't be too pert neither, I beseech thee. Thou wilt not find thy Master's Sister half so ready to take thy Freedoms, as thy mannerly Master is!—So, a little of that Modesty and Humility that my Mother's Waiting-maid used to shew, will become thee better than the Airs thou givest thyself, since my Mother's Son has taught thee to forget thyself.

I would beg, said I, one Favour of your Ladyship, that if you would have me keep my Distance, you will not forget your own Degree.—Why, suppose, *Miss Pert*, I should forget my Degree, wouldst thou not keep thy Distance then?

If you, Madam, said I, lessen the Distance yourself, you will descend to my Level, and make an Equality, which I don't presume to think of; for I can't descend lower than I am,—at least in your Ladyship's Esteem!

Did I not tell you, *Jackey*, said she, that I should have a Wit to talk to?—He, who swears like a Gentleman, at every Word, rapt out an Oath, and said, drolling, I think, Mrs. *Pamela*, if I may be so bold as to say so, you should know you are speaking to Lady *Davers!*—Sir, said I, I hope there was no Need for your Information, and so I can't thank you for it; especially as you seem to think it wants an Oath to convince me of it.

He look'd more foolish than I at this, if possible, not expecting such a Reprimand—And said at last, Why, Mrs. *Pamela*, you put me half out of Countenance with your witty Reproof!—Sir, said I, you seem quite a fine Gentleman, and it will not be easily done, I dare say.

How now, Pert-ones, said my Lady, do you know who you talk to?—I think I do not, Madam, reply'd I: And, for fear I should forget myself more, I'll withdraw. Your Ladyship's Servant, said I, and was going: But she rose, and gave me a Push, and pull'd a Chair, and setting the Back against the Door, sat down in it.

Well, said I, I can bear any thing at your Ladyship's Hands; but I was ready to cry tho'. And I went, and sat down, and fann'd myself at the other End of the Room.

Her Woman, who stood all the Time, said softly, Mrs. *Pamela*, you should not sit in my Lady's Presence. And my Lady, tho' she did not hear her, said, You shall sit down, Child, in the Room where I am, when I give you Leave.

So I stood up, and said, When your Ladyship will hardly permit me to stand, one might be indulg'd to sit down. But I ask'd you, said she, Whither your Master is gone? To one Mr. *Carlton*, Madam, said I, about eighteen Miles off, who is very sick. And when does he come home?— This Evening, Madam, said I. And where are you going? To a Gentleman's House in the Town, Madam. And how was you to go?—In the Chariot, Madam.—Why, you must be a Lady in time, to be sure!—I believe you'd become a Chariot mighty well, Child!—Was you ever out in it, with your Master?

Pray your Ladyship, said I, be pleased to ask half a dozen such Questions together; because one Answer may do for all!—Why, Boldface, said she, you'll forget your Distance, and bring me to your Level before my Time.

So I could no longer refrain Tears, but said, Pray your Ladyship, let me ask what I have done to be thus severely treated? I never did your Ladyship any Harm. And if you think I am deceived, as you was pleas'd to hint, I should be more intitled to your Pity than your Anger.

She arose, and took me by the Hand, and led me to her Chair, and then sat down; and still holding my Hand, said, Why, *Pamela*, I did indeed pity you while I thought you innocent; and when my Brother seiz'd you, and brought you down hither, without your Consent, I was concern'd for you. And I was still more concern'd for you, and lov'd you, when I heard of your Virtue and Resistance, and your virtuous Efforts to get away from him. But when, as I fear, you have suffer'd yourself to be prevail'd upon, and have lost your Innocence, and added another to the Number of the Fools he has ruin'd, *(This shock'd me a little!)* I cannot help shewing my Displeasure to you.

Madam, reply'd I, I must beg no hasty Judgment; I have not lost my Innocence!—Take care, take care, *Pamela*, said she!—Don't lose your Veracity, as well as your Honour!—Why are you here, when you are at full Liberty to go whither you please?—I will make one Proposal to you, and if you are innocent, I am sure you'll accept it. Will you go and live with me?—I will instantly set out with you, in my Chariot, and not stay half an Hour longer in this House, if you'll go with me.—Now, if you're innocent, and willing to keep so, deny me, if you can.

I am innocent, Madam, reply'd I, and willing to keep so; and yet I cannot consent to this. Then, said she, very mannerly, Thou lyest, Child, that's all; and I give thee up!

And so she arose, and walk'd about the Room in great Wrath. Her Nephew and her Woman said, Your Ladyship's very good; 'tis a plain Case; a very plain Case!

I would have remov'd the Chair, to have gone out, but her Nephew came and sat in it. This provok'd me; for I thought I should be unworthy of the Honour I was rais'd to, tho' I was afraid to own it, if I did not shew some Spirit; and I said, What, Sir, is your Pretence in this House, to keep me a Prisoner here? Because, said he,—I like it.—Do you so, Sir? reply'd I: If that's the Answer of a Gentleman to such a one as I, it would not, I dare say, be the Answer of a Gentleman to a Gentleman.—My Lady! my Lady! said he, a Challenge, a Challenge, by Gad! No, Sir, said I, I am of a

Sex that gives no Challenges; and you think so too, or you would not give this Occasion for the Word.

Said my Lady, Don't be surpriz'd, Nephew; the Wench could not talk thus, if she had not been her Master's Bed-fellow.—*Pamela, Pamela*, said she, and tapp'd me upon the Shoulder, two or three times, in Anger, thou hast lost thy Innocence, Girl; and thou hast got some of thy bold Master's Assurance, and art fit to go any-whither.—Then, and please your Ladyship, said I, I am unworthy of your Presence, and desire I may quit it.

No, reply'd she, I will know first what Reason you can give for not accepting my Proposal, if you are innocent? I can give, said I, a very good one; but I beg to be excus'd. I will hear it, said she. Why then, answer'd I, I should perhaps have less Reason to like this Gentleman, than where I am.

Well then, said she, I'll put you to another Trial. I'll set out this Moment with you to your Father and Mother, and give you up safe to them. What do you say to that?—Ay, Mrs. *Pamela*, said her Nephew, now what does your Innocence say to that?—'Fore Gad, Madam, you have puzzled her now.

Be pleas'd, Madam, said I, to call off this fine Gentleman. Your Kindness in these Proposals makes me hope you will not have me baited. I'll be d---- said he, if she does not make me a Bull-dog! Why she'll toss us all by-and-by! Sir, said I, you indeed behave as if you were in a Bear-garden.[1]

Jackey, be quiet, said my Lady. You only give her a Pretence to evade my Questions. Come, answer me, *Pamela*. I will, Madam, said I, and it is thus: I have no Occasion to be beholden to your Ladyship for this Honour; for I am to set out to-morrow Morning on the Way to my Parents.—Now again, thou lyest, Wench.—I am not of Quality, said I, to answer to such Language.—Once again, said she, provoke me not, by these Reflections, and this Pertness; if thou dost, I shall do something by thee unworthy of myself. That, thinks I, you have done already; but I ventur'd not to say so. But who is to carry you, said she, to your Father and Mother? Who my Master pleases, Madam, said I. Ay, said she, I doubt not, thou wilt do every thing he pleases, if thou hast not already. Why now tell me, *Pamela*, from thy Heart, hast thou not been in Bed with thy Master? Ha, Wench!—I was quite shock'd at this, and said, I wonder how your Ladyship can use me thus!—I am sure you can expect no Answer; and my Sex, and my tender Years, might exempt me from such Treatment, with a Person of your Ladyship's Birth and Quality, and who, be the Distance ever so great, is of the same Sex with me.

Thou art a confident Wench, said she, I see!—Pray, Madam, said I, let me beg you to permit me to go. I am waited for in the Town to Dinner. No, reply'd she, I can't spare you, and whoever you are to go to, will excuse you, when they are told 'tis I that commands you not to go;—and you may excuse it too, young Lady *Wou'd-be,*[1] if you consider that 'tis the unexpected Coming of your late Lady's Daughter, and your Master's Sister, that commands your Stay.

But a Pre-engagement, your Ladyship will consider, is something!—Ay, so it is; but I know not what Reason Waiting-maids have to assume these Airs of *Pre-engagements!*—Oh *Pamela, Pamela,* I am sorry for thy thus aping thy Betters, and giving thyself such Airs; I see thou'rt quite spoil'd! Of a modest, innocent Girl, that thou wast, and humble too, thou now art fit for nothing in the World, but what I fear thou art.

Why, please your Ladyship, said her Kinsman, what signifies all you say? The Matter's over with her, no doubt; and she likes it; and she is in a Fairy-dream, and 'tis pity to awaken her before her Dream's out.—Bad as you take me to be, Madam, said I, I am not used to such Language or Reflections as this Gentleman gives me; and I won't bear it.

Well, *Jackey,* said she, be silent; and shaking her Head, Poor Girl, said she!———What a sweet Innocence is here destroy'd!—A thousand Pities!— I could cry over her, if that would do her good! But she is quite lost, quite undone; and then has assum'd a Carriage upon it, that all those Creatures are distinguish'd by!—

I cry'd sadly for Vexation; and said, Say what you please, Madam: If I can help it, I will not answer another Word.—

Mrs. *Jewkes* came in, and ask'd, If her Ladyship was ready for Dinner. She said, Yes. I would have gone out with her; but my Lady said, taking my Hand, she could not spare me. And, Miss, said she, you may pull off your Gloves, and lay your Fan by, for you shan't go; and if you behave well, you shall wait upon me at Dinner, and then I shall have a little further Talk with you.

Mrs. *Jewkes* said to me, Madam, may I speak one Word with you?—I can't tell, Mrs. *Jewkes,* said I; for my Lady holds my Hand, and you see I am a kind of Prisoner.

What you have to say, Mrs. *Jewkes,* said she, you may speak before me. But she went out, and seem'd vex'd for me; and she says, I look'd like the very Scarlet.

The Cloth was laid in another Parlour, and for three Persons, and she led me in: Come, my little Dear, said she, with a Sneer, I'll hand you in, and I wou'd have you think it as well as if it was my Brother.

What a sad Case, thought I, should I be in, if I were as naughty as she thinks me! It was bad enough as it was.

Jackey, said my Lady, come, let us go to Dinner. She said to her Woman, Do you, *Beck*, help *Pamela* to 'tend us; we will have no Men-fellows.—Come, my young Lady, shall I help you off with your white Gloves?—I have not, Madam, said I, deserv'd this at your Ladyship's Hands.

Mrs. *Jewkes* coming in with the first Dish, she said, Do you expect any body else, Mrs. *Jewkes*, that you lay the Cloth for three?—Said she, I hop'd your Ladyship and Madam would have been so well reconcil'd, that she would have sat down too.—What means the clownish Woman? said my Lady, in great Disdain: Could you think the Creature should sit down with me.—She does, Madam, and please your Ladyship, with my Master.—I doubt it not, good Woman, said she, and lyes with him too, does she not? Answer me, Fat-face!—How these Ladies are privileg'd!

If she does, Madam, said she, there may be a Reason for it, perhaps! And went out.—So, said she, has the Wench got thee over too!—Come, my little Dear, pull off thy Gloves, I say; and off she pull'd my Left Glove herself, and 'spy'd my Ring. O my dear God! said she, if the Wench has not got a Ring!—Well, this is a pretty Piece of Foolery, indeed! Dost know, my Friend, that thou art miserably trick'd!—And so, poor Innocent, thou hast made a fine Exchange, hast thou not? Thy Honesty for this Bauble! And I'll warrant, my little Dear has topp'd her Part, and paraded it like any real Wife; and so mimicks still the Condition!—Why, said she, and turn'd me round, thou art as mincing as any Bride! No wonder thou art thus trick'd out, and talkest of thy *Pre-engagements!*—Pr'ythee, Child, walk before me to that Glass, survey thyself, and come back to me, that I may see how finely thou canst act the Theatrical Part given thee!

I was then resolv'd to try to be silent; although most sadly vex'd.—So I went and sat me down in the Window, and she took her Place at the upper End of the Table; and her sawcy *Jackey*, fleering at me most provokingly, sat down by her.—Said he, Shall not the Bride sit down by us, Madam? Ay, well thought of, said my Lady: Pray, Mrs. Bride, your Pardon for sitting down in your Place?—I said nothing.

Said she, with a poor Pun, Thou hast some Modesty, however, Child! For thou canst not *stand it*, so must *sit down*, tho' in my Presence!—I still kept my Seat, and said nothing.—Thinks I, this is a sad Thing, and I am

hinder'd too from shewing my Duty where it is most due, and shall have
Anger there too, may-be, if my dear Master should be there before me!—
So she eat some Soup, as did her Kinsman; and then as she was cutting up
a Fowl, said, If thou *long'st*, my little Dear, I will help thee to a Pinion, or
Breast, or any thing. But may-be, Child, said he, thou likest the Rump,
shall I bring it thee? And then laugh'd like an Idiot, for all he is a Lord's
Son, and may be a Lord himself.—For he is the Son of the Lord ——;
and his Mother, who was Lord *Davers's* Sister, being dead, he has receiv'd
what Education he has, from Lord *Davers's* Direction. Poor Wretch! for
all his Greatness! he'll ne'er die for a Plot,—at least of his own hatching.
If I could then have gone up, I would have given you his Picture. But for
one of 25 or 26 Years of Age, much about the Age of my dear Master, he
is a most odd Mortal.

Pamela, said my Lady, help me to a Glass of Wine. No, *Beck*, said she,
you shan't; for she was offering to do it. I will have my Lady Bride confer
that Honour upon me; and then I shall see if she can *stand up*. I was silent,
and never stirr'd.

Dost hear, *Chastity?* said she. Help me to a Glass of Wine, when I bid
thee.—What! not stir! Then I'll come and help thee to one. Still I stirr'd
not, and fanning myself, continu'd silent. Said she, When I have ask'd thee,
Meek-ones, half a dozen Questions together, I suppose thou wilt answer
them all at once! Pretty Creature, is not that it?

I was so vex'd, I bit a Piece of my Fan out, not knowing what I did; but
still I said nothing, and did nothing but flutter it, and fan myself.

I believe, said she, my next Question will make up half a dozen; and
then, Modest-ones, I shall be intitled to an Answer.

He arose, and brought the Bottle and Glass, Come, said he, Mrs. Bride,
be pleas'd to help my Lady, and I will be your Deputy. Sir, reply'd I, it is
in a good Hand; help my Lady yourself.—Why, Creature, said she, dost
thou think thyself above it?—And then flew into a Passion, Insolence!
continued she, this Moment, when I bid you, know your Duty, and give
me a Glass of Wine; or—

So, I took a little Spirit then—thinks I, I can but be beat—If, said I, to
attend your Ladyship at Table, or even kneel at your Feet, was requir'd of
me, I would most gladly do it, were I only the Person you think me; but,
if it be to triumph over one who has received Honours, that she thinks
requires her to act another Part, not to be utterly unworthy of them, I must
say, I cannot do it.

She seem'd quite surpriz'd, and look'd now upon her Kinsman, and then
upon her Woman.—I'm astonish'd! I'm quite astonish'd!—Well then, I

suppose you would have me conclude you my Brother's Wife; wou'd you not?

Your Ladyship, said I, compels this from me!—Well, return'd she, but dost thou thyself think thou art so?—Silence, said her Kinsman, gives Consent.[1] 'Tis plain enough she does. Shall I rise, Madam, and pay my Duty to my new Aunt?

Tell me, said my Lady, what, in the Name of Impudence, possesses thee, to dare to look upon thyself as my Sister?—Madam, reply'd I, that is a Question will better become your most worthy Brother to answer, than me?

She was rising in great Wrath; but her Woman said, Good your Lady-ship; you'll do yourself more Harm, than her; and if the poor Girl has been deluded so, as you have heard, with the Sham-marriage, she'll be more deserving of your Ladyship's Pity than Anger. True, *Beck*, very true, said my Lady; but there's no bearing the Impudence of the Creature mean-time.

I would have gone out at the Door, but her Kinsman run and set his Back against it. I expected bad Treatment from her Pride and violent Temper; but this was worse than I could have thought of. And I said to him, Sir, when my Master comes to know your rude Behaviour, you will, may-be, have Cause to repent it. And went and sat down in the Window again.

Another Challenge, by Gad! said he; but I am glad she says her *Master!*—You see, Madam, she herself does not believe she is marry'd, and so has not been so much deluded as you think for. And coming to me with a most barbarous Air of Insult, he said, kneeling on one Knee before me; My new Aunt, your *Blessing*, or your *Curse*, I care not which; but quickly give me one or other, that I may not lose my Dinner!

I gave him a most contemptuous Look: Tinsel'd Toy, said I, (for he was lac'd all over) Twenty or Thirty Years hence, when you are *at Age*, I shall know how to answer you better; mean-time, sport with your Footmen, and not me! And so I remov'd to another Window nearer the Door, and he look'd like a sad Foolish, as he is.

Beck, Beck, said my Lady, this is not to be borne! Was ever the like heard! Is my Kinsman and Lord *Davers's* to be thus used by such a Slut? And was coming to me: And indeed I began to be afraid; for I have but a poor Heart, after all. But Mrs. *Jewkes*, hearing high Words, came in again, with the second Course, and said, Pray your Ladyship, don't so discompose yourself. I am afraid this Day's Business will make Matters wider than ever between your good Ladyship and your Brother: For my Master doats upon Madam.

Woman, said she, do thou be silent! Sure, I, that was born in this House, may have some Privilege in it, without being talk'd to by the saucy Servants in it!

I beg Pardon, Madam, reply'd Mrs. *Jewkes*; and turning to me, said, Madam, my Master will take it very ill, if you make him wait for you thus. So I rose to go out; but my Lady said, If it was only for *that* Reason, she shan't go.—And went to the Door, and shut it, and said to Mrs. *Jewkes*, Woman, don't come again till I call you; and coming to me, took my Hand, and said, Find your Legs, Miss, if you please.

I stood up, and she tapp'd my Cheek! Oh! says she, that scarlet Glow shews what a rancorous little Heart thou hast, if thou durst shew it; but come this way. And so led me to her Chair: Stand there, said she, and answer me a few Questions while I dine, and I'll dismiss thee, till I call thy impudent Master to Account; and then I'll have you Face to Face, and all this Mystery of Iniquity shall be unravell'd; for, between you, I will come to the Bottom of it.

When she had sat down, I mov'd to the Window on the other Side the Parlour, looking into the private Garden; and her Woman said, Mrs. *Pamela*, don't make my Lady angry. Stand by her Ladyship, as she bids you. Said I, Pray, good now, let it suffice you to attend your *Lady's* Commands, and don't lay *yours* upon *me*.—Your Pardon, sweet Mrs. *Pamela*, said she. Times are much alter'd with you, I'll assure you! Said I, Her Ladyship has a very good Plea to be free in the House that she was *born* in. But you may as well confine your Freedoms to the House in which you had your *Breeding*. Why, how now, Mrs. *Pamela*, said she! Since you provoke me to it, I'll tell you a Piece of my Mind. Hush, hush, *good Woman*, said I, alluding to my Lady's Language to Mrs. *Jewkes*; my Lady wants not your Assistance!—Besides, I can't scold!

The Woman was ready to stutter with Vexation; and Lord *Jackey* laugh'd as if he would burst his Sides; G— d— me, *Beck*, said he, you'd better let her alone to my Lady here; for she'll be too many for twenty such as you and I.—And then he laugh'd again, and repeated— *I can't scold*, quoth-a! but, by Gad, Miss, you can speak d—d spightful Words, I can tell you that!—Poor *Beck!* poor *Beck!*—'Fore Gad, she's quite dumb-founder'd!

Well, but, *Pamela*, said my Lady, come hither, and tell me truly: Dost thou think thyself really marry'd?—Said I, and approach'd her Chair, My good Lady, I will answer all your Commands, if you'll have Patience with me, and not be so angry as you are; but I can't bear to be us'd thus by this Gentleman, and your Ladyship's Woman. Child, said she, thou art very impertinent to my Kinsman; thou can'st not be civil to me; and my Ladyship's Woman is much thy Betters. But that's not the Thing!—Dost thou think thou art really marry'd?

I see, Madam, said I, you are resolv'd not to be pleas'd with *any* Answer I shall return: If I should say, I am not, then your Ladyship will call me hard Names, and perhaps I should tell a Fib. If I should say, I am, your Ladyship will ask how I have the Impudence to be so,—and will call it a Sham-marriage. I will, said she, be answer'd more directly. Why, what, and please your Ladyship, does it signify what I think? Your Ladyship will believe as you please.

But canst thou have the Vanity, the Pride, the Folly, said she, to think thyself actually marry'd to *my* Brother? He is no Fool, Child; and Libertine enough of Conscience; and thou art not the first in the List of his credulous Harlots.—Well, well, said I, (and was in a sad Flutter) as I am easy and pleas'd with my Lot, pray your Ladyship let me continue so, as long as I can. It will be Time enough for me to know the worst, when the worst comes. And if it will be so bad, your Ladyship should pity me, rather than thus torment me before my Time.

Well, said she, but dost not think I am concern'd that a young Wench, whom my poor dear Mother lov'd so well, should thus cast herself away, and suffer herself to be deluded and undone, after such a noble Stand as thou mad'st for so long a Time?

I think myself far from being deluded and undone, and please your Ladyship, and am as innocent and virtuous as ever I was in my Life. Thou lyest, Child, said she. So your Ladyship told me *twice* before!

She gave me a Slap on the Hand for this; and I made a low Curchee, and said, I humbly thank your Ladyship!—but I could not refrain Tears. And added, Your dear Brother, Madam, however, won't thank your Ladyship for this Usage of me, tho' I do. Come a little nearer me, my Dear, said she, and thou shalt have a little more than *that* to tell him of, if thou think'st thou hast not made Mischief enough already between a Sister and Brother. But, Child, if he was here, I would serve thee worse, and him too. I wish he was, said I.—Dost thou threaten me, Mischief-maker, and insolent as thou art?

Now, pray your Ladyship, said I, (but got to a little Distance) be pleas'd to reflect upon all that you have said to me, since I have had the *Honour*, or rather *Misfortune*, to come into your Presence; whether you have said *one* Thing befitting your Ladyship's Degree to me, even supposing I was the Wench, and the Creature, you suppose me to be?—Come hither, my pert Dear, reply'd she; come but within my Reach for one Moment, and I'll answer thee as thou deservest.

To be sure she meant to box my Ears. But I should be unworthy of my happy Lot, if I could not shew some Spirit.

When the Cloth was taken away, I said, I suppose I may now depart your Presence, Madam? I suppose not, said she. Why, I'll lay thee a Wager, Child, thy Stomach's too full to eat, and so thou may'st fast till thy mannerly Master comes home.

Pray your Ladyship, said her Woman, let the poor Girl sit down at Table with Mrs. *Jewkes* and me.—Said I, you are very kind, Mrs. *Worden*; but Times, as you said, are much alter'd with me; and I have been of late so much honour'd by better Company, that I can't stoop to yours.

Was ever such Confidence, said my Lady! Poor *Beck*, poor *Beck*, said her Kinsman; why, she beats you quite out of the Pit!¹—Will your Ladyship, said I, be pleased to tell me how long I am to tarry? For you'll please to see by that Letter, that I am oblig'd to attend my Master's Commands. And so I gave her the dear Gentleman's Letter from Mr. *Carlton*'s, which I thought would make her use me better, as she might judge by it of the Honour done me by him. Ay, said she, this is my worthy Brother's Hand. It is directed to Mrs. *Andrews*. That's to you, I suppose, Child? And so she read on, making Remarks as she went along, in this manner:

My dearest PAMELA,—"Mighty well!"—*I hope my not coming home this Night will not frighten you!*—"Vastly tender, indeed!—And did it frighten you, Child!"—*You may believe I can't help it.* "No, to be sure!—A Person in thy Way of Life, is more tenderly used than an honest Wife. But mark the End of it!"—*I could have wish'd,* "Prythee, *Jackey*, mind this," *we* "mind the significant *We*," *had not engaged to the good Neighbourhood, at Sir* Simon's *for to-morrow Night.*——"Why, does the good Neighbourhood, and does Sir *Simon*, permit thy Visits, Child? They shall have none of mine then, I'll assure them!" *But I am so desirous to set out on* Wednesday *for the other House*—"So, *Jackey*, we but just nick'd it, I find."—*that, as well as in Return for the Civilities of so many good Friends, who will be there on purpose, I would not put it off.*—"Now mind, *Jackey*."—*What I beg of you,*—"Mind the Wretch, that could use me and your Uncle, as he has done; he is turn'd Beggar to this Creature!" *I beg of you, therefore, my Dear,* "My *Dear!* there's for you!—I wish I may not be quite sick before I get thro'."—*What I beg of you, therefore, my Dear,* [and then she look'd me full in the Face] *is, that you will go in the Chariot to Sir* Simon's, *the sooner in the Day, the better;*—"Dear Heart! and why so, when WE were not expected till Night? Why, pray observe the Reason—Hem!" [said she] *Because you will be diverted with the Company;* "Mighty kind indeed!"——*who all,* "*Jackey, Jackey*, mind this,"—*who all so much admire you.* "Now he'd ha' been hang'd to have said so complaisant a thing, had he been marry'd, I'm sure!"—"Very true, Aunt, said he: A plain Case that!"—[Thinks I, that's hard upon poor Matrimony, tho'. I hope my Lady don't find it so. But I durst not speak out.] *Who all so much admire you,* [said she] "I must repeat that—Pretty Miss—I wish thou wast as *admirable* for thy Virtue, as for that Baby-face of thine!"—*And I hope to join you there by your Tea-time, in the Afternoon!*—"So, you're in very good Time, Child, an Hour or two hence, to answer all your important Pre-engagements!"—*which will be better than going home, and returning with you; as it will be six Miles Difference to me; and I know the good Company will excuse my Dress on the Occasion.* "Very true, any Dress is good enough, I'm sure, for such Company as *admire* thee, Child, for a Companion in thy ruin'd State!—*Jackey, Jackey,* mind, mind again! more fine things still." *I count every Hour of this little Absence for a Day;*—"There's for you! Let me repeat it," *I count every Hour of this little Absence for a Day!*—"Mind too the Wit of the good Man! One may see Love is a new thing to him. Here is a very tedious time gone since he saw his Deary; no less than, according to *his* amorous Calculation, a Dozen Days and Nights, at least! and yet, TEDIOUS as it is, it is but a LITTLE ABSENCE. Well said, my good accurate and consistent Brother.—But wise Men in Love, are always the greatest Simpletons!—But now comes the Reason, why this LITTLE Absence, which, at the same time, is so GREAT an Absence, is so *tedious.*" FOR *I am,* "Ay, now for it!"—*with the utmost Sincerity, My dearest Love,* "Out upon DEAREST LOVE! I shall never love the Word again! Pray bid your Uncle never call me Dearest Love, *Jackey!*"—*For Ever Yours!*—"But, Brother, thou lyest!—Thou knowest thou dost.—And so, my good Lady *Andrews,* or what shall I call you? Your *dearest Love* will be *for Ever Yours!* And hast thou the Vanity to believe this!—But stay, here is a Postscript. The poor Man knew not when to have done to his *dearest Love.*—He's sadly in for't, truly! Why, *his dearest Love,* you are mighty happy in such a Lover!"—*If you could go to dine with them,*—"Cry your Mercy, my *dearest Love,* now comes the Pre-engagement!" *it will be a Freedom that will be very pleasing to them, and the more as they don't expect it.*

Well, so much for this kind Letter! But you see you cannot honour this admiring Company with this little-expected, and, but in Complaisance to his Folly, I dare say, little-desired Freedom. And I cannot forbear *admiring* you so much myself, my *dearest Love,* that I will not spare you at all, this whole Evening. For 'tis a little hard, if thy Master's Sister may not be blest a little bit with thy charming Company.

So I found I had shewed her my Letter to very little Purpose, and repented it several times, as she read on.—Well then, I hope, said I, your Ladyship will give me Leave to send my Excuses to your good Brother, and say, that your Ladyship is come, and is so fond of me, that you will not let me leave you.—Pretty Creature! said she; and wantest thou thy good Master to come, and quarrel with his Sister on thy Account?—But thou shalt not stir from my Presence; and I would now ask thee, What it is thou meanest by shewing me this Letter?—Why, Madam, said I, to shew your Ladyship how I was engaged for this Day and Evening.—And for nothing else? said she. Why, I can't tell, Madam, said I: But if you can collect from it any other Circumstances, I might hope I should be not the worse treated.

I saw her Eyes began to sparkle with Passion; and she took my Hand, and said, grasping it very hard, I know, confident Creature, that you shew'd it me to insult me!—You shew'd it me, to let me see, that he could be civiller to a Beggar-born, than to me, or to my good Lord *Davers!*—You shew'd it me, as if you'd have me be as credulous a Fool as yourself, to believe your true Marriage, when I know the whole Trick of it, and have Reason to believe you do too; and you shew'd it me, to upbraid me with his stooping to such painted Dirt, to the Disgrace of a Family, ancient and untainted beyond most in the Kingdom; and now will I give thee One hundred Guineas for one bold Word, that I may fell thee at my Foot.

Was not this very dreadful! To be sure, I had better have kept the Letter from her. I was quite frighten'd!—And this fearful Menace, and her fiery Eyes, and rageful Countenance, made me lose all my Courage!—So I said, weeping, Good your Ladyship, pity me!—Indeed I am honest; indeed I am virtuous; indeed I would not do a bad thing for the World.

Tho' I know, said she, the whole Trick of thy pretended Marriage, and thy foolish Ring here, and all the rest of the wicked Nonsense; yet I should not have Patience with thee, if thou but offerest to let me know thy Vanity prompts thee to *believe* thou art marry'd to *my* Brother!—I could not bear the Thought!—So take care, *Pamela*; take care, beggarly Brat; take care.

Good your Ladyship, said I, spare my dear Parents. They are honest and industrious: They were once in a very creditable Way, and never were Beggars. Misfortunes may attend any body: And I can bear the cruellest Imputations on myself, because I know my Innocence; but upon such honest, industrious Parents, who lived thro' the greatest Trials, without being beholden to any thing but God's Blessing, and their own hard Labour; I cannot bear Reflection.

What! art thou setting up for a Family, Creature as thou art! God! give me Patience with thee! I suppose my Brother's Folly for thee, and his Wickedness together, will, in a little while, occasion a Search at the Herald's-office,[1] to set out thy wretched Obscurity. Provoke me, I desire thou wilt. One hundred Guineas will I give thee, to say but thou thinkest thou art marry'd to my Brother!

Your Ladyship, I hope, won't kill me. And since nothing I can say, will please; but your Ladyship is resolved to quarrel with me; since I must not say what I think, on one hand nor another, whatever your Ladyship designs by me, be pleased to do, and let me depart your Presence!

She gave me a Slap on the Hand, and reached to box my Ear; but Mrs. *Jewkes* hearkening without, and her Woman too, they both came in at that Instant; and Mrs. *Jewkes* said, pushing herself in between us, Your Ladyship knows not what you do. Indeed you don't. My Master would never forgive me, if I suffer'd, in his House, one he so dearly loves, to be so used; and it must not be, tho' you are Lady *Davers*. Her Woman too interposed, and told her, I was not worth her Ladyship's Anger. But she was like a Person beside herself.

I offer'd to go out, and Mrs. *Jewkes* took my Hand, to lead me out: But her Kinsman set his Back against the Door, and put his Hand to his Sword, and said, I should not go, till his Aunt permitted it. He drew it half-way; and I was so terrified, that I cry'd out, Oh! the Sword! the Sword! and, not knowing what I did, I run to my Lady herself, and clasp'd my Arms about her, forgetting, just then, how much she was my Enemy, and said, sinking on my Knees, Defend me, good your Ladyship! The Sword! the Sword!—Mrs. *Jewkes* said, Oh! my Lady will fall into Fits; but Lady *Davers* was, herself, so startled at the matter being carry'd so far, that she did not mind her Words, and said, *Jackey*, don't draw your Sword!—You see, as great as her Spirit is, she can't bear that.

Come, said she, be comforted; he shan't fright you!—I'll try to overcome my Anger, and will pity you. So, Wench, rise up, and don't be foolish. Mrs. *Jewkes* held her Salts to my Nose, and I did not faint. And my Lady said, Mrs. *Jewkes*, if *you* would be forgiven, leave *Pamela* and me by ourselves; and, *Jackey*, do you withdraw; only you, *Beck*, stay.

So I sat down in the Window, all in a sad Fluster; for, to be sure, I was sadly frighted.—Said her Woman, You should not sit in my Lady's Presence, Mrs. *Pamela*. Yes, let her sit till she is a little recover'd of her Fright, said my Lady, and set my Chair by her. And so she sat over-against me, and said, To be sure, *Pamela*, you have been very provoking with your Tongue, to be sure you have, as well upon my Nephew, (who is a Man of Quality too) as me. And, palliating her cruel Usage, and beginning, I suppose, to think herself, she had carry'd it further than she could answer it to her Brother, she wanted to lay the Fault upon me; Own, said she, you have been very saucy, and beg my Pardon, and beg *Jackey's* Pardon; and I will try to pity you: For you are a sweet Girl, after all;—if you had but held out, and been honest.

'Tis injurious to me, Madam, said I, to imagine I am not honest!— Said she, Have you not been a-bed with my Brother? tell me that.—Your Ladyship, reply'd I, asks your Questions in a strange Way, and in strange Words.

Oh! your Delicacy is wounded, I suppose, by my plain Question!—This Niceness will soon leave you Wench: It will indeed. But answer me directly. Said I, Then your Ladyship's next Question will be, Am I marry'd? And you won't bear my Answer to that,——and will beat me again.

I han't beat you yet; have I, *Beck?* said she. So you want to make out a Story, do you?—But, indeed, I can't bear thou should'st so much as *think* thou art *my* Sister. I know the whole Trick of it; and so, 'tis my Opinion, dost thou! It is only thy little Cunning, that it may look like a Cloak to thy yielding, and get better Terms from him. Pr'ythee, pr'ythee, Wench, thou seest I know the World a little;—almost as much at Thirty-two, as thou dost at Sixteen.—Remember that!

I rose from the Window, and walking to the other End of the Room, Beat me again, if you please, said I; but I must tell your Ladyship, I scorn your Words, and am as much marry'd as your Ladyship!

At that she run to me, but her Woman interposed again; Let the vain wicked Creature go from your Presence, Madam, said she. She is not worthy to be in it. She will but vex your Ladyship. Stand away, *Beck*, said she. That's an Assertion that I would not take from my Brother. I can't bear it. As much marry'd as I!—Is that to be borne? But if the Creature believes she is, Madam, said her Woman, she is to be as much pity'd for her Credulity, as despised for her Vanity.

I was in hopes to have slipt out of the Door; but she caught hold of my Gown, and pulled me back. Pray your Ladyship, said I, don't kill me!—I have done no Harm.—But she lock'd the Door, and put the Key in her Pocket. So seeing Mrs. *Jewkes* before the Window, I lifted up the Sash, and said, Mrs. *Jewkes*, I believe it would be best for the Chariot to go to your Master, and let him know, that Lady *Davers* is here; and I cannot leave her Ladyship.

She was resolved to be displeased, let me say what I would. Said she, No, no; he'll then think that I make the Creature my Companion, and know not how to part with her. I thought your Ladyship, reply'd I, could not have taken Exceptions at this Message. Thou knowest nothing, Wench, said she, of what belongs to People of Condition: How shouldst thou? Nor, thought I, do I desire it, at this Rate.

What shall I say, Madam? said I. Nothing at all, reply'd she; let him expect his *Dearest Love*, and be disappointed; it is but adding a few more *Hours*, and he will make every one *a Day*, in his amorous Account.—Mrs. *Jewkes* coming nearer me, and my Lady walking about the Room, being then at the End, I whisper'd, Let *Robert* stay at the Elms; I'll have a Struggle for't by-and-by.

As much marry'd as I! repeated she.—The Insolence of the Creature!— And so she walk'd about the Room, talking to herself, to her Woman, and now-and-then to me; but seeing I could not please her, I thought I had better be silent. And then it was, Am I not worthy an Answer? If I speak, said I, your Ladyship is angry at me, tho' ever so respectfully; if I do not, I cannot please: Would your Ladyship tell me but how I shall oblige you, and I would do it with all my Heart?

Confess the Truth, said she, that thou'rt an undone Creature; hast been in Bed with thy Master; and art sorry for it, and for the Mischief thou hast occasion'd between him and me; and then I'll pity thee, and persuade him to pack thee off, with a hundred or two of Guineas, and some honest Farmer may take Pity of thee, and patch up thy Shame, for the sake of the Money; and if nobody will have thee, thou must vow Penitence, and be as humble as I once thought thee.

I was quite sick at Heart, at all this passionate Extravagance, and to be hinder'd from being where was the Desire of my Soul, and afraid too of incurring my dear Master's Displeasure; and, as I sat, I saw it was no hard matter to get out of the Window, into the Front-yard, the Parlour being even with the Yard, and so have a fair Run for it; and after I had seen my Lady at the other End of the Room again, in her Walks, having not pulled down the Sash, when I spoke to Mrs. *Jewkes*, I got upon the Seat, and whipt out in a Minute, and ran away as hard as I could drive, my Lady calling after me to return, and her Woman at the other Window: But two of her Servants appearing at her crying out, and she bidding them stop me, I said, Touch me at your Peril, Fellows; but their Lady's Commands would have prevail'd on them, had not Mr. *Colbrand*, who, it seems, had been kindly order'd, by Mrs. *Jewkes*, to be within Call, when she saw how I was treated, come up, and put on one of his deadly fierce Looks, the only time, I thought, it ever became him, and said, He would *chine*[1] the Man, that was his Word, who offer'd to touch his Lady; and so he run along-side of me; and I heard my Lady say, The Creature flies like a Bird! And, indeed, Mr. *Colbrand*, with his huge Strides, could hardly keep pace with me; and I never stopt till I got to the Chariot; and *Robert* had got down, seeing me running at a Distance, and held the Door in his Hand, with the Step ready down; and in I jumpt, without touching the Step, saying, Drive me, drive me, as fast as you can, out of my Lady's Reach! And he mounted, and *Colbrand* said, Don't be frighten'd, Madam; nobody shall hurt you.—And shut the Door, and away *Robert* drove; but I was quite out of Breath, and did not recover it, and my Fright, all the Way.

Mr. *Colbrand* was so kind, but I did not know it till the Chariot stopt at Sir *Simon's*, to step up behind the Coach, lest, as he said, my Lady should send after me; and he told Mrs. *Jewkes*, when he got home, that he never saw such a Runner as me, in my Life.

When the Chariot stopt, which was not till Six o'Clock, so long did this cruel Lady keep me, Miss *Darnford* run out to me; O, Madam, said she, ten times welcome! but you'll be beat, I can tell you; for here has been the 'Squire come these two Hours, and is very angry at you.

That's hard indeed, said I!—Indeed I can't afford it!—for I hardly knew what I said, having not recover'd my Fright. Let me sit down, Miss, anywhere, said I; for I have been sadly off. So I sat down, and was quite sick with the Hurry of my Spirits, and lean'd upon her Arm.

Said she, Your Lord and Master came in very moody; and when he had staid an Hour, and you not come, he began to fret, and said, He did not expect so little Complaisance from you. And he is now sat down, with great Persuasions, to a Game at Loo.[1]—Come, you must make your Appearance, Lady fair; for he's too sullen to attend you, I doubt.

You have no Strangers, have you, Miss, said I?—Only two Women Relations from *Stamford*, reply'd she, and an humble Servant of one of them.—Only all the World, Miss! said I.—What shall I do, if he be angry? I can't bear that.

Just as I had said so, came in Lady *Darnford* and Lady *Jones*, to chide me, as they said, for not coming sooner. And before I could speak, came in my dear Master. I ran to him. How d'ye, *Pamela*, said he, and saluted me, with a little more Formality than I could well bear.—I expected half a Word from me, when I was so complaisant to your Choice, would have determin'd you, and that you'd been here to Dinner;—and the rather, as I made my Request a reasonable one, and what, I thought, would be agreeable to you. O dear Sir, said I, pray, pray hear me, and you'll pity me, and not be displeased: Mrs. *Jewkes* will tell you, that as soon as I had your kind Commands, I said, I would obey you, and come to Dinner with these good Ladies; and so prepared myself instantly, with all the Pleasure in the World. Lady *Darnford* and Miss said, I was their Dear!—Look you, said Miss, did I not tell you, Stately-ones, that something must have happen'd? But O these Tyrants! these Men!

Why, what hinder'd it, my Dear? said he: Give yourself Time; you seem out of Breath!—O Sir, said I, Out of Breath! well I may!—For, just as I was ready to come away, who should drive into the Court-yard, but Lady *Davers!*—Lady *Davers!* Nay, then, my sweet Dear, said he, and kissed me more tenderly, hast thou had a worse Trial than I wish thee, from one of the haughtiest Women in *England*, tho' my Sister!—For she, too, my *Pamela*, was spoiled by my good Mother!—But have you seen her?

Yes, Sir, said I, and more than seen her!—Why, sure, said he, she has not had the Insolence to strike my Girl!—Sir, said I, but tell me you forgive me; for indeed I could not come sooner; and these good Ladies but excuse me; and I'll tell you all another time; for to take up the good Company's Attention now, will spoil their Pleasantry, and be to them, tho' more important to me, like the Lady's broken China, you caution'd me about.

That's a dear Girl! said he; I see my Hints are not thrown away upon you; and I beg Pardon for being angry at you; and, for the future, will stay till I hear your Defence before I judge you. Said Miss *Darnford*, This is a little better! To own a Fault, is some Reparation; and what every lordly Husband will not do. He said, But tell me, my Dear, Did Lady *Davers* offer you any Incivility? O Sir, reply'd I, she is your Sister, and I must not tell you all; but she has used me very severely. Did you tell her, said he, you was marry'd?—Yes, Sir, I did at last: But she will have it, 'tis a Sham-marriage, and that I am a vile Creature: And she was ready to beat me, when I said so; for she could not have Patience that I should be deem'd her Sister, as she said.

How unlucky it was, reply'd he, I was not at home?—Why did you not send to me here? Send, Sir! I was kept Prisoner by Force. They would not let me stir, or do you think, I would have been hinder'd from obeying you? Nay, I told them, that I had a Pre-engagement; but she ridiculed me, and said, Waiting-maids talk of Pre-engagements! and then I shew'd her your kind Letter; and she made a thousand Remarks upon it, and made me wish I had not. In short, whatever I could do or say, there was no pleasing her; and I was a *Creature*, and *Wench*, and all that was naught. But you must not be angry with her, on my Account.

Well, but, said he, I suppose she hardly asked you to dine with her; for she came before Dinner, I suppose, if it was soon after you had received my Letter? No, Sir, dine with my *Lady!* no indeed! Why, she would make me wait at Table upon her, with her Woman, because she would not expose herself and me before the Men-servants; which, you know, Sir, was very good of her Ladyship.

Well, said he, but *did* you wait at Table upon her? Would you have had me, Sir? said I.—Only, *Pamela*, reply'd he, if you did, and knew not what belong'd to your Character, as my Wife, I shall be very angry with you. Sir, said I, I did not; but refused it, out of Consideration of the Dignity you have raised me to; else, Sir, I could have waited on my Knees upon your Sister.

Now, said he, you confirm my Opinion of your Prudence and Judgment. She is an insolent Woman, and shall dearly repent it. But, Sir, she is to be excus'd, because she won't believe I am indeed marry'd; so don't be too angry at her Ladyship.

He said, Ladies, pray don't let us keep you from the Company; I'll only ask a Question or two more, and attend you. Said Lady *Jones*, I so much long to hear this Story of poor Madam's Persecution, that if it was not improper, I should be glad to stay. Miss *Darnford* would stay for the same Reason; my Master saying, he had no Secrets to ask, and that it was kind of them to interest themselves in my Grievances.

But Lady *Darnford* went in to the Company, and told them the Cause of my Detention; for, it seems, my dear Master loved me too well, to keep to himself the Disappointment my not being here to receive him, had given him; and they had all given the two Miss *Boroughs*'s, and Mr. *Perry*, the *Stamford* Guests, such a Character of me, that they said they were impatient to see me.

Said my Master, But, *Pamela*, you said, *They* and *Them*; Who had my Sister with her, besides her Woman? Her Nephew, Sir, and three Footmen on Horseback; and she and her Woman were in her Chariot and Six.

That's a sad Coxcomb, said he: How did he behave to you?—Not extraordinarily, Sir; but I should not complain; for I was even with him; because I thought I ought not to bear with him as with my Lady.

By Heaven! said he, if I knew he behav'd unhandsomely to my Jewel, I'd send him home to his Uncle without his Ears. Indeed, Sir, return'd I, I was as hard upon him, as he was upon me. Said he, 'Tis kind to make the best for them. But I believe I shall make them dearly repent their Visit, if I find their Behaviour to call for my Resentment.

But, sure, my Dear, you might have got away when you went to your own Dinner? Indeed, Sir, said I, her Ladyship locked me in, and would not let me stir.—So you han't eat any Dinner? No, indeed, Sir, nor had a Stomach to any. My poor Dear! said he. But then, how got you away at last?—O, Sir, reply'd I, I jump'd out of the Parlour Window, and run away to the Chariot, which had waited for me several Hours, by the Elm-walk, from the Time of my Lady's coming (for I was just going, as I said); and Mr. *Colbrand* saw me thro' her Servants, whom she call'd to, to stop me; and was so kind to step behind the Chariot, unknown to me, and saw me safe here.

I'm sure, said he, these insolent Creatures must have treated you vilely. But tell me, What Part did Mrs. *Jewkes* act in this Affair? A very kind Part, Sir, said I, in my Behalf; and I shall thank her for it. Sweet Creature, said he, thou makest the best for every body; but I hope she deserves it; for she knew you are married.—But come, we'll now join the Company, and try to forget all you have suffer'd, for two or three Hours, that we may not fill the Company with our Concerns; and resume the Subject as we go home. And you shall find, I will do you Justice as I ought. But you forgive me, Sir, said I, and are not angry? Forgive you, my Dear! return'd he.—I hope you forgive me!—I shall never make you Satisfaction for what you have suffer'd *from* me, and *for* me! And with those Words, he led me into the Company.

He very kindly presented me to the two Stranger Ladies, and the Gentleman, and them to me; and Sir *Simon*, who was at Cards, rose from Table, and saluted me: Adad! Madam, said he, I'm glad to see you here. What, it seems you have been a Prisoner! 'Tis well you was, or your Spouse and I should have sat in Judgment upon you, and condemned you to a fearful Punishment for your first Crime of *Læsæ Majestatis*[1] (I had this explained to me afterwards, as a sort of Treason against my Liege Lord and Husband). For we Husbands, hereabout, said he, are resolv'd to turn over a new Leaf with our Wives, and *your* Lord and Master shall shew us the Way, I can tell you that. But I see by your Eyes, my sweet Culprit, added he, and your Complection, you have had sour Sauce to your sweet Meat.[2]

Miss *Darnford* said, I think we are oblig'd to our sweet Guest, at last; for she was forced to jump out at a Window to come to us. Indeed! said Mrs. *Peters*;—and my Master's Back being turn'd, says she, Lady *Davers*, when a Maiden, was always vastly passionate; but a very good Lady when it was over. And she'd make nothing of slapping her Maids about, and begging their Pardons afterwards, if they took it patiently; otherwise she used to say, The *Creatures* were even with her.

Ay, said I, I have been a many *Creatures* and *Wenches*, and I know not
what; for these were the best of her Names. And I thought I ought to act
up to the Part her dear Brother has given me; and so, truly, I have but just
escaped a good Cuffing.

Miss *Boroughs* said to her Sister, as I heard, but she did not design it,
What a sweet Creature is this! And then she takes so little upon her, is so
free, so easy, and owns the Honour done her so obligingly! Said Mr. *Perry*,
softly, The loveliest Person I ever saw! Who could have the Heart to be
angry with her one Moment?

Says Miss *Darnford*, Here, my dearest Neighbour, these Gentry are
admiring you strangely; and Mr. *Perry* says, you are the loveliest Lady he
ever saw; and says it to his own Mistress's Face too, I'll assure you—Or
else, says Miss *Boroughs*, I should think he much flatter'd me.

O Miss, return'd I, you are exceedingly obliging; but your kind Opinion
ought to learn me Humility, and to reverence so generous a Worth as can
give a Preference against yourself, where it is so little due. Indeed, Madam,
said Miss *Nanny Boroughs*, I love my Sister well; but it would be a high
Compliment to any Lady, to be deem'd worthy of a second or third Place
after you.

There is no answering such Politeness, said I: I am sure Lady *Davers*,
was very cruel to keep me from such kind Company. 'Twas our Loss,
Madam, said Miss *Darnford*. I'll allow it, said I, in Degree, Miss; for you
have all been deprived, several Hours, of an humble Admirer.

Mr. *Perry* said, I never before saw so young a Lady shine forth with such
Graces of Mind and Person. Alas! Sir, said I, my Master coming up, Mine
is but a borrow'd Shine, like that of the Moon: Here is the Sun, to whose
fervent Glow of Generosity I owe all the faint Lustre that your Goodness
is pleased to look upon with so much kind Distinction.

Mr. *Perry* was pleased to hold up his Hands; and the Ladies look'd
upon one another. And my Master said, hearing part of the last Sentence,
What's the pretty Subject, that my *Pamela* is displaying, so sweetly, her
Talents upon?

Oh! Sir, said Mr. *Perry*, I will pronounce you the happiest Gentleman
in *England*. And I, said Miss *Boroughs*; And I, said Miss *Darnford*; And I,
said each of the other.

My Master said, most generously, Thank ye, Thank ye, Thank ye, all
round, my dear Friends. I know not your Subject; but if you believe me
so, for a single Instance of this dear Girl's Goodness, what must I think
myself, when blest with a thousand Instances, and experiencing it in every
single Act and Word! I do assure you, my *Pamela*'s Person, all lovely as

PAMELA; OR, VIRTUE REWARDED

PAMELA; OR, VIRTUE REWARDED

you see it, is far short of her Mind; That first impress'd me in her Favour; but that only made me her *Lover*. But they were the Beauties of her Mind, that made me her *Husband*; and proud, my sweet Dear, said he, pressing my Hand, am I of that Title.

Well, said Mr. *Perry*, very kindly and politely, Excellent as your Lady is, I know not the Gentleman that could deserve her, but that one, who could say such just and such fine things.

I was all abash'd; and took Miss *Darnford*'s Hand, and said, Save me, dear Miss, by your sweet Example, from my rising Pride. But could I deserve half these kind things, what a happy Creature should I be! Said Miss *Darnford*, You deserve them all, indeed you do.

The greatest Part of the Company being sat down to Loo, my Master being press'd, said, he would take one Game at Whist;[1] but had rather be excused too, having been up all Night; and I asked how his Friend did? We'll talk of that, said he, another time; which, and his Seriousness, made me fear the poor Gentleman was dead, as it prov'd.

We cast in,[2] and Miss *Boroughs* and my Master were together, and Mr. *Perry* and I; and I had all four Honours the first time, and we were up at one Deal. Said my Master, An honourable Hand, *Pamela*, should go with an honourable Heart; but you'd not have been up, if a Knave had not been one. Whist, Sir, said Mr. *Perry*, you know, was a Court Game originally, and the Knave, I suppose, signified always the prime Minister.[3]

'Tis well, said my Master, if now there is but One Knave in a Court, out of Four Persons, take the Court thro'.

The King and Queen, Sir, said Mr. *Perry, can* do no Wrong, you know. So there are Two that *must* be good out of Four; and the Ace seems too plain a Card to mean much Hurt.

We compliment the King, said my Master, in that manner; and 'tis well to do so, because there is something sacred in the Character. But yet, if Force of Example be consider'd, it is going a great way; for certainly a good Master makes a good Servant, generally speaking.

One thing, added he, in regard to the Ace; I have always look'd upon that plain and honest-looking Card, in the Light you do. And have consider'd Whist as an *English* Game in its Original; which has made me fonder of it than of any other. For, by the Ace, I have always thought the Laws of the Land denoted; and, as the Ace is above the King or Queen, and wins them; I think the Law should be thought so too; tho', may-be, I shall be deem'd a *Whig* for my Opinion.[4]

I shall never play at Whist, said Mr. *Perry*, without thinking of this, and shall love the Game the better for the Thought; tho' I am no Party-man.

Nor I, said my Master; for I think the Distinctions of *Whig* and *Tory* odious; and love the one or the other, only as they are honest and worthy Men; and have never, (nor ever shall, I hope) given a Vote, but according to what I thought was for the publick Good, let either *Whig* or *Tory* propose it.[1]

I wish, Sir, reply'd Mr. *Perry*, all Gentlemen, in your Station, would act so. If there was no undue Influence, said my Master, I am willing to think so well of all Mankind, that I believe they generally would.

But you see, said he, by my *Pamela's* Hand, when all the Court-cards get together, and are acted by *one Mind*, the Game is usually turn'd accordingly. Tho' now-and-then, too, it may be so circumstanced, that *Honours* will do them no Good; and they are forced to depend altogether upon *Tricks*.

I thought this way of Talking prettier than the Game itself. But I said, Tho' I have won the Game, I hope, Sirs, I am no *Trickster*. No, said my Master, God forbid but *Court-cards* should *sometimes* win with *Honour!* But you see, for all that, your Game is as much owing to the *Knave*, as the *King*; and you, my Fair-one, lost no Advantage, when it was put into your Power.

Else, Sir, said I, I should not have done Justice to my Partner: You are certainly right, *Pamela*, reply'd he; tho' you thereby beat your Husband. Sir, said I, You may be my Partner next, and I must do Justice, you know. Well, said he, always chuse so worthy a Friend, as Chance has given you for a Partner, and I shall never find Fault with you, do what you will.

Mr. *Perry* said, You are very good to me, Sir; and Miss *Boroughs*, I observed, seem'd pleas'd with the Compliment to her humble Servant; by which I saw she esteem'd him, as he seems to deserve. Dear-sirs! said I, how much better is this, than to be lock'd in by Lady *Davers?*

The Supper was brought in sooner on my Account, because I had had no Dinner; and there passed very agreeable Compliments on the Occasion. Lady *Darnford* would help me first, because I had so long fasted, as she said. Sir *Simon* would have placed himself next me: And my Master said, he thought it was best, where there was an equal Number of Ladies and Gentlemen, that they should sit intermingled, that the Gentlemen might be employ'd in helping and serving the Ladies. Lady *Darnford* said, She hoped Sir *Simon* would not sit above any Ladies, at his own Table especially. Well, said he, I shall sit over-against her however; and that's as well.

My dearest Sir could not keep his Eye off me, and seem'd generously to be delighted with all I did, and all I said; and every one was pleased to see his kind and affectionate Behaviour to me.

Lady *Jones* brought up the Discourse about Lady *Davers* again; and my Master said, I fear, *Pamela*, you have been hardly used, more than you'll say. I know my Sister's passionate Temper too well, to believe she could be over-civil to you, especially as it happen'd so unluckily that I was out. If, added he, she had had no Pique to you, my Dear, yet what has passed between her and me, has so exasperated her, that I know she would have quarrel'd with my *Horse*, if she had thought I valued it, and nobody else was in her way. Dear Sir, said I, don't say so of good Lady *Davers*.

Said he, Why, my Dear, I know she came on purpose to quarrel; and had she not found herself under a very violent Uneasiness, after what had passed between us, and my Treatment of her Lord's Letter, she would not have offer'd to come near me. What sort of Language had she for me, *Pamela?* O, Sir, very good, only *her well-manner'd Brother*, and such as that!

Only, said he, 'tis taking up the Attention of the Company disagreeably, or I could tell you almost every Word she said. Lady *Jones* wish'd to hear a further Account of my Lady's Conduct, and most of the Company join'd with her, particularly Mrs. *Peters*; who said, That as they knew the Story, and Lady *Davers*'s Temper, tho' she was very good in the main, they could wish to be so agreeably entertain'd, if he and I pleas'd; because they imagin'd I should have no Difficulties after this.

Tell me then, *Pamela*, said he, did she lift up her Hand at you? Did she strike you? But I hope not! A little Slap of the Hand, said I, or so!—Insolent Woman! She did not, I hope, offer to strike your Face? Why, said I, I was a little saucy once or twice, and she would have given me a Cuff on the Ear, if her Woman and Mrs. *Jewkes* had not interpos'd? Why did you not come out at the Door? Because, said I, her Ladyship sat her Chair against it, one while, and another while lock'd it; else I offer'd, several times, to get away.

She knew I expected you here? You say, you shew'd her my Letter to you? Yes, Sir, said I; but I had better not; for she was then more exasperated, and made strange Comments upon it. I doubt it not, said he; but, did she not see, by the kind Epithets in it, that there was room to think we were marry'd? O, Sir, reply'd I, and made the Company smile, she said, For that very Reason, she was sure I was not marry'd.

That's like my Sister! said he, exactly like her; and yet she lives very happily herself. For her poor Lord never contradicts her. Indeed he *dare* not.

You was a great many *Wenches*, was you not, my Dear? for that's a great Word with her.—Yes, Sir, said I, *Wenches* and *Creatures* out of Number;

and worse than all that. What? tell me, my Dear. Sir, said I, I must not have you angry with Lady *Davers*. While you are so good to me, 'tis all nothing, only the Trouble that I cannot be suffer'd to shew how much I honour her Ladyship, as your Sister.

Well, said he, you need not be afraid to tell me: I must love her, after all; tho' I shall not be pleas'd with her on this Occasion. And I know it is her mistaken Love for me, that makes her so uneasy; and, after all, she comes, I know, to be reconciled to me; tho' it must be thro' a good hearty Quarrel first. For she can shew a deal of Sun-shine; but it must be always after a Storm. And I'll love her dearly, if she has not been, and will not be, too hard upon my Dearest.

Mr. *Peters* said, Sir, you are very good, and very kind. I love to see this Complaisance to your Sister, tho' she be in Fault, so long as you can shew it with so much Justice to the sweetest Innocence and Merit in the World. By all that's good, Mr. *Peters*, said he, I'd present my Sister with One thousand Pounds, if she would kindly take my dear *Pamela* by the Hand, and wish her Joy, and call her Sister!—And yet I should be unworthy of the dear Creature that smiles upon me there, if it was not principally for her sake, and the Pleasure it would give her, that I say this: For I will never be thoroughly reconciled to my Sister, till she does; for I most sincerely think, as to myself, that my dear Spouse, there she sits, does me more Honour in her new Relation, than she receives from me!

Sir, said I, I am overwhelm'd with your Goodness!—And my Eyes were filled with Tears of Joy and Gratitude. And all the Company, with one Voice, blessed him. And Lady *Jones* was pleased to say, The Company and Behaviour of you two happy Ones to each other, are the most edifying I ever knew. I am always improv'd when I see you. How happy would every good Lady be with such a Gentleman, and every good Gentleman with such a Lady!—In short, you seem made for one another.

O, Madam, said I, you are so kind, so good to me, that I know not how to thank you enough. Said she, You deserve more than I can express; for, to all who know your Story, you are a matchless Person. You are an Ornament to our Sex, and your Virtue, tho' your dear Spouse is so excellent and generous as he is, has met with no more than its due Reward. And God long bless you together.

You are, said my dearest Sir, very good to me, Madam, I am sure. I have taken Liberties in my former Life, that deserved not so much Excellence. I have offended extremely, by Trials glorious to my *Pamela*, but disgraceful to me, against a Virtue that I now consider as almost sacred; and I shall not think I deserve her, till I can bring my Manners, my Sentiments, and my

Actions, to a Conformity with her own. And, in short, my *Pamela*, said he, I want you to be nothing but what you are, and have been. You cannot be better; and if you could, it would be but filling me with Despair to attain the awful Heights of Virtue, at which you are arrived. Perhaps, added the dear Gentleman, the Scene I have beheld within these twelve Hours, has made me more serious than otherwise I should have been; but I'll assure you, before all this good Company, I speak the Sentiments of my Heart; and those not of this Day only.

What a happy Daughter is yours, O my dear Father and Mother! I owe it all to God's Grace, and yours and my good Lady's Instructions; and to these let me always look back with grateful Acknowledgments, that I may not impute to myself, and be proud, my very great Happiness.

The Company were so kindly pleas'd with our Concerns, and my dear Master's Goodness, that he observing their Indulgence, and being himself curious to know what had pass'd between my Lady and me, repeated his Question, What she had call'd me besides Wench and Creature? And I said, My Lady, supposing I was wicked, lamented over me very kindly, my Depravity and Fall, and said what a thousand Pities it was, so much Virtue, as she was pleas'd to say, was so destroy'd, and that I had yielded after so noble a Stand, as she said.

Excuse me, Gentlemen and Ladies, said I; you know my Story, it seems; and I am commanded by one, who has a Title to all my Obedience, to proceed.

They gave all of them Bows of Approbation, that they might not interrupt me; and I continued my Story.—

I told her Ladyship, continued I, that I was still innocent, and would be so, and it was injurious to suppose me otherwise! Why, tell me, Wench, said she,—but I think I must not tell you what she said. Yes, do, said my Master, to clear my Sister; we shall think it very bad else.

I held my Hand before my Face, and said, Why, she said, Tell me, Wench, hast thou not been a-bed with thy Master!—That she said.— And when I said, she ask'd strange Questions, and in strange Words, she ridicul'd my Delicacy, as she call'd it, and said my Niceness would not last long. She said, I must know I was not really marry'd, that my Ring was only a Sham, and all was my Cunning to cloak my yielding, and get better Terms: She said, she knew the World as much at Thirty-two, as I did at Sixteen; and bid me remember that.

I took the Liberty to say, (but I got a good way off) That I scorn'd her Ladyship's Words, and was as much marry'd as her Ladyship. And then, Good-sirs, I had certainly been cuff'd, if her Woman had not interposed, and told her I was not worth her Anger; and that I was as much to be pitied for my Credulity, as despis'd for my Vanity.

My poor *Pamela*, said my Master, this was too-too hard upon you! O Sir, said I, how much easier it was to me, than if it had been so!—That would have broke my Heart quite!—For then I should have deserv'd it all, and worse; and these Reproaches, added to my own Guilt, would have made me truly wretched!

Lady *Darnford*, at whose Right-hand I sat, kissed me with a kind of Rapture, and call'd me a sweet Exemplar for all my Sex. Mr. *Peters* said very handsome Things. So did Mr. *Perry*; and Sir *Simon* had Tears in his Eyes, and said to my Master, Why, Neighbour, Neighbour, this is excellent, by my Troth. I believe there is something in Virtue, that we had not well considered. On my Soul there has been but one Angel come down for these thousand Years, and you have got her.

Well, my Dearest, said my Master, pray proceed with your Story till we have done Supper, since the Ladies seem pleas'd with it. Why, Sir, said I, her Ladyship went on in the same manner; but said one time, (and held me by the Hand) she would give me a hundred Guineas for one provoking Word, or if I would but say, I *believ'd* myself marry'd, that she might fell me at her Foot. But, Sir, you must not be angry with her Ladyship. She call'd me *Painted Dirt, Baby-face, Waiting-maid, Beggar-brat,* and *Beggar-born*; but I said, as long as I knew my Innocence, I was easy in every thing, but to have my dear Parents abused. I said, they were never Beggars, nor beholden to any body; nor to any thing but God's Grace, and their own Labour: That they once lived in Credit; that Misfortunes might befal any body; and that I could not bear they should be treated so undeservedly.

Then her Ladyship said, Ay, she supposed my Master's Folly would make us now set up for a Family, and that the Herald's Office would shortly be search'd to make it out.

Exactly my Sister again! said he. So you could not please her any way?

No, indeed, Sir. When she commanded me to fill her a Glass of Wine, and would not let her Woman do it, she ask'd, If I was above it? I then said, If, to attend your Ladyship at Table, or even kneel at your Feet, was requir'd of me, I would most gladly do it, were I only the Person you think me. But, if it be to triumph over one, who has received Honours that she thinks require from her another Part, that she may not be utterly unworthy of them, I must say, I cannot do it. This quite astonish'd her Ladyship; and a little before, her Kinsman brought me the Bottle and Glass, and requir'd me to fill it for my Lady at her Command, and call'd himself my Deputy;

and I said, 'Tis in a good Hand; help my Lady yourself. So, Sir, added I, you see I could be a little saucy upon Occasion.

You please me well, my *Pamela*, said he. This was quite right. But proceed.

Her Ladyship said, She was astonish'd! adding, She suppos'd I would have her look upon me as her Brother's Wife: And ask'd me, What, in the Name of Impudence, possessed me, to *dare* to look upon myself as her Sister! And I said, That was a Question better became her most worthy Brother to answer than me. And then I thought I should have had her Ladyship upon me; but her Woman interposed.

I afterwards told Mrs. *Jewkes* at the Window, That since I was hinder'd from going to you, I believ'd it was best to let *Robert* go with the Chariot, and say, Lady *Davers* was come, and I could not leave her Ladyship. But this did not please, and I thought it would, too; for she said, No, no, he'll think I make the Creature my Companion, and know not how to part with her.

Exactly, said he, my Sister again!

And she said, I knew nothing what belong'd to People of Condition; how should I?—What *shall* I say, Madam? said I. Nothing at all, answer'd she; let him expect his *dearest Love*, alluding to your kind Epithet in your Letter, and be disappointed; it is but adding a few more Hours to this heavy Absence, and every one will become a Day in his amorous Account.

So, to be short, I saw nothing to be done, and I fear'd, Sir, you would wonder at my Stay, and be angry; and I watch'd my Opportunity, while my Lady, who was walking about the Room, was at the further End; and the Parlour being a Ground-floor in a manner, I jump'd out of the Window, and run for it.

Her Ladyship call'd after me; so did her Woman; and I heard her say, I flew like a Bird; and she call'd to two of her Servants in Sight to stop me; but I said, Touch me at your Peril, Fellows. And Mr. *Colbrand* having been planted at hand by Mrs. *Jewkes*, (who was very good in the whole Affair, and incurr'd her Ladyship's Displeasure, once or twice, by taking my Part, seeing how I was us'd) put on a fierce Look, cock'd his Hat with one Hand, and put t'other on his Sword, and said, He would chine the Man who offer'd to touch his Lady. And so he ran a long-side of me, and could hardly keep Pace with me:—And here, my dear Sir, concluded I, I am, at yours, and the good Company's Service.

They seem'd highly pleas'd with my Relation; and my Master said, he was glad Mrs. *Jewkes* behav'd so well, as also Mr. *Colbrand*. Yes, Sir, said

I, when Mrs. *Jewkes* interposed once, her Ladyship said, It was hard, she, who was born in that House, could not have some Privilege in it, without being talk'd to by the saucy Servants. And she call'd her another time *Fat-face*, and *woman'd* her most violently.

Well, said my Master, I am glad, my Dear, you have had such an Escape. My Sister was always passionate, as Mrs. *Peters* knows. And my poor Mother had enough to do with us both. For we neither of us wanted Spirit; and when I was a Boy, I never came home from School or College, for a few Days, but tho' we long'd to see one another before, yet ere the first Day was over, we had a Quarrel; for she being seven Years older than me, was always for domineering over me, and I could not bear it. And I used, on her frequently quarrelling with the Maids, and being always a Word and a Blow,[1] to call her Captain *Bab*; for her Name is *Barbara*. And when my Lord *Davers* courted her, my poor Mother has made up Quarrels between them three times in a Day; and I used to tell her, she would certainly beat her Husband, marry whom she would, if he did not beat her first, and break her Spirit.

Yet has she, continued he, very good Qualities. She was a dutiful Daughter, is a good Wife; she is bountiful to her Servants, firm in her Friendships, charitable to the Poor, and, I believe, never any Sister better loved a Brother, than she me: And yet, she always lov'd to vex and teaze me; and as I would bear a Resentment longer than she, she'd be one Moment the most provoking Creature in the World, and the next would do any thing to be forgiven; and I have made her, when she was the Aggressor, follow me all over the House and Garden to be upon good Terms with me.

But this Case piques her the more, because she had found out a Match for me, in the Family of a Person of Quality, and had set her Heart upon bringing it to Effect, and had even proceeded far in it, without my Knowledge, and brought me into the Lady's Company, unknowing of her Design: But I was then averse to Matrimony at all; and was angry at her proceeding in it so far without my Privity[2] or Encouragement: And she cannot, for this Reason, bear the Thoughts of my being now marry'd; and to her Mother's Waiting-maid too, as she reminds my dear *Pamela*, when I had declin'd her Proposal with the Daughter of a noble Earl.

This is the whole Case, said he; and allowing for the Pride and Violence of her Spirit, and that she knows not, as I do, the transcendent Excellencies of my dear Spouse, and that all her View, in her own Conception, is, mine and my Family's Honour, she is a little to be allow'd for. Tho' never fear, my *Pamela*, but that I, who never had a Struggle with her, that I did not get the better, will do you Justice, and myself too.

This Account of Lady *Davers* pleas'd every body, and was far from being to her Ladyship's Disadvantage in the main: And I would do any thing in the World to have the Honour to be in her Ladyship's good Graces. Yet I fear it will not be easily, if at all effected. But I will proceed:

After Supper, nothing would serve Miss *Darnford* and Miss *Boroughs*, but we must have a Dance, and Mr. *Peters*, who plays a good Fiddle, urg'd it forward; my dear Master, tho' in a Riding-dress, danc'd (and danc'd sweetly) with Miss *Boroughs*.

Sir *Simon*, for a Gentleman of his Years, danc'd well, and took me out; but put on one of his free Jokes, that I was fitter to dance with a younger Gentleman; and he would have it, tho' I had not danc'd since my dear Lady's Death to signify, except once or twice to please Mrs. *Jervis*, and indeed believ'd all my dancing Days over, that as my Master and I were the best Dancers, we should dance once together *before* Folks, as the odd Gentleman said; and my dear Sir was pleas'd to oblige him: And he afterwards danc'd with Miss *Darnford*, who I think has much more Skill and Judgment than I; tho' they compliment me with an easier Shape and Air.

We left the Company, with great Difficulty, at about Eleven, my dear Master having been up all Night before, and we being at the greatest Distance from Home; tho' they seem'd inclinable not to break up so soon, as they were Neighbours; and the Ladies said they long'd to hear what would be the End of Lady *Davers*'s Interview with her Brother.

My Master said, He fear'd we must not now think of going next Day to *Bedfordshire*, as we had intended, and perhaps might see them again. And so we took Leave, and set out for Home; where we arriv'd not till Twelve o' Clock; and found Lady *Davers* had gone to Bed about Eleven, wanting sadly that we should come home first; but so did not I.

Mrs. *Jewkes* told us, That my Lady was sadly fretted, that I had got away so; and seem'd a little apprehensive of what I would say of the Usage I had receiv'd from her. She ask'd Mrs. *Jewkes*, If she thought I was really marry'd? And Mrs. *Jewkes* telling her, Yes, she fell into a Passion, and said, Begone, bold Woman; I cannot bear thee. See not my Face till I send for thee. Thou hast been very impudent to me once or twice to-day already, and art now worse than ever. She said, She would not have told her Ladyship, if she had not ask'd her; and was sorry she had offended.

She sent for her at Supper-time; Said she, I have another Question to ask thee, Woman, and tell me Yes, if thou darest. Was ever any thing so odd?—Why then, said Mrs. *Jewkes*, I will say No, before your Lady-ship speaks.—My Master laugh'd, Poor Woman! said he.—She call'd her *insolent*, and *Assurance*;[1] and said, Begone, bold Woman as thou art;—but come hither. Dost thou know if that young Harlot is to lie with my Brother to-night?

She said, she knew not what to answer, because she had threaten'd her, if she said Yes. But at last, my Lady said, I will know the Bottom of this Iniquity. I suppose they won't have so much Impudence to lie together, while I'm in the House; but I dare say they have been Bed-fellows.

Said she, I will lie to-night in the Room I was born in; so get that Bed ready. That Room being our Bed-chamber, Mrs. *Jewkes*, after some Hesitation, reply'd, Madam, my Master lies there, and has the Key. I believe, Woman, said she, thou tellest me a Story. Indeed Madam, said she, he does; and has some Papers there he will let nobody see; for Mrs. *Jewkes* said, she fear'd she would beat her, if she went up, and found by my Cloaths, and some of my Master's, how it was.

So she said, I will then lie in the best Room, as it is called; and *Jackey* shall lie in the little green Room adjoining to it. Has thy Master got the Key of those?—No, Madam, said Mrs. *Jewkes*; I will order them to be made ready for your Ladyship.

And where dost thou lay thy pursy Sides, said she? Up two Pair of Stairs, Madam, next the Garden. And where lies the young Harlotry, continued she? Sometimes with me, Madam, said she. And sometimes with thy virtuous Master, I suppose, said my Lady.—Ha, Woman! what say'st thou? I must not speak, said Mrs. *Jewkes*. Well, thou mayst go, said she; but thou hast the Air of a Secret-keeper[2] of that sort: I dare say thou'lt set the good Work forward most cordially. Poor Mrs. *Jewkes!* said my Master, and laugh'd most heartily.

This Talk we had whilst we were undressing. So she and her Woman lay together in the Room my Master lay in before I was happy.

I said, Dear Sir, pray in the Morning let me lock myself up in the Closet, as soon as you rise; and not be call'd down for ever so much; for I am afraid to see her Ladyship: And I will employ myself about my Journal, while these Things are in my Head. Don't be afraid, my Dear, said he; am not I with you?

Mrs. *Jewkes* pity'd me for what I had undergone in the Day; and I said, We won't make the worst of it to my dear Master, because we won't exasperate where we would reconcile; but, added I, I am much oblig'd to you, Mrs. *Jewkes*, and I thank you. Said my Master, I hope she did not beat your Lady, Mrs. *Jewkes?* Not much, Sir, said she; but I believe I sav'd my Lady once: Yet, added she, I was most vex'd at the young Lord. Ay, Mrs. *Jewkes*, said my Master, let me know his Behaviour. I can chastise him, tho' I cannot my Sister, who is a Woman; let me therefore know the Part he acted.

Nothing, my dear Sir, said I, but Impertinence, if I may so say, and Foolishness, that was very provoking; but I spar'd him not, and so there is no Room, Sir, for your Anger. No, Sir, said Mrs. *Jewkes*, nothing else indeed.

How was her Woman? said my Master. Pretty impertinent, reply'd Mrs. *Jewkes*, as Ladies Women will be. But, said I, you know she sav'd me once or twice. Very true, Madam, return'd Mrs. *Jewkes*. And she said to me at Table, continued she, that you was a sweet Creature; she never saw your Equal; but that you had a Spirit, and she was sorry you answer'd her Lady so, who never bore so much Contradiction before. I told her, added Mrs. *Jewkes*, that if I was in your Ladyship's Place, I should have taken much more upon me, and that you was all Sweetness. And she said, I was got over, she saw.

TUESDAY *Morning, the Sixth of my Happiness.*[1]

My Master had said to Mrs. *Jewkes*, That he should not rise till Eight or Nine, as he had sat up all the Night before; but it seems, my Lady, knowing he usually rose about Six, got up soon after that Hour, rais'd her Woman, and her Nephew; having a whimsical Scheme in her Head, to try to find whether we were in Bed together: And at about half an Hour after Six, she rapt at our Chamber-door.

My Master was wak'd at the Noise, and asked who was there? Open the Door, said she; open it this Minute! I said, clinging about his Neck, Dear, dear Sir, pray, pray don't!—O save me, save me! Don't fear, *Pamela*, said he. The Woman's mad, I believe.

But he call'd out, Who are you? What do you want?—You know my Voice well enough, said she!—I *will* come in!—Pray, Sir, said I, don't let her Ladyship in.—Don't be frighted, my Dear, said he; she thinks we are not marry'd, and are afraid to be found a-bed together. I'll let her in; but she shan't come near my Dearest.

So he slipt out of Bed, and putting on some of his Cloaths, and Gown, and Slippers, he said, What bold body dares disturb my Repose thus? and open'd the Door. In rush'd she; I'll see your Wickedness, said she, I will! In vain shall you think to hide it from me!——What should I hide? said he. How dare you set a Foot into my House after the Usage I have receiv'd from you?—I had cover'd myself over Head and Ears, and trembled every Joint. He look'd and 'spy'd her Woman, and Kinsman, in the Room, she crying out, Bear Witness, *Jackey*; bear Witness, *Beck*; the Creature is now in his Bed. And not seeing the young Gentleman before, who was at the Feet of the Bed, he said, How now, Sir? What's your Business in this Apartment! Begone this Moment!—And he went away directly.

Beck, said my Lady, you see the Creature is in his Bed. I do, Madam, answer'd she. My Master came to me, and said, Ay look, *Beck*, and bear Witness; here is my *Pamela!*—My dear Angel, my lovely Creature, don't be afraid; look up, and see how frantickly this Woman of Quality behaves.

At that I just peep'd, and saw my Lady, who could not bear this, coming to me; and she said, Wicked abandon'd Wretch, vile Brother, to brave me thus! I'll tear the Creature out of Bed before your Face, and expose you both as you deserve.

At that he took her in his Arms, as if she had been nothing, and carrying her out of the Room, she cry'd out, *Beck, Beck!* help me, *Beck*; the Wretch is going to fling me down Stairs. Her Woman ran to him, and said, Good Sir, for God's sake, do no Violence to my Lady: Her Ladyship has been ill all Night.

He sat her down in the Chamber she lay in, and she could not speak for Passion. Take care of your Lady, said he; and when she has render'd herself more worthy of my Attention, I'll see her; till then, at her Peril, and yours too, come not near my Apartment. And so he came to me, and with all the sweet soothing Words in the world, pacify'd my Fears, and gave me Leave to go to write in my Closet, as soon as my Fright was over, and to stay there till Things were more calm. And so he dress'd himself, and went out of the Chamber, permitting me, at my Desire, to fasten the Door after him.

At Breakfast-time my Master tapp'd at the Door, and I said, Who's there? I, my Dearest, said he. Oh! then, reply'd I, will I open it with Pleasure. I had wrote on a good deal; but I put it by when I ran to the Door. I would have lock'd it again, when he was in; but he said, Am not I here! Don't be afraid. Said he, Will you come down to Breakfast, my Love? O no, dear Sir, said I; be pleas'd to excuse me. Said he, I cannot bear the Look of it, that the Mistress of my House should breakfast in her Closet, as if she durst not come down, and I in it!—O dearest Sir, reply'd I, pray pass that over for my sake; and don't let my Presence aggravate your Sister, for a kind Punctilio. Then, my Dear, said he, I shall breakfast with you here. No, pray, dear Sir, answer'd I, breakfast with your Sister.

That, my Dear, reply'd he, will too much gratify her Pride, and look like a Slight to you.—Dear Sir, said I, your Goodness is too great, for me to want punctilious Proofs of it. Pray oblige her Ladyship. She is your Guest; surely, Sir, you may be freest with your dutiful Wife!

She is a strange Woman, said he: How I pity her!—She has thrown herself into a violent Fit of the Colick, thro' Passion: And is but now, her Woman says, a little easier. I hope, Sir, said I, when you carry'd her Ladyship out, you did not hurt her. No, reply'd he, I love her too well. I sat her down in the Apartment she had chosen; and she but now desires to see me, and that I will breakfast with her, or refuses to touch any thing. But, if my Dearest please, I will insist it shall be with you at the same time.

O no, no, dear Sir, said I; I should never forgive myself, if I did. I would on my Knees beg her Ladyship's Goodness to me, now I am in your Presence, tho' I thought I ought to carry it a little stiff when you was absent, for the sake of the Honour you had done me. And, dear Sir, if my deepest Humility will please, permit me to shew it.

You shall do nothing, return'd he, unworthy of my Wife, to please the proud Woman!—But I will, however, permit you to breakfast by yourself this once, as I have not seen her since I have used her in so barbarous a manner, as I understand she exclaims I have; and as she will not eat any thing, unless I give her my Company.—So he saluted me, and withdrew, and I lock'd the Door after him again for Fear.

Mrs. *Jewkes*, soon after, rapp'd at my Door. Who's there? said I. Only I, Madam. So I open'd the Door. 'Tis a sad Thing, Madam, said she, you should be so much afraid in your own House. She brought me some Chocolate and Toast; and I ask'd her about my Lady's Behaviour. She said, She would not suffer any body to attend but her Woman, because she would not be heard what she had to say; but she believ'd, she said, her Master was very angry with the young Lord, as she call'd her Kinsman; for as she pass'd by the Door, she heard him say, in a high Tone, I hope, Sir, you did not forget what belongs to the Character you assume: or to that Effect.—

About one o'Clock, my Master came up again, and he said, Will you come down to Dinner, *Pamela*, when I send for you? Whatever you command, Sir, I must do: But my Lady won't desire to see me. No matter whether she will or no. But I will not suffer that she shall prescribe her insolent Will to my Wife, and in your own House too.—I will by my Tenderness to you, mortify her Pride, and it cannot be done so well as to her Face.

Dearest Sir, said I, pray indulge me, and let me dine here by myself. It will make my Lady but more inveterate.—Said he, I have told her we are marry'd. She is out of all Patience about it, and yet pretends *not* to believe it. Upon that I tell her, Then she shall have it her own way, and that I am *not*. And what has she to do with it either way? She has scolded and begg'd, commanded and pray'd, bless'd me, and curs'd me, by Turns, twenty times, in these few Hours. And I have sometimes soothed her, sometimes storm'd at her, sometimes argued, sometimes raged; and at last I left her, and took a Turn in the Garden for an Hour to compose myself, because you should not see how the foolish Woman ruffled me; and just now, I came out, seeing her coming in.

Just as he had said so, I cry'd, Oh! my Lady, my Lady! for I heard her Voice in the Chamber, saying, Brother, Brother, one Word with you!— Stopping in Sight of the Closet where I was. He stept out, and she went up to the Window that looks towards the Garden, and said, Mean Fool that I am, to follow you up and down the House in this manner, tho' I am shunn'd and avoided by you! You a Brother!—you a Barbarian!—Is it possible we could be born of one Mother?

Why, said he, do you charge me with a Conduct to you, that you bring upon yourself?—Is it not surprizing, that you should take Liberties with me, that the dear Mother you have nam'd, never gave you an Example for to any of her Relations?—Was it not sufficient, that I was insolently taken to Task by you in your Letters, but my Retirements must be invaded? My House insulted? And, if I have one Person dearer to me than another, that that Person must be singled out for an Object of Violence?

Ay, said she, that one Person is the Thing!—But tho' I came up with a Resolution to be temperate, and to expostulate with you on your avoiding me so unkindly, yet cannot I have Patience to look upon that Bed in which I was born, and to be made the guilty Scene of your Wickedness with such a ——

Hush! said he, I charge you, call not the dear Girl by any Name unworthy of her. You know not, as I told you, her Excellence; and I desire you'll not repeat the Freedoms you have taken below.

She stamp'd with her Foot, and said, God give me Patience! So much Contempt to a Sister that loves you so well; and so much Tenderness to a vile -----

He put his Hand before her Mouth, Be silent, said he, once more, I charge you. You know not the Innocence you abuse so freely; I ought not, neither will I bear it.

She sat down, and fann'd herself, and burst into Tears, and such Sobs of Grief, or rather Passion, that griev'd me to hear; and I sat and trembled sadly.—

He walk'd about the Room, in great Anger; and at last said, Let me ask you, Lady *Davers*, why I am thus insolently to be called to Account by you. Am I not independent? Am I not of Age? Am I not at Liberty to please myself?—Would to God, that instead of a Woman and my Sister, any Man breathing had dar'd, whatever his Relation under that of a Father, to give himself half the Airs you have done!—Why did you not send of this accursed Errand your Lord, who could write me such a Letter as no Gentleman should write, nor any Gentleman tamely receive? He should have seen the Difference.

We all know, said she, that since your *Italian* Duel, you have commenc'd a Bravo;[1] and all your Airs breathe as strongly of the Manslayer as of the Libertine. This, said he, I will bear; for I have no Reason to be asham'd of that Duel,[2] nor the Cause of it; since it was to save a Friend; and because 'tis levell'd at myself only: But suffer not your Tongue to take too great a Liberty with my *Pamela*.

She interrupted him, in a violent Burst of Passion. If I bear this, said she, I can bear any thing!—O the little Strumpet!—He interrupted her then, and said wrathfully, Begone, rageful Woman, begone this Moment from my Presence! Leave my House this Instant!—I renounce you, and all Relation to you; and never more let me see your Face, or call me Brother. And took her by the Hand to lead her out. She laid hold of the Curtains of the Window, and said, I will not go! you shall not force me from you thus ignominiously in the Wretch's Hearing, and suffer *her* to triumph over me in your barbarous Treatment of me.

Not considering any thing, I run out of the Closet, and threw myself at my dear Master's Feet, as he held her Hand, in order to lead her out; and I said, Dearest Sir, let me beg, that no Act of Unkindness, for my sake, pass between so worthy and so near Relations. Dear, dear Madam, said I, and clasp'd her Knees, pardon and excuse the unhappy Cause of all this Evil; on my Knees I beg your Ladyship to receive me to your Grace and Favour, and you shall find me incapable of any Triumph but in your Ladyship's Goodness to me.

Creature, said she, art *thou* to beg an Excuse for me!—Art *thou* to implore my Forgiveness! Is it to *thee* I am to owe the Favour that I am not cast headlong from my Brother's Presence! Begone to thy Corner, Wench; begone, I say, lest thy Paramour kill me for trampling thee under my Foot.

Rise, my dear *Pamela*, said my Master; rise, dear Life of my Life, and expose not so much Worthiness to the ingrateful Scorn of so violent a Spirit. And so he led me to my Closet again, and there I sat and wept.

Her Woman came up, just as he had led me to my Closet, and was returning to her Lady; and she very humbly said, Excuse my Intrusion, good Sir!—I hope I may come to my Lady. Yes, Mrs. *Worden*, said he, you may come in, and pray take your Lady down Stairs with you, for fear I should too much forget what belongs either to my Sister or myself!

I began to think (seeing her Ladyship so outrageous with her Brother) what a happy Escape I had had the Day before, tho' hardly enough us'd in Conscience too, as I thought.

Her Woman begg'd her Ladyship to walk down, and she said, *Beck*, seest thou that Bed? That was the Bed that I was born in; and yet that was the Bed, thou sawest as well as I, the wicked *Pamela* in this Morning, and this Brother of mine just risen from her!

True, said he; you both saw it, and 'tis my Pride that you *could* see it. 'Tis my Bridal-bed, and 'tis abominable, that the Happiness I knew before you came hither, should be so barbarously interrupted.

Swear to me but, thou bold Wretch, said she; swear to me, that *Pamela Andrews* is really and truly thy lawful Wife, without Sham, without Deceit, without Double-meaning, and I know what I have to say.

I'll humour you for once, said he; and then swore a solemn Oath, that I was. And, said he, did I not tell you so at first?

I cannot yet believe you, said she, because, in this Particular, I had rather have called you *Knave* than *Fool*.[1]—Provoke me not too much, said he; for if I should as much forget myself as you have done, you'd have no more of a Brother in me, than I have a Sister in you!

Who marry'd you? said she; tell me that: Was it not a broken Attorney in a Parson's Habit? Tell me truly, in the Wench's Hearing. When she's undeceiv'd, she'll know how to behave herself better! Thank God, thought I, it is not so.

No, said he, and I'll tell you, that I bless God, I abhorred that Project, before it was brought to bear; and Mr. *Williams* marry'd us.—Nay then, said she—but answer me another Question or two, I beseech you. Who gave her away? Parson *Peters*, said he. Where was the Ceremony perform'd? In my own little Chapel, which you may see, as it was put in Order on purpose.

Now, said she, I begin to fear there is something in it! But who was present? said she. Methinks, reply'd he, I look like a fine Puppy, to suffer myself to be thus interrogated by an insolent Sister. But, if you must know, Mrs. *Jewkes* was present. O the Procuress, said she! But nobody else? Yes, said he, all my Heart and Soul!

Wretch! said she! And what would thy Father and Mother have said, had they lived to this Day? Their Consents, reply'd he, I should have thought it my Duty to ask; but not yours, Madam.

Suppose, said she, I had marry'd my Father's Groom! what would you have said to that?—I could not have behav'd worse, reply'd he, than you have done. And would you not have thought, said she, I had deserv'd it?

Said he, Does your Pride let you see no Difference in the Case you put? None at all, said she. Where can the Difference be between a Beggar's Son marry'd by a Lady; or a Beggar's Daughter made a Gentleman's Wife?

Then I'll tell you, reply'd he; The Difference is, a Man ennobles the Woman he takes, be she *who* she will; and adopts her into his own Rank, be it *what* it will: But a Woman, tho' ever so nobly born, debases herself by a mean Marriage, and descends from her own Rank, to his she stoops to.

When the noble Family of *Stuart* ally'd itself into the low Family of *Hyde*, (comparatively low, I mean) did any body scruple to call the Lady Royal Highness, and Duchess of *York?*[a] And did any body think her Daughters, the late Queen *Mary* and Queen *Anne*, less Royal for that?

When the broken-fortun'd Peer goes into the City to marry a rich Tradesman's Daughter, be he Duke or Earl, does not his Consort immediately become ennobled by his Choice? and who scruples to call her Lady Duchess, or Countess?

But when a Duchess, or Countess Dowager, descends to mingle with a Person of obscure Birth, does she not then degrade herself? and is she not effectually degraded? And will any Duchess or Countess rank with her?

Now, Lady *Davers*, do you not see a Difference between my marrying my dear Mother's beloved and deserving Waiting-maid, with a Million of Excellencies about her, and such Graces of Mind and Person, as would adorn any Distinction; and your marrying a sordid Groom, whose constant Train of Education, Conversation, and Opportunities, could possibly give him no other Merit, than that which must proceed from the vilest lowest Taste, in his sordid Dignifier?

O the Wretch! said she, how he finds Excuses to palliate his Meanness!

Again, said he, let me observe to you, Lady *Davers*, when a Duke marries a private Person, is he not still her Head, by virtue of being her Husband?

But, when a Lady descends to marry a Groom, is not that Groom her Head, as her Husband? And does not that Difference strike you? For what Lady of Quality ought to respect another, who has made so sordid a Choice, and set a Groom above her? For, would not that be to put that Groom upon a Par with themselves?—Call this Palliation, or what you will; but if you see not the Difference, you are blind, and a very unfit Judge for yourself, much more unfit to be a Censurer of me.

I'd have you, said she, publish your fine Reasons to the World, and they will be sweet Encouragements to all the young Gentlemen that read them, to cast themselves away on the Servant-wenches in their Families.

Not at all, Lady *Davers*, reply'd he: For, if any young Gentleman stays till he finds such a Person as my *Pamela*; so inrich'd with the Beauties of Person and Mind, so well accomplish'd, and so fitted to adorn the Degree she is raised to, he will stand as easily acquitted, as I shall be to all the World that sees her, except there be many more Lady *Davers*'s than I apprehend can possibly be met with.

And so, return'd she, you say, You are actually and really marry'd, honestly, or rather foolishly, marry'd to this Slut?

I am indeed, said he, if you presume to call her so! And why should I not, if I please? Who is there ought to contradict me? Whom have I hurt by it?—Have I not an Estate, free and independent? Am I likely to be beholden to you, or any of my Relations? And why, when I have a Sufficiency in my own single Hands, should I scruple to make a Woman equally happy, who has all I want? For Beauty, Virtue, Prudence, and Generosity too, I will tell you, she has more than any Lady I ever saw. Yes, Lady *Davers*, she has all these *naturally*; they are *born* with her; and a few Years Education, with her Genius, has done more for her, than a whole Life has done for others.

No more, no more, I beseech you, said she; thou surfeitest me, honest Man, with thy weak Folly. Thou art worse than an Idolater; thou hast made a graven Image, and thou fallest down and worshippest the Works of thine own Hands; and, *Jeroboam* like, would have every body else bow down before thy Calf![1]

Well said, Lady *Davers!* Whenever your Passion suffers you to descend to Witticism, 'tis almost over with you. But, let me tell you, tho' I worship myself this sweet Creature that you call such Names, I want nobody else to do it; and should be glad you had not intruded upon me, to interrupt me in the Course of our mutual Happiness.

Well said, well said, my kind, my well-manner'd Brother! said she. I shall, after this, very little interrupt your mutual Happiness, I'll assure you.

I thought you a Gentleman once, and prided myself in my Brother; but I'll say with the Burial Service, *Ashes to Ashes, and Dirt to Dirt!*[1]

Ay, said he, Lady *Davers*, and there we must all end at last; you with all your Pride, and I with my plentiful Fortune, must come to it; and then where will be your Distinction? Let me tell you, except you and I both mend our Manners, tho' you have been no Duellist, no Libertine, as you call me, this amiable Girl, whom your Vanity and Folly so much despises, will out-soar us both, infinitely out-soar us; and He that judges best, will give the Preference where due, without Regard to Birth or Fortune.

Egregious Preacher, said she! What, my Brother already turn'd *Puritan!*—See what Marriage and Repentance may bring a Man to! I heartily congratulate this Change!—Well, said she, and came towards me, and I trembled to see her coming; but her Brother followed to observe her, and I stood up at her Approach, and she said, Give me thy Hand, Mrs. *Pamela*, Mrs. *Andrews*, Mrs. —— what shall I call thee!—Thou hast done Wonders in a little time: Thou hast not only made a Rake a Husband; but thou hast made a Rake a Preacher! But take care, added she, after all, in ironical Anger, and tapp'd me on the Neck, take care that thy Vanity begins not where his ends; and that thou callest not thyself my Sister!

She shall, I hope, Lady *Davers*, said he, when she can make as great a Convert of you from Pride, as she has of me from Libertinism.

Mrs. *Jewkes* just then came up, and said, Dinner was ready. Come, my *Pamela*, said my dear Master; you desired to be excus'd from breakfasting with us; but I hope you'll give Lady *Davers* and me your Company to Dinner.

How dare you insult me thus? said my Lady.—How dare you, said he, insult me by your Conduct in my own House, after I have told you I am marry'd? How dare you think of staying here one Moment, and refuse my Wife the Honours that belong to her, as such?

Merciful God! said she, give me Patience! and held her Hand to her Forehead.

Pray, Sir, dear Sir, said I, excuse me; don't vex my Lady.—Be silent, my dear Love, said he; you see already what you have got by your sweet Condescension. You have thrown yourself at her Feet, and, insolent as she is, she has threaten'd to trample upon you. She'll ask you presently, if she is to owe her Excuse to your Interposition; and yet nothing else can make her forgiven.

Poor Lady! she could not bear this, and, as if she was discomposed, she ran to her poor grieved Woman, and took hold of her Hand, and said, Lead me down, lead me down, *Beck!* Let us instantly quit this House, this cursed House, that once I took Pleasure in; order the Fellows to get ready, and I will never see it, nor its Owner, more. And away she went down Stairs, in a great Hurry. And the Servants were order'd to make ready for their Departure.

I saw my Master was troubled, and I went to him, and I said, Pray, dear Sir, follow my Lady down, and pacify her. 'Tis her Love to you.—Poor Woman! said he, I am concern'd for her! But I insist upon your coming down, since Things are gone so far. Her Pride will get new Strength else, and we shall be all to begin again.

Dearest, dear Sir, said I, excuse me going down this once! Indeed, my Dear, I won't, reply'd he. What! shall it be said, that my Sister shall scare my Wife from my Table, and I present?—No, I have borne too much already; and so have you. And I charge you come down, when I send for you.

He departed, saying these Words, and I durst not dispute; for I saw, he was determin'd. And there is as much Majesty as Goodness in him; as I have often had Reason to observe, tho' never more, than on the present Occasion with his Sister. Her Ladyship instantly put on her Hood and Gloves, and her Woman ty'd up a Handkerchief full of Things; for her principal Matters were not unpack'd, and her Coachman got her Chariot ready, and her Footmen their Horses, and she appear'd resolved to go. But her Kinsman and Mr. *Colbrand* had taken a Turn together, somewhere; and she would not come in, but sat fretting on a Seat in the Fore-yard, with her Woman by her; and at last said, to one of the Footmen, Do you, *James*, stay, to attend my Nephew; and we'll take the Road we came.

Mrs. *Jewkes* went to her Ladyship, and said, Your Ladyship will be pleas'd to stay Dinner; 'tis just coming upon Table. No, said she, I have enough of this House! I have indeed. But give my Service to your Master, and I wish him happier than he has made me.

He had sent for me down, and I came, tho' unwillingly, and the Cloth was laid in the Parlour I had jump'd out of; and there was my Master walking about it. Mrs. *Jewkes* came in, and asked, If he pleas'd to have Dinner brought in? for my Lady would not come in, but desired her Service, and wish'd him happier than he had made her. He seeing at the Window, when he went to that Side of the Room, all ready to go, stept out to her, and said, Lady *Davers*, if I thought you would not be harden'd rather than soften'd by my Civility, I would ask you to walk in, and at least let your Kinsman and Servants dine before they go. She wept, and turn'd her Face from him to hide it; he took her Hand, and said, Come,

Sister, let me prevail upon you: Walk in. No! said she, don't ask me.—I
wish I could hate you, as much as you hate me!—You do, said he, and
a great deal more, I'll assure you; or else you'd not vex me as you do.—
Come, pray, walk in. Don't ask me, said she. Her Kinsman just then
return'd: Why, Madam, said he, your Ladyship won't go till you have
din'd, I hope. No, *Jackey*, said she, I can't stay; I'm an *Intruder* here, it
seems!—Think, said my Master, of the Occasion you gave for that Word.
Your violent Passions are the only *Intruders!* Lay them aside, and never
Sister was dearer to a Brother. Don't say such another Word, said she,
I beseech you; for I am too easy to forgive you any thing, for one kind
Word!—You shall have One hundred, said he, nay, Ten thousand, if they
will do, my dear Sister. And kissing her, he added, Pray give me your
Hand. *John*, said he, put up the Horses; you are all as welcome to me, for
all your Lady's angry with me, as at any Inn you can put up at. Come,
Mr. *H.* said he, lead your Aunt in; for she won't permit that Honour
to me.

This quite overcame her; and she said, giving her Brother her Hand,
Yes, I will, and you shall lead me any-whither!—and kiss'd him. But don't
think, said she, I can forgive you neither. And so he led her into the Parlour
where I was. But, said she, why do you lead me to this Wench? 'Tis my
Wife, my dear Sister; and if you will not love her, yet don't forget common
Civilities to her, for your own sake.

Pray, Madam, said her Kinsman, since your Brother is pleas'd to own
his Marriage, we must not forget common Civilities, as the 'Squire says.
And, Sir, added he, permit me to wish you Joy. Thank you, Sir, said he.
And may I, said he, looking at me? Yes, Sir, reply'd my Master. So he
saluted me, very complaisantly, and said, I vow to Gad, Madam, I did not
know this Yesterday; and, if I was guilty of a Fault, I beg your Pardon.

My Lady said, Thou'rt a good-natur'd foolish Fellow; thou mightst have
sav'd this nonsensical Parade, till I had given thee Leave. Why, Aunt, said
he, if they're actually marry'd, there's no Help for't, and we must not make
Mischief between Man and Wife.

But, Brother, said she, do you think I'll sit at Table with the Creature?
No contemptuous Names I beseech you, Lady *Davers!* I tell you she is
really my Wife; and I must be a Villain to suffer her to be ill used. She has
no Protector but me; and, if you will permit her, she will always love and
honour you.—Indeed, indeed, I will, Madam, said I.

I cannot, I wo'not sit down at Table with her, said she: *Pamela*, I hope
thou dost not think I will? Indeed, Madam, said I, if your good Brother
will permit it, I will attend your Chair all the time you dine, to shew my

Veneration for your Ladyship, as the Sister of my kind Protector. See, said he, her Condition has not altered her; but I cannot permit in her a Conduct unworthy of my Wife, and I hope my Sister would not expect it neither.

Let her leave the Room, reply'd she, if I must stay. Indeed, you're out of the Way, Aunt, said her Kinsman; that is not right, as Things stand. Said my Master, No, Madam, that must not be; but if it must be so, we'll have two Tables; you and your Nephew shall sit at one, and my Spouse and I at the other: And then see what a Figure your unreasonable Punctilio will make you cut.—She seem'd irresolute, and he sat her down at the Table, the first Course, which was Fish, being brought in. Where, said she to me, wouldst thou presume to sit? Wouldst have me give *Place* to thee *too*, Wench?—Come, come, said my Master, I'll put that out of Dispute: and so sat himself down by her Ladyship, at the upper End of the Table, and plac'd me on his Left-hand. Excuse me, my Dear, said he, this once excuse me!—Oh! your cursed Complaisance, said she, to such a —— Hush, Sister! Hush, said he! I will not bear her to be spoken slightingly of! 'Tis enough, that to oblige your violent and indecent Caprice, you make me compromise with you thus.

Come, Sir, added he, pray take your Place next your gentle Aunt!—*Beck*, said she, do you sit down by *Pamela* there, since it must be so; we'll be hail Fellow all!¹ With all my Heart, reply'd my Master: I have so much Honour for all the Sex, that I would not have the meanest Person of it stand, while I sit, had I been to have made the Custom. Mrs. *Worden*, pray sit down. Sir, said she, I hope I shall know my Place better.

My Lady sat considering, and then lifting up her Hands, said, Lord! what will this World come to?—To nothing but what's very good, reply'd my Master, if such Spirits as Lady *Davers*'s do but take the Rule of it. Shall I help you, Sister, to some of that Carp? Help your Beloved, said she! That's kind, said he!—Now, that's my good Lady *Davers*. Here, my Love, let me help you, since my Sister desires it!—Mighty well! return'd she, mighty well!—But sat on one Side, turning from me, as it were.

Dear Aunt, said her Kinsman, let's see you buss and be Friends; since 'tis so, what signifies it? Hold thy Fool's Tongue, said she! Is thy Tone so soon turn'd since Yesterday? Said my Master, I hope nothing affronting was offer'd Yesterday to my Wife in her own House. She hit him a good smart Slap on the Shoulder; Take that, impudent Brother, said she. I'll *Wife* you, and in *her own* House! She seem'd half afraid; but he, in very good Humour, kiss'd her, and said, I thank you, Sister, I thank you. But I have not had a Blow from you before of some Time!

'Fore Gad, Sir, said her Kinsman, 'tis very kind of you to take it so well. Her Ladyship is as good a Woman as ever liv'd; but I have had many a Cuff from her myself.

I won't put it up neither, said my Master, except you'll assure me, you have seen her serve her Lord so.

I press'd my Foot to his, and said, softly, Don't, dear Sir!—What, said she, is the Creature begging me off from Insult? If *his* Manners won't keep him from outraging me, I wo'not owe his Forbearance to *thee*, Wench.

Said my Master, and put some Fish on my Lady's Plate, Well, does Lady *Davers* use the Word *Insult!*—But, come, let me see you eat one Mouthful, and I'll forgive you; and he put the Knife in one of her Hands, and the Fork in the other. As I hope to live, said he, I cannot bear this silly Childishness, for nothing at all. I am quite asham'd of it.

She put a little Bit to her Mouth, but put it down in her Plate again: I cannot eat, said she; I cannot swallow, I'm sure. It will certainly choak me. He had forbid his Men-servants to come in, that they might not behold the Scene he expected; and rose from Table himself, and fill'd a Glass of Wine, her Woman offering, and her Kinsman rising to do it. Mean-time, his Seat between us being vacant, she turn'd to me, How now, Confidence, said she, darest thou sit next *me?* Why dost thou not rise, and take the Glass from thy Property?[1]

Sit still, my Dear, said he, I'll help you both. But I arose; for I was afraid of a good Cuff; and said, Pray, Sir, let me help my Lady! So you shall, reply'd he, when she's in a Humour to receive it as she ought. Sister, said he, with a Glass in his Hand, Pray drink; you'll perhaps eat a little Bit of something then. Is this to insult me, said she?—No, really, return'd he; but to incite you to eat; for you'll be sick for want of it.

She took the Glass, and said, God forgive you, wicked Wretch, for your Usage of me this Day!—This is a little as it used to be!—I once had your Love;—and now it is changed; and for who? that vexes me! And wept so, she was forced to set down the Glass.

You don't do well, said he. You neither treat me like your Brother, nor a Gentleman; and if you would suffer me, I would love you as well as ever.—But, for a Woman of Sense and Understanding, and a fine-bred Woman, as I once thought my Sister, you act quite a childish Part. Come, added he, and held the Glass to her Lips, let your Brother, that you once lov'd, prevail on you to drink this Glass of Wine.—She then drank it. He kiss'd her, and said, Oh! how Passion deforms the noblest Minds! You have lost a good deal of that Loveliness that used to adorn my Sister. And let me persuade you to compose yourself, and be my Sister again!—For Lady *Davers* is indeed a fine Woman, and has a Presence as majestick for a Lady, as her dear Brother has for a Gentleman.

He then sat down between us again, and said, when the second Course came in, Let *Abraham* come in, and wait. I touch'd his Toe again; but he minded it not; and I saw he was right; for her Ladyship began to recollect herself, and did not behave half so sorrowfully before the Servants, as she had done; and help'd herself with some little Freedom; but she could not forbear a strong Sigh and a Sob, now-and-then. She call'd for a Glass of the same Wine she had drank before. Said he, shall I help you again, Lady *Davers?*—and rose at the same time, and went to the Side-board, and filled her a Glass. Indeed, said she, I love to be sooth'd by my Brother!—Your Health, Sir!

Said my Master to me with great Sweetness, My Dear, now I'm up, I'll fill for you!—I must serve *both* Sisters alike! She look'd at the Servant, as if he were a little Check upon her, and said to my Master, How now, Sir!—Not that you know of. He whisper'd her, Don't shew any Contempt before my Servants to one I have so deservedly made their Mistress. Consider 'tis done.—Ay, said she, that's the Thing that kills me.

He gave me a Glass; My good Lady's Health, Sir, said I, and stood up.—That won't do, said she, leaning towards me, softly; and was going to say, Wench, or Creature, or some such Word. And my Master, seeing *Abraham* look towards her, her Eyes being red and swell'd, said, Indeed, Sister, I would not vex myself about it, if I was you. About what, said she? Why, reply'd he, about your Lord's not coming down, as he had promised. He sat down, and she tapp'd him on the Shoulder: Ah! Wicked-one, said she, nor will that do neither!—Why, to be sure, added he, it would vex a Lady of your Sense and Merit, to be slighted, if it was so; but I am sure my Lord loves you, as well as you love him; and you know not what may have happen'd.

She shook her Head, and said, That's like your Art!—This makes one amaz'd you should be so caught!—Who, my Lord caught! said he; no, no! he'll have more Wit than so! But I never heard you was jealous before. Nor, said she, have you any Reason to think so now! Honest Friend, you need not wait, said she; my Woman will help us to what we want. Yes, let him, reply'd he. *Abraham*, fill me a Glass. Come, said my Master, Lord *Davers* to you, Madam: I hope he'll take care he is not found out!—You're very provoking, Brother, said she. I wish you was as good as Lord *Davers.*—But don't carry your Jest too far. Well, said he, 'tis a tender Point, I own. I've done!

By these kind Managements the Dinner passed over better than I expected. And when the Servants were withdrawn, my Master said, still keeping his Place between us, I have a Question to ask you, Lady *Davers*; and that is, If you'll bear me Company to *Bedfordshire.* I was intending to set out thither to-morrow. But I'll tarry your Pleasure, if you'll go with me.

Is thy Wife, as thou callest her, to go along with thee, Friend? said she. Yes, to be sure, answer'd he, my dear Quaker Sister,[1] and took her Hand, and smil'd. And wouldst have me parade it with her on the Road?—Hay!—And make one to grace her Retinue?—Hay!—Tell me how thou'dst chalk it out,[2] if I would do as thou wouldst have me, honest Friend!

He clasped his Arms about her, and kissed her: You are a dear saucy Sister, said he; but I must love you!—Why, I'll tell you how I'd have it. Here shall you, and my *Pamela*—Leave out *my*, I desire you, if you'd have me sit patiently. No, said he, I can't do that. Here shall you, and my *Pamela*, go together in your Chariot, if you please; and she will then appear as one of your Retinue; and your Nephew and I will sometimes ride, and sometimes go into my Chariot, to your Woman.

Shouldst thou like this, Creature? said she to me.—If your Ladyship think it not too great an Honour for me, Madam, said I. Yes, reply'd she, but my Ladyship does think it would be too great an Honour.

Now I think of it, said he, this must not be, neither; for without you'd give her the Hand, in your own Chariot, my Wife would be thought your Woman, and that must not be. Why, that would, may-be, said she, be the only Inducement for me to bear her near me, in my Chariot.—But, how then?—Why then, when we came home, we'd get Lord *Davers* to come to us, and stay a Month or two.

And what if he was to come?—Why I would have you, as I know you have a good Fancy, give *Pamela* your Judgment on some Patterns I expect from *London*, for Cloaths.—Provoking Wretch! said she; now I wish I may keep my Hands to myself. I don't say it to provoke you, said he, nor ought it to do so. But when I tell you, I am marry'd, Is it not a Consequence, that we must have new Cloaths?

Hast thou any more of these obliging things to say to me, Friend? said she. I will make you a Present, return'd he, worth your Acceptance, if you will grace us with your Company at Church, when we make our Appearance!—Take that, said she, if I die for't; Wretch that thou art! And was going to hit him a great Slap, but he held her Hand. Her Kinsman said, Dear Aunt, I wonder at you! why all these are things of Course.

I begg'd Leave to withdraw; and, as I went out, my good Master said, There's a Person! There's a Shape! There's a Sweetness! O Lady *Davers!*

were you a Man, you would doat on her, as I do. Yes, said the naughty Lady, so I should, for my Harlot, but not for a Wife. I turn'd, on this, and said, Indeed your Ladyship is cruel; and well may Gentlemen take Liberties, when Ladies of Honour say such things! And I wept, and added, Your Ladyship's Influence, if your good Brother were not the most generous of Men, would make me very unhappy.

No Fear, Wench; no Fear, said she: Thou'lt hold him, as long as any body can, I see that!—Poor *Sally Godfrey* never had half the Interest in him, I'll assure you!

Stay, my *Pamela*, said he, in a Passion; stay, when I bid you. You have heard, this Day, two vile Charges upon me! I love you with such a true Affection, that I ought to say something before this malicious Accuser, that you may not think your consummate Virtue link'd to too black a Villain.

Her Nephew seem'd uneasy, and blam'd her much; and I came back, but trembled as I stood; and he sat me down, and said, taking my Hand, I have been accused, my Dear, as a Dueller, and now as a Profligate, in another Sense! and there was a Time, I should not have received these Imputations with so much Concern as I now do, when I would wish, by degrees, by a Conformity of my Manners to your Virtue, to shew every one the Force your Example has upon me. But this briefly is the Case of the first.

I had a Friend, who had been basely attempted to be assassinated by Bravoes, hir'd by a Man of Title in *Italy*, who, like many other Persons of Title, had no Honour; and at *Padua*, I had the Fortune to disarm one of these Bravoes in my Friend's Defence, and made him confess his Employer; and him, I own, I challeng'd. At *Sienna* we met, and he dy'd in a Month after, of a Fever, but, I hope, not occasion'd by the slight Wounds he had receiv'd from me, tho' I was obliged to leave *Italy* upon it, sooner than I intended, because of his numerous Relations, who looked upon me as the Cause of his Death. Tho' I pacify'd them by a Letter I wrote them from *Inspruck*, acquainting them with the Baseness of the Deceased; and they followed me not to *Munich*, as they had intended.

This is one of the good-natur'd Hints, that might shock your Sweetness on reflecting that you are yoked with a Murderer. The other—Nay, Brother, said she, say no more. 'Tis your own Fault if you go further. She shall know it all, said he; and I defy the utmost Stretch of your Malice.

When I was at College, I was well received by a Widow Lady, who had several Daughters, and but small Fortunes to give them; and the old Lady set one of them; a deserving good Girl she was; to draw me in to a Marriage with her, for the sake of the Fortune I was Heir to; and contriv'd many Opportunities to bring us and leave us together. I was not then of Age; and the young Lady, not half so artful as her Mother, yielded to my Addresses, before the Mother's Plot could be ripen'd, and so utterly disappointed it. This, my *Pamela*, is the *Sally Godfrey* this malicious Woman, with the worst Intentions, has inform'd you of. And whatever other Liberties I may have taken; for perhaps some more I have, which, had she known, you had heard of, as well as this; I desire Heaven will only forgive me till I revive its Vengeance by the like Offences, in Injury to my *Pamela.*

And now, my Dear, you may withdraw; for this worthy Sister of mine has said all the Bad she knows of me; and what, at a proper Opportunity, when I could have convinced you, that they were not my *Boast*, but my *Concern*, I should have acquainted you with, myself; for I am not fond of being thought better than I am: Tho', I hope, from the Hour I devoted myself to so much Virtue, to that of my Death, my Conduct shall be irreproachable.

She was greatly mov'd at this, and the noble Manner in which the dear Gentleman own'd and repented of his Faults; and gushed out into Tears, and said, No, don't yet go, *Pamela*, I beseech you. My Passion has carry'd me too far a great deal; and coming to me, she took my Hand, and said, You must stay to hear me beg his Pardon, and so took his Hand—But, to my Concern, (for I was grieved for her Ladyship's Grief) he burst from her; and went out of the Parlour into the Garden, in a violent Rage, that made me tremble. Her Ladyship sat down, and leaned her Head against my Bosom, and made my Neck wet with her Tears, holding me by my Hands; and I wept for Company.——Her Kinsman walked up and down the Parlour, in a sad Fret; and going out afterwards, he came in, and said, The 'Squire has order'd his Chariot to be got ready, and won't be spoken to by any body. Where is he? said she—Walking in the Garden till 'tis ready, reply'd he.

Well, said she, I have indeed gone too far. I was bewitched! And now, said she, malicious as he calls me, will he not forgive me for a Twelvemonth: For I tell you, *Pamela*, if ever you offend, he will not easily forgive. I was all delighted, tho' sad, to see her Ladyship so good to me. Will you venture, said she, to accompany me to him!—Dare you follow a Lion in his Retreats?—I'll attend your Ladyship, said I, where-ever you command. Well, Wench, said she, *Pamela*, I mean, thou art very good in the main!—I should have lov'd thee as well as my Mother did—if—but 'tis all over now! Indeed you should not have marry'd my Brother! But come, I must love him! Let's find him out. And yet will he now use me worse than a Dog!—I should not, added she, have so much exasperated him: For whenever I have, I have always had the worst of it. He knows I love him!

In this manner her Ladyship talk'd to me, leaning on my Arm, and walked into the Garden. I saw he was still in a Tumult, as it were; and he took another Walk to avoid us.—She call'd after him, and said, Brother, Brother, Let me speak to you!—One Word with you! And as we made haste towards him, and came near to him; I desire, said he, That you'll not oppress me more with your Follies and your Violence. I have borne too much with you. And I will vow for a Twelvemonth, from this Day—Hush, said she, don't vow, I beg you; for too well will you keep it, I know by Experience, if you do: You see, said she, I stoop to ask *Pamela* to be my Advocate. Sure that will pacify you!

Indeed, said he, I desire to see neither of you, on such an Occasion; and let me only be left to myself; for I will not be intruded upon thus; and was going away.—But she said, One Word first, I desire—If you'll forgive me, I'll forgive you!—What, said the dear Man, haughtily, will you forgive me!—Why, said she, for she saw him too angry to mention his Marriage, as a Subject that requir'd her Pardon,—I will forgive you all your bad Usage of me this Day.

I will be serious with you, Sister, said he: I wish you most sincerely well; but let us, from this Time, study so much one another's Quiet, as never to come near one another more.—Never? said she.—And can you desire this, barbarous Brother! can you?—I can, I do, said he; and I have nothing to do, but hide from you, not a Brother, but a Murderer, and a Profligate, unworthy of your Relation; and let me be consign'd to Penitence for my past Evils: A Penitence however, that shall not be broken in upon by so violent an Accuser.

Pamela, said he, and made me tremble, How dare you approach me, without Leave, when you see me thus disturb'd!—Never, for the future, come near me, while I am in these Tumults, unless I send for you.

Dear Sir! said I——Leave me, interrupted he. I will set out for *Bedfordshire* this Moment: What! Sir, said I, without me?—What have I done! You have too meanly, said he, for my Wife, stooped to this furious Sister of mine; and, till I can recollect, I am not pleased with you: But *Colbrand* shall attend you, and two other of my Servants; and Mrs. *Jewkes* shall wait upon you part of the Way. And I hope, you'll find me in a better Disposition to receive you there, than I am at parting with you here.

Had I not hoped, that this was partly put on to intimidate my Lady, I believe I could not have borne it: But it was grievous to me; for I saw he was most sincerely in a Passion.

I was afraid, said she, he would be angry at you, as well as me; for well do I know his unreasonable Violence, when he is moved. But one Word,

Sir, said she; Pardon *Pamela*, if you won't me; for she has committed no Offence, but that of Good-nature to me, and at my Request. I will begone myself, directly, as I was about to do, had you not prevented me.

I prevented you, said he, thro' Love; but you have stung me for it, thro' Hatred. But as for my *Pamela*, I know, besides the present Moment, I cannot be angry with her; and therefore I desire her never to see me on such Occasions, till I can see her in the Temper I ought to be in when so much Sweetness approaches me. 'Tis therefore, I say, my Dearest, leave me now.

But, Sir, said I, must I leave you, and let you go to *Bedford* without me! O dear Sir, how can I?——Said my Lady, You may go to-morrow, both of you, as you had design'd, and I will go away this Afternoon; and since I cannot be forgiven, I will try to forget I have a Brother.

May I, Sir, said I, beg all your Anger on myself, and to be reconciled to your good Sister? Presuming *Pamela!* reply'd he, and made me start, art thou then so hardy, so well able to sustain a Displeasure, which, of all things, I expected, from thy Affection and thy Tenderness, thou wouldst have wished to avoid?—Now, said he, and took my Hand, and, as it were, tost it from him, begone from my Presence, and reflect upon what you have said to me!

I was so frighted, for then I saw he took amiss what I said, that I took hold of his Knees, as he was turning from me, and I said, Forgive me, good Sir; you see I am not so hardy! I cannot bear your Displeasure! And was ready to sink.

His Sister said, Only forgive *Pamela*; 'tis all I ask!——You'll break her Spirit quite!——You'll carry your Passion as much too far as I have done!——I need not say, said he, how well I love her: but she must not intrude upon me at such times as these!——I had intended, as soon as I could have quell'd, by my Reason, the Tumults you had caused by your Violence, to have come in, and taken such a Leave of you both, as might become a Husband and a Brother; but she has, unbidden, broken in upon me, and must take the Consequence of a Passion, which, when raised, is as uncontroulable as your own.

Said she, Did I not love you so well, as Sister never loved a Brother, I should not have given you all this Trouble. And did I not, said he, love you better than you are resolv'd to deserve, I should be indifferent to all you say. But this last Instance, (after the Duelling-story, which you would not have mention'd, had you not known it is always matter of Concern for me to think upon) of poor *Sally Godfrey*, is a Piece of Spite and Meanness, that I can renounce you my Blood for.

Well, said she, I am convinced it was wrong. I am asham'd of it myself. 'Twas poor, 'twas mean, 'twas unworthy of your Sister: And 'tis for this Reason I stoop to follow you, to beg your Pardon, and even to procure for my Advocate one, that I thought had some Interest in you, if I might have believed your own Professions to her; which now I shall begin to think made purposely to insult me.

I care not what you think!——After the Meanness you have been guilty of, I can only look upon you with Pity. For, indeed, you have fallen very low with me.

'Tis plain I have, said she. But, I'll begone.—And so, Brother, let me call you so this once! God bless you! And, *Pamela*, said her Ladyship, God bless you! And kissed me, and wept.

I durst say no more; and my Lady turning from him, he said, Your Sex is the D——l; how strangely can you discompose, calm, and turn, as you please, us poor Weathercocks of Men! Your last kind Blessing to my *Pamela*, I cannot stand! Kiss but each other again. And he then took both our Hands, and join'd them; and my Lady saluting me again, with Tears on both sides, he put his kind Arms about each of our Waists, and saluted us with great Affection, saying, Now, God bless you both, the two dearest Creatures I have in the World.

Well, said she, you will quite forget my Fault about Miss —— He stopt her, before she could speak the Name, and said, For ever forget it!—And, *Pamela*, I'll forgive you too, if you don't again make my Displeasure so light a thing to you, as you did just now!

Said my Lady, She did not make your Displeasure a light thing to her; but the heavier it was, the higher Compliment she made me, that she would bear it all, rather than not see you and me reconciled. No matter for that, said he: It was either an Absence of Thought, or a Slight, by Implication at least, that my Niceness could not bear from her Tenderness. For, looked it not presuming, that she could stand my Displeasure, or was sure of making her Terms when she pleas'd? Which, fond as I am of her, I assure her, will not be always, in wilful Faults, in her own Power.

Nay, said my Lady, I can tell you, *Pamela*, you have a Gentleman here in my Brother; and you may expect such Treatment from him, as that Character, and his known good Sense and Breeding, will always oblige him to shew: But *if* you offend, the Lord have Mercy upon you!— You see how it is by poor me!—And yet, I never knew him forgive so soon.

I am sure, said I, I will take care as much as I can! for I have been frighted out of my Wits, and had offended before I knew where I was.

So happily did this Storm blow over; and my Lady was quite subdu'd and pacify'd. When we came out of the Garden, his Chariot was ready; and he said, Well, Sister, I had most assuredly gone away towards my other House, if things had not taken this happy Turn; and if you please, instead of it, you and I will take an Airing: And pray, my Dear, said he to me, bid Mrs. *Jewkes* order Supper by Eight o'Clock, and we shall then join you.

Sir, added he, to her Nephew, will you take your Horse, and escorte us. I will, said he; and am glad, at my Soul, to see you all so good Friends.—So my dear lordly Master (O my dear Parents! he is very dreadful when he pleases, I see!—But, I hope, I shall never incur his Anger) handed my Lady into his Chariot, and her Kinsman, and his Servant, rode after them; and I went up to my Closet, to ruminate on these things. And, foolish thing that I am, this poor Miss *Sally Godfrey* runs in my Head!——How soon the Name and Quality of a Wife gives one Privileges, in one's own Account!—Yet, methinks, I want to know more about her; for, is it not strange, that I, who lived Years in the Family, should have heard nothing of this? But I was so constantly with my Lady, that I might the less hear of it; for she, I dare say, never knew it, or she would have told me.

But I dare not ask him about the poor Lady—Yet I wonder what became of her? Whether she be living? And whether any thing came of it?—— May-be I shall hear full soon enough:—But I hope not to any bad Purpose.

As to the other unhappy Case, I know it was talk'd of, that in his Travels, before I was taken into the Family long, he had one or two Broils; and, from a Youth, he was always remarkable for Courage, and is reckon'd a great Master of his Sword. God grant he may never be put to use it! And that he may be always preserved in Honour and Safety!

About Seven o'Clock, my Master sent word, that he would have me not expect him to Supper. For that he and my Lady his Sister, and Nephew, were prevailed upon to stay with Lady *Jones*; and that Lady *Darnford*, and Mr. *Peters*'s Family, had promised to meet them there. I was glad that they did not send for me; and the rather, as I hoped those good Families, being my Friends, would confirm my Lady a little in my Favour; and so I follow'd my Writing closely.

About Eleven o'Clock they return'd. I had but just come down, having tir'd myself with my Pen, and was sitting talking with Mrs. *Jewkes* and Mrs. *Worden*, whom I would, tho' unwillingly on their Sides, make sit down over-against me. Mrs. *Worden* asked me Pardon, in a good deal of

Confusion, for the Part she had acted against me; saying, That Things had been very differently represented to her; and that she little thought I had been marry'd, and that she was behaving so rudely to the Lady of the House.

I said, I took nothing amiss, and very freely forgave her; and hoped my new Condition would not make me forget how to behave properly to every one; but that I must endeavour to act not unworthy of it, for the Honour of the Gentleman who had so generously raised me to it.

Mrs. *Jewkes* said, that my Situation gave me great Opportunities of shewing the Excellency of my Nature, that I could forgive Offences against me so readily, as she for her own Part, must always, she said, acknowledge, with Confusion of Face.

People, said I, Mrs. *Jewkes*, don't know how they shall act, when their Wills are in the Power of their Superiors; and I always thought one should distinguish between Acts of Malice, and of implicit Obedience; tho', at the same time, a Person should know how to judge between Lawful and Unlawful. And even the Great, continued I, tho' at present angry they are not obey'd, will afterwards have no ill Opinion of a Person for withstanding them in their unlawful Commands.

Mrs. *Jewkes* seem'd a little concern'd at this; and I said, I spoke chiefly from my own Experience; for that I might say, as they both knew my Story, that I had not wanted both for Menaces and Temptations; and had I comply'd with the one, or been intimidated by the other, I should not have been what I was.

Ah! Madam, said Mrs. *Jewkes*, I never knew any body like you: And I think your Temper sweeter since the happy Day, than before; and that, if possible, you take less upon you than before.

Why, a good Reason, said I, may be assigned for that: I thought myself in Danger: I look'd upon every one as my Enemy; and it was impossible that I should not be fretful, uneasy, jealous. But when my dearest Sir had taken from me the Ground of my Uneasiness, and made me quite happy, I should have been very blameable if I had not shewn a satisfy'd and easy Mind, and a Temper that should engage every one's Respect and Love at the same time, if possible: And so much the more, as it was but justifying, in some sort, the Honour I had received; for the fewer Enemies I made myself, the more I engaged every one to think, that my good Benefactor had been less to blame in descending as he has done.

This way of talking pleas'd them both very much; and they made me many Compliments upon it, and wished me to be always happy, as, they said, I so well deserved.

We were thus engaged, when my Master and his Sister, and her Nephew, came in. And they made me quite alive, in the happy Humour in which they all return'd. The two Women would have withdrawn; but my Master said, Don't go, Mrs. *Worden*; Mrs. *Jewkes*, pray stay; I shall speak to you presently. So he came to me, and saluting me, said, Well, my dear Love, I hope I have not trespass'd upon your Patience, by an Absence longer than we design'd. But it has not been to your Disadvantage; for tho' we had not your Company, we have talked of nobody else but you.

My Lady came up to me, and said, Ay, Child, you have been all our Subject. I don't know how it is; but you have made two or three whole Families, in this Neighbourhood, as much your Admirers, as your Friend here.

My Sister, said he, has been hearing your Praises, *Pamela*, from half a score Mouths, with more Pleasure than her Heart will easily let her express.

My good Lady *Davers*'s Favour, said I, and the Continuance of yours, Sir, would give me more Pride than that of all the rest of the World put together.

Well, Child, said she, proud Hearts don't come down all at once; tho' my Brother here has, this Day, set mine a good many Pegs lower than I ever knew it: But I will say, I wish you Joy with my Brother; and so kissed me.

My dear Lady, said I, you for ever oblige me!—I shall now believe myself quite happy. This was all I wanted to make me so!—And, I hope, I shall always, thro' my Life, shew your Ladyship, that I have the most grateful and respectful Sense of your Goodness.

But, Child, said she, I shall not give you my Company when you make your Appearance. Let your own Merit make all your *Bedfordshire* Neighbours your Friends, as it has done here, by your *Lincolnshire* ones; and you'll have no need of my Countenance, nor any body's else.

Now, said her Nephew, 'tis my Turn; I wish you Joy with all my Soul, Madam; and, by what I have seen, and by what I have heard, 'fore Gad, I think you have met with no more than you deserve; and so all the Company says, where we have been. And pray forgive all my Nonsense to you.

Sir, said I, I shall always, I hope, respect as I ought, so near a Relation of my good Lord and Lady *Davers*; and I thank you for your kind Compliment.

Gad, *Beck*, said he, I believe you've some Forgiveness too to ask; for we were all to blame, to make Madam, here, fly the Pit, as she did! Little did we think we made her quit her own House.

Thou always, said my Lady, say'st too much or too little.

Mrs. *Worden* said, I have been treated with so much Goodness and Condescension, since you went, that I have been beforehand, Sir, in asking Pardon for myself.

So my Lady sat down with me half an Hour, and told me how her Brother had carry'd her a fine Airing, and had quite charm'd her with his kind Treatment of her; and had much confirm'd her in the good Opinion she had begun to entertain of my discreet and obliging Behaviour: But, continued she, when he would make me visit, without intending to stay, my old Neighbours, (for, said she, Lady *Jones* being nearest, we visited her first; and she scrap'd all the rest of the Company together) they were all so full of your Praises, that I was quite borne down; and, truly, it was *Saul* among the Prophets!

You may believe how much I was delighted with this; and I spar'd not my due Acknowledgments.

When her Ladyship took Leave, to go to-bed, she said, Good-night to you, heartily, and to your good Man. I kiss'd you when I came in, out of Form; but I now kiss you out of more than Form, I'll assure you.

Join with me, my dear Parents, in my Joy for this happy Turn; the contrary of which, I so much dreaded, and was the only Difficulty I had to labour with!—This poor Miss *Sally Godfrey*, I wonder what's become of her, poor Soul!—I wish he would, of his own Head, mention her again.— Not that I am *very* uneasy neither.—You'll say, I must be a little saucy, if I was.

My dear Master gave me an Account, when we went up, of the Pains he had taken with his beloved Sister, as he himself styled her; and of all the kind Things the good Families had said in my Behalf; and that he observ'd she was not so much displeas'd with hearing them, as she was at first; when she would not permit any body to speak of me as his Wife. And that my Health, as his Spouse, being put; when it came to her, she drank it; but said, Come, Brother, here's your *Pamela* to you.—But I shall not know how to stand this Affair, when the Countess -------- and the young Ladies come to visit me. It was with one of those young Ladies, that she was so fond of promoting a Match with her Brother.—Lady *Betty*, I know, said she, will rally me smartly upon it; and you know, Brother, she wants neither Wit, nor Satire. He said, I hope, Lady *Betty*, whenever she marries, will meet with a better Husband than I should have made her; for, on my Conscience, I think, I should hardly have made a tolerable one to any but *Pamela*.

He told me, That they rallied him on the Stateliness of his Temper; and said, They saw he would make an exceeding good Husband where he was;

but it must be owing to my Meekness,[1] more than his Complaisance; for, said Miss *Darnford*, I could see, well enough, when your Ladyship detained her, tho' he had but hinted his Desire of finding her at our House, he was so out of Humour at her supposed Non-complaisance, that mine and my Sister's Pity for her was much more engag'd than our Envy.

Ay, said my Lady, he is too lordly a Creature, by much, and can't bear Disappointment, and never could.

Said he, Well, Lady *Davers*, you should not, of all Persons, find Fault with me; for I bore a great deal from you, before I was at all angry.

Yes, reply'd she; but when I had gone a little too far, as I own I did, you made me pay for it severely enough! You know you did, Sauce-box. And the poor thing too, added she, that I took with me for my Advocate, so low had he brought me! he treated in such a manner, as made my Heart ach for her: But part was *Art*, I know, to make me think the better of her.

Indeed, Sister, said he, there was very little of that; for, at that time, I cared not what you thought, nor had Complaisance enough to have given a Shilling for your good or bad Opinion of her or me. And, I own, I was displeased to be broken in upon, after your Provocations, by either of you; and she must learn that Lesson, never to come near me, when I am in those Humours; which shall be as little as possible; for, after a-while, if let alone, I always come to myself, and am sorry for the Violence of a Temper so like my dear Sister's here: And, for this Reason, think it is no matter how few Witnesses I have of its Intemperance, while it lasts; especially since every Witness, whether they merit it or not, as you see in my *Pamela*'s Case, must be a Sufferer by it, if, unsent for, they come in my Way.

He repeated the same Lesson to me again, and inforc'd it; and own'd, that he was angry with me in Earnest, just then; tho' more with himself, afterwards, for being so: But when, *Pamela*, said he, you wanted to transfer all my Displeasure upon yourself, it was so much braving me with your Merit, as if I must soon end my Anger, if placed there; or it was making it so light to you, that I was truly displeased. For, continued he, I cannot bear that you should wish, on any Occasion whatever, to have me angry with you, or not to value my Displeasure, as the heaviest Misfortune that could befal you.

But, Sir, said I, you know, that what I did was to try to reconcile my Lady, and as she herself observ'd, it was paying her a high Regard. It was so, reply'd he; but never think of making a Compliment to her, or any body living, at my Expence. Besides, she had behav'd herself so intolerably, that I began to think you had stooped too much, and more than I ought to permit my Wife to do; and Acts of Meanness are what I can't endure in any body, but especially where I love; and as she had been guilty of a very signal one, I had much rather have renounced her, at that time, than have been reconciled to her.

Sir, said I, I hope I shall always comport myself so, as not wilfully to disoblige you for the future; and the rather do I hope this, as I am sure I shall want only to *know* your Pleasure, to *obey* it. But this Instance shews me, that I may *much* offend, without designing it in the *least*.

Now, *Pamela*, reply'd he, don't be too serious; I hope I shan't be a very tyrannical Husband to you. Yet do I not pretend to be perfect, or to be always govern'd by Reason in my first Transports; and I expect, from your Affection, that you will bear with me when you find me wrong. I have no ingrateful Spirit, and can, when cool, enter as impartially into myself, as most Men; and then I am always kind and acknowledging, in proportion as I have been out of the Way.

But, to convince you, my Dear, continued he, of your Fault, (I mean, with regard to the Impetuosity of my Temper; for there was no Fault in your Intention, *that* I acknowledge) I'll observe only, that you met, when you came to me, while I was so out of Humour, a Reception you did not expect, and a harsh Word or two, that you did not deserve. Now, had you not broken in upon me, while my Anger lasted, but stay'd till I had come to you, or sent to desire your Company, you'd have seen none of this; but that affectionate Behaviour, that, I doubt not, you'll always merit, and I shall always take Pleasure in expressing; and in *this Temper* shall you always find a *proper Influence* over me: But you must not suppose, whenever I am out of Humour, that, in opposing yourself to my Passion, you oppose a proper Butt to it; but when you are so good, like the slender Reed, to bend to the Hurricane, rather than, like the sturdy Oak, to resist it,[1] you will always stand firm in my kind Opinion, while a contrary Conduct would uproot you, with all your Excellencies, from my Soul.

Sir, said I, I will endeavour to conform myself, in all things, to your Will. I make no Doubt, but you will: And I'll endeavour to make my Will as conformable to Reason as I can. And, let me tell you, that this Belief of you, is one of the Inducements I have had to marry at all. For nobody was more averse to this State than myself; and now we're upon this Subject, I'll tell you why I was so averse.

We People of Fortune, or such as are born to large Expectations, of both Sexes, are generally educated wrong. You have occasionally touch'd upon this, *Pamela*, several times in your Journal, so justly, that I need say the less to you. We are usually so headstrong, so violent in our Wills, that we very little bear Controul.

Humour'd by our *Nurses*, thro' the Faults of our Parents, we practise first upon them; and shew the *Gratitude* of our Dispositions, in an Insolence that ought rather to be check'd and restrain'd, than encouraged.

Next, we are to be indulged in every thing at School; and our *Masters and Mistresses* are rewarded with further grateful Instances of our boisterous Behaviour.

But, in our wise Parents Eyes, all looks well, all is forgiven and excus'd; and for no other Reason, but because we are *Theirs*.

Our next Progression is, we exercise our Spirits, when brought home, to the Torment and Regret of our *Parents themselves*, and torture their Hearts by our undutiful and perverse Behaviour to them; which, however ingrateful in us, is but the natural Consequence of their culpable Indulgence to us, from Infancy upwards.

And then, next, after we have, perhaps, half broken their Hearts, a *Wife* is look'd out for: Convenience, or Birth and Fortune, are the first Motives, Affection the last (if it is at all consulted): And two People thus educated, thus trained up in a Course of unnatural Ingratitude, and who have been headstrong Torments to every one who has had a Share in their Education, as well as to those to whom they owe their Being, are brought together; and what can be expected, but that they should pursue, and carry on, the same comfortable Conduct, in Matrimony, and join most heartily to plague one another? And, in some measure, indeed, this is right, because hereby they revenge the Cause of all those who have been aggrieved and insulted by them, upon one another.

The Gentleman has never been controuled: The Lady has never been contradicted.

He cannot bear it from one whose new Relation, he thinks, should oblige her to shew a quite contrary Conduct.

She thinks it very barbarous, now, for the *first* time, to be opposed by a Man, from whom she expected nothing but Tenderness.

So great is the Difference, between what they both expect *from* one another, and what they both find *in* each other, that no wonder Misunderstandings happen; that these ripen to Quarrels; that Acts of Unkindness pass, which, even had the first Motive to their Union been *Affection*, as usually it is not, would have effaced all manner of tender Impressions on both sides.

Appeals to Parents or Guardians often ensue: If, by Mediation of Friends, a Reconciliation takes place, it hardly ever holds; for why? The Fault is in the Minds of *both*, and *neither* of them will think so; so that the Wound (not permitted to be probed) is but skinn'd over, and rankles still at the Bottom, and at last breaks out with more Pain and Anguish than before. Separate Beds are often the Consequence; perhaps Elopements; if not, an unconquerable Indifference, possibly Aversion. And whenever, for Appearance-sake, they are obliged to be together, every one sees, that the yawning Husband, and the vapourish[1] Wife, are truly insupportable to one another; but, separate, have freer Spirits, and can be tolerable Company.

Now, my Dear, I would have you think, and, I hope, you will have no other Reason, that had I marry'd the first Lady in the Land, I would not have treated her better than I will my *Pamela*. For my Wife *is* my Wife; and I was the longer in resolving on the State, because I knew its Requisites, and doubted my Conduct in it.

I believe I am more nice than many Gentlemen; but it is because I have been a close Observer of the Behaviour of wedded Folks, and hardly have ever seen it to be such as I could like in my own Case. I shall, possibly, give you Instances, of a more particular Nature, of this, as we are *longer*, and, perhaps, I might say, *better* acquainted.

Had I marry'd with the Views of most Gentlemen, and with such as my good Sister (supplying the Place of my Father and Mother) would have recommended, I had wedded a fine Lady, brought up pretty much in my own Manner, and used to have her Will in every thing.

Some Gentlemen can come into a Compromise; and, after a few Struggles, sit down tolerably contented. But, had I marry'd a Princess, I could not have done so. I must have loved her exceedingly well, before I had consented to knit the Knot with her, and preferr'd her to all her Sex; for without this, *Pamela*, Indifferences, if not Disgusts, will arise in every wedded Life, that could not have made me happy at home; and there are fewer Instances, I believe, of Mens loving better after Matrimony, than of Womens; the Reasons of which 'tis not my present Purpose to account for.

Then I must have been morally sure, that she preferr'd me to all Men; and, to convince me of this, she must have lessen'd, not aggravated, my Failings; she must have borne with my Imperfections; she must have watch'd and study'd my Temper; and if ever she had any Points to carry, any Desire of overcoming, it must have been by Sweetness and Complaisance; and yet not such a slavish one, as should make her Condescension seem to be rather the Effect of her Insensibility,[2] than Judgment or Affection.

She should not have given Cause for any Part of my Conduct to her, to wear the least Aspect of Compulsion or Force. The Word *Command*, on my Side, or *Obedience*, on hers, I would have blotted from my Vocabulary. For this Reason I should have thought it my Duty to have desired nothing of her, that was not significant, reasonable, or just; and that then she should, on hers, have shewn no Reluctance, Uneasiness, or Doubt, to oblige me, even at half a Word.

I would not have excus'd her to let me twice injoin the same thing, while I took such care to make her Compliance with me reasonable, and such as should not destroy her own free Agency, in Points that ought to be allow'd her. And if I was not always right, that yet she would bear with me, if she saw me set upon it; and expostulate with me on the right side of Compliance; for that would shew me, (supposing *small Points* in Dispute, from which the greatest Quarrels, among *Friends*, generally arise) that she differ'd from me, not for *Contradiction-sake*, but desir'd to convince me for *my own*; and that I should, another time, take better Resolutions.

This would be so obliging a Conduct, that I should, in Justice, have doubled my Esteem for one, who, to humour me, could give up her own Judgment; and I should see she could have no other View in her Expostulations, after her Compliance had passed, than to rectify my Notions for the future; and it would have been impossible then, but I must have paid the greater Deference to her Opinion and Advice in more momentous Matters.

In all Companies she must have shewn, that she had, whether I deserved it altogether, or not, a high Regard and Opinion of me; and this the rather, as that such a Conduct in her, would be a Reputation and Security to herself; for if ever we Rakes attempt a marry'd Lady, our first Encouragement, exclusive of our own Vanity, arises from the indifferent Opinion, Slight, or Contempt she expresses for her Husband.

That therefore she would draw a kind Veil over my Faults; that such as she could not hide, she would extenuate: That she would place my better Actions in an advantageous Light, and shew, that I had *her* good Opinion, at least, whatever Liberties the *World* took with my Character.

She must have valued my Friends for *my* sake; been chearful and easy, whomever I had brought home with me; and whatever Faults she had observed in me, have never blamed me before Company; at least, with such an Air of Superiority as should have shewn she had a better Opinion of her own Judgment, than mine.

Now, my *Pamela*, this is but a faint Sketch of the Conduct I must have expected from my Wife, let her Quality have been what it would, or have lived with her on bad Terms. Judge then, if, to me, a Lady of the modish Taste could have been tolerable.

The Perverseness and Contradiction I have too often seen, in some of my Visits, even among People of Sense, as well as Condition, had prejudiced me to the marry'd State; and, as I knew I could not bear it, surely I was in the right to decline it; and you see, my Dear, that I have not gone among this Class of People for a Wife; nor know I indeed, where, in any Class, I could have sought one, or had one, suitable to my Mind, if not you. For here is my Misfortune; I could not have been contented to have been *but moderately happy* in a Wife.

Judge you, from all this, if I could very well bear, that you should think yourself so well secur'd of my Affection, that you could take the Faults of others upon yourself; and, by a supposed supererogatory Merit,[1] think your Interposition sufficient to atone for the Faults of others.

Yet am I not perfect myself: No, I am greatly imperfect. Yet will I not allow, that my Imperfections shall excuse those of my Wife, or make her think I ought to bear Faults in her, that she can rectify, because she bears greater from me.

Upon the Whole, I may expect, that you will bear with me, and study my Temper, *till*, and only *till*, you see I am capable of returning Insult for Obligation; and till you think that I shall be of a gentler Deportment, if I am roughly used, than otherwise. One thing more I will add, That I should scorn myself, if there was one Privilege of your Sex, that a Princess might expect, as my Wife, to be indulg'd in, that I would not allow to my *Pamela*. For you are the Wife of my Affections: I never wish'd for one before you, nor ever do I hope to have another!

I hope, Sir, said I, my future Conduct——Pardon me, said he, my Dear, for interrupting you; but it is to assure you, that I am so well convinc'd of your affectionate Regards for me, that I know I might have spared the greatest Part of what I have said: And indeed, it must be very bad for both of us, if I should have Reason to think it *necessary* to say so much. But one thing has brought on another; and I have rather spoken what my Niceness has made me *observe* in *other* Families, than what I *fear* in *my own*. And therefore, let me assure you, I am thoroughly satisfy'd with your Conduct hitherto. You shall have no Occasion to repent it. And you shall find, tho' greatly imperfect, and passionate, on particular Provocations, (which yet I will try to overcome) that you have not a brutal or ungenerous Husband, who is capable of offering Insult for Condescension, or returning Evil for Good.

I thank'd him for these kind Rules, and generous Assurances; and assured him, that they had made so much Impression on my Mind, that these, and his most agreeable Injunctions before given me, and such as he should hereafter be pleased to give me, should be so many Rules for my future Conduct.

And I am glad of the Method I have taken of making a Journal of all that passes in these first Stages of my Happiness, because it will sink the Impression still deeper; and I shall have recourse to them for my better Regulation, as often as I shall mistrust my Memory.

Let me see: What are the Rules I am to observe from this awful Lecture? Why, these:

1. That I must not, when he is in great Wrath with any body, break in upon him, without his Leave.——*Well, I'll remember it, I warrant. But yet I fansy this Rule is almost peculiar to himself.*
2. That I must think his Displeasure the heaviest thing that can befal me. *To be sure I shall.*
3. And so that I must not wish to incur it, to save any body else. *I'll be further if I do.*
4. That I must never make a Compliment to any body at his Expence.
5. That I must not be guilty of any Acts of wilful Meanness! *There is a great deal meant in this; and I'll endeavour to observe it all. To be sure, the Occasion on which he mentions this, explains it; that I must say nothing, tho' in Anger, that is spiteful or malicious; that is disrespectful or undutiful, and such-like.*
6. That I must bear with him, even when I find him in the wrong. *This is a little hard, as the Case may be!*
   I wonder whether poor Miss Sally Godfrey be living or dead!
7. That I must be as flexible as the Reed in the Fable, lest, by resisting the Tempest, like the Oak, I be torn up by the Roots. *Well! I'll do the best I can!—There is no great Likelihood, I hope, I should be too perverse; yet, sure, the Tempest will not lay me quite level with the Ground neither.*
8. That the Education of young People of Condition is generally wrong. Memorandum, *That if any Part of Childrens Education[1] fall to my Lot, I never indulge or humour them in things that they ought to be restrain'd in.*
9. That I accustom them to bear Disappointments and Controul.
10. That I suffer them not to be too much indulged in their Infancy.
11. Nor at School.
12. Nor spoil them when they come home.
13. For that Children generally extend their Perverseness from the Nurse to the Schoolmaster; from the Schoolmaster to the Parents.
14. And, in their next Step, as a proper Punishment for all, make their own Selves unhappy.

15. That undutiful and perverse Children make bad Husbands and Wives: *And, collaterally, bad Masters and Mistresses.*

16. That not being subject to be controuled early, they cannot, when marry'd, bear one another.

17. That the Fault lying deep, and in the Minds of each, neither will mend it.

18. Whence follow Misunderstandings, Quarrels, Appeals, ineffectual Reconciliations, Separations, Elopements—or, at best, Indifference; perhaps, Aversion.—Memorandum, *A good Image of unhappy Wedlock, in the Words* YAWNING HUSBAND *and* VAPOURISH WIFE, *when* together:—*But* separate, *both quite alive.*

19. Few marry'd Persons behave as he likes!—*Let me ponder this with Awe and Improvement.*

20. Some Gentlemen can compromise with their Wives for Quietness-sake; but he can't.—*Indeed I believe that's true!—I don't desire he should.*

21. That Love before Marriage is absolutely necessary.

22. That there are fewer Instances of Mens than Womens loving better after Marriage.—*But why so? I wish he had given his Reasons for this! I fansy they would not have been to the Advantage of his own Sex.*

23. That a Woman give her Husband Reason to think she prefers him before all Men. *Well, to be sure this should be so.*

24. That if she would overcome, it must be by Sweetness and Complaisance; *that is, by* yielding, *he means, no doubt.*

25. Yet not such a slavish one neither, as should rather seem the Effect of her Insensibility, than Judgment or Affection!

26. That the Words COMMAND and OBEY shall be blotted out of his Vocabulary. *Very good!*

27. That a Man should desire nothing of his Wife but what is significant, reasonable, just. *To be sure that is right.*

28. But then, that she must not shew Reluctance, Uneasiness, or Doubt, to oblige him; and that too at half a Word; and must not be bid twice to do one thing.—*But may not there be some Occasions, where this may be a little dispens'd with? But he says afterwards, indeed,*

29. That this must be only while he took care to make her Compliance reasonable, and consistent with her free Agency, in Points that ought to be allow'd her.—*Come, this is pretty well, considering.*

30. That if the Husband be *set* upon a wrong Thing, she must not dispute with him, but do it, and expostulate afterwards.—*Good-sirs! I don't know what to say to this!—It looks a little hard, methinks!—This would*

bear a smart Debate, I fansy, in a Parliament of Women.[1]—But then he says,

31. Supposing they are only small Points that are in Dispute.—*Well, this mends it a little. For small Points, I think, should not be stood upon.*

32. That the greatest Quarrels among Friends, *and Wives and Husbands are or should be Friends,* arise from small Matters.—*I believe this is very true; for I had like to have had Anger here, when I intended very well.*

33. That a Wife should not desire to convince her Husband for CONTRADICTION sake; but for HIS OWN. *As both will find their Account in this, if one does; I believe 'tis very just.*

34. That in all Companies a Wife must shew Respect and Love to her Husband.

35. And this for the sake of her own Reputation and Security; for,

36. That Rakes cannot have a greater Encouragement to attempt a marry'd Lady's Virtue, than her slight Opinion of her Husband. *To be sure, this stands to Reason, and is a fine Lesson.*

37. That a Wife should therefore draw a kind Veil over her Husband's Faults.

38. That such as she could not conceal, she should extenuate.

39. That his Virtues she should place in an Advantageous Light.

40. And shew the World, that he had HER good Opinion at least.

41. That she must value his Friends for *his* sake.

42. That she must be chearful and easy in her Behaviour, to whomsoever he brings home with him.

43. That whatever Faults she sees in him, she never blames him before Company.

44. At least, with such an Air of Superiority, as if she had a less Opinion of his Judgment than her own.

45. That a Man of nice Observation cannot be contented to be only *moderately* happy in a Wife.

46. That a Wife take care how she ascribe supererogatory Merit to herself; so as to take the Faults of others upon her.—*Indeed, I think it is well if we can bear our own! This is of the same Nature with the Third. And touches upon me on the present Occasion, for this wholsome Lecture.*

47. That *his* Imperfections must not be a Plea for *hers. To be sure, 'tis no matter how good the Women are; but 'tis to be hoped, Men will allow a little. But, indeed, he says,*

48. That a Husband who expects all this, is to be incapable of returning Insult for Obligation, or Evil for Good; and ought not to abridge her of any Privilege of her Sex.

Well, my dear Parents, I think this last Rule crowns the rest, and makes them all very tolerable; and a generous Man, and a Man of Sense, cannot be too much obliged. And, as I have this Happiness, I shall be very unworthy, if I do not always so *think*, and so *act*.

Yet, after all, you'll see I have not the easiest Task in the World. But I know my own Intentions, that I shall not wilfully err; and so fear the less.

Not one Hint did he give, that I durst lay hold of, about poor Miss *Sally Godfrey*. I wish my Lady had not spoken of it. For it has given me a Curiosity that is not quite so pretty in me; especially so early in my Nuptials, and in a Case so long ago past. Yet he intimated too, to his Sister, that he had had other Faults, (of this Sort, I suppose) that had not come to her Knowledge!—But I make no Doubt, he has seen his Error, and will be very good for the future. I wish it, and pray it may be so, for his own dear sake!

WEDNESDAY, the Seventh.

When I arose in the Morning, I went to wait on Lady *Davers*, seeing her Door open; and she was in Bed, but awake, and talking to her Woman. I said, I hope I don't disturb your Ladyship: No, not at all, said she; I am glad to see you. How do you?—Well, added she, when do you set out for *Bedfordshire?* I said, I can't tell, Madam. It was design'd as to-day; but I have heard no more of it.

Sit down, said she, on the Bed-side.—I find, by the Talk we had Yesterday and last Night, you have had but a poor Time of it, *Pamela*, (I must call you so yet, said she) since you was brought to this House, till within these few Days. And Mrs. *Jewkes* too has given *Beck* such an Account, as makes me pity you.

Indeed, Madam, said I, if your Ladyship knew all, you *would* pity me; for never poor Creature was so hard put to it. But I ought to forget it all now, and be thankful.

Why, said she, as far as I can find, 'tis a Mercy you are here now. I was sadly moved with some part of your Story. And you have really made a noble Defence, and deserve the Praises of all our Sex.

It was God enabled me, Madam, reply'd I. Why, said she, 'tis the more extraordinary, because, I believe, if the Truth was known, you lov'd the Wretch not a little. While my Trials lasted, Madam, said I, I had not a *Thought* of *any thing*, but to preserve my Innocence; much less of Love.

But tell me truly, said she, Did you not love him all the time? I had always, Madam, answer'd I, a great Reverence for my Master, and thought all his good Actions doubly good; and for his naughty ones, tho' I abhorr'd his Attempts upon me, yet I could not hate him; and always wish'd him well; but I did not know that it was Love. Indeed I had not the Presumption!

Sweet Girl! said she; that's prettily said: But when he found he could not gain his Ends, and begun to be sorry for your Sufferings, and to admire your Virtue, and to profess honourable Love to you, What did you think?

Think, and please your Ladyship! I did not know what to think! I could neither hope, nor believe so great an Honour would fall to my Lot; and I fear'd more from his Kindness, for some time, than I had done from his Unkindness: And having had a private Intimation, from a kind Friend, of a Sham-marriage intended, by means of a Man who was to personate a Minister, it kept my Mind in too much Suspense, to be greatly overjoy'd at his kind Declaration.

Said she, I think he *did* make two or three Attempts upon you in *Bedfordshire?* Yes, Madam, said I, he was very naughty, to be sure!

And *here*, he proposed Articles to you, I understand? Yes, Madam, reply'd I; but I abhorr'd so much the Thoughts of being a kept Creature, that I rejected them with great Boldness; and was resolved to die before I would consent to them.

He afterwards attempted you, I think; Did he not? O, yes, Madam! said I, a most sad Attempt he made; and I had like to have been lost; for Mrs. *Jewkes* was not so good as she should have been. And so I told her Ladyship that sad Offer, and how I fell into Fits; and that they, believing me dying, forbore. Any Attempts after this base one? said she.

He was not so good as he should have been, return'd I, once, in the Garden, afterwards; but I was *so* watchful, and *so* ready to take the Alarm!

But, said she, did he not threaten you, at times, and put on his stern Airs, every now-and-then?—Threaten, Madam! reply'd I; yes, I had enough of that!—I thought I should have dy'd for Fear, several times. How could you bear that? said she: For he is a most daring and majestick Mortal! He has none of your puny Hearts, but as courageous as a Lion; and, Boy and Man, never fear'd any thing. I myself, said she, have a pretty good Spirit; but when I have made him truly angry, I have always been forced to make it up with him, as well as I could. For, Child, he is not one that is easily reconciled, I'll assure you.

But, after he had profess'd honourable Love to you, Did he never attempt you again? No, indeed, Madam, he did not. But he was a good while struggling with himself, and with his Pride, as he called it, before he could stoop so low; and consider'd, and consider'd again: And once, upon my saying but two or three Words, that displeas'd him, when he was very kind to me, he turn'd me out of Doors, in a manner, at an Hour's Warning; for he sent me above a Day's Journey towards my Father's; and then sent a Man and Horse, Post-haste, to fetch me back again; and has been exceedingly kind and gracious to me ever since, and made me happy.

That sending you away, said she, one Hour, and sending after you the next, is exactly like my Brother; and 'tis well if he don't turn you off twice or thrice before a Year come about, if you vex him: And he would have done the same by the first Lady in the Land, if he had been marry'd to her. Yet has he his Virtues, as well as his Faults; for he is generous, nay, he is noble in his Spirit; hates little dirty Actions; he delights in doing Good: But does not pass over a wilful Fault easily. He is wise, prudent, sober and magnanimous; and will not tell a Lye, nor disguise his Faults; but you must not expect to have him all to yourself, I doubt.

But I'll no more harp upon this String:[1] You see how he was exasperated at me; and he seem'd to be angry at you too; tho' something of it was Art, I believe.

Indeed, Madam, said I, he has been pleased to give me a most noble Lecture; and I find he was angry with me in Earnest, and that it will not be an easy Task to behave unexceptionably to him: For he is very nice and delicate in his Notions, I perceive; but yet, as your Ladyship says, exceeding generous.

Well, says she, I'm glad thou hadst a little bit of his Anger, else I should have thought it Art; and I don't love to be treated with low Art, any more than he; and I should have been vex'd, if he had done it by me.

But I understand, Child, says she, that you keep a Journal of all Matters that pass, and he has several times found means to get at it: Should you care I should see it? It could not be to your Disadvantage; for I find it had no small Weight with *him* in your Favour; and I should take great Pleasure to read all his Stratagems, Attempts, Contrivances, Menaces, and Offers to you, on one hand; and all your pretty Counter-plottings, which he much praises, your resolute Resistance, and the noble Stand you have made to preserve your Virtue; and the Steps by which his Pride was subdued, and his Mind induced to honourable Love, till you were made what you now are: For it must be a rare, an uncommon Story; and will not only give me great Pleasure in reading, but will intirely reconcile me to the Step he has taken. And that, let me tell you, is what I never thought to be; for I had gone a great way in bringing about a Match with him and Lady *Betty* ------; and had said so much of it, that the Earl, her Father, approv'd of it; and so did the Duke of -------, her Uncle; and Lady *Betty* herself was not averse: And now shall I be hunted to Death about it; and this has made me so outrageous as you have seen me upon the Matter. But when I can find, by your Writings, that your Virtue is but suitably rewarded, it will be not only a good Excuse for me, but for him, and make me love you.

There is nothing that I would not do, said I, to oblige your Ladyship; but my poor Father and Mother (who would rather have seen me buried quick[1] in the Earth, than to be seduced by the greatest of Princes) have them in their Hands at present; and your dear Brother has bespoken them, when they have done reading them; but if he gives me Leave, I will shew them to your Ladyship with all my Heart; not doubting your generous Allowances, as I have had his; tho' I have treated him very freely all the way, while he had naughty Views; and that your Ladyship would consider them as the naked Sentiments of my Heart, from Time to Time, deliver'd to those, whose Indulgence I was sure of; and for whose Sight, only, they were written.

Give me a Kiss now, said her Ladyship, for your chearful Compliance; for I make no doubt my Brother will consent I shall see them, because they must needs make for *your* Honour; and I see he loves you better than any one in the World.

I have heard, continued her Ladyship, a mighty good Character of your Parents, as industrious, honest, sensible, good Folks, who know the World; and, as I doubt not my Brother's Generosity, I am glad they will make no ill Figure in the World's Eye.

Madam, said I, they are the honestest, the lovingest, and the most conscientious Couple breathing. They once lived creditably; brought up a great Family, of which I am the youngest; but had Misfortunes, thro' their doing beyond their Power for two unhappy Brothers, who are both dead, and whose Debts they stood bound for, and so became reduced, and, by harsh Creditors, (where most of the Debts were not of their own contracting) turn'd out of all; and having, without Success, try'd to set up a little Country School, (for my Father understood a little of Accompts, and wrote a pretty good Hand) forced to take to hard Labour; but honest all the Time; contented; never repining; and loving to one another; and, in the midst of their Poverty and Disappointments, above all Temptation; and all their Fear was, that I should be wicked, and yield to Temptation, for the sake of worldly Riches: And to God's Grace, and their good Lessons, and those I imbib'd from my dear good Lady, your Ladyship's Mother, it is that I owe the Preservation of my Innocence, and the happy Station I now am exalted to.

She was pleased to kiss me again, and said, There is such a noble Simplicity in thy Story, such an honest Artlesness in thy Mind, and such a sweet Humility in thy Deportment, notwithstanding thy present Station, that I believe I shall be forced to love thee, whether I will or not: And the Sight of your Papers, I dare say, will crown the Work, will disarm my Pride, banish my Resentment on Lady *Betty*'s account, and justify my Brother's Conduct; and, at the same time, redound to your own everlasting Honour, as well as to the Credit of our Sex: And so I make no doubt but my Brother will let me see them.

Mrs. *Worden*, said my Lady, I can say any thing before you; and you will take no Notice of our Conversation; but I see you are much touched with it: Did you ever hear any thing prettier, more unaffected, sincere, free, easy?—No, never, Madam, answer'd she, in my Life; and it is a great Pleasure, to see so happy a Reconciliation taking Place, where there is so much Merit.

I said, I have discover'd so much Prudence in Mrs. *Worden*, that, as well for that, as for the Confidence your Ladyship places in her, I have made no Scruple of speaking my Mind freely before her; and of blaming my dear Master, while he was blame-worthy, as well as acknowledging his transcendent Goodness to me since; which, I am sure, exceeds all I can ever deserve. May-be not, said my Lady. I hope you'll be very happy in one another; and I'll now rise, and tell him my Thoughts, and ask him to let me have the reading of your Papers; for I promise myself much Pleasure in them; and shall not grudge a Journey, and a Visit to you, to the other House, to fetch them.

Your Ladyship's Favour, said I, was all I had to wish for; and if I have that, and the Continuance of your dear Brother's Goodness to me, I shall be easy under whatever else may happen.

And so I took my Leave, and withdrew; and she let me hear her say to Mrs. *Worden*, 'Tis a charming Creature, Mrs. *Worden*!—I know not which excels, her Person or her Mind!—And so young a Creature too!—Well may my Brother love her!

I am afraid, my dear Father and Mother, I shall now be too proud indeed.—I had once a good mind to have asked her Ladyship about Miss *Sally Godfrey*; but I thought it was better let alone, as she did not mention it herself. May-be, I shall hear it too soon. But I hope not!—I wonder, tho', whether she be living or dead!

We breakfasted together with great good Temper; and my Lady was very kind, and asking my good Master, he gave Leave, very readily, she should see all my Papers, when you return'd them to me; and he said, He was sure, when she came to read them, she would say, that I had well deserv'd the Fortune I had met with, and would be of Opinion, that, all the Kindness of his future Life would hardly be a sufficient Reward for my Virtue, and make me Amends for my Sufferings.

My Lady resolving to set out the next Morning, to return to her Lord, my Master order'd every thing to be made ready for his doing the like, to *Bedfordshire*; and this Evening our good Neighbours will sup with us, to take Leave of my Lady and us.

WEDNESDAY Night.

Nothing particular having passed at Dinner and Supper, but the most condescending Goodness, on my Lady's side, to me; and the highest Civilities from Mr. *Peters*'s Family; from Lady *Jones*, from Sir *Simon*'s Family, *&c.* and reciprocal good Wishes all round; and a Promise obtain'd from my Benefactor, that he would endeavour to pass a Fortnight or three Weeks in these Parts, before the Winter set in; I shall conclude this Day with observing, that I disposed of the Money my Master was so good to put into my Hands, in the Method he was pleased to direct; and I gave Mrs. *Jewkes* hers, in such a manner, as highly pleased her; and she wished me, with Tears, all kind of Happiness; and pray'd me to forgive her all her past Wickedness to me, as she herself called it. I begg'd Leave of my Master to present Mrs. *Worden* with Five Guineas, for a Pair of Gloves; which he said was well thought of.

SATURDAY.

On *Thursday* Morning my Lady set out for her own Seat; and my good Sir and I, attended by Mr. *Colbrand*, *Abraham* and *Thomas*, for this dear House. Her Ladyship parted with her Brother and me with great Tenderness, and made me promise to send her my Papers; which I find she intends to entertain Lady *Betty* with, and another Lady or two, her Intimates, as also her Lord; and hopes to find, as I believe, in the Reading of them, some Excuse for her Brother's Choice.

My dearest Master has been all Love and Tenderness on the Road, as he is in every Place, and on every Occasion. And Oh! what a delightful

Change was this Journey, to that which, so contrary to all my Wishes, and so much to my Apprehensions, carry'd me hence to the *Lincolnshire* House! And how did I bless God at every Turn, and at every Stage!

We did not arrive here till yesterday Noon. *Abraham* rode before, to let them know we were coming. And I had the Satisfaction to find every body there I wished to see. When the Chariot enter'd the Court-yard, I was so strongly impress'd with the Favour and Mercies of God Almighty, on remembring how I was sent away the last time I saw this House; the Leave I took; the Dangers I had encounter'd; a poor cast-off Servant Girl; and now returning a joyful Wife, and the Mistress, thro' his Favour, of the noble House I was turn'd out of; that I was hardly able to support the Joy I felt in my Mind on the Occasion. He saw how much I was moved, and tenderly ask'd me, why I seem'd so affected? I told him, and lifted his dear Hand to my Lips, and said, O, Sir! God's Mercies, and your Goodness to me, on entering this dear, dear Place, are above my Expression! I can hardly bear the Thoughts of them!—He said, Welcome, thrice welcome, Joy of my Life! to your own House: And kissed my Hand in Return. All the common Servants stood at the Windows, as unseen as they could, to observe us. He took my Hand, with the most condescending Goodness in the World, and, with great Complaisance, led me into the Parlour, and kissed me with the greatest Ardour. Welcome again, my dearest Spouse, said he, a thousand times welcome, to the Possession of a House that is not more mine than yours.

I threw myself at his Feet: Permit me, dear Sir, thus to bless *God*, and thank *you*, for all *his* Mercies, and *your* Goodness. O may I so behave, as not to be *utterly unworthy*; and then how *happy* shall I be! God give me, my Dearest, said he, Life and Health to reward all your Sweetness: And no Man can be then so blest as I!

Where (said he to *Abraham*, who passed by the Door, Where) is Mrs. *Jervis?*—She bolted in! Here, good Sir, said she, here, good Madam, am I, waiting impatiently, till called for, to congratulate you both!—I ran to her, and clasp'd my Arms about her Neck, and kissed her: O my dear Mrs. *Jervis!* said I, my other dear Mother! receive your happy, happy *Pamela:* And join with me to bless God, and bless our Master, for all these great Things!—I was ready to sink into her Arms thro' Excess of Joy, to see the dear good Woman, who had been so often a mournful Witness of my Distress, as now of my Triumph!—Dearest Madam, said she, you do me too much Honour. Let my whole Life shew the Joy I take in your deserv'd good Fortune, and in my Duty to you, for the early Instance I received of your Goodness in your kind Letter. O, Mrs. *Jervis*, reply'd I,

There all Thanks are due, both from you and me: For our dear Master granted me this Blessing, as I may justly call it, the very first Moment I begg'd it of him. Your Goodness, Sir, said she, I will for ever acknowledge; and I beg Pardon for the wrong Step I made, in applying to my Lady *Davers.*—He was so good as to salute her, and said, All's over now, Mrs. *Jervis*; and I shall not remember you *ever* disoblig'd me. I always respected you, and shall now, more and more, value you, for the sake of that dear good Creature, that, with Joy unfeign'd, I can call my Wife. God bless your Honour, for ever! said she; and many, *many* happy Years may ye live together, the Envy and Wonder of all who know you!

But where, said my dear Master, is honest *Longman?* and where is *Jonathan?*—Come, Mrs. *Jervis*, said I, you shall shew me them, and all the good Folks, presently; and let me go up with you to behold the dear Apartments, which I have seen *before* with such different Emotions to what I shall *now* do.

We went up; and in every Room, the Chamber I took Refuge in, when my Master pursu'd me, my Lady's Chamber, her Dressing-room, Mrs. *Jervis's* Room, not forgetting her Closet, my own little Bed-chamber, the Green-room, and in each of the others, I kneeled down severally, and blessed God for my past Escapes, and present Happiness; and the good Woman was quite affected with the Zeal and Pleasure with which I made my thankful Acknowledgments to the Divine Goodness. O my excellent Lady! said she, you are still the same good, pious, humble Soul I knew you; and your Marriage has added to your Graces, as I hope it will to your Blessings.

Dear Mrs. *Jervis*, said I, you know not what I have gone thro'! You know not what God has done for me! You know not what a happy Creature I am now! I have a thousand, thousand things to tell you; and a whole Week would be too little, every Moment of it spent in relating to you what has befallen me, to make you acquainted with it all. We shall be sweetly happy together, I make no doubt. But I charge you, my dear Mrs. *Jervis*, whatever you call me before Strangers, that when we are by ourselves, you call me nothing but *your Pamela.* For what an ingrateful Creature should I be, who have receiv'd so many Mercies at the Hand of God, if I attributed them not to his Divine Goodness, but assumed to myself insolent Airs upon them! No, I hope, I shall be more and more thankful, as I am more and more blest; and more humble, as God, the Author of all my Happiness, shall more distinguish me.

We went down again to the Parlour, to my dear Master. Said he, Call in again Mr. *Longman*; he longs to see you, my Dear. He came in: God

bless you, my sweet Lady, said he; as now, God be praised, I may call you.
Did I not tell you, Madam, that Providence would find you out? O, Mr.
Longman, said I, God be praised for all his Mercies!——I am rejoiced to
see you; and I laid my Hand on his, and said, Good Mr. *Longman*, how
do you do!—I must always value you; and you don't know how much of
my present Happiness I owe to the Sheets of Paper, and Pens and Ink you
furnish'd me with. I hope, my dear Sir and you are quite reconciled.—O
Madam, said he, how good you are!—Why, I cannot contain myself for
Joy! and then he wiped his Eyes, good Man!

Said my Master, Yes, I have been telling Mr. *Longman*, that I am obliged
to him for his ready Return to me; and that I will intirely forget his Appeal
to Lady *Davers*; and I hope he'll find himself quite as easy and happy as
he wishes.——My Partner here, Mr. *Longman*, I dare promise you, will
do all she can to make you so. God bless you both together! said he. 'Tis
the Pride of my Heart to see this!—I return'd with double Delight, when
I heard the blessed News; and I am sure, Sir, said he, mark old *Longman*'s
Words, God will bless you for this every Year more and more!—You don't
know how many Hearts you have made happy by this generous Deed!—I
am glad of it, said my dear Master; I am sure I have made my own happy:
And, Mr. *Longman*, tho' I must think you SOMEBODY, yet, as you are
not a young Man, and so won't make me jealous, I can allow you to wish
my dear Wife Joy in the tenderest manner. Adad, Sir, said he, I am sure
you rejoice me with your Favour: 'Twas what I long'd for, but durst not
presume. My Dear, said my Master, receive the Compliment of one of the
honestest Hearts in *England*, that always rever'd your Virtues!—And the
good Man saluted me with great Respect; and said, God in Heaven bless
you both, and kneeled on one Knee. I must quit your Presence! Indeed I
must!—And away he went.

Your Goodness, Sir, said I, knows no Bounds! O may my Gratitude
never find any!—I saw, said my Master, when the good Man approach'd
you, that he did it with so much Awe and Love mingled together, that
I fansied he long'd to salute my Angel; and I could not but indulge his
honest Heart. How bless'd am I, said I, and kiss'd his Hand—And indeed
I make nothing now of kissing his dear Hand, as if it was my own!

When honest old Mr. *Jonathan* came in to attend at Dinner, so clean,
so sleek, and so neat, as he always is, with his silver Hair, I said, Well,
Mr. *Jonathan*, how do you? I am glad to see you?—You look as well as
ever, thank God! O dear, Madam! said he, better than ever, to have such
a blessed Sight!—God bless you and my good Master!—and I hope, Sir,
said he, you'll excuse all my past Failings. Ay, that I will, *Jonathan*, said he;

because you never had any, but what your Regard for my dear Spouse here was the Occasion of. And now I can tell you, you can never err, because you cannot respect her too much. O Sir, said he, your Honour is exceeding good. I'm sure I shall always pray for you both.

After Dinner Mr. *Longman* coming in, and talking of some Affairs under his Care, he said afterwards, All your Honour's Servants are now happy; for *Robert*, who left you, had a pretty little Fortune fallen to him, or he never would have quitted your Service. He was here but Yesterday, to enquire when you and my Lady return'd hither; and hop'd he might have Leave to pay his Duty to you both. Ay, said my Master, I shall be glad to see honest *Robin*; for that's another of your Favourites, *Pamela.*—It was high time, I think, I should marry you, were it but to engage the Respects of all my Family to myself. There are, Sir, said I, ten thousand Reasons why I should rejoice in your Goodness.

But I was going to say, said Mr. *Longman*, That all your Honour's old Servants are now happy, but one. You mean *John Arnold?* said my Master. I do, indeed, said he, if you'll excuse me, Sir. O said I, I have had my Prayer for poor *John* answer'd, as favourably as I could wish.—Why, said Mr. *Longman*, to be sure poor *John* has acted no very good Part, take it all together; but he so much honour'd you, Sir, and so much respected you, Madam, that he would have been glad to have been obedient to both; and so was faithful to neither. But indeed the poor Fellow's Heart's almost broke, and he won't look out for any other Place; and says, he must live in your Honour's Service, or he must die wretched very shortly. Mrs. *Jervis* was there when this was said; Indeed, says she, the poor Man has been here every Day since he heard the Tidings that have rejoiced us all; and he says, he hopes he shall yet be forgiven. Is he in the House now? said my Master. He is, Sir; and was here when your Honour came in, and play'd at hide-and-seek to have one Look at you both when you alighted; and was ready to go out of his Wits for Joy, when he saw your Honour hand my Lady in. *Pamela*, said my dear Master, you're to do with *John* as you please. You have full Power. Then pray Sir, said I, let poor *John* come in.

The poor Fellow came in, with so much Confusion, that I have never seen a Countenance that express'd so lively Consciousness of his Faults, and mingled Joy and Shame. How do you do, *John?* said I; I hope you're very well!—The poor Fellow could hardly speak, and look'd with Awe upon my Master, and Pleasure upon me. Said my Master, Well, *John*, there is no room to say any thing to a Man that has so much Concern already: I am told you will serve me whether I will or not; but I turn you over altogether to my Spouse here. And she is to do by you as she pleases. You see, *John*, said I, your good Master's Indulgence. Well may I forgive, that have so generous an Example. I was always persuaded of your honest Intentions, if you had known how to distinguish between your Duty to your Master, and your Good-will to me: You will now have no more Puzzles on that Account, from the Goodness of your dear Master. I shall be but too happy said the poor Man. God bless your Honour! God bless you, Madam!—I now have the Joy of my Soul, in serving you both; and I will make the best of Servants, to my Power. Well then, *John*, said I, your Wages will go on, as if you had not left your Master: May I not say so, Sir? said I. Yes, surely, my Dear, reply'd he, and augment them too, if you find his Duty to you deserves it. A thousand Million of Thanks, said the poor Man: I am very well satisfy'd, and desire no Augmentation; and so he withdrew overjoy'd; and Mrs. *Jervis* and Mr. *Longman* were highly pleas'd; for tho' they were incens'd against him for his Fault to me, when Matters look'd badly for me, yet they, and all his Fellow-servants, always lov'd *John*.

When Mr. *Longman* and Mrs. *Jervis* had din'd, they came in again, to know if he had any Commands; and my dear Master filling a Glass of Wine, said, Mr. *Longman*, I am going to toast the happiest and honestest Couple in *England*, my dear *Pamela*'s Father and Mother.—Thank you, dear Sir, said I.

Said he, I think that little *Kentish* Purchase wants a Manager; and as it is a little out of *your* Way, Mr. *Longman*, I have been purposing, if I thought Mr. *Andrews* would accept of it, that he should enter upon *Hodges*'s Farm, that was, and so manage for me that whole little Affair; and we will well stock the Farm for him, and make it comfortable; and I think, if he will take that Trouble upon him, it will be an Ease to you, and a Favour to me.

Your Honour, said he, cannot do a better thing; and I have had some Inkling given me, that you might, if you pleased, augment that Estate, by a Purchase, of equal Amount, contiguous to it; and as you have so much Money to spare, I can't see your Honour can do better. Well, said he, let me have the Particulars another time, and we will consider about it. But my Dear, added he, you'll mention this to your Father, if you please.

I have too much Money, Mr. *Longman*, continu'd he, lies useless; tho', upon this Occasion, I shall not grudge laying out as much in Liveries, and other things, as if I had marry'd a Lady of a Fortune equal, if possible, to my *Pamela*'s Merit; and I reckon you have a good deal in Hand. Yes, Sir, said he, more than I wish I had. But I have a Mortgage in View, if you don't buy that *Kentish* thing, that I believe will answer very well; and when Matters are riper, will mention it to your Honour.

I took with me to *Lincolnshire*, said my Master, upwards of Six hundred Guineas, and thought to have laid most of them out there (Thank God, thought I, you did not! for he offer'd me Five hundred of them, you know!) But I have not laid out above Two hundred and fifty of them; so Two hundred I left there in my Escritoire; because I shall go again for a Fortnight or so, before Winter; and Two hundred I have brought with me. And I have Money, I know not what, in three Places here; the Account of which is in my Pocket-book, in my Library.

You have made some little Presents, *Pamela*, to my Servants there, on our Nuptials; and these Two hundred that I have brought up, I will put into your Disposal, that, with some of them, you shall do here as you did there.

I am asham'd, good Sir, said I, to be so costly and so worthless! Pray, my Dear, said he, say not a Word of that.

Said Mr. *Longman*, Why, Madam, with Money in Stocks, and one thing or another, his Honour could buy half the Gentlemen round him. He wants not Money, and lays up every Year. And it would have been pity, but his Honour should have wedded just as he has. Very true, Mr. *Longman*, said my Master; and pulling out his Purse, said, Tell out, my Dear, Two hundred Guineas, and give me the rest.—I did so. Now, said he, take them yourself, for the Purposes I mentioned. But, Mr. *Longman*, do you, before Sun-set, bring my dear Girl Fifty Pounds, which is due to her this Day, by my Promise; and every three Months, from this Day, pay her Fifty Pounds more; which will be Two hundred Pounds *per Annum*; and this is for her to lay out at her own Discretion, and without Account, in such a way, as shall derive a Blessing upon us all: For she was my Mother's Almoner, and shall be mine, and her own too.—I'll go for it this Instant, said Mr. *Longman*.

When he was gone, I looked upon my dear generous Master, and on Mrs. *Jervis*; and he gave me a Nod of Assent; and I took Twenty Guineas, and said, Dear Mrs. *Jervis*, accept of this; which is no more than my generous Master order'd me to present to Mrs. *Jewkes*, for a pair of Gloves, on my happy Nuptials, and so you, who are so much better intitled to them, by the Love I bear you, must not refuse them.

Said she, Mrs. *Jewkes* was on the Spot, Madam, at the happy Time. Yes, said my Master, but *Pamela* would have rejoiced to have had you there instead of her. That I should, Sir, reply'd I, or instead of any body except my own Mother. She gratefully accepted them, and thank'd us both: But I don't know what she should thank *me* for; for I was not worth a fourth Part of them myself.

I'd have you, my Dear, said he, in some handsome manner, as you know how, oblige *Longman* to accept of the like Present.

Mr. *Longman* return'd from his Office, and brought me the fifty Pounds, saying, I have enter'd this new Article with great Pleasure. *To my Lady— Fifty Pounds, to be paid the same Sum quarterly.* O Sir, said I, what will become of me to be so poor in myself, and so rich in your Bounty.—It is a Shame to take all that your profuse Goodness would heap upon me thus: But indeed it shall not be without Account.—Make no Words, my Dear, said he. Are you not my Wife? And have I not endow'd you with my Goods? and, hitherto, this is a very small Part.

Mr. *Longman*, said I, and Mrs. *Jervis*, you both see how I am even oppress'd with unreturnable Obligations. God bless the Donor, and God bless the Receiver! said Mr. *Longman*; I am sure they will bring back good Interest; for, Madam, you had ever a bountiful Heart; and I have seen the Pleasure you used to take to dispense my late Lady's Alms and Donations.

I'll warrant, Mr. *Longman*, said I, notwithstanding you are so willing to have me take large Sums for nothing at all, I should affront you, if I asked you to accept from me a Pair of Gloves only, on Account of my happy Nuptials. He seem'd not readily to know how to answer, and my Master said, If Mr. *Longman* refuse you, my Dear, he may be said to refuse your first Favour. On that I put twenty Guineas in his Hand; but he insisted upon it, that he would take but Five. I said, I must desire you to oblige me, Mr. *Longman*, or I shall think I have affronted you. Well, if I must, said he, I know what I know. What is that, Mr. *Longman*, said I?—Why, Madam, said he, I will not lay it out till my young Master's Birth Day, which I hope will be within this Twelve-month.

Not expecting any thing like this from the old Gentleman, I look'd at my Master, and then blush'd so, I could not hold up my Head. Charmingly said, Mr. *Longman*, said my Master, and clasped me in his Arms; O my dear Life! God send it may be so.—You have quite delighted me, Mr. *Longman!* Tho' I durst not have said such a Thing for the World.—Madam, said the old Gentleman, I beg your Pardon; I hope no Offence. But I'd speak it ten times in a Breath to have it so, take it how you please, as long as my good Master takes it so well. Mrs. *Jervis*, said my Master, this is an over-nice dear Creature; you don't know what a Life I have had with her, even on this side Matrimony.—Said Mrs. *Jervis*, I think Mr. *Longman* says very well; I am sure I shall hope for it too.

Mr. *Longman*, who had struck me of a Heap, withdrawing soon after, my Master said, Why, My Dear, you can't look up! The old Man said nothing shocking. I did not expect it, tho', from him, said I. I was not aware but of some innocent Pleasantry. Why, so it was, said he, both innocent and pleasant. And I won't forgive you, if you don't say as he says. Come, speak before Mrs. *Jervis*. May every thing happen, Sir, said I, that will give *you* Delight!—That's my dear Love, said he, and kiss'd me with great Tenderness.

When the Servants had dined, I desired to see the Maidens, and all Four came up together. You are welcome home, Madam, said *Rachel*; We rejoice all to see you here, and more to see you our Lady. O my good old Acquaintances, said I, you see how good God, and the best of Gentlemen have been to me! O I joy to see you! How do you do, *Rachel*? How do you, *Jane*? How do you do, *Hannah*? How do you do, *Cicely*? And I took each of them by the Hand, and could have kissed them.—For, said I to myself, I kissed you all last time I saw you, in Sorrow; why should I not kiss you all with Joy? But I forbore in Honour of their dear Master's Presence.

They seem'd quite transported with me; and my good Master was pleas'd with the Scene. See here, my Lasses, said he, your Mistress! I need not bid you respect her; for you always lov'd her; and she'll have it as much in her Power as Inclination to be kind to the Deserving. Indeed, said I, I shall always be a kind Friend to you; and your dear good Master, has order'd me to give each of you this, that you may rejoice with me, on my Happiness. And so I gave them five Guineas a-piece; and said God bless you every one. I am over-joy'd to see you!—And they withdrew with the greatest Gratitude and Pleasure, praying for us both.

I turn'd to my dear Master, 'Tis to you, dear Sir, said I, next to God, who put it into your generous Heart, that all my Happiness is owing! That my Mind thus overflows with Joy and Gratitude! And I would have kissed his Hand; but he clasped me in his Arms, and said, You deserve it, my Dear! You deserve it all. Mrs. *Jervis* came in; said she, I have seen a very affecting Sight; you have made your Maidens quite happy, Madam, with your Kindness and Condescension! I saw them all Four, as I came by the Hall Door, just got up from their Knees, praising and praying for you both! Dear good Bodies, said I; and did *Jane* pray too? God return their Prayers upon themselves, I say.

My Master sent for *Jonathan*, and I held up all the Fingers of my two Hands; and my Master giving a Nod of Approbation as he came in, I said, Well, Mr. *Jonathan*, I could not be satisfy'd without seeing you in Form, as it were, and thanking you for all your past Good-will to me. You'll accept of *that* for a Pair of Gloves, on this happy Occasion; and I gave him ten Guineas, and took his honest Hand between both mine: God bless you, said I, with your Silver Hairs, so like my dear Father!—I shall always value such a good old Servant of the best of Masters!—He said, O such Goodness! Such kind Words!—It is Balm to my Heart! Blessed be God I have lived to this Day!—And his Eyes swam in Tears, and he withdrew.—My Dear, said my Master, you make every one happy!—O Sir, said I, 'tis you, 'tis you; and let my grateful Heart always spring to my Lips, to acknowledge the Blessings you heap upon me.

Then in came *Harry*, and *Isaac*, and *Benjamin*, and the two Grooms of this House, and *Arthur* the Gardener, for my dear Master had order'd them by Mrs. *Jervis* thus to be marshall'd out; and he said, Where's *John?* Poor *John* was asham'd, and did not come in till he heard himself call'd for. I said to them, How do you do, *Henry?* How do you do, *Isaac?* How do you do, *Benjamin?* How do you do, *Arthur?* And you, and you, *Richard* and *Roger?* God bless you every one. My Master said, I have given you a Mistress, my Lads, that is the Joy of my Heart. You see her Goodness and Condescension! Let your Respects to her be but answerable, and she'll be proportionably as great a Blessing to you all as she is to me. *Harry* said, In the Names of all your Servants, Sir, I bless your Honour and your good Lady: And it shall be all our Studies to deserve her Ladyship's Favour, as well as your Honour's. And so I gave every one five Guineas, to rejoice, as I said, in my Happiness.

When I came to *John*, I said, I saw you before, *John*; but I again tell you, I am glad to see you. He said, he was quite asham'd and confounded. O, said I, forget every thing that's past, *John!*—Your dear good Master will, and so will I. For God has wonderfully brought about all these Things, by the very Means I once thought most grievous. Let us therefore look forward, and be only asham'd to commit Faults for the Time to come. For they may not always be attended with like happy Consequences.

Arthur, said my Master, I have brought you a Mistress that is a great Gardener. She'll shew you a new Way to plant Beans. And never anybody had such a Hand at improving a Sun-flower, as she!—O Sir, Sir, said I; but yet a little dash'd; all my Improvements in every kind of Thing are owing to you, I am sure!—And so I think I was even with the dear Man, and yet appear'd grateful before his Servants. They withdrew, blessing us both, as the rest had done.

And then came in the Postilion,[1] and two Helpers, (for my Master has both here, and at *Lincolnshire*, fine Hunting-horses, and it is the chief Sport he takes Delight in) as also the Scullion-boy;[2] And I said, How do you, all of you? And how dost do, *Tommy?* I hope you're very good. Here, your dear Master has order'd you something a piece, in Honour of me. And my Master holding three Fingers to me, I gave the Postilion and Helpers three Guineas each, and the little Boy two; and bid him let his poor Mother lay it out for him, for he must not spend it idly. Mr. *Colbrand, Abraham* and *Thomas*, I had before presented at t'other House.

And when they were all gone, but Mrs. *Jervis*, I said, And now, dearest Sir, permit me on my Knees, thus, to bless you, and pray for you. And Oh, may God crown you with Length of Days, and Increase of Honour; and may your happy, happy *Pamela*, by her grateful Heart, appear always worthy in your dear Eyes, tho' she cannot be so in her own, nor in those of any others!

Mrs. *Jervis*, said my Master, you see the Excellency of this sweet Creature! And when I tell you, that the Charms of her Person, all lovely as she is, bind me not so strongly to her as the Graces of her Mind, congratulate me, that my Happiness is built on so stable a Basis!—Indeed I do, most sincerely, Sir, said she!—This is a happy Day to me.

I stept into the Library, while he was thus pouring out his Kindness for me to Mrs. *Jervis*; and bless'd God there on my Knees, for the Difference I now found to what I had once known in it.—And when I have done the same in the first Scene of my Fears, the once frightful Summer-house, I shall have gone thro' most of my distressful Scenes with Gratitude; but shall never forbear thanking God in my Mind, for his Goodness to me in every one. Mrs. *Jervis* I find, had whisper'd him what I had done above, and he saw me on my Knees, with my Back towards him, unknown to me; but softly put to the Door again, as he had open'd it a little Way. And I said, not knowing he had seen me, You have some charming Pictures here, Sir:—Yes, said he, my dear Life, so I have; but none equal to that, which your Piety affords me!—And may the God you delight to serve bless more and more my dear Angel. Sir, said I, you are all Goodness!—I hope, reply'd he, after your sweet Example, I shall be better and better!—Do you think, my dear Father and Mother, there ever was so happy a Creature as I! To be sure it would be very ingrateful to think with Uneasiness, or any thing but Compassion, of poor Miss *Sally Godfrey*.

He order'd *Jonathan* to let the Evening be pass'd merrily, but wisely, as he said, with what every one liked, whether Wine or *October*.[1]

He was pleased afterwards to lead me up Stairs, and gave me Possession of my Lady's Dressing-room and Cabinet, and her fine Repeating-watch[2] and Equipage;[3] and in short of a complete Set of Diamonds, that were his good Mother's; as also of the two Pair of Diamond Ear-rings, the two Diamond Rings, and Diamond Necklace he mention'd in his naughty Articles, which her Ladyship had intended for Presents to Miss *Tomlins*, a rich Heiress that was proposed for his Wife, when he was just come from his Travels; but which went off, after all was agreed upon on both the Friends Sides, because he approv'd not her Conversation; and she had, as he told his Mother, too masculine an Air; and he never could be brought to see her but once, tho' the Lady lik'd him very well. He presented me also with her Ladyship's Books, Pictures, Linnen, Laces, &c. that were in her Apartments, and bid me call those Apartments mine. O give me, my good God, Humility and Gratitude!

SUNDAY Night.

This Day, as Matters could not be ready for our Appearance at a better Place, we staid at home; and my dear Master imploy'd himself a good deal in his Library. And I have been taken up pretty much, I hope, as I ought to be, in Thankfulness, Prayer, and Meditation in my newly presented Closet: And I hope God will be pleas'd to give a Blessing to me; for I have the Pleasure to think I am not puffed up with this great Alteration; and yet am not wanting to look upon all these Favours and Blessings in the Light wherein I ought to receive them, both at the Hands of God, and my dear Benefactor.

We din'd together with great Pleasure, and I had in every Word and Action, all the Instances of Kindness and Affection that the most indulg'd Heart could wish. He said he would return to his Closet again; and at Five o' Clock would come and take a Walk with me in the Garden, and so retir'd as soon as he had din'd; and I went up to mine.

About Six he was pleas'd to come up to me, and said, Now, my Dear, I will attend you for a little Walk in the Garden; and I gave him my Hand with great Pleasure. This Garden is much better cultivated than the *Lincolnshire* one; but that is larger; and has nobler Walks in it; and yet here is a pretty Canal in this, and a Fountain, and Cascade. We had a deal of sweet Conversation as we walk'd; and, after we had taken a Turn round, I bent towards the little Garden, and when I came near the Summer-house, took the Opportunity to slip from him, and just whipt up the Steps of this once frightful Place, and kneeled down, and said, I bless thee, O God, for my Escapes, and for thy Mercies! O let me always possess a grateful and humble Heart! And I whipt down again, and join'd him; and he hardly missed me.

Several of the neighbouring Gentry sent their Compliments to him on his Return, but not a Word about his Marriage, particularly 'Squire *Arthur,* 'Squire *Towers,* 'Squire *Brooks,* and 'Squire *Martin* of the Grove.

MONDAY.

I had a good deal of Employment in chusing Patterns for my new Cloaths. He thought nothing too good; but I thought every thing I saw was; and he was so kind, to pick out Six of the richest, for me to chuse three Suits out of, saying, we would furnish ourselves with more in Town, when we went thither. One was a white flower'd with Gold most richly; and he was pleased to say, that as I was a Bride, I should make my Appearance in that the following *Sunday.* And so we shall have in two or three Days, from several Places, nothing but Mantua-makers and Taylors at Work. Bless me! what a chargeable, and what a worthless Hussy I am, to the dear Gentleman!—But his Fortune and Station require a great deal of it; and his Value for me, will not let him do less than if he had marry'd a Fortune equal to his own; and then, as he says, it would be a Reflection upon him if he did.—And so I doubt it will be as it is: For, either way, the World will have something to say. He made me also chuse some very fine Laces, and Linen; and has sent a Message on purpose, with his Orders, to hasten all down; what can be done in Town, as the Millenary Matters, *&c.* to be completed there, and sent by particular Messengers, as done. All to be here, and finished by *Saturday* Afternoon without fail.

I send away *John* this Morning, with some more of my Papers to you, and with the few he will give you, separate. My Desire is, that you will send me all the Papers you have done with, that I may keep my Word with Lady *Davers*; to beg the Continuance of your Prayers and Blessings; to hope you will give me your Answer about my dear Benefactor's Proposal of the *Kentish* Farm; to beg you to buy two Suits of Cloaths, each, of the finest Cloth for you, my dear Father, and of a creditable Silk for my dear Mother; and good Linen, and every thing answerable; and that you will, as my dearest Sir bid me say, let us see you here, as soon as possible, and he will have his Chariot come for you, when you tell *John* the Day. Oh! how I long to see you both, my dear good Parents, and to share with you my Felicities!

You will have, I am sure, the Goodness to go to all your Creditors, which are chiefly those of my poor unhappy Brothers, and get an Account of all you are bound for; and every one shall be paid to the utmost Farthing, and Interest besides, tho' some of them have been very cruel and unrelenting.— But they are all intitled to their own, and shall be thankfully paid.

Now I think of it, *John* shall take my Papers down to this Place; that you may have something to amuse you of your dear Child's, instead of those you part with; and I will continue writing till I am settled, and you are determin'd; and then I shall apply myself to the Duties of the Family, in order to become as useful to my dear Benefactor, as my small Abilities will let me.

If you think a Couple of Guineas will be of Use to Mrs. *Mumford*, who I doubt has not much aforehand,[1] pray give them to her, from me, (and I will return them to you) as for a Pair of Gloves on my Nuptials: And look thro' your poor Acquaintance, and Neighbours, and let me have a List of such honest, industrious Poor, as may be true Objects of Charity; and have no other Assistance; particularly such as are blind, lame, or sickly, with their particular Cases; and also, such poor Families and House-keepers as are reduced by Misfortunes, as ours was, and where a great Number of Children may keep them from rising to a State of tolerable Comfort: And I will chuse as well as I can; for I long to be making a Beginning, with the kind Quarterly Benevolence my dear good Benefactor has bestowed on me for such good Purposes.

I am resolv'd to keep Account of all these Matters, and Mr. *Longman* has already furnish'd me with a Vellum-book of all white Paper; some Sides of which I hope soon to fill, with the Names of proper Objects: And tho' my dear Master has given me all this without Account, yet shall he see, (but nobody else) how I lay it out, from Quarter to Quarter; and I will, if any be left, carry it on, like an Accomptant, to the next Quarter, and strike a Ballance four times a Year, and a general Ballance at every Year's End.—And I have written in it, *Humble* RETURNS *for* DIVINE MERCIES; and lock it up safe in my newly presented Cabinet.

I intend to let Lady *Davers* see no further of my Papers, than to her own angry Letter to her Brother; for I would not have her see my Reflections upon it; and she'll know, down to that Place, all that's necessary for her Curiosity, as to my Sufferings, and the Stratagems used against me, and the honest Part God enabled me to act: And I hope, when she sees them all, she will be quite reconcil'd; for she will see it is all God Almighty's Doings; and that a Gentleman of his Parts and Knowledge was not to be drawn in by such a poor young Body as me. I will detain *John* no longer. He will tell you to read this last Part first, and while he stays. And so with my humble Duty to you both, and my dear Sir's kind Remembrance, I rest,

Your ever dutiful and gratefully happy Daughter.

WEDNESDAY Evening.

Honoured Father and Mother,

I will now proceed with my Journal.

On *Tuesday* Morning, my dear Sir rode out, attended by *Abraham*; and he brought with him to Dinner Mr. *Martin* of the Grove, and Mr. *Arthur*, and Mr. *Brooks*, and one Mr. *Chambers*; and he stept up to me, and said he had rode out too far to return to Breakfast; but he had brought with him some of his old Acquaintance, to dine with me. Are you sorry for it, *Pamela*, said he? I remembered his Lessons, and said, No, sure, Sir; I can't be angry at any thing you are pleas'd to do. Said he, you know Mr. *Martin*'s Character, and have severely censur'd him in one of your Letters, as one of my Brother Rakes, and for his three Lyings-in.—

He then gave me the following Account, how he came to bring them. Said he, 'I met them all at Mr. *Arthur*'s, and his Lady asked me, if I was really marry'd? I said, Yes, really. And to who, said Mr. *Martin?* Why, reply'd I, bluntly, to my Mother's Waiting-maid. They could not tell what to say to me, hereupon, and look'd one upon another. And I saw I had spoil'd a Jest, from each. Mrs. *Arthur* said, You have indeed, Sir, a charming Creature as ever I saw, and she has mighty good Luck. Ay, said I; and so have I. But I shall say the less, because a Man never did any thing of this Nature, that he did not think he ought, if it were but in Policy, to make the best of it. Nay, said Mr. *Arthur*, if you have sinn'd, it is with your Eyes open: For you know the World as well as any Gentleman of your Years in it.

'Why, really, Gentlemen, said I, I should be glad to please all my Friends; but I can't expect, till they know my Motives and Inducements, that it will be so immediately. But I do assure you, I am exceedingly pleased myself; and, that, you know, is most to the Purpose.

'Said Mr. *Brooks*, I have heard my Wife praise your Spouse that is, so much, for Beauty and Shape, that I wanted to see her of all Things. Why, reply'd I, if you'll all go and take a Dinner with me, you shall see her with all my Heart. And, Mrs. *Arthur*, will you bear us Company? No, indeed, Sir, said she. What, I'll warrant, my *Wife* will not be able to reconcile you to my *Mother's Waiting-maid*; is not that it? Tell Truth, Mrs. *Arthur*. Nay, said she, I shan't be backward to pay your Spouse a Visit, in Company of the neighbouring Ladies; but for one single Woman to go, on such a sudden Motion too, with so many Gentlemen, is not right. But that need not hinder you, Gentlemen. So, said he, the rest sent, that they should not dine at home; and they, and Mr. *Chambers*, a Gentleman lately settled in these Parts, one and all came with me: And so, my Dear, concluded he, when you make your Appearance next *Sunday*, you're sure of a Party in your Favour; for all that see you must esteem you.'

He went to them; and when I came down to Dinner, he was pleased to take me by the Hand, at my Entrance into the Parlour, and said, My dear Love, I have brought some of my good Neighbours to take a Dinner with you. I said, You are very good, Sir!—My Dear, this Gentleman is Mr. *Chambers*; and so he presented every one, to me; and they saluted me, and wish'd us both Joy.

Mr. *Brooks* said, I, for my Part, wish you Joy most heartily. My Wife told me a good deal of the Beauties of your Person; but I did not think we had such a Flower in our County. Sir, said I, your Lady is very partial to me; and you are so polite a Gentleman, that you will not contradict your good Lady.

I'll assure you, Madam, return'd he, you have not hit the Matter at all; for we contradict one another twice or thrice a Day. But the Devil's in't if we are not agreed in so clear a Case.

Said Mr. *Martin*, Mr. *Brooks* says very true, Madam, in both respects (meaning his Wife's and his own Contradiction to one another, as well as in my Favour); for, added he, they have been marry'd some Years.

As I had not the best Opinion of this Gentleman, nor his Jest, I said, I am almost sorry, Sir, for the Gentleman's Jest upon himself and his Lady; but I think it should have reliev'd him from a greater Jest, your pleasant Confirmation of it.—But still, the Reason you give that it may be so, I hope, is the Reason that may be given that it is not so,—to wit, That they have been married some Years.

Said Mr. *Arthur*, Mr. *Martin*, I think the Lady has very handsomely reprov'd you. I think so too, said Mr. *Chambers*; and it was but a very indifferent Compliment to a Bride. Said Mr. *Martin*, Compliment or not, Gentlemen, I have never seen a Matrimony of any time standing, that it was not so, little or much. But I dare say, it will never be so here.

To be sure, Sir, said I, if it was, I must be the ungratefullest Person in the World, because I am the most obliged Person in it. That Notion, said Mr. *Arthur*, is so excellent, that it gives a moral Certainty, that it never can.

Sir, said Mr. *Brooks*, to my dear Sir, softly, You have a most accomplish'd Lady, I do assure you, as well in her Behaviour and Wit, as in her Person, call her what you please. Why, my dear Friend, said my Master, I must tell you, That her Person made me her Lover; but her Mind made her my Wife.

The first Course coming in, my dear Sir led me himself to my Place; and set Mr. *Chambers*, as the greatest Stranger, at my Right-hand, and Mr. *Brooks* at my Left; and Mr. *Arthur* was pleased to observe, much to my Advantage, on the Ease and Freedom with which I behav'd myself, and helped them; and said, He would bring his Lady to be a Witness, and a Learner both, of my Manner. I said, I should be proud of any Honour Lady *Arthur* would vouchsafe to do me; and if I once could promise myself the Opportunity of his good Lady's Example, and those of the other Gentlemen present, I should have the greater Opinion of my Worthiness to sit in the Place I fill'd, at present, with much Insufficiency.

Mr. *Arthur* drank to my Health and Happiness, and said, my Wife told your Spouse, Madam, You had very good Luck in such a Husband; but I now see who has the best of it. Said Mr. *Brooks*, Come, come, let's make no Compliments; for the plain Truth of the Matter is, our good Neighbour's Generosity and Judgment have met with so equal a Match, in his Lady's Beauty and Merit, that I know not which has the best Luck. But may you be both long happy together, say I! And so he drank a Glass of Wine.

My dear Sir, who always takes Delight to have me praised, seemed much pleased with our Conversation; and he said the kindest, tenderest, and most respectful Things in the World to me. Insomuch, that the rough Mr. *Martin* said, Did you ever think our good Friend here, who used to ridicule Matrimony so much, would have made so complaisant a Husband? How long do you intend, Sir, that this shall hold? As long as my good Girl deserves it, said he, and that I hope will be for ever. But, continued he, you need not wonder I have changed my Mind as to Wedlock; for I never expected to meet with one whose Behaviour and Sweetness of Temper was so well adapted to make me happy.

After Dinner, and having drank good Healths to each of their Ladies, I withdrew; and they sat and drank two Bottles of Claret apiece, and were very merry; and went away, full of my Praises, and vowing to bring their Ladies to see me.

John having brought me your kind Letter, my dear Father, I told my good Master, after his Friends were gone, how gratefully you received his generous Intentions as to the *Kentish* Farm, and promised your best Endeavours to serve him in that Estate; and that you hoped your Industry and Care would be so well employ'd in it, that you should be very little troublesome to him as to the liberal Manner in which he had intended to add to a Provision, that of itself exceeded all your Wishes. He was very well pleased with your chearful Acceptance of it.

I am glad your Engagements in the World lie in so small a Compass: As soon as you have gotten an Account of them exactly, you will be pleased to send it me, with the List of the poor Folks you are so kind to promise to procure me.

I think, as my dear Master is so generous, you should think nothing that is plain too good. Pray, don't be afraid of laying out upon yourselves. My dear Sir intends that you shall not, when you come to us, return to your old Abode, but stay with us, till you set out for *Kent*; and so you must dispose of yourselves accordingly. And, I hope, my dear Father, you have quite left off all Slavish Business. As Farmer *Jones* has been kind to you, as I have heard you say, pray, when you take Leave of them, present them with three Guineas worth of good Books, such as a Family-Bible, a Common-Prayer, a Whole Duty of Man,¹ or any other you think will be acceptable; for they live a great way from Church; and in Winter, the Ways from their Farm thither are impassable.

He has brought me my Papers safe: And I will send them to Lady *Davers* the first Opportunity, down to the Place I mentioned in my last.

My dear Sir, just now tells me, that he will carry me in the Morning a little Airing, about ten Miles off, in his Chariot and Four, to Breakfast at a Farm-house, noted for a fine Dairy, and where, now-and-then, the neighbouring Gentry of both Sexes resort, for that Purpose. And he will send *Abraham* on Horse-back, before us; to let the good Folks know it.

THURSDAY.

We set out at about half an Hour after Six, accordingly, and driving pretty smartly, got at this truly neat House at half an Hour after Eight, and found *Abraham* there; and I was much pleas'd with the Neatness of the good Woman, and Daughter, and Maid; and he was so good as to say he would now-and-then take a Turn with me to the same Place, and on the same Occasion, as I seem'd to like it; for that it would be a pretty Exercise, and procure us Appetites to our Breakfasts, as well as our Return would to our Dinners. But I find this was not (tho' a very good Reason) the only one for which he gave me this agreeable Airing; as I shall acquaint you.

We were prettily receiv'd and entertain'd here, and an Elegance ran through every thing, Persons as well as Furniture, yet all plain. And my Master said to the good Housewife, Do your young Boarding-school Ladies still at times continue their Visits to you, Mrs. *Dobson?* Yes, Sir, said she, I expect three or four of them every Minute.

There is, my Dear, said he, within three Miles of this Farm, a very good Boarding-school for Ladies: The Governess of it keeps a Chaise and Pair, which is to be made a double Chaise² at Pleasure; and in Summer-time, when the Misses perform their Tasks to Satisfaction, she favours them with an Airing to this Place, three or four at a Time; and after they have breakfasted, they are carried back: And this serves both for a Reward, and for Exercise; and the Misses who have this Favour are not a little proud of it; and it brings them forward in their respective Tasks.

A very good Method, Sir, said I. And just as we were talking, the Chaise came in with four Misses, all pretty much of a Size, and a Maid-servant to attend them. They were shewn another little neat Apartment, that went thro' ours, and made their Honours[1] very prettily, as they passed by us. I went into the Room to them, and asked them Questions about their Work, and their Lessons; and what they had done to deserve such a fine Airing and Breakfasting; and they all answer'd me very prettily. And pray, little Ladies, said I, what may I call your Names? One was called Miss *Burdoff*, one Miss *Nugent*, one Miss *Booth*, and the fourth Miss *Goodwin*. I don't know which, said I, is the prettiest; but you are all best, my little Dears; and you have a very good Governess to indulge you with such a fine Airing, and such delicate Cream, and Bread and Butter. I hope you think so too.

My Master came in, and I had no Mistrust in the World; and he kissed each of them; but look'd more wistfully on Miss *Goodwin*, than any of the others; but I thought nothing just then: Had she been called Miss *Godfrey*, I had hit upon it in a trice.

When we went from them, he said, Which do you think the prettiest of those Misses? Really, Sir, reply'd I, it is hard to say; Miss *Booth* is a pretty brown Girl, and has a fine Eye; Miss *Burdoff* has a great deal of Sweetness in her Countenance, but not so regularly featur'd. Miss *Nugent* is very fair: And Miss *Goodwin* has a fine black Eye, and is besides, I think, the genteelest shap'd Child; but they are all pretty.

The Maid led them into the Garden, to shew them the Bee-hives; and Miss *Goodwin* made a particular fine Curchee to my Master; and I said, I believe Miss knows you, Sir; and taking her by the Hand, I said, Do you know this Gentleman, my pretty Dear?——Yes, Madam, said she, It is my own dear Uncle. I clasp'd her in my Arms, O why did you not tell me, Sir, said I, that you had a Niece among these little Ladies? And I kissed her, and away she tript, after the others.

But pray, Sir, said I; How can this be?—You have no Sister nor Brother, but Lady *Davers!*——How can this be?

He smiled; and then I said, O my dear Sir, tell me now of a Truth, Does not this pretty Miss stand in a nearer Relation to you, than as a Niece?—I know she does! I know she does! And I embrac'd him as he stood.

'Tis even so, my Dear, reply'd he; and you remember my Sister's good-natur'd Hint of Miss *Sally Godfrey!* I do well, Sir! answer'd I. But this is

Miss *Goodwin*. Her Mother chose that for her, said he, because she should not be called by her own.

Well, said I, excuse me, Sir, I must go and have a little Prattle with her. I'll send for her in again, reply'd he; and in she came, in a Moment. I took her in my Arms, and said, O my charming Dear! will you love me?—Will you let me be your Aunt? Yes, Madam, answer'd she, with all my Heart! And I will love *you* dearly! But I mustn't love my Uncle! Why so? said he. Because, reply'd she, you would not speak to me at first!—And because you would not let me call you, Uncle; (for it seems she was bid not, that I might not guess at her presently) and yet, said the pretty Dear, I had not seen you a great while, so I hadn't!

Well, *Pamela*, said he, now can you allow me to love this little Innocent? Allow you, Sir! reply'd I; you would be very barbarous if you did not; and I should be more so, if I did not further it all I could, and love the little Lamb myself, for your sake, and for her own sake; and in Compassion to her poor dear Mother, tho' unknown to me. And Tears stood in my Eyes.

Said he, Why, my Love, are your Words so kind, and your Countenance so sad?—I drew to the Window, from the Child, and said, Sad it is not, Sir; but I have a strange Grief and Pleasure mingled at once in my Breast, on this Occasion: It is indeed a twofold Grief, and a twofold Pleasure. As how, my Dear? said he.—Why, Sir, said I, I cannot help being grieved for the poor Mother of this sweet Babe, to think, if she be living, that she must call her chiefest Delight her Shame; if she be no more, that she must have sad Remorses on her poor Mind, when she came to leave the World, and her little Babe: And, in the second Place, I grieve, that it must be thought a Kindness to the dear little Soul, not to let her know how near the dearest Relation she has in the World is to her!—Forgive me, dear Sir, I say not this to reproach you, in the least. Indeed, I don't. And I have a twofold Cause of Joy; first, That I have had the Grace to escape the like Unhappiness with this poor Gentlewoman; and next, That this Discovery has given me an Opportunity to shew the Sincerity of my grateful Affection for you, Sir, in the Love I will always express to this dear Child!

And then I stept to her again, and kissed her; and said, Join with me, my pretty Love, to beg your dear Uncle to let you come home, and live with your new Aunt! Indeed, my little Precious, I'll love you dearly!

Will you, Sir, said the little Charmer, will you let me go and live with my Aunt?

You are very good, my *Pamela*, said he.—And I have not once been deceived in the Hopes my fond Heart had entertained of your Prudence.——But will you, Sir, said I, will you grant me this Favour!—I shall most sincerely love the little Charmer; and all I am capable of doing for her, both by Example and Affection, shall most cordially be done.—My dearest Sir, added I, oblige me in this thing! I think already my Heart is set upon it!—What a sweet Employment and Companionship shall I have!

We'll talk of this some other Time, reply'd he; but I must, in Prudence, put some Bounds to your amiable Generosity. I had always intended to surprize you into this Discovery; but my Sister led the Way to it, out of a Poorness in her Spite, that I could not brook; and tho' you have pleased me beyond Expression, in your Behaviour on this Occasion; yet I can't say, that you have gone much beyond my Expectations; for I have such an high Opinion of you, that I think nothing could have shaken it, but a contrary Conduct to this you have express'd on so tender a Circumstance.

Well, Sir, said the dear little Miss, then you won't let me go home with my Aunt, will you? I'm sure she'll love me! When you break up next, my Dear, said he, if you're a good Girl, you shall make your new Aunt a Visit. She made a low Curchee, Thank you, Sir, said she. Yes, my Dear, said I, and I'll get you some fine things against the Time. I'd have brought you some now, had I known I should have seen my pretty Love! Thank you, Madam, return'd she.

How old, Sir, said I, is Miss? Between Six and Seven, answer'd he. Was she ever, Sir, said I, at your House? My Sister, reply'd he, carry'd her there once, as a little Relation of her Lord's. I remember, Sir, said I, a little Miss; and Mrs. *Jervis* and I took her to be a Relation of Lord *Davers's*.

My Sister, said he, knew the whole Secret from the Beginning; and it made her a great Merit with me, that she kept it from the Knowledge of my Father, who was then living, and of my Mother, to her Dying-day; tho' she descended so low, in her Rage, to hint the Matter to you.

The little Misses took their Leaves soon after; and I know not how, but I am strangely affected with this dear Child. I wish he would be so good as to let me have her home. It would be a great Pleasure to have such a fine Opportunity, oblig'd as I am, to shew my Love for himself, in my Fondness for this dear Miss.

As we came home together in the Chariot, he gave me the following Particulars of this Affair, additional to what he had before mention'd.

That this Lady was of a good Family, and the Flower of it: But that her Mother was a Person of great Art and Address, and not altogether so nice in the Particular between himself and Miss, as she ought to have been. That, particularly, when she had Reason to find him unsettled and wild, and her Daughter in more Danger from him, than he was from her; yet she encouraged their Privacies; and even, at last, when she had Reason to

apprehend, from their being surpriz'd together, in a way not so creditable
to the Lady, that she was far from forbidding their private Meetings; on
the contrary, that on a certain Time, she had set one, that had formerly
been her Footman, and a Half-pay Officer,¹ her Relation, to watch an
Opportunity, and to frighten him into a Marriage with the Lady. That
accordingly, when they had surpriz'd him in her Chamber, just as he had
been let in, they drew their Swords upon him, and threaten'd instantly to
kill him, if he did not promise Marriage on the Spot; and that they had a
Parson ready below Stairs, as he found afterwards. That then he suspected,
from some strong Circumstances, that Miss was in the Plot; which so
enraged him, with their Menaces together, that he drew, and stood upon
his Defence, and was so much in Earnest, that the Man he push'd into
the Arm, and disabled; and pressing pretty forward upon the other, as he
retreated, he rushed in upon him, near the Top of the Stairs, and push'd
him down one Pair, and he was much hurt with the Fall:—Not but that,
he said, he might have paid for his Rashness; but that the Business of
his Antagonists was rather to frighten than kill him. That, upon this, in
the Sight of the old Lady, the Parson she had provided, and her other
Daughters, he went out of their House, with bitter Execrations against
them all.

That after this, designing to break off all Correspondence with the
whole Family, and Miss too, she found means to engage him to give
her a Meeting at *Woodstock*, in order to clear herself. That, poor Lady!
she there was obliged, naughty Creature as he was! to make herself quite
guilty of a worse Fault, in order to clear herself of a lighter. That they
afterwards met at *Godstow* often, at *Woodstock*, and every neighbouring
Place to *Oxford*; where he was then studying, as it prov'd, guilty Lessons,
instead of improving ones; till, at last, the Effect of their frequent Interviews
grew too obvious to be concealed. That the young Lady then, when she
was not fit to be seen, for the Credit of the Family, was confin'd, and all
manner of Means were used, to induce him to marry her. That, finding
nothing would do, they at last resolved to complain to his Father and
Mother. But that he made his Sister acquainted with the Matter, who
then happen'd to be at home, and, by her Management and Spirit, their
Intentions of that sort, were frustrated; and seeing no Hopes, they agreed
to Lady *Davers*'s Proposals, and sent poor Miss down to *Marlborough*,²
where, at her Expence, which he answer'd to her again, she was provided
for, and privately lay-in. That Lady *Davers* took upon herself the Care of
the Little-one, till it came to be fit to be put to the Boarding-school, where
it now is; and that he had settled upon the dear little Miss such a Sum of

Money, as the Interest of it would handsomely provide for her; and the
Principal would be a tolerable Fortune, fit for a Gentlewoman, when she
came to be marriageable. And this, my Dear, said he, is the Story in brief.
And I do assure you, *Pamela*, added he, I am far from making a Boast of,
or taking a Pride in, this Affair: But since it has happen'd, I can't say, but I
wish the poor Child to live, and be happy; and I must endeavour to make
her so.

Sir, said I, to be sure you should; and I shall take a very great Pride to
contribute to the dear little Soul's Felicity, if you will permit me to have
her home.—But, added I, does not Miss know any thing who are her
Father and Mother?—I wanted him to say, if the poor Lady was living or
dead.—No, answer'd he. Her Governess has been told, by my Sister, That
she is the Daughter of a Gentleman and his Lady, who are related, at a
Distance, to Lord *Davers*, and now live in *Jamaica*;[1] and she calls me Uncle,
only because I am the Brother to Lady *Davers*, whom she calls Aunt, and
who is very fond of her; as is also my Lord, who knows the whole Matter;
and they have her, at all her little School Recesses, at their House, and are
very kind to her.

I believe, added he, the Truth of the Matter is very little known or
suspected; for as her Mother *is* of no mean Family, her Friends endeavour
to keep it secret, as much as I; and Lady *Davers*, till her Wrath boil'd over,
t'other Day, had manag'd the Matter very dexterously and kindly.

The Words, Mother *is* of no mean Family, gave me not to doubt the
poor Lady was living. And I said, But how, Sir, can the dear Miss's poor
Mother be content to deny herself the Enjoyment of so sweet a Child?—
Ay, *Pamela*, reply'd he, now *you* come in; I see you want to know what's
become of the poor Mother!—'Tis natural enough you should; but I was
willing to see how the little Suspence would operate upon you.—Dear Sir,
said I—Nay, reply'd he, 'tis very natural, my Dear! I think you have had
a great deal of Patience, and are come at this Question so fairly, that you
deserve to be answer'd.

You must know then, there is some Foundation for saying, That her
Mother, at least, lives in *Jamaica*; for there she does live, and very happily
too. For you must know, that she suffer'd so much in Childbed, that nobody
expected her Life; and this, when she was up, made such an Impression
upon her, that she dreaded nothing so much as the Thoughts of returning
to her former Fault; and to say the Truth, I had intended to make her
a Visit as soon as her Month was well up.[2] And so, unknown to me,
she engaged herself to go to *Jamaica*, with two young Ladies, who were
born there; but were returning to their Friends, after they had been four

Years in *England* for their Education; and recommending to me, by a very moving Letter, her little Baby, and that I would not suffer it to be called by her Name, but *Goodwin*, that her Shame might be the less known, for hers and her Family's sake; she got her Friends to assign her Five hundred Pounds, in full of all her Demands upon her Family, and went up to *London*, and imbarked, with her Companions, at *Gravesend*, and so sailed to *Jamaica*; where she is since well and happily marry'd; passing, to her Husband, for a young Widow, with one Daughter, which her first Husband's Friends take care of, and provide for. And so, you see, *Pamela*, that in the whole Story on both sides, the Truth is as much preserv'd as possible.

Poor Lady! said I; how her Story moves me!—I am glad she is so happy at last! And, my Dear, said he, Are you not glad she is so far off too?—As to that, Sir, said I, I cannot be sorry, to be sure, as she is so happy; which she could not have been here. For, Sir, I doubt, you would have proceeded with your Temptations, if she had not gone; and it shew'd she was much in Earnest to be good, that she could leave her native Country, leave all her Relations, leave you that she so well lov'd, leave her dear Baby, and try a new Fortune, in a new World, among quite Strangers, and hazard the Seas; and all to preserve herself from further Guiltiness!—Indeed, indeed, Sir, said I, I bleed for what her Distresses must be in this Life: I am grieved for her poor Mind's Remorse, thro' her Childbed Terrors, which could have so great and so worthy an Effect upon her afterwards; and I honour her Resolution; and should rank such a returning dear Lady in the Class of those who are most virtuous, and doubt not God Almighty's Mercies to her; and that her present Happiness is the Result of his gracious Providence, blessing her Penitence and Reformation.—But, Sir, said I, Did you not once see the poor Lady after her Lying-in?

I did not believe her so much in Earnest, answer'd he; and I went down to *Marlborough*, and heard she was gone from thence to *Calne*.[1] I went to *Calne*, and heard she was gone to *Reading*, to a Relation's there. Thither I went, and heard she was gone to *Oxford*. I follow'd; and there she was; but I could not come at her Speech.

She at last received a Letter from me, begging a Meeting with her; for I found her Departure with the Ladies was resolved on; and that she was with her Friends only to take Leave of them, and receive her agreed-on Portion: And she appointed the *Saturday* following, and that was *Wednesday*, to give me a Meeting at the old Place, at *Woodstock*.

Then, added he, I thought I was sure of her, and doubted not I should spoil her intended Voyage. I set out on *Thursday* to *Gloucester*, on a Party of

Pleasure; and on *Saturday* I went to the Place appointed, at *Woodstock*; but when I came there, I found a Letter instead of my Lady; and when I open'd it, it was to beg my Pardon for deceiving me. Expressing her Concern for her past Fault; her Affection to me; and the Apprehension she had, that she should be unable to keep her good Resolves if she met me: That she had set out the *Thursday* for her Embarkation; for that she fear'd nothing else could save her; and had appointed this Meeting on *Saturday*, at the Place of her former Guilt, that I might be suitably impress'd upon the Occasion, and pity and allow for her; and that she might get three or four Days start of me, and be quite out of my Reach. She recommended again, as upon the Spot where the poor Little-one ow'd its Being, my Tenderness to it, for her sake: and that was all she had to request of me, she said; but would not forget to pray for me in all her own Dangers, and in every Difficulty she was going to encounter.

I wept at this moving Tale: And did not this impress you much, my dear Sir, said I? Surely, such an affecting Lesson as this, on the very guilty Spot too, (I admire the dear Lady's pious Contrivance!) must have had a great Effect upon you. One would have thought, Sir, it was enough to reclaim you for ever. All your naughty Purposes, I make no Doubt, were quite chang'd. Why, my Dear, said he, I was much mov'd, you may be sure, when I came to reflect: But, at first, I was so assur'd of being a successful Tempter, and spoiling her Voyage, that I was vexed, and much out of Humour; but when I came to reflect, as I said, I was quite overcome with this Instance of her Prudence, her Penitence, and her Resolution; and more admir'd her than I had ever done. Yet I could not bear she should so escape me neither; so much overcome me, as it were, in an heroical Bravery; and I hasten'd away, and got a Bill of Credit of Lord *Davers*, upon his Banker in *London*, for Five hundred Pounds, and set out for that Place; having called at *Oxford*, and got what Light I could, as to where I might hear of her there.

When I arriv'd in Town, which was not till *Monday* Morning, I went to a Place called *Crosby-square*,[1] where the Friends of the two Ladies liv'd. She had set out, in the Flying-coach,[2] on *Tuesday*; got to the two Ladies that very Night; and, on *Saturday*, had set out, with them, for *Gravesend*, much about the Time I was expecting her at *Woodstock*.

You may suppose, that I was much affected, my Dear, with this. However, I got my Bill of Credit converted into Money; and I set out, with my Servant, on *Monday* Afternoon, and reached *Gravesend* that Night; and there I understood that she and the two Ladies had gone on Board from the very Inn I put up at, in the Morning; and the Ship waited only for the Wind, which then was turning about in its Favour.

I got a Boat directly, and put on Board the Ship, and asked for Mrs. *Godfrey.* But judge you, my dear *Pamela*, her Surprize and Confusion when she saw me. She had like to have fainted away. I offer'd any Money to put off the Sailing till next Day, but it would not be comply'd with; and fain would I have got her on Shore, and promised to attend her, if she would go over Land, to any Part of *England* the Ship would touch at. But she was immoveable.

Every one concluded me her humble Servant; and were touched at the moving Interview; the young Ladies, and their Female Attendants especially. With great Difficulty, upon my solemn Assurances of Honour, she trusted herself with me in one of the Cabins; and there I try'd, what I could, to prevail upon her to quit her Purpose: But all in vain: She said, I had made her quite unhappy by this Interview! She had Difficulties enough upon her Mind before; but now I had imbitter'd all her Voyage, and given her the deepest Distress.

I could prevail upon her, but for one Favour, and that with the greatest Reluctance; which was, to accept of the Five hundred Pounds, as a Present from me; and she promised, at my earnest Desire, to draw upon me for a greater Sum, as a Person that had her Effects in my Hands, when she arriv'd, if she should find it convenient for her. In short, this was all the Favour I could procure; for she would not promise so much as to correspond with me; and was determin'd on going; and, I believe, if I would have marry'd her, which yet I had not in my Head, she would not have been diverted from her Purpose.

But how, Sir, said I, did you part? I would have sailed with her, answer'd he, and been landed at the first Port in *England*, or *Ireland*, I cared not which, they should put in at. But she was too full of Apprehensions to admit it; and the rough Fellow of a Master, Captain they call'd him, (but, in my Mind, I could have thrown him overboard) would not stay a Moment, the Wind and Tide being quite fair, and was very urgent with me to go ashore, or to go the Voyage; and being impetuous in my Temper, *spoilt, you know, my Dear, by my Mother*, and not used to Controul, I thought it very strange that Wind and Tide, or any thing else, should be preferr'd to me, and my Money: But so it was, I was forced to go, and so took Leave of the Ladies and the other Passengers; wish'd them a good Voyage; gave Five Guineas among the Ship's Crew, to be good to the Ladies; and took such a Leave as you may better imagine, than I express. She recommended, once more, to me, the dear Guest, as she called her, the Ladies being present, and thanked me for all these Instances of my Regard, which, she said, would leave a strong Impression on her Mind; and, at parting, she threw her Arms about my Neck, and we took such a Leave, as affected every one present, Men, as well as Ladies.

So, with a truly heavy Heart, I went down the Ship's Side to my Boat; and stood up in it, looking at her, as long as I could see her, and she at me, with her Handkerchief at her Eyes; and then I gaz'd at the Ship, *till* and *after* I had landed, as long as I could discern the least Appearance of it; for she was under Sail, in a manner, when I left her: And so I return'd, highly disturb'd, to my Inn.

I went to-bed, but rested not; return'd to *London* the next Morning; and set out that Afternoon again, for the Country. And so much, my Dear, for poor *Sally Godfrey*.—She sends, I understand, by all Opportunities, with the Knowledge of her Husband, to learn how her Child, by her first Husband, does; and has the Satisfaction to know she is happily provided for. And, about half a Year ago, her Spouse sent a little Negro Boy, of about ten Years old, as a Present, to wait upon her. But he was taken ill of the Small-pox, and died in a Month after he was landed.

Sure, Sir, said I, your generous Mind must have been long affected with this melancholy Case, and all its Circumstances. It hung upon me, indeed, some time, said he; but I was full of Spirits and Inconsideration. I went soon after to travel; a hundred new Objects danced before my Eyes, and kept Reflection from me. And, you see, I had, five or six Years afterwards, and even before that, so thoroughly lost all the Impressions you talk of, that I doubted not to make my *Pamela* change her Name, without either Act of Parliament or Wedlock, and be *Sally Godfrey* the Second.

O you dear naughty Gentleman! said I, this seems but too true! But I bless God that it is not so!—I bless God for your Reformation, and that for your own dear sake, as well as mine!

Well, my Dear, said he, and I bless God for it too!—I do most sincerely!—And 'tis my greater Pleasure, because I have, as I hope, seen my Error so early; and that, with such a Stock of Youth and Health of my Side, in all Appearance, I can truly abhor my past Liberties, and pity poor *Sally Godfrey*, from the same Motives that I admire my *Pamela's* Virtues; and resolve, by the Grace of God, to make myself as worthy of them as possible: And I will hope, my Dear, your Prayers for my Pardon and my Perseverance, will be of no small Efficacy on this Occasion.

These agreeable Reflections, on this melancholy, but instructive, Story, brought us in View of his own House; and we alighted, and took a Walk in the Garden till Dinner was ready. And now we are so busy about making ready for our Appearance, that I shall hardly have time to write till that be over.

MONDAY Morning.

Yesterday we set out, attended by *John, Abraham, Benjamin* and *Isaac*, in fine new Liveries, in the best Chariot, which had been new clean'd, and lin'd, and new harness'd; so that it look'd like a quite new one: But I had no Arms to quarter[1] with my dear Spouse's; tho' he jocularly, upon my taking Notice of my Obscurity, said, that he had a good mind to have the Olive-branch,[2] which would allude to his Hopes, quarter'd for mine. I was dress'd in the Suit I mention'd, of White flower'd with Gold, and a rich Head-dress, and the Diamond Necklace, Ear-rings, &c. I also mention'd before. And my dear Sir, in a fine laced silk Waistcoat, of blue Paduasoy,[3] and his Coat a pearl-colour'd fine Cloth, with gold Buttons and Button-holes, and lin'd with white Silk; and he look'd charmingly indeed. I said, I was too fine, and would have laid aside some of the Jewels; but he said, It would be thought a Slight to me from him, as his Wife; and tho', as I apprehended, it might be, that People would talk as it was, yet he had rather they should say any thing, than that I was not put upon an equal Foot, as his Wife, with any Lady he might have marry'd.

It seems, the neighbouring Gentry had expected us; and there was a great Congregation; for (against my Wish) we were a little of the latest; so that, as we walked up the Church to his Seat, we had abundance of Gazers, and Whisperers: But my dear Master behav'd with so intrepid an Air, and was so chearful and complaisant to me, that he did Credit to his kind Choice, instead of shewing as if he was asham'd of it; and as I was resolved to busy my Mind intirely with the Duties of the Day, my Intentness on that Occasion, and my Thankfulness to God, for his unspeakable Mercies to me, so took up my Attention, that I was much less concern'd than I should otherwise have been, at the Gazings and Whisperings of the Ladies and Gentlemen, as well as of the rest of the Congregation; whose Eyes were all turn'd to our Seat.

When the Sermon was ended, we staid the longer, because the Church should be pretty empty; but we found great Numbers at the Church Doors, and in the Church Porch; and I had the Pleasure of hearing many Commendations, as well of my Person, as my Dress and Behaviour, and not one Reflection, or Mark of Disrespect. 'Squire *Martin*, who is single,

Mr. *Chambers*, Mr. *Arthur*, and Mr. *Brooks*, with their Families, were all there: And the four Gentlemen came up to us, before we went into the Chariot, and, in a very kind and respectful manner, complimented me, and my dear Sir; and Mrs. *Arthur*, and Mrs. *Brooks*, were so kind as to wish me Joy; and Mrs. *Brooks* said, You sent my Spouse, Madam, home, t'other Day, quite charm'd with that easy and sweet Manner, which you have convinced a thousand Persons, this Day, is so natural to you.

You do me great Honour, Madam, reply'd I. Such a good Lady's Approbation must make me too sensible of my Happiness. My dear Master handed me into the Chariot, and stood talking with Sir *Thomas Atkyns*, at the Door of it, (who was making him abundance of Compliments, and is a very ceremonious Gentleman, a little to Extremes) and I believe, to familiarize me to the Gazers, which concern'd me a little. For I was dash'd to hear the Praises of the Country People, and to see how they crouded about the Chariot. Several poor People begg'd my Charity, and I beckon'd *John* with my Fan, and said, Divide, in the further Church-Porch, that Money to the Poor, and let them come to-morrow Morning to me, and I will give them something more, if they don't importune me now.——So I gave him all the Silver I had, which happen'd to be between twenty and thirty Shillings; and this drew away from me, their clamorous Prayers for Charity.

Mr. *Martin* came up to me on the other side of the Chariot, and lean'd on the Door, while my Master was talking to Sir *Thomas*, from whom he could not get away, and said, By all that's good, you have charm'd the whole Congregation. Not a Soul but is full of your Praises. My Neighbour knew, better than any body could tell him, how to chuse for himself. Why, said he, the Dean himself look'd more upon you than his Book.

O Sir, said I, you are very encouraging to a weak Mind! I vow, said he, I say no more than's Truth: I'd marry to-morrow, if I was sure of meeting with a Person of but one half of the Merit you have. You are, said he, and 'tis not my way to praise too much, an Ornament to your Sex, an Honour to your Spouse, and a Credit to Religion!—Every body is saying so, added he; for you have, by your Piety, edified the whole Church.

As he had done speaking, the Dean himself complimented me, that the Behaviour of so sweet a Bride would be very edifying to his Congregation, and encouraging to himself. Sir, said I, you are very kind. I hope I shall not behave unworthy of the good Instructions I shall have the Pleasure to receive from so worthy a Divine. He bow'd, and went on.

Sir *Thomas* then apply'd to me, my Master stepping into the Chariot, and said, I beg Pardon, Madam, for detaining your good Spouse from you.

But I have been saying, he is the happiest Man in the World. I bow'd to him; but I could have wish'd him further, to make me sit so in the Notice of every one; which, for all I could do, dash'd me not a little.

Mr. *Martin* said to my Master, If you'll come to Church every *Sunday*, with your charming Lady, I will never absent myself, and she'll give a good Example to all the Neighbourhood. O, my dear Sir, said I, to my Master, You know not how much I am obliged to good Mr. *Martin*. He has, by his kind Expressions, made me dare to look up with Pleasure and Gratitude.

Said my Master, My dear Love, I am very much oblig'd, as well as you, to my good Friend Mr. *Martin*. And he said to him, We will constantly go to Church, and to every other Place, where we can have the Pleasure of seeing Mr. *Martin*.

Mr. *Martin* said, Gad, Sir, you are a happy Man; and I think your Lady's Example has made you more polite, and handsome too, than I ever knew you before, tho' we never thought you unpolite neither. And so he bow'd, and went to his own Chariot; and as we drove away, the People kindly blessed us, and called us a charming Pair. As I have no other Pride, I hope, in repeating these things, than in the Countenance the general Approbation gives to my dear Master for his stooping so low, you will excuse me for it, I know.

In the Afternoon, we went again to Church, and a little early, at my Request; but the Church was quite full, and soon after even crowded; so much does Novelty, the more's the Pity! attract the Eyes of Mankind. 'Squire *Martin* came in, after us, and made up to our Seat, and said, If you please, my dear Friend, I will take my Seat with you this Afternoon. With all my Heart, said my Master. I was sorry for it; but was resolved my Duty should not be made second to Bashfulness, or any other Consideration; and when Divine Service began, I withdrew to the further End of the Pew, and left the Gentlemen in the Front; and they behav'd quite suitably, both of them, to the Occasion. I mention this the rather, because Mr. *Martin* was not very noted for coming to Church, or Attention when there, before.

The Dean preached again, which he was not used to do, out of Compliment to us; and an excellent Sermon he made on the relative Duties of Christianity;[1] and it took my peculiar Attention; for he made many fine Observations on the Subject. Mr. *Martin* address'd himself twice or thrice to me, during the Sermon; but he saw me so wholly engross'd with hearkening to the good Preacher, that he forbore interrupting me; yet I took care, according to my dear Sir's Lesson, formerly, to observe to him a

chearful and obliging Behaviour, as one of his Friends and Intimates. My
Master ask'd him to give him his Company to Supper; and he said, I am
so taken with your Lady, that you must not give me too much Encouragement; for I shall be always with you, if you do. He was pleased to say,
You cannot favour us with too much of your Company; and as I have left
you in the Lurch, in your single State, I think you will do well to oblige
us as much as you can; and who knows but my Happiness may reform
another Rake? *Who* knows?—said Mr. *Martin*—Why, I know!—for I am
more than half reform'd already.

At the Chariot-door, Mrs. *Arthur*, Mrs. *Brooks*, Mrs. *Chambers*, were
brought to me, by their respective Spouses; and presently, the witty Lady
Towers, who banter'd me before, (as I once told you) join'd them; and
Mrs. *Arthur* said, She wished me Joy: And that all the good Ladies, my
Neighbours, would collect themselves together, and make me a Visit. This,
said I, will be an Honour, Madam, that I can never enough acknowledge.
It will be very kind so to countenance a Person, who will always study to
deserve your Favour, by the most respectful Behaviour.

Lady *Towers* said, My dear Neighbour, you want no Countenance; your
own Merit is sufficient. I had a slight Cold, that kept me at home in the
Morning; but I heard you so much talk'd of, and prais'd, that I resolved
not to stay away in the Afternoon. And I join in the Joy every one gives
you. She turn'd to my Master, and said, You are a sly Thief, as I always
thought you. Where have you stolen this Lady! And now, how barbarous
is it, thus, unawares in a manner, to bring her here upon us, to mortify
and eclipse us all!—You are very kind, Madam, said he, that you, and all
my worthy Neighbours, see with my Eyes. But had I not known she had
so much Excellency of Mind and Behaviour, as would strike every body in
her Favour at first Sight, I should not have dared to class her with such of
my worthy Neighbours, as now so kindly congratulate us both.

I own, said she, softly, I was one of your Censurers; but I never lik'd
you so well in my Life, as for this Action, now I see how capable your
Bride is of giving Distinction to any Condition.—And coming to me, My
dear Neighbour, said she, excuse me for having but in my Thought, the
Remembrance that I have *seen you formerly*, when, by your sweet Air, and
easy Deportment, you so much surpass us all, and give Credit to your
present happy Condition.

Dear good Madam, said I, how shall I suitably return my Acknowledgments! But it will never be a Pain to me to look back upon my *former Days*,
now I have the kind Allowance and Example of so many worthy Ladies to

support me in the Honours to which the most generous of Men has raised me.

Sweetly said! she was pleased to say. If I was in another Place, I would kiss you for that Answer. Oh! happy, happy, Mr. *B.* said she to my Master; what Reputation have you not brought upon your Judgment!—I won't be long before I see you, added she, I'll assure you, if I come by myself. That shall be your own Fault, Madam, said Mrs. *Brooks*, if you do.

And so they took Leave; and I gave my Hand to my dear Sir, and said, How happy have you made me, generous Sir!—And the Dean, who was just come up, heard me, and said, And how happy you have made your Spouse, I'll venture to pronounce, is hard to say, from what I observe of you both. I curt'sy'd, and blush'd, not thinking any body heard me. And my Master telling him he should be glad of the Honour of a Visit from him; he said, He would pay his Respects to us, the first Opportunity, and would bring his Wife and Daughter to attend me. I said, That was doubly kind; and I should be very proud of cultivating so worthy an Acquaintance. I thanked him for his fine Discourse; and he thanked me for my Attention to it, which he called Exemplary: And so my dear Sir handed me into the Chariot; and we were carried home, *both* happy, and *both* pleased, thank God!

Mr. *Martin* came in the Evening, with another Gentleman, his Friend, one Mr. *Dormer*; and he entertained us with the favourable Opinion, he said, every one had of me, and of the Choice my good Benefactor had made.

This Morning the Poor came, according to my Invitation; and I sent them away with glad Hearts, to the Number of Twenty-five. They were not above Twelve or Fourteen, on *Sunday*, that *John* divided the Silver I gave among them; but others got hold of the Matter, and made up to the above Number.

TUESDAY.

My generous Master has given me, this Morning, a most considerate, but yet, from the Nature of it, melancholy Instance of his great Regard for my Unworthiness, which I never could have wished, hoped for, or even thought of.

He took a Walk with me, after Breakfast, into the Garden; and a little Shower falling, he led me, for Shelter, into the little Summer-house, in the private Garden, where he formerly gave me Apprehensions; and sitting down by me, he said, I have now finish'd all that lies on my Mind, my Dear, and am very easy: For have you not wonder'd, that I have so much employ'd myself in my Library? Been so much at home, and yet not in your Company?——No, Sir, said I, I have never been so impertinent as to wonder at any thing you please to employ yourself about; nor would give way to a Curiosity that should be troublesome to you: And besides, I know your large Possessions, and the Method you take of looking yourself into your Affairs, must needs take up some Portions of your Time, that I ought to be very careful how I invade.

Well, said he, but I'll tell you what has been my last Work: I have taken it into my Consideration, that, at present, my Line is almost extinct; and a great Part of my Estate, in case I die without Issue, will go to another Line; and other Parts of my personal Estate, will go into such Hands, as I should not care my *Pamela* should lie at their Mercy. I have therefore, as human Life is uncertain, made such a Disposition of my Affairs, as will make you absolutely independent and happy; as will secure to you the Power of doing a great deal of Good; and living as a Person ought to do, who is my Relict;[1] and shall put it out of any body's Power to molest your Father and Mother, in the Provision I design them, for the Remainder of their Days: And I have finish'd all this very Morning, except to naming Trustees for you; and if you have any body you would confide in more than another, I would have you speak.

I was so touch'd with this mournful Instance of his excessive Goodness to me, and the Thoughts necessarily flowing from the solemn Occasion, that I was unable to speak, and at last reliev'd my Mind by a violent Fit of weeping; and could only say, clasping my Arms around the dear generous Gentleman! How shall I support this! So very cruel, yet so very kind!

Don't, my Dear, said he, be concern'd at what gives me Pleasure. I am not the nearer my End, for having made this Disposition; but I think the putting off these material Points, when so many Accidents every Day happen, and Life is so precarious, is one of the most inexcusable Things in the World. And there are so many important Points to be thought of, when Life is drawing to its utmost Verge; and the Mind may be so agitated and unfit, that it is a most sad thing to put off, to that Time, any of those Concerns, which more especially require a considerate and composed Frame of Temper, and perfect Health and Vigor to manage.

My poor Friend, Mr. *Carlton*, who died in my Arms so lately, and had a Mind disturb'd by worldly Considerations on one side, a Weakness of Body, thro' his Distemper's Violence, on another, and the Concerns of still as much more Moment, as the Soul is to the Body, on a third, made so great an Impression upon me then, that I was the more impatient to come to this House, where were most of my Writings, in order to make the Disposition I have now perfected: And since it is grievous to my dear Girl, I will think myself of such Trustees, as shall be most for her Benefit. I have only therefore to assure you, my Dear, that in this Instance, as I will do in every other I can think of, I have studied to make you quite easy, free, and independent. And because I shall avoid all Occasions, for the future, which may discompose you, I have but one Request to make; which is, That if it please God, for my Sins, to separate me from my dearest *Pamela*, that you will only resolve not to marry *one* Person; for I would not be such an *Herod*,[1] as to restrict you from a Change of Condition with any other, however reluctantly I may think of any other Person succeeding me in your Esteem.

I could not answer, and thought my Heart would have burst. And he continued, To conclude at once, a Subject that is so grievous to you, I will tell you, my *Pamela*, that this Person is Mr. *Williams*: And now I will acquaint you with my Motive for this Request; which is wholly owing to my Niceness, and to no Dislike I have for him, or Apprehension of any Likelihood that it will be so: But, methinks, it would reflect a little upon my *Pamela*, if she was to give way to such a Conduct, as if she had marry'd a Man for his *Estate*, when she had rather have had *another*, had it not been for *that*; and that now, the World will say, she is at Liberty to pursue her Inclination, the Parson is the Man!——And I cannot bear even the most distant Apprehension, that I had not the Preference with you, of any Man living, let me have been what I would; as I have shewn my dear Life, that I have preferr'd her to all her Sex, of whatever Degree.

I could not speak, might I have had the World; and he took me in his Arms, and said, I have now spoken all my Mind, and expect no Answer; and I see you too much mov'd to give me one.——Only forgive me the Mention, as I have told you my Motive; which as much affects your Reputation as my Niceness; and offer not at an Answer;—only say, You forgive me. And I hope I have not one discomposing thing to say to my Dearest, for the rest of my Life; which, I pray God, for both our sakes, to lengthen for many happy Years.

Grief still choaked up the Passage of my Words; and he said, The Shower is over, my Dear, let us walk out again.——He led me by the Hand,

and I would have spoke; but he said, I will not hear my dear Creature say any thing: To hearken to your Assurance of complying with my Request, would look as if I doubted you, and wanted it. I am confident I needed only to speak my Mind, to be observed by you; and I shall never more think of the Subject, if you don't remind me of it. He then most sweetly chang'd the Discourse.

Don't you with Pleasure, my Dear, said he, take in the delightful Fragrance that this sweet Shower has given to these Banks of Flowers? Your *Presence* is so enlivening to me, that I could almost fansy, that what we owe to the *Shower*, is owing to *That*: And all Nature, methinks, blooms around me, when I have my *Pamela* by my Side. You are a Poetess, my Dear; and I will give you a few Lines,[1] that I made myself on such an Occasion as this I am speaking of, the Presence of a sweet Companion, and the fresh Verdure, that, after a Shower succeeding a long Draught, shew'd itself throughout all vegetable Nature. And then in a sweet and easy Accent, (with his dear Arms about me as we walk'd) he sung me the following Verses; of which he afterwards favour'd me with a Copy.

I.

All Nature blooms when you appear;
The Fields their richest Liv'ries wear;
Oaks, Elms and Pines, blest with your View,
Shoot out fresh Greens, and bud anew.
   The varying Seasons you supply;
   And when you're gone, they fade and die.

II.

Sweet Philomel, *in mournful Strains,*
To you appeals, to you complains.
The tow'ring Lark, on rising Wing,
Warbles to you, your Praise does sing;
   He cuts the yielding Air, and flies
   To Heav'n, to type[2] your future Joys.

III.

The purple Violet, damask Rose,
Each to delight your Senses blows.
The Lilies ope', as you appear,
And all the Beauties of the Year
   Diffuse their Odors at your Feet,
   Who give to ev'ry Flow'r its Sweet.

IV.

For Flow'rs and Women are ally'd;
Both, Nature's Glory, and her Pride!
Of ev'ry fragrant Sweet possest,
They bloom but for the Fair One's Breast;
   And to the swelling Bosom born,
   Each other mutually adorn.

Thus sweetly did he palliate the Woes, which the Generosity of his Actions, mix'd with the Solemness of the Occasion, and the strange Request he had vouchsafed to make me, had occasion'd. And all he would permit me to say, was, That I was not displeased with him!—Displeased with you, dearest Sir! said I: Let me thus testify my Obligations, and the Force all your Commands shall have upon me. And I took the Liberty to clasp my Arms about his Neck, and kissed him.

But yet my Mind was pained at times, and has been to this Hour.— God grant that I may never see the dreadful Moment, that shall shut up the precious Life of this excellently generous Benefactor of mine! And—but I cannot bear to suppose—I cannot say more on such a deep Subject!

Oh! what a poor thing is human Life in its best Enjoyments!—subjected to *imaginary* Evils, when it has no *real* ones to disturb it! and that can be made as effectually unhappy by its Apprehensions of remote Contingencies, as if it was struggling with the Pangs of a present Distress! This, duly reflected upon, methinks, should convince every one, that this World is not a Place for the immortal Mind to be confined to; and that there must be an Hereafter, where the *whole* Soul shall be satisfy'd.

But I shall get out of my Depth; my shallow Mind cannot comprehend, as it ought, these weighty Subjects: Let me, therefore, only pray, that after having made a grateful Use of God's Mercies here, I may, with my dear Benefactor, rejoice in that happy State, where is no Mixture, no Unsatisfiedness; and where all is Joy, and Peace, and Love, for evermore!

I said, when we sat at Supper, The charming Taste you gave me, Sir, of your poetical Fancy, makes me sure you have more Favours of this Kind, to delight me with, if you please; and may I beg to be indulged on this agreeable Head?—Hitherto, said he, my Life has been too much a Life of Gaiety and Action, to be busy'd so innocently. Some little Essays I have now-and-then attempted; but very few have I completed. Indeed I had not Patience nor Attention enough to hold me long to any one thing.

Now-and-then, perhaps, I may occasionally shew you what I have attempted. But I never could please myself in this way.

FRIDAY.

We were Yesterday favour'd with the Company of almost all the neighbouring Gentry, and their good Ladies, who, by Appointment with one another, met to congratulate our Happiness. Nothing could be more obliging, more free and affectionate, than the Ladies; nothing more polite than the Gentlemen. All was perform'd, (for they came to Supper,) with Decency and Order, and much to every one's Satisfaction, which was principally owing to good Mrs. *Jervis's* Care and Skill; who is an excellent Manager.

For my part, I was dress'd out, only to be admir'd, as it seems; and truly, if I had not known, that I did not make *myself*, as you, my dear Father, once hinted to me; and if I had had the Vanity to think as well of myself, as the good Company was pleased to do, I might possibly have been proud. But I know, as my Lady *Davers* said, tho' in Anger, yet in Truth, that I am but *a poor Bit of painted Dirt.* All that I value myself upon, is, that God has raised me to a Condition to be useful in my Generation, to better Persons than myself. This is my Pride: And I hope this will be *all* my Pride. For what was I of myself!—All the Good I can do, is but a poor third-hand Good; for my dearest Master himself is but the Second-hand. GOD, the All-gracious, the All-good, the All-bountiful, the All-mighty, the All-merciful GOD, is the First: To HIM, therefore, be all the Glory!

As I expect the Happiness, the unspeakable Happiness, my ever-dear and ever-honour'd Father and Mother, of enjoying you both here, under this Roof, so soon, (and pray let it be as soon as you can) I will not enter into the Particulars of the last agreeable Evening: For I shall have a thousand things, as well as that, to talk to you upon. I fear you will be tir'd with my Prattle when I see you!

I am to return these Visits singly; and there were Eight Ladies here, of different Families. Dear Heart, I shall find enough to do!—I doubt my Time will not be so well filled up, as I once promised my dear Sir!—But he is pleas'd, chearful, kind, affectionate! O what a happy Creature am I!—May I be always thankful to GOD, and grateful to *him!*—When all these tumultuous Visitings are over, I shall have my Mind, I hope, subside into a Family Calm, that I may make myself a little useful to the

Houshold of my dear Master; or else I shall be an unprofitable Servant
indeed!

Lady *Davers* sent this Morning her Compliments to us both, very affec-
tionately; and her Lord's good Wishes and Congratulations. And she
desir'd my Writings *per* Bearer; and says, she will herself bring them to me
again, with Thanks, as soon as she has read them; and she and her Lord
will come and be *my* Guests (that was her particularly kind Word) for a
Fortnight.

I have now but one thing to wish for, and then, methinks, I shall be
all Ecstasy; and that is, Your Presence, both of you, and your Blessings;
which I hope you will bestow upon me every Morning and Night, till you
are settled in the happy manner my dear Spouse has intended.

Methinks I want sadly your List of the honest and worthy Poor; for the
Money lies by me, and brings me no Interest. You see I am become a mere
Usurer; and want to make Use upon Use: And yet, when I have done all, I
cannot do so much as I ought. God forgive my Imperfections!

I tell my dear Sir, I want another Dairy-house Visit. To be sure, if he
won't, at *present*, permit it, I shall, if it please God to spare us, tieze him
like any over-indulged Wife, if, as the dear Charmer grows *older*, he won't
let me have the Pleasure of forming her tender Mind, as well as I am able,
lest, poor little Soul! she fall into such Snares as her unhappy dear Mother
fell into. I am providing a Power of pretty Things for her, against I see her
next, that I may make her love me, if I can.

Just now I have the blessed News, that you will set out, for this happy
House, on *Tuesday* Morning. The Chariot shall be with you without fail.
God give us a happy Meeting! O, how I long for it! Forgive your impatient
Daughter, who sends this, to amuse you on your Journey; and desires
to be

Ever most dutifully Yours.

Here end the Letters of the incomparable P A M E L A to her Father and
Mother. For, as they arriv'd at their Daughter's House on *Tuesday* Evening
in the following Week, she had no Occasion to continue her Journal longer.

The good old Couple were receiv'd, by her, with the utmost Joy and
Duty; and with great Goodness and Complaisance by her generous Spouse.
And having resided there till every thing was put in Order for them at the
Kentish Estate, they were carried down thither by the 'Squire himself,
and their Daughter, and put into Possession of the pretty Farm he had

designed for them. In which they long liv'd comfortably, doing Good by their Examples, and their judicious Charities, to all about them.

They constantly, twice in every Year, for a Fortnight together, so long as they liv'd, visited their dear Daughter; and once a Year, at least, for a Week at a time, were visited by them again: And the 'Squire having added, by new Purchases, to that Estate, they, by their Diligence, augmented the Value of it, and deserved of him the Kindness he shew'd them.

As for the excellent PAMELA, she enjoy'd, for many Years, the Reward of her Virtue, Piety and Charity; exceedingly beloved by both Sexes, and by all Degrees; and was look'd upon as the Mirror of her Age and Sex.

She made her beloved Spouse happy in a numerous and hopeful Progeny. And he made her the best and fondest of Husbands; and, after her Example, became remarkable for Piety, Virtue, and all the Social Duties of a Man and a Christian. And they charm'd every one within the Circle of their Acquaintance, by the Sweetness of their Manners, the regular Order and Oeconomy of their Household; by their chearful Hospitality, and a diffusive Charity to all worthy Objects within the Compass of their Knowledge.

She was regularly visited by the principal Ladies in the Neighbourhood; who were fond of her Acquaintance, and better'd by her Example.

Lady *Davers* became one of her sincerest and most affectionate Admirers. And her Lord, in a manner, doated upon her.

The poor little Miss *Goodwin* was, after a while, given up to her Wishes and Importunities, in order to be form'd by her Example; and, in Process of Time, was joined in Marriage with a Gentleman of Merit and Fortune, to whom she made an excellent Wife.

Having thus brought this little History to a happy Period, the Reader will indulge us in a few brief Observations, which naturally result from it; and which will serve as so many Applications, of its most material Incidents, to the Minds of the Youth of both Sexes.

First, then, in the Character of the GENTLEMAN, may be seen that of a fashionable Libertine, who allow'd himself in the free Indulgence of his Passions, especially as to the Fair Sex; and found himself supported in his daring Attempts, by an affluent Fortune in Possession, a personal Bravery, as it is called, readier to give than take Offence, and an imperious Will; yet as he betimes sees his Errors, and reforms in the Bloom of Youth, an edifying Lesson may be drawn from it, for the Use of such as are born to large Fortunes; and who may be taught, by his Example, the inexpressible Difference between the Hazards and Remorse which attend a profligate Course of Life; and the Pleasures which flow from virtuous Love, and virtuous Actions.

The Generosity of his Mind; his Sobriety, as to *Wine* and *Hours*; his prudent Oeconomy and Hospitality; the Purity and Constancy of his Affection, after his Change; his polite Behaviour to his *Pamela*; his generous Provision for her, in case he had died; his Bounty to her Parents, attended with such Marks of Prudence as made them useful to *himself*, as well as render'd *them* happy; and shew'd he was not acted merely by a blind and partial Passion; are so many Instances worthy of being remember'd in his Favour, and of being imitated, in Degree, by all such as are circumstanced as he was.

In the Character of Lady DAVERS, let the Proud and the High-born see the Deformity of unreasonable Passion, and how weak and ridiculous such Persons must appear, who suffer themselves, as is usually the Case, to be hurried from one Extreme to another; from the Height of Violence, to the most abject Submission; and subject themselves to be out-done by the humble Virtue they so much despise.

Let good CLERGYMEN, in Mr. WILLIAMS, see that whatever Displeasure the doing of their Duty may give, for a Time, to their proud Patrons, Providence will, at last, reward their Piety, and turn their Distresses to Triumph; and make them even *more* valued for a Conduct that gave Offence while the Violence of Passion lasted, than if they had meanly stoop'd to flatter or sooth the Vices of the Great.

In the Examples of good old ANDREWS, and his WIFE, let those, who are reduced to a low Estate, see, that Providence never fails to reward their Honesty and Integrity; and that God will, in his own good Time, extricate them, by means unforeseen, out of their present Difficulties, and reward them with Benefits unhop'd-for.

The UPPER SERVANTS of great Families may, from the odious Character of Mrs. *Jewkes*, and the amiable ones of Mrs. *Jervis*, Mr. *Longman*,

&c. learn what to avoid, and what to chuse, to make themselves valued and esteem'd by all who know them.

And, from the double Conduct of poor *John*, the L O W E R   S E R V A N T S may learn Fidelity, and how to distinguish between the lawful and unlawful Commands of a Superior.

The poor deluded Female, who, like the once unhappy Miss G O D F R E Y, has given up her Honour, and yielded to the Allurements of her designing Lover, may learn from her Story, to stop at the *first Fault*; and, by resolving to repent and amend, see the Pardon and Blessing which await her Penitence, and a kind Providence ready to extend the Arms of its Mercy to receive and reward her returning Duty. While the abandon'd Prostitute, pursuing the wicked Courses, into which, perhaps, she was at first *inadvertently* drawn, hurries herself into filthy Diseases, and an untimely Death; and, too probably, into everlasting Perdition afterwards.[1]

Let the *desponding Heart* be comforted by the happy Issue which the Troubles and Trials of the lovely P A M E L A met with, when they see, in her Case, that no Danger nor Distress, however inevitable or deep to their Apprehensions, can be out of the Power of Providence to obviate or relieve; and which, as in various Instances in her Story, can turn the most seemingly grievous Things to its own Glory, and the Reward of suffering Innocence; and that, too, at a Time when all human Prospects seem to fail.

Let the *Rich*, and those who are *exalted* from a *low* to a *high Estate*, learn from her, that they are not promoted only for a *single Good*; but that Providence has raised them, that they should dispense to all within their Reach, the Blessings it has heaped upon them; and that the greater the Power is to which G O D has raised them, the greater is the Good that will be expected from them.

From the low Opinion she every-where shews of herself, and her attributing all her Excellencies to her pious Education, and her Lady's virtuous Instructions and Bounty; let Persons, even of *Genius* and *Piety*, learn, not to arrogate to themselves those Gifts and Graces, which they owe least of all to themselves: Since the Beauties of Person are frail, and it is not in our Power to give them to ourselves, or to be either prudent, wise, or good, without the Assistance of Divine Grace.

From the same good Example, let *Children* see what a Blessing awaits their Duty to their Parents, tho' ever so low in the World: And that the only Disgrace is to be dishonest; but none at all to be poor.

From the *Oeconomy* she purposes to observe in her Elevation, let even *Ladies of Condition* learn, that there are Family Employments in which they may, and ought to, make themselves useful, and give good Examples to their Inferiors, as well as Equals. And that their Duty to God, Charity to the Poor and Sick, and the different Branches of Houshold Management, ought to take up the most considerable Portions of their Time.

From her signal *Veracity*, which she never forfeited, in all the Hardships she was try'd with, tho' her Answers, as she had Reason to apprehend, would often make against her; and the Innocence she preserved throughout all her Stratagems and Contrivances to save herself from Violation; Persons, even *sorely tempted*, may learn to preserve a sacred Regard to *Truth*; which always begets a Reverence for them, even in the corruptest Minds.

In short,

Her obliging Behaviour to her Equals, before her Exaltation; her Kindness to them afterwards; her forgiving Spirit, and her Generosity;

Her Meekness, in every Circumstance where her Virtue was not concern'd;

Her charitable Allowances for others, as in the Case of Miss *Godfrey*, for Faults she would not have forgiven in herself;

Her Kindness and Prudence to the Offspring of that melancholy Adventure;

Her Maiden and Bridal Purity, which extended as well to her Thoughts as to her Words and Actions;

Her signal Affiance in God;

Her thankful Spirit;

Her grateful Heart;

Her diffusive Charity to the Poor, which made her blessed by them whenever she appear'd abroad;

The chearful Ease and Freedom of her Deportment;

Her Parental, Conjugal and Maternal Duty;

Her Social Virtues;

Are all so many signal Instances of the Excellency of her Mind; which may make her Character worthy of the Imitation of her Sex, from low to high Life. And the Editor of these Sheets will have his End, if it inspires a laudable Emulation in the Minds of any worthy Persons, who may thereby intitle themselves to the Rewards, the Praises, and the Blessings, by which she was so deservedly distinguished.

FINIS.

INTRODUCTION TO THE SECOND EDITION OF *PAMELA: OR, VIRTUE REWARDED* (1741)

The second edition of *Pamela: or, Virtue Rewarded* was published on 14 February 1741. It featured a new introduction, consisting mostly of excerpts of letters to Richardson from Aaron Hill, in which Hill answered objections to the novel and its heroine raised by other readers; it concluded with a commendatory poem, also by Hill. Its length and additive, pastiche-like structure may be explained by the fact that Richardson had as much as a sheet (twelve leaves or twenty-four pages) to fill up and kept adding materials until he ran out of space. Hill's peculiar style and cantankerous tone became fodder for detractors of the novel, beginning with Henry Fielding, who, in *Shamela* (published 2 April 1741), took aim not only at the hypocritical posturing of Richardson's heroine, but also at the bathetic earnestness of her most enthusiastic apologist.

INTRODUCTION TO THIS SECOND EDITION.

The kind Reception which this Piece has met with from the Publick, (a large Impression having been carried off in less than Three Months) deserves not only Acknowlegdment, but that some Notice should be taken of the Objections that have hitherto come to hand against a few Passages in it, that so the Work may be rendered as unexceptionable as possible, and, of consequence, the fitter to answer the general Design of it; which is to promote Virtue, and cultivate the Minds of the Youth of both Sexes.

But Difficulties having arisen from the different Opinions of Gentlemen, some of whom applauded the very Things that others found Fault with, it was thought proper to submit the Whole to the Judgment of a Gentleman of the most distinguish'd Taste and Abilities; the Result of which will be seen in the subsequent Pages.

We begin with the following Letter[1], at the Desire of several Gentlemen, to whom, on a very particular Occasion, it was communicated, and who wish'd to see it prefixed to the New Edition. It was directed,

To the Editor of PAMELA.

Dear Sir,

You have agreeably deceiv'd me into a Surprize, which it will be as hard to express, as the Beauties of PAMELA. Though I open'd this powerful little Piece with more Expectation than from common Designs, of like Promise, because it came from *your* Hands, for my *Daughters*[2], yet, who could have dreamt, he should find, under the modest Disguise of a *Novel*, all the *Soul* of Religion, Good-breeding, Discretion, Good-nature, Wit, Fancy, Fine Thought, and Morality?—I have done nothing but read it to others, and hear others again read it, to me, ever since it came into my Hands; and I find I am likely to do nothing else, for I know not how long yet to come: because, if I lay the Book down, it comes after me.——When it has dwelt all Day long upon the Ear, It takes Possession, all Night, of the Fancy.——It has Witchcraft in every Page of it: but it is the Witchcraft of Passion and Meaning. Who is there that will not despise the false, empty *Pomp* of the Poets, when he observes in this little, unpretending, mild Triumph of *Nature*, the whole Force of Invention and Genius, creating new Powers of Emotion, and transplanting *Ideas* of *Pleasure* into that unweeded low Garden the *Heart*, from the dry and sharp *Summit of Reason?*

Yet, I confess, there is *One*, in the World, of whom I think with still greater Respect, than of PAMELA: and That is, of the wonderful AUTHOR of PAMELA.—Pray, Who is he, Dear Sir? and where, and how, has he been able to hide, hitherto, such an encircling and all-mastering Spirit? He possesses every Quality that ART could have charm'd by: yet, has lent it to, and conceal'd it in, NATURE.—The Comprehensiveness of his Imagination must be truly prodigious!—It has stretch'd out this diminutive mere *Grain of Mustard-seed*[3], (a poor Girl's little, innocent, Story) into a Resemblance of That *Heaven*, which the Best of Good Books has compar'd it to.—All the Passions are His, in their most close and abstracted Recesses: and by selecting the most delicate, and yet, at the same time, most powerful, of their Springs, thereby to act, wind, and manage, the Heart, He *moves* us, every where, with the Force of a TRAGEDY.

What is there, throughout the *Whole*, that I do not sincerely admire!——I admire, in it, the strong distinguish'd Variety, and picturesque glowing Likeness to *Life*, of the Characters. I know, hear, see, and live among 'em All: and, if I cou'd paint, cou'd return you their *Faces*. I admire, in it, the noble Simplicity, Force, Aptness, and Truth, of so many modest, oeconomical, moral, prudential, religious, satirical, and cautionary, *Lessons*; which are introduc'd with such seasonable Dexterity, and with so polish'd and exquisite a Delicacy, of Expression and Sentiment, that I am only apprehensive, for the *Interests* of *Virtue*, lest some of the *finest*, and *most touching*, of those elegant Strokes of Good-breeding, Generosity, and Reflection, shou'd be lost, under the too gross Discernment of an unfeeling Majority of Readers; for whose Coarseness, however, they were kindly design'd, as the most useful and charitable Correctives.

One of the best-judg'd Peculiars, of the Plan, is, that These Instructions being convey'd, as in a Kind of Dramatical Representation, by those beautiful *Scenes*, Her own Letters and Journals, who acts the most moving and suffering *Part*, we feel the Force in a threefold Effect,—from the Motive, the Act, and the Consequence.

But what, above All, I am charm'd with, is the amiable *Good-nature* of the AUTHOR; who, I am convinc'd, has one of the best, and most generous Hearts, of Mankind: because, mis-measuring *other* Minds, by *His Own*, he can draw Every thing, to Perfection, but *Wickedness*.——I became inextricably in *Love* with this delightful Defect of his Malice;—for, I found it owing to an *Excess* in his *Honesty*. Only observe, Sir, with what *virtuous Reluctance* he complies with the Demands of his Story, when he stands in need of some blameable Characters. Tho' his Judgment compels him to mark 'em with disagreeable Colourings, so that they make an odious Appearance at first, He can't forbear, by an unexpected and gradual Decline from Themselves, to soften and transmute all the Horror conceiv'd for their Baseness, till we are arriv'd, through insensible Stages, at an Inclination to forgive it intirely.

I must venture to add, without mincing the matter, what I really believe, of this Book.—It will live on, through Posterity, with such unbounded Extent of Good Consequences, that Twenty Ages to come may be the Better and Wiser, for its Influence. It will steal first, imperceptibly, into the Hearts of the *Young* and the *Tender*: where It will afterwards guide and moderate their Reflections and Resolves, when grown Older. And, so, a gradual moral Sunshine, of un-austere and compassionate *Virtue*, shall break out upon the *World*, from this TRIFLE (for such, I dare answer for the *Author*, His Modesty misguides him to think it).— No Applause therefore can be too *high*, for *such Merit*. And, let me abominate the contemptible *Reserves of mean-spirited Men*, who while they but *hesitate* their

Esteem, with Restraint, can be fluent and uncheck'd in their *Envy.*—In an Age so deficient in Goodness, Every such Virtue, as That of this Author, is a salutary *Angel,* in *Sodom*[1]. And *One* who cou'd stoop to conceal, a Delight he receives from the *Worthy,* wou'd be equally capable of submitting to an Approbation of the *Praise* of the *Wicked.*

I was thinking, just now, as I return'd from a *Walk* in the *Snow,* on that *Old Roman Policy*[2], of Exemptions in Favour of Men, who had given a few, bodily, Children to the Republick.—What superior Distinction ought *our* Country to find (but that *Policy* and *We* are at Variance) for Reward of this *Father, of Millions of* MINDS, which are to owe new Formation to the future Effect of his Influence!

Upon the whole, as I never met with so pleasing, so honest, and so truly deserving a Book, I shou'd never have done, if I explain'd All my Reasons for admiring its Author.—If it is not a *Secret,* oblige me so far as to tell me his *Name:*[3] for since I feel him the *Friend* of my Soul, it would be a Kind of Violation to retain him a *Stranger.*—I am not able to thank you enough, for this highly acceptable Present. And, as for my Daughters, They have taken into their Own Hands the Acknowledgment due from their Gratitude[4]. I am,

Dec. 17,   DEAR SIR,
    1740.   *Your,* &c.

Abstract of a second Letter from the same Gentleman.[5]

'—No Sentiments which I have here, or in my last, express'd, of the sweet *Pamela,* being more than the bare Truth, which every Man must feel, who lends his Ear to the inchanting Prattler, why does the Author's Modesty mislead his Judgment, to suspect the Style wants Polishing?—No, Sir, there is an *Ease,* a *natural Air,* a dignify'd *Simplicity,* and measured Fullness, in it, that, resembling Life, outglows it! He has reconciled the *Pleasing* to the *Proper.* The *Thought* is every-where exactly *cloath'd* by the *Expression:* And becomes its Dress as roundly, and as close, as *Pamela* her Country-habit. Remember, tho' she put it on with humble Prospect, of descending to the Level of her Purpose, it *adorn'd* her, with such unpresum'd *Increase* of Loveliness; sat with such neat Propriety of Elegant Neglect about her, that it threw out All her Charms, with tenfold, and resistless Influence.—And so, dear Sir, it will be always found.—When modest Beauty seeks to hide itself by casting off the *Pride* of *Ornament,* it but displays itself without a *Covering:* And so, becoming more distinguished, by its Want of *Drapery,* grows *stronger,* from its *purpos'd Weakness.*'

There were formed by an anonymous Gentleman[1], the following Objections to some Passages in the Work.

1. That the Style ought to be a little raised, at least so soon as *Pamela* knows the Gentleman's Love is honourable, and when her Diffidence[2] is changed to Ease: And from about the fourth Day after Marriage, it should be equal to the Rank she is rais'd to, and charged to fill becomingly.

2. That to avoid the Idea apt to be join'd with the Word *'Squire*, the Gentleman should be styled Sir *James*, or Sir *John*, &c. and Lady *Davers* in a new Edition might procure for him the Title of a Baronet.

3. That if the sacred Name were seldomer repeated, it would be better; for that the Wise Man's Advice is, *Be not righteous over-much*[3].

4. That the Penance which *Pamela* suffers from Lady *Davers* might be shorten'd: That she is too timorous after owning her Marriage to that Lady, and ought to have a little more Spirit, and get away sooner out at the Window, or call her own Servants to protect, and carry her to her Husband's Appointment.

5. That Females are too apt to be struck with Images of Beauty; and that the Passage where the Gentleman is said to span the Waist of *Pamela* with his Hands[4], is enough to ruin a Nation of Women by Tight-lacing.

6. That the Word *naughty* had better be changed to some other, as *Bad, Faulty, Wicked, Vile, Abominable, Scandalous:* Which in most Places would give an Emphasis, for which recourse must otherwise be had to the innocent Simplicity of the Writer; an Idea not necessary to the Moral of the Story, nor of Advantage to the Character of the Heroine.

7. That the Words[5], *p. 305. Foolish Thing that I am*, had better be *Foolish that I am.* The same Gentleman observes by way of *Postscript*, that Jokes are often more severe, and do more Mischief, than more solid Objections; and would have one or two Passages alter'd, to avoid giving Occasion for the Supposition of a double Entendre, particularly in two Places which he mentions, *viz. p.* 175. *and* 181.

He is pleased to take notice of several other Things of less Moment, some of which are merely typographical; and very kindly expresses, on the Whole, a high Opinion of the Performance, and thinks it may do a great deal of Good: For all which, as well as for his Objections, the Editor gives him very sincere Thanks.

Others are of Opinion, That the Scenes in many Places, in the Beginning especially, are too low; and that the Passions of Lady Davers, *in particular, are carried too high, and above Nature.*

And others have intimated, That Pamela *ought, for Example sake, to have discharg'd Mrs.* Jewkes *from her Service.*

These are the most material Objections that have come to hand, all which are considered in the following Extracts from some of the most beautiful Letters that have been written in any Language:

'The Gentleman's Advice[1], not to alter *Pamela* at all, was both friendly, and solidly just. I run in, with full Sail, to his Anchorage, that the low Scenes are no more out of Nature, than the high Passions of proud Lady *Davers*. Out of Nature, do they say? 'Tis my Astonishment how Men of Letters can read with such absent Attention! They are so far from *Out of Nature*, They are absolute *Nature herself!* or, if they must be confess'd her *Resemblance*; they are *such* a Resemblance, at least, as our *true Face* gives our *Face* in the *Looking-glass*.

'I wonder indeed, what it is, that the Gentlemen, who talk of *Low* Scenes, wou'd desire should be understood by the Epithet?—Nothing, properly speaking, is *low*, that suits well with the Place it is rais'd to.——The Passions of Nature are the same, in the *Lord*, and his *Coach-man*. All, that makes them seem different consists in the *Degrees*, in the *Means*, and the *Air*, whereto or wherewith they indulge 'em. If, in painting Distinctions like these, (which arise but from the Forms of Men's Manners, drawn from *Birth*, *Education*, and *Custom*) a Writer *falls short* of his Characters, there his Scene is a low one, indeed, whatever high Fortune it flatter'd. But, to imagine that Persons of Rank are above a Concern for what is thought, felt, or acted, by others, of their Species, between whom and themselves is *no Difference*, except such as was owing to Accident, is to reduce Human Nature to a Lowness,—*too low* for the *Truth* of her *Frailty*.—

'In *Pamela*, in particular, we owe All to her *Lowness*. It is to the docile Effects of this Lowness of *that amiable Girl*, in her Birth, her Condition, her Hopes, and her Vanities, in every thing, in short, but her *Virtue*,—that her Readers are indebted, for the moral *Reward*, of that *Virtue*. And if we are to look for the *Low* among the Rest of the Servants, less lovely tho' they are, than a *Pamela*, there is something however, so glowingly painted, in the Lines whereby the Author has mark'd their Distinctions——Something, so movingly forceful, in the *Grief* at their *Parting*, and *Joy* at the happy *Return*,—Something so finely, at once, and so strongly and feelingly, *varied*, even in the smallest and least promising, little Family Incidents! that I need only appeal from the *Heads*, to the *Hearts* of the Objectors themselves, whether these are *low* Scenes to be censur'd?

'And as for the opposite Extreme they wou'd quarrel with, the high-passion'd, and un-tam'd Lady *Davers*,—I cou'd direct 'em to a Dozen or two of *Quality Originals*, from whom (with Exception perhaps of her *Wit*) one wou'd swear the Author had taken her Copy.—What a Sum might these Objectors ensure, to be paid, by the *Husbands* and *Sons*, of such termagant, hermaphrodite Minds, upon their making due Proof, that they were no longer to be found, in the Kingdom!

'I know, you are too just to imagine me capable of giving any other Opinion than my best-weigh'd and true one. But, because it is fit you should have *Reasons*, in Support of a Judgment that can neither deserve nor expect an implicit Reception, I will run over the Anonymous Letter I herewith return you; and note with what Lightness even Men of *good-natur'd* Intention fall into *Mistakes*, by Neglect in too hasty Perusals, which their Benevolence wou'd take Pleasure in blushing at, when they discover their Weakness, in a cooler Revisal.

'The Writer of this Letter is for having the Style *rais'd*, after *Pamela's* Advance in her Fortune. But surely, This was hasty Advice: because, as the Letters are writ to her Parents, it wou'd have look'd like forgetting, and, in some sort, insulting, the Lowliness of their inferior Condition, to have assum'd a new Air in her Language, in Place of retaining a steady Humility. But, here, it must not be pass'd unobserv'd, that in her Reports of Conversations that follow'd her Marriage, she *does*, aptly and beautifully, heighten her Style, and her Phrases: still returning however to her decent Simplicity, in her Addresses to her Father and Mother.

'I am against giving a Gentleman (who has ennobled himself, by reforming his Vices, and rewarding the Worth of the *Friendless*) the unnecessary new Toy of a *Title*. It is all strong in Nature, as it stands in the Letters: and I don't see how Greatness, from Titles, can add Likeness or Power, to the Passions. So complete a Resemblance of *Truth* stands in need of no borrow'd Pretensions.

'The Only of this Writer's Objections, which, I think, carries Weight, is That, which advises some little *Contraction* of the Prayers, and Appeals to the Deity. I say *little* Contraction: for they are nobly and sincerely pathetic. And I say it only in Fear, lest, if fansied too long, by the fashionably *Averse* to the Subject, Minds, which most want the *purpos'd Impression*, might hazard the *Loss* of its *Benefit*, by passing over those pious Reflections, which, if shorter, would catch their Attention.

'Certainly, the Gentleman's Objection against the Persecution that *Pamela* suffers from Lady *Davers*, in respect to the Relation this Madwoman bears to the *Brother*, is the rashest of All his Advices! And when he thinks she ought rather to have assum'd the Protection of her Servants, he seems unaware of the probable *Consequence*; where there was a Puppy, of Quality, in the Case, who had, even without Provocation, drawn his Sword on the poor passive PAMELA. Far from bearing a Thought of exciting an abler Resentment, to the Danger of a Quarrel with so worthless a Coxcomb, how charmingly natural, apprehensive, and generous, is her Silence (during the Recital she makes of her Sufferings) with regard to this *masculine* Part of the Insult! as also her Prevention of Mrs. *Jewkes's* less delicate Bluntness, when she was beginning to complain of the whelp Lord's Impertinence!

'If I were not afraid of a *Pun*, I shou'd tell the anonymous Letter-writer, that he made a too *tight-laced* Objection, where he quarrels with the spann'd Waist of

Pamela. What, in the Name of Unshapeliness! cou'd he find, to complain of, in a beautiful Girl of Sixteen, who was born *out of Germany*, and had not, yet, reach'd ungraspable *Roundness!*——These are wonderful Sinkings from Purpose where a Man is considering such mental, and passionate Beauties, as this Gentleman profess'd to be touch'd by!

'But, when he goes on, to object against the Word *naughty*, (as apply'd in the Phrase *naughty Master*) I grow mortified, in Fear for our human Sufficiency, compar'd with our Aptness to blunder! For, here, 'tis plain, this Director of Another's Discernment is quite blind, Himself, to an Elegance, one wou'd have thought it *impossible* not to be struck by?—Faulty, wicked, abominable, scandalous, (which are the angry Adjectives, he prefers to that sweet one) wou'd have carried Marks of her Rage, not Affliction—whereas *naughty* contains, in One single significant Petulance, twenty thousand inexpressible Delicacies!—It insinuates, at once, all the beautiful Struggle, between her Contempt of his Purpose, and tender Regard for his Person; her Gratitude to Himself and his Family; her Recollection of his superior Condition.—There is in the elegant Choice of this half-kind, half-peevish, *Word*, a never-enough to be prais'd speaking Picture of the Conflict betwixt her Disdain, and her Reverence! See, Sir, the Reason I had, for apprehending some Danger that the refin'd Generosity in many of the most charming of the Sentiments wou'd be *lost*, upon the too coarse Conception of some, for whose Use the Author intended them.

'It is the same Case again, in *foolish Thing that I am!* which this nice, un-nice, Gentleman wou'd advise you to change, into *foolish that I am!* He does not seem to have tasted the pretty Contempt of Herself, the submissive *Diminutive*, so distant from Vanity, yet allay'd by the gentle Reluctance in Self-condemnation;—and the other fine Touches of Nature: which wou'd All have been lost, in the grave, sober Sound of his *Dutch Emendation*[1].

'As to his Paragraph in *Postscript*, I shall say the less of it, because the Gentleman's own good Sense seems to confess, by the Place he has chosen to rank it in, that it ought to be turn'd out of Doors, as too *dirty* for the rest of his Letter.—In the Occasions he is pleas'd to discover for *Jokes*, I either find not, that he has any Signification at all, or such vulgar, coarse-tasted Allusions to loose low-life Idioms, that *not* to understand what he means, is both the cleanliest, and prudentest Way of confuting him.

'And now, Sir, you will easily gather how far I am from thinking it needful to change any thing in *Pamela*. I would not scratch such a beautiful Face, for the *Indies!*

'You can hardly imagine how it charms me to hear of a Second Edition already! but the News of still new upon new ones, will be found no Subject of Wonder. As 'tis sure, that no Family is without Sisters, or Brothers, or Daughters, or Sons, who can *read*; or wants Fathers, or Mothers, or Friends, who can *think*; so equally certain it is, that the Train to a Parcel of Powder does not run on with more natural Tendency, till it sets the whole Heap in a Blaze, than that *Pamela*, inchanting from Family to Family, will overspread all the Hearts of the Kingdom.

'As to the Objection of those warm Friends to *Honesty*, who are for having *Pamela* dismiss Mrs. *Jewkes*; there is not One, among All these benevolent Complainers, who wou'd not discern himself to have been, *laudably*, in the *wrong*, were he only to be ask'd this plain Question—Whether a Step, both ill-judg'd, and undutiful, had not been the Reverse of a PAMELA's Character?—Two or three times over, Mr. B—— had inform'd her, that Mrs. *Jewkes* and Himself having been equally involv'd in *One Guilt*, she must forgive, or condemn, *Both together*. After this, it grew manifest *Duty* not to treat her with Marks of Resentment.— And, as here was a visible Necessity to appear not desirous of turning her away, so, in point of mere *Moral* Regard to the bad Woman Herself, it was nobler, to retain her, with a Prospect of correcting, in Time, her loose Habit of thinking, than, by casting her off, to the licentious Results of her Temper, abandon her to Temptations and Danger, which a Virtue like PAMELA's cou'd not wish her expos'd to[1].'

The Manner in which this admirable Gentleman gives his Opinion of the Piece, and runs thro' the principal Characters, is so masterly, that the Readers of Pamela *will be charm'd by it, tho' they should suppose, that his inimitable Benevolence has overvalu'd the Piece itself.*

'Inspir'd, without doubt, by some Skill, more than human, and comprehending in an humble, and seemingly artless, Narration, a Force that can tear up the Heart-strings, this Author has prepar'd an enamouring *Philtre* for the Mind, which will excite such a *Passion* for Virtue, as scarce to leave it in the Power of the *Will* to neglect her.

'*Longinus*[2], I remember, distinguishing by what Marks we may know the *Sublime*, says, it is chiefly from an Effect that will follow the Reading it: a delightfully-adhering Idea, that clings fast to the Memory; and from which it is difficult for a Man to disengage his Attention.—If *this* is a Proof of the *Sublime*, there was never *Sublimity* so lastingly felt, as in PAMELA!

'Not the Charmer's own prattling Idea stuck so close to the Heart of her Master, as the Incidents of her Story to the Thoughts of a Reader.—The Author transports, and transforms, with a Power more extensive than *Horace*[3] requires, in his POET!—

'Mr. B——, and the Turns of his Passions—and the Softness, yet Strength, of their amiable Object—after having given us the most masterly Image of Nature, that ever was painted! take Possession of, and *dwell in*, the Memory.

'And there, too, broods the kind and the credulous Parson WILLIAMS's *Dove*, (without *serpentine* Mixture) hatching *Pity* and *Affection*, for an Honesty so sincere, and so silly!

'There too, take their Places All the *lower* Supports of this beautiful Fabrick.——

'I am sometimes transform'd into plain Goodman ANDREWS, and sometimes the good Woman, his Wife.

'As for old Mr. LONGMAN, and JONATHAN, the Butler, they are sure of me both, in their Turns.

'Now and-then, I am COLBRAND the *Swiss*: but, as *broad* as *I stride*, in that Character, I can never escape Mrs. JEWKES: who often keeps me awake in the Night—

'Till the Ghost of Lady DAVERS, drawing open the Curtains, scares the *Scarer*, of me, and of PAMELA!——

'And, then, I take Shelter with poor penitent JOHN, and the rest of the *Men* and the *Maids*, of all whom I may say, with compassionate *Marcia*,

'——*The Youths* DIVIDE *their Reader*[1].'

And this fine Writer adds:

'I am glad I made War, in my last, upon the Notion of altering the Style: for, having read it twice over since then, (and to Audiences, where the *Tears* were applausively eloquent) I could hardly, here and there, find a Place, where one Word *can* be chang'd for a better. There are some indeed, where 'twere *possible* to leave out, a few, without making a Breach in the Building. But, in short, the Author has put so bewitching a Mixture together, of the *Rais'd* with the *Natural*, and the *Soft* with the *Strong* and the *Eloquent*—that never Sentiments were finer, and fuller of Life! never any were utter'd so sweetly!—Even in what relates to the pious and frequent Addresses to God, I now retract (on these two last Revisals) the Consent I half gave, on a *former*, to the anonymous Writer's Proposal, who advis'd the Author to *shorten* those Beauties.——Whoever considers his *Pamela* with a View to find Matter for Censure, is in the Condition of a passionate Lover, who breaks in upon his Mistress, without Fear or Wit, with Intent to accuse her, and quarrel—He came to her with Pique in his Purpose; but his *Heart* is too hard for his *Malice*—and he goes away more enslav'd, for complaining.'

The following delightful Story[2], *so admirably related, will give great Pleasure to the Reader; and we take the Liberty of inserting it, for that very Reason.*

'What a never-to-be satisfied *Length* has this Subject always the Power of attracting me into! And yet, before I have done, I must by your means tell the Author a *Story*, which a Judge not so skilful in Nature as he is, might be in Danger perhaps of mistaking, for a trifling and silly one. I expect it shou'd give him the clearest Conviction, in a Case he is subject to question.

'We have a lively little Boy in the Family, about seven Years old—but, alas for him, poor Child! quite unfriended; and born to no Prospect. He is the Son of an honest, poor Soldier, by a Wife, grave, unmeaning, and innocent. Yet the Boy, (see the Power of connubial *Simplicity*) is so pretty, so genteel, and gay-spirited, that we have made him, and design'd him, our *own*, ever since he could totter, and waddle. The wanton Rogue is half Air: and every Motion he acts by has a Spring, like *Pamela*'s when she threw down the Card-table. All this Quickness, however, is temper'd by a good-natur'd Modesty: so that the wildest of his Flights are thought rather diverting than troublesome. He is an hourly Foundation for Laughter, from the Top of the House to the Parlours: and, to borrow an Attribute from the Reverend Mr. *Peters*, (tho' without any Note of his Musick) *plays a very good* FIDDLE in the Family. I have told you the History of this *Tom-tit* of a Prater, because, ever since my first reading of PAMELA, he puts in for a Right to be *one* of her Hearers; and, having got half her Sayings by heart, talks in no other Language but hers: and, what really surprises, and has charm'd me into a *certain* Fore-taste of her Influence, he is, at once, become fond of his Book; which (before) he cou'd never be brought to attend to—that *he may read* PAMELA, he says, *without stopping*. The first Discovery we made of this Power over so unripe and unfix'd an Attention, was, one Evening, when I was reading her Reflections at the *Pond* to some Company. The little rampant Intruder, being kept out by the Extent of the Circle, had crept under my Chair, and was sitting before me, on the Carpet, with his Head almost touching the Book, and his Face bowing down toward the Fire.—He had sat for some time in this Posture, with a Stillness, that made us conclude him asleep: when, on a sudden, we heard a Succession of heart-heaving Sobs; which while he strove to conceal from our Notice, his little Sides swell'd, as if they wou'd burst, with the throbbing Restraint of his Sorrow. I turn'd his innocent Face, to look toward me; but his Eyes were quite lost, in his *Tears*: which running down from his Cheeks in free Currents, had form'd two sincere little Fountains, on that Part of the Carpet he hung over. All the Ladies in Company were ready to devour him with Kisses: and he has, since, become doubly a Favourite—and is perhaps the youngest of *Pamela*'s Converts.

The same incomparable Writer has favour'd us with an Objection, that is more material than any we have mention'd; which cannot be better stated nor answer'd, than in his own beautiful Words; viz[1].

'An Objection is come into my Thoughts, which I should be glad the Author would think proper to obviate in the Front of the Second Edition.

'There are Mothers, or Grandmothers, in all Families of affluent Fortune, who, tho' they may have none of Lady *Davers*'s *Insolence*, will be apt to feel one of her *Fears*,—that the Example of a Gentleman so amiable as Mr. *B*— may be follow'd, by the *Jackies, their Sons*, with too blind and unreflecting a Readiness. Nor does the Answer of that Gentleman to his Sister's Reproach come quite up to the Point they will rest on. For, tho' indeed it is true, all the World wou'd acquit the best Gentleman in it, if he married *such* a Waiting-maid as *Pamela*, yet, there is an ill-discerning Partiality, in Passion, that will overthrow all the Force of that Argument: because *every belov'd Maid will be* PAMELA, in a Judgment obscur'd by her Influence.

'And, since the Ground of this Fear will *seem* solid, I don't know how to be easy, till it is shewn (nor ought it to be left to the Author's Modesty) that they who consider his Design in that Light will be found but short-sighted Observers.

'Request it of him then to suffer it to be told them, that not a limited, but general, Excitement to Virtue was the first and great End to his Story: And that this Excitement must have been deficient, and very imperfectly offer'd, if he had not look'd quite *as low as he cou'd* for his Example: because if there had been any Degree or Condition, more remote from the Prospect than that which he had chosen to work on, that Degree might have seem'd out of Reach of the Hope, which it was his generous Purpose to encourage.—And, so, he was under an evident *Necessity* to find such a Jewel in a *Cottage*: and expos'd, too, as she was, to the severest Distresses of Fortune, with Parents unable to support their own Lives, but from the daily hard Product of *Labour*.

'Nor wou'd it have been sufficient to have plac'd her thus *low* and *distressful*, if he had not also suppos'd her a *Servant*: and that too in some elegant Family; for if she had always remain'd a Fellow-cottager with her Father, it must have carried an Air of Romantick Improbability to account for her polite Education.

'If she had *wanted* those Improvements, which she found means to acquire in her *Service*, it wou'd have been very unlikely, that she shou'd have succeeded so well; and had destroy'd *one* great *Use* of the Story, to have allow'd such uncommon Felicity to the Effect of mere *personal Beauty*.—And it had not been *judicious* to have represented her as educated in a superior Condition of Life with the proper Accomplishments, before she became reduc'd by Misfortunes, and so not a Servant, but rather an Orphan under hopeless Distresses—because Opportunities which had made it no Wonder how she came to be so winningly qualified, wou'd have lessen'd her Merit in being so. And besides, where had then been the purpos'd Excitement of Persons in PAMELA's Condition of Life, by an Emulation of her Sweetness, Humility, Modesty, Patience, and Industry, to attain some faint Hope of arriving, in time, within View of *her* Happiness?——And what a delightful

Reformation shou'd we see, in all Families, where the Vanity of their *Maids* took no Turn toward Ambition to *please*, but by such innocent Measures, as PAMELA's!

'As it is clear, then, the Author was under a Necessity to suppose her a *Servant*, he is not to be accountable for mistaken Impressions, which the Charms he has given her may happen to make, on wrong Heads, or weak Hearts, tho' in Favour of Maids the Reverse of her Likeness.

'What is it then (they may say) that the Lowness, and Distance of *Pamela's* Condition from the Gentleman's who married her, proposes to teach the *Gay World*, and the *Fortunate?—It is this*—By Comparison with that infinite Remoteness of her Condition from the Reward which her Virtue procur'd her, one great *Proof* is deriv'd, (which is Part of the *Moral* of PAMELA) that Advantages from *Birth*, and Distinction of *Fortune*, have no Power at all, when consider'd against those from *Behaviour*, and Temper of *Mind*: because where the *Last* are *not added*, all the *First* will be boasted in vain. Whereas she who possesses the Last finds *no Want* of the First, in her Influence.

'In *that* Light alone let the Ladies of *Rank* look at PAMELA.—Such an alarming Reflection as that will, at the same time that it raises the Hope and Ambition of the *Humble*, correct and mortify the Disdain of the *Proud*. For it will compel them to observe, and acknowledge, that 'tis the Turn of their *Mind*, not the Claims of their *Quality*, by which (and which only) Womens Charms can be lasting: And that, while the *haughty Expectations*, inseparable from an elevated Rank, serve but to multiply its Complaints and Afflictions, the Condescensions of *accomplish'd Humility*, attracting Pity, Affection, and Reverence, secure an hourly Increase of Felicity.—So that the *moral Meaning* of PAMELA's Good-fortune, far from tempting young Gentlemen to marry *such* Maids as are found in their Families, is, by teaching Maids *to deserve to be Mistresses*, to stir up Mistresses *to support their Distinction.*'

We shall only add, That it was intended to prefix two neat Frontispieces[1] *to this Edition, (and to present them to the Purchasers of the first) and one was actually finished for that Purpose; but there not being Time for the other, from the Demand for the new Impression; and the Engraving Part of that which was done (tho' no Expence was spared) having fallen very short of the Spirit of the Passages they were intended to represent, the Proprietors were advised to lay them aside. And were the rather induced to do so, from the following Observation of a most ingenious Gentleman, in a Letter to the Editor.* "I am so jealous, *says he*, in Behalf of our *inward* Idea of PAMELA's Person, that I dread *any* figur'd Pretence to Resemblance. For it will be pity to look at an *Air*, and imagine it *Hers*, that does not carry some such elegant Perfection of Amiableness, as will be sure to find place in the *Fancy*[2]."

VERSES, sent to the Bookseller, for the Unknown Author of the beautiful new Piece call'd *PAMELA*[1].

Blest be thy pow'rful Pen, whoe'er thou art,
Thou skill'd, great Moulder *of the master'd Heart!*
Where hast thou lain conceal'd!—or why thought fit,
At this dire Period, to unveil *thy Wit?*
 O! late *befriended Isle! had this broad Blaze,*
With earlier Beamings, bless'd our Fathers *Days,*
The Pilot Radiance, pointing out the Source,
Whence public Health derives its vital Course,
Each timely Draught some healing Power had shown,
Ere gen'ral Gangrene *blacken'd, to the* Bone.
But, fest'ring now, beyond all Sense of Pain,
'Tis hopeless: *and the Helper's Hand is* vain.
 Sweet Pamela! *forever-blooming Maid!*
Thou dear, unliving, yet immortal, Shade!
Why are thy Virtues scatter'd to the Wind?
Why are thy Beauties flash'd upon the Blind?
 What, tho' thy flutt'ring Sex might learn, from thee,
That Merit *forms a Rank, above* Degree?
That Pride, too conscious, falls, from ev'ry Claim,
While humble Sweetness climbs, beyond its Aim?
What, tho' Religion, smiling from thy Eyes,
Shews her plain Power, *and charms without* Disguise?
What, tho' thy warmly-pleasing moral Scheme
Gives livelier Rapture, than the Loose can dream?
What, tho' thou build'st, by thy persuasive Life,
Maid, Child, Friend, Mistress, Mother, Neighbour, Wife?
Tho' Taste like thine each Void of Time, can fill,
Unsunk by Spleen, unquicken'd by Quadrille!
What, tho' 'tis thine to bless the lengthen'd Hour !
Give Permanence *to Joy, and* Use *to Pow'r?*
Lend late-felt Blushes to the Vain *and* Smart?
And squeeze cramp'd Pity from the Miser's *Heart?*
What, tho' 'tis thine to hush the Marriage Breeze,
Teach Liberty to tire, *and Chains to* please?
Thine tho', from Stiffness to divest Restraint,
And, to the Charmer, reconcile the Saint?
Tho' Smiles and Tears obey thy moving Skill,
And Passion's ruffled Empire waits thy Will?
Tho' thine the fansy'd Fields of flow'ry Wit,
Thine, Art's whole Pow'r, in Nature's Language writ!
Thine, to convey strong Thought, with modest Ease,
And, copying Converse, *teach its* Style *to please?*
Tho' thine each Virtue, that a God *cou'd lend?*

Thine, ev'ry Help, that ev'ry Heart, can mend?
'Tis Thine in vain!——*Thou wak'st a* dying *Land:*
And lift'st departed Hope, *with fruitless Hand:*
Death has NO CURE. *Thou hast* mis-tim'd *thy Aim;*
Rome *had her* GOTHS: *and all, beyond, was* Shame.

EXPLANATORY NOTES
TO INTRODUCTION
TO SECOND EDITION

Page 464

1 *the following Letter*: Written by Aaron Hill, this letter, with minor changes, is included in *The Works of the Late Aaron Hill, Esq.* (1753), II, pp. 286–91; and, reduced to four short paragraphs, in Barbauld's edition of Richardson's *Correspondence*, I, pp. 53–5. No manuscript copy seems to have survived.

2 *for my Daughters*: Hill's unmarried daughters, Astræa and Minerva, with whom Hill was then residing in Plaistow, Essex. At Hill's request, Richardson would send him 'new Books' lately published in London to serve, in Hill's words to Richardson on 27 September 1739, as 'an agreeable Amusement in some of [my] weak, vacant, Hours'. *Pamela* was one of those books. In a letter dated 8 December 1740, Richardson asks Hill to seek from 'your young Ladies... [Acceptance] of the two volumes which accompany', adding that 'they were tolerably received by the Publick'.

3 *Grain of Mustard-seed... Heaven*: See Matthew 13:31: 'The kingdom of heaven is like to a grain of mustard seed, which a man took, and sowed in his field'. Cf. Mark 4:30–2; Luke 13:18–19. In *Shamela*, Fielding changes the phrase in parentheses to 'a poor Girl's little, &c.' (p. 156), thus stretching into obscenity Hill's dubious biblical parallel.

Page 466

1 *Angel, in Sodom*: Hill is alluding to the two angels, in Genesis 19, who warn Lot to flee with his family before the city's destruction. Attacking the novel in *The Virgin in Eden* (1741), Charles Povey plays on Hill's biblical allusion and suggests that Pamela 'may be compar'd to one of the fair Apples of *Sodom*, beautiful for the Eye to behold, but Stains and Rottenness within' (p. 70).

2 *Old Roman Policy*: To increase the number of Roman citizens, Augustus enacted a 'Statute which oblig'd the several Orders to marry', granting substantial rewards to those who complied and imposing harsh penalties on those who did not (Suetonius, *The Lives of the Twelve Caesars*, trans. Jabez Hughes, 2nd edn (1726), I, p. 86).

3 *tell me his Name*: Richardson acknowledged his authorship of the novel in a letter to Hill on 22 December 1740.

4 *Acknowledgment... Gratitude*: On 17 December 1740, Astræa Hill wrote to Mrs Richardson that 'My Sister, and I, are extremely obliged to your good Mr. Richardson, for so wise, and so sweet, a Companion, as Pamela.'

5 *Abstract . . . same Gentleman*: A manuscript copy of this letter, dated 29 December 1740, is in FM XVI, 1, fols. 37–8. In his later trembling hand, Richardson wrote, right above the date, 'Too high Praise'. This letter is reprinted, with cuts that include this paragraph, in Hill, *Works*, II, pp. 292–5.

Page 467

1 *anonymous Gentleman*: In a letter, dated 15 November 1740, addressed to Charles Rivington (1688–1742), one of the publishers of the novel; the manuscript copy of this letter is in FM XVI, 1, fols. 33–4. For this letter and Richardson's reaction to it, including his unsuccessful attempt to identify its author, see General Introduction, pp. lii–liii.

2 *her Diffidence*: This correction appears for the first time in the sixth duodecimo edition of 1746 ('his Diffidence', 2–5).

3 *Be not righteous over-much*: Ecclesiastes 7:16. This text had recently been at the centre of a very public homiletic spat, with which the 'anonymous Gentleman' (who may have been a clergyman) was very likely acquainted. In 1739, Joseph Trapp (1679–1747) had preached four sermons – published as *The Nature, Folly, Sin, and Dangers of being Righteous over-much* – attacking 'the Doctrines and Practices Of certain Modern Enthusiasts' (title page), particularly those of the itinerant Methodist preacher, George Whitefield; Whitefield had retaliated with *An Explanatory Sermon on that Mistaken Text, Be not Righteous over-much* (1739). In *Shamela*, Parson William preaches 'an excellent Sermon' on this text (p. 171). In *Pamela in Her Exalted Condition*, Richardson looks back to these criticisms of his novel's (and heroine's) quasi-Methodist tendencies when Mr. B., 'pleas'd with [Pamela's] Manner, beheld the good Effects, and countenanc'd me by his Praises and his Endearments, *as* acting discreetly, *as* not falling into Enthusiasm, and (as he used to say) *as* not aiming at being *righteous over-much*' (IV, p. 391).

4 *Hands*: Corrected in fourth edition ('Hand', 2–3). This change restores the correct reading from the 'anonymous' letter as well as the text of *Pamela*.

5 *That the Words*: The page numbers here are keyed to the first edition of the novel (pp. 402, 318, and 321, respectively, in the Cambridge text above). For Richardson's responses to these objections, see General Introduction, p. lxvi.

Page 468

1 *The Gentleman's Advice*: In the opening paragraph of this letter (dated 6 January 1741), Hill identifies this 'gentleman' as Richardson's 'hearty good Friend . . . Doct^r. Slocock', who had recently recommended *Pamela* from his pulpit, adding that 'I am charmed by the brave Independence of Taste in this generous Doctor.' On Benjamin Slocock (1691–1753) and his controversial role in promoting the novel, see General Introduction, pp. li–lii. Extracts from the letter of 6 January 1741 conclude with the paragraph beginning 'You can hardly imagine' and ending with 'all the Hearts of the Kingdom'.

Page 470

1 *Dutch Emendation*: As Keymer notes, 'Dutch scholarship and commentary [were] prover-bial for humourless pedantry' (p. 539). Dullness seems to have been a national charac-teristic, as Fielding suggests in the preface to *The Tragedy of Tragedies* (1731), where H. Scriblerus Secundus observes that the play 'hath . . . been translated into *Dutch*, and cel-ebrated with great Applause at *Amsterdam* (where Burlesque never came) by the Title of *Mynheer Vander Thumb*, the Burgomasters receiving it with that reverent and silent

Attention, which becometh an Audience at a deep Tragedy' (Henry Fielding, *Plays Volume One 1728–1731*, ed. Thomas Lockwood (Oxford: Clarendon Press, 2004), p. 541).

Page 471

1 *wish her expos'd to*: This paragraph and subsequent extracts (down to the paragraph ending with 'more enslav'd, for complaining') come from Hill's letter of 15 January 1741.

2 *Longinus*: The 'true Sublime', writes Longinus, 'is grand and lofty, which the more we consider, the greater Ideas we conceive of it; whose Force we cannot possibly withstand; which immediately sinks deep, and makes such Impressions on the Mind as cannot be easily worn out or effaced' (*Dionysius Longinus on the Sublime*, trans. William Smith (1739), section vii, p. 15).

3 *Horace*: Hill is here thinking of Horace's instructions to the poet in the *Ars Poetica*, particularly those passages (e.g., lines 99–103) in which Horace focuses on the affective power of poetry and on how the poet must labour to achieve it: ''Tis not enough, All elegantly wrought / Appear; a Spirit must there reign throughout, / As shall command your Audience, charm the Heart, / And any Passion, you will, impart. / As we with others laugh, so weep we too; / But e'er I weep, yourself the way must shew' (*Horace of the Art of Poetry, in English Numbers* (1735), p. 11).

Page 472

1 *The Youths ... Reader*: Marcia is Cato's daughter in Addison's *Cato. A Tragedy* (1713). Hill is adapting Lucia's words to Marcia: 'The Youths have equal Share / In *Marcia*'s Wishes, and divide their Sister' (I.vi.34–5).

2 *delightful Story*: This story, told in what might be a second letter Hill wrote to Richardson on 29 December 1740, is printed in Barbauld's edition of Richardson's *Correspondence*, I, pp. 55–8. The 'lively little Boy' was Harry Campbell, who served as Richardson's apprentice (without paying a fee) from 1751 to 1758; he set up as a printer in Popping's Alley, near Richardson's own press, and 'was one of the two witnesses to Richardson's will and the one member of his plant, besides his foreman, who received by that will a mourning ring' (Sale (1950), p. 21). See *Stationers' Company Apprentices 1701–1800*, ed. D. F. McKenzie (The Oxford Bibliographical Society, 1978), under apprentices for Samuel Richardson, entry 6768: 'Henry Campbell; John [father's name]; Portsmouth; G[loucester]; 7 May 1751; 3 Oct. 1758; 7. [years as apprentice] n.m. [no money]' (p. 290).

Page 473

1 *beautiful Words; viz.*: This extract (concluding with the paragraph ending '*to support their Distinction*') might be from Hill's letter of 15 January 1741, from which four manuscript pages are missing. There is no printed version of these paragraphs, either in Barbauld's *Correspondence* or in Hill's *Works*.

Page 475

1 *two neat Frontispieces*: According to Eaves and Kimpel (pp. 127, 188), Richardson had commissioned William Hogarth (1697–1764) to represent two scenes from the novel: of Pamela by the pond and of Pamela with her three bundles. Hill mentions these frontispieces in the same letter of 29 December 1740 in which he tells the story of Harry Campbell: 'The designs you have taken for frontispieces, seem to have been very judiciously chosen; upon pre-supposition that Mr. Hogarth is able (and if any-body is,

it is he), to teach pictures to speak and to think' (*Correspondence*, I, p. 56). The 'finished'
frontispiece has apparently not survived.

2 *in the Fancy."*: This paragraph is taken from a letter dated 9 February 1741, printed in Hill,
  Works, II, pp. 297–302; the paragraph is on p. 301. A fragment from this letter is in FM
  XIII, 2, fol. 45; another partial state, misdated 'December 1740', appears in Barbauld's
  Correspondence, I, pp. 59–66. Barbauld's version contains another reading scene featuring
  little Harry Campbell; one of the two illustrated books Harry is reading in bed is very
  likely Richardson's edition of *Æsop's Fables*, which Richardson had sent him as a gift.

Page 476

1 *VERSES... PAMELA*: Written by Aaron Hill. A manuscript copy is in FM XVI, 1,
  fols. 40–1; it appears in Hill, *Works*, III, pp. 348–50. As Keymer observes (p. 539), the
  eighth line of the poem seems to have troubled Richardson, who changed Hill's original
  'Wealth' to 'Health'; in the fifth edition of the novel, 'vital' became 'moral'. The 'Verses'
  were reprinted, along with Hill's letter of 17 December 1740, in *The Weekly Miscellany* on
  Saturday, 28 February 1741, two weeks after the publication of the second edition of the
  novel. This was the third of three puff pieces on the novel placed in this publication, the
  first being the letter of 11 October 1740 that became part of the novel's original preface.
  The second was another letter, on 13 December 1740, alluding to the first: 'You inserted
  a short Letter concerning a new Performance, intitled, *PAMELA*, or *Virtue Rewarded*.
  The Design is undeniably laudable, and, I think, the Execution shews a Genius. Perhaps
  I may, at my Leisure, send you some critical Remarks upon it. In the meantime, I should
  be glad if you'd publish the EDITOR's *Preface* and *Recapitulation* of the Uses that the
  Reader may make of it.' Both the preface and the 'recapitulation' (from the end of the
  novel) follow in their entirety.

CONTENTS
FROM
OCTAVO EDITION
(1742)

The octavo edition of *Pamela* Richardson published in May 1742 was notable not only because of its high-quality paper and illustrations by Hayman and Gravelot, but also because it was fronted by a detailed table of contents of all four volumes. In his addendum to the preface, Richardson explains that he has omitted the commendatory letters as well as introduction present in previous editions because of the 'kind Reception these Volumes have met with' and the fact that 'the most material Objections answer'd in the *Introductory Preface*, are taken notice of and obviated in the Third Volume' (Preface, p. viii). Instead, 'their place is supply'd, not unusefully, it is presum'd, by the following Epitome of the Work' (ibid.). Though not so detailed as Richardson's 'Index or Table of Contents' to *The Negotiations of Sir Thomas Roe* (1740), which had been singled out for particular praise by the reviewer of that volume in *The History of the Works of the Learned* (May 1740), the 'epitome' of *Pamela* indicates to the reader that this is not merely a novel but an important 'Work'. *Pamela*, in short, is worthy of serious critical attention and, therefore, merits the kind of critical apparatus accorded the papers and correspondence of a celebrated English diplomat. The contents of the first two volumes are reproduced below; the contents of the third and fourth volumes appear in *Pamela in Her Exalted Condition*.

CONTENTS
OF THE
FOUR VOLUMES.

It is thought proper to prefix to this Edition the following ample Table of CONTENTS, *which may serve to revive the Memory of the principal Matters in the Minds of those who* have *read them, and to give an easy and clear View of what they contain, to those who have* not, *nor perhaps have Leisure to peruse them; at least, so carefully as may be necessary to answer the End of their Publication: And which, at the same time, will serve as a* copious INDEX *to direct the Reader where to find the most material Passages, as well as give an Idea of the entertaining and instructive Variety to be found in the Work.*

VOL. I.

Her JOURNAL,

The JOURNAL *continued.*

CONTENTS *of* VOL. II.

The JOURNAL *Continued*.

MONDAY. Mrs. *Jewkes* insults her on her Departure. Her wicked Hints to her Master in her hearing. He rebukes her for them. *Pamela* blesses him on her Knees for it.—Wonders she could be so loth to leave the House.—The Chariot drives away with her. She can hardly think but she is in a Dream all the time.— A Copy of her Master's Letter to her, deliver'd at a certain Distance, 'full of Tenderness and Respect, declaring his honourable Intentions to her, had she not unseasonably, in the midst of his Kindness to her, preferred going to her

ILLUSTRATIONS FROM OCTAVO EDITION (1742)

The octavo edition featured twenty-nine engravings, depicting scenes from the novel, by Hubert François Gravelot (1699–1773; also known as Henri Gravelot) and Francis Hayman (1708–76), with seven appearing in each of the first three volumes and eight in the fourth. Because no correspondence or other papers have survived, we do not know the terms of Richardson's dealings with Gravelot and Hayman, or the extent to which the author prescribed or did not prescribe the choice of scenes to be represented or the mode of their representation. The critical consensus is that Richardson indeed played a major role in the illustrations of his novel. The fourteen engravings from the first two volumes are reproduced here; the fifteen engravings from the third and fourth volumes appear in *Pamela in Her Exalted Condition*. The seven engravings from the first volume face pages 4, 123, 151, 214, 290, 358, and 373 in the octavo text (these are located in the Cambridge Edition at 10, 73, 88, 121, 161, 197, 207). Gravelot engraved all of them and designed the illustration facing p. 373; Hayman designed the other six. The seven engravings from the second volume face pages 32, 89, 175, 249, 267, 305, and 404 in the octavo text (in the Cambridge Edition: 241, 272, 318, 357, 366, 386, 439). Hayman designed the illustration facing p. 267; Gravelot designed the other six and engraved all seven.

2 Engraving by Hubert Gravelot, facing Vol. I, p. 4 of octavo edition (1742) of
Pamela: or, Virtue Rewarded

3 Engraving by Hubert Gravelot, facing Vol. I, p. 123 of octavo edition (1742) of
Pamela: or, Virtue Rewarded

4 Engraving by Hubert Gravelot, facing Vol. I, p. 151 of octavo edition (1742) of
Pamela: or, Virtue Rewarded

5 Engraving by Hubert Gravelot, facing Vol. I, p. 214 of octavo edition (1742) of
Pamela: or, Virtue Rewarded

6 Engraving by Hubert Gravelot, facing Vol. I, p. 290 of octavo edition (1742) of
Pamela: or, Virtue Rewarded

7 Engraving by Hubert Gravelot, facing Vol. I, p. 358 of octavo edition (1742) of
Pamela: or, Virtue Rewarded

Vol. I. p. 373.

H. Gravelot inv. et sculp.

8 Engraving by Hubert Gravelot, facing Vol. I, p. 373 of octavo edition (1742) of
Pamela: or, Virtue Rewarded

Vol. II. p. 32.

H. Gravelot inv. sc.

9 Engraving by Hubert Gravelot, facing Vol. II, p. 32 of octavo edition (1742) of
Pamela: or, Virtue Rewarded

10 Engraving by Hubert Gravelot, facing Vol. II, p. 89 of octavo edition (1742) of
Pamela: or, Virtue Rewarded

11 Engraving by Hubert Gravelot, facing Vol. II, p. 175 of octavo edition (1742) of
Pamela: or, Virtue Rewarded

Vol. II. p. 249.

H. Gravelot inv&. sculps.

12 Engraving by Hubert Gravelot, facing Vol. II, p. 249 of octavo edition (1742) of
Pamela: or, Virtue Rewarded

13 Engraving by Hubert Gravelot, facing Vol. II, p. 267 of octavo edition (1742) of
Pamela: or, Virtue Rewarded

14 Engraving by Hubert Gravelot, facing Vol. II, p. 305 of octavo edition (1742) of
Pamela: or, Virtue Rewarded

15 Engraving by Hubert Gravelot, facing Vol. II, p. 404 of octavo edition (1742) of
Pamela: or, Virtue Rewarded

EMENDATIONS

In this list of emendations, the reading adopted in the Cambridge text is recorded to the left of the bracket, followed by the number of the edition from which it is taken, followed in turn by the rejected reading from the first edition. The wavy or swung dash (∼) represents the word (or, in some instances, words) in the lemma to the left of the bracket, with the caret denoting missing punctuation.

12.25 should be robb'd] 2; should robb'd 1
13.14 fear any thing.] 2; ∼. 1
15.25 *dutiful Daughter.*] 2; ∼. 1
20.1 not of *mine.*] 2; ∼. 1
20.4 always scribbling] 2; alwas scribbling 1
36.6 she had it, I can't] 2; she had, it I can't 1
60.7 the worst of all] 2; the the worst of all 1
62.29 LETTER XXVII] 8vo; LETTER XXVI 1–5
66.11 LETTER XXVIII] 8vo; LETTER XXVII 1–5
70.9 LETTER XXIX] 8vo; LETTER XXVIII 1–5
72.17 see 'em] 2; see'em 1
76.4 fluster'd as I have] 2; fluster'd as as I have 1
76.13 LETTER XXX] 8vo; LETTER XXIX 1–5
80.1 LETTER XXXI] 8vo; LETTER XXX 1–5
91.1 LETTER XXXII] 8vo; LETTER XXXI 1–5
93.35 Sweet-meats] 4; Sweat-meats 1–3
95.16 Daughter] 2; Daughters 1
101.13 Duty to my Master;] 2; ∼,, 1
105.35 in me] 3; to me 1–2
122.23 Are there any] 2; Are there are any 1
124.6 nothing). 'And] 2; nothing)'. 'And 1
135.26 that if I can] 2; that (gap) I can 1

143.3 getting] 3; get-/ing 1–2
149.11 discover something. And] 2; ∼· ∼ 1
153.32 judge] 2; iudge 1
162.32 cry'd out] 3; cry'd, out 1–2
166.5 to be borne] 2; to borne 1
178.5 cover'd as this] 2; cover'd at this 1
187.10 said I] 2; said, I 1
188.25 Grimace) he] 2; Grimace he) 1
188.29 sitting on] 2; setting on 1
194.5 bid you.] 2; bid you? 1
216.25 tell] 2; telll 1
225.12 Leave of, to delay] 2; ∼. ∼ 1
225.13 crying. Pray] 2; ∼· ∼ 1
225.36 to be sure] 2; to he sure 1
226.25 lifted up, O] 2; ∼. ∼ 1
227.17 Handkerchief] 3; Handerchief 1–2
230.12 to be sure] 2; to sure 1
235.37 fetching-up] 2; fetch-/up 1
247.20 Setness] 2; Settness 1
255.30 against any] 2; againstany 1
256.6 if you] 2; ifyou 1
265.17 reply'd] 2; repl'yd 1
322.18 last my best] 2; last by best 1
326.10 yourself] 2; youself 1
326.18 Twenty Guineas] 2; Twenty Gineas 1
337.6 innumerable] 2; inumerable 1
353.18 reply'd I] 2; reply' I 1
363.40 Reflection.] 2; ∼· 1
365.20 almost as much] 2; almost at much 1
366.18 thou'rt] 2; thou't 1
375.23 Goodness] 2; Goodneess 1
377.32 me to fill] 2; me for fill 1
378.33 Affair, and] 2; Affair,) and 1
382.11 return'd] 2: retturn'd 1
384.38 Will to my Wife] 2; Will my Wife 1
385.23 Retirements] 2; Retiretments 1
391.10 Indeed] 2; In deed 1
391.29 I have indeed.] 2; ∼· 1
392.2 and a great deal] 2; and great deal 1
397.1 as I do.] 2; ∼· 1

399.1 leaning on my Arm] 2; learning on my Arm 1
414.36 *to be hoped*] 2; *to he hoped* 1
416.26 Attempts] 2; Attemps 1
422.40 he longs] 2; he ongs 1
424.31 said my] 2; said said my 1
427.21 Favour. On] 2; ~,~ 1
430.9 by her] 2; byher 1
433.24 see no] 2; seeno 1
433.31 drawn in] 2; drawnin 1
435.20 not so,—to wit] 2; ~.~ 1
435.23 reprov'd you. I] 2; ~,~ 1
438.29 believe] 2; believ'd 1
440.14 love me] 2; loves me 1
451.13 him he should] 2; him he he should 1
461.23 herself;] 2; ~. 1

WORD-DIVISION

Hyphenated compounds in which both elements are capitalized are not included. Compounds hyphenated at the end of the line in the copy-text as well as in the Cambridge Edition are marked with an asterisk.

1. The following compounds, or possible compounds, are hyphenated at the end of the line in the present edition.

4.16	much-wanted
5.25	high-meriting
7.12	un-amiable
9.17	Death-bed
21.40, 32.36, 39.23, 56.20	Summer-house
31.10	Dressing-room
31.29	any-where
41.25	Night-gown
48.2	Fellow-servants
59.6	To-morrow
69.24	Hard-heartedness
69.28	Ads-heartlikins
73.19	*April*-day
87.16	Day-light
94.21	Church-dyal
95.37	well-behav'd
103.1	House-maid
119.21	School-time
138.16	Half-pence
154.24	Over-security
156.31	Handkerchiefs
165.24	Sham-marriage

169.15, 220.13	to-morrow
174.25	whenever
175.33	humble-born
181.10	Chit-chat
*225.23	by-and-by
244.5, 304.9	where-ever
269.2	Iron-gate
274.10	whatever
274.32	Upper-end
286.17	Communion-picture
293.19	somebody
318.10	wherewith
320.19	Hunting-note
342.33	Coach-horse
377.21	*Beggar-brat*
391.22	somewhere
413.14	Quietness-sake
438.39	good-natur'd
*447.14	Button-holes
456.21	Second-hand
456.22	All-mighty

2. The following compounds, or possible compounds, are hyphenated at the end
   of the line in the copy-text. The forms recorded below are those adopted in
   the Cambridge Edition; they are derived, when possible, from other instances
   found within the line in the copy-text. Though retaining their hyphens in
   the instances recorded below, 'House-keeper' and 'over-joy'd' appear in both
   forms, as 'House-keeper' and 'over-joy'd' as well as 'Housekeeper' and 'overjoy'd',
   within the line in the copy-text.

7.1, 91.13	withstand
17.33	everlasting
27.22	Summer-house
37.33	Ill-will
44.4	To-morrow
44.23, 50.24, 337.4	may-be
45.22	sweet-temper'd
48.9, 225.23, 292.16, 345.10	by-and-by
51.20	Necklace
52.2	Under-petticoat
54.5	Doating-piece

54.6, 458.3	Fortnight
54.34, 225.7, 268.34	House-keeper
59.22	over-joy'd
62.18, 242.34	overcome
65.29	Lyings-in
65.38	alack-a-day
69.38	hard-hearted
72.31	Closet-work
73.18	Shoe-buckle
77.19	sweet-fac'd
90.8	well-nigh
90.32	Journal-wise
100.19	Court-yard
104.7	here-and-there
117.21, 166.4	such-like
125.13	thereabouts
137.23	to-night
137.26	Sealing-wax
138.26	Snuff-box
142.24	Head-piece
149.15	*Plaything*
157.12	Neck-handkerchief
162.39	Witchcrafts
175.33	Ear-rings
176.19	Free-will
182.34, 187.11, 302.22, 354.28, 448.17	to-morrow
182.35	withstood
183.5	Besure
184.14	Cherry-brandy
184.18, 184.19, 187.10	to-bed
187.7	Right-hand
199.12	overheard
207.2	Rose-bush
207.5	Gypsey-like
210.29	half-angry
212.29	open-hearted
215.32	Fox-hunters
239.12	Good-for-nothingness
239.21	*high-minded*
240.8, 258.35, 360.8, 416.13	Sham-marriage
244.9, 307.16, 437.16	now-and-then
244.10	Over-flowings
256.4	Lumber-room

256.10	Great-grandfather's
268.29	Neckcloth
268.32	brow-beaten
272.26	scarce-believing
276.5	wrong-timed
281.12	Brook-side
284.6	overcoming
292.35	Common-prayer
297.33	*Sun-flower*
299.26	Supper-time
299.39	Cherry-brandy
302.16	to-day
307.26	Honey-flowing
309.40	Godmother
311.27	Out-houses
315.32	Headcloths
316.19, 327.6, 327.27	Dinner-time
318.24	evermore
320.19	Hunting-note
330.40	overwhelm'd
337.16	out-does
339.39	Clockwork
350.16	Stair-case
350.38	a-bed
367.1	along-side
367.21	any-where
377.3	too-too
380.35	Begone
390.8	out-soar
395.26	Wicked-one
404.3	withdrawn
419.19	blame-worthy
426.8	Pocket-book
430.37	Dressing-room
432.9	Mantua-makers
433.4	aforehand
433.9	House-keepers
437.16	Farm-house
444.32	*Crosby-square*
447.14	pearl-colour'd
447.14	Button-holes

BIBLIOGRAPHICAL DESCRIPTIONS OF
EARLY EDITIONS

This bibliography is arranged chronologically. It includes bibliographical descriptions of all eight duodecimo editions (up to 1762), the French edition published with Richardson's approval in October 1741, the octavo edition (1742), and the 'fourteenth' (1801) and 'fifteenth' (1810) editions; the last two, though published several decades after his death, nonetheless belong to a line of textual transmission that can be traced, through his daughters, back to Richardson. Editions or abridgements of the novel appearing in Dublin, North America (including Benjamin Franklin's), or London (after 1762) are not described because there is no evidence that Richardson was involved in their publication. Because the eight duodecimo editions of the first two volumes constitute one line of textual transmission, beginning with the second edition every bibliographical description indicates how that particular edition resembles, or differs from, its predecessor. Thus, the description of the third edition builds on the description of the second edition, the fourth on the third, and so on.

I   FIRST EDITION, 1741
[PUBLISHED 6 NOVEMBER 1740], 2 VOLS., 12°

Volume I

Title page: A reproduction of the title page of the first edition appears before the present text.

Collation: 12° A^8 (–A1) B–N^{12} O^4 = 155 leaves; $1–6 (–A2, 5, 6, O3, 4); $1 includes signature title 'VOL. I.'

Notes: Page 16 is misnumbered 61; LETTERS XXVII–XXXII are misnumbered LETTERS XXVI–XXXI; 5 is missing in pagination of p. 295. Sale (1936) notes that A1 of Vol. I 'was undoubtedly used for the title-page of Vol. II' (p. 14). Press figure H166-5, present in other copies I have examined, has been cut out of the Newberry Library copy.

Contents: [i] Title; [ii] blank; [iii]–vi preface, with caption title ([iii]) PREFACE | BY THE | EDITOR.; vii–xiv letters to the editor, with caption titles (vii) *To the Editor of the Piece intitled*, PAMELA; | *or*, VIRTUE Rewarded.; and (x) *To my worthy Friend, the Editor of* | PAMELA, *&c*.; [1]–296 Text, with caption title ([1]) *PAMELA*; | OR, | VIRTUE Rewarded. | [long rule] | *In a Series of* FAMILIAR LETTERS, &c. | [long rule] |; 296 *The END of* VOL. I.

Running heads: PREFACE.; *To the Editor of* PAMELA.; *PAMELA*; Or, | VIRTUE Rewarded.; *PAMELA*, &c. (p. 296)

Press figures: Axii-4; C46-4; D69-5; E94-I; F118-2; G142-4; H166-5; I182-I; K213-5; K214-2; L238-4; M264-5; N288-I

Catchword variants: p. vi *om*.; xiv *PAMELA:* (*PAMELA*;); 6 LET- (LETTER); 7 LET- (LETTER); 10 LET- (LETTER); 15 LET- (LETTER); 23 LET- (LETTER); 39 LET- (LETTER); 42 LET- (LETTER); 43 them (themselves); 53 LET- (LETTER); 57 LET- (LETTER); 58 them- (themselves); 80 LET- (LETTER); 101 Yester- (Yesterday); 107 *om*.; 125 a Let- (a Letter); 138 faith- (faithfully); 140 laugh- (laughing); 146 *Long*- (*Longman*); 170 *FRI*- (*FRIDAY*); 186 bring- (bringing); 198 Neces- (Necessaries); 209 Tempta- (Temptations); 212 *MON*- (*MONDAY*); 215 after- (afterwards); 216 WELL ('WELL); 224 *THURS*- (*THURSDAY*); 238 *MON*- (*MONDAY*); 250 *there*- (*therefore*); 252 'ficien- ('ficiencies); 255 'im- ('impossible), *mar*- (*marry'd*); 260 may- (may-be); 263 *SUN*- (*SUNDAY*); 283 *WED*- (*WEDNESDAY*)

Ornaments: Maslen R049, R443, A3ʳ; Maslen R236, A5ʳ; Maslen R181, A6ᵛ; Maslen R280, A8ᵛ; Maslen R064, R492, B1ʳ; Maslen R388, O4ᵛ

Volume II

Title page: Same as Vol. I, except omits 'A Narrative... should *instruct*.' and 'In Two VOLUMES.'; 'VOL. II.' instead of 'VOL. I.'

Collation: 12° [A]1 (= A1 of Vol. I) B–R¹² S⁶ = 199 leaves; $1–6 (–S4, 5, 6); $1 includes signature title 'VOL. II.'

Notes: Press figure L240-5 is not present in Cornell University Library and National Library of Scotland copies. Cornell University Library copy has press figure S392-5; this press figure also appears in Library of Scotland copy but is missing from other copies I have examined, including Princeton University Library and

Newberry Library. Press figure R374-4 is missing from Library of Scotland copy but is present in other copies I have examined, including Cornell, Princeton, and Newberry.

Contents: [i] Title; [ii] blank; [1]–396 Text, with caption title [1] *PAMELA*; | OR, | Virtue Rewarded. | [long rule] | VOL. II. | [long rule] | *The* Journal *continued*. | [long rule]; 396 *FINIS*.

Running heads: *PAMELA*; Or, | Virtue *Rewarded*.; *PAMELA*, &c. (p. 396)

Press figures: B16-I; B22-2; C48-4; D64-5; E94-2; F118-I; G142-I; G144-4; H166-I; H168-I; I190-4; K214-5; L240-5; N288-5; O310-4; P334-2; Q358-4; R374-4

Catchword variants: p. 2 Inno- (Innocence); 6 Adven- (Adventure); 11 *SATUR-* (*SATURDAY*); 20 some- (sometimes); 39 'Justifi- ('Justification); 47 Wo- (Woman); 52 'Dis- ('Disgrace); 53 'Fel- ('Fellow); 61 con- (convinced); 79 *THURS-* (*THURSDAY*); 126 man- (manner); 137 *WHEN* (I. *WHEN*); 153 break- (breakfasting); 158 I can- (I cannot); 165 a Whis- (a Whisper); 182 Good- (Goodness); 199 Sur- (Surname); 215 unpro- (unprovided); 226 Crea- (Creature); 249 Con- (Confess); 278 Stop- (Stopping); 284 them- (themselves); 321 Elope- (Elopements); 329 Senti- (Sentiments); 349 *SUN-* (*SUNDAY*); 355 *Cham-* (*Chambers*); 368 Rela- (Relations); 384 discom- (discomposing); 387 *FRI-* (*FRIDAY*); 393 distin- (distinguish)

Ornaments: Maslen R051, R444, B1ʳ

Copy: Newberry Library (Chicago) VAULT Case 3A 881 v 1–2

ESTC: T111392

2   SECOND EDITION, 1741
[PUBLISHED 14 FEBRUARY 1741], 2 VOLS., 12°

Volume I

Title page: Same as first edition, except 'In order to cultivate the Principles of Virtue | and Religion in the Minds of the YOUTH | of BOTH SEXES.' and adds, below 'In Two Volumes.', '| [long rule] | The Second Edition. | To which are prefixed, Extracts from several curious | Letters written to the *Editor* on the Subject. | [long rule] | VOL. I.'

Collation: 12° A⁸ (–A1) a¹² B–N¹² O⁴ = 167 leaves; $1–6 (–A2, 5, 6, O3, 4); $1 includes signature title 'Vol. I.'

Notes: LETTER XXV is misnumbered LETTER XII; LETTERS XXVI–XXXII are misnumbered XXV–XXXI; p. 295 is misnumbered 293.

Contents: [i] Title; [ii] blank; [iii]–vi preface, with caption title ([iii]) PREFACE | BY THE | EDITOR.; vii–xiv letters to the editor, with caption titles (vii) *To the Editor of the Piece intitled*, PAMELA; | *or*, VIRTUE Rewarded.; and (x) *To my worthy Friend, the Editor of* | PAMELA.; xv–xxxvii introduction, with caption title (xv) INTRODUCTION | TO THIS | SECOND EDITION.; xxxvii–xxxviii verses; [1]–296 Text, with caption title ([1]) *PAMELA*; | OR, | VIRTUE Rewarded. | [long rule] | *In a Series of* FAMILIAR LETTERS, &c. | [long rule]; 296 *The END of* VOL. I.

Running heads: PREFACE.; *To the Editor of* PAMELA.; Introduction *to the* | SECOND EDITION.; Introduction *to*, &c. (p. xxxvi); *PAMELA*; Or, | VIRTUE *Rewarded.*; *PAMELA*, &c. (p. 296)

Press figures: axxvi-5

Catchword variants: p. vi *om.*; xiv INTRO- (INTRODUCTION); xxxviii PA- (*PAMELA*); 6 LET- (LETTER); 7 LET- (LETTER); 10 LET- (LETTER); 15 LET- (LETTER); 23 LET- (LETTER); 39 LET- (LETTER); 42 LET- (LETTER); 43 them- (themselves); 53 LET- (LETTER); 57 LET- (LETTER); 58 them- (themselves); 80 LET- (LETTER); 101 Yester- (Yesterday); 138 faith- (faithfully); 140 laugh- (laughing); 170 *FRI- (FRIDAY)*; 173 I But (I but); 174 to ('to); 186 bring- (bringing); 195 her (her,); 197 'say ('say); 198 Neces- (Necessaries); 209 to ('to); 212 *MON- (MONDAY)*; 215 after- (afterwards); 216 WELL ('WELL); 220 hanging (banging ['banging' is incorrect]); 224 *THURS- (THURS-DAY)*; 238 *MON- (MONDAY)*; 250 *there- (therefore)*; 252 'ficien- (ficiencies); 255 'im- ('impossible), *mar- (marry'd)*; 260 may- (may-be); 263 *SUN- (SUNDAY)*; 264 Night, ('Night,); 283 *WED- (WEDNESDAY)*

Ornaments: Maslen R049, R443, A3ʳ; Maslen R236, A5ʳ; Maslen R181, A6ᵛ; Maslen R280, A8ᵛ; Maslen R091, R452, a1ʳ; Maslen R188, a12ʳ; Maslen R067, R484, B1ʳ; Maslen R388, O4ᵛ

Volume II

Title page: Same as Vol. I, except 'In order to cultivate the Principles of | VIRTUE and RELIGION in the Minds of | the YOUTH of BOTH SEXES.; omits 'A Narrative... should *instruct.*' and 'To which . . . on the Subject.'; 'VOL. II.' instead of 'VOL. I.'

Collation: 12° [A]1 (= A1 of Vol. I) B–R¹² S⁶ = 199 leaves; $1–6 (–S4, 5, 6); $1 includes signature title 'VOL. II.'

Notes: Page 177 is misnumbered 187; p. 242 is misnumbered 142.

Contents: [i] Title; [ii] blank; [1]–396 Text, with caption title [1] *PAMELA*; | OR, | VIRTUE Rewarded. | [long rule] | VOL. II. | [long rule] | *The* JOURNAL *continued.* | [long rule]; 396 *FINIS.*

Running heads: *PAMELA*; Or, | VIRTUE *Rewarded.*; *PAMELA*, &c. (p. 396)

Press figures: D50-5; E85-4; E87-4; F111-4; F120-4; G132-4; H168-4; K216-5; L240-5; M264-5; R382-4

Catchword variants: p. 3 Mrs. (*Jervis*); 6 Adven- (Adventure); 9 *Jewkes*; ('*Jewkes*;); 11 *SATUR-* (*SATURDAY*); 20 some- (sometimes); 39 'Justifi- ('Justification); 47 Wo- (Woman); 52 'Dis- ('Disgrace); 53 'Fel- ('Fellow); 55 *And* (*And*,); 61 con- (convinced); 79 *THURS-* (*THURSDAY*); 126 man- (manner); 137 *WHEN* (I. *WHEN*); 153 break- (breakfasting); 158 I can- (I cannot); 165 a Whis- (a Whisper); 181 *Abra-* (*Abraham*); 183 possibly (Possibly); 199 Sur- (Surname); 215 unpro- (unprovided); 226 Crea- (Creature); 249 Con- (Confess); 278 stop- (stopping); 284 them- (themselves); 321 Elope- (Elopements); 329 Senti- (Sentiments); 336 you (you,); 349 *SUN-* (*SUNDAY*); 368 Rela- (Relations); 384 discom- (discomposing); 387 *FRI-* (*FRIDAY*); 393 distin- (distinguish)

Ornaments: Maslen R381 [A]1ʳ; Maslen R068, R460, B1ʳ

Copy: Newberry Library (Chicago) Case Y155 R4086 v 1–2

ESTC: 110967

3   THIRD EDITION, 1741
[PUBLISHED 12 MARCH 1741], 2 VOLS., 12°

Volume I

Title page: Same as second edition, except 'The THIRD EDITION.' instead of 'The SECOND EDITION.'

Collation: Same as second edition.

Notes: LETTERS XXVI–XXXII are misnumbered LETTERS XXV–XXXI; p. 60 is misnumbered 90; p. 169 is misnumbered 269; p. 295 is misnumbered 293. Sale (1936) notes that Richardson printed signatures A, a, and O of this volume (p. 18). The rest of this volume and all of Vol. II (except for the title page) seem to be by other printers or presses. Signatures B and C of this volume were printed by William Bowyer (as attested by his ornaments 41 and 235 on B1^r).

Contents: Same as second edition, except caption title (xv) 'INTRODUCTION | TO THE | SECOND EDITION.'

Running heads: Same as second edition.

Press figures: axxxvi-I; J192-I

Catchword variants: Same as second edition, except corrections to p. 173 I but (I but); 174 'to ('to); 197 'say ('say); and 264 'Night, ('Night,)

Ornaments: Maslen R049, R443, A3^r; Maslen R236, A5^r; Maslen R181, A6^v; Maslen R280, A8^v; Maslen R091, R452, a1^r; Maslen R188, a12^r; Maslen R388, O4^v. Maslen identifies ornaments on B1^r as William Bowyer's ornaments 41 and 235 (p. 131).

Volume II

Title page: Same as second edition, except 'The THIRD EDITION.' instead of 'The SECOND EDITION.'

Collation: Same as second edition.

Contents: Same as second edition.

Running heads: Same as second edition.

Press figures: B2-3; B21-3; D50-2; D69-2; E95-I; F110-I; G130-I; H154-I; H156-2; I172-4; I190-5; K196-4; K198-4; L218-4; L232-4; M255-4; M261-2; P327-5

Catchword variants: Same as second edition, except corrections to p. 9 *'Jewkes*; ('*Jewkes*;); 47 Woman, (Woman,); and 183 possibly (possibly)

Ornaments: Maslen R381, [A]1^r; unidentified ornaments on B1^r

Copy: Cornell University Library (Rare) PR3664. P2 1741d v 1-2

ESTC: T111393

4   FOURTH EDITION, 1741
[PUBLISHED 5 MAY 1741], 2 VOLS., 12°

Volume I

Title page: Same as third edition, except 'The FOURTH EDITION.' instead of 'The THIRD EDITION.'

Collation: Same as third edition.

Notes: LETTERS XXVI–XXXII are misnumbered LETTERS XXV–XXXI. Sale (1936) notes that 'the type pages used for printing the eight leaves of signature A of the fourth edition were the same as those used for the second and third' (p. 19). The rest of the type pages were reset. Based on identification of his ornaments, Richardson printed signatures A through C and O. The remaining signatures were probably the work of other (unidentified) printers or presses.

Contents: Same as third edition, except extracts from letters to the editor end in the middle of p. xxxvi and Hill's verses begin at the top of p. xxxvii.

Running heads: Same as third edition.

Press figures: B22-4; C46-4; G142I; K206I; M264-5; N286-I

Catchword variants: p. vi, *om*.; xiv INTRO- (INTRODUCTION); xxviii '*of* (*of*); xxxviii *PA- (PAMELA)*; 6 LET- (LETTER); 7 LET- (LETTER); 10 LET- (LETTER); 15 LET- (LETTER); 23 LET- (LETTER); 39 LET- (LETTER); 42 LET- (LETTER); 43 them- (themselves); 53 LET- (LETTER); 57 LET- (LETTER); 58 them- (themselves); 80 LET- (LETTER); 92 and (and,); 101 Yester- (Yesterday); 131 *Dear*, ('*Dear*); 138 faith- (faithfully); 140 laugh- (laughing); 151 *om*.; 170 *FRI- (FRIDAY)*; 184 X. *Yea* (X. *Yes*); 186 bring- (bringing); 191 *Mrs.* ('*Mrs.*); 198 Neces- (Necessaries); 212 *MON- (MONDAY)*; 215 after- (afterwards); 216 WELL ('WELL); 224 *THURS- (THURSDAY)*; 225 tions. (tions:); 238 *MON- (MONDAY)*; 250 *there- (therefore)*; 255 'im- ('impossible), *mar- (marry'd)*; 260 may- (may-be); 263 *SUN- (SUNDAY)*; 283 *WED- (WEDNESDAY)*

Ornaments: Maslen R049, R443, A3^r; Maslen R236, A5^r; Maslen R181, A6^v; Maslen R280, A8^v; Maslen R069, R471, a1^r; Maslen R383, a11^v; Maslen R184, a12^r; Maslen R384, a12^v; Maslen R067, R485, B1^r; Maslen R388, O4^v

Volume II

Title page: Same as third edition, except 'The FOURTH EDITION.' instead of 'The THIRD EDITION.'

Collation: Same as third edition.

Notes: Ornaments on B1^r not identified as Richardson's. Richardson may have printed only the title page of this volume. Pages 289, 292, 293, 296, 297, 300, 301, 304, 305, 308, 309, 312 are misnumbered 265, 268, 269, 272, 273, 276, 277, 280, 281, 284, 285, 288, respectively; page 365 is not paged.

Contents: Same as third edition.

Running heads: Same as third edition.

Press figures: C48-*; D70-*; E94-*; F120-*; G130-I; H154-I; M261-3; M262-2; O310-I; P334-5; Q358-4

Catchword variants: Same as third edition, except p. 197 'You, ('you,)

Ornaments: Maslen R381, [A]1ʳ; unidentified ornaments on B1ʳ

Copy: Princeton University Library (Ex) 3907.7.369.11 v 1–2 (Both title pages of these volumes bear signature 'Jane Collier', as do the title pages of the third and fourth volumes that complete the set. The third and fourth volumes are from the first edition.)

ESTC: T132466

5   FIFTH EDITION, 1741
[PUBLISHED 22 SEPTEMBER 1741], 2 VOLS., 12°

Volume I

Title page: Same as fourth edition, except 'The FIFTH EDITION.' instead of 'The FOURTH EDITION.'

Collation: Same as fourth edition.

Notes: LETTERS XXVI–XXXII are misnumbered LETTERS XXV–XXXI. Long rules separate letters in this volume. Page 138 is misnumbered 158.

Contents: Same as fourth edition, except that caption title (xv) changed to 'INTRODUCTION | TO THE | PRESENT EDITION.'

Running heads: Same as fourth edition, except 'Introduction *to the* | PRESENT EDITION.' instead of 'Introduction *to the* | SECOND EDITION.'

Press figures: xxvii-4; D62-I; E84-2; E94-4; L240-5; M254-I; M256-2; N286-4

Catchword variants: p. v *CON- (CONFIDENT)*; xiv *INTRO- (INTRODUC-TION)*; xxii 'I won- ('I wonder); xxix 'Now- ('Now-and-then); 6 LET- (LET-TER); 7 LET- (LETTER); 10 LET- (LETTER); 15 LET- (LETTER); 23 LET- (LETTER); 39 LET- (LETTER); 42 LET- (LETTER); 43 them- (them-selves); 53 LET- (LETTER); 57 LET- (LETTER); 58 them- (themselves); 80 LET- (LETTER); 101 Yester- (Yesterday); 138 faith- (faithfully); 140

laugh- (laughing); 143 here- (here-and-there); 170 *FRI- (FRIDAY)*; 186 bring-(bringing); 191 *Mrs.* ('Mrs.); 198 Neces- (Necessaries); 212 *MON- (MONDAY)*; 215 after- (afterwards); 224 *THURS- (THURSDAY)*; 238 *MON- (MONDAY)*; 250 *there- (therefore)*; 255 'im- ('impossible), *mar- (marry'd)*; 260 may- (may-be); 263 *SUN- (SUNDAY)*; 276 you r (your); 278 Mrs, (Mrs.); *WED- (WEDNESDAY)*

Ornaments: Maslen R049, R443, A3^r; Maslen R298, A4^v; Maslen R236, A5^r; Maslen R250, A6^v; Maslen R349, A8^v; Maslen R069, R492, a1^r; Maslen R349, a11^v; Maslen R236, a12^r; Maslen R280, a12^v; Maslen R067, R481, B1^r; R388, O4^v

Volume II

Title page: Same as fourth edition, except 'The FIFTH EDITION.' instead of 'The FOURTH EDITION.'

Collation: Same as fourth edition.

Notes: 9 is missing in pagination of p. 379.

Contents: Same as fourth edition.

Running heads: Same as fourth edition.

Press figures: B12-2; B14-1; D69-3; E88-4; F112-1; F118-2; G136-2; G142-1; H166-3; K214-3; K216-4; L240-3; M242-5; M253-1; N286-1; O304-1; P314-2

Catchword variants: p. 6 Adven- (Adventure); 11 *SATUR- (SATURDAY)*; 20 some-(sometimes); 39 'Justifi- ('Justification); 52 'Dis- ('Disgrace); 53 'Fel- ('Fellow); 61 con- (convinced); 66 vour (vour,); 79 *THURS- (THURSDAY)*; 158 I can-(I cannot); 181 *Abra- (Abraham)*; 199 Sur- (Surname); 215 unpro- (unprovided); 226 Crea- (Creature); 231 te (tell); 249 Con- (Confess); 278 stop- (stopping); 284 them- (themselves); 309 Form (Form;); 321 Elope- (Elopements); 329 Senti-(Sentiments); 336 you (you,); 349 *SUN- (SUNDAY)*; 353 will (I will); 369 Rela-(Relations); 384 discom- (discomposing); 387 *FRI- (FRIDAY)*; 389 it. (it,); 393 distin- (distinguish)

Ornaments: Maslen R381 [A]1^r; Maslen R052, R467, B1^r

Copy: Cornell University Library (Rare) PR3664. P2 1741f v 1–2

ESTC: T058976

5B   FRENCH TRANSLATION, 1741
[PUBLISHED 23 OCTOBER 1741], 2 VOLS., 12°

Volume I

Title page: PAMELA; | OU | La Vertu Recompensée. | Traduit de L'ANGLOIS. | En Deux Tomes. | [ornament] | A LONDRES, | Chez Thomas Woodward, au Croissant entre | les Portes du Temple; | Et Jean Osborn, à la Boule d'Or, dans | Pater Noster Row, près de S. Paul. | M DCC XLI.

Collation: 12° [A]² a⁶ (–a6) B–P¹² Q⁸ = 183 leaves; $1–6 (–A2, a4, a5, B6, C6, Q5, 6; C3 missigned B3); $1 (–D1) includes signature title 'Tom. I.'

Notes: One leaf is missing from signature a; it was probably used for title page of Vol. II. Editor's preface begins on p. [xi], as the printer seems to have anticipated a longer preface by the translator. Printer's ornaments in this volume are by William Bowyer, with ornament numbers recorded below referring to K. I. D. Maslen, *The Bowyer Ornament Stock* (Oxford Bibliographical Society, Bodleian Library, 1973). An entry dated 19 August 1741 in Bowyer's ledgers (for 1,500 copies) seems to refer to this volume. Variant title page, with only Osborn's name on it, fronts what are either copies of this edition or a second impression; this title page also features Bowyer's ornament 179.

Contents: [i] Title; [ii] blank; [iii–iv] translator's preface, with caption title ([iii]) PREFACE.; [xi]–xii preface, with caption title ([xi]) PREFACE | DE | L'EDITEUR.; xiii–xx letters to the editor, with caption titles (xiii) *A L'Editeur du Livre intitulé* Pamela; | *ou*, La Virtu Recompense´e. and ([xv]) *A mon digne Ami, l'Editeur de* Pamela.; [1]–351 Text, with caption title [1] *PAMELA*; | OU | La Vertu Recompensée.; 351 FIN du Iᵉ TOME.; [352] *BOOKS printed for, and sold by* J. Osborn, *at the* Golden-Ball *in* Paternoster-Row.

Running Heads: PREFACE.; PAMELA; Ou, | la Vertue Recompense´e.

Press figures: None.

Catchword variants: p. [iv] *om.*; xiii inter- (interressantes); xx *PA-* (*PAMELA*); 36 ren- (renvoyer); 57 ap- (appartement); 116 Pre- (Premiérement); 118 s'éva- (s'évanouissent); 127 Cela (Voilá); 152 coup (conp ['conp' is incorrect]); 219 se (propose); 235 diffi- (difficultez); 279 J'ajou- (J'ajouteray); 297 con- (convient); 301 actu- (actuallement); 304 pronon- (prononcerois); 337 répondis- (répondis-je); 341 dintin- (distinguées); 351 *om.*

Ornaments: Maslen B179, [A]1^r; Maslen B64, a1^r; Maslen B94 (similar to or same as Maslen R236?), a2^r; Maslen B85 (similar to or same as Maslen R221?), a3^v; Maslen B41, Maslen B217, B1^r; Maslen B179, Q8^r

Volume II

Title page: PAMELA: | OU | LA VERTU RECOMPENSE´E | Traduit de L'ANGLOIS. | TOME II. | [ornament] | A LONDRES, | Chez JEAN OSBORN, Libraire, à la Boule d'Or, | dans Pater-Noster-Row, près de S. PAUL. | M DCC XLI.

Collation: 12° [A]1 (= a6 of Vol. I?) B–U^{12} X^1 = 230 leaves; $1–6; $1 (–T1) includes signature title 'TOME II.'

Notes: Printer's ornaments in this volume not identified as Bowyer's by Maslen. This volume might have been printed by another printer (or group of printers).

Contents: [i] Title; [ii] blank; [1]–458 Text, with caption title [1] PAMELA; | OU | La VERTU Récompensée. | [long rule] | TOME SECOND. | [long rule] | Continuation du JOURNAL. | [long rule]; 458 F I N.

Running heads: PAMELA; ou, | LA VERTU RECOMPENSE´E.; PAMELA. (p. 458)

Press figures: B21-3; B22-3; C34-2; D70-2; E86-2; F98-3; G144-1; H146-3; H168-2; I182-3; K214-2; L238-5; M264-5; N274-2; O310-3; P335-1; Q351-2; R375-3; S386-3; T410-2; U442-1

Catchword variants: p. 5 d'éxa- (d'éxaminer); 15 com- (commencez); 29 riva (arriva); 53 à Ro (à Robin); 55 lettre- (letter-là); 66 peut- (peut-être); 95 moins (Au moins); 101 con- (connoissance); 105 con- (conduire); 111 vois- (vois-je); 115 m'êm- (m'empêcher); 117 tre- (tre-regarder); 136 ajouta- (ajouta-t'il); 161 géné- (généreux); 166 Mesde- (Mesdemoiselles); 218 met- (mettre); 219 S'imagi- (S'imaginant); 227 vou- (voulois); 232 mau- (mauvais); 245 con- (conserver); 246 nom- (nombreuse); 259 "diver- ("divertirez); 268 inno- (innocente); 281 *om.*; 291 Con- (Confesse); 318 con- (continua); 337 puis- (puis-je); 341 chagrine! (me chagrine!); 382 honorable (honorablement); 387 Wor- (Worden); 403 Jan- (Janneton); 415 que ("que); 440 jouta- (jouta-t'il)

Ornaments: Unidentified printer's ornament, [A]1^r; two unidentified printer's ornaments, B1^r

Copy: Bodleian Library (University of Oxford) Vet. A4 f464

ESTC: T170831

6   SIXTH EDITION, 1742
[PUBLISHED 8 MAY 1742], 4 VOLS., 8°

Volume I

Title page: PAMELA:| OR, | VIRTUE Rewarded. | In a SERIES of | FAMILIAR LETTERS | From a Beautiful | Young DAMSEL to her PARENTS: | And afterwards, | In her EXALTED CONDITION, | BETWEEN | HER, and Persons of *Figure* and *Quality*, | UPON THE | Most Important and Entertaining SUBJECTS, | In GENTEEL LIFE. | [long rule] | IN FOUR VOLUMES. | [long rule] | Publish'd in order to cultivate the Principles of VIRTUE | and RELIGION in the Minds of the YOUTH of | BOTH SEXES. | [long rule] | The SIXTH EDITION, Corrected. | And Embellish'd with COPPER PLATES, Design'd and | Engrav'd by Mr. HAYMAN, and Mr. GRAVELOT. | [long rule] | VOL. I. | To which is prefixed, An Ample TABLE of CONTENTS; | Being, An EPITOME of the *Work*. | [long rule] | *LONDON:* | Printed for S. RICHARDSON; | And Sold by J. OSBORN, in *Pater-noster Row*; and JOHN | RIVINGTON, in *St. Paul's Church-Yard*. | [short rule] | M.DCC.XLII.

Collation: 8° A⁴ a–b⁸ c² B–Cc⁸ Dd⁴ = 226 leaves + 7 leaves of engraved illustrations; $1–4 (–A1, 3, 4, c2, Dd3, 4; A3 signed A2); $1 includes signature title 'VOL. I.'

Contents: [i] Blank; [ii] royal licence; [iii] title; [iv] blank; v–viii preface, with caption title (v) PREFACE | BY THE | EDITOR.; [i]–xxxvi contents, with caption title ([i]) CONTENTS | OF THE | FOUR VOLUMES.; [1]–407 Text, with caption title ([1]) PAMELA; | OR, | VIRTUE Rewarded. | [long rule] | *In a Series of* FAMILIAR LETTERS, &c. | [long rule]; 407 *The End of* VOL. I.; [408] blank.

Running heads: PREFACE.; *The* CONTENTS: *Being* | *An* EPITOME *of the Work.*; *The* CONTENTS: *Being*, &c. (p. xxxvi); *PAMELA*; or, | VIRTUE *Rewarded*.

Press figures: axiv-1; bxxx-4; cxxxvi-1; C24-2; D48-4; E63-4; F66-3; G95-2; H98-3; I114-1; K132-1; L158-4; M162-2; N191-3; O207-1; P219-3; Q239-2; S260-2; S270-4; T285-4; U301-4; Y331-1; Z350-4; Aa363-3; Bb383-5; Cc386-1

Catchword variants: p. viii CON- (CONTENTS); iii Con- (Conduct); ix THURS- (THURSDAY); xiii Gentle- (Gentleman); xxv XLI (XLI.); xxxii ---Ac- (---Acquaints); xxxvi PA- (PAMELA); 4 LET- (LETTER); 7 LET- (LETTER); 10 LET- (LETTER); 28 LET- (LETTER); 37 threw- (threw-to); 89 LET- (LETTER); 102 LET- (LETTER); 116 LET- (LETTER); 179 Mrs (Mrs.); 196 TUES- (TUESDAY); 202 den- (den-door); 211 "De- ("Dependence); 238

SUN- (*SUNDAY*); 246 *MON-* (*MONDAY*); 251 ALACK- (ALACK-A-DAY); 257 *TUES-* (*TUESDAY*); 258 I EXPO- (I EXPOSTULATED) 281 *THURS-* (*THURS-DAY*); 299 *THURS-* (*THURSDAY*); 332 *TUES-* (*TUESDAY*); —I (----I); 371 *FRI-* (*FRIDAY*); 391 won't (you); 405 Ihave (I have)

Illustrations: Seven engravings facing pp. 4, 123, 151, 214, 290, 358, 373. Hubert Gravelot engraved all of them and designed the illustration facing p. 373; Francis Hayman designed the other six. Reproduced in Appendix III.

Volume II

Title page: Same as Vol. I, except 'In FOUR VOLUMES.' instead of 'IN FOUR VOLUMES.'; 'VOL. II.' instead of 'VOL. I.'; omits 'To which is prefixed, An Ample TABLE of CONTENTS; | Being, An EPITOME of the *Work*.'; 'Richardson:' instead of 'Richardson;'

Collation: 8° [A]² B–Ee⁸ Ff⁴ = 222 leaves + 7 leaves of engraved illustrations; $1–4 (–Ff3, 4); $1 includes signature title 'VOL. II.'

Notes: Page 296 is misnumbered 269.

Contents: [i] Blank; [ii] royal licence; [iii] title; [iv] blank; [1]–438 Text, with caption title ([1]) *PAMELA*; | OR, | VIRTUE Rewarded. | [long rule] | VOL. II. | [long rule] | *The* JOURNAL *Continued*. | [long rule]; 438 *The END of* VOL. II.; [439] *BOOKS printed for, and sold by* J. OSBORN, *at the* | Golden Ball, *in* Pater-noster Row.; [440] *BOOKS printed for* JOHN RIVINGTON, *at the* | Bible *and* Crown, *in* St. Paul*'s* Church-Yard.

Running heads: *PAMELA*; or, | VIRTUE *Rewarded*.; *PAMELA*, &c. (p. 438)

Press figures: B14-4; D34-1; E61-5; F66-2; F80-4; G82-1; I116-4; K143-2; L150-5; N192-4; O194-5; P223-1; P224-6; Q233-5; R253-2; S270-4; T286-1; U303-2; X312-5; Y329-3; Z349-4; Aa362-1; Bb370-2; Cc398-4; Dd409-3; Ee422-5

Catchword variants: p. 11 *MON-* (*MONDAY*); 37 yoursef: (yourself:); 47 you (Pen); 88 *Jewkes*, (*Jewkes*); 98 *SATUR-* (*SATURDAY*); 119 My (My); 188 *FRI-* (*FRI-DAY*); 279 turn'd (turned); 310 Hands: (Hands;); 330 I PRE- (I PREVENTED); 375 after- (afterwards); 394 *WED-* (*WEDNESDAY*); 413 tion (tion:); 419 *MON-* (*MONDAY*)

Illustrations: Seven engravings facing pp. 32, 89, 175, 249, 267, 305, 404. Hayman designed the illustration facing p. 267; Gravelot designed the other six and engraved all seven. Reproduced in Appendix III.

Copy: Princeton University Library (Ex) 3907.7.369 v 1–2

ESTC: T128629

6B SIXTH EDITION, 1746
[PUBLISHED 16–18 OCTOBER 1746], 4 VOLS., 12°

Volume I

Title page: Same as fifth edition, except 'Now first Published,' instead of 'Now first Published'; 'In FOUR VOLUMES.' instead of 'In TWO VOLUMES.'; 'The SIXTH EDITION.' instead of 'The FIFTH EDITION.'; and changes in colophon 'Printed for J. OSBORN, in *Pater-noster Row*; and | J. and J. RIVINGTON, in *St. Paul's Church-Yard.* | [short rule] | M DCC XLVI.'

Collation: Same as fifth edition.

Notes: Page 1, unpaged in first five editions, is paged [I]. LETTERS XXVI–XXXII are misnumbered LETTERS XXV–XXXI. As in fifth edition, long rules separate letters in this volume. Vols. I and II of this edition were combined with Vols. III and IV, 'The FOURTH EDITION, *Corrected.*', to complete the set of four volumes advertised in the *General Evening Post* on 16–18 October 1746. Vols. III and IV are dated 1742; bibliographical descriptions of these volumes appear in *Pamela in Her Exalted Condition.*

Contents: Same as fifth edition.

Running heads: Same as fifth edition.

Press figures: B22-I; C46-I; D70-4; E86-3; F118-3; G141-I; H159-4; I170-4; K208-7; L230-4; M250-3; N286-3; N288-4

Catchword variants: p. v CON- (*CONFIDENT*); xiv INTRO- (*INTRODUC-TION*); xxii 'I won- ('I wonder); xxix 'Now- ('Now-and-then); 6 LET- (LET-TER); 7 LET- (LETTER); 10 LET- (LETTER); 15 LET- (LETTER); 23 LET- (LETTER); 39 LET- (LETTER); 42 LET- (LETTER); 43 them- (themselves); 53 LET- (LETTER); 57 LET- (LETTER); 58 them- (themselves); 80 LET- (LETTER); 85 Sauce- (Sauce-box); 101 Yester- (Yesterday); 114 I (It); 124 ab ject (abject); 138 faith- (faithfully); 140 laugh- (laughing); 170 *FRI-* (*FRIDAY*); 186 bring- (bringing); 191 *Mrs.* ('Mrs.); 198 Neces- (Necessaries); 212 *MON-* (*MON-DAY*); 215 after- (afterwards); 219 Well (Well,); 224 *THURS-* (*THURSDAY*); 238 *MON-* (*MONDAY*); 250 *there-* (*therefore*); 255 'im- ('impossible), *mar-* (*marry'd*); 260 may- (may-be); 263 *SUN-* (*SUNDAY*); 283 *WED-* (*WEDNESDAY*)

Ornaments: Maslen R049, R432, A3^r; Maslen R280, A4^v; Maslen R269, A5^r; Maslen R208, A6^v; Maslen R298, A8^v; Maslen R069, R473, a1^r; Maslen R349, a11^v; Maslen R185, a12^r; Maslen R353, a12^v; Maslen R049, R484, B1^r; Maslen R287, O4^v

Volume II

Title page: Same as fifth edition, except 'In FOUR VOLUMES.' instead of 'In Two VOLUMES.'; 'The SIXTH EDITION.' instead of 'The FIFTH EDITION.'; colophon same as Vol. I.

Collation: Same as fifth edition.

Notes: Page 1, unpaged in first five editions, is paged 1.

Contents: Same as fifth edition.

Running heads: Same as fifth edition.

Press figures: B24-3; C46-4; D63-4; E82-4; F117-I; G135-3; H158-I; I190-3; K202-3; L239-4; M262-I; N266-4; P336-3; Q358-3; R383-4; S386-3

Catchword variants: p. 6 Adven- (Adventure); 11 *SAT- (SATURDAY)*; 20 some- (sometimes); 39 'Justifi- ('Justification); 45 Safety, ('Safety); 52 'Dis- ('Disgrace); 53 'Fel- ('Fellow); 61 con- (convinced); 79 *THURS- (THURSDAY)*; 158 I can- (I cannot); 181 *Abra- (Abraham)*; 199 Sur- (Surname); 215 unpro- (unprovided); 226 Crea- (Creature); 249 Con- (Confess); 263 Sir (Sir,); 278 stop- (stopping); 309 Form (Form;); 321 Elope- (Elopements); 329 Senti- (Sentiments); 336 you (you,); 349 *SUN- (SUNDAY)*; 358 *om.*; 368 Rela- (Relations); 369 me. (me:); 384 discom- (discomposing); 387 *FRI- (FRIDAY)*; 393 distin- (distinguish)

Ornaments: Maslen R381, [A]1^r; Maslen R054, R444, B1^r

Copy: Cornell University Library (Rare) PR3664 .P2 1746 v 1–2

ESTC: T149952

7   SEVENTH EDITION, 1754
[NO DATE OF PUBLICATION FOUND], 4 VOLS., 12°

Volume I

Title page: Same as sixth duodecimo edition (1746), except '*PAMELA*,' instead of '*PAMELA*.'; 'The SEVENTH EDITION.' instead of 'The SIXTH EDITION.';

and changes in colophon 'Printed for JAMES HODGES, near *London-Bridge*; and | J. and J. RIVINGTON, in *St. Paul's Church-Yard.* | [short rule] | M.DCC.LIV.'

Collation: Same as 1746 edition, except A⁸ (–A2).

Notes: As in 1746 edition, page 1 is paged [I]. LETTERS XXVI–XXXII are misnumbered XXV–XXXI. As in fifth and 1746 editions, long rules separate letters in this volume. Title page of Vol. I is printed on [A]1; title page of Vol. II is printed on A2 (in the Cornell copy, a thin slice of the cut A2 leaf protrudes from the binding). Vols. I and II of this edition were published with the 'fifth edition' of Vols. III and IV. Bibliographical descriptions of Vols. III and IV appear in *Pamela in Her Exalted Condition*.

Contents: Same as 1746 edition.

Running heads: Same as 1746 edition.

Press figures: I183-7; M263-7; N287-7

Catchword variants: Same as 1746 edition, except p. 131 *Dear*, (*Dear*) and 268 every- (every-body); and corrections to p. 114 It (It); 124 abject (abject); and 219 Well, (Well,)

Ornaments: Maslen R067, R457, A3ʳ; Maslen R388, A4ᵛ; Maslen R183, A5ʳ; Maslen R223, A6ᵛ; Maslen R316, A8ᵛ; Maslen R069, R479, a1ʳ; Maslen R272, a11ᵛ; Maslen R180, a12ʳ; Maslen R353, a12ᵛ; Maslen R067, R473, B1ʳ; Maslen R273, O4ᵛ

Volume II

Title page: Same as 1746 edition, except 'The SEVENTH EDITION.' instead of 'The SIXTH EDITION.'; colophon same as Vol. I, except '*Church Yard.*' instead of '*Church-Yard.*'

Collation: Same as 1746 edition, except [A]1 (= A2 of Vol. II).

Notes: Page 1 not paged, as in all prior duodecimo editions except 1746.

Contents: Same as 1746 edition.

Running heads: Same as 1746 edition.

Press figures: C46-6; F106-7; H166-7

Catchword variants: Same as 1746, except p. 88 Thought (Thoughts) and 257 Her (Here); and corrections to p. 45 'Safety ('Safety); 309 Form; (Form;), 336 you, (you,); 358 us, (us,); and 369 me: (me:)

Ornaments: Maslen R313, [A]1ʳ; Maslen R069, R473, B1ʳ

Copy: Cornell University Library (Rare) PR3664 .P2 1754 v 1–2

ESTC: N37980

8   EIGHTH EDITION, 1762
[PUBLISHED 28 OCTOBER 1761], 4 VOLS., 12°

Volume I

Title page: Same as seventh edition, except '*PAMELA*,' instead of '*PAMELA*;'; 'PUBLISHED,' instead of 'Now first Published,'; 'A NARRATIVE which has its Foundation in TRUTH; | and at the same time that it agreeably entertains, by a Variety | of *curious* and *affecting* INCIDENTS, is entirely divested of all | those Images, which in too many Pieces calculated for Amuse- | ment only, tend to *inflame* the Minds they should *instruct*.'; 'The EIGHTH EDITION.' instead of 'The SEVENTH EDITION.'; and changes in colophon '[long double rule] | *LONDON:* | Printed for HENRY WOODFALL, JOHN RIVINGTON, | WILLIAM JOHNSTON, JOSEPH RICHARDSON, and | STANLEY CROWDER and C°. | [short rule] | M.DCC.LXII.'

Collation: 12° A⁴ a¹² B–N¹² O⁴ = 164 leaves; $1–6 (–A3, 4, O3, 4); $1 (–a1) includes signature title 'VOL. I.'

Notes: In this edition, the introduction, printed on twelve leaves in previous duodecimo editions, is reduced by two leaves. As a result, the letter addressed '*To my worthy Friend the Editor of* PAMELA.' moves from signature A to the first two leaves of signature a. LETTERS XXVI–XXXII are misnumbered XXV–XXXI. The long rules separating letters in the fifth, sixth (duodecimo), and seventh editions are omitted. Page 122 is misnumbered 722; p. 127 is misnumbered 121. Vols. I and II of this edition were published with the 'eighth edition' of Vols. III and IV; there is no 'sixth' or 'seventh' edition of the continuation. Bibliographical descriptions of Vols. III and IV appear in *Pamela in Her Exalted Condition*.

Contents: [i] Title; [ii] blank; [iii]–iv preface; vi–xii letters to the editor; xiii–xxx introduction; xxxi–xxxii verses; [1]–296 Text; 296 *The END of* VOL. I.

Running heads: Same as seventh edition.

Press figures: aх-10; B14-2; C47-2; D70-2; E88-4; F110-4; G130-4; H157-4; I189-5; L239-5; N287-3

Catchword variants: p. xii INTRO- (INTRODUCTION); xxi cause (cause,); xxx VERSES (VERSES); 6 LET- (LETTER); 7 LET- (LETTER); 10 LET- (LETTER); 15 LET- (LETTER); 23 LET- (LETTER); 39 LET- (LETTER); 42 LET- (LETTER); 43 them- (themselves); 53 LET- (LETTER); 57 LET- (LETTER); 58 them- (themselves); 73 with- (without); 74 In- (Instantly); 80 LET- (LETTER); 85 Sauce- (Sauce-box); 87 con- (continued); 101 Yester- (Yesterday); 128 and- (and-then); 138 faith- (faithfully); 170 *FRI- (FRIDAY)*; 185 ano- (another); 186 bring- (bringing); 191 *Mrs.* ('*Mrs.*); 200 Witch- (Witchcraft); 212 *MON- (MONDAY)*; 215 after- (afterwards); 224 *THURS- (THURSDAY)*; 234 Witch- (Witchcrafts); 238 *MON- (MONDAY)*; 250 *there- (therefore)*; 255 tho' (though); 260 may- (may-be); 263 *SUN- (SUNDAY)*; 276 any- (any-thing); 283 *WEDNES- (WEDNESDAY)*; 284 good- (good-lack)

Ornaments: Maslen R051, R485, A2^r; Maslen R312, A3^r; Maslen R169, A3^v; Maslen R180, a1^r; Maslen R148, R481, a3^r; Maslen R180, a12^r; Maslen R381, a12^v; Maslen R049, R439, B1^r; Maslen R273, O4^v

Volume II

Title page: Same as seventh edition, except 'PUBLISHED,' instead of 'Now first Published,'; 'In order to cultivate the Principles of VIRTUE | and RELIGION in the Minds of the YOUTH | of BOTH SEXES.'; 'The EIGHTH EDITION.' instead of 'The SEVENTH EDITION.'; colophon same as Vol. I, except 'CROWDER and Co.' instead of 'CROWDER and C°.'

Collation: 12° [A]1 B–R^{12} S^6 (–S6) = 198 leaves; $1–6 (–S4, 5); $1 includes signature title 'VOL. II.'

Notes: Title page probably printed on S6; in previous duodecimo editions title page of Vol. II was apparently printed on leaf of signature A of Vol. I. This volume is one leaf shorter than the second volume of previous duodecimo editions because it omits paragraphs detailing the future lives of the novel's principal characters (which are depicted in volumes 3 and 4). This is the only duodecimo edition that is presented as a continuous four-volume set (in previous duodecimo editions the last page of Vol. II ends with '*FINIS.*'. o is missing in pagination of p. 80.

Contents: [i] Title; [ii] blank; [1]–394 Text; 394 END *of* VOL. II.

Running heads: Same as seventh edition, except '*PAMELA*; Or,' (p. 394)

Press figures: B4-5; C45-5; D63-4; E85-3; F106-5; G130-3; H157-3; I190-6; K214-5; L229-5; M261-3; N286-4; O301-4; P335-3; Q360-4; R370-5; S386-4

Catchword variants: p. 6 Adven- (Adventure); 11 *SATUR- (SATURDAY)*; 20 some- (sometimes); 23 'any- ('any-thing); 39 'Justifi- ('Justification); 52 'Dis- ('Disgrace); 55 *And* (*And,*); 57 him, (him); 61 con- (convinced); 79 *THURS- (THURSDAY)*; 158 I can- (I cannot); 181 *Abra- (Abraham)*; 182 I can- (I cannot); 197 'you ('you,); 199 Sur- (Surname); 215 unpro- (unprovided); 226 Crea- (Creature); 249 Con- (Confess); 278 stop- (stopping); 306 a Per- (a Person); 321 Elope- (Elopements); 329 Senti- (Sentiments); 346 Good- (Goodness); 349 *SUN- (SUNDAY)*; 384 discom- (discomposing)

Ornaments: Maslen R313, [A]1ʳ; Maslen R049, R451, B1ʳ

Copy: Cornell University Library (Rare) PR3664 .P2 1762 v 1–2

ESTC: N26227

9   'FOURTEENTH' EDITION, 1801
[PUBLISHED MARCH 1801], 4 VOLS., 12°

Volume I

Title page: PAMELA; | OR, | VIRTUE REWARDED. | IN A | SERIES OF LETTERS | FROM A BEAUTIFUL | YOUNG DAMSEL TO HER PARENTS: | AND AFTERWARDS | *IN HER EXALTED CONDITION,* | BETWEEN | HER, AND PERSONS OF FIGURE AND QUALITY, | UPON THE | MOST IMPORTANT AND ENTERTAINING | SUBJECTS, IN GENTEEL LIFE. | [short rule] | IN FOUR VOLUMES. | VOL. I. | [long double rule] | PUBLISHED IN ORDER TO CULTIVATE THE PRINCI- PLES | OF VIRTUE AND RELIGION IN THE MINDS OF THE | YOUTH OF BOTH SEXES. | [long double rule] | A NEW EDITION, BEING THE FOURTEENTH, | WITH NUMEROUS CORRECTIONS AND ALTER- ATIONS. | [short rule] | London: | Printed for J. Johnson, G. G. and J. Robinson, R. Baldwin, | W. J. and J. Richardson, F. and C. Rivington, Ogilvy and | Son, Otridge and Son, P. Macqueen, J. Nunn, W. Lane, | G. Wilkie, Vernor and Hood, Lackington, Allen, and Co. | Cadell and Davies, C. Law, Longman and Rees, T. Hurst, | and J. Wallis. | [short rule] | 1801.

Collation: 12° a⁶ B–O¹² P⁶ = 168 leaves; $1–6 (–a4, 5, 6, P4, 5, 6); $1 includes signature title 'VOL. I.'; P6ʳ has signature line '*Printed by G. Woodfall, No. 22, Paternoster-row, London.*'

Notes: Page 279 is misnumbered 297.

Contents: [i] Title; [ii] ENTERED AT STATIONERS' HALL. | PRINTED BY G. WOODFALL, NO. 22, PATERNOSTER-ROW.; [iii] *ADVERTISE-MENT* | TO THE | FOURTEENTH EDITION. | [rule] |; [iv]–v preface, with caption title [iv] PREFACE | BY | *THE EDITOR.* | [short double rule]; vi–xii CONTENTS.; [1]–323 Text, with caption title [1] PAMELA; | OR, | VIRTUE REWARDED. | [short double rule] | IN A SERIES OF FAMILIAR LETTERS. | VOL. I. | [double rule]; 323 THE END OF VOL. I.; [324] blank.

Running heads: PREFACE BY THE EDITOR.; CONTENTS.; PAMELA; | OR, VIRTUE REWARDED. ('PAMELA.' pp. 112, 114)

Press figures: avii-5; B13-5; B14-4; C34-4; C45-5; D69-I; D71-5; E82-3; F104-3; F106-I; G142-5; G144-4; H167-5; I190-3; I192-4; K202-3; L230-4; L240-5; M244-5; M262-4; N286-4; O310-4; P319-5

Catchword variants: p. 8 LET- (LETTER); 11 LET- (LETTER); 15 LET- (LETTER); 23 stra- (stratagem); 25 sub- (subtle); 33 com- (compelling); 36 LET- (LETTER); 37 *om.*; 66 Im- (Impertinence); 68 LET- (LETTER); 74 LET- (LETTER); 101 ment. (ment,); 108 *om.*; 136 Never- (Nevertheless); 152 'No- ('Nothing); 162 THURS- (THURSDAY); 163 Hey- (Hey-day!); 196 doubt- (doubtful); 213 're- ('receiv'd); 216 'dis- ('dishonour); 240 sham- (sham-marriage); 246 By- (By-the-way); 252 my (soul); 277 com- (compliance); 279 [misnumbered 297] WED-(WEDNESDAY); 283 WED- (WEDNESDAY)

Volume II

Title page: Same as Vol. I, except 'VOL. II.' instead of 'VOL. I.'

Collation: 12° [A]1 b² B–O¹² P³ = 162 leaves; $1–6 (–b2, P3; C9 missigned C3); $1 includes signature title 'VOL. II.'; P3ʳ has signature line, below long rule, '*Printed by G. Woodfall, No. 22, Paternoster-row, London.*'

Contents: [i] Title; [ii] ENTERED AT STATIONERS' HALL. | PRINTED BY G. WOODFALL, NO. 22, PATERNOSTER-ROW.; iii–v CONTENTS.; [vi] blank; [1]–317 Text, with caption title [1] PAMELA; | OR, | VIRTUE REWARDED. | [short double rule] | VOL. II. | THE JOURNAL CONTINUED. | [short double rule] |; 317 THE END OF VOL. II.; [318] blank.

Running heads: CONTENTS.; PAMELA; | OR, VIRTUE REWARDED.

Press figures: biv-I; B16-5; C26-4; D64-4; D70-5; E85-I; E87-5; F110-I; G141-3; G142-5; G146-I; H168-4; I182-5; K214-4; L229-5; L234-3; M254-3; M256-5; N274-5; N288-3; O303-I

Catchword variants: p. 11 Mon- (Monday); 12 Bran- (Brandon); 15 *om.*; 21 *om.*; 68 I re- (I referred); 91 con- (consisting); 95 WHEN (I. WHEN); 101 *om.*; 102 I an- (I answered); 105 Mon- (Monday); 115 Wed- (Wednesday); 123 Thurs- (Thursday); 154 *om.*; 183 *MY* (*My*); 224 men- (men-servants); 276 hall- (hall-door)

Copy: Princeton University Library (Ex) PR3664 .P35 1801 v 1–2

10   'FIFTEENTH' EDITION, 1810
[PUBLICATION DATE NOT FOUND], 4 VOLS., 12°

Volume I

Title page: Same as 1801 edition, except '*IN HER EXALTED CONDITION* | BETWEEN | HER AND PERSONS OF FIGURE AND QUALITY, | UPON THE | MOST IMPORTANT AND ENTERTAINING | SUBJECTS IN GENTEEL LIFE. | [short rule] | IN FOUR VOLUMES. | VOL. I. | [long double rule] | PUBLISHED IN ORDER TO CULTIVATE THE PRIN-CIPLES OF VIRTUE | AND RELIGION IN THE MINDS OF THE | YOUTH OF BOTH SEXES. | [long double rule] | A NEW EDITION, BEING THE FIFTEENTH, | WITH NUMEROUS CORRECTIONS AND ALTERATIONS. | [short rule] | *LONDON:* | Printed for F. C. and J. Rivington, W. Otrige and Son, | W. Lowndes, Wilkie and Robinson, J. Nunn, J. Walker, | Lackington, Allen and Co. C. Law, Longman, Hurst, | Rees, and Orme, Cadell and Davies, B. Crosby and Co. | J. Richardson, J. M. Richardson, R. Scholey, and New- | man and Co. | [short rule] | 1810.

Collation: 12° [A]⁴ B–Z⁶ Aa–Cc⁶ Dd–Ee⁴ = 162 leaves; $1–3 (–Dd3, Ee2, Ee3); $1 includes signature title 'VOL. I.' (–C1, D1, F1, G1, I1, K1, M1, N1, P1, Q1, S1, T1, X1, Y1, Aa1, Bb1, Dd1); Dd4ᵛ has signature line '[rule] | G. Woodfall, Printer, Paternoster-row, | London.'

Contents: [i] Title; [ii] ENTERED AT STATIONERS' HALL. | PRINTED BY G. WOODFALL, NO. 22, PATERNOSTER-ROW, LONDON.; [iii] *ADVERTISEMENT* | TO THE | FOURTEENTH EDITION. | [short double rule]; [iv] blank; [v]–[vii] preface, with caption title [v] PREFACE | BY | *THE EDITOR.* | [short double rule] |; [viii] blank; [1]–308 Text, with caption title [1] PAMELA; | OR, | VIRTUE REWARDED. | [short double rule]; 308 THE END OF VOL. I.; [309]–[316] CONTENTS.

Running heads: PREFACE BY THE EDITOR.; PAMELA; | OR, VIRTUE REWARDED.; PAMELA. (p. 308); CONTENTS.

Press figures: B12-6; G67-7; K107-7; N144-7; Q170-7; R191-6; S199-7; U223-7; X238-6; Bb278-6; Bb282-7; Cc290-2; Dd305-4

Catchword variants: No catchwords in this volume.

Volume II

Title page: Same as Vol. I, except '*IN HER EXALTED CONDITION*,' and 'VOL. II.' instead of 'VOL. I.'

Collation: 12° [A]¹ B–Z⁶ Aa–Cc⁶ Dd–Ee² = 155 leaves; $1–3 (–Dd2, Ee2; T3 missigned 3); $1 includes signature title 'VOL. II.' (–C1, D1, F1, G1, I1, K1, M1, N1, P1, Q1, S1, T1, X1, Y1, Aa1, Bb1, Dd1); Dd2ᵛ has signature line "[rule] | G. Woodfall, Printer, | Paternoster-row, London.'

Contents: [i] Title; [ii] ENTERED AT STATIONERS' HALL. | PRINTED BY G. WOODFALL, NO. 22, PATERNOSTER-ROW, LONDON.; [1]–304 Text, with caption title [1] PAMELA; | OR, | VIRTUE REWARDED. | [short double rule] | THE JOURNAL CONTINUED. | [short double rule]; 304 THE END OF VOL. II.; [305]–[308] CONTENTS.

Running heads: PAMELA; | OR, VIRTUE REWARDED.; PAMELA. (p. 304); CONTENTS.

Press figures: C16-6; G62-7; I86-7; L114-2; P163-2; P164-7; T206-2; U228-6; Z254-6; Cc290-6; Cc300-7

Catchword variants: No catchwords in this volume.

Copy: Princeton University Library (Ex) 2008–0045N v. 1–2

EXPLANATORY NOTES

Page 3

1 *the Parental, the Filial, and the Social Duties*: Richardson here places *Pamela* within a tradition of works dealing with proper Christian conduct, particularly as it pertains to the individual's obligations within his or her familial and social circles. The most popular of these works was *The Whole Duty of Man*, which, along with the Bible and the Book of Common Prayer, Pamela later recommends be given to a farmer's family (see p. 437 and note below). Richardson was probably also acquainted with William Fleetwood's *The Relative Duties of Parents and Children, Husbands and Wives, Masters and Servants* (1705). The fourth edition of this work had been published in 1732 by a group of booksellers that included John Osborn and Charles Rivington. Both *The Whole Duty* and *The Relative Duties* have on their title pages the phrase, 'Necessary for all Families', a variant of which ('Necessary to be had in all Families') appears on the title page of *Shamela*. Richardson printed Patrick Delany's *Fifteen Sermons upon Social Duties* for John Rivington, Charles's son, in 1744 (Maslen, p. 78, item 217). Richardson's purpose in *Pamela* is thus similar to that enunciated in the preface to *Familiar Letters*: 'The Writer [who] is no Friend to long Prefaces... has endeavour'd... to inculcate Principles of *Virtue* and *Benevolence*; to describe *properly*, and recommend *strongly*, the SOCIAL and RELATIVE DUTIES...' (*EW*, p. 324). Cf. *Clarissa*: 'in all the *relative*, in all the *social* and, what is still beyond both, in all our *superior* duties' (I, p. 181); and *SCG*: 'a man cannot be defective in *any* of the social duties' (II, p. 318).

2 *sensible Reader*. A reader possessing not only sensibility, and thus capable of sympathetic identification with the feelings of others, but also good sense, intelligence, and judgment. This kind of appeal was a commonplace of the period. See, for example, Eliza Haywood, *The Injur'd Husband* (1722): 'But setting aside these Reflections, which the sensible Reader need not be put in mind of...' (*Secret Histories, Novels, and Poems*, 3rd edn (1732), II, p. 238); and Colley Cibber, *An Apology for the Life of Colley Cibber* (1740): 'If these Facts seem too trivial for the Attention of a sensible Reader, let it be consider'd, that they are not chosen Fictions, to *entertain*, but Truths necessary to *inform* him...' (p. 197). Henry Fielding appeals to the 'sensible Reader' in the prefaces to both *Joseph Andrews* and *Tom Jones*, as well as in the concluding paragraph of the opening chapter of Book XII in *Amelia*.

Page 5

1 *That it will appear from several Things . . . intended by the Publication*: On the origins of the story, see General Introduction, pp. xxxii–xxxv.

2 *a neighbouring Nation*: France.

3 *J.B.D.F.*: Jean Baptiste de Freval was a French writer and translator then working in London. For his relations with Richardson, see General Introduction, pp. xlix–l. The original version of this letter is in FM XVI, 1, fol. 13.

Page 7

1 *Magazine*: Repository, storehouse.

2 *Whip-syllabub*: Whipped syllabub, a sweetened drink made of milk or cream, beaten into a froth. In a figurative sense, an unsubstantial piece of writing; the *OED* cites this passage as illustration. Cf. *Clarissa*: 'I read to her [Clarissa] such parts of your letters as I *could* read to her; and I thought it was a good test to distinguish the froth and whipt-syllabub in them from the cream, in what one *could* and *could* not read to a woman of so fine a mind . . .' (Belford to Lovelace, VII, p. 117).

Page 8

1 *Your affectionate Friend, &c.*: Probably the Reverend William Webster (1689–1758), editor of *The Weekly Miscellany*, in which this letter, with minor variants, had been originally published on 11 October 1740. On Richardson and Webster, see General Introduction, pp. xlix–l.

Page 9

1 *cast Accompts*: To sum up or reckon accounts.

2 *Paper so blotted*: Cf. *Pamela 2*, in which the former Sally Godfrey, writing from Jamaica, asks Pamela to 'let my Tears in these Blots speak the rest' (IV, p. 287). In *Clarissa*, Mrs. Harlowe's 'open slip of paper' to her daughter is 'blister'd with a mother's tear' (II, p. 46); later in the novel, asserting that she is 'but a cypher', Clarissa laments that 'these griefs . . . will sometimes burst into tears; and these mingling with my ink, will blot my paper' (IV, p. 2). In *SCG*, Harriet Byron apologizes to Mrs. Selby for 'this great blot—Forgive it—It *would* fall—My pen found it, before I saw it' (II, p. 25); later on, writing to Lucy, Mrs. Selby's niece, Harriet once again cannot control her emotions: 'Fie upon it!—Why this involuntary tear? You will see it by the large blot it has made, if I did not mention it' (III, p. 218). Women are not alone in providing such visual evidence of deep feeling. Having just copied Clarissa's moving fragments and letter after the rape, Lovelace remarks to Belford, 'the paper, thoul't see, is blister'd with the tears even of the harden'd transcriber' (V, p. 244).

3 *Clog*: Burden or encumbrance.

4 *Linen*: Articles of clothing made of this fabric but in this instance, given Mr. B.'s phrasing ('my Linen'), probably a reference to his undergarments, such as his shirts; Pamela makes this distinction below (p. 20). In *A Present for a Servant Maid: or, the Sure Means of Gaining Love and Esteem* (1743), Eliza Haywood offers detailed 'Directions how to manage Linnen for the Wash' (pp. 72–5).

Page 10

1 *Mourning*: Clothes (usually black) worn by mourners or, as Johnson defines it, 'the dress of sorrow'.

2 *Four golden Guineas*: Minted in 1663 for use in the Africa trade, these gold pieces were originally worth 20 shillings (the equivalent of an English pound); their value fluctuated according to market conditions and speculation until the guinea was fixed at 21 shillings in 1717.

Page 15

1 *Four Holland ones*: Holland was a linen fabric, so called because originally made in the province of Holland in the Netherlands; cambric was a kind of fine linen, originally made at Cambrai in France, or an imitation made of hard-spun cotton yarn. Shifts were women's undergarments or chemises made of linen, cotton, or similar fabric. Handkerchiefs were squares of linen, silk, or other fabric for wiping the face, nose, and eyes; they could also be worn as kerchiefs about the neck or to cover the head.

Page 16

1 *Mort*: A great quantity or number.

2 *Closet*: A small room used for privacy or retirement.

3 *fine Flanders lac'd Headcloths*: Headdresses or caps edged with Flanders lace. Topknots were bows of ribbons worn by ladies on the top of their heads.

Page 20

1 *flowering*: Embellishing or adorning with flowers or floral design. The *OED* cites this passage as illustration.

Page 21

1 *stand in your own Light*: Proverbial (Tilley, L276; *ODEP*, s.v. 'light').

2 *Earnest*: Sum of money paid, as an initial instalment, to secure a bargain or contract.

Page 22

1 *my grey Russet*: Rustic dress made of coarse reddish brown or (in this case) grey homespun woollen cloth.

Page 24

1 *Toilet*: Dressing-table.

Page 26

1 *Baggage*: 'A worthless woman . . . so called, because such women follow [military] camps' (Johnson). See p. 226 and note below.

2 *Gypsey*: A contemptuous term for a woman, as being cunning or deceitful.

Page 29

1 *Angels . . . defend me*: Pamela's adaptation of Hamlet's startled words upon seeing his father's ghost for the first time: 'Angels and ministers of grace defend us!' (*Hamlet*, I.iv.39). The line is accurately quoted by Clementina during her 'mad scene' in *SCG*

(III, p. 118). The line is cited in *The Spectator*, no. 44 (Friday, 20 April 1711), a possible source for Richardson other than the play itself. As far as I have been able to determine, this is the first citation of it in a novel. For later citations, see, for example, Laurence Sterne, *The Life and Opinions of Tristram Shandy, Gentleman* (1759–67), ed. Melvyn New (Gainesville: University Presses of Florida, 1978), pp. 176, 230; and Tobias Smollett, *The Life and Adventures of Sir Launcelot Greaves* (1762), ed. Robert Folkenflik and Barbara Laning Fitzpatrick (Athens, GA, and London: The University of Georgia Press, 2002), p. 142.

2 *Lucretia*: Virtuous wife of Lucius Tarquinius Collatinus, a Roman nobleman. After her brutal rape by Sextus Tarquinius, son of Lucius Tarquinius Superbus, she urged her family to seek revenge and stabbed herself to death. Lucius Junius Brutus then led a rebellion that toppled the Tarquins from power and established the Roman republic in 509 BC. Exemplifying admirable resistance to tyranny, Lucretia's story appeared in Livy's history of Rome and Ovid's *Fasti*, and was often retold in the Renaissance, for instance in Shakespeare's *The Rape of Lucrece* (1594). In the early eighteenth century, it was usually included in compilations of lives of worthy women such as *Female Excellency: or, the Ladies Glory*, attributed to Robert Burton, and *The Female Orators: or, the Courage and Constancy of divers Famous Queens and Illustrious Women*, 'English'd from the French Edition of Monsieur [actually Madame] De Scudery'. Third editions of both of these works were published in 1728 by Arthur Bettesworth, one of the booksellers for whom Richardson printed. For references to Lucretia in *Clarissa*, see, for example, IV, p. 267; V, pp. 242 and 252; and VII, p. 338.

3 *a pretty Story in Romance*: Mr. B.'s words echo those of Captain Clerimont in one of his asides to Biddy Tipkin during the 'Painter Scene' in Sir Richard Steele's *The Tender Husband: or, The Accomplish'd Fools* (1705): 'and, Madam, tho' our Amours can't furnish out a Romance, they'll make a very pretty Novel' (*The Plays of Richard Steele*, ed. Shirley Strum Kenny (Oxford: Clarendon Press, 1971), IV.ii.210–11). Mr. B. alludes to this passage again on p. 215. *The Tender Husband* is one of the plays Mr. and Mrs. B. attend in London in the sequel. At the request of Lady Davers, Pamela records her thoughts on the performance; while her review is mixed, she commends the 'Painter's Scene' as 'entertaining' (*Pamela 2*, IV, p. 107). *The Tender Husband* seems to have made an impression on Richardson, with references to it also appearing in *Clarissa* (e.g., III, p. 197 and VII, p. 340) and *SCG* (e.g., III, p. 222 and V, p. 388).

4 *stretch'd out at my Length*: The anonymous author of *Pamela Censured* (1741) observed that 'the Idea of peeping thro' a Key-hole to see a fine Woman extended on a Floor in a Posture that must naturally excite Passions of Desire, may indeed be read by one in his *grand Climacteric* without ever wishing to see one in the same situation, but the Editor of *Pamela* directs himself to the *Youth* of both Sexes' (p. 31). In the fifth edition, Pamela falls on her face – Richardson, Eaves and Kimpel quip, 'was presumably innocent of perversions' (p. 129) – but reassumes her original posture in the 1801 edition.

Page 30

1 *Smelling-bottle*: A vial or bottle containing smelling salts.

2 *Chariot and Four*: A light four-wheeled carriage with only back seats, drawn by four horses.

Page 31

1 *unjust Judge*: As Keymer notes (p. 527), perhaps a reference to the 'unjust Judge' in Luke 18:6, who 'feared not God, neither regarded man' (Luke 18:2).

2 *Passing-bell*: 'The bell which rings at the hour of departure, to obtain prayers for the passing soul: often used for the bell which rings immediately after death' (Johnson).

Page 34

1 *Staff... Comfort too*: See Psalms 23:4: 'Yea, though I walk through the valley of the shadow of death, I will fear no evil: for thou art with me; thy rod and thy staff they comfort me.'

Page 35

1 *against*: By the time that.

Page 37

1 *Coach*: A large carriage, with facing seats.

Page 40

1 *Power*: A large quantity or amount.

2 *Foolatum*: Humorous form of fool. The *OED* cites this passage as illustration.

Page 41

1 *Linsey-woolsey*: A coarse textile fabric, woven from a mixture of wool and flax.

Page 42

1 *Calicoe*: 'An Indian stuff made of cotton, sometimes stained with gay and beautiful colours' (Johnson). Robings and facings were trimming materials.

2 *Camlet*: 'A kind of stuff originally made by a mixture of silk and camel's hair; it is now made with wool and silk' (Johnson).

3 *Swan-skin*: Fine thick kind of flannel. The *OED* cites this passage as illustration.

4 *Scots Cloth*: A cheap textile fabric resembling fine linen; also known as Scotch cloth.

5 *round-ear'd Caps*: Caps or coifs curved around the ears. The *OED* cites this passage as the first example of this usage. The second example, from *Joseph Andrews*, refers to Fanny who, on the day she weds Joseph, wears 'one of her own short round-ear'd Caps'. Fanny is also wearing a shift, 'which *Pamela* presented her', as well as 'a Pair of fine white Thread Stockings', another present from Pamela, but these 'were all she would accept' (*Joseph Andrews*, p. 342).

6 *white Clocks*: Ornamental patterns embroidered or knitted in silk threads on the sides of stockings.

Page 46

1 *Wafers*: Small discs of gelatine or of flour mixed with gum and colouring matter, used for sealing letters or attaching papers.

2 *tro'*: Short for 'I trow' or 'trow you' and probably meaning 'I suppose' or 'do you suppose?' The *OED* cites this passage as illustration.

Page 48

1 *owe themselves a Spight*: Do themselves an injury.

Page 49

1 *Clacks*: Tongues (in a contemptuous sense); the *OED* cites this passage as illustration. Johnson defines 'clack' as 'any thing that makes a lasting and importunate noise; generally used, in contempt, for the tongue'.

Page 50

1 *out of Door*: Amnon, son of David, fell in love with his sister, Tamar. In spite of her pleas, he, 'being stronger than she, forced her, and lay with her. Then Amnon hated her exceedingly; so that the hatred wherewith he hated her *was* greater than the love wherewith he had loved her. And Amnon said unto her, Arise, be gone' (2 Samuel 13:14–15).

Page 51

1 *Muslin Tucker*: A piece or frill of lace, worn within or around the top of the bodice.

Page 53

1 *Bite*: 'A cheat; a trick; a fraud; in low and vulgar language' (Johnson).

2 *nor forbear her*: Mr. B.'s 'Strange Words' are actually derived from the Stoic philosopher Epictetus. See, for example, 'The Life of Epictetus, From *Monsieur* Boilieau' in George Stanhope, *Epictetus His Morals, with Simplicius His Comments*, 4th edn (1721), p. xv: '*Epictetus* made all Philosophy to consist in Continence and Patience, for which reason he had always those two words in his Mouth, *Bear and Forbear:* Words, which in *Greek* have a peculiar Elegance, there being but the difference of a single Letter between them.' Richardson quotes the phrase in *Familiar Letters* (1741), Letter XLIX, 'To a Brother too captious to bear himself the Ridicule he practises upon others': 'The Philosopher says, That to *Bear* and *Forbear*, are the highest Points of Wisdom' (*EW*, p. 378). It also appears in *Pamela 2* (III, p. 207) and *Clarissa* (VII, p. 368).

Page 54

1 *Justice of Peace*: An inferior magistrate appointed to preserve the peace in a county, town, or other district. If persuaded of their guilt, he would commit persons accused of major crimes to stand trial before a judge and jury; he could also summarily convict offenders accused of minor infractions. In the country, these judicial duties were performed by owners of large estates such as Mr. B.

Page 56

1 *Peace against him*: Because acting under the authority of the local justice of the peace, a petty constable or headborough (parish officer) would be powerless to assist Pamela in her legal complaint against Mr. B.

Page 57

1 *Confederations*: Johnson defines 'confederation' as 'League; compact of mutual support; alliance', with one of his illustrative examples – drawn from *Eikon Basilike* (1649), a work purportedly written by King Charles I and published a few days after his

execution – pointing to another, older sense of the word (also noted in the *OED*) as 'conspiracy': 'Nor can those confederations or designs be durable, when subjects make bankrupt of their allegiance.' Mrs. Jervis might, therefore, be using the word as a synonym for Pamela's 'Designs' earlier in their conversation. Cf. Pamela's later question to Mrs. Jewkes: 'are you afraid I should confederate with them [the other servants] to commit a Robbery upon my Master?' (p. 116); and Mr. B.'s comments to Pamela: 'And, in this Suspense, I suppose, some of your Confederates, *Pamela*, (for we have been a Couple of Plotters, tho' your Virtue and Merit have engag'd you faithful Friends and Partisans, which my Money and Promises could hardly do) one way or other got Knowledge of it . . .' (p. 249). Finding herself in a situation similar to Pamela's, Clarissa laments to Anna Howe, 'for he [Clarissa's brother] has found means to confederate all the family against me' (I, p. 85), adding, in a later letter to the same correspondent, a complaint against 'those who take so much pains to confederate every one against me' (I, p. 163). As usual with Clarissa, she seems to be alluding to a biblical passage (a passage also cited by Johnson, to illustrate the adjective 'confederate') – 'For they have consulted together with one consent: they are confederate against thee' (Psalms 83:5) – which captures the double sense of the word, as both 'alliance' and 'conspiracy'. 'Confederations' was changed to 'Considerations' in the second edition, a reading retained in all subsequent lifetime editions as well as in 1801 and 1810.

Page 58

1 *Morning Gown*: 'A loose gown worn before one is fully dressed' (Johnson). Pamela is wearing slippers or very loose shoes (hence 'slip-shod').

Page 62

1 *God's Grace is not confin'd to Space*: Pamela is echoing the proverb, 'In space comes grace' (Tilley, S697–8; *ODEP*, s.v. 'space').

Page 63

1 *Chaise*: 'A carriage of pleasure drawn by one horse' (Johnson).
2 *Birth-day Suit*: A costly dress worn at court to celebrate a royal birthday.

Page 64

1 *Ad's my Heart*: God save my heart. By mimicking the antiquated oaths of such old country folk as Mr. Longman, Mr. B. is perhaps mocking the pretensions to gentility of the rustic Pamela.

Page 65

1 *as quick another Way*: Mr. B. puns on 'quick' with child or pregnant. Alert, as usual, to such possibilities, the anonymous author of *Pamela Censured* sneered that 'here's Virtue encouraged with a Vengeance and the most obscene Idea express'd by a double Entendre, which falls little short of the coarsest Ribaldry' (p. 44). The offending passage remained in all editions issued during Richardson's lifetime; Richardson's daughters, rather than Richardson himself, were probably responsible for its removal from the 1801 edition.
2 *Lyings-in*: Childbirths.

Page 68

1 *Ads-bobbers*: God's mockers.

Page 69

1 *Elbow Chair*: 'A chair with arms to support the elbows' (Johnson).
2 *Ads-heartlikins*: God's little heart.

Page 70

1 *Cot*: Cottage.
2 *Plain-work*: 'Needlework as distinguished from embroidery' (Johnson).

Page 71

1 *Grasshopper in the Fable*: In a note to this passage in the fifth edition, Richardson refers the reader to his own revision of Sir Roger L'Estrange's translation of *Æsop's Fables*, published on 20 November 1739, ten days after he began writing the first draft of *Pamela*. 'An ANT and a GRASS-HOPPER' is fable 164 in Richardson's edition.
2 *a good Bishop . . . into the lighted Candle*: Sabor suggests that 'Pamela has probably been reading John Foxe's *Book of Martyrs* (1563), in which Thomas Bilney (who was not, however, a bishop) places his hand in a candle in preparation for his death by burning' (p. 522, n. 80). Keymer advances another possibility, also in Foxe's collection, Archbishop Thomas Cranmer's 'famous mortification, in 1556, of the hand with which he had signed a recantation' (p. 528). Pamela might also have been reading one of several compilations of Protestant martyrs' lives, distilled mostly from Foxe, issued by early eighteenth-century booksellers eager to capitalise on the renewed popularity of Foxe's book. One such compilation – Henry Bilton's *The History of the English Martyrs* (1720), published by (among others) Arthur Bettesworth and Charles Rivington (the latter one of the publishers of *Pamela*) – contains accounts of both Bilney and Cranmer. While the account of Bilney omits the anecdote of the candle, that of Archbishop Cranmer concludes with his last heroic act: 'he stretch'd out his Arm, and put his Right Hand in the Flame, which he held there so stedfast and immoveable, (saving that once with the same Hand he wip'd his Face) that all Men might see his Hand burn'd before his Body was touch'd' (p. 244). Sabor notes another possible source – also included in Bilton's book – in the story of Thomas Tomkins who, imprisoned by Bishop Bonner for his beliefs, underwent a similar ordeal: 'the Bishop finding *Tomkins* to continue as he was wont, stedfast in the Defence of his Faith, the Bishop took *Tomkins* by the Fingers, and held his Hand directly over the Flame of a Wax Candle that was burning on the Table, to try his Courage' (*The History of the English Martyrs*, pp. 101–2). While Tomkins did not burn his own finger, the details of his story also fit Pamela's recollection.
3 *Beechen Trencher*: A plate or platter made of beech wood.
4 *City Mouse . . . same Book of Fables*: Pamela is alluding to fable 11 in Richardson's edition of *Æsop's Fables*.

Page 72

1 *a little Time for reading*: In writing about Pamela's desire to find 'time for reading', Richardson might have been remembering his years as a printer's apprentice when, as he would confide to Stinstra on 2 June 1753, 'I stole from the Hours of Rest and Relaxation, my Reading Times for Improvement of my Mind.'
2 *Sash-door*: A door with a sash-window in it.

Page 73

1 *Night-gown*: 'A loose gown used for undress' (Johnson); Johnson defines 'undress' as 'a loose or negligent dress'. The *OED* records as obsolete another sense, perhaps applicable to the grander versions of this garment Pamela later wears: 'A kind of gown worn by women in the 18th cent., originally as an evening dress'. See pp. 240 and 315 below.

2 *Callimancoe*: Variant spelling of calamanco, a glossy woollen stuff from Flanders.

3 *Point of Equity and Conscience*: This phrase establishes a specific legal context for Pamela's quasi-judicial presentation of her case. As Nathan Bailey defines it in his *Universal Etymological English Dictionary*, a court of equity 'is the Court of *Chancery*, in which the Rigour of the Common Law, and the Severity of other Courts, is moderated, and where Controversies are supposed to be determined according to the exact Rules of Equity and Conscience'. According to Sale (1950, p. 148) and Maslen (p. 57, item 15), Richardson printed letters L through S of the second edition (1724) of Bailey's *Dictionary*. Pamela's questioning of her three bundles rehearses a common fairy-tale motif, whose most memorable appearance in English literature, the testing of Portia's three caskets in *The Merchant of Venice*, might have inspired Richardson's writing of this scene.

Page 75

1 *Hips and Haws*: Fruits of roses and hawthorns.

2 *Pig-nuts*: Edible tubers. Johnson defines 'pignut' as 'an earth nut' and cites as sole illustration Caliban's 'And I with my long nails will dig thee pig-nuts' (*The Tempest*, II.ii.168).

3 *Fetch*: Trick.

Page 85

1 *Body Coachman*: A coachman reserved for personal attendance or use.

Page 87

1 *sat out*: Past tense of 'set out'. Although the *OED* notes that this usage was 'frequent in inferior writers of the second half of the 18th c.', it was not necessarily considered impolite in Richardson's time. However, Richardson changed 'sat out' in the second edition to 'set out'; two other instances of 'sat out' occur below (pp. 94, 322), also changed to 'set out' in the second edition. On p. 286, Pamela uses 'sat' as past tense for 'set' ('I first sat my Foot in it'); this clause remained unchanged in the second edition but was changed to 'I first set my Foot in it' in the third. I have found no instances of this usage in *Pamela in Her Exalted Condition* and *Clarissa*, but, in the duodecimo first edition of *Grandison*, there are at least two. In Vol. IV, letter 23, Harriet writes, 'O Lucy, Sir Charles Grandison is gone! Gone indeed! He sat out at three this morning...' This reading remains unchanged in the simultaneously published octavo 'second' edition as well as the third. In Vol. VI, letter 50, Lady G. comments on Mr. Selby's inability to keep track of the 'subjects' of his conversation, so that 'before uncle Selby is aware of it, he finds himself in one (subject) that he had not in his head when he sat out'. The octavo 'second' edition reads 'when he set out', but the third edition has 'when he sat out'.

Page 92

1 *mody*: Fashionable, modish. The *OED* cites this passage as illustration.

Page 93

1 *Diet-bread*: Special bread prepared for invalids or persons under a dietetic regimen. Canary wine is a light sweet wine from the Canary Islands.

Page 94

1 *Jehu-like*: Fast or furiously, alluding to 'the driving of Jehu the son of Nimshi; for he driveth furiously' (2 Kings 9:20).

2 *Bait*: 'A refreshment on a journey' (Johnson).

Page 95

1 *laying Middle and both Ends together*: Reaching a conclusion by lining up the evidence. Cf. George Psalmanazar, *Memoirs of ****, Commonly known by the Name of George Psalmanazar, A Reputed Native of Formosa* (1764): 'The same lectures were read and expounded to all alike, and in the usual course, so that those who came not at the very beginning, had no other chance, but at the end, to put middle and both ends together...' (p. 98). The phrase seems to have been coined by Richardson; other than this use by Psalmanazar, I have found no other instances of it. Psalmanazar knew *Pamela* and Richardson well. Richardson consulted him about the continuation of the novel and, in response, Psalmanazar sent him a long letter, running to several pages in manuscript, in which the heroine describes a scene in which she and Lady Davers argue over Pamela's 'Charities'. Richardson was not impressed by Psalmanazar's attempt to write in Pamela's manner, scrawling on the margins of the letter such comments as 'Ridiculous & improbable, like the whole of it' and 'O! Mr. Psalmanazar!!!' (FM XVI, 1, fols. 27–33).

Page 96

1 *cordial Water*: A spirituous drink for restoring strength. Johnson defines 'cordial' as 'a medicine that increases the force of the heart, or quickens the circulation'.

Page 98

1 *to bait*: To break a journey to feed and rest the horses (see p. 94, n. 2 above).

Page 100

1 *If ackins*: In faith.

2 *brown nodding Horrors*: As Keymer suggests (p. 528), Pamela might be recalling Dryden's translation of Virgil's *Aeneid* (1697), VII.40–1 ('a Wood / Which thick with Shades, and a brown Horror, stood') as well as Milton's *Comus* (1634), lines 37–9 ('this drear Wood, / The nodding horror of whose shady Brows / Threats the forlorn and wand'ring Passenger'). Richardson here anticipates the ominous landscapes and lonely mansions of the Gothic novel.

3 *wip'd his Mouth*: Declared his own innocence. Cf. Proverbs 30:20: 'Such *is* the way of an adulterous woman; she eateth, and wipeth her mouth, and saith, I have done no wickedness.'

Page 101

1 *May-game*: Object of mirth or ridicule, laughing-stock.

Page 104

1 *at a Jirk*: Quickly, suddenly.

Page 105

1 *pursy*: Fat, corpulent. The *OED* cites this passage as illustration.

Page 113

1 *Argus*: In Greek mythology, Argos Panoptes ('all-seeing') was a giant with one hundred eyes set by Hera to watch over Io, who had been transformed into a cow, to thwart the amorous advances of Zeus. After Argos was lulled to sleep and (by Zeus's orders) slain by Hermes, Hera placed his one hundred eyes on the peacock's tail. A version of this story appears in the first book of Ovid's *Metamorphoses*.

Page 114

1 *Hussy*: A case for needles, thread, and other sewing implements.

Page 116

1 *Property*: As Keymer suggests (p. 528), Pamela's declaration of self-ownership might derive from Locke's *The Second Treatise of Government* (1690), paragraph 27: 'Though the Earth, and all inferior Creatures be common to all Men, yet every Man has a *Property* in his own *Person*. This no Body has any Right to but himself' (John Locke, *Two Treatises of Government*, ed. Peter Laslett, 2nd edition (Cambridge University Press, 1970), p. 305). Whereas Pamela sees her situation as servant (albeit one without wages) in Lockean, contractual terms, guaranteeing her rights as a free individual subject, Mrs. Jewkes invokes a Filmerian, paternalistic model in which the head of the family is entitled to absolute rule over all members of his household. As Locke explains, '*Master* and *Servant* are Names as old as History, but given to those of far different condition; for a Free-man makes himself a Servant to another, by selling him for a certain time, the Service he undertakes to do, in exchange for Wages he is to receive: And though this commonly puts him into the Family of his Master, and under the ordinary Discipline thereof; yet it gives the Master but a Temporary Power over him, and no greater, than what is contained in the *Contract* between 'em' (paragraph 85, p. 340). Locke summarises the limits on the power of the master of a family in the next paragraph.

2 *Jezebel*: Wicked wife of Ahab, king of Israel (see 1 Kings 16:31, 19:1–2, 21:5–25; 2 Kings 9:30–7); hence a name for an evil woman.

Page 117

1 *Settle-bench*: A long wooden bench, usually with arms and high back extending to the ground. The *OED* cites this passage as illustration.

2 *in a great Pucker*: A state of agitation. This passage is the first example of this colloquial expression cited in the *OED*.

Page 119

1 *Can*: 'A cup; generally a cup made of metal, or some other matter other than earth' (Johnson).

Page 120

1 *Horse-beans*: Coarse beans, used to feed horses and cattle.

Page 121

1 *five Ells*: About 19 feet. An English ell equalled 45 inches.

Page 123

1 *Planting, &c.*: Mrs. Jewkes is presumably using 'Planting' (i.e., 'planting men') as a vulgar expression for sexual intercourse. The expression was usually attributed to Diogenes. See, for example, Bayle's *Dictionary*: 'Diogenes embracing a woman in the middle of the streets, being asked what he did? answered... *I plant a man*' (2nd edn (1734–8), III, p. 460; note to article on Hipparchia). In *The Guardian*, no. 155 (Tuesday, 8 September 1713), Addison refers to this story, observing that '*Hipparchia*, the famous She-Cynick... arrived at such a Perfection in her Studies, that she Conversed with her Husband, or Man-planter, in broad Day-light, and in the open Streets'; Addison is using 'converse' in the double sense of talking to as well as having sexual intercourse with. In *The Spectator*, no. 203 (Tuesday, 23 October 1711), Addison condemns the 'Tribe' of seducers of 'unfortunate Females' (*Spectator*, II, p. 295) and proposes that, as punishment, these men be sent to the American colonies 'in the Phrase of *Diogenes* to *Plant Men*' (p. 297).

Page 127

1 *cunning as a Serpent*: A recollection of Jesus' words to his disciples (Matthew 10:16): 'Behold, I send you forth as sheep in the midst of wolves: be ye therefore wise as serpents, and harmless as doves.' But her reversal of clauses and pejorative 'cunning' indicate that Mrs. Jewkes might be thinking of serpents more along the lines of Genesis 3:1: 'Now the serpent was more subtil than any beast of the field which the Lord God had made.'

Page 129

1 *thus I turn'd it*: Paula R. Backscheider places Pamela's poetic effort in a long-standing tradition of paraphrasing or adapting biblical Psalms; see *Eighteenth-Century Women Poets and Their Poetry: Inventing Agency, Inventing Genre* (Baltimore: The Johns Hopkins University Press, 2005), especially pp. 132–3. On the popularity of Psalm 137, see Hannibal Hamlin, *Psalm Culture and Early Modern English Literature* (Cambridge University Press, 2004), Chapter 7, 'Psalm 137: singing the Lord's song in a strange land', pp. 218–52. A translation of Psalm 137, attributed to Sir Philip Sidney, appears at the end of the third volume (which Richardson printed) of *The Works of the Honourable Sir Philip Sidney* (1724). For a reading of Pamela's 'turning' of this Psalm, see Michael Austin, 'Lincolnshire Babylon: Competing Typologies in Pamela's 137th Psalm', *Eighteenth-Century Fiction* 12 (2000), 501–14.

2 *B——n-hall*: 'Brandon-hall' in the 1801 edition, suggesting that, by analogy with Grandison Hall where Sir Charles Grandison resides, Brandon is Mr. B.'s surname.

Page 135

1 *Consent of Twain*: As Sabor (pp. 525–6, n. 136) and Keymer (p. 529) note, this saying appears in the 'Moral' (p. 232) of a story told in Sir John Harrington's edition (1591) of Ariosto's *Orlando Furioso* (Book XXVIII), where it translates a line from Ovid: 'Non

caret effectu, quod volvere duo' (*Amores*, II.iii.6). In *Clarissa*, Lovelace reminds Belford of this same story: 'Thou remembrest the Host's tale in Ariosto. And *thy* experience, as well as *mine*, can furnish out twenty *Fiametta's* in proof of the imbecility of the sex' (V, p. 273).

Page 138

1 *Band*: A collar worn round the neck; as part of a clerical dress, a pair of strips hanging down in front.

Page 139

1 *in a sweet Pickle*: Proverbial for awkward predicament (Tilley, P276; *ODEP*, s.v. 'pickle').

2 *my Heart up at my Mouth*: Proverbial expression for being afraid, fearful (Tilley, H331; *ODEP*, s.v. 'heart').

Page 142

1 *grabbling*: Groping or feeling eagerly with his hands.

2 *Head-piece*: Head, as the seat of the intellect. The *OED* cites this passage as illustration.

Page 145

1 *Gainsborough*: A town in Lincolnshire.

Page 146

1 *meanest Slave*: As Lori Humphrey Newcomb has argued, this statement recalls, in its antithetical structure, the rhetoric of the heroine of *Dorastus and Fawnia*, the usual title given, after 1632, to the many versions of Robert Greene's popular prose romance, *Pandosto: The Triumph of Time* (1588); see *Reading Popular Romance in Modern England* (New York: Columbia University Press, 2002), especially pp. 230–40. As Newcomb suggests, Pamela's words most closely resemble those uttered by Fawnia, in response to Pandosto's offer of '*Dignities and Riches*' in exchange for her virtue, in Hugh Stanhope's *The Fortunate and Unfortunate Lovers: or, the History of the Lives, Fortunes, and Adventures of Dorastus and Fawnia, Hero and Leander* (1735): 'I have a Monarch's Soul, though the Gods have been pleased to cover it with *Plebean Clay*' (p. 47). 'Hugh Stanhope' was a pseudonym for William Bond, Aaron Hill's collaborator in *The Plain Dealer* (1724–5), a newspaper printed by Richardson; two of the publishers of *The Fortunate Lovers*, Arthur Bettesworth and Charles Hitch, were associated with Richardson. The fire scene in *Clarissa* purportedly begins, as Lovelace writes to Belford, because of 'the carelessness of Mrs. Sinclair's cook-maid, who, having sat up to read the simple history of Dorastus and Faunia, when she should have been in bed, had set fire to an old pair of callicoe window-curtains' (IV, p. 291).

Page 149

1 *Fool's Plaything*: In general terms, a toy or trinket, but the insult might also include a more pointed reference to the baton or stick, usually topped by a head with asses' ears, carried by a court jester; this particular fool's plaything was also known as a 'bauble', a word appearing in the next paragraph.

2 *Action of Debt*: At the bequest of their creditors, debtors could be arrested and imprisoned, without trial, until they discharged their debts. Henry Fielding is reputed to have written

Shamela (1741) to pay his way out of a sponging house, a place of preliminary confinement for debtors kept by a bailiff or sheriff's officer.

3 *Gewgaw*: 'A showy trifle; a toy; a bauble; a splendid plaything' (Johnson).

Page 150

1 *Colbrand*: A name probably derived from *The Famous History of Guy Earle of Warwick*, one of the popular penny romances Henry Fielding facetiously praises, in the opening chapter of *Joseph Andrews* (1742), for their 'excellent Use and Instruction, finely calculated to sow the Seeds of Virtue in Youth, and very easy to be comprehended by Persons of moderate Capacity' (p. 18). As D. C. Muecke has noted, the description of the giant Colbrond in the 1607 edition of *Guy of Warwick* as 'that same Monster of a man he found, / Treading at every step two yards of ground' might be the source of Colbrand's 'running with his long Legs, well nigh two Yards at a Stride' in *Pamela* (p. 166); see 'Beauty and Mr. B.', *Studies in English Literature* 7 (1967), 467–74 (p. 469). Colbrand is also mentioned in Shakespeare's *King John* (I.i.225) and *Henry VIII* (V.iii.22).

2 *speaking Picture*: This phrase appears in Sidney's *Defence of Poesy* (1595): 'Poesy therefore, is an Art of *imitation*; for so *Aristotle* termeth it in the word μίησις (*mimesis*), that is to say, A representing, counterfeiting, or figuring forth, to speak metaphorically. A speaking *picture* with this end, To teach and delight' (*The Works of the Honourable Sir Philip Sidney*, III, p. 10; each work in this volume is separately paginated). In his subsequent discussion of the third kind of mimetic poets, whom he calls the 'right poets', Sidney cites the representation of Lucretia, to whom Mr. B. has earlier alluded (p. 29), as illustration of their artistic achievement. As noted in the General Introduction (p. xxxix, n. 20), Richardson printed this volume of Sidney's *Works*.

3 *echo . . . fantastical Innocence*: Mr. B. here mocks the complaints of seduced and abandoned women. In the sixth book of Ovid's *Metamorphoses*, for example, after being raped by Tereus and immediately before he cuts off her tongue, Philomela promises that she will not remain silent: '*inplebo silvas et conscia saxa movebo*' (line 547). In Samuel Garth's edition – which includes translations by (among others) Addison, Dryden, Gay, and Pope – this line is rendered by Samuel Croxall as 'My mournful Voice the pitying Rocks shall move, / And my Complainings (shall) echo thro' the Grove' (4th edn (1736), I, p. 229). In Eliza Haywood's *Love in Excess* (1719), after being nearly 'ruined' by the irresistible D'Elmont, Amena bemoans her fate with 'piteous Lamentations' (*Secret Histories, Novels, and Poems*, I, p. 27).

Page 153

1 *lawless Tyranny*: By using these politically loaded words, Pamela continues her earlier Lockean argument against Mr. B.'s abuse of his authority as both master and magistrate. As Locke asserts, '*Where-ever Law ends, Tyranny begins*, if the Law be transgressed to another's harm. And whosoever in Authority exceeds the Power given him by the Law, and makes use of the Force he has under his Command, to compass that upon the Subject, which the Law allows not, ceases in that to be a Magistrate, and acting without Authority, may be opposed, as any other Man, who by force invades the Right of another' (*The Second Treatise of Government*, paragraph 202, pp. 418–19).

Page 154

1 *Bag*: 'An ornamental purse of silk tied to men's hair' (Johnson).

2 *Stamford*: A town in Lincolnshire.

3 *Bears, and Lions, and Tygers*: As Keymer notes (p. 529), Pamela here anticipates Clarissa's confused recollection, in the third of her 'mad' papers, of 'A Lady (who) took a great fancy to a young Lion, or a Bear, I forget which—But a Bear, or a Tyger, I believe, it was' (V, p. 235).

Page 155

1 *Leads*: Sheets or strips of lead used to cover a roof.

2 *a great Captain*: Unidentified, but both Alexander and Julius Caesar, in accounts by Plutarch, are credited with feats of swimming under enemy attack: 'What can be more astonishing than his Passage over the *Granicus*? *Alexander* there looks more like one possessed, than a Man of Sense and Reason... At last after infinite Hazards and through the midst of a shower of Darts, he reached the opposite Banks, where he engaged the Enemy, and obtained a signal Victory... With *Alexander*'s Passage over the *Granieus* [sic]... may be opposed that Exploit of *Cæsar*, who in the War of *Alexandria* ran a much greater Risque when he... launched... into the Sea to swim to his Ships riding at Anchor a great ways off, tho' he was exposed all the while to the Enemies Darts and Javelins' (*Plutarch's Lives... Translated from the Greek. With Notes Historical and Critical From M. Dacier* (1727), VI, pp. 218–20). Caesar's 'exploit' appears with a few more details, some of which are similar to those in Pamela's account of the 'great Captain', in Aaron Crossly's *The Signification Of most Things that are born in Heraldry* (Dublin, 1724), p. 48: '*Julius Caesar*... at the Battle of *Alexandria*, on a Bridge, being abandon'd by his People, for the Multitude of his Enemies which oppressed them; when he might no longer sustain the Shot of *Darts* and *Arrows*, he boldly leap'd into the Sea, and diving under Water, escap'd the Shot, and swam the Space of two hundred Paces to one of his Ships, drawing his Coat-Armour in his Teeth, on his Back, after him, which marvellously defended him from their *Arrows*, so as they were both preserved.'

Page 156

1 *fast*: I.e., fast asleep.

Page 157

1 *broke*: Bruised, scraped.

Page 159

1 *Highway Interrment*: An allusion to the old custom of burying the body of a suicide, with a wooden stake driven through it, at a crossroads. See Giles Jacob, *A New Law-Dictionary*: 'By Custom and Practice, the Bodies of *Felo's de se's* are buried in the Highway' (3rd edn (1736), last line of definition of 'felo de se').

Page 160

1 *This Act of Despondency... no Forgiveness*: In this dialogue with herself, Pamela is recalling traditional Christian arguments against suicide. William Fleetwood's *The Relative Duties of Parents and Children* (see p. 3, n. 1 above), for example, concludes with three sermons 'Upon the Case of SELF-MURDER' (title page). Fleetwood mentions as a possible deterrent the denial of 'Christian Burial' to suicides who, according to Church and State law, 'should be put into the Earth, and left there with a lasting Mark of Infamy... [with]

a *Stake driven through them*, which [is] not to be removed' (p. 52). However, as Fleetwood sympathetically but regretfully adds, 'these Penalties' are often not enforced because of verdicts of '*Distracted*' and the intervention of friends and relatives who, just as Pamela earlier imagines Mr. B. will do for her, spare the culprit and thus unwittingly encourage such acts of self-destruction. Both Sabor (p. 527, n. 163) and Keymer (p. 530) hear echoes of Sidney's *Arcadia* in Pamela's meditation.

Page 161

1 *carry'd away . . . by some Angel*: While sleeping between two soldiers, bound by two chains, with keepers stationed at the door, St Peter was released from prison by 'the angel of the Lord' on the same night that Herod intended to 'bring him forth to the people' for trial (Acts 12:3–11).

Page 162

1 *Out-offices*: The *OED* defines 'offices' as 'the parts of a house, or buildings attached to a house, specially devoted to household work or service, or to storage, etc.; *esp.* the kitchen and rooms connected with it, as pantry, scullery, cellars, laundry, etc.; (also) the stables, outhouses, barns, and cowsheds of a farm'.

2 *Hap*: Lot, fortune, luck.

3 *Billet*: A thick stick, meant to be used as a weapon, or a big piece of firewood.

Page 163

1 *Family Plaister*: Homemade version of a solid or semi-solid medicinal substance, usually spread on a piece of muslin or similar material, placed on a wound to close it.

2 *Spoon-meat*: Soft or liquid food, taken with a spoon, for infants or invalids.

Page 165

1 *sell his Wife*: As Keymer notes, 'though outside the law, and mainly confined to the lower classes, wife-selling was an established practice . . . as a form of ritual divorce' (p. 530). Instances of wife-selling were sometimes cited in the newspapers. See, for example, *The True Briton* (31 March 1796): 'A few days since, a steel-burner, of Sheffield, sold his wife for Sixpence, to a fellmonger of the same place. She was delivered to the purchaser with a halter around her neck, and the Clerk of the Market received four-pence for toll.—If this summary mode of transferring *conjugal* property were legalized, how greatly would the number of Divorces increase.'

Page 167

1 *Handle*: Excuse, pretext, 'that of which use is made' (Johnson).

Page 170

1 *Accusation of the Wolf*: Pamela misremembers the details of fable 29 in Richardson's edition of *Æsop's Fables*. The plaintiff is not a wolf but a dog; the defendant, a sheep, is convicted on the testimony of 'three positive Witnesses, the Wolf, the Kite, and the Vulture' (*EW*, p. 153).

2 *Reflection*: Mr. B. is alluding to a specific kind of publication containing thoughts or observations (i.e., 'reflections') on philosophical, religious, or literary topics. A 'reflection' could also follow a tale or story, to provide further elaboration on the practical lesson

(or lessons) adduced in the 'moral'. The 'reflection' following fable 29 in Richardson's edition begins by pointing out that 'no Innocence can be safe, when Power and Malice are in Confederacy against it' (*EW*, p. 154). Mr. B. is also glancing at another sense of 'reflection', as a statement or comment meant to cast aspersions on a person's character.

Page 171

1 *Secrets of all Hearts*: This phrase appears in 'The Form of Solemnization of Matrimony' in *The Book of Common Prayer* (see p. 317, n. 1 below).

Page 172

1 *Grimace*: Affectation or pretence.

Page 173

1 *as Samson was*: See Judges 16:25–7. While making sport for the amusement of the Philistines, Samson manages to take 'hold of the two middle pillars upon which the house stood', fatally bringing it down upon himself and his captors (Judges 16:29–30).

Page 177

1 *a certain great Commander*: The Roman general and consul, Manius Curius Dentatus (d. 270 BC), was legendary for his temperance and integrity as well as for having risen from humble origins to assume high public office. The story Pamela might have in mind here is told in the Life of Cato the Censor in Plutarch's *Lives*, but Richardson probably knew it in the version (adapted from Plutarch) appearing in Nathaniel Hooke's *The Roman History, from the Building of Rome to the Ruin of the Commonwealth* (1738), sold by his associates Bettesworth and Hitch: 'This *Consul* was remarkable for living, without ostentation, in that voluntary Poverty, which some Philosophers have with great vanity cried up and recommended. The *Samnite* Deputies found him sitting on a sorry wooden seat near a fire, dressing his own dinner, which consisted only of some roots; and they offered him a present of a considerable sum of Money. *Curius* expressed his indignation by a disdainful smile. "Without doubt, said he, my indigence makes you hope that you may corrupt me: But you are mistaken. I had rather be the commander of rich men, than be rich my self. Take away that metal, which men make use of only to their destruction, and go tell your nation, that they will find it as difficult to bribe me, as to conquer me"' (I, p. 566). Like Pamela, the besieged Clarissa thinks of 'the old Roman and his lentiles' (*Clarissa*, I, p. 130). I have been unable to find an account of this incident in which Dentatus eats lentils – his meagre fare usually consists of turnips, parsnips, or just plain, generic roots – but his co-consul at the time of his triumph over the Samnites was named Lentulus.

Page 179

1 *where I can command*: A possible echo (noted by Keymer, p. 531) of Shakespeare's Richard II's 'We were not born to sue, but to command' (*Richard II*, I.i.196).

Page 180

1 *Nonsuch*: A person who has no equal (i.e., to whom none can be compared).

Page 184

1 *'bating*: Except for, abating.

Page 185

1 *was a Bye-word*: Cf. Richard Sympson's remarks on his cousin Gulliver: 'the Author was so distinguished for his Veracity, that it became a sort of Proverb among his Neighbours at *Redriff*, when any one affirm'd a Thing, to say, it was as true as if Mr. *Gulliver* had spoke it' (*Gulliver's Travels* (1726), p. vi). Richardson was one of the printers of an abridgement of *Gulliver's Travels* published in 1727 (Maslen, p. 143, items 810, 811), which, however, omits 'The Publisher to the Reader' in which Sympson's remarks appear.

Page 188

1 *don't stand dilly-dallying*: Cf. Humphry's words in Steele's *The Tender Husband*: 'Why should I stand shilly-shally like a Country Bumpkin' (III.i.168–9); ''Tis certainly the foolishest thing in the World to stand shilly-shally about a Woman, when one has a Mind to marry her' (IV.ii.144–6).

2 *I talked quite wild*: For a written representation, typographically rendered, of 'wild' speech, see Clarissa's 'fragments' after her rape by Lovelace (*Clarissa*, V, pp. 234–9). After being 'pressed' and 'bruised' by the villainous Sir Hargrave Pollexfen, Harriet Byron reports to Lucy Selby that 'I talked half wildly', concluding 'my head swam; my eyes failed me; and I fainted quite away' (*SCG*, I, p. 221).

Page 193

1 *Paw of the Lion and the Bear*: See 1 Samuel 17:36–7: 'Thy servant slew both the lion and the bear: and this uncircumcised Philistine shall be as one of them, seeing he hath defied the armies of the living God. David said moreover, The LORD that delivered me out of the paw of the lion, and out of the paw of the bear, he will deliver me out of the hand of this Philistine.'

Page 196

1 *Affiance*: 'Trust in the divine promises and protection' (Johnson).

Page 202

1 *struck all of a Heap*: Paralysed; prostrated mentally; caused to collapse.

2 *saluted*: Kissed.

Page 207

1 *cramp*: Difficult to make out or understand.

Page 208

1 *Billet*: A small piece of paper; a short, informal letter.

Page 209

1 *broken*: Bankrupt.

Page 213

1 *it does not appear so in the Text*: By asking Mr. B. to adhere to the literal sense of her letters, Pamela reveals to him (or so he infers) her 'knowledge' of the central tenet of Protestant biblical exegesis. Opposing what they saw as the unwarranted proliferation of allegorical readings of Scripture typical of the Catholic exegetical tradition, Protestant

theologians stipulated that no interpretation or comment is valid unless unequivocally derived from the words on the page.

Page 214

1 *Punctilio*: A thing of no importance; a trifle.

Page 215

1 *pretty Novel*: Although Richardson does not use 'romance' or 'novel' to label his own works of prose fiction, he allows Mr. B., at several points in the narrative, to disclose that he is familiar with this species of writing and that, as a result, he views his struggles with Pamela in romantic or novelistic terms. Pamela appears to agree when she muses that 'my Story surely would furnish out a surprizing kind of Novel, if it was to be well told' (see p. 228, below).
2 *chop Logick*: Engage in sophistry.
3 *dull as a Beetle*: Proverbial (Tilley, B220; *ODEP*, s.v. 'beetle').
4 *clouterly*: Clumsy, awkward, clownish.

Page 216

1 *no Jesuit ever went beyond you*: The Society of Jesus, a religious order founded by Saint Ignatius of Loyola in 1534 to defend Roman Catholicism against the Reformers, was notoriously linked with casuistry, equivocation, and other forms of verbal mystification.

Page 217

1 *escape the Question*: Judicial examination by torture. Mr. B. might be alluding specifically to the method of interrogation, known as putting or giving the question, associated with the Spanish Inquisition.
2 *we press him to Death*: By the 1740s, the punishment of *peine forte et dure* was rarely used in England and was abolished by statute in 1772. It was designed to wring confessions from persons arraigned for felonies who refused to confess or testify by placing heavy iron weights on their chests. Sabor (p. 529, n. 206) cites two cases – one recent, the other after the publication of the novel – in which this form of torture had been used, as reported in *London Magazine* (21 August 1735) and *Universal Spectator*, no. 674 (October 1741). See John H. Langbein, *Torture and the Law of Proof: Europe and England in the Ancien Regime* (University of Chicago Press, 1977), pp. 74–7; and J. M. Beattie, *Crime and Courts in England, 1660–1800* (Oxford: Clarendon Press, 1986), pp. 337–8. Beattie notes that 'prisoners were pressed to death in Surrey in the 1660s and the 1720s' (p. 337, n. 54).

Page 224

1 *Mother spoil'd him at first*: Cf. Lovelace to Belford: 'Why, why, did my mother bring me up to bear no controul?' (*Clarissa*, VII, p. 326).

Page 226

1 *Bag and Baggage*: 'The goods that are to be carried away' (Johnson). Originally a military phrase denoting all the property of an army or of a soldier; here, used pejoratively to indicate that Pamela has been sent packing, with good riddance. The *OED* cites this passage as illustration.

2 *old murmuring Israelites*: Forgetting God's deliverance from their Egyptian captivity, the Israelites ungratefully grumbled to Moses about their fleshless diet of manna in the wilderness: 'We remember the fish, which we did eat in Egypt freely; the cucumbers, and the melons, and the leeks, and the onions, and the garlick' (Numbers 11:5).

Page 227

1 *Tennis-ball of Fortune*: A proverbial expression, meant to convey the uncertainty of human life. In a series of 'considerations' on 'what is man', Jane Barker, for instance, writes that 'Man is a Tennis-Ball of Fortune, a Shuttle-cock of Folly, a Mark for Malice' (*The Lining of the Patch-Work Screen* (1726), p. 169). Anticipating Pamela's association of tennis-ball with 'Sporting-piece', William Oldys, in a biography of Sir Walter Ralegh, cites the words of one of his sources to illustrate the precariousness of Ralegh's colourful life: ''Tis observable, that Sir *Walter Ralegh* was in and out at court so often, that he was commonly call'd the *Tennis-Ball of Fortune* which she delighted to sport with' (Sir Walter Ralegh, *The History of the World*, 11th edn (1736), I, p. lxxvi). Attempting to account for his peregrinations, a later eighteenth-century novel hero offers an interesting variation on the tennis-ball motif while relating a dream his mother had while she was pregnant with him: 'She dreamed, she was delivered of a tennis-ball, which the devil . . . struck so forcibly with a racket, that it disappeared in an instant . . .' (Tobias Smollett, *Roderick Random* (1748), p. 2).

Page 228

1 *Mockado*: Mockery, derision. The *OED* cites this passage as the first example of this usage.

Page 235

1 *burnt Wine*: Heated wine.

2 *fetching-up*: Making up for. The *OED* cites this passage as illustration.

Page 236

1 *Sack-whey*: A medicinal beverage, made by mixing sack, a white wine originally imported from Spain or the Canary Islands, with whey, the serum or watery part of milk. Writing to Richardson on 12 January 1739/40, George Cheyne prescribes to his friend and patient 'a good Dose of Spirit of Hartshorn, 40 or 50 Drops in Half a Pint of warm Sack Whey [to] make you sleep and lie more comfortable and warmer at least during this extreme Season'.

Page 238

1 *said the Philosopher*: Diogenes the Cynic, having been discovered looking at a pile of bones by Alexander the Great, said to him that he could not distinguish between the bones of Alexander's father and those of his slaves. Lovelace refers to the same story in *Clarissa*: 'There is no difference to be found between the skull of king Philip and that of another man' (V, p. 226).

Page 239

1 *the Poet*: The author of these lines remains unidentified, though Keymer (p. 532) plausibly nominates Richardson himself as a candidate. The poem, without the closing couplet,

also appears in the 'reflection' following fable 194 ('A Lion, Ass, and Hare') in Richardson's edition of *Æsop's Fables* (*EW*, p. 281) and, as part of a longer poem, in *Pamela 2* (III, p. 360). It is reprinted, unattributed, with minor alterations in one line and again without the closing couplet – suggesting that the source might be *Æsop's Fables* rather than *Pamela* – in *Little Master's Miscellany, or, Divine and Moral Essays in Prose and Verse, Adapted to the Capacities, and Design'd for the Improvement of the Youth of Both Sexes* (1746), pp. 53–4.

Page 242

1 *the Chace, the Green, and the Assemblée*: The hunt, the bowling-green, and the assembly, the last a meeting of polite persons of both sexes for the sake of conversation, gallantry, or play.

2 *Hybla*: An ancient town in Sicily, famous in classical times for the sweetness of the honey produced on its neighbouring hills.

Page 247

1 *Secretary*: A style of handwriting used chiefly in legal documents from the fifteenth to the seventeenth century; a kind of black-letter type imitating this style.

Page 249

1 *first Men of the Law*: Keymer (p. 533) plausibly suggests that Mr. B. is referring here to Edward Hyde (1609–74), who engineered the secret marriage of his daughter Anne (1637–71) to the Duke of York (later James II) in September 1660. Hyde had been appointed Lord Chancellor in 1658 and became the first Earl of Clarendon in 1661. Mr. B. later cites the Hyde family as a prominent example of upward mobility through marriage (see p. 388 below).

2 *out of the way*: Mistaken (i.e., away from the right path).

Page 260

1 *French Telemachus*: *Les Avantures de Télémaque fils d'Ulysse* (1699), a didactic prose epic written by François de Salignac de la Mothe-Fénelon (1651–1715), French theologian and Archbishop of Cambrai (after 1695). Richardson was one of the printers of an English translation of this work published in 1728 (Maslen, p. 84, items 273, 274).

2 *Cast*: A ride or lift in a conveyance.

Page 267

1 *Go...Night*: This poem, omitted in the 1801 edition, is by Aaron Hill (1685–1750); a version of it, titled 'The Messenger', appeared in *The Works of the Late Aaron Hill, Esq.* (1753), I, pp. 155–6.

Page 271

1 *Quadrille*: A card game, played by four persons, with forty cards, the eights, nines, and tens being discarded.

Page 275

1 *touch any Key*: As the ensuing banter suggests, Sir Simon is punning obscenely on the word 'key'. See Eric Partridge, *A Dictionary of Slang and Unconventional English*, 8th

edn, ed. Paul Beale (London: Routledge, 1984; repr. 2002): 'The penis: C18–early 20: sometimes euph., but gen. low coll.' (s.v. 'key', 2).

2 *They blush, because they understand*: Jonathan Swift, *Cadenus and Vanessa* (1713; published 1726), line 171. In a letter to Lady Bradshaigh (22 April 1752), while discussing Lord Orrery's recently published *Memoirs of the Life and Writings of Jonathan Swift*, Richardson refers to this poem as 'that really pretty piece of his'.

Page 277

1 *Jacob's Ladder*: See Genesis 28:12: 'And he [Jacob] dreamed, and behold a ladder set up on the earth, and the top of it reached to heaven: and behold the angels of God ascending and descending on it.'

Page 279

1 *Jephtha's Daughters*: See Judges 11:30–40. In exchange for victory over Ammon's children, Jephthah vows to sacrifice to God 'whatsoever cometh forth of the doors of my house to meet me'. Jephthah is greeted by his only child, a daughter, who requests that, before her death, she be 'let . . . alone two months, that I may go up and down upon the mountains, and bewail my virginity'.

2 *mantua*: A mantua was a loose gown worn by women.

Page 280

1 *over-against*: Opposite, facing.

Page 281

1 *Boileau's Lutrin*: *Le Lutrin* (1674–83), a mock-heroic poem by Nicolas Boileau-Despréaux (1636–1711); it describes the ludicrous quarrel between two clergymen over the placement of a lectern in a chapel.

Page 284

1 *capping Compliments . . . Verses*: To 'cap' verses, as Johnson explains, is 'to name alternately verses beginning with a particular letter' or, more generally, 'to name alternately', with the purpose of topping the previous verse (or, in this instance, compliment) and thus having the last word. The *OED* cites this passage as illustration.

Page 285

1 *prevented*: Anticipated.

2 *unsearchable Wisdom of God*: See Romans 11:33: 'O the depth of the riches both of the wisdom and knowledge of God! how unsearchable *are* his judgments, and his ways past finding out!'

Page 286

1 *There is . . . not Repentance*: Slightly altered version of Luke 15:7: 'I say unto you, that likewise joy shall be in heaven over one sinner that repenteth, more than over ninety and nine just persons, which need no repentance.'

Page 287

1 *Now lettest . . . thy Salvation*: These words are spoken by the just and devout Simeon while holding the child Jesus in his arms. See Luke 2:29–30: 'Lord, now lettest thou thy servant depart in peace, according to thy word. For my eyes have seen thy salvation.'

2 *My Soul . . . low Degree*: These sentences are quoted or adapted from Luke 1:46 ('And Mary said, "My soul doth magnify the Lord . . . "'); 48 ('For he hath regarded the low estate of his handmaiden; for behold, from henceforth all generations shall call me blessed'); and 52 ('He hath put down the mighty from their seats, and exalted them of low degree').

3 *Book of Ruth*: Ruth the Moabitess, a virtuous widow who gleaned the fields to support her family, is 'purchased' by the wealthy Boaz to be his wife; she gives birth to a child, Obed, who, in the concluding words of the book, 'begat Jesse, and Jesse begat David' (Ruth 4:22). Both Matthew and Luke, in their genealogies of Jesus, name David as his ancestor. Mr. Andrews's hint of a biblical parallel for his daughter thus complements Pamela's own linking of herself to 'the blessed Virgin'.

Page 288

1 *a fine Drab*: A suit made of a dull light brown or yellowish brown cloth.

Page 290

1 *Staves*: Stanzas, verses.

Page 292

1 *the common Translation*: *The Whole Booke of Psalmes*, a metrical translation by Thomas Sternhold and John Hopkins, was first published in 1562 and reprinted many times before the end of the eighteenth century; all the Psalms cited in this section of the novel come from this work. It was also known as the Old Version, to distinguish it from *A New Version of the Psalms of David*, by Nahum Tate and Nicholas Brady, published in 1696.

Page 295

1 *Sons of Edom . . . insulting Babylonians*: See Psalms 137:7–9: 'Remember, O LORD, the children of Edom in the day of Jerusalem; who said, "Rase it, rase it: even to the foundation thereof". O daughter of Babylon, who art to be destroyed: happy *shall he be*, that rewardeth thee as thou hast served us. Happy *shall he be* that taketh and dasheth thy little ones against the stones.'

Page 301

1 *Thursday*: According to Eaves and Kimpel, Thursday was 'one of Mrs. Richardson's two lucky days. Richardson fairly often made private references in his works, and it is likely that he was permitting himself a little fun with his wife's superstition' (p. 485). *Pamela* was published on Thursday, 6 November 1740 (as advertised in that day's issue of *The Daily Gazetteer*).

Page 304

1 *close up*: Hidden.

Page 305

1 *the grand Tour*: A tour of the principal cities and places of interest in Europe, taken by young men of birth and fortune as part of their education. For a concise, informative account of this custom, see Bruce Redford, *Venice & the Grand Tour* (New Haven, CT: Yale University Press, 1996). Like Mr. B., Lovelace and Sir Charles Grandison have made the grand tour. In the sequel, Mr. B. takes Pamela on a 'tour' of France and Italy (as well as other locations, both foreign and domestic) to further her education. At the same time, however, Pamela (and Mr. B.) echo detractors of the grand tour in their discussion of the dubious benefits of Italian opera: 'Mr. B. says, sometimes, that this Taste [for '*Italian* Opera'] is almost the only good Fruit our young Nobility gather, and bring home from their foreign Tours; and that he found the *English* Nation much ridicul'd on this Score by those very People who are benefited by the Depravity. And if this be the best, what must the other Qualifications be, which they bring home?— Yet every one does not return with so little Improvements, it is to be hop'd' (*Pamela 2*, IV, p. 111).

Page 313

1 *conning*: Committing to memory, usually by repeating the words of a text to oneself either silently or out loud. Cf. Viola's boast before delivering Orsino's speech to Olivia: 'I have taken great pains to con it' (*Twelfth Night*, I.v.174).

Page 314

1 *dark Bosom of Futurity*: Cf. Belford's comment on the moving style of Clarissa's letters: 'How much more lively and affecting, for that reason, must her stile be, than all that can be read in the dry, narrative, unanimated stile of persons relating difficulties and dangers surmounted! The minds of such not labouring in suspense, not tortured by the pangs of uncertainty about events still hidden in the womb of fate...' (*Clarissa*, VI, p. 336). Richardson cites this passage from Belford's letter in his preface to the third edition of *Clarissa* (published in 1751) to explain the affective power of the novel's 'dramatic' narrative (p. viii).

Page 315

1 *throb, throb, throb*: Cf. Anna Howe's insinuation (with a passing glance at the 'earthly Lover' in *The Rape of the Lock*) that Clarissa is attracted to Lovelace: 'Yet, my dear, don't you find at your heart somewhat unusual make it go throb, throb, throb, as you read just here?' (*Clarissa*, I, p. 62). Clarissa is emphatic in her denial: 'Indeed, my dear, THIS man is not THE man. I have great objections to him. My heart *throbs* not after him' (I, p. 64).

Page 317

1 *the solemn Words*: Pamela is recalling the following sentence from 'The Form of Solemnization of Matrimony' in *The Book of Common Prayer* (1738): 'I Require and charge you both (as ye will answer at the dreadful day of judgement, when the secrets of all hearts shall be disclosed) that if either of you know any Impediment why ye may not be lawfully joined together in Matrimony, ye do now confess it.'

Page 318

1 *I made a Curchee*: Writing to Sarah Chapone on 18 April 1752 regarding Clarissa's refusal of Solmes, Richardson observes: 'You will allow that there are Hundreds (more's the Pity!) who are prevailed upon, & even compelled, to marry the Person they dislike. But how few of those Hundreds are there, who when led to the Altar, & hearing the Vow read, withdraw their Hands and refuse the Engagement; Who say, No instead of the assenting Bow or Courtesy, which the Minister always watches for, and expects not the Negative!'

Page 319

1 *Sack... Sugar*: Mrs. Jewkes is offering Pamela a fortified version of a traditional refreshment, consisting in this case of a piece of toast, spiced with nutmeg, sweetened with sugar, and immersed in sack (see p. 236, n. 1 above).

Page 320

1 *beat up*: Arouse, disturb, visit unceremoniously. The *OED* cites this passage as illustration.

Page 334

1 *Scale of Beings*: A graduated series of beings from the lowest forms to the highest, proving the plenitude or fullness of the universe, and, in a Christian context, the providential design of God's Creation. Cf. *The Spectator*, no. 519 (Saturday, 25 October 1712): 'If the Scale of Being rises by such a regular Progress, so high as Man, we may by a Parity of Reason suppose that it still proceeds gradually through those Beings which are of a Superior Nature to him, since there is an infinitely greater Space and Room for different Degrees of Perfection, between the Supreme Being and Man, than between Man and the most despicable Insect' (*Spectator*, IV, p. 348). This commonplace theological idea was also represented by the image of a chain, as in Pope's *An Essay on Man* (1733): 'Vast Chain of Being! which from God began, / Natures Ethereal, human, Angel, Man, / Beast, bird, fish, insect; what no Eye can see, / No Glass can reach: from Infinite to thee, / From thee to Nothing!' (Epistle I.237–41). On this topic, see Arthur O. Lovejoy, *The Great Chain of Being: A Study of the History of an Idea* (Cambridge, MA: Harvard University Press, 1936).
2 *a mere Cypher*: An arithmetical symbol or character which, though having no value in itself, increases the value of another figure when placed on its right side. Cf. Clarissa's lament to Anna Howe: 'I am but a cypher, to give him significance, and myself pain' (*Clarissa*, IV, p. 2).
3 *Depart, ye Cursed*: See Matthew 25:41: 'Then shall he say also unto them on the left hand, Depart from me, ye cursed, into everlasting fire, prepared for the devil and his angels.' Jesus is here describing the fate of the damned at the Last Judgment.

Page 335

1 *these Reflections*: While writing her 'Reflections', Pamela is probably thinking of the moral of the parable of the talents: 'For unto every one that hath shall be given, and he shall have abundance: but from him that hath not shall be taken away even that which he hath' (Matthew 25:29). Jesus tells this parable just before his description of the Last Judgment, from which Pamela has earlier quoted.

2 *the best of Men*: This phrase appears frequently in *Grandison* to refer to the titular hero—so frequently, in fact, that it prompted Austen to parody its use in 'Evelyn' (see Jane Austen, *Juvenilia*, ed. Peter Sabor (Cambridge University Press, 2006), pp. 229–40).

Page 340

1 *Every one mend one*: Mr. B. is recalling the proverb, 'If every man mend one all shall be mended' (Tilley, M196; *ODEP*, s.v. 'mend'). In *Pamela 2*, it is Lady Davers who remembers this 'good Lesson': 'What remains then . . . but that we take the World as we find it? Give Praise to the Good, Dispraise to the Bad; and every one try to mend *one?*' (III, p. 282).

Page 341

1 *the old Parthians*: Parthian horsemen discharged their arrows at their enemies while moving backward in real or pretended flight. Cf. the pedantic Mr. Walden's retort to Harriet Byron in *SCG*: 'I have discovered you, Madam, to be a *Parthian* Lady. You can fight flying' (I, p. 68).

Page 344

1 *spanning my Waste with his Hands*: An 'anonymous Gentleman', as he is called in the introduction to the second edition of *Pamela*, raised 'Objections to some Passages in the Work' (see p. 467) in a letter (dated 15 November 1740) sent to Charles Rivington, one of the publishers of the novel. One of his objections is aimed directly at this particular passage: 'This Expression is enough to ruin a Nation of Women—I am certain when the Author considers, he will alter it.' Richardson never altered this passage.

Page 345

1 *officiously*: Attentively or obligingly; also, dutifully (i.e., fulfilling her duties as a servant by doing good offices).
2 *Rhenish*: Wine produced in the Rhine region.

Page 347

1 *the Ringers, at the Town*: Celebrations of the B.s' wedding were apparently not confined to fictional bell-ringers. For the story of country villagers who rang church bells upon hearing of Pamela's wedding, see Alan Dugald McKillop, 'Wedding Bells for Pamela', *Philological Quarterly* 28 (1949), 323–5.

Page 350

1 *the right Side the Hedge*: On the safe side, with the hedge acting as a protective barrier against danger; a proverbial expression (*ODEP*, s.v. 'hedge').
2 *I am sick . . . I'm dying*: Possibly an allusion to Pope, *Epistle to Dr. Arbuthnot* (1735), line 2: 'Tye up the knocker, say I'm sick, I'm dead.' See Marie E. McAllister, 'Popean Echoes in *Pamela*: The Lady Davers Scene', *Papers on Language and Literature* 28 (1992), 374–8.

Page 351

1 *Fool's Paradise*: A state of illusory happiness (Tilley, F523; *ODEP*, s.v. 'Fool's paradise').

Page 354

1 *Bear-garden*: A place set aside for the exhibition of rough sports; it takes its name from bear-baiting, the 'sport' of setting dogs to attack a bear chained to a stake.

Page 355

1 *Lady Wou'd-be*: A reference to Lady Would-be, wife of Sir Politick Would-be in Ben Jonson's *Volpone* (1606).

Page 358

1 *Silence . . . gives Consent*: Proverb (Tilley, S446; *ODEP*, s.v. 'silence').

Page 361

1 *she beats . . . the Pit*: I.e., cockpit. Lord Jackey here uses an expression associated with cock-fighting, still popular at the time of the novel's writing, though it declined in popularity towards the end of the century and was outlawed by the Victorians. Lord Jackey's subsequent reference to cock-fighting on p. 404 ('fly the Pit') appears as an illustrative example in the *OED*.

Page 364

1 *Herald's-office*: The Herald's College, or College of Arms, was founded in 1483, to record pedigrees and grant armorial bearings; the Herald's Office was the office of this royal corporation.

Page 366

1 *chine*: To break the chine or back of. The *OED* cites this passage as an example of this usage.

Page 367

1 *Game at Loo*: Abbreviated form of lanterloo, a round card game played by any number of players. In five-card loo, for example, the Jack of Clubs or 'Pam' is the highest card. A player who loses or breaks any of the rules of the game is 'looed' and required to pay a certain sum or 'loo' to the pool.

Page 370

1 *Læsæ Majestatis*: Lese-majesty, in civil law, is any offence against the sovereign or treason. The term comes from the French *lèse-majesté*, itself derived from the Latin *læsa majestas*, meaning hurt or violated majesty.

2 *sour Sauce to your sweet Meat*: Sir Simon is echoing the proverb, 'Sweet meat must have sour sauce' (Tilley, M839; *ODEP*, s.v. 'meat').

Page 372

1 *Whist*: A card game (also known as 'whisk') ordinarily played by four players, teaming up in pairs, with partners facing each other across the card table. One of the suits, usually determined by the last card dealt, is designated 'trumps', with points scored according to the number of tricks won. In some versions of the game, points are also scored by tallying up the 'honours' or highest trumps held by each pair of partners. The immense popularity of this game in the early 1740s prompted Horace Walpole to lament to Sir Horace Mann,

in a letter dated 9 December 1742, that 'Whisk has spread an universal opium over the whole nation; it makes Courtiers and Patriots sit down to the same pack of cards' (*Horace Walpole's Correspondence with Sir Horace Mann*, ed. W. S. Lewis, Warren Hunting Smith and George L. Lam (New Haven, CT: Yale University Press, 1954), II, p. 124).

2 *cast in*: I.e., chose partners at cards. The *OED* cites this passage as an example of this obsolete usage.

3 *the prime Minister*: Mr. Perry is referring to Sir Robert Walpole (1676–1745), a favourite target of Opposition writers, who served as 'prime Minister' (an epithet then used pejoratively) from 1721 until his fall from power in 1742.

4 *a Whig for my Opinion*: In *The Second Treatise of Government*, paragraph 200, Locke offers a succinct enunciation of this 'Whig' principle: 'Thus that Learned King [James I] who well understood the Notions of things, makes the difference betwixt a *King* and a *Tyrant* to consist only in this, That one makes the Laws the Bounds of his Power, and the Good of the Publick, the end of his Government; the other makes all give way to his own Will and Appetite' (p. 418).

Page 373

1 *let either Whig or Tory propose it*: Keymer (pp. 535–6) notes similarities between these professions of impartiality and those Lord M. attributes to his 'old friend Archibald Hutcheson' in *Clarissa*: 'I look upon an administration, as intitled to every vote I can with good conscience give it; for a House of Commons should not needlessly put drags upon the wheels of Government: And, when I have not given it my vote, it was with regret: And, for my Country's sake, I wish'd with all my heart, the measure had been such as I could have approved' (IV, p. 186). Hutcheson (*c*.1660–1740), a Tory MP for Hastings (1713–27), wrote several anti-Walpole pamphlets in the early 1720s which Richardson printed (see Maslen, pp. 95–8, items 372–90).

Page 379

1 *a Word and a Blow*: Proverbial (Tilley, W763; *ODEP*, s.v. 'blow').

2 *Privity*: Private knowledge or cognizance.

Page 381

1 *Assurance*: Impudence, presumption, 'want of modesty' (Johnson); by extension, in this instance, an impudent woman.

2 *Secret-keeper*: Bawd, procuress.

Page 382

1 *TUESDAY… Happiness*: This is the second journal entry dated '*TUESDAY Morning*' (the first appears on p. 348). In the octavo edition of 1742, Richardson changes the first instance to '*MONDAY Morning, Eleven o'Clock*', but chronological inconsistencies remain in subsequent editions. In a final attempt to correct these inconsistencies, the 1801 edition alters the hour from '*Eleven o'Clock*' to '*Seven o'Clock*'.

Page 386

1 *Bravo*: 'A man who murders for hire' (Johnson).

2 *that Duel*: Like Sir Richard Steele, Richardson was vehemently opposed to duelling, calling challenges in *SCG* 'those polite *invitations to murder*' ('A Concluding Note by

the Editor', VI, p. 301). He also condemns duelling in the Conclusion to *Clarissa*, but apparently not forcefully enough for some of his readers, whom he addresses in a footnote appearing at the end of the Conclusion in the third edition: 'Several worthy persons have wished, that the heinous Practice of Duelling had been more forcibly discouraged, by way of Note, at the Conclusion of a Work designed to recommend the *highest and most important Doctrines of Christianity*. It is humbly presumed, that those persons have not sufficiently attended to what is already done on that subject in Vol. II. p. 60. and in Vol. VIII. Letters x. xxxvii. xxxviiii. Xxxix' (*Clarissa*, 3rd edn (1751), VIII, p. 276). See also the 'Six Original Letters upon Duelling', published posthumously in the *Candid Review* for March 1765 (I, 227–31) and there attributed to Richardson. Richardson's family denied his authorship of these letters, but Alexander Pettit, in his General Introduction to *EW*, supports the attribution.

Page 387

1 *Knave than Fool*: The fool–knave pairing is proverbial; see, for example, Tilley, K129 ('More knave than fool') and K144 ('Knaves and fools divide the world'); *ODEP*, s.v. 'knave'. It appears most famously in the definition of happiness in Swift's *A Tale of a Tub* (1704): 'This is the sublime and refined Point of Felicity, called, *the Possession of being well deceived*; The Serene Peaceful State of being a Fool among Knaves' (p. 175). Pamela uses the fool–knave opposition in the sequel (IV, p. 109) to comment on the dubious morality of *The Tender Husband*.

Page 388

1 *Duchess of York*: In September 1660, the Duke of York (the future James II) secretly married Anne, the daughter of Edward Hyde (1609–74), then a commoner but soon ennobled and created Earl of Clarendon by Charles II in 1661. Given the controversy and scandal surrounding this marriage, Mr. B.'s allusion to it is puzzling; it is unlikely that Richardson meant his readers to recall the sordid details of this affair at this point in the narrative – though, if Keymer is correct in his surmise, that is precisely what Mr. B. had earlier done (see p. 249 and n. above). On this topic, see Carolyn D. Williams, 'Pamela and the Case of the Slandered Duchess', *Studies in English Literature* 29 (1989), 515–33.

Page 389

1 *Jeroboam . . . before thy Calf*: See 1 Kings 12:28: 'Whereupon the king [Jeroboam] took counsel, and made two calves *of* gold, and said unto them, It is too much to go up to Jerusalem: behold thy gods, O Israel, which brought thee up out of the land of Egypt.' God punishes Jeroboam for the 'sin' of commanding his people to worship false idols (29–30).

Page 390

1 *Dirt to Dirt*: The words from 'The Order for the Burial of the Dead' in *The Book of Common Prayer* are not 'dirt to dirt' but 'dust to dust'.

Page 393

1 *hail Fellow all*: Mr. B. is alluding to the proverb, 'Hail fellow well met' (Tilley, H15; *ODEP*, s.v. 'fellow').

Page 394

1 *Property*: Not so much in the sense of possession – though that sense is certainly implied – but, meant as a greater insult, denoting 'a person or thing to be made use of; an instrument or tool' (*OED*).

Page 396

1 *my dear Quaker Sister*: Founded by George Fox in 1648–50, the Society of Friends advocated equality and peaceful principles. Its members, commonly (and sometimes pejoratively) known as Quakers, dressed simply and spoke in a plain and (to outsiders' ears) affected manner punctuated by the words – *friend, thee, thou* – Lady Davers uses here to mock what she perceives as her brother's hypocritical self-righteousness. This accusation of Quakerism looks back to her earlier characterization of Mr. B. as an 'Egregious [Puritan] Preacher' (p. 390).

2 *chalk it out*: To trace or mark out (as with chalk) a path or course to be followed. Cf. Clarissa's exclamation to Anna Howe: 'What an exertion of independency does it chalk out for me!' (*Clarissa*, II, p. 238) and Harriet's injunction to Clementina: 'Lay down your own plan, dear Lady: Chalk out your future steps' (*SCG*, VI, p. 259). For other instances of this expression, see *Clarissa*, III, p. 242; V, p. 299; VI, p. 293; and *SCG*, II, p. 336.

Page 405

1 *Saul among the Prophets*: See 1 Samuel 10:10–12, 19:24. Sabor (p. 536, n. 332) cites another reference to this biblical proverb in Richardson's contribution to *The Rambler*, no. 97 (19 February 1751): 'even a *Saul* was once found prophesying among the prophets whom he had set out to destroy'.

Page 406

1 *owing to my Meekness*: This is an assessment of Pamela's character with which Richardson, in defending the ending of his second novel, would later agree: 'I had given in the Story of Pamela what is called a happy Issue. It was, however, owing to her implicit Submission to a lordly and imperious Husband, who hardly deserved her, that she was happy; a Submission which every Woman could not have shewn' ('Hints of Prefaces for Clarissa', FM XV, 3, fol. 2). Cf. Richardson's letter to Solomon Lowe on 21 January 1748/9: 'In the proud and haughty Mr. B. in Pamela, I had done something of what Mr. C[oope]r would have done in Clarissa. It is apparent by the whole Tenor of Mr. B.'s Behaviour to Pamela after Marriage, that nothing but such an implicit Obedience, and slavish Submission, as Pamela shewed to all his Injunctions and Dictates, could have made her *tolerably* happy, even with a *Reformed* Rake . . . Let me observe, Sirs, that Rakes and Free-livers, well as the Women generally love them, are jealous of their Prerogatives, and Tyrants of course.'

Page 407

1 *to resist it*: See Richardson's edition of *Æsop's Fables*, no. 163, 'An O A K *and a* W I L L O W ': 'In a Controversy betwixt an Oak and a Willow, the Oak upbraided the Willow, that it was weak and wavering, and gave way to every Blast; while he scorn'd, he said, to bend to the most raging Tempests, which he despis'd as they whistled by him. Some very little while after this Dispute, it blew a most violent Storm. The Willow ply'd and gave way to

the Gust, and still recover'd it self again, without receiving any Damage: But the Oak, stubbornly resisting the Hurricane, was torn up by the Roots' (*EW*, p. 256).

Page 409

1 *vapourish*: Afflicted with the 'vapours' or 'diseases caused by flatulence, or by diseased nerves; hypochondriacal maladies; melancholy; spleen' (Johnson).

2 *Insensibility*: 'Stupidity; dulness of mental perception' as well as 'torpor; dulness of corporal sense' (Johnson).

Page 411

1 *supererogatory Merit*: The Roman Catholic doctrine of supererogation stipulates that good works performed beyond what God requires become a store of merit, which the Church may then dispense to others to make up for their deficiencies. In *Pamela 2*, Pamela writes to Miss Darnford, 'I hope I shall not be thought ridiculous, or as one who aims at Works of Supererogation, for what I think is very short of my Duty' (III, p. 247); Clarissa declares to Lovelace that 'I aim not at works of supererogation' (*Clarissa*, IV, p. 165). Cf. Mr. Selby's humorous quip to Harriet about her relatives: 'they attribute to themselves some merit from the relation they stand to you. *Supererogatorians* all of them (I *will* make words whenever I please) with their *attributions* to you' (*SCG*, I, p. 32). Later in the novel, Harriet quotes Mr. Grandison's compliment to Sir Charles: 'let me be allowed to believe the Roman Catholic doctrine of Supererogation; and let me express my hope, that I your kinsman may be the better for your good works' (II, p. 149).

Page 412

1 *Childrens Education*: Part of the education of the B.s' children does indeed fall to Pamela's lot in the second part of the novel. To guide her in this task, Mr. B. gives Pamela a copy of Locke's *Some Thoughts Concerning Education* (1693), on which she comments extensively, at times disagreeing with – and offering correctives to – the philosopher's pedagogical principles.

Page 414

1 *Parliament of Women*: Probably derived from Aristophanes' *Parliament of Women*, a facetious or satirical name traditionally given to a usually fictitious body, to whose deliberations cases of love, marriage, and politics would be referred. See, for example, Mrs. Modern's comments in Henry Fielding's *The Modern Husband* (1732): 'to see what empty Politicians Men are found, when they oppose their weak Heads to ours! On my Conscience, a Parliament of Women would be of very great Service to the Nation' (IV, iii), in *Plays Volume Two 1731–1734*, ed. Thomas Lockwood (Oxford: Clarendon Press, 2007), p. 260. As Keymer (p. 536) and Sabor (p. 537, n. 338) point out, Richardson referred to his women correspondents in the 1750s – with whom he discussed questions of love, courtship, and marriage – as the 'female senate' or 'little senate'.

Page 417

1 *harp upon this String*: Proverbial (Tilley, S936; *ODEP*, s.v. 'string').

Page 418

1 *quick*: Alive.

Page 429

1 *Postilion*: 'One who guides the first pair of a set of six horses in a coach' (Johnson).

2 *Scullion-boy*: A scullion is 'the lowest domestick servant, that washes the kettles and the dishes in the kitchen' (Johnson).

Page 430

1 *October*: Ale brewed in October.

2 *Repeating-watch*: A watch (or clock) that strikes the hours by compression of a spring.

3 *Equipage*: Articles for personal ornament or use.

Page 433

1 *aforehand*: 'By a previous provision' (Johnson); prepared or provided for the future. The *OED* cites this passage as illustration.

Page 437

1 *Whole Duty of Man*: First published in 1657, *The Whole Duty of Man* was a popular devotional treatise outlining the obligations of Christians to God and to themselves as well as to their families and neighbours; it was attributed to Richard Allestree (1621/2–81), a royalist clergyman who was appointed chaplain to King Charles II in 1663 and provost of Eton in 1665; he was also Regius Professor of Divinity at Oxford University. *The Whole Duty of Man* is one of the 'good Books' Joseph Andrews has read while serving in Sir Thomas Booby's family (*Joseph Andrews*, p. 24); it is also found among the volumes of Shamela's eclectic library, 'with only the Duty to one's Neighbour, torn out' (*Shamela*, p. 181).

2 *double Chaise*: I.e., a chaise drawn by four horses.

Page 438

1 *made their Honours*: Curtsied.

Page 441

1 *Half-pay Officer*: An officer in the army or navy, when not in actual service or after retirement, would receive half his usual wages.

2 *Marlborough*: A town in Wiltshire.

Page 442

1 *Jamaica*: Captured from the Spanish by an English expedition led by Admiral William Penn and General Robert Venables in 1655, Jamaica had become by the time of *Pamela*'s writing a prosperous colony and a centre of British trade in the Americas. Known primarily for its produce of sugar, spices, coffee, and rum, the island also had a reputation for lawlessness, lack of schools, unhealthy conditions, and cruel treatment of slaves. These issues are discussed in *A New History of Jamaica*, whose second edition Richardson printed in 1740 (Maslen, p. 102, item 436). Attributed to 'Charles Leslie, a Jamaican', this informative work consists of '*Thirteen Letters from a Gentleman in that* Island *to his Friend in* London' (p. 1), in which the author, while granting the difficulties of life in Jamaica, offers a compelling case for increasing emigration from Britain to such a strategically situated and commercially important outpost of the British empire.

2 *her Month was well up*: The usual period of confinement for women during and after childbirth was one month.

Page 443
1 *Calne*: A town in Wiltshire.

Page 444
1 *Crosby-square*: Located off Bishopsgate, a square of good houses inhabited by gentry and merchants.
2 *Flying-coach*: The ordinary designation for a swift stage coach in the seventeenth and eighteenth centuries. The *OED* cites this passage as an illustrative example of this usage.

Page 447
1 *no Arms to quarter*: It was customary for a well-born wife to have her family's coat of arms added, in alternate quarters, to her husband's hereditary coat of arms.
2 *Olive-branch*: To serve as a symbol for their children. See Psalms 128:3: 'Thy wife *shall be as a fruitful vine by the sides of thine house: thy children like olive plants round about thy table.*'
3 *Paduasoy*: A strong corded or gros-grain silk fabric, worn by both men and women in the eighteenth century.

Page 449
1 *relative Duties of Christianity*: See p. 3, n. 1 above. As William Fleetwood observes in his epistolary preface to his congregation, '*the Design of Christianity is to make People happy in this World, as well as in* another: *And the Way it takes to do this, is to make them good and virtuous whilst they live, by the Discharge of all the Relations they stand in to each other, whether Natural, Civil, or Contracted*; i.e., *by performing their Duty to their Neighbour. And therefore, if I can help to make you* good Relations, *you will, I know, be so far* good Christians' (*The Relative Duties of Parents and Children* [p. ii]).

Page 452
1 *Relict*: Widow.

Page 453
1 *such an Herod*: See Richardson's own footnote in *SCG* to IV, p. 350: 'Herod directed, that his Mariamne should be put to death, that she might not be the wife of any other man, if he returned not alive from the court of Augustus Cæsar, before whom he was cited to answer for his conduct, which had been obnoxious to that Prince, in the contest between him and Antony for the empire of the world.' Eventually the jealous Herod had his wife executed. Cf. Anna Howe's warning to Clarissa that Lovelace loves her 'with *such* a love as Herod loved his Mariamne' (*Clarissa*, IV, p. 340). The story of Herod and Mariamne appears in Josephus' *Antiquities of the Jews* (Book XV, chapters iv and xi). This chronicle, under the title *Of the Jewish Antiquities*, is included in *The Works of Flavius Josephus*, translated by Sir Roger L'Estrange; Richardson was among the printers of the fifth edition (1733) of this compilation (Maslen, p. 99, item 404). Writing on jealous husbands, Addison features the story, 'as I have collected it out of *Josephus*' (*Spectator*, II, p. 176), at the conclusion of *The Spectator*, no. 171 (Saturday, 15 September

1711). As Keymer notes (p. 537), *Mariamne. A Tragedy* (1723), a play by Elijah Fenton (1683–1730), had been acted three times at Covent Garden in 1739 (13 March, 9 April, 15 September).

Page 454

1 *give you a few Lines*: Sabor (p. 538, n. 368) suggests that this poem might be by Richardson himself, while Keymer (p. 537), noting similarities between it and 'Celia, in the Garden', tentatively assigns it to Aaron Hill. For 'Celia, in the Garden', see *The Works of the Late Aaron Hill, Esq.* (1753), III, pp. 145–6.

2 *type*: Johnson defines 'type' as 'that by which something is prefigured' and cites illustrative examples from Milton's *Paradise Lost* and Tillotson's sermons, thus tracing the word to its origins in biblical hermeneutics, particularly that branch of it known as typology. At times in the novel, Richardson seems to be pointing towards a typological relation between Pamela and biblical characters – for example when she likens herself to the 'old murmuring *Israelites*' (p. 226) – but, except for scattered references, there is no evidence to support that he is using biblical typology in any systematic way to structure her story. On this topic, see Albert J. Rivero, 'Typology, History, and Blake's *Milton*', *Journal of English and Germanic Philology* 81 (1982), 30–46; and Paul J. Korshin, *Typologies in England, 1650–1820* (Princeton University Press, 1982).

Page 460

1 *into everlasting Perdition afterwards*: Penelope Aubin expresses similar views on this subject in her preface to *The Life and Adventures of the Lady Lucy* (1726): 'But let me give this Word of Advice to the vicious Woman; let her Station be ever so great and high in the World, nay, let her Crimes be ever so well concealed from human Eyes; yet, like *Henrietta*, she will be unfortunate in the End, and her Death, like her's, will be accompanied with Terrors, and a bitter Repentance shall attend her to the Grave: Whilst the virtuous shall look Dangers in the Face unmoved, and putting their whole trust in the Divine Providence, shall be delivered, even by miraculous Means; or dying with Comfort, be freed from the Miseries of this Life, and go to taste eternal Repose' (Penelope Aubin, *A Collection of Entertaining Histories and Novels* (1739), II, p. [79]).

INDEX